SQL Programming Joes 2 Pros

Programming & Development for
Microsoft SQL Server 2008

(SQL Exam Prep Series 70-433 Volume 4 of 5)

By
Rick A. Morelan
MCDBA, MCTS, MCITP, MCAD, MOE, MCSE, MCSE+I

ISBN: 1451579489
EAN-13: 978-145-157-9482
Rick A. Morelan
Rick@Joes2Pros.com

Table of Contents

About the Authors

Rick A Morelan

In 1994, you could find Rick Morelan braving the frigid waters of the Bering Sea as an Alaska commercial fisherman. His computer skills were non-existent at the time, so you might figure such beginnings seemed unlikely to lead him down the path to SQL Server expertise at Microsoft. However, every computer expert in the world today woke up at some point in their life knowing nothing about computers. They say luck is what happens when preparation meets opportunity. In the case of Rick Morelan, people were a big part of his good luck.

Making the change from fisherman seemed scary and took daily schooling at Catapult Software Training Institute. Rick got his lucky break in August 1995, working his first database job at Microsoft. Since that time, Rick has worked more than 10 years at Microsoft and has attained over 30 Microsoft technical certifications in applications, networking, databases and .NET development.

Pinal Dave

Pinal works as a Technology Evangelist (Database and BI) with Microsoft India. He has been a part of the industry for more than seven years. During his career he has worked both in India and the US, mostly working with SQL Server Technology - right from version 6.5 to its latest form. Pinal has worked on many performance tuning and optimization projects for high transactional systems. He received his Master of Science from the University of Southern California and a Bachelors of Engineering from Gujarat University. Additionally, he holds many Microsoft certificates. He has been a regular speaker at many international events like TechEd, SQL PASS, MSDN, TechNet and countless user groups.

Pinal frequently writes at http://blog.sqlauthority.com on various subjects regarding SQL Server technology and Business Intelligence. His passion for the community drives him to share his training and knowledge. Before joining Microsoft, he was awarded the Microsoft Most Valuable Professional (MVP) in SQL Server Technology for three continuous years for his outstanding community service and evangelizing SQL Server technology. He was also awarded the Community Impact Award – Individual Contributor. When he is not in front of a computer, he is usually travelling to explore hidden treasures in nature.

Acknowledgements

As a book with a supporting web site, illustrations, media content and software scripts, it takes more than the usual author, illustrator, and editor to put everything together into a great learning experience. Since my publisher has the more traditional contributor list available, I'd like to recognize the core team members:

Editor: Jessica Brown
Cover Illustration: Jungim Jang
Technical Review: Tom Ekberg, Joel Heidal
Software Design Testing: Irina Berger
Index: Denise Driscoll
User Acceptance Testing: Michael McLean, Simon Nicholson
Website & Digital Marketing: Gaurav Singhal

Thank you to all the teachers at Catapult Software Training Institute in the mid-1990s. What a great start to open my eyes. It landed me my first job at Microsoft by August of that year.

A giant second wind came from Koenig-Solutions, which gives twice the training and attention for half the price of most other schools. Mr. Rohit Aggarwal is the visionary founder of this company based in New Delhi, India. Rohit's business model sits students down one-on-one with experts. Each expert dedicates weeks to help each new IT student succeed. The numerous twelve-hour flights I took to India to attend those classes were pivotal to my success. Whenever a new generation of software was released, I got years ahead of the learning curve by spending one or two months at Koenig.

Dr. James D. McCaffrey at Volt Technical Resources in Bellevue, Wash., taught me how to improve my own learning by teaching others. You'll frequently see me in his classroom because he makes learning fun. McCaffrey's unique style boosts the self-confidence of his students, and his tutelage has been essential to my own professional development. His philosophy inspires the *Joes 2 Pros* curriculum.

Preface

If you have the equivalent knowledge of the first three books in the *Joes 2 Pros* book series (*Beginning SQL Joes 2 Pros, SQL Queries Joes 2 Pros, and SQL Architecture Basics Joes 2 Pros*), then you have good knowledge of queries and how SQL stores and retrieves data. Many of the programming objects of this book will reference and build upon architecture concepts you covered in the *SQL Architecture Basics Joes 2 Pros* book.

In *SQL Queries Joes 2 Pros*, we continued to build our large JProCo database one chapter at a time. When you are a part of building something, you comprehend each new level of complexity that is added. Afterward, you're able to stand back and say, "I built that and understand how it works!" In *SQL Architecture Basics Joes 2 Pros*, we got under the hood and became acquainted with the physical structure of SQL Server and best practices for keeping our databases and indexes well-tuned for performance. In this volume, we will add a host of new objects to the JProCo database and will also tackle key topics, such as error handling and the new Change Tracking and Change Data Capture features debuted in SQL Server 2008.

Most of the programming objects have code inside them that resemble advanced queries from *SQL Queries Joes 2 Pros*. Since tasks need to get done at all hours of the day and night, you need to create programming objects that act on the data in the way that meets your organization's needs. Programming objects interact with the data to protect it and modify it at the right time and in the right way.

Introduction

Many SQL Server developer job openings refer to skills with larger database or complex databases. A database can be complex without being very large, and *vice versa*. If you have ever seen a database that has no user input and does not allow any updates (just inserts from feeds), then you know sometimes a giant database is little more than a big relational storage area. Many companies need to track updates, approvals, time changes, historical changes, and currency conversions based on real time market rates. In short, every database is a combination of data and actions and tells a story about the business or organization it represents.

Most actions within a database take place many times to satisfy many customers or partners. The SQL developer needs to be able to create processes for the working database by using one of many programming objects (like functions, stored procedures, constraints, or triggers). By creating objects that talk with SQL Server, you control the way other programs (like applications or web pages) can interconnect. These external programs only need to call on the names of your programming objects by name rather than needing to submit large pieces of advance code. This limited number of handshakes to SQL often represents a safe and pre-set way into SQL and keeps data better protected.

Programming objects are the building blocks for software and business intelligence applications. Throughout your SQL development career, most of the code you write will be contained in these objects.

Once you learn how programming objects work in SQL Server, you are in control of how things run on your system. These objects become tools you wield in order to enforce business rules within your database. Sometimes a valid SQL statement might be one you never want to run. Some tables may have data that is not allowed to be changed or duplicated. With objects like constraints and triggers, you can make your own rules about which actions are allowed – and which are forbidden – within your database.

Skills Needed for this Book

If you have no SQL coding knowledge, then I recommend you first get into the groove of the *Beginning SQL 2008 Joes 2 Pros* book (ISBN 1-4392-5317-5). If you already have basic SQL skills and want to get really good at writing queries, then I recommend *SQL Queries Joes 2 Pros* (ISBN 1-4392-5318-2) as your best starting point before tackling the programming topics. For all the lessons to make sense in this book, you will need to know what SQL is thinking and how it makes decisions. The *SQL Architecture Basics Joes 2 Pros* (ISBN 1-4515-7946-2) book is needed so the programming objects make sense.

The discussion of SQL architectural concepts and the index lessons presented in *SQL Architecture Basics* are the ideal preparation for the programming topics contained in this SQL Programming volume. As this series precisely follows my MCTS preparatory course, I have carefully sequenced the chapters and topics to build upon each other. However, intermediates and developers with a good handle on T-SQL and SQL query writing should be able to approach the programming topics without much difficulty.

About this Book

My understanding of the engine in my car is very limited, yet I benefit everyday from its underlying complexity because I know how to operate the pedals, steering wheel, and other devices of the car. I don’t need to be an expert at a car’s construction to use it effectively. Very few people in the company will actually want or need direct access to SQL Server. Rather, their goal will be to have your work benefit them, their people, and their business but without needing to understand the complexity of SQL Server or T-SQL. By developing programming objects that their applications get to use, very advanced perspectives of the data will be used by many people within your company.

Data needs to be useful to a business. In the *Beginning SQL Joes 2 Pros* book the very first chapter talked about turning data into information. For the large part we saw how to do that in the *SQL Queries Joes 2 Pros* book. Data has been around for thousands of years but quick business information (reports) from that data has only become instantaneous in the last few decades. Having access to the right information is complex but crucial to business. SQL Programming is your chance to bridge this critical gap of information to the right people.

Most of the exercises in this book are designed around proper database practices in the workplace. The workplace also offers common challenges and process changes over time. For example, it is good practice to use numeric data for IDs. If you have ever seen a Canadian postal code (zip code), you can understand the need for character data in relational information. You will occasionally see an off-the-beaten-path strategy demonstrated so you know how to approach a topic in a job interview or workplace assignment.

Note: For purposes of keeping code examples as short and readable as possible for students, in many cases throughout the series I use simple naming when calling database objects, including referenced objects. However, the recommended best practice is to use two-part naming (particularly when calling stored procedures and referenced tables) because it consumes fewer SQL Server system resources. This is discussed in detail by Pinal Dave in Chapter 13.

I'm often asked about the Points to Ponder feature, which is popular with both beginners and experienced developers. Some have asked why I don't simply call it a "Summary Page." While it's true that the Points to Ponder page generally captures key points from each section, I frequently include options or technical insights not contained in the chapter. Often these are points which I or my students have found helpful and which I believe will enhance your understanding of SQL Server.

The *Joes 2 Pros* series began in the summer of 2006. The project started as a few easy-to-view labs to transform the old, dry text reading into easier and fun lessons for the classroom. The labs grew into stories. The stories grew into chapters. In 2008, many people whose lives and careers had been improved through my classes convinced me to write a book to reach out to more people. In 2009 the first book began in full gear until its completion (*Beginning SQL Joes 2 Pros*, ISBN 1-4392-5317-5) and three books later, the adventure continues.

How to Use the Downloadable Companion Files

Clear content and high-resolution multimedia videos coupled with code samples will take you on this journey. To give you all this and save printing costs, all supporting files are available with a free download from www.Joes2Pros.com. The breakdown of the offerings from these supporting files is listed below:

Training videos: To get you started, the first four chapters are in video format for free downloading. Videos show labs and demonstrate concepts. Ranging from 3-15 minutes in length, they use special effects to highlight key points. There is even a "Setup" video that shows you how to download and use all other files. You can go at your own pace and pause or replay within lessons as needed.

Answer Keys: The downloadable files also include an answer key. You can verify your completed work against these keys. Another helpful use is these coding answers are available for peeking if you get really stuck.

Resource files: If you are asked to import a file into SQL Server, you will need that resource file. Located in the resources sub-folder from the download site are your practice lab resource files. These files hold the few non-SQL script files needed for some labs. Please note that no resource files are needed for Volume 4, *SQL Programming Joes 2 Pros.*

Lab setup files: SQL Server is a database engine and we need to practice on a database. The Joes 2 Pros Practice Company database is a fictitious travel booking company whose name is shortened to the database name of JProCo. The scripts to set up the JProCo database can be found here.

Chapter review files: Ready to take your new skills out for a test drive? We have the ever popular Bug Catcher game located here.

What This Book is Not

This is not a memorization book. Rather, this is a skills book to make preparing for the certification test a familiarization process. This book prepares you to apply what you've learned to answer SQL questions in the job setting. The highest hopes are that your progress and level of SQL knowledge will soon have business managers seeking your expertise to provide the reporting and information vital to their decision making. It's a good feeling to achieve and to help at the same time. Many students commented that the training method used in *Joes 2 Pros* was what finally helped them achieve their goal of certification.

When you go through the *Joes 2 Pros* series and really know this material, you deserve a fair shot at SQL certification. Use only authentic testing engines drawing on your skill. Show you know it for real. At the time of this writing, MeasureUp® at http://www.measureup.com provides a good test preparation simulator. The company's test pass guarantee makes it a very appealing option.

Chapter 1. Constraints

When I was a little kid, the watchwords "buckle up" could always be heard whenever we got into the family car. Public service ad campaigns were popular at that time, and I recall commercials and billboards with slogans like "always wear safety belts" or "use your safety constraints."

Nowadays, it's a well known fact that safety constraints (like seat belts) in automobiles or airplanes save lives. Emergency response teams and healthcare professionals save the lives of individuals rescued from accidents, even if people did not use their safety constraints. However, the best practice is to buckle up and try to prevent calamities from occurring in the first place.

The same is true with databases. Utilizing database constraints can help you avoid "accidents" which can harm your data. Constraints can save you time, because you won't need to spend time removing bad data from your system. Like vehicle safety constraints, they are designed to prevent bad things from happening.

This chapter will explore the types of constraints that help keep your database safe and also help maintain data integrity. Since the syntax for adding most of these constraints at the time of table creation is fairly straightforward (e.g., we've already added primary keys to most of the tables we created in Volumes 2 and 3 of the *Joes 2 Pros SQL Series*), we will examine each constraint in the more advanced context of modifying existing tables and constraints. The final section of the chapter will demonstrate the syntax and tips for creating each of the constraints on brand new tables.

***READER NOTE:** In order to follow along with the examples in the first section of Chapter 1, please run the setup script SQLProgrammingChapter1.0Setup.sql. The setup scripts for this book are posted at Joes2Pros.com.*

Data Types

Suppose we use the smallmoney data type for a field called HourlyRate. Just to test this, try entering the word 'Peanuts' into the PayRate.HourlyRate field (see Figure 1.1). *SQL Server rejects this entry because the smallmoney data type will only allow numeric values into this field.*

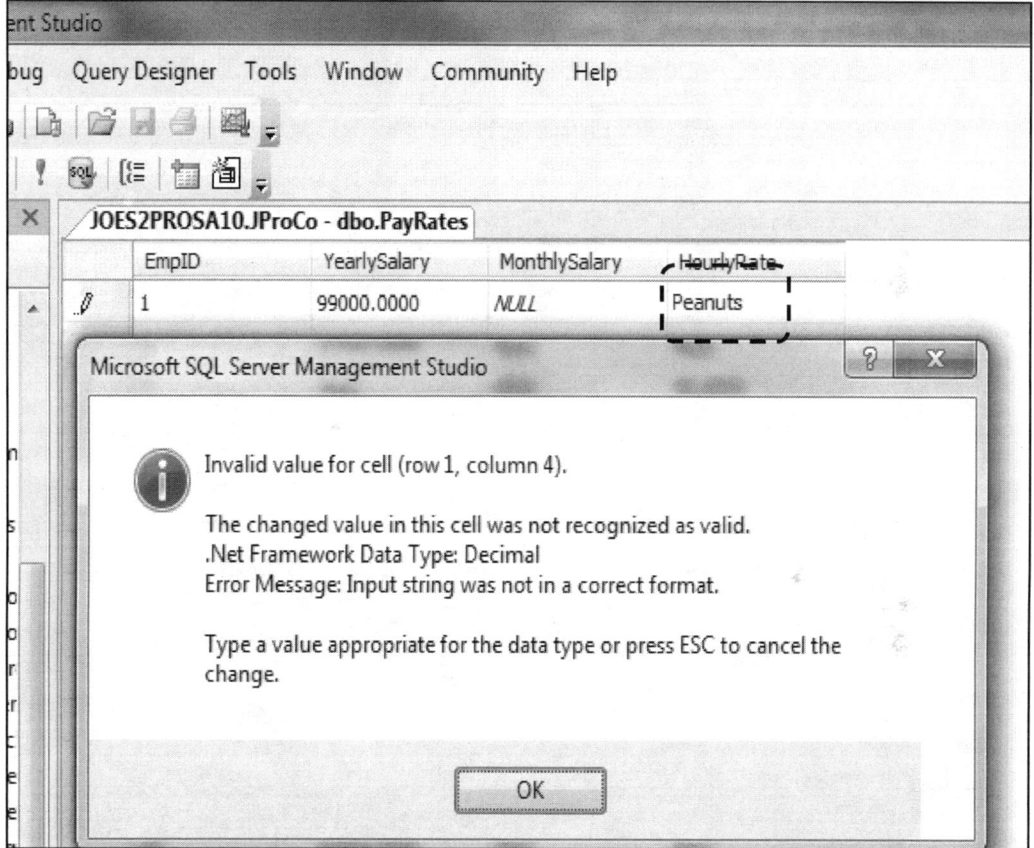

Figure 1.1 The smallmoney data type constrains the values that can be entered into the field.

Notice that entering the letter P in Peanuts (and all the other letters) will be rejected by the HourlyRate field. In this situation, data types are the first line of defense in constraining bad data and ensuring field inputs are valid.

Data types are the simplest and most frequently used **constraints**. They are the only constraint which can blanket every field in every table of your database.

Primary Keys

Perhaps the most commonly used and talked about constraint is the **primary key**. A primary key prevents duplicates and ensures that all records have their own distinct values. Primary keys don't allow nulls, so you are guaranteed that each record has its own unique populated value.

A glance at the dbo.StateList table of the JProCo database shows us we have 53 records. All states and territories listed in this table have values for the StateID field, the StateName field, the RegionName field, and the LandMass field.

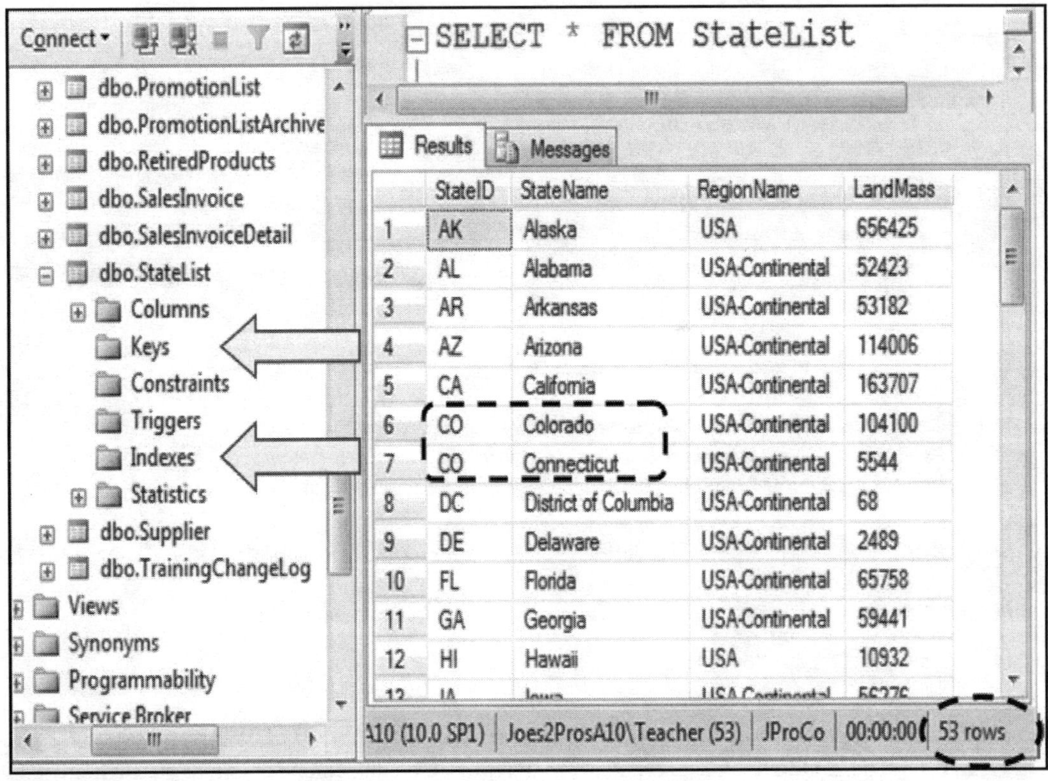

Figure 1.2 The StateList table has no indexes or keys.

When we look at the metadata for this table, we see it has no keys and no indexes. That can be risky, as evidenced by the mistakes shown in Rows 6 and 7. In Figure 1.2 you can see both Colorado and Connecticut are abbreviated as "CO." There are no constraints preventing duplicate StateID records from being entered into this table.

The NH-New Hampshire record is also listed twice (Figure 1.3). It's clearly time to scrub this data and remove duplicates from the StateList table.

30	NE	Nebraska	USA-Continental	77358
31	NH	New Hampshire	USA-Continental	9351
32	NJ	New Jersey	USA-Continental	8722
33	NH	New Hampshire	USA-Continental	9351
34	NM	New Mexico	USA-Continental	121593

Figure 1.3 The NH–New Hampshire record is duplicated in the StateList table.

Let's fix the CO Colorado/Connecticut problem and the New Hampshire duplicate with two different statements. In Figure 1.4, the UPDATE statement corrects the StateID of Connecticut to be abbreviated as CT.

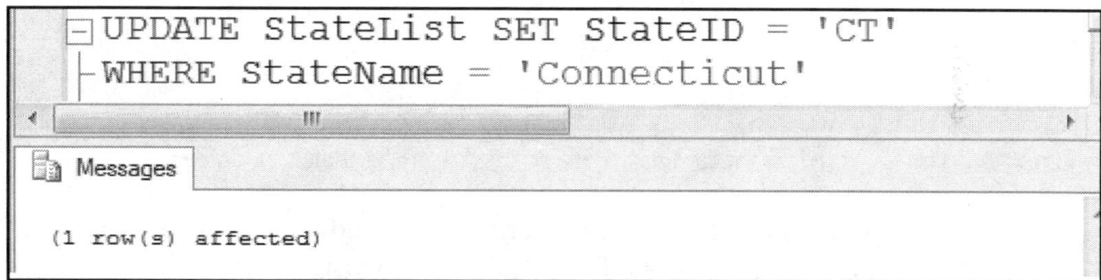
UPDATE StateList SET StateID = 'CT'
WHERE StateName = 'Connecticut'
Messages
(1 row(s) affected)

Figure 1.4 Updating Connecticut to have the StateID of "CT" eliminates one of the duplicates.

To ensure we get rid of just one of the two New Hampshire records, we will combine a DELETE statement with the TOP keyword (Figure 1.5).

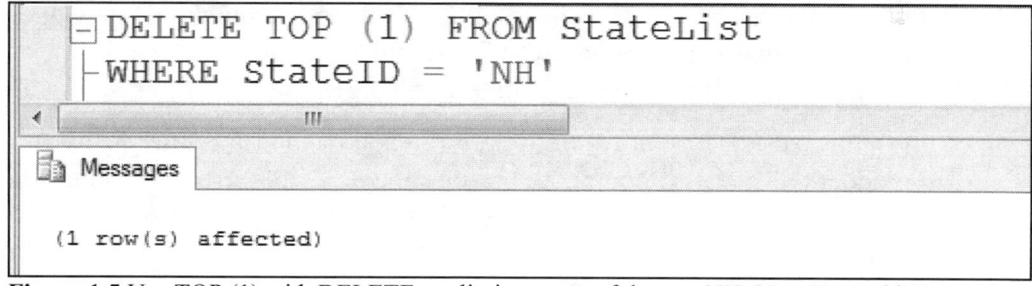
DELETE TOP (1) FROM StateList
WHERE StateID = 'NH'
Messages
(1 row(s) affected)

Figure 1.5 Use TOP (1) with DELETE to eliminate one of the two NH–New Hampshire records.

Finally, our review of the StateList data reveals that our lack of constraints allowed in a record (the Virgin Islands) which actually doesn't belong in our StateList table. The name may begin with "US", but since the Virgin Islands are a territory and not a state (see Figure 1.6), we must delete this record (see Figure 1.7).

```
SELECT * FROM StateList
WHERE RegionName NOT LIKE 'USA%'
```

	StateID	StateName	RegionName	LandMass
1	VI	US Virgin Islands	Other	-1545

Figure 1.6 Our lack of constraints allowed a record which didn't belong in the StateList table.

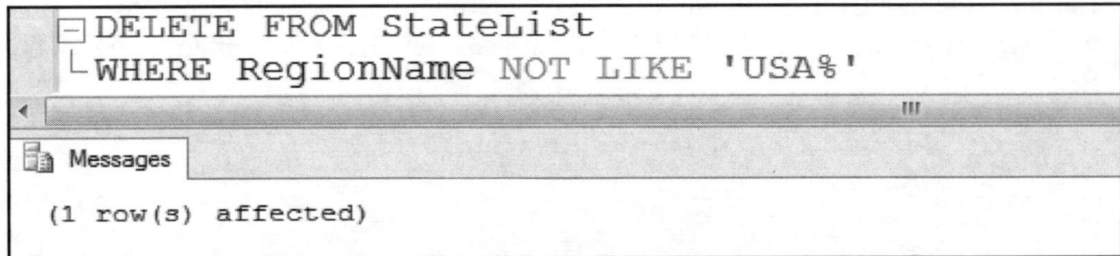
DELETE FROM StateList
WHERE RegionName NOT LIKE 'USA%'
Messages
(1 row(s) affected)

Figure 1.7 The Virgin Islands record has been removed from the StateList table.

With one UPDATE and two DELETE operations, we now have 51 records in StateList (i.e., the 50 states and the District of Columbia).

Creating Primary Keys on Existing Tables

Our StateList data is now scrubbed but we need to prevent bad records (e.g., duplicate StateID records) from entering the table in the future. A primary key on the StateID field of the StateList table would have prevented the duplicate values issue. With this primary key added, SQL Server will not allow any accidental or intentional duplication of values in the StateID field.

Since this table is used constantly, we'd prefer to add the constraint to the existing table in production (versus dropping and re-building the table). We will alter the table and add a primary key constraint on the StateID field (Figure 1.8). A good naming convention is to use PK for "primary key" plus the table name and the field name. In this case, we will name the primary key **PK_StateList_StateID**. You can also specify whether this primary key will create a clustered or non-clustered index, as well as whether to sort StateID values in ascending or descending order. We will add this primary key as a clustered index in ascending order.

(*Note:* If no clustered index already exists on the table, then adding a primary key constraint will generate a clustered index by default. However, you may choose to specify a non-clustered index for the primary key.)

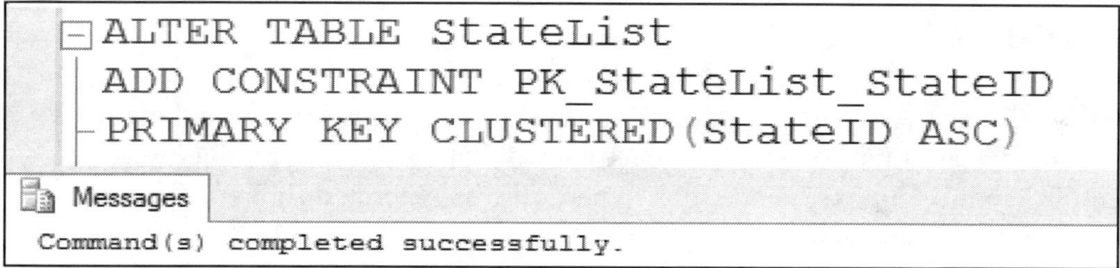

```
ALTER TABLE StateList
ADD CONSTRAINT PK_StateList_StateID
PRIMARY KEY CLUSTERED(StateID ASC)
```


Figure 1.8 The PK_StateList_StateID primary key is created on the dbo.StateList table.

After running the code (in Figure 1.8), open Object Explorer to find the primary key we just created. Beneath the JProCo database, expand the Tables folder and navigate to the dbo.StateList table. Expand the Keys folder and note that the primary key PK_StateList_StateID is present (Figure 1.9). (Right-click dbo.StateList to refresh its folders, as needed.) As well, observe that the Indexes folder has a new clustered index named for the primary key.

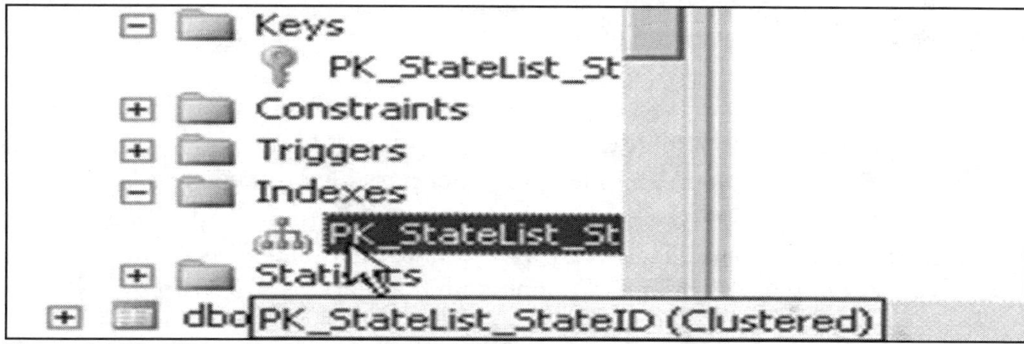

Figure 1.9 The Object Explorer shows us the creation of the primary key and a clustered index.

The purpose of PK_StateList_StateID is to prevent duplicate StateID values from entering our table. To confirm whether this really protects the StateList table, Figure 1.10 attempts to change the StateList.StateID field of the Connecticut record back to CO. The error message demonstrates that PK_StateList_StateID has detected a violation and will prevent the update from running (see Figure 1.10).

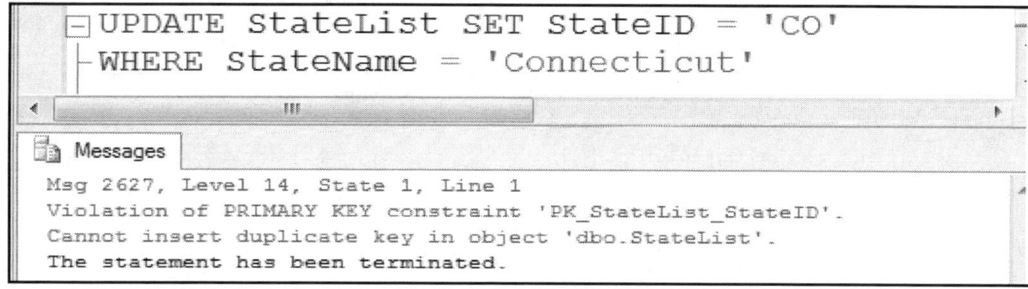

```
UPDATE StateList SET StateID = 'CO'
WHERE StateName = 'Connecticut'
```


Figure 1.10 PK_StateList_StateID prevents duplicate StateID values in the StateList table.

Check Constraints

My old track coach would tell us to give 110% effort. However, had my math teacher heard this, he would have explained that a percentage value exceeding 100% in this context is actually a hyperbolic, exaggerated figure. It implies that you will give all you have, but then somehow you will give 10% more than "all." Does that mean 110% is always an incorrect value? No, it depends on the situation. For example, this year's sales could be 110% of last year's sales. The range of acceptable values defined for a field depends upon the context.

Let's consider negative numbers for a moment. If a form asked for my height in inches, and I wrote -67.5, you would think this was either a typo or a joke. That figure would be easily accepted by a decimal or float data type, but in the context of height, a negative number simply isn't acceptable. A person's height will always be a positive number, never a negative number. For that reason, a "Height" field in a database should be restricted to only positive values. If you want to add your own logic on top of a data type, you can use what is known as a **check constraint**.

Returning to the StateList table, all is well with respect to protection from the risk of duplicate StateID values. But there are other possible erroneous updates or inserts we haven't yet prevented. For example, the "District of Columbia" consists of 68 square miles of land. However, we see a negative LandMass value for a few records, including the District of Columbia, in the StateList field (Figure 1.11).

```
SELECT * FROM StateList
WHERE LandMass < 0
```

Results | Messages

	StateID	StateName	RegionName	LandMass
1	DC	District of Columbia	USA-Continental	-68
2	DE	Delaware	USA-Continental	-2489
3	RI	Rhode Island	USA-Continental	-1545

Figure 1.11 Some records (e.g., District of Columbia) show a negative LandMass number.

Similar to the concept of height, there really is no such thing as a negative land mass (coastal erosion anomalies aside). We know that the absolute value for each LandMass number in our table is correct, so we essentially just need to change any negative figures to positive numbers (e.g., -68 should be 68). The UPDATE statement below (Figure 1.12) multiplies the LandMass value by -1 where the existing LandMass value is < 0 (less than zero). The SELECT query in Figure 1.12 shows that no negative LandMass values remain following the update.

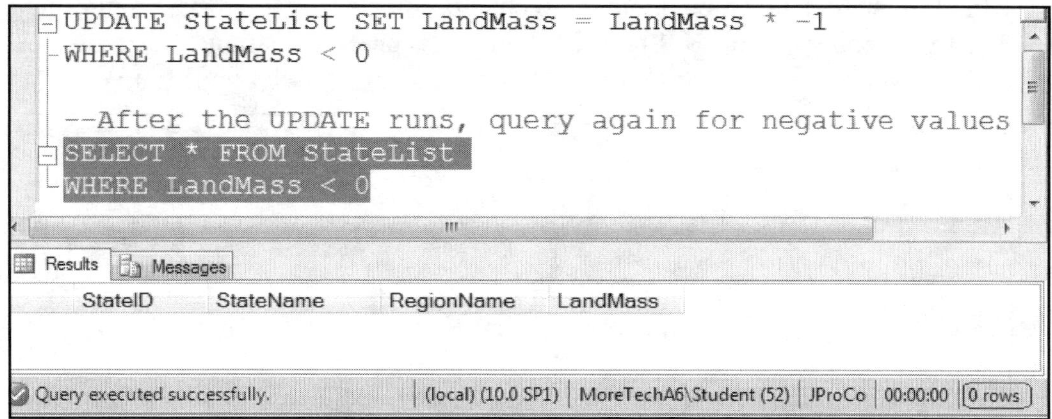
```
UPDATE StateList SET LandMass = LandMass * -1
WHERE LandMass < 0

--After the UPDATE runs, query again for negative values
SELECT * FROM StateList
WHERE LandMass < 0
```


Figure 1.12 There are no negative LandMass values remaining in the StateList table.

Creating Check Constraints

Our LandMass data has been scrubbed and now we want to create the check constraint to maintain this field's data integrity during future inserts or updates. Last time we used a primary key to prevent bad entries in StateID, but that won't solve the LandMass problem. A primary key wouldn't prevent negative values. As well, a primary key would enforce uniqueness of each LandMass value. This would be incorrect business logic, because it is perfectly acceptable for two states to have the same LandMass.

We want SQL Server to say "Yes" to duplicate LandMass values but "No" to any update or insert resulting in a negative LandMass value. The check constraint in Figure 1.13 will check to see if the value is positive before accepting the transaction. The preferred naming convention for the check constraint is similar to the primary key convention. CK for check (constraint) plus the table name and the fieldname, with each part separated by an underscore: **CK_StateList_LandMass**.

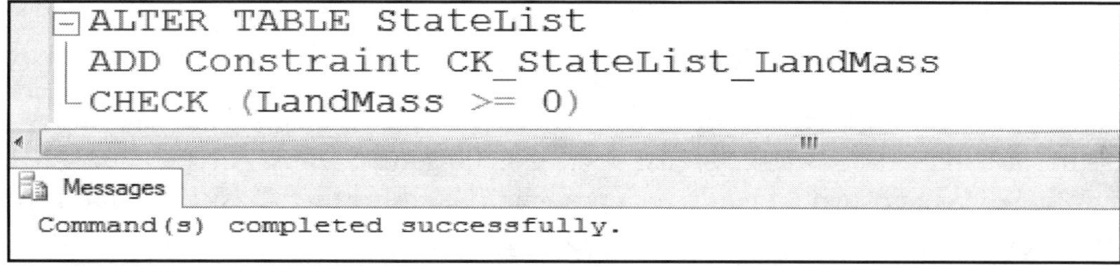
```
ALTER TABLE StateList
ADD Constraint CK_StateList_LandMass
CHECK (LandMass >= 0)
```


Figure 1.13 Use an ALTER TABLE statement to add a new constraint to an existing table.

To prove that our check constraint will prevent DML statements which try to introduce negative LandMass numbers, we will run a quick test. Below you see an UPDATE statement which attempts to change some of the LandMass values into negative numbers. The CK_StateList_LandMass check constraint guards against updates which would result in invalid LandMass values (see Figure 1.14).

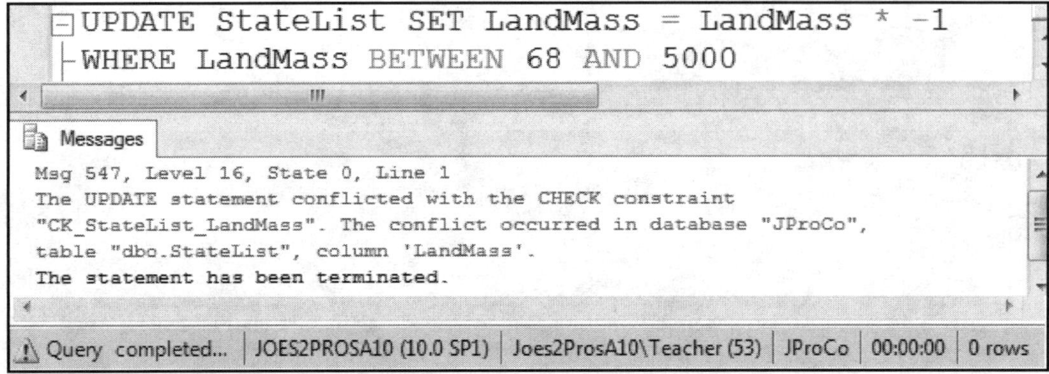

Figure 1.14 Trying to update the LandMass field to a negative number no longer works.

Figure 1.15 shows the CK_StateList_LandMass check constraint that we just added. In Object Explorer, expand the "Tables" folder of the JProCo database and expand Constraints. *Note:* You may need to right-click to refresh the Constraints folder and see newly created items.

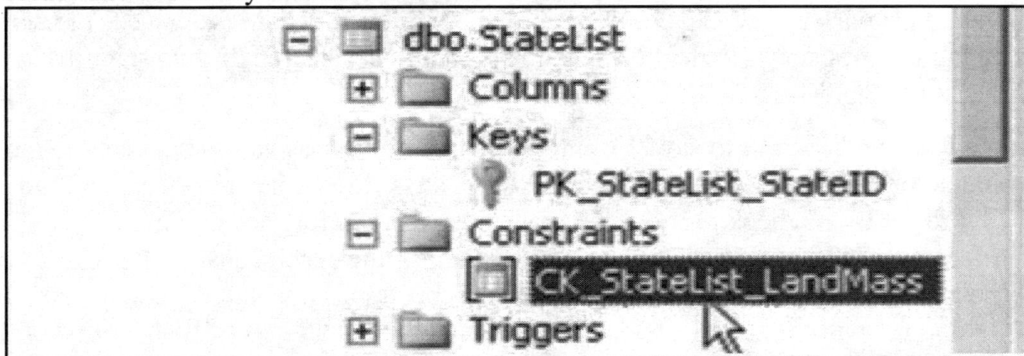

Figure 1.15 The CK_StateList_LandMass check constraint is inside the Constraints folder (a.k.a., the Constraints node) of the StateList table.

Let's consider other errors which could occur in our LandMass data. Our largest current LandMass is Alaska at just over 650,000 square miles. A typo adding one or two extra zeros would really be a problem (i.e., distorting Alaska's LandMass to either 6 million or 65 million miles). Let's attempt a bad UPDATE to help us recognize that our check constraint isn't currently protecting our table from these kinds of mistakes (Figure 1.16).

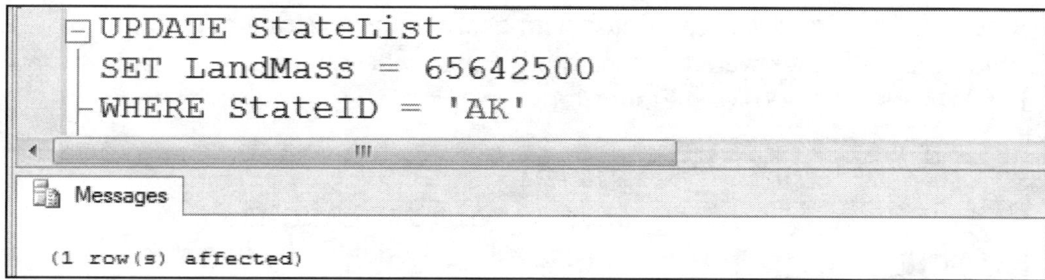
```
UPDATE StateList
SET LandMass = 65642500
WHERE StateID = 'AK'
```
Messages

(1 row(s) affected)

Figure 1.16 The CK_StateList_LandMass does not prevent overly large values.

Since the UPDATE succeeded, our StateList table now incorrectly indicates that Alaska's LandMass exceeds 65 million square miles. While constraints can't guard against all potential data integrity problems, we should constrain the upper limit of the LandMass field to disallow such glaringly large, erroneous values.

Before proceeding, let's reset Alaska's LandMass back to its proper value:

```
UPDATE StateList
SET LandMass = 656425
WHERE StateID = 'AK'
```

Changing Existing Check Constraints

We want to add another **condition** to CK_StateList_LandMass, our existing check constraint for the LandMass field. *Note:* While SQL Server Management Studio (SSMS) offers some options for adding, modifying, and deleting check constraints by clicking through the Object Explorer interface, all of our solutions will be based in T-SQL code.

There isn't a T-SQL statement which allows us to directly modify our existing check constraint. But we can easily accomplish our purpose by dropping the current constraint object and then rebuilding it with both conditions (values for LandMass must be non-negative and less than 2 million square miles).

Run the DROP CONSTRAINT statement (see Figure 1.17).

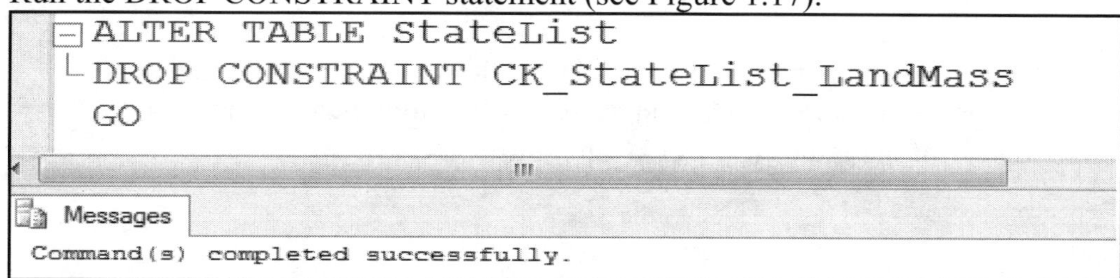
```
ALTER TABLE StateList
DROP CONSTRAINT CK_StateList_LandMass
GO
```
Messages

Command(s) completed successfully.

Figure 1.17 Code to drop the CK_StateList_LandMass constraint.

Re-create CK_StateList_LandMass with expressions covering both of the conditions which we want the constraint to prevent (LandMass >= 0 and LandMass < 2000000) (see Figure 1.18).

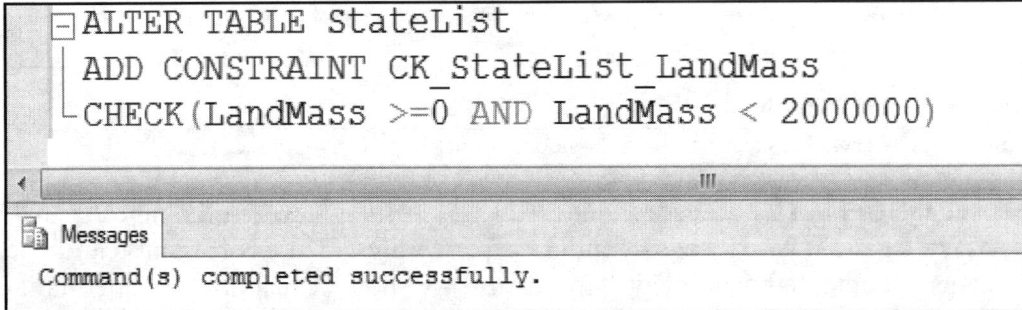

Figure 1.18 Re-create the CK_StateList_LandMass check constraint to only allow values between 0 and 2 Million.

To test whether our revised constraint works, let's reattempt our earlier UPDATE statements (which we ran in Figures 1.14 and 1.16).

Our first condition (LandMass >= 0) is enforced by the revised check constraint. Non-negative values are disallowed for the LandMass field (see Figure 1.19).

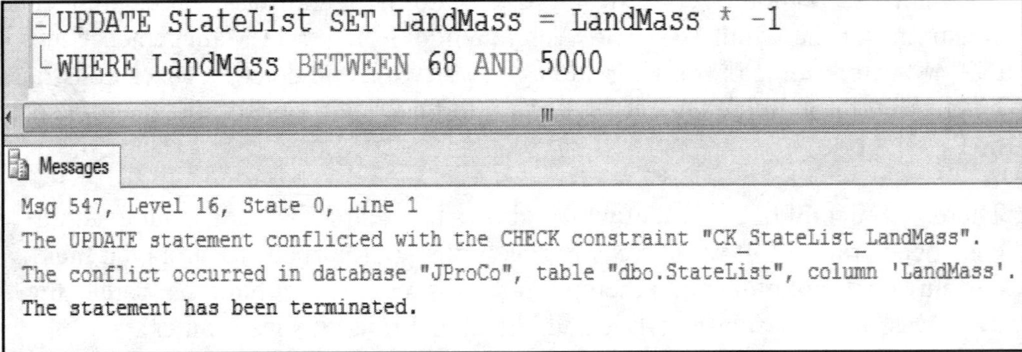

UPDATE StateList SET LandMass = LandMass * -1
WHERE LandMass BETWEEN 68 AND 5000
Messages
Msg 547, Level 16, State 0, Line 1
The UPDATE statement conflicted with the CHECK constraint "CK_StateList_LandMass".
The conflict occurred in database "JProCo", table "dbo.StateList", column 'LandMass'.
The statement has been terminated.

Figure 1.19 The check constraint blocks any DML statement which would place negative values in the LandMass field.

Our second requirement (LandMass < 2000000) is similarly enforced by the revised check constraint. Values in excess of 2 million (square miles) are disallowed for the LandMass field (see Figure 1.20).

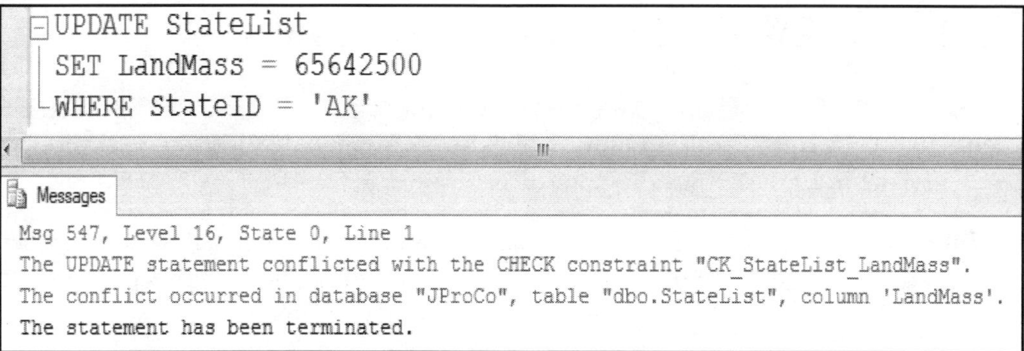

Figure 1.20 The check constraint blocks any DML statement which would place values greater than 2 million in the LandMass field.

You may also wish to perform additional testing to observe the check constraint allows valid transactions into the StateList table. Afterward, remember to rerun the setup script SQLProgrammingChapter1.0Setup.sql (i.e., to reset your StateList table) before performing any examples involving the StateList table.

Lab 1.1: Introduction to Constraints

Lab Prep: Before you can begin the lab, you must have SQL Server installed and have run the script SQLProgrammingChapter1.1Setup.sql. View the lab video instructions in Lab1.1_IntroductionToConstraints.wmv.

Skill Check 1: Create a primary key constraint called PK_RetiredProducts_ProductID on the RetiredProducts table, so that duplicates are prevented from occurring in the ProductID field. Make sure the primary key also creates a clustered index.

dbo.RetiredProducts
Columns
Keys
PK_RetiredProducts_ProductID
Constraints
Triggers
Indexes
PK_RetiredProducts_ProductID (Clustered)
Statistics

Figure 1.21 Skill Check 1.

Skill Check 2: Create a primary key constraint on the ID field of the HumanResources.RoomChart table. Make sure the primary key also creates a clustered index.

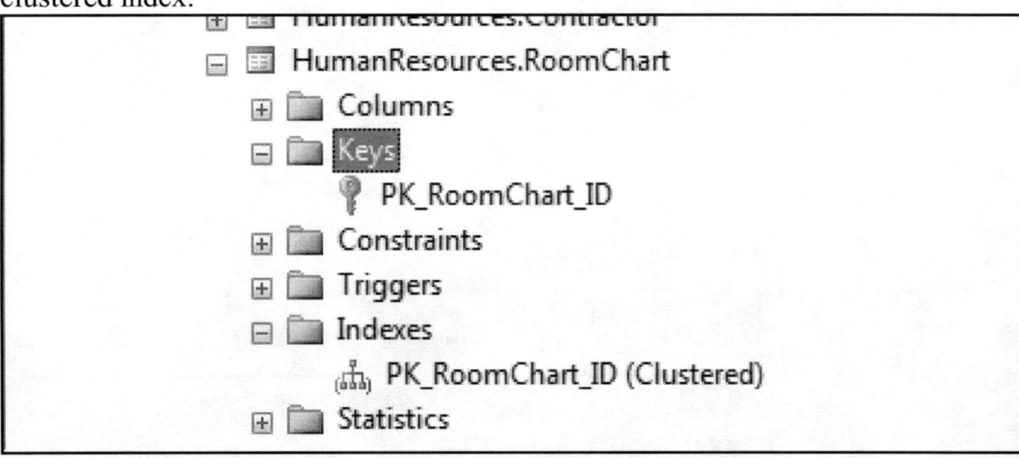

Figure 1.22 Skill Check 2.

Skill Check 3: Create a CHECK constraint to make sure that the UnitDiscount field of the SalesInvoiceDetail table does not allow negative values. Test your constraint by trying to update the UnitDiscount field with a negative value.

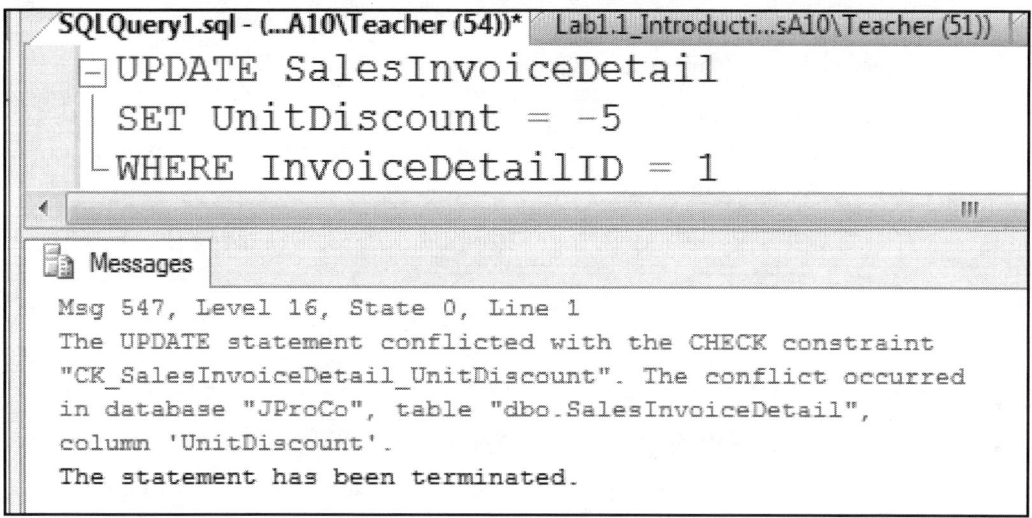
SQLQuery1.sql - (...A10\Teacher (54))*
Lab1.1_Introducti...sA10\Teacher (51))
UPDATE SalesInvoiceDetail
SET UnitDiscount = -5
WHERE InvoiceDetailID = 1
Messages
Msg 547, Level 16, State 0, Line 1
The UPDATE statement conflicted with the CHECK constraint "CK_SalesInvoiceDetail_UnitDiscount". The conflict occurred in database "JProCo", table "dbo.SalesInvoiceDetail", column 'UnitDiscount'.
The statement has been terminated.

Figure 1.23 Skill Check 3.

Skill Check 4: Create a constraint called CK_SalesInvoice_PaidDate, for the SalesInvoice table, which checks to see that the PaidDate is never earlier than the OrderDate. The PaidDate can be the same as the OrderDate or it can be any date subsequent to the OrderDate. Test your code by trying to update a PaidDate value to occur before the OrderDate for InvoiceID 1.

Skill Check 5: On the MgmtTraining table, create a check constraint called CK_MgmtTraining_ApprovedDate that only allows ApprovedDate values of '1/1/2006' or newer.

Skill Check 6: On the StateList table, create a check constraint called CK_StateList_Region, which only allows RegionName values that start with 'USA'.

Answer Code: The T-SQL code to this lab can be found in the downloadable files in a file named Lab1.1_IntroductionToConstraints.sql.

Introduction to Constraints - Points to Ponder

1. Data integrity is the consistency and accuracy of the data which is stored in a database.
2. Good data integrity produces high quality, reliable data.
3. A constraint is a table column property which performs data validation. Using constraints, you can maintain database integrity by preventing invalid data from being entered.
4. Constraints can be added to, or dropped from, tables using the ALTER TABLE statement.
5. You can add constraints to a table that already has data.
6. A table can only have one primary key.
7. Primary keys cannot accept null values, but unique indexes can.
8. A check constraint restricts the values that users can enter into a particular column during INSERT and UPDATE statements.
9. Column level check constraints restrict the values that can be stored in a column.
10. Table level check constraints reference multiple columns in the same table to allow for cross-referencing and comparison of values.
11. A check constraint can be any logical expression that returns true or false.
12. ***Tip***: If necessary, you can temporarily disable a CHECK constraint. *However, data integrity will not be enforced while the constraint is disabled.* Disabling and enabling constraints is outside of the scope of this book.

Unique Constraints

Since we created a primary key on the StateID field, no StateID value can be repeated. Thus, we have ensured each StateID value will be unique. In other words, two states will never have the same StateID (see Figure 1.24).

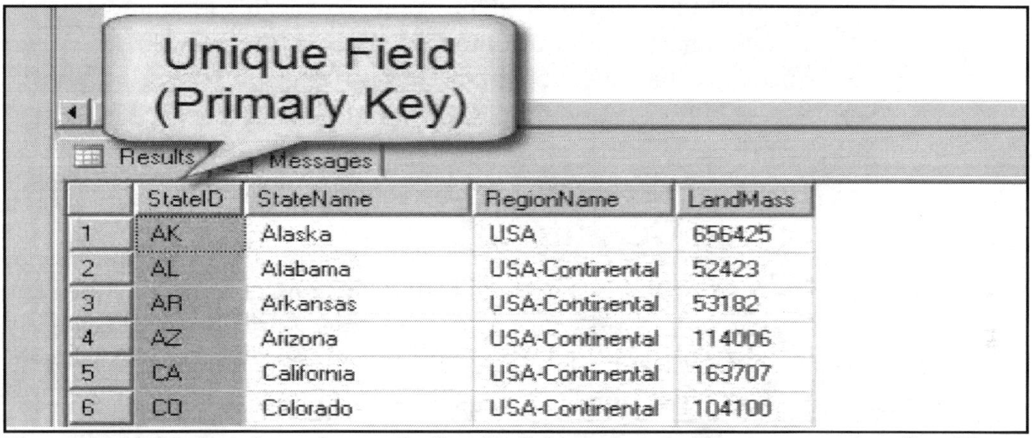

Unique Field (Primary Key)

Results | Messages

	StateID	StateName	RegionName	LandMass
1	AK	Alaska	USA	656425
2	AL	Alabama	USA-Continental	52423
3	AR	Arkansas	USA-Continental	53182
4	AZ	Arizona	USA-Continental	114006
5	CA	California	USA-Continental	163707
6	CO	Colorado	USA-Continental	104100

Figure 1.24 With the primary key on the StateID field, each record has its own unique StateID.

However, there is no constraint on the StateName field. Currently the only requirement for a StateName value is that it be compatible with a varchar(50) data type or that it be null. We would like to ensure uniqueness for each StateName value. Since a table may only have one primary key, and StateList already has a primary key (StateID), we'll need another way to ensure uniqueness of this field.

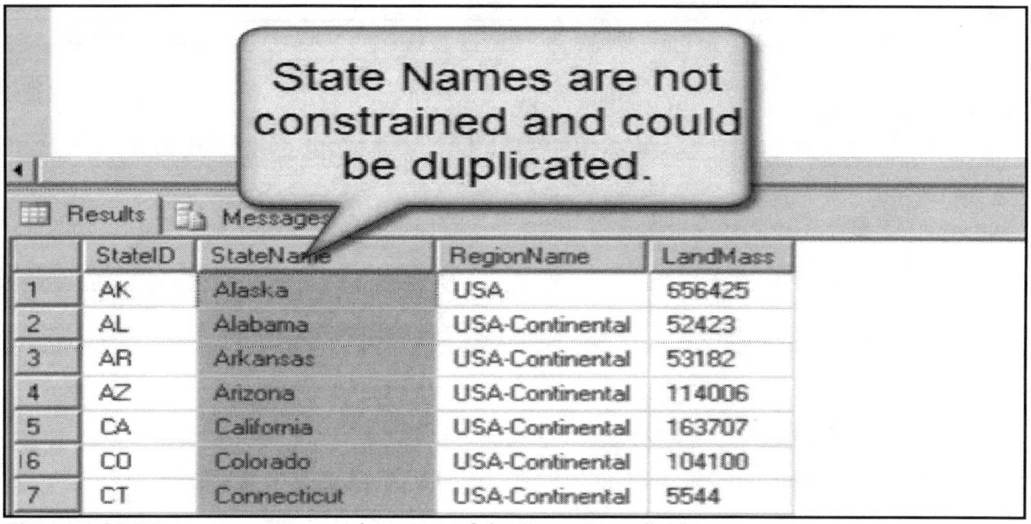

State Names are not constrained and could be duplicated.

Results | Messages

	StateID	StateName	RegionName	LandMass
1	AK	Alaska	USA	656425
2	AL	Alabama	USA-Continental	52423
3	AR	Arkansas	USA-Continental	53182
4	AZ	Arizona	USA-Continental	114006
5	CA	California	USA-Continental	163707
6	CO	Colorado	USA-Continental	104100
7	CT	Connecticut	USA-Continental	5544

Figure 1.25 We want to ensure uniqueness of the StateName field.

While tables are limited to a single primary key field, SQL Server allows multiple *unique constraints* to be added to a table.

Comparing Unique Constraints to Primary Keys

Unique constraints have two main differences versus primary keys:

1) Unique constraints will allow a null value. If a field is nullable then a unique constraint will allow at most one null value (i.e., since all values must be unique).
2) SQL Server allows many unique constraints per table where it allows just one primary key per table.

Creating Unique Constraints

Now let's write the statement which will add a unique constraint to the StateName field. Our object name will begin with UQ (for **unique constraint**) but otherwise will follow the naming convention for the other constraints which we've built in this chapter: UQ_TableName_FieldName (see Figure 1.26).

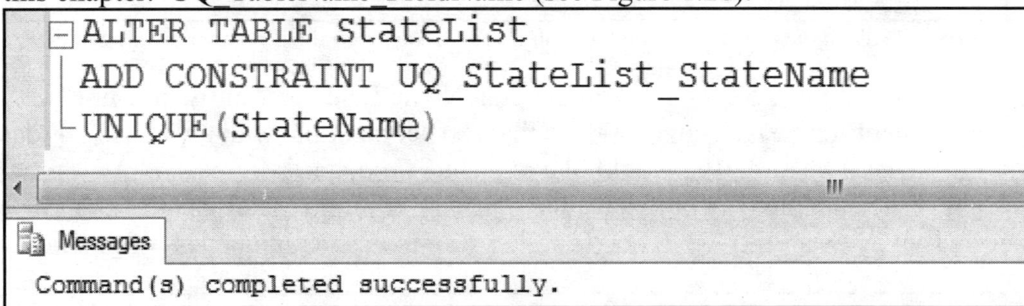

Figure 1.26 Code to create a unique constraint on the StateName field of the StateList table.

Let's test our new constraint by attempting to insert a record which would duplicate the StateName Alaska. Success! The constraint disallows the insert.

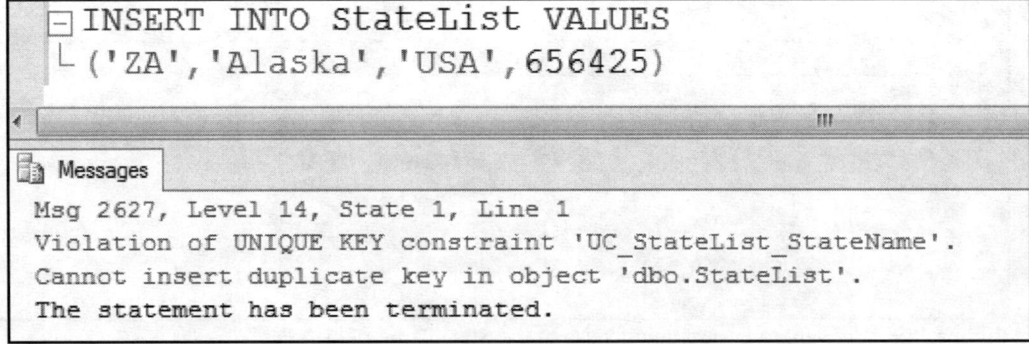

Figure 1.27 The unique constraint does not allow you to insert 'Alaska' twice.

Let's turn to the RoomChart table for our next example. An earlier Skill Check exercise added a primary key constraint to the ID field (as shown in Figure 1.22). Suppose we are given a new requirement that no two RoomDescription values should be duplicated in the RoomChart table (see Figure 1.28).

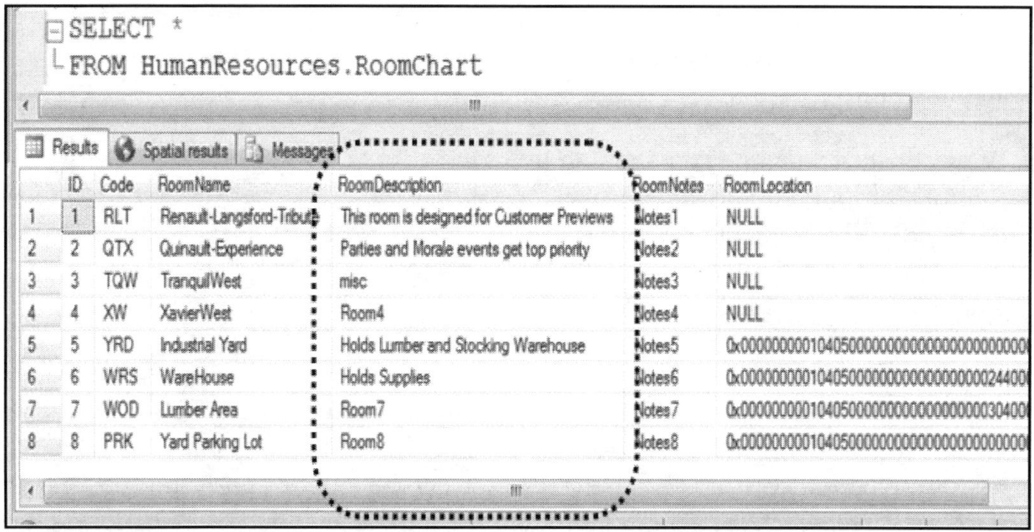
SELECT *
FROM HumanResources.RoomChart
Results
Spatial results
Messages

	ID	Code	RoomName	RoomDescription	RoomNotes	RoomLocation
1	1	RLT	Renault-Langsford-Tribut	This room is designed for Customer Previews	Notes1	NULL
2	2	QTX	Quinault-Experience	Parties and Morale events get top priority	Notes2	NULL
3	3	TQW	TranquilWest	misc	Notes3	NULL
4	4	XW	XavierWest	Room4	Notes4	NULL
5	5	YRD	Industrial Yard	Holds Lumber and Stocking Warehouse	Notes5	0x000000000104050000000000000000000000000
6	6	WRS	WareHouse	Holds Supplies	Notes6	0x000000000104050000000000000000024400
7	7	WOD	Lumber Area	Room7	Notes7	0x000000000104050000000000000000030400
8	8	PRK	Yard Parking Lot	Room8	Notes8	0x000000000104050000000000000000000000000

Figure 1.28 No two RoomDescription fields can be the same in the RoomChart table.

We need to add a unique constraint to the RoomDescription field. Our new unique constraint, UQ_RoomChart_RoomDescription, will prevent duplicate descriptions from appearing in this field (see Figure 1.29).

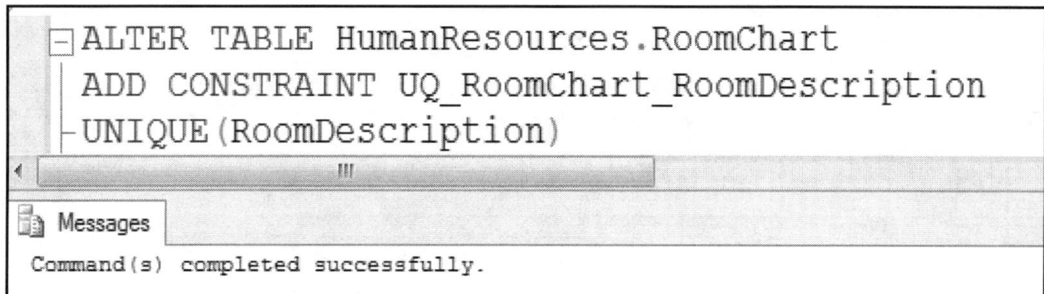
ALTER TABLE HumanResources.RoomChart
ADD CONSTRAINT UQ_RoomChart_RoomDescription
UNIQUE(RoomDescription)
Messages
Command(s) completed successfully.

Figure 1.29 Code to add a unique constraint to the RoomDescription field of the RoomChart table.

Unique Constraint Considerations

Open Object Explorer and look at the details for the HumanResources.RoomChart table. The Columns folder contains the specifics for each field in the RoomChart table (field name, data type, and nullability).

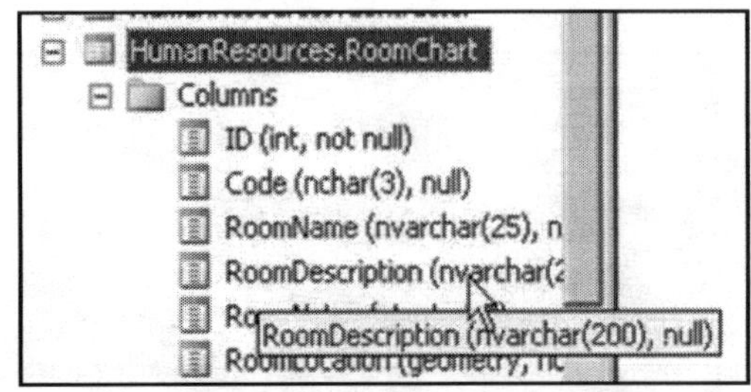

Figure 1.30 RoomDescription is an nvarchar(200) field that can take up to 400 bytes in your memory page.

We just added a unique constraint to the RoomDescription field, which is an nvarchar(200). Thus far, that's the biggest field to which we've added a unique constraint. Each value in this field could take up to 400 bytes.

Suppose we receive an additional requirement saying that no two RoomNotes values may be duplicated. The RoomNotes field is an nText Data type. When you try to run the ALTER TABLE statement adding the unique constraint, you get an error message which references a problem with the data type. ***You can't put a unique constraint on a field having a data type over 900 bytes.***

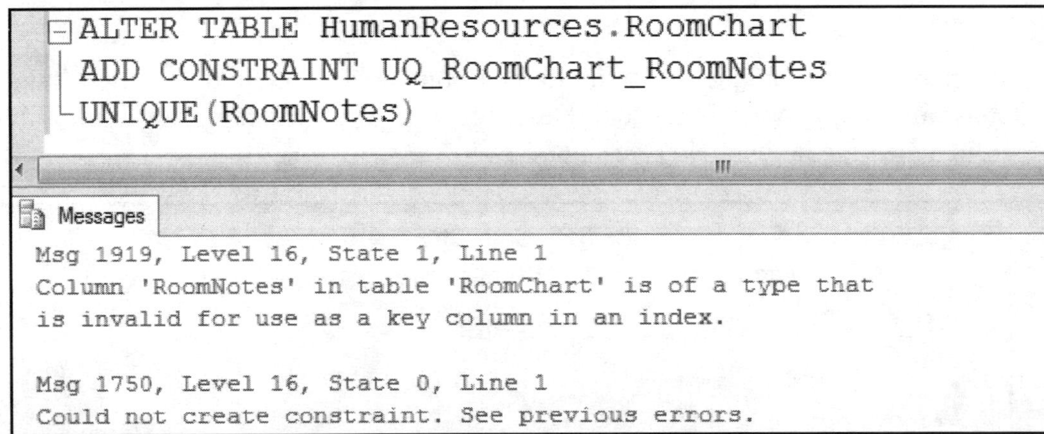

ALTER TABLE HumanResources.RoomChart
ADD CONSTRAINT UQ_RoomChart_RoomNotes
UNIQUE(RoomNotes)
Messages
Msg 1919, Level 16, State 1, Line 1
Column 'RoomNotes' in table 'RoomChart' is of a type that
is invalid for use as a key column in an index.
Msg 1750, Level 16, State 0, Line 1
Could not create constraint. See previous errors.

Figure 1.31 A unique constraint can't be added to a field with a data type over 900 bytes.

Unique constraints are limited to data types that are 900 bytes, or less. Examples of data types that cannot be made into a unique constraint are: Text, nText, Image, Geography, nvarchar(max) and varchar(max), varchar (901) and higher, and nvarchar (451) and higher.

Lab 1.2: Unique Constraints

Lab Prep: Before you can begin the lab, you must have SQL Server installed and have run the script SQLProgrammingChapter1.2Setup.sql. It is recommended that you view the lab video instructions in Lab1.2_UniqueConstraints.wmv.

Skill Check 1: Create a unique constraint called UQ_RoomChart_RoomName on the RoomName field of the RoomChart table. Verify your new constraint in the Object Explorer.

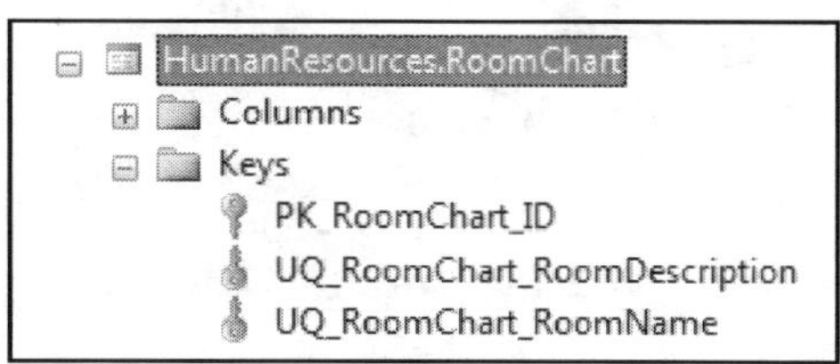

Figure 1.32 Skill Check 1.

Skill Check 2: Create a unique constraint called UQ_MgmtTraining_ClassName on the ClassName field of the MgmtTraining table. Verify your new constraint in the Object Explorer.

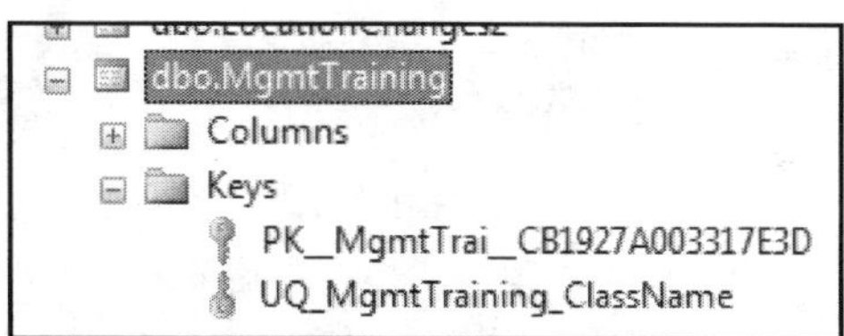

Figure 1.33 Skill Check 2

Skill Check 3: Management wants unique constraints on the HumanResources.Vendor table. They say the Email will never be duplicated and neither will Description. Write the code to create one of these constraints and a comment on why the other is not possible. *(Note: There is no result figure for Skill Check 3, since it would give away the answer.)*

Answer Code: The T-SQL code to this lab can be found in the downloadable files in a file named Lab1.2_UniqueConstraints.sql.

Unique Constraints - Points to Ponder

1. Unique constraints ensure a column will never contain duplicate values.
2. Unique constraints will allow up to one null value.
3. If your data type does not allow nulls and you put a unique constraint on it, then your field will have no null values.
4. A table can have only one primary key but it may have many unique constraints.
5. Indexes on fields cannot include LOB types like text, varchar(max), image, and XML.
6. Unique constraints cannot be placed on fields using the sparse data type feature. (The sparse data option is covered in *Joes 2 Pros* Volume 3, Chapter 4.)
7. Unique constraints can be applied on a composite of multiple fields to ensure uniqueness of records.
   Example: City + State in the StateList table.

Default Constraints

Another useful tool for protecting table data is the establishment of **default values** wherever possible.

Until this point in the *Joes 2 Pros* series, most of the values we've entered into empty fields have been our own user-supplied values or a function (e.g., CURRENT_TIMESTAMP). The only alternative we've seen is the possible use of a null value (i.e., assuming the field is nullable). (Chapter 3 in *SQL Queries Joes 2 Pros* (Volume 2) explores the use and functionality of null fields.) Non-nullable fields are helpful for steering your users into providing data, rather than leaving null values. A field having some data is usually preferable to no data, but you have no guarantee the data will be clean (i.e., free of typos or errors) or even meaningful.

Even if the default value is a temporary placeholder (as we will see in our first example), supplying a default value reduces the likelihood of null values in your data because you've offered users a reasonable value for those fields.

Defaults are the only type of constraints which don't actually restrict data entry. Unless the default value is the only possible value for a field, users are able to enter their own value.

Creating and Using Default Constraints

A default constraint may be added to a field in an existing table (using ALTER TABLE), or it may be added to a field at the time you create a table (using CREATE TABLE – this will be shown in the final section of this chapter).

Our first example will add a default constraint to the Status field of the Employee table. As we can see from the current dataset, the status for most of our employees is "Active" (see Figure 1.34). Recall that the newest hires (i.e., Janis Smith and Phil Wilconkinski) arrived two years ago (both were hired in 2009 during the production of *SQL Queries Joes 2 Pros (Volume 2))*. JProCo is currently experiencing an upswing in activity and needs to hire a number of additional people. They have developed a thorough orientation and onboarding process to ramp up new hires on the company's business and processes, as well as role-specific training.

The new Status category "Orientation" has been added to the business requirements for the Employee table. All new hire records will receive the "Orientation" Status by default. After each employee completes the extensive onboarding process, the Status will be upgraded to "Active."

```
SELECT * FROM Employee
```

Results | Messages

	EmpID	LastName	FirstName	HireDate	LocationID	ManagerID	Status	HiredOffset	TimeZone
1	1	Adams	Alex	2001-01-01...	1	11	Active	2001-01-01...	-08:00
2	2	Brown	Barry	2002-08-12...	1	11	Active	2002-08-12...	-08:00
3	3	Osako	Lee	1999-09-01...	2	11	Active	1999-09-01...	-05:00
4	4	Kennson	David	1996-03-16...	1	11	Has Tenure	1996-03-16...	-08:00
5	5	Bender	Eric	2007-05-17...	1	11	Active	2007-05-17...	-08:00
6	6	Kendall	Lisa	2001-11-15...	4	4	Active	2001-11-15...	-08:00
7	7	Lonning	David	2000-01-01...	1	11	On Leave	2000-01-01...	-08:00
8	8	Marshbank	John	2001-11-15...	NULL	4	Active	2001-11-15...	-06:00
9	9	Newton	James	2003-09-30...	2	3	Active	2003-09-30...	-05:00
10	10	O'Haire	Terry	2004-10-04...	2	3	Active	2004-10-04...	-05:00
11	11	Smith	Sally	1989-04-01...	1	NULL	Active	1989-04-01...	-08:00
12	12	O'Neil	Barbara	1995-05-26...	4	4	Has Tenure	1995-05-26...	-08:00
13	13	Wilconkinski	Phil	2009-06-11...	1	11	Active	2009-06-11...	-08:00
14	14	Smith	Janis	2009-10-18...	1	4	Active	2009-10-18...	-08:00

Figure 1.34 The Status field of the Employee table is upgraded to 'Active' after Orientation.

First we will alter the Employee table to add this default constraint on the Status field. Then we will add several of JProCo's new hires to the Employee table.

The syntax to add the *default constraint* is similar to the other constraints we create in this chapter. We begin with an ALTER TABLE statement, an ADD CONSTRAINT clause which names the constraint (DF_TableName_FieldName), and finally a clause which defines the specific behavior of the constraint. In this case, the specific behavior is that "Orientation" will be the default value for the Status field (see Figure 1.35).

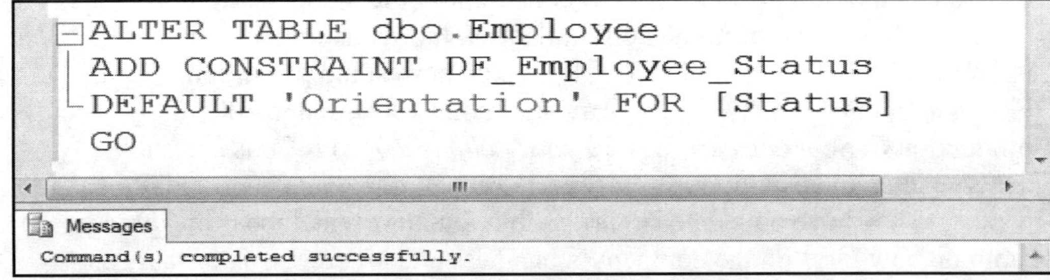

```
ALTER TABLE dbo.Employee
ADD CONSTRAINT DF_Employee_Status
DEFAULT 'Orientation' FOR [Status]
GO
```

Messages

```
Command(s) completed successfully.
```

Figure 1.35 The default constraint, DF_Employee_Status, is created.

When you type this code into your query window, try removing the delimiting brackets around the keyword Status and notice that it turns blue. This is because

Status is a reserved keyword. In this instance (Figure 1.35), SQL Server will allow the statement to complete even without the brackets. But because this isn't always the case, the best practice recommendation is to bracket reserved words when you use them as names of database objects (e.g., the State field, the Grant table, and the Status field). This also helps keep the color scheme of your coding consistent (e.g., keywords appear in one color, db objects appear in another color, and so forth).

Before we see DF_Employee_Status in action, let's briefly look at the changes visible in SSMS following the creation of this new default constraint (see Figure 1.36). The only change to the Object Explorer tree appears to be the addition of DF_Employee_Status in the Constraints folder of the Employee table. The design view of the Employee table hasn't changed (upper right corner of Figure 1.36). However, the Column Properties tab now shows the Default Value ("Orientation").

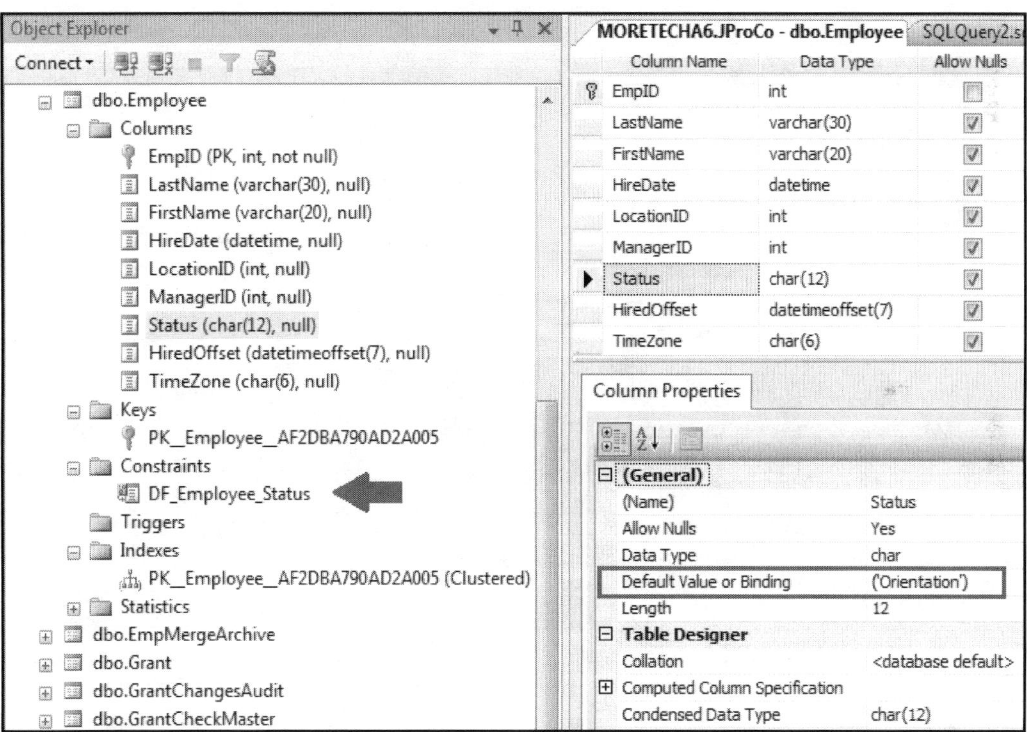

Figure 1.36 The Object Explorer tree and the design view of dbo.Employee following creation of the default constraint DF_Employee_Status.

Let's begin by adding the newest JProCo hire and see the effect of our new default constraint (see Figure 1.37). Tess Jones is the employee and she will work in the Seattle office (Location 1) for Manager 11. Since Tess hasn't yet completed the orientation process, her Status must be the default value ("Orientation").

In order to better visualize each field and value, we've copied the Column names from the Object Explorer (click and drag the Columns folder icon into the query window) and are inserting the values by name, instead of position (see Figure 1.37). (*Note:* Inserting values by name and by position is covered in *SQL Queries Joes 2 Pros*, Chap 3, p. 116.)

After running the INSERT INTO statement, we run the SELECT query (shown in the lower query window) to see all 15 Employee records, including Tess Jones and her Status value of "Orientation" (see Figure 1.37).

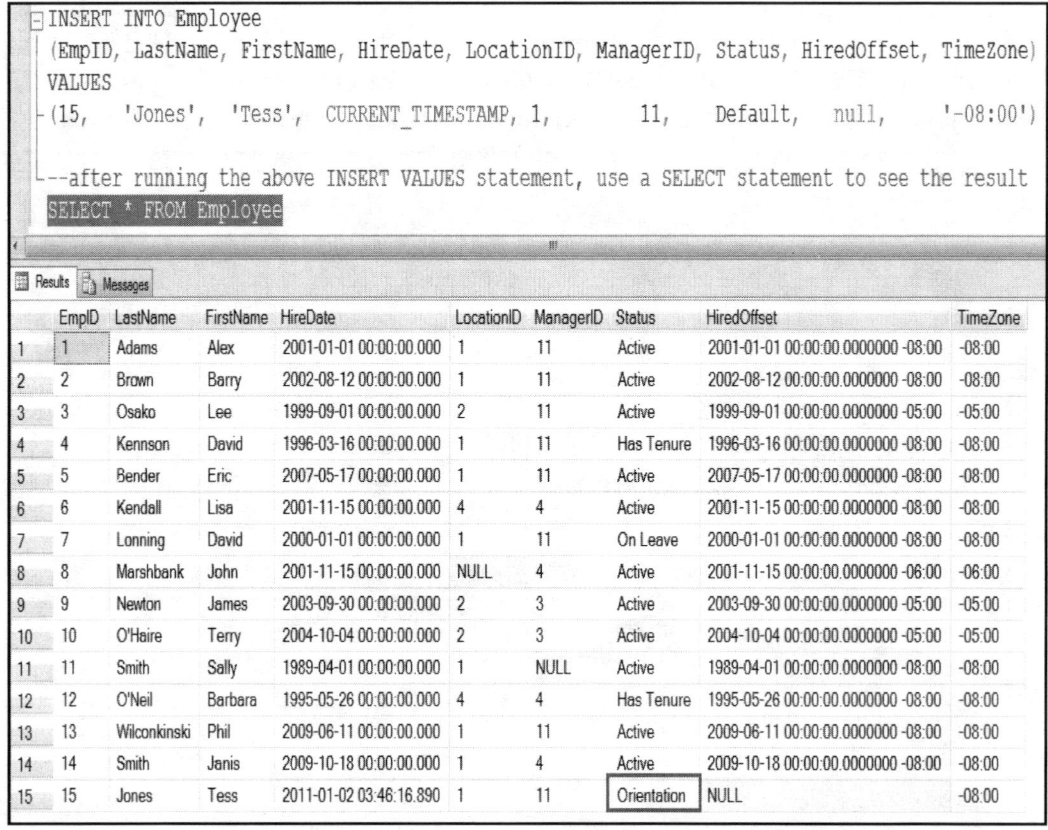

```
INSERT INTO Employee
(EmpID, LastName, FirstName, HireDate, LocationID, ManagerID, Status, HiredOffset, TimeZone)
VALUES
(15,    'Jones',   'Tess',   CURRENT_TIMESTAMP, 1,        11,    Default,   null,      '-08:00')

--after running the above INSERT VALUES statement, use a SELECT statement to see the result
SELECT * FROM Employee
```

Results | Messages

	EmpID	LastName	FirstName	HireDate	LocationID	ManagerID	Status	HiredOffset	TimeZone
1	1	Adams	Alex	2001-01-01 00:00:00.000	1	11	Active	2001-01-01 00:00:00.0000000 -08:00	-08:00
2	2	Brown	Barry	2002-08-12 00:00:00.000	1	11	Active	2002-08-12 00:00:00.0000000 -08:00	-08:00
3	3	Osako	Lee	1999-09-01 00:00:00.000	2	11	Active	1999-09-01 00:00:00.0000000 -05:00	-05:00
4	4	Kennson	David	1996-03-16 00:00:00.000	1	11	Has Tenure	1996-03-16 00:00:00.0000000 -08:00	-08:00
5	5	Bender	Eric	2007-05-17 00:00:00.000	1	11	Active	2007-05-17 00:00:00.0000000 -08:00	-08:00
6	6	Kendall	Lisa	2001-11-15 00:00:00.000	4	4	Active	2001-11-15 00:00:00.0000000 -08:00	-08:00
7	7	Lonning	David	2000-01-01 00:00:00.000	1	11	On Leave	2000-01-01 00:00:00.0000000 -08:00	-08:00
8	8	Marshbank	John	2001-11-15 00:00:00.000	NULL	4	Active	2001-11-15 00:00:00.0000000 -06:00	-06:00
9	9	Newton	James	2003-09-30 00:00:00.000	2	3	Active	2003-09-30 00:00:00.0000000 -05:00	-05:00
10	10	O'Haire	Terry	2004-10-04 00:00:00.000	2	3	Active	2004-10-04 00:00:00.0000000 -05:00	-05:00
11	11	Smith	Sally	1989-04-01 00:00:00.000	1	NULL	Active	1989-04-01 00:00:00.0000000 -08:00	-08:00
12	12	O'Neil	Barbara	1995-05-26 00:00:00.000	4	4	Has Tenure	1995-05-26 00:00:00.0000000 -08:00	-08:00
13	13	Wilconkinski	Phil	2009-06-11 00:00:00.000	1	11	Active	2009-06-11 00:00:00.0000000 -08:00	-08:00
14	14	Smith	Janis	2009-10-18 00:00:00.000	1	4	Active	2009-10-18 00:00:00.0000000 -08:00	-08:00
15	15	Jones	Tess	2011-01-02 03:46:16.890	1	11	Orientation	NULL	-08:00

Figure 1.37 Using the Default keyword in this insert statement has the same effect as explicitly inserting the value "Orientation" into the Status field.

Notice that the TimeZone field indicates that nearly all of JProCo's employees work in the same timezone (-08:00, signifying GMT minus 8 hours, which corresponds to Pacific Time and includes the west coasts of the U.S. and Canada).

Before we add our next new hire record, we will add the default value of -08:00 to the TimeZone field. The ALTER TABLE statement to accomplish this is similar to the statement we ran to create the default constraint on the Status field (shown in Figure 1.35). Run the code you see here to create DF_Employee_TimeZone (see Figure 1.38).

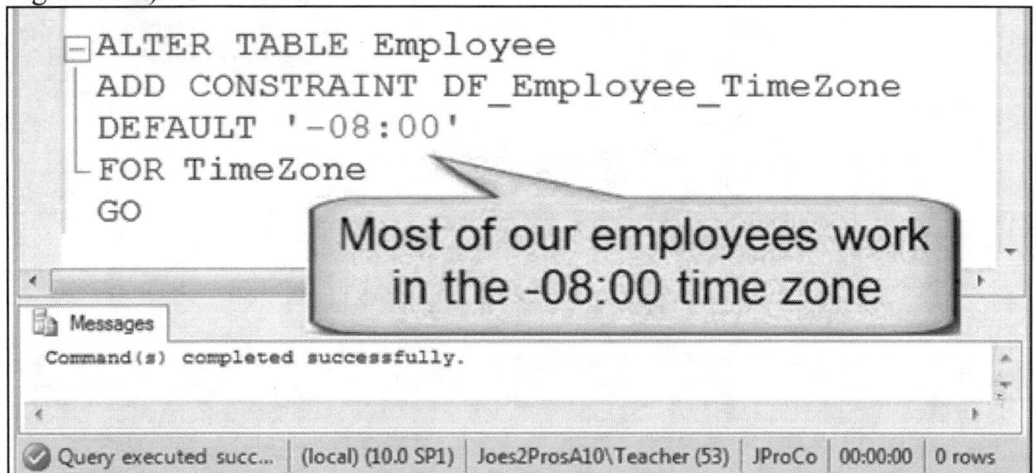

ALTER TABLE Employee
ADD CONSTRAINT DF_Employee_TimeZone
DEFAULT '-08:00'
FOR TimeZone
GO
Most of our employees work in the -08:00 time zone
Messages
Command(s) completed successfully.
Query executed succ... | (local) (10.0 SP1) | Joes2ProsA10\Teacher (53) | JProCo | 00:00:00 | 0 rows

Figure 1.38 The code to create -08:00 as the default for the TimeZone field of the Employee table.

When we add our next new hire record (for Nancy Biggs), we're able use both of our defaults. Nancy's initial status is Orientation, and she will work in the Seattle Headquarters, which is in the -8:00 time zone. The second default keyword will use the value from the DF_Employee_TimeZone default constraint (see Figure 1.39).

```
INSERT INTO Employee
(EmpID, LastName, FirstName, HireDate, LocationID, ManagerID, Status, HiredOffset, TimeZone)
VALUES
(16,   'Biggs',  'Nancy', CURRENT_TIMESTAMP, 1,        11,    Default,  null,      Default)
```

Messages

(1 row(s) affected)

Figure 1.39 We want -08:00 to be the default value for the last field of the Employee table.

Let's run a SELECT statement to see all 16 records in the Employee table, including the new record for Nancy Biggs. Notice that Nancy's TimeZone value is -08:00, as we expected (see Figure 1.40).

```
SELECT * FROM Employee
```

Results | Messages

	EmpID	LastName	FirstName	HireDate	LocationID	ManagerID	Status	HiredOffset	TimeZone
1	1	Adams	Alex	2001-01-01...	1	11	Active	2001-01-01 ...	-08:00
2	2	Brown	Barry	2002-08-12...	1	11	Active	2002-08-12 ...	-08:00
3	3	Osako	Lee	1999-09-01...	2	11	Active	1999-09-01 ...	-05:00
4	4	Kennson	David	1996-03-16...	1	11	Has Tenure	1996-03-16 ...	-08:00
5	5	Bender	Eric	2007-05-17...	1	11	Active	2007-05-17 ...	-08:00
6	6	Kendall	Lisa	2001-11-15...	4	4	Active	2001-11-15 ...	-08:00
7	7	Lonning	David	2000-01-01...	1	11	On Leave	2000-01-01 ...	-08:00
8	8	Marshbank	John	2001-11-15...	NULL	4	Active	2001-11-15 ...	-06:00
9	9	Newton	James	2003-09-30...	2	3	Active	2003-09-30 ...	-05:00
10	10	O'Haire	Terry	2004-10-04...	2	3	Active	2004-10-04 ...	-05:00
11	11	Smith	Sally	1989-04-01...	1	NULL	Active	1989-04-01 ...	-08:00
12	12	O'Neil	Barbara	1995-05-26...	4	4	Has Tenure	1995-05-26 ...	-08:00
13	13	Wilconkinski	Phil	2009-06-11...	1	11	Active	2009-06-11 ...	-08:00
14	14	Smith	Janis	2009-10-18...	1	4	Active	2009-10-18 ...	-08:00
15	15	Jones	Tess	2011-01-02...	1	11	Orientation	NULL	-08:00
16	16	Biggs	Nancy	2011-01-02...	1	11	Orientation	NULL	-08:00

Figure 1.40 Nancy Biggs' record shows both default values, Orientation and -08:00.

Dynamic Defaults

You may notice that each employee record includes their HireDate as well as a HiredOffset value, which is a combination of HireDate + TimeZone.

A default constraint can make coding of dynamic values much easier for reuse. Our next step will be to add a default constraint to the HiredOffset field. Being able to type "Default" in an INSERT statement rather than a lengthy expression saves us a significant number of keystrokes and is a great use of the default constraint.

Alter the Employee table to add a constraint named **DF_Employee_HiredOffset** where the value will be an expression using the ToDateTimeOffset function with the Current_Timestamp property (Figure 1.41).

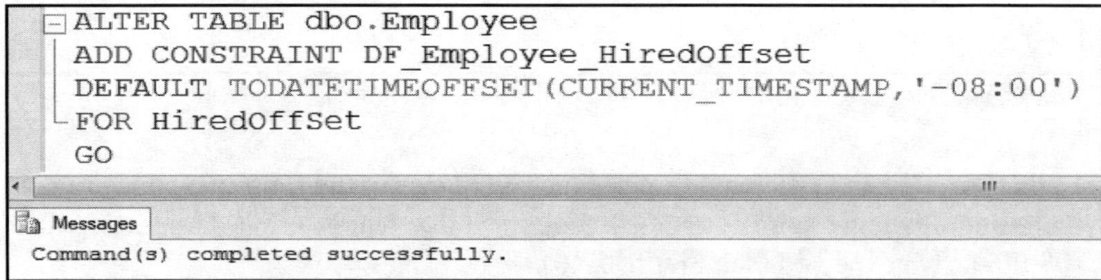

```
ALTER TABLE dbo.Employee
ADD CONSTRAINT DF_Employee_HiredOffset
DEFAULT TODATETIMEOFFSET(CURRENT_TIMESTAMP,'-08:00')
FOR HiredOffSet
GO
```

Messages

```
Command(s) completed successfully.
```

Figure 1.41 The default constraint, DF_Employee_HiredOffset, is created.

We will now add the next new JProCo employee, Wendy Downs. Since Wendy will also work in the Seattle Headquarters office, we can use all three default values in her INSERT INTO statement (see Figure 1.42).

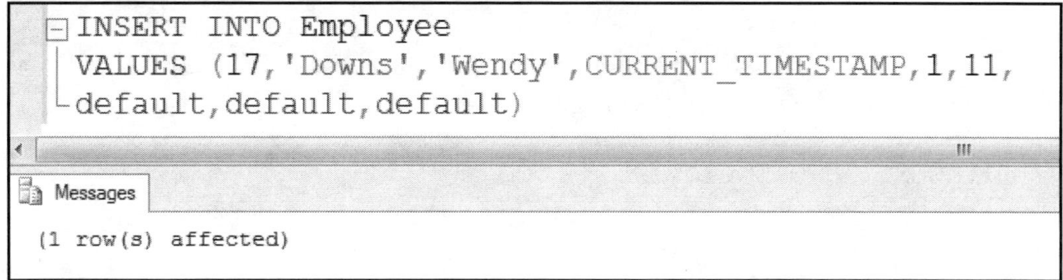

```
INSERT INTO Employee
VALUES (17,'Downs','Wendy',CURRENT_TIMESTAMP,1,11,
default,default,default)
```

Messages

```
(1 row(s) affected)
```

Figure 1.42 Wendy's INSERT statement utilizes the default value for three fields.

Let's rerun a SELECT statement to see all 17 records in the Employee table (see Figure 1.43). We see all of Wendy's values appearing, as expected.

```
SELECT * FROM Employee
```

Results | Messages

	EmpID	LastName	FirstName	HireDate	LocationID	ManagerID	Status	HiredOffset	TimeZon
1	1	Adams	Alex	2001-01-01 ...	1	11	Active	2001-01-01 ...	-08:00
2	2	Brown	Barry	2002-08-12 ...	1	11	Active	2002-08-12 ...	-08:00
3	3	Osako	Lee	1999-09-01 ...	2	11	Active	1999-09-01 ...	-05:00
4	4	Kennson	David	1996-03-16 ...	1	11	Has Tenure	1996-03-16 ...	-08:00
5	5	Bender	Eric	2007-05-17 ...	1	11	Active	2007-05-17 ...	-08:00
6	6	Kendall	Lisa	2001-11-15 ...	4	4	Active	2001-11-15 ...	-08:00
7	7	Lonning	David	2000-01-01 ...	1	11	On Leave	2000-01-01 ...	-08:00
8	8	Marshbank	John	2001-11-15 ...	NULL	4	Active	2001-11-15 ...	-06:00
9	9	Newton	James	2003-09-30 ...	2	3	Active	2003-09-30 ...	-05:00
10	10	O'Haire	Terry	2004-10-04 ...	2	3	Active	2004-10-04 ...	-05:00
11	11	Smith	Sally	1989-04-01 ...	1	NULL	Active	1989-04-01 ...	-08:00
12	12	O'Neil	Barbara	1995-05-26 ...	4	4	Has Tenure	1995-05-26 ...	-08:00
13	13	Wilconkinski	Phil	2009-06-11 ...	1	11	Active	2009-06-11 ...	-08:00
14	14	Smith	Janis	2009-10-18 ...	1	4	Active	2009-10-18 ...	-08:00
15	15	Jones	Tess	2011-01-02 ...	1	11	Orientation	NULL	-08:00
16	16	Biggs	Nancy	2011-01-02 ...	1	11	Orientation	NULL	-08:00
17	17	Downs	Wendy	2011-01-02 ...	1	11	Orientation	2011-01-02 ...	-08:00

Figure 1.43 Wendy's record appears as we expected. The default value was inserted for 3 fields.

Overriding Default Constraints

To insert a record with a value other than the default, simply include the explicit value in the INSERT statement.

We will test this by attempting to insert a test record with "HIRE DELAYED" as the value for the Status field (see Figure 1.44).

```
INSERT INTO Employee
VALUES (98,'Test','InsertRecord',CURRENT_TIMESTAMP,1,11,
'HIRE DELAYED',default,default)
```

Messages

```
(1 row(s) affected)
```

Figure 1.44 We want to override the default value of the Status field.

Our test inserted the value, as we expected. The Status value of our test record is "HIRE DELAYED" (see Figure 1.45).

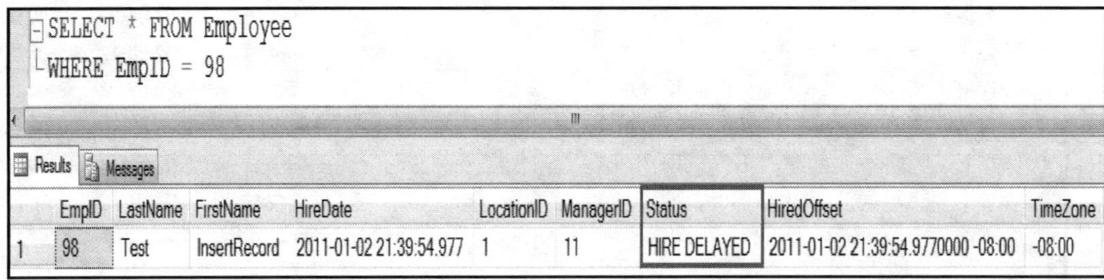

Figure 1.45 Our explicit value ("Hired Delayed") overrode the default.

Removing Default Constraints

The code syntax shown here will remove a default constraint, in case you no longer wish to have the default enabled on your field (see Figure 1.46).

```
ALTER TABLE dbo.Employee
DROP DF_Employee_Status
GO

ALTER TABLE dbo.Employee
DROP DF_Employee_HiredOffset
GO
```

Messages

Command(s) completed successfully.

Figure 1.46 The code syntax for removing default constraints.

This inserted test record includes the default keyword for the two fields (Status and HiredOffset) which no longer have default constraints (see Figure 1.47).

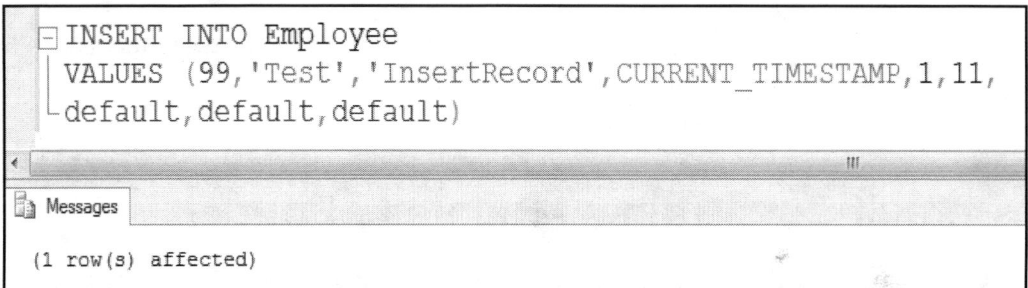
INSERT INTO Employee
VALUES (99,'Test','InsertRecord',CURRENT_TIMESTAMP,1,11,
default,default,default)
Messages
(1 row(s) affected)

Figure 1.47 We will insert a test record to see the effect of removing the default from two fields.

The keyword "Default" in the insert statement results in a null value for both fields (see Figure 1.48).

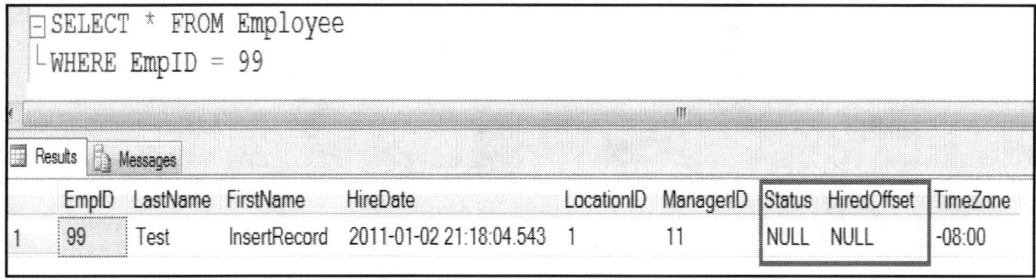
SELECT * FROM Employee
WHERE EmpID = 99
Results
Messages

	EmpID	LastName	FirstName	HireDate	LocationID	ManagerID	Status	HiredOffset	TimeZone
1	99	Test	InsertRecord	2011-01-02 21:18:04.543	1	11	NULL	NULL	-08:00

Figure 1.48 The default keyword added nulls to the fields after 2 default constraints were removed.

Lab 1.3: Default Constraints

Lab Prep: Before you can begin the lab, you must have SQL Server installed and have run the script SQLProgrammingChapter1.3Setup.sql. View the lab video instructions in Lab1.3_DefaultConstraints.wmv.

Skill Check 1: Create a default constraint named DF_Employee_LocationID that sets the default for the LocationID field of the Employee table to 1.

Skill Check 2: Create a default constraint that sets the UnitDiscount field of the SalesInvoiceDetail table to 0 (zero). Use proper naming conventions for your constraint.

Skill Check 3: Create a default constraint that sets the OrderDate field of the SalesInvoice table to the current date and time using the Current_Timestamp property.

Answer Code: The T-SQL code to this lab can be found in the downloadable files in a file named Lab1.3_DefaultConstraints.sql.

Default Constraints - Points to Ponder

1. A default constraint enters a value in a column when one is not specified in an INSERT or UPDATE statement.
2. The ALTER TABLE statement modifies a table definition by altering, adding, or dropping columns and constraints, reassigning partitions, or disabling or enabling constraints and triggers.
3. Default constraints can be created on fields in your table.
4. The DEFAULT keyword defines a value that is used if the user doesn't specify a value for the column.
5. Defaults may not be added to timestamp data types or to identity fields.
6. Defaults are the only type of constraints which don’t actually restrict data entry.

Data Integrity

Dictionary definitions of the term "integrity" include helpful terms like incorruptibility, soundness, and wholeness. In the world of relational databases, the term "data integrity" denotes a system of processes and constraints established to ensure that data remains intact, adheres to business rules, and is not adversely impacted (i.e., corrupted) by user input or by database operations. The specific requirements to uphold data integrity will vary from database to database according to the purpose of the database and its attendant level of complexity and criticality.

Constraints are objects which support and enforce data integrity. Each of the constraints we've explored in this chapter plays a role in your data integrity strategy, which should be executed on three levels: *domain integrity*, *entity integrity*, and *referential integrity*.

1) **Domain integrity.** Only values which meet the criteria of the column should be allowed into the table. In other words, *domain integrity* is achieved when constraints ensure that each value allowed to be inserted into a column falls within the *domain* of acceptable values for the column. Check constraints help enforce domain integrity by rejecting any DML statement which would introduce unacceptable values.
2) **Entity integrity.** This principle defines each row as a unique entity in a table. Primary keys and unique constraints enforce *entity integrity.* They evaluate each proposed value, compare it to the set of existing values, and disallow any statement which would introduce an unacceptable value (i.e., null or non-unique).
3) **Referential integrity.** This principle involves fields which are present across your database tables. The foreign key constraint enforces the rule that columnar values referenced by another column (often within another table) must be in sync with the chief instance of the field. This is frequently accomplished with the help of lookup or mapping tables. *Example:* Each record in the Employee table includes the LocationID for the site where the employee works. LocationID is a primary key in the Location table. The Location table is the source of the master Location data – any column which references location data must look to the Location table in order to ensure that it contains accurate location data. The LocationID field in the Employee table is a foreign key. This foreign key ensures that only values from Location.LocationID will be allowed into the Employee.LocationID field. The foreign key constraint will reject any DML statement which introduces a LocationID not found in Location.LocationID.

Since we've become well-versed in the various types of data constraints (data types, primary keys, check constraints, unique constraints, and default constraints), this will speed our comprehension of implementing data integrity methodology in our data model and database design. This section will also demonstrate the mechanics of foreign key constraints.

Domain Integrity

Recall the check constraint we enabled earlier on the StateList table, CK_StateList_LandMass. It allows only non-negative (>=0) values and those which are less than 2 million (square miles).

These constraints enforce our rules for valid data which should be allowed into the StateList table – good data is allowed in and bad data is kept out. This constraint preserves *domain integrity* in the StateList table (see Figures 1.49).

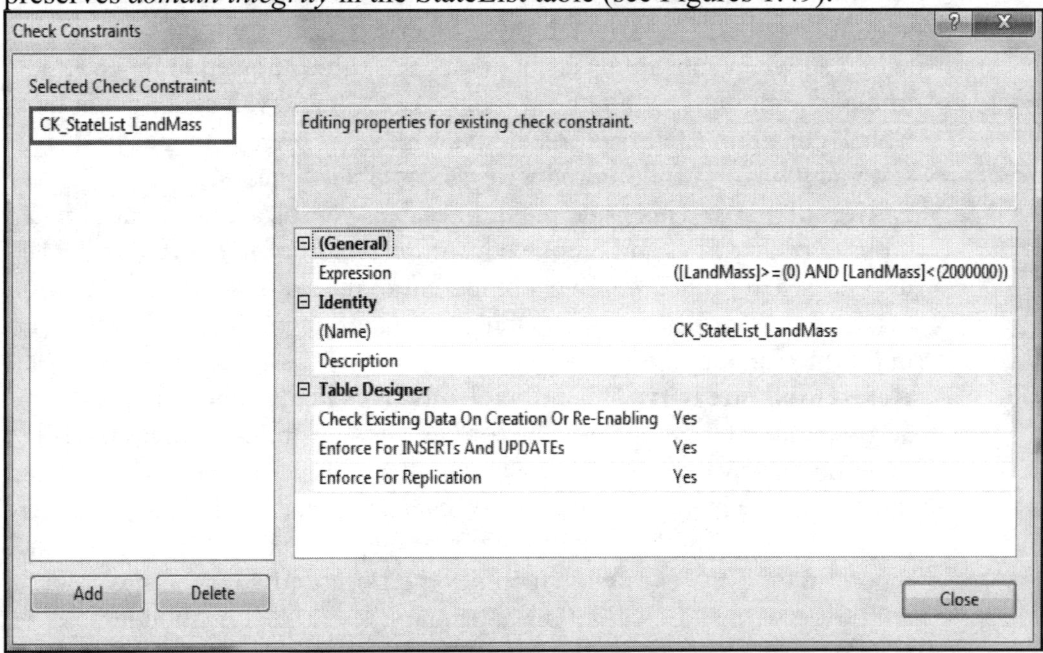

Figure 1.49 The check constraint CK_StateList_LandMass was created earlier in Figure 1.18.

(*Note:* The Check Constraints dialog showing the properties in Figure 1.49 may be seen by right-clicking the constraint in Object Explorer > Modify.)

The check constraint CK_StateList_LandMass blocks any DML statement which would place values greater than 2 million in the LandMass field.

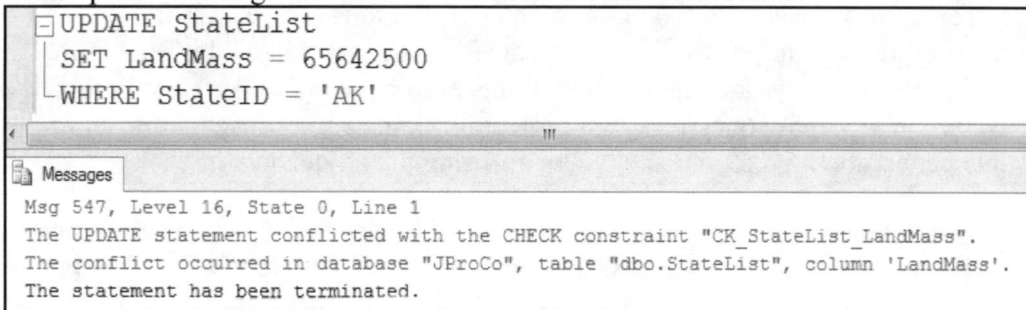

```
UPDATE StateList
SET LandMass = 65642500
WHERE StateID = 'AK'
```

Messages

```
Msg 547, Level 16, State 0, Line 1
The UPDATE statement conflicted with the CHECK constraint "CK_StateList_LandMass".
The conflict occurred in database "JProCo", table "dbo.StateList", column 'LandMass'.
The statement has been terminated.
```

Figure 1.50 The check constraint enforces domain integrity.

Before the CK_StateList_LandMass check constraint allows a value into the LandMass field, it confirms whether the proposed value meets the criteria.

Negative values and values >2 million are not allowed. This check constraint enforces *domain integrity*.

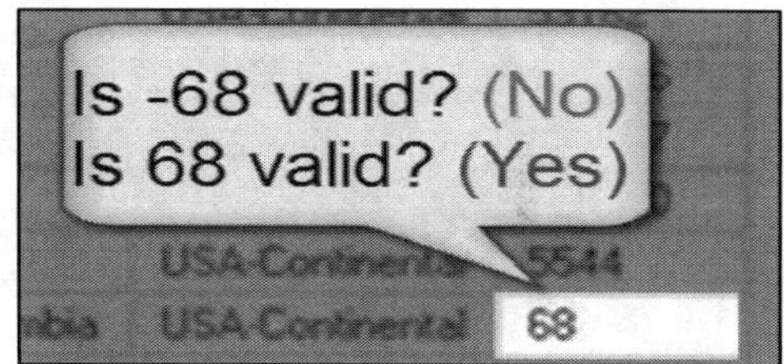

Figure 1.51 Negative numbers are not valid values for the LandMass field.

```
SELECT * FROM StateList
```

Results | Messages

StateID	StateName	RegionName	LandMass
AK	Alaska	USA	656425
AL	Alabama	USA-Continental	52423
AR	Arkansas	USA-Continental	53182
AZ	Arizona	USA-Continental	114006
CA	California	USA-Continental	163707
CO	Colorado	USA-Continental	104100
CO	Connecticut	USA-Continental	5544
DC	District of Columbia	USA-Continental	68
DE	Delaware	USA-Continental	2489
FL	Florida	USA-Continental	65758
GA	Georgia	USA-Continental	59441

Figure 1.52 A partial view of the dataset contained in the StateList table, which is protected by a check constraint. It is also protected by a primary key & unique constraint, which enforce *entity integrity*.

Entity Integrity

Because we've been focused on domain integrity, thus far we have ignored the primary key constraint which is also protecting the StateList table (see Figure 1.53). Primary keys and unique constraints enforce *entity integrity*. Whereas *domain integrity* is concerned with protecting single values in a column, *entity integrity* is about protecting a table by ensuring the uniqueness of each record.

PK_StateList_StateID is responsible for ensuring that each StateID value is unique and non-null. With each value you attempt to add to the StateID field, the primary key checks all the existing values to confirm that the proposed value isn't already present in the field.

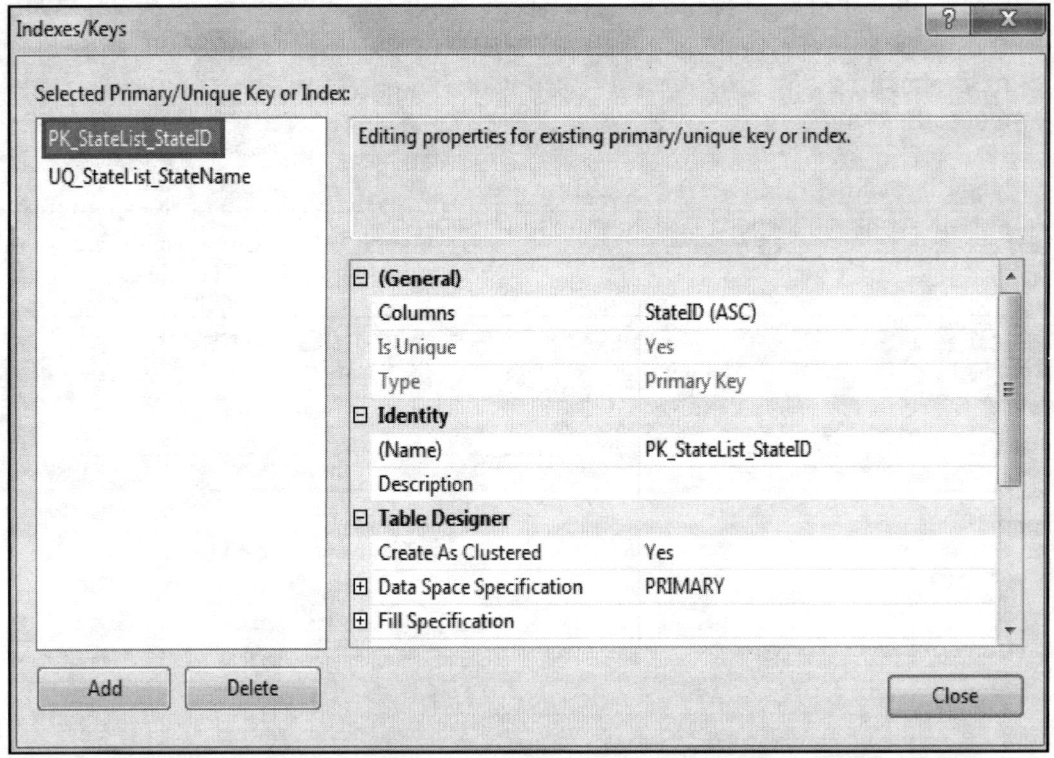

Figure 1.53 The primary key constraint PK_StateList_StateID ensures *entity integrity*.

The Indexes/Keys dialog (Figures 1.53 and 1.54) may be seen by right-clicking either constraint in the Object Explorer > Modify to open the design table interface. Right click in the design table UI > Indexes/Keys.

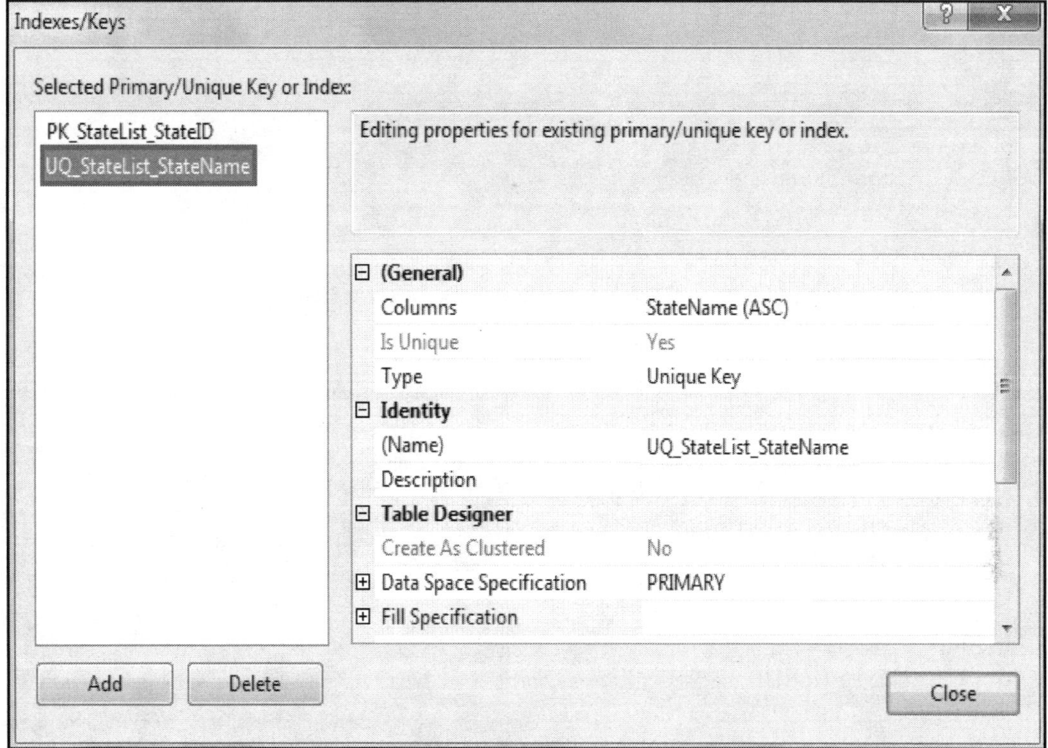

Figure 1.54 The unique constraint UQ_StateList_StateName was originally created in Figure 1.26.

Readers who have previously worked hands-on with relational databases will already be aware of the heavy emphasis placed on having a primary key for every table in your database. By ensuring uniqueness and non-nullability for each value of the StateID field, we eliminate the possibility of duplicate records in the StateList table. This ensures the integrity of the StateList entity. (Later in the discussion of referential integrity, we will also see that assuring integrity of the StateList entity at the field and table levels also helps ensure integrity of StateList in relation to other entities in the database.)

As we saw earlier (originally shown in Figure 1.10), this primary key constraint (PK_StateList_StateID) violation prevented the duplicate StateID value "CO" from entering the StateList table. The primary key rejects the value and effectively disallows the update (see Figure 1.55).

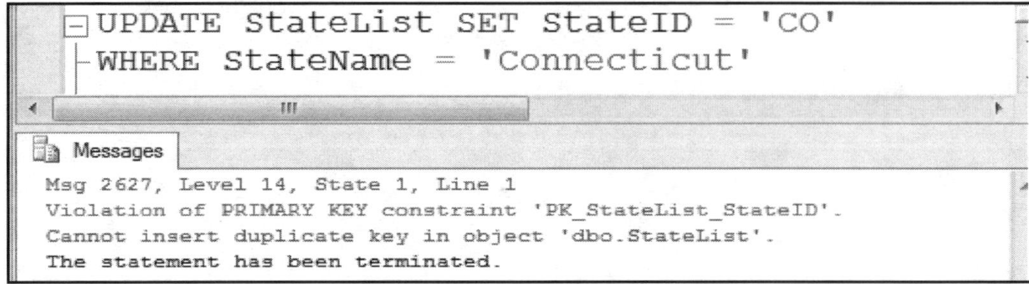

UPDATE StateList SET StateID = 'CO'
WHERE StateName = 'Connecticut'
Messages
Msg 2627, Level 14, State 1, Line 1
Violation of PRIMARY KEY constraint 'PK_StateList_StateID'.
Cannot insert duplicate key in object 'dbo.StateList'.
The statement has been terminated.

Figure 1.55 PK_StateList_StateID rejects this duplicate StateID value.

Notice the possible insert shown here (Figure 1.56) and consider whether this insert would be allowed. Currently there is no "TU" value existing in the StateID field; neither is there a "Tuskani" value in the StateName field. The value of 84,956 (square miles) fulfills the criteria for the LandMass field.

Yes, this insert would be allowed. Despite the fact that three of four fields each have constraints, an incorrect record could still slip into our table. Yikes!

TU | Tuskani | USA-NA | 84956

	StateID	StateName	RegionName	LandMass
1	AK	Alaska	USA	656425
2	AL	Alabama	USA-Continental	52423
3	AR	Arkansas	USA-Continental	53182
4	AZ	Arizona	USA-Continental	114006
5	CA	California	USA-Continental	163707
6	CO	Colorado	USA-Continental	104100
7	CT	Connecticut	USA-Continental	5544
8	DC	District of Columbia	USA-Continental	68
9	DE	Delaware	USA-Continental	2489
10	FL	Florida	USA-Continental	65758
11	GA	Georgia	USA-Continental	59441
12	HI	Hawaii	USA	10932
13	IA	Iowa	USA-Continental	56276
14	ID	Idaho	USA-Continental	83574
15	IL	Illinois	USA-Continental	57918

Figure 1.56 The primary key will check for an existing value 'TU' in the StateID field to enforce entity integrity.

This example illustrates that even a well-devised plan for data integrity can't prevent all unforeseen data. This brings us back to our seatbelt analogy. Implementing constraints as part of a comprehensive data integrity strategy is necessary – just as wearing seatbelts is legally required (and if you reside someplace where this isn't a legal requirement, you should be smart and wear them anyway!). But protecting your data also requires human intelligence and review – in the workplace, these are known as "sanity checks" of your data.

A helpful way of thinking about *entity integrity* is that "entities" are the main players in your business and thus are represented by the major tables in your database. For example, the entities in JProCo are Employee, Location, Customer, CurrentProducts, Grant, and Supplier. Fields are attributes of the entities (e.g., the attributes of each employee record are Name, ManagerID, HireDate, etc.). The

Employee table is the definitive source of information for our employees, so it's important that there be no duplicate records and that the data remain clean. The same is true for Location, Customer, and so forth.

The same is just as true for our StateList table, even though it is essentially a resource table. Other tables or objects relying on the StateList table depend upon the StateList data to be accurate. Adhering to the guideline that each table in your database should have a primary key is a smart way to keep your data safe and ensure uniqueness of each record in every table.

Referential Integrity

The concept of *referential integrity* is tied closely to our next topic, *foreign keys.* Whereas *domain integrity* is concerned with protecting the values in a column, and *entity integrity* requires that each record in a table be unique, *referential integrity* is about ensuring that your clean entity data (i.e., table data) remains just as squeaky clean and intact when it appears in other tables – in other words, when it is *referenced* by columns which most often are in other tables. Later you will see that foreign keys work hand-in-glove with primary keys in their enforcement of referential integrity.

Let's look at two related tables, Employee and Location (shown respectively in the upper and lower portions of Figure 1.57).

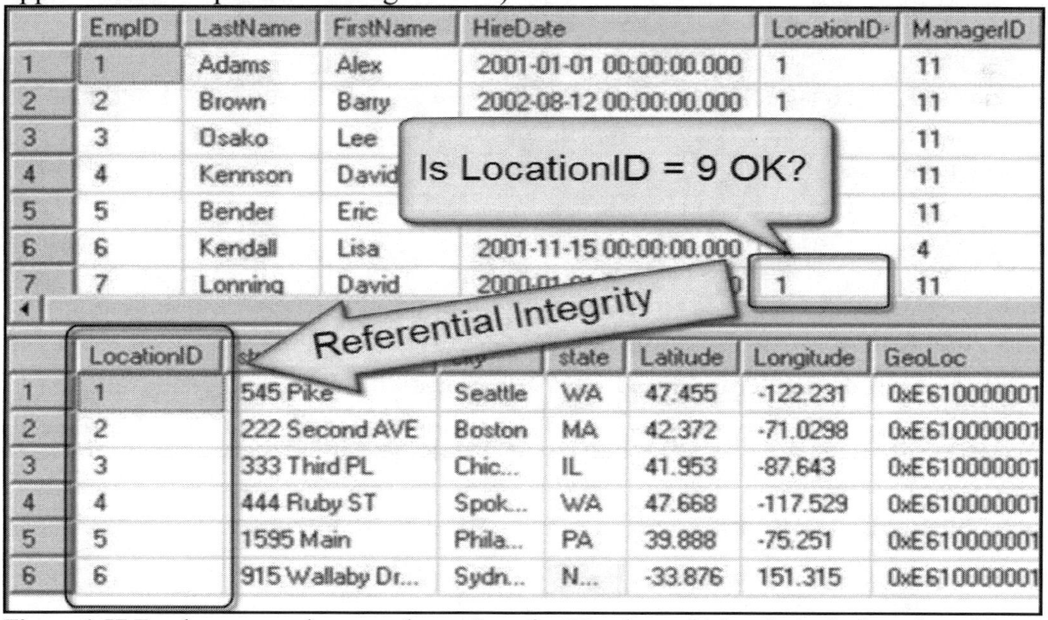

	EmpID	LastName	FirstName	HireDate	LocationID	ManagerID
1	1	Adams	Alex	2001-01-01 00:00:00.000	1	11
2	2	Brown	Barry	2002-08-12 00:00:00.000	1	11
3	3	Osako	Lee			11
4	4	Kennson	David			11
5	5	Bender	Eric			11
6	6	Kendall	Lisa	2001-11-15 00:00:00.000		4
7	7	Lonning	David	2000-01-0	1	11

Is LocationID = 9 OK?

Referential Integrity

	LocationID	st		state	Latitude	Longitude	GeoLoc
1	1	545 Pike	Seattle	WA	47.455	-122.231	0xE610000001
2	2	222 Second AVE	Boston	MA	42.372	-71.0298	0xE610000001
3	3	333 Third PL	Chic...	IL	41.953	-87.643	0xE610000001
4	4	444 Ruby ST	Spok...	WA	47.668	-117.529	0xE610000001
5	5	1595 Main	Phila...	PA	39.888	-75.251	0xE610000001
6	6	915 Wallaby Dr...	Sydn...	N...	-33.876	151.315	0xE610000001

Figure 1.57 Employee records may only use LocationID values which exist in the Location table.

The Location table is the definitive source for location information in the JProCo database. Any location data which is referenced by other tables must originate in the Location table. JProCo currently has six office locations. If the address or other vital information for a location changes (e.g., a new office is added, an office is closed), the data must first be updated in the Location table before it can cascade out to the other tables.

As illustrated in Figure 1.57, any value added to Employee.LocationID must be contained in the Location.LocationID field. In other words, the only legitimate values for LocationID are 1 through 6. Thus, if we enter a new employee record with a LocationID of 9, that data would be incorrect.

Similarly, the only legitimate values for the Employee.ManagerID field are those contained in the Employee.EmpID field. If an insert to the Employee table were to accept a non-existent ManagerID (e.g., 111), then the Employee table data would become incorrect (i.e., unusable due to invalid data) and *referential integrity* would be violated.

For a database to have sound data integrity, the principles of domain integrity, entity integrity, and referential integrity must be upheld. Since SQL Server is an RDMS (relational database management system), it offers many tools and prompts for enforcing data integrity in as systematic a way as possible.

Foreign Key Constraints

Foreign key constraints enforce *referential integrity*. The referential integrity topic mentioned that foreign keys and primary keys work hand-in-glove. The foreign key builds upon the primary key and *entity integrity* you have established in each of your database tables.

A simple way to think of a foreign key is that, essentially, it is another field which has a corresponding primary key field. Every foreign key field refers to another column which is a primary key field, most often in another table. The Employee.LocationID field references the Location.LocationID field (the Employee table is the *referencing table* and Location is the *referenced table* – the one which contains the definitive instance of the Location data).

Compare the two instances of the LocationID field in Figure 1.58 (Location.LocationID and Employee.LocationID). One noticeable difference between the primary key (Location.LocationID) versus the foreign key (Employee.LocationID) is that the values are non-unique in the foreign key. The master version of the location data in the Location table (i.e., the *referenced table*) contains one unique record for each JProCo office. However, the Employee table (i.e., the *referencing table*) naturally reflects many employees working at each location. In other words, the Location and Employee entities have a 1:Many relationship ("one-to-many relationship"). Notice that the same is true for Employee and Grant – one employee may have many grants (see Figure 1.58).

PK	GrantID	GrantName	FK EmpID	Amount
1	001	92 Purr_Scents %% team	7	4750.00
2	002	K-Land fund trust	2	15750.00
3	003	Robert@BigStarBank.com	7	18100.00
4	005	BIG 6's Foundation%	4	21000.00
5	006	TALTA_Kishan International	3	18100.00
6	007	Ben@MoreTechnology.com	10	41000.00
7	008	www.@-Last-U-Can-Help.com	7	25000.00
8	009	Thank you @.com	11	21500.00
9	010	Just Mom	5	9900.00
10	011	Big Giver Tom	7	95900.00
11	012	Mega Mercy	9	55000.00

Primary key

Foreign key

	EmpID	LastName	FirstName	HireDate	LocationID	ManagerID
1	1	Adams	Alex	2001-01-01 00:00:00.000	1	11
2	2	Brown	Barry	2002-08-12 00:00:00.000	1	11
3	3	Osako	Lee	1999-09-01 00:00:00.000	2	11
4	4	Kennson	David	1996-03-16 00:00:00.000	1	11
5	5	Bender	Eric	2007-05-17 00:00:00.000	1	11
6	6	Kendall	Lisa	2001-11-15 00:00:00.000	4	4
7	7	Lonning	David	2000-01-01 00:00:00.000	1	11

Primary key

	LocationID	street	city	state	Latitude	Longitude	GeoLoc
1	1	545 Pike	Seattle	WA	47.455	-122.231	0xE610000001
2	2	222 Second AVE	Boston	MA	42.372	-71.0298	0xE610000001
3	3	333 Third PL	Chic...	IL	41.953	-87.643	0xE610000001
4	4	444 Ruby ST	Spok...	WA	47.668	-117.529	0xE610000001
5	5	1595 Main	Phila...	PA	39.888	-75.251	0xE610000001
6	6	915 Wallaby Dr...	Sydn...	N...	-33.876	151.315	0xE610000001

Figure 1.58 The primary key (PK) and foreign key (FK) relationships between columns contained in the Grant, Employee, and Location tables.

Currently we don't actually have a foreign key constraint added to the Employee.LocationID field. But irrespective of whether this field does or doesn't contain the foreign key constraint object, the rules of a relational database require that the field must logically behave in the same fashion. In other words, the Employee.LocationID field may contain only those values found in the Location.LocationID field. If a location is removed from the Location table (e.g., if JProCo closed its Boston office), then no employee records in the Employee table could legitimately have Boston (LocationID 2) as their location. If a new JProCo location is added, then that value becomes available for use by the Employee table.

Before we look at the mechanics of adding the foreign key to the Employee table, let's attempt to add some incorrect data, so that we can get a better sense of how foreign keys can protect our data. We will attempt to add an employee record having a LocationID value of 11, which we know doesn't exist (see Figure 1.59). Since JProCo doesn't yet have a Location 11, this record should be disallowed.

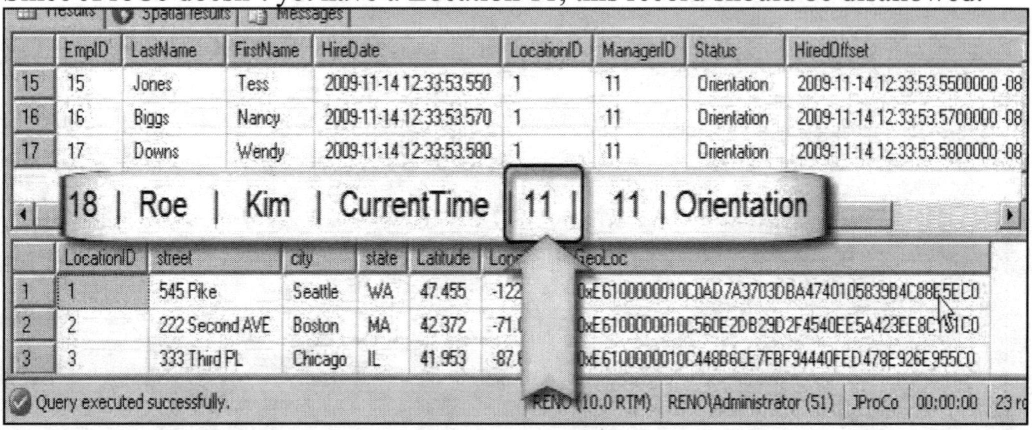

Results | Spatial results | Messages

	EmpID	LastName	FirstName	HireDate	LocationID	ManagerID	Status	HiredOffset
15	15	Jones	Tess	2009-11-14 12:33:53.550	1	11	Orientation	2009-11-14 12:33:53.5500000 -08
16	16	Biggs	Nancy	2009-11-14 12:33:53.570	1	11	Orientation	2009-11-14 12:33:53.5700000 -08
17	17	Downs	Wendy	2009-11-14 12:33:53.580	1	11	Orientation	2009-11-14 12:33:53.5800000 -08

18 | Roe | Kim | CurrentTime | 11 | 11 | Orientation

	LocationID	street	city	state	Latitude	Lon…	GeoLoc
1	1	545 Pike	Seattle	WA	47.455	-122	…xE6100000010C0AD7A3703DBA4740105839B4C88E5EC0
2	2	222 Second AVE	Boston	MA	42.372	-71.…	…xE6100000010C560E2DB29D2F4540EE5A423EE8C1[illegible]1C0
3	3	333 Third PL	Chicago	IL	41.953	-87.…	…xE6100000010C448B6CE7FBF94440FED478E926E955C0

Query executed successfully. RENO (10.0 RTM) RENO\Administrator (51) JProCo 00:00:00 23 r…

Figure 1.59 We are going to attempt to insert LocationID 11 for a new employee, knowing there is no LocationID 11 existing in the Location table.

However, the Employee table allows the bad data to be inserted into the LocationID field. Because the LocationID field of the *referencing table* contains a value not found in the LocationID field of the *referenced table*, referential integrity has been violated.

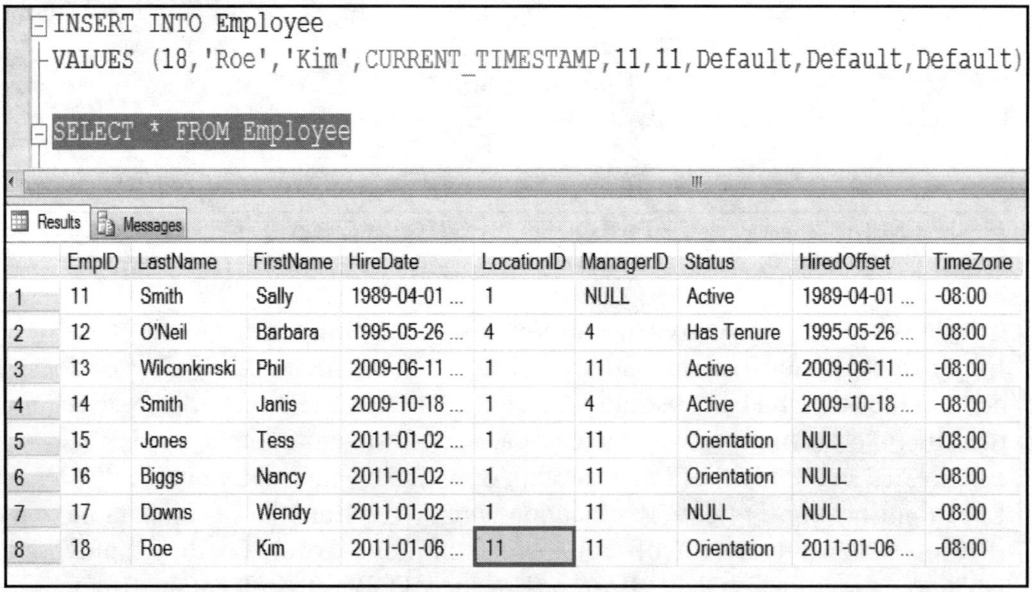

```
INSERT INTO Employee
VALUES (18,'Roe','Kim',CURRENT_TIMESTAMP,11,11,Default,Default,Default)

SELECT * FROM Employee
```

Results | Messages

	EmpID	LastName	FirstName	HireDate	LocationID	ManagerID	Status	HiredOffset	TimeZone
1	11	Smith	Sally	1989-04-01 ...	1	NULL	Active	1989-04-01 ...	-08:00
2	12	O'Neil	Barbara	1995-05-26 ...	4	4	Has Tenure	1995-05-26 ...	-08:00
3	13	Wilconkinski	Phil	2009-06-11 ...	1	11	Active	2009-06-11 ...	-08:00
4	14	Smith	Janis	2009-10-18 ...	1	4	Active	2009-10-18 ...	-08:00
5	15	Jones	Tess	2011-01-02 ...	1	11	Orientation	NULL	-08:00
6	16	Biggs	Nancy	2011-01-02 ...	1	11	Orientation	NULL	-08:00
7	17	Downs	Wendy	2011-01-02 ...	1	11	NULL	NULL	-08:00
8	18	Roe	Kim	2011-01-06 ...	11	11	Orientation	2011-01-06 ...	-08:00

Figure 1.60 The insertion of the LocationID 11 value was allowed since there is no foreign key to enforce referential integrity.

Delete the Employee 18 record (Figure 1.61), so that we can create the foreign key.

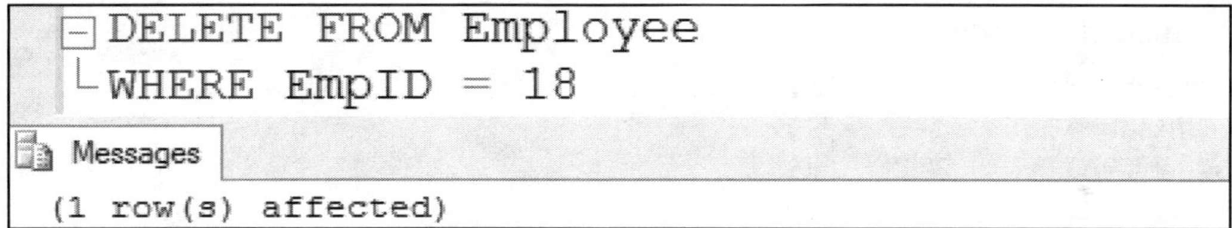

Figure 1.61 We must first delete the bad record before we can create the foreign key constraint.

Run this code to add the FK_Employee_Location_LocationID constraint to the Employee table and disallow invalid inserts (Figure 1.62).

```
ALTER TABLE Employee
ADD CONSTRAINT FK_Employee_Location_LocationID
FOREIGN KEY (LocationID)
REFERENCES Location(LocationID)
```

Messages

```
Command(s) completed successfully.
```

Figure 1.62 This code creates the foreign key FK_Employee_Location_LocationID.

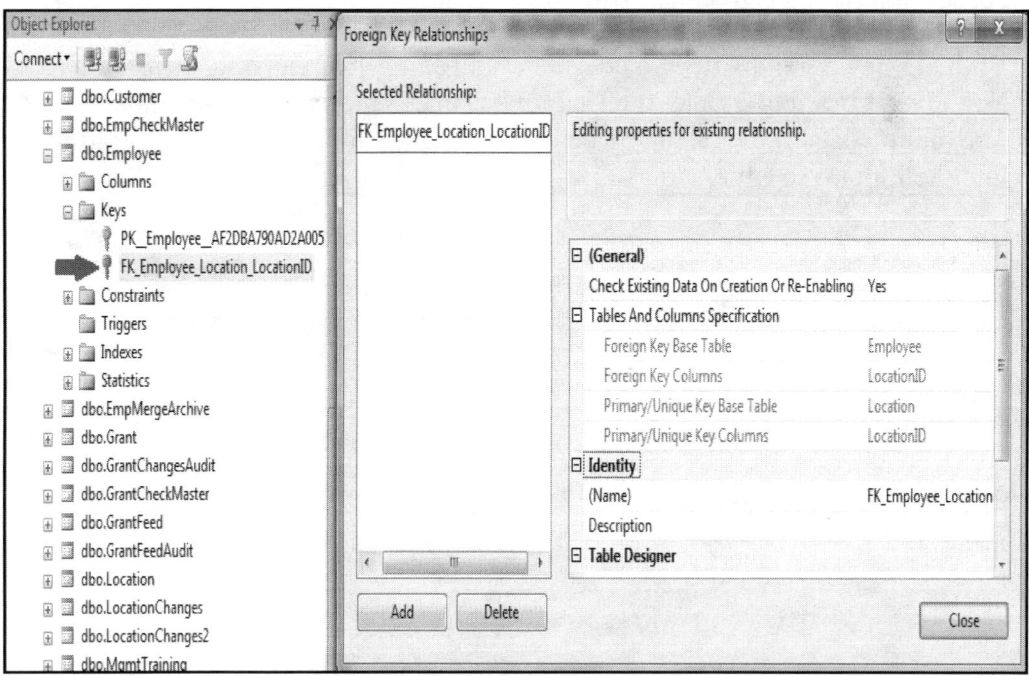

Figure 1.63 The Object Explorer view of the new foreign key (right-click on the object > Modify).

After you create the foreign key constraint, it's worthwhile taking a moment to view it in Object Explorer. The foreign key has a grey key icon and has been created in the Keys folder of the Employee table. The Foreign Key Relationships dialog displays metadata about the constraint and its options.

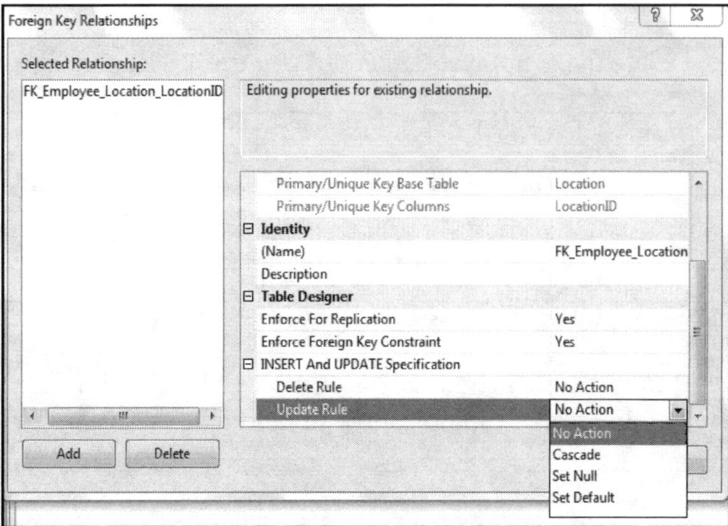

Figure 1.64 The Foreign Key Relationships dialog.

(*Note:* Because the footprint of the Foreign Key Relationships dialog doesn't fully expand, it's difficult to adequately display these options in a figure.)

Following the creation of FK_Employee_Location_LocationID, each update to a LocationID value in the Employee table will only be allowed by this foreign key constraint if it is in agreement with the Location.LocationID field.

With our new foreign key in place and establishing referential integrity on the Employee.LocationID field, the Employee table is protected against false LocationID data. Observe that when you reattempt to insert the bad LocationID into the Employee table, it disallows the insert (see Figure 1.65).

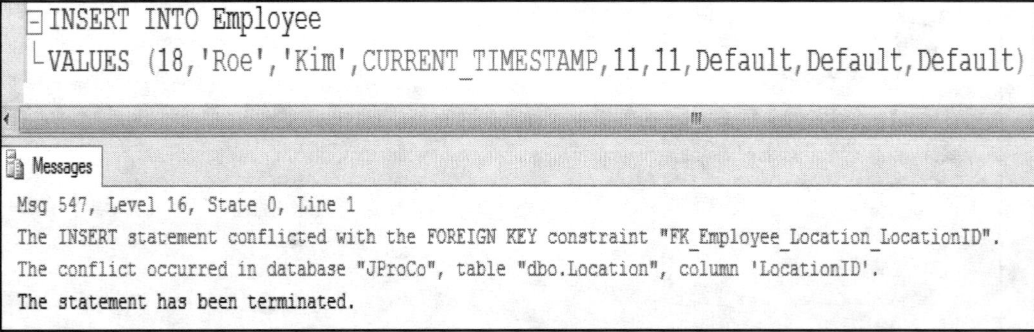

Figure 1.65 The FK_Employee_Location_LocationID constraint will not insert LocationID 11.

Using the WITH NOCHECK Option

Recall that earlier (Figures 1.63 and 1.64) we looked at the Foreign Key Relationships dialog in SSMS (SQL Server Management Studio) and we reviewed the metadata for FK_Employee_Location_LocationID.

You may have noticed the Yes/No option that determines whether or not to "Check Existing Data On Creation Or Re-Enabling" (see Figure 1.66). This option defaults to "Yes" – at the time you create the constraint, it first checks the existing data to confirm that all values in the field are legitimate.

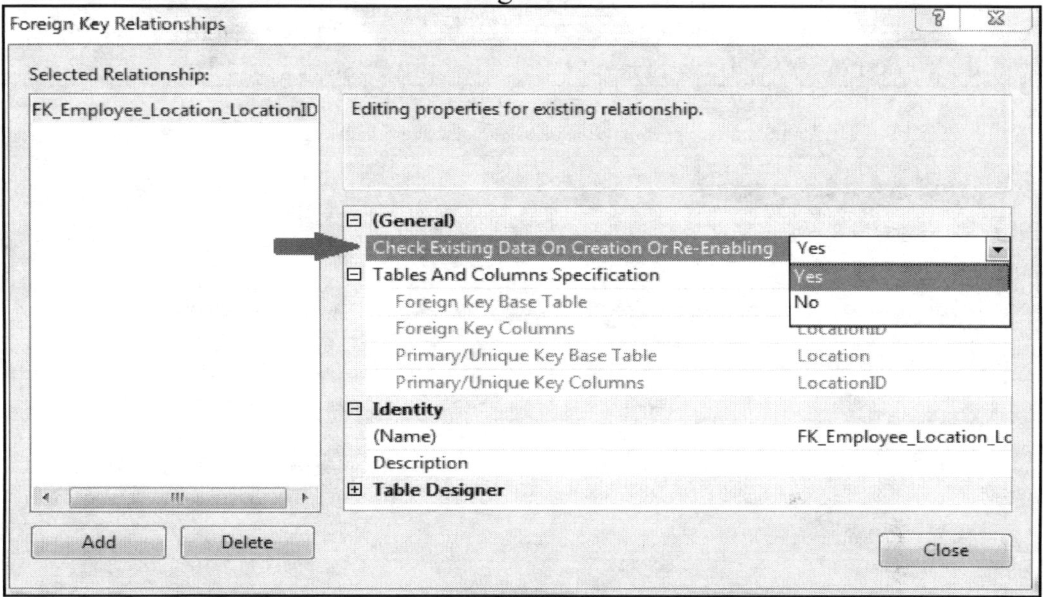

Figure 1.66 The options and metadata for FK_Employee_Location_LocationID.

Prior to creating the foreign key constraint, we removed the record containing false data (i.e., LocationD 11) (as we saw in Figure 1.61).

Our next example will take us back to the point prior to the creation of the constraint. We want to create the constraint again, but this time we will have it skip the step of validating the existing data before creating the foreign key.

Run the code to remove the foreign key constraint (see Figure 1.67).

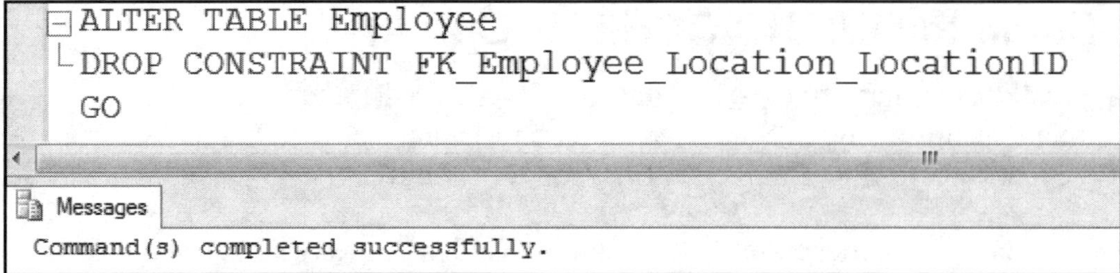

Figure 1.67 This code drops the foreign key constraint.

Run this code which inserts some bad data into the Employee table. As we know, the value of 13 is not an actual LocationID, but we are intentionally inserting it in order to demonstrate the WITH NOCHECK option (see Figure 1.68).

```
INSERT INTO Employee  --Insert Employee record, LocationID 13
VALUES (19,'Testing','Data',CURRENT_TIMESTAMP,13,11,Default,Default,Default)

SELECT * FROM Employee
```

Results | Messages

	EmpID	LastName	FirstName	HireDate	LocationID	ManagerID	Status	HiredOffset	TimeZone
1	11	Smith	Sally	1989-04-01...	1	NULL	Active	1989-04-01 ...	-08:00
2	12	O'Neil	Barbara	1995-05-26...	4	4	Has Tenure	1995-05-26 ...	-08:00
3	13	Wilconkinski	Phil	2009-06-11...	1	11	Active	2009-06-11 ...	-08:00
4	14	Smith	Janis	2009-10-18...	1	4	Active	2009-10-18 ...	-08:00
5	15	Jones	Tess	2011-01-07...	1	11	Orientation	2011-01-07 ...	-08:00
6	16	Biggs	Nancy	2011-01-07...	1	11	Orientation	2011-01-07 ...	-08:00
7	17	Downs	Wendy	2011-01-07...	1	11	Orientation	2011-01-07 ...	-08:00
8	18	Roe	Kim	2011-01-07...	1	11	Orientation	2011-01-07 ...	-08:00
9	19	Testing	Data	2011-01-07...	13	11	Orientation	2011-01-07 ...	-08:00

Figure 1.68 Because we've temporarily removed the protection of the foreign key, the Employee table allowed the insertion of our bad data (i.e., LocationID 13).

Create the foreign key constraint using WITH NOCHECK (see Figure 1.69).

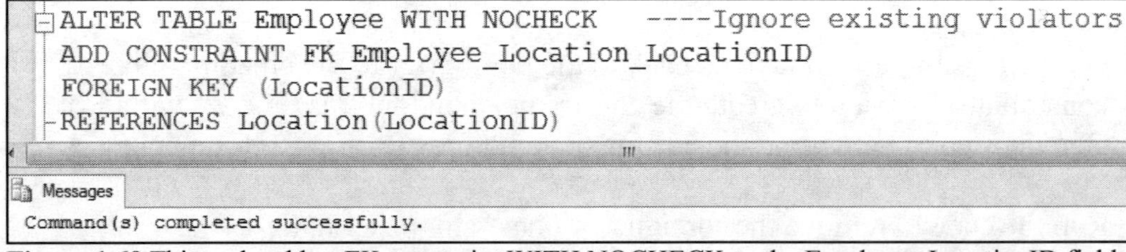

ALTER TABLE Employee WITH NOCHECK   ----Ignore existing violators
ADD CONSTRAINT FK_Employee_Location_LocationID
FOREIGN KEY (LocationID)
REFERENCES Location(LocationID)
Messages
Command(s) completed successfully.

Figure 1.69 This code adds a FK constraint WITH NOCHECK to the Employee.LocationID field.

When we check the Object Explorer, we see the newly created constraint. The WITH NOCHECK option allowed FK_Employee_Location_LocationID to be created, despite the invalid value (13) present in the Employee.LocationID field (see Figure 1.70). The Foreign Key Relationships dialog now shows a "No" for the Check Existing Data option (see Figure 1.71).

dbo.Employee
- Columns
- Keys
  - PK_Employee_AF2DBA790AD2A005
  - FK_Employee_Location_LocationID
- Constraints
- Triggers
- Indexes
- Statistics

dbo.EmpMergeArchive
dbo.Grant
dbo.GrantChangesAudit
dbo.GrantCheckMaster
dbo.GrantFeed
dbo.GrantFeedAudit
dbo.Location
dbo.LocationChanges

```
SELECT * FROM Employee
```

	EmpID	LastName	FirstName	HireDate	LocationID	ManagerID	Status	HiredOffset	TimeZone
1	11	Smith	Sally	1989-04-01...	1	NULL	Active	1989-04-01 ...	-08:00
2	12	O'Neil	Barbara	1995-05-26...	4	4	Has Tenure	1995-05-26 ...	-08:00
3	13	Wilconkinski	Phil	2009-06-11...	1	11	Active	2009-06-11 ...	-08:00
4	14	Smith	Janis	2009-10-18...	1	4	Active	2009-10-18 ...	-08:00
5	15	Jones	Tess	2011-01-07...	1	11	Orientation	2011-01-07 ...	-08:00
6	16	Biggs	Nancy	2011-01-07...	1	11	Orientation	2011-01-07 ...	-08:00
7	17	Downs	Wendy	2011-01-07...	1	11	Orientation	2011-01-07 ...	-08:00
8	18	Roe	Kim	2011-01-07...	1	11	Orientation	2011-01-07 ...	-08:00
9	19	Testing	Data	2011-01-07...	13	11	Orientation	2011-01-07 ...	-08:00

Figure 1.70 The OE view of the new foreign key, alongside the bad data (LocationID 13).

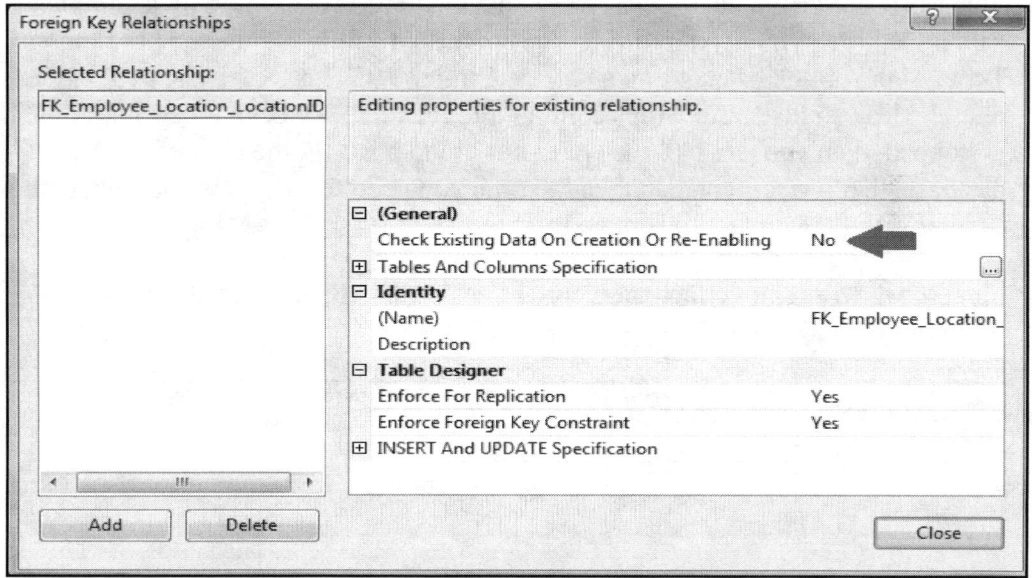

Figure 1.71 The FK Relationships dialog showing "Check Existing Data" option is "No."

Our demonstration is complete – we now have the foreign key constraint enabled on the Employee.LocationID field, and we have one bad record in our Employee table. Let's consider how this unusual situation may occur in our database within a production environment – in other words, how the WITH NOCHECK may come in handy in the workplace setting.

We know the best practice is to establish data constraints as early as possible in the life cycle of our tables. However, we don't always encounter "best case" scenarios with our data or databases. (*Example*: if your database is dependent upon data coming from other systems, new schema or data changes may be requested which require new tables or modification of your existing data constraints.) Our demonstration simulates a situation where you discover bad data coming into a field. You need to add a constraint to the field, but if you stop and attempt to scrub out the bad data prior to adding the constraint, even more bad data could enter your table while you take the time needed to investigate and scrub the data.

The flexibility of the WITH NOCHECK option allows you to add the constraint immediately without having to first correct all of your data. This immediately halts the flow of bad data into the field. Obviously you should also correct the existing data as quickly as possible, but the more pressing urgency is to stop more bad data from entering your table.

This is not unlike the classic leaky rowboat analogy. When triaging a complex data issue, often you need multiple steps in order to fully handle the problem. Think of the option of enabling a data constraint WITH NOCHECK as a way to plug the leak so that water stops coming into the boat. Once that perilous situation is stopped, then you can bail the water out of the boat. In the case of your database, that's when you can take the time you need for analysis and remediation or removal of the bad data from your table.

Finally, we will remove the bad record (LocationID 13) from the Employee table (see Figure 1.72).

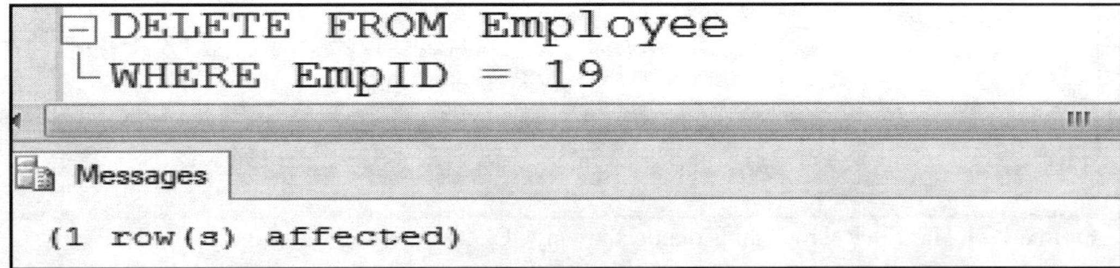
DELETE FROM Employee
WHERE EmpID = 19
Messages
(1 row(s) affected)

Figure 1.72 This code removes from the Employee table the bad record we added during our demonstration.

Lab 1.4: Foreign Key Constraints

Lab Prep: Before you can begin the lab, you must have SQL Server installed and have run the SQLProgrammingChapter1.4Setup.sql script. View the lab video instructions in Lab1.4_ForeignKeyConstraints.wmv.

Skill Check 1: Create a foreign key relationship called FK_Grant_Employee_EmpID that ensures all EmpID values entered into the Grant table are from valid values listed in the Employee table.

Skill Check 2: You notice that your invoice numbers range from 1 to 1885. Someone entered a record into the SalesInvoiceDetail table referring to Invoice 2000. Tomorrow you will investigate what to do with that record. In the meanwhile, establish referential integrity between SalesInvoice and SalesInvoiceDetail so that only InvoiceID values listed in SalesInvoice will be allowed into the SalesInvoiceDetail table.

Skill Check 3: Add a foreign key so the ProductID field of the SalesInvoiceDetail table references the ProductID of the CurrentProducts table.

Answer Code: The T-SQL code to this lab can be found in the downloadable files in a file named Lab1.4_ForeignKeyConstraints.sql.

Foreign Key Constraints - Points to Ponder

1. Foreign keys are constraints that compare values between one column and another.
2. Setting up a foreign key relationship enforces what is known as referential integrity.
3. The foreign key field of a table must be the same data type when referencing the primary key table. For example, the LocationID field of the Employee table is a CHAR(3), if the LocationID of the Location table was an INT then you could not create this reference.
4. You can use a FOREIGN KEY to specify that a column allows only those values contained in the referenced table (a.k.a., the base table).
5. You can create constraints using:
    a. The CONSTRAINT keyword in the CREATE TABLE statement at the time you create the table.
    b. The CONSTRAINT keyword in the ALTER TABLE statement after you have created the table.
6. Data integrity is the consistency and accuracy of the data which is stored in a database. In relational databases, the three types of data integrity are:
    a. Domain Integrity (data type, check constraint)
    b. Entity Integrity (primary key, unique constraint)
    c. Referential Integrity (handled by foreign key constraint)
7. If you don't want to check the existing data at the time you create the foreign key, then specify WITH NOCHECK.

Creating Tables with Constraints

Our earlier examples created or modified constraints on existing tables. This section will demonstrate the code syntax for creating these constraints at the time you create your tables.

PK_TravelTrip_TripID is a primary key constraint on the TripID field. From our work in *SQL Architecture Basics Joes 2 Pros* (Chapter 8), we know the CLUSTERED keyword specifies that the records of the table will be physically ordered by TripID. Substitute the NONCLUSTERED keyword, if you do not wish the records to be physically ordered by TripID (see Figure 1.73).

```
CREATE TABLE Sales.TravelTrip
(
TripID INT NOT NULL,
TripName varchar(100),
EmpID int NULL
CONSTRAINT PK_TravelTrip_TripID PRIMARY KEY CLUSTERED (TripID ASC)
)
GO
```

```
Messages
Command(s) completed successfully.
```

Figure 1.73 The Sales.TravelTrip table is created with the primary key constraint on TripID.

An alternate syntax for adding a primary key in your CREATE TABLE statement is shown below (see Figure 1.74). This syntax also specifies a unique constraint (UQ_TravelTrip_TripName), so that the values of the TripName field will be unique. ***Note***: If you want to run this code make sure you first drop the Sales.TravelTrip table [DROP TABLE Sales.TravelTrip].

```
CREATE TABLE Sales.TravelTrip
(
TripID INT PRIMARY KEY NONCLUSTERED,
TripName varchar(100) CONSTRAINT UQ_TravelTrip_TripName UNIQUE,
EmpID int NULL
)
GO
```

```
Messages
Command(s) completed successfully.
```

Figure 1.74 Shown here: 1) alternate code syntax for creating a primary key on a new table; 2) use of NONCLUSTERED; 3) code syntax for creating a unique constraint on a new table.

Observe that we chose not to customize the name for our primary key on the TripID field (Figure 1.74). Instead we allowed SQL Server to create the key using its own convention (PK_First8CharOfTableName_AlphanumericID). If you later wish to customize the appearance of your key (i.e., to include the FieldName), right-click on the key in Object Explorer and choose the Rename option. As you change the name of the key (or constraint), SQL Server will follow suit and automatically rename the index to match your custom name (see Figure 1.75).

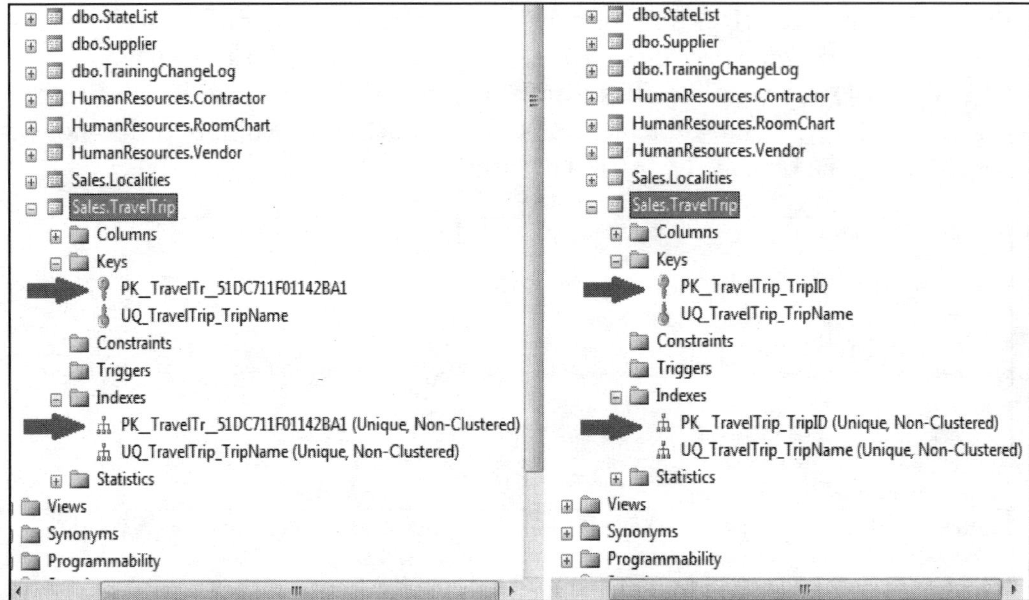

Figure 1.75 You can customize the names of your Keys and Constraints in Object Explorer.

Default constraint values may be defined at the time of table creation (Figure 1.76).

```
CREATE TABLE  Sales.TravelerProfile
 (First_Name char(30),
  Last_Name char(60),
  Mailing_Address char(50) DEFAULT 'Unknown',
  City char(50) DEFAULT 'Seattle',
  Country char(30),
  Birth_Date date)
GO
```

Messages

```
Command(s) completed successfully.
```

Figure 1.76 The syntax for defining default constraint values at the time of table creation.

After creating the Sales.TravelerProfile table, the values for the default constraints (Mailing_Address 'Unknown', City 'Seattle') may be seen by opening Object Explorer > Databases > Tables > right-click Sales.TravelerProfile > Design. Click the City field in the design interface in order to display the Column Properties tab for the City field (see Figure 1.77).

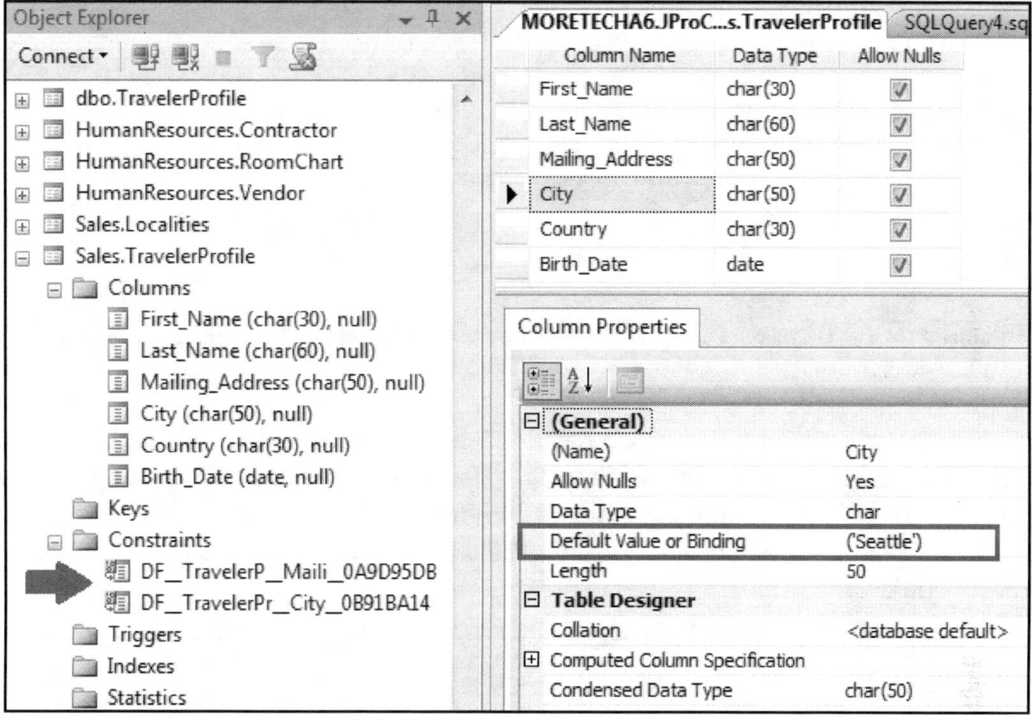

Figure 1.77 The Object Explorer view of the default constraints and values defined in Figure 1.76.

Check constraints may also be added to a table at the time of its creation. In Figure 1.78 we add the CK_TravelTrip_EndDate check constraint, which ensures that the EndDate for a trip can't occur earlier than the StartDate.

```
CREATE TABLE Sales.TravelTrip
(
TripID INT NOT NULL,
TripName varchar(100) CONSTRAINT UQ_TravelTrip_TripName UNIQUE,
StartDate datetime NOT NULL,
EndDate datetime NOT NULL,
Complaint bit NOT NULL,
EmpID int NULL
CONSTRAINT PK_TravelTrip_TripID PRIMARY KEY CLUSTERED (TripID ASC),
CONSTRAINT CK_TravelTrip_EndDate CHECK (EndDate>=StartDate)
)
GO
```

Messages

Command(s) completed successfully.

Figure 1.78 The CK_TravelTrip_EndDate check constraint is added during the creation of the Sales.TravelTrip table.

Foreign key constraints may also be added at the time of table creation. Here we see FK_TravelTrip_Employee_EmpID added as a foreign key referencing the EmpID field of the Employee table (see Figure 1.79). For this to run, the Employee table must already have been created. If the Employee table does not exist, then you would get an error.

```
CREATE TABLE Sales.TravelTrip
(
TripID INT NOT NULL,
TripName varchar(100) CONSTRAINT UQ_TravelTrip_TripName UNIQUE,
StartDate datetime NOT NULL,
EndDate datetime NOT NULL,
Complaint bit NOT NULL,
EmpID int NULL
CONSTRAINT PK_TravelTrip_TripID PRIMARY KEY CLUSTERED (TripID ASC),
CONSTRAINT CK_TravelTrip_EndDate CHECK (EndDate>=StartDate),
CONSTRAINT FK_TravelTrip_Employee_EmpID FOREIGN KEY (EmpID) REFERENCES Employee(EmpID)
)
GO
```

Messages

Command(s) completed successfully.

Figure 1.79 FK_TravelTrip_Employee_EmpID is added at the time of table creation.

Lab 1.5: Creating Table Constraints

Lab Prep: Before you can begin the lab, you must have SQL Server installed and have run the SQLProgrammingChapter1.5Setup.sql script.

Skill Check 1: Create the dbo.Contestant table and insert the three records seen in the figure below.

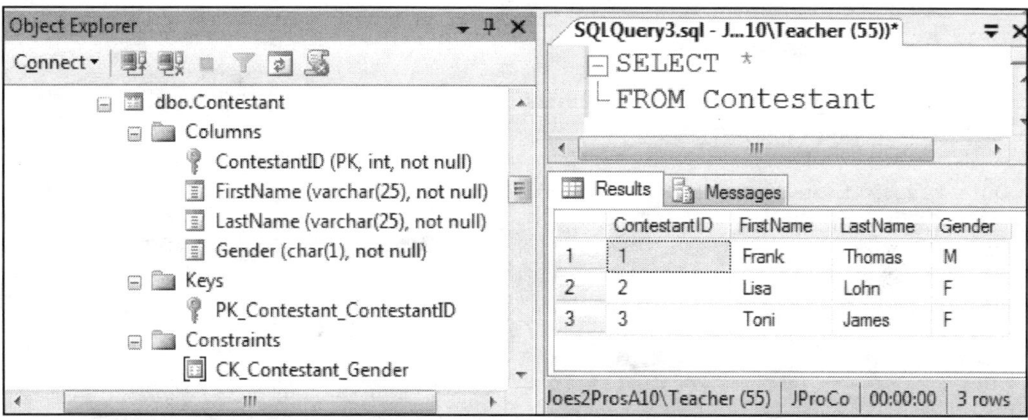

Figure 1.80 The table design including keys and constraints for Skill Check 1.

Your checklist to complete this code should include the following:

- All fields should not allow nulls.
- The ContestantID should be the primary key using the naming convention of PK_*Tablename*_*Fieldname*.
- A check constraint on the Gender field should only allow an F or an M.
- Test your check constraint by attempting to insert Sam Haas with a gender value of 'O' and verify that it fails.

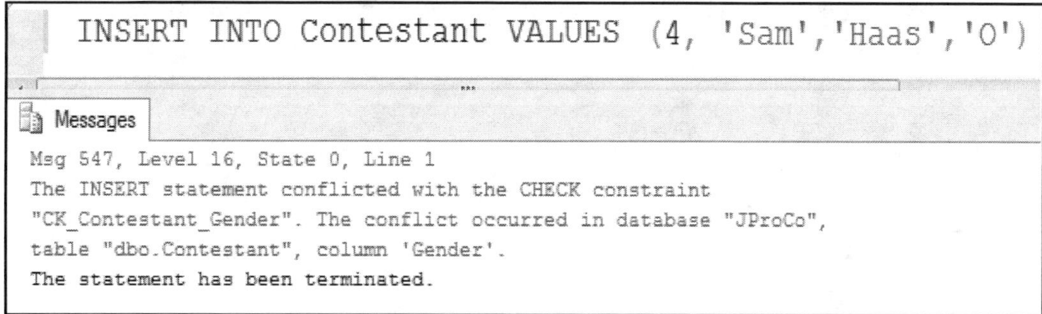

Figure 1.81 Test the check constraint which prevents the gender value of 'O' from being entered.

Creating Table Constraints - Points to Ponder

1. You can create constraints while creating a new table using the CREATE TABLE statement.
2. When an INSERT, UPDATE, or DELETE statement violates a constraint, then the statement is terminated with an error.
3. Creating a unique constraint creates an index. By default this index will be nonclustered.
4. Creating a primary key constraint creates an index. By default this index will be clustered.
5. Foreign keys are constraints that compare values between columns (usually, but not always, of different tables).

Chapter Glossary

Check constraint: an object on a SQL Server table that places a condition to verify valid data during inserts or updates.
Composite key (also known as *compound key*): two or more fields that when combined uniquely identify a row.
Condition: a rule which you want a constraint to enforce (*examples:* all height values must be positive; LandMass values must be non-negative and < 2 million; a numeric data type can ensure that no character data is entered into a number field).
Data integrity: the consistency and accuracy of the data which is stored in a database.
Default constraint: inserts a specific value into a field when the input is left blank for the field.
Domain integrity: every accepted value is verified by the rules set forth on the field.
Foreign key: constraints that compare values between other fields
Primary key: an object on a SQL Server table that specifies which fields must have unique, non-null values for each record.
Referenced table: also known as *base table*. This specifies an enumerated set of acceptable values that can be used.
Referencing table: a table that is being used by another object in SQL Server.
Referential integrity: a guideline that says valid values are only values from a referenced table.
Table constraint: object on a table that disallows unacceptable data from entering the table.
Unique constraint: SQL Object that ensures that no duplicate values are entered in specific columns.
WITH NOCHECK: an option available when creating a constraint that allows existing data to be out of compliance with the constraint. All new data coming in will be in compliance with the constraint.

Chapter One - Review Quiz

1.) Data types help to enforce what type of data integrity?

O a. Entity Integrity
O b. Domain Integrity
O c. Referential Integrity

2.) How many primary keys can a table have?

O a. Depends on your ANSI null settings
O b. Up to 1
O c. Up to as many fields as you have
O d. No limit

3.) A check constraint…
O a. must be present on every table in your database.
O b. can be a logical expression.
O c. must be purchased from Microsoft as a middleware component from a third party before you can use it.

4.) Foreign keys are used to enforce referential integrity. What does referential integrity do?

O a. Assigns values between tables to save the user time
O b. Compares values to different fields to run complex calculations in place of methods
O c. Compares values between the fields of two tables to limit the acceptable values which may be used

5.) Which column cannot have a unique constraint?
O a. ISBN INT NULL
O b. ISBN nchar(100) NULL
O c. ISBN nvarchar(100) NULL
O d. ISBN nvarchar(max) NULL.

6.) You tried to set up a foreign key constraint to limit LocationID values of your Employee table to valid values listed in the Location.LocationID field. Where do you place the foreign key?

O a. On the Employee.LocationID field.
O b. On the Location.LocationID field.

7.) You have a database with two tables named Employee and Location. Both tables have a field called LocationID. You need to ensure that all Locations listed in the Employee table have a corresponding LocationID in the Location table? How do you enforce this type of integrity?

O a. JOIN
O b. DDL Trigger
O c. Foreign key constraint
O d. Primary key constraint

8.) You have a table named Feedback that contains every record of how a customer felt about their purchase. One field is called Complaint, where 0 is no complaint and 1 is a complaint. You also have a field called Rating that ranges from 0 to 100. If a customer complains they should not be giving a perfect rating of 100. If they complain then they can enter a score between 0 and 90. If they don't then it can be between 1 and 100. Which check constraint would you use?

O a. CHECK (Rating BETWEEN 1 and 100)
O b. CHECK (Rating <=90 AND Complaint = 1)
O c. CHECK ((Rating BETWEEN 1 and 90 AND Complaint = 1))
OR (Rating BETWEEN 1 and 100 AND Complaint = 0))
O d. CHECK ((Rating BETWEEN 1 and 90 AND Complaint = 1)
AND (Rating BETWEEN 1 and 100 AND Complaint = 0))

9.) You have a table named Customer. You need to ensure that customer data in the table meets the following requirements:

- Credit limit must be zero unless customer identification has been verified.
- Credit limit must be less than 25,000.

Which check constraint should you use?

O a. CHECK (CreditLimit BETWEEN 1 AND 25000 AND 0)
O b. CHECK (PreApproved = 1 AND CreditLimt BETWEEN 1 AND 25000)
O c. CHECK ((CreditLimit = 0 AND PreApproved = 0) OR (CreditLimit BETWEEN 1 AND 25000 AND PreApproved = 1))
O d. CHECK ((CreditLimit = 0 AND PreApproved = 0) AND (CreditLimit BETWEEN 1 AND 25000 AND PreApproved = 1))

10.) Which two column definitions could have a unique constraint?

□ a. Nvarchar(100) NULL
□ b. Nvarchar(max) NOT NULL
□ c. Nvarchar(100) NOT NULL
□ d. Nvarchar(100) SPARSE NOT NULL

11.) You are developing a new database. The database contains two tables named InvoiceDetail and Product. You need to ensure that all ProductIDs referenced in the InvoiceDetail table have a corresponding record in the ProductID field of the Product table. Which method should you use?

O a. JOIN
O b. DDL Trigger
O c. Foreign key constraint
O d. Primary key constraint

Answer Key

1.) b 2.) b 3.) b 4.) c 5.) d 6.) a 7.) c 8.) c 9.) c 10) a, c 11) c

Bug Catcher Game

To play the Bug Catcher game, run the file BugCatcher_Chapter1Constraints.pps from the BugCatcher folder of the companion files found at www.Joes2Pros.com.

Chapter 2. After Triggers

Back in high school during Track & Field competition, I knew to listen for a starting siren or whistle to cue me that it was time to take off running. Of all the noises coming from the outdoors, the stadium, the team, or the crowd, I was focused and listening intently for that one sound. You could say there was a **trigger** in my head waiting for that event.

In this analogy, the starting sound was the *event* and in my mind was a *trigger* that fired off a command telling my legs to take me as fast as possible down and around the track. I never ran before that starting sound event for fear of disqualification.

Based on events which take place in your database, you can have SQL Server "listen" for just the ones that should signal when it's time for actions to run automatically. **After triggers** are essentially stored procedures that run after an event occurs.

There are three types of after triggers: after insert triggers, after delete triggers, and after update triggers. For short, these are referred to as insert triggers, update triggers, and delete triggers. In this chapter we will examine all three types of after triggers.

READER NOTE: *In order to follow along with the examples in the first section of Chapter 2, please run the setup script SQLProgrammingChapter2.0Setup.sql. The setup scripts for this book are posted at Joes2Pros.com.*

Insert Triggers

The first type of trigger we will examine is the **insert trigger**. Since our first examples will be based on the Employee table data, query your Employee table and confirm you have the same 17 employee records shown below (see Figure 2.1). (If not, please run the setup script SQLProgrammingChapter2.0Setup.sql.) Our most recent hire is Employee 17 (Wendy Downs), who is still in orientation.

```
SELECT * FROM Employee
```

Results | Messages

	EmpID	LastName	FirstName	HireDate	LocationID	ManagerID	Status	HiredOffset	TimeZone
1	1	Adams	Alex	2001-01-01 ...	1	11	Active	2001-01-01...	-08:00
2	2	Brown	Barry	2002-08-12 ...	1	11	Active	2002-08-12...	-08:00
3	3	Osako	Lee	1999-09-01 ...	2	11	Active	1999-09-01...	-05:00
4	4	Kennson	David	1996-03-16 ...	1	11	Has Tenure	1996-03-16...	-08:00
5	5	Bender	Eric	2007-05-17 ...	1	11	Active	2007-05-17...	-08:00
6	6	Kendall	Lisa	2001-11-15 ...	4	4	Active	2001-11-15...	-08:00
7	7	Lonning	David	2000-01-01 ...	1	11	On Leave	2000-01-01...	-08:00
8	8	Marshbank	John	2001-11-15 ...	NULL	4	Active	2001-11-15...	-06:00
9	9	Newton	James	2003-09-30 ...	2	3	Active	2003-09-30...	-05:00
10	10	O'Haire	Terry	2004-10-04 ...	2	3	Active	2004-10-04...	-05:00
11	11	Smith	Sally	1989-04-01 ...	1	NULL	Active	1989-04-01...	-08:00
12	12	O'Neil	Barbara	1995-05-26 ...	4	4	Has Tenure	1995-05-26...	-08:00
13	13	Wilconkinski	Phil	2009-06-11 ...	1	11	Active	2009-06-11...	-08:00
14	14	Smith	Janis	2009-10-18 ...	1	4	Active	2009-10-18...	-08:00
15	15	Jones	Tess	2010-12-29 ...	1	11	Orientation	2010-12-29...	-08:00
16	16	Biggs	Nancy	2010-12-29 ...	1	11	Orientation	2010-12-29...	-08:00
17	17	Downs	Wendy	2010-12-29 ...	1	11	Orientation	2010-12-29...	-08:00

Query executed successfully. | (local) (10.0 SP1) | MoreTechA6\Student (54) | JProCo | 00:00:00 | 17 rows

Figure 2.1 Our most recent employee is EmpID 17, Wendy Downs.

We want to have two identical tables called Employee and EmployeeHistory. Attempting to query the EmployeeHistory table (which does not yet exist) gets an error message (Figure 2.2). We can confirm in the Object Explorer that we see an Employee table but no EmployeeHistory table.

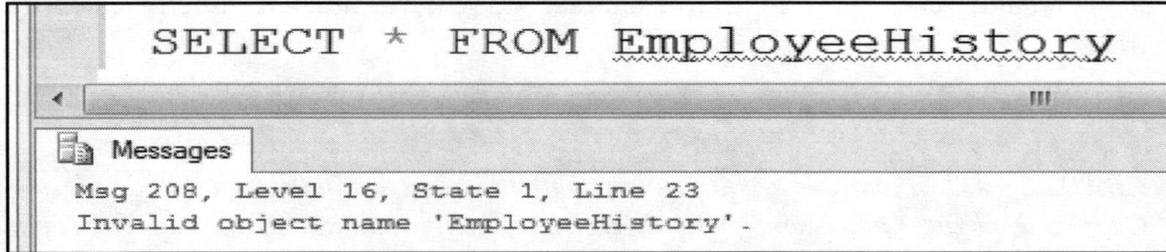
SELECT * FROM EmployeeHistory
Messages
Msg 208, Level 16, State 1, Line 23
Invalid object name 'EmployeeHistory'.

Figure 2.2 There is no table called EmployeeHistory in the JProCo database.

One way to create the Employee table would be to run a CREATE TABLE statement and then insert the records. (An easy way to obtain the code for an existing table is to right click it in Object Explorer > Script Table as > CREATE To > New Query Editor Window. This gives you the table's structure, and then you need to insert the values.) However, a SELECT INTO statement is a quicker process and is a commonly used technique for quickly copying a table *(including all its data)*. Be aware that the SELECT INTO statement doesn't support the creation of clustered indexes. Our trigger example in this section would work fine without a clustered index, but we will briefly digress to show you this useful technique.

Recall that the Employee table has a primary key on the EmpID field. In Object Explorer, expand the dbo.Employee object and notice the primary key (Figure 2.3). Alternatively, you can right click dbo.Employee to see the design of the Employee table where the key symbol denotes the primary key on the EmpID field.

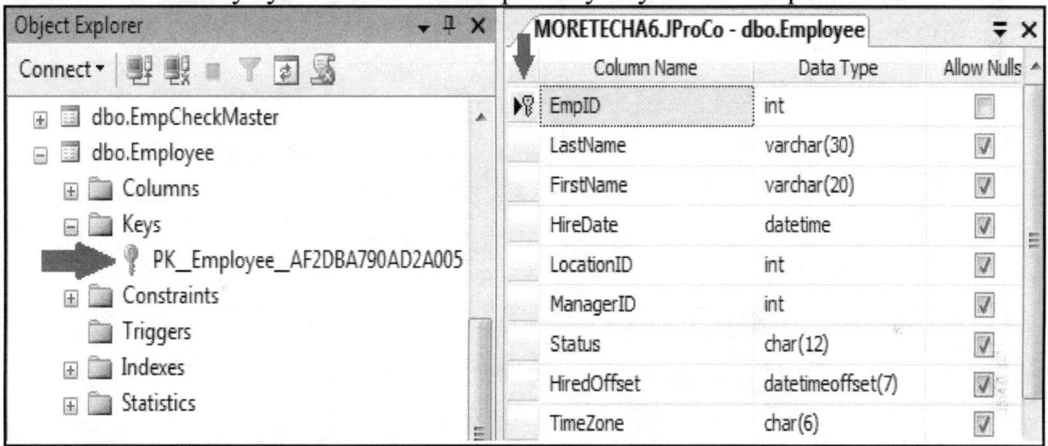

Figure 2.3 There is a primary key constraint on the EmpID field of the Employee table.

Run the SELECT INTO statement you see here (Figure 2.4). The ORDER BY clause isn't essential. However, it will make our creation of the clustered index on the EmployeeHistory table run more quickly.

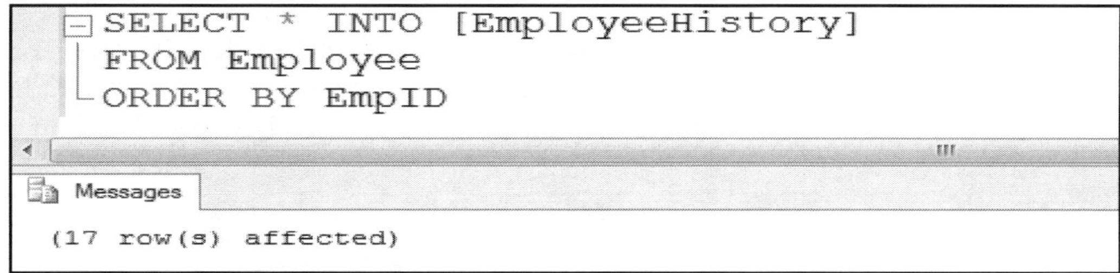

Figure 2.4 The EmployeeHistory table is a copy of the Employee table and all its records.

We have successfully created the EmployeeHistory table, which is a copy of the Employee table and all of its records. At this point, we could move ahead with our main example, which is to create a trigger. (And in many cases in the job setting, once you've completed the SELECT INTO statement, you can roll forward.) However, since the EmployeeHistory table doesn't contain a clustered index, any new records added will not necessarily be ordered by EmpID.

If we check Object Explorer, we will see the EmployeeHistory table shows no primary key and no clustered index (see Figure 2.5).

Our next step will be to add a primary key on EmpID. Adding this clustered index will ensure records in the EmployeeHistory table will always appear in order according to EmpID (see Figure 2.6).

(*Note:* If for some reason we didn't want EmpID to be a primary key, we could accomplish our goal by creating a unique clustered index on EmpID.)

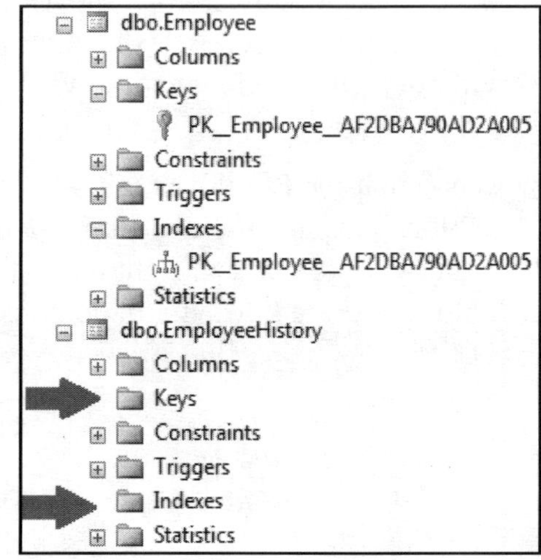

Figure 2.5 The EmployeeHistory table has no PK.

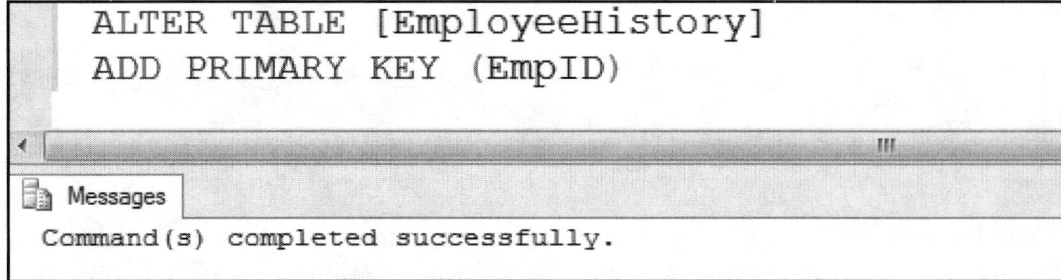

Figure 2.6 We are adding a unique clustered index by making EmpID a primary key field.

The two tables are currently in sync and each contains precisely the same 17 records. If we inserted an 18th record into the Employee table but did not take the time to write the same insert for the EmployeeHistory table, they would no longer be in sync.

To demonstrate how these two tables can get out of sync with an INSERT statement, let's add a new record to the Employee table. A new employee named Rainy Walker (EmpID 18) was hired on January 1, 2010. Rainy will work for Manager 11 in Location 1. To keep things simple, we will use the default values for the last three fields of this record (Figure 2.7).

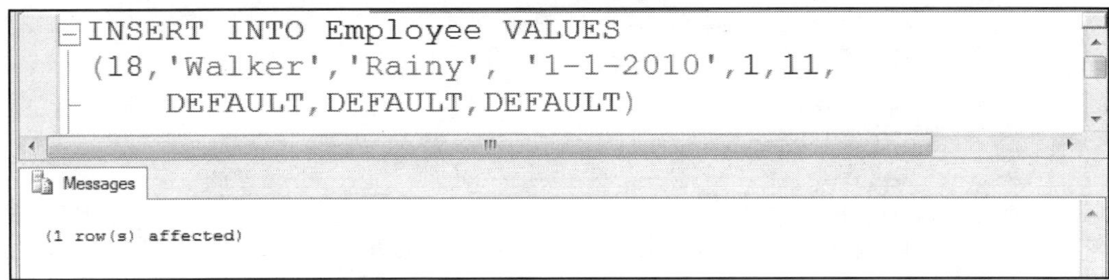
INSERT INTO Employee VALUES
(18,'Walker','Rainy', '1-1-2010',1,11,
DEFAULT,DEFAULT,DEFAULT)
Messages
(1 row(s) affected)

Figure 2.7 EmpID 18 is inserted into the Employee table.

After you get the "1 row(s) affected" message, you should see 18 records in the Employee table. A SELECT query confirms it has 18 records, and the EmployeeHistory table still has 17 records (see Figure 2.8). The EmployeeHistory should have the same number of records as the Employee table, so we need to identify and deal with the missing record.

```
SELECT * FROM Employee
SELECT * FROM EmployeeHistory
```

Results | Messages

	EmpID	LastName	FirstName	HireDate	LocationID	ManagerID	Status	HiredOffset
17	17	Downs	Wendy	2010-09-25 15:42:22.940	1	11	Orientation	2010-09-25 15:42:22.940000
18	18	Walker	Rainy	2010-01-01 00:00:00.000	1	11	Orientation	2010-09-25 16:04:14.223000

	EmpID	LastName	FirstName	HireDate	LocationID	ManagerID	Status	HiredOffset
16	16	Biggs	Nancy	2010-09-25 15:42:22.917	1	11	Orie...	2010-09-25 15:42:22.9170000 -08
17	17	Downs	Wendy	2010-09-25 15:42:22.940	1	11	Orie...	2010-09-25 15:42:22.9400000 -08

Figure 2.8 EmpID 18 is in the Employee table but not the EmployeeHistory table.

We know exactly which record is missing, since we caused the mismatch. But in the real world you won't always be so lucky. If you inherited this asynchronous data problem and needed to find out which record was missing, it would take some investigation. You can always run an unmatched query. A left outer join of the

Employee table to the EmployeeHistory table on the EmpID field will get all matching and non-matching records. To look for every record where the Employee table does not have a matching record in the EmployeeHistory table, we look for a null in the EmployeeHistory table. The result of the unmatched query shows that the one missing record is EmpID 18 (see Figure 2.9).

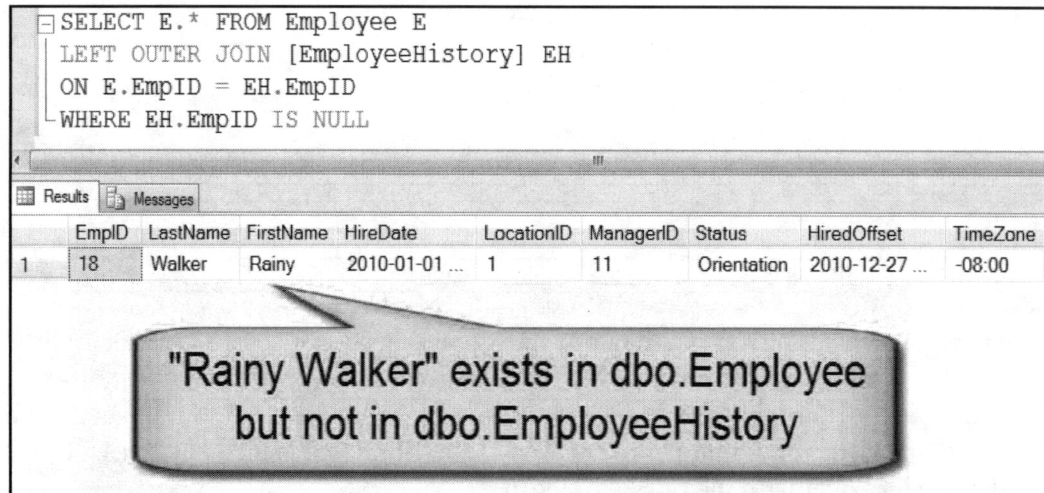

Figure 2.9 The unmatched query shows the record missing from the Employee table.

Employee 18's record needs to be inserted into the EmployeeHistory table. A quick way to accomplish this is to simply add an INSERT statement to our existing query (Figure 2.10). To confirm your tables are back in sync, you can repeat the mismatch query (Figure 2.9). You can also repeat the SELECT queries (Figure 2.8).

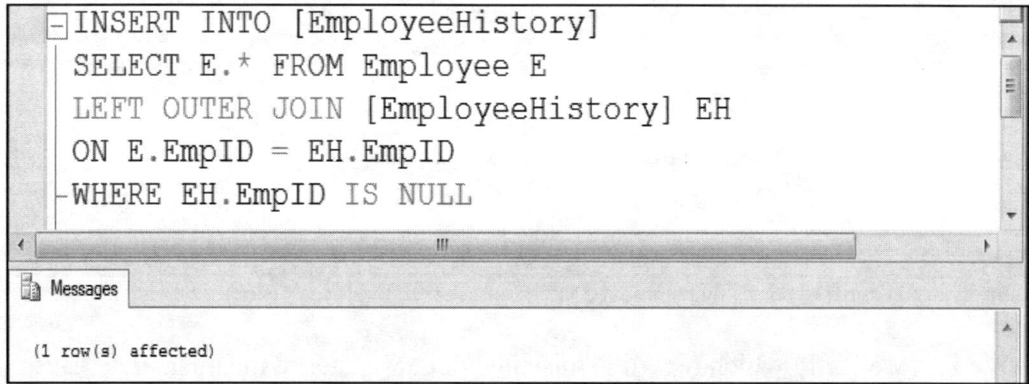

Figure 2.10 The unmatched query record(s) can be combined with an INSERT statement.

Coding the After Insert Trigger

The Employee and EmployeeHistory tables were out of sync for a short period of time. Two INSERT statements were needed because we have two tables that need the same records. The first INSERT statement put the record in the Employee table; the second INSERT statement put the same record into the EmployeeHistory table. To ensure that the data for these two tables remains synchronized, we would need the two INSERT statements to run at the same time. *Therefore, our goal is to have all inserts from the Employee table also affect the EmployeeHistory table.*

We can tell the Employee table that as soon as it encounters an insert, it should immediately invoke another INSERT statement to the Employee History table. An object that runs an action after an event (e.g., after an insert to the Employee table) is known as an **after trigger**. An **after trigger** is actually a stored procedure which runs after a specified event occurs. In this example, the specified event will be an insert into the Employee table.

We're going to create a trigger called trg_InsertEmployee which awaits an insert to the Employee table (Figure 2.11). This trigger will run after the insert happens. Figure 2.11 outlines the code we will need for this trigger.

```
CREATE TRIGGER trg_InsertEmployee
ON dbo.Employee
AFTER INSERT AS
 BEGIN
    --Insert code to run here
 END
```

Figure 2.11 Code to start your CREATE TRIGGER statement.

Between the BEGIN and END keywords, we're going to write code to INSERT INTO dbo.EmployeeHistory the same records which are inserted into the Employee table. Behind the scenes, all rows affected by the insert to dbo.Employee will go into the "Inserted" table. Thus, we can pull those same rows from the Inserted table in order to populate the EmployeeHistory table (see Figure 2.12). *(For more on the memory resident Inserted and Deleted tables, refer to Volume 2, Chapter 14.)*

```
CREATE TRIGGER trg_InsertEmployee
ON dbo.Employee
AFTER INSERT AS
 BEGIN
    INSERT INTO dbo.EmployeeHistory
    SELECT * FROM Inserted
 END
```

Messages

Command(s) completed successfully.

Figure 2.12 The Inserted table will contain the records from the INSERT statement that fired off the trigger.

Once you see the "Command(s) completed successfully" confirmation, the trigger will be visible in Object Explorer (see Figure 2.13).

This trigger should run the moment after we insert any records into the Employee table. It's always a good idea to test your code, which we will do by inserting a new record.

Figure 2.13 Our new trigger shows in Object Explorer.

Figure 2.14 shows an insert for a new record, Employee #19. Notice we see two "1 row(s) affected" confirmation messages. The first reflects our insert into the Employee table. The second message is confirmation that the record was inserted into the EmployeeHistory table as a result of the trigger.

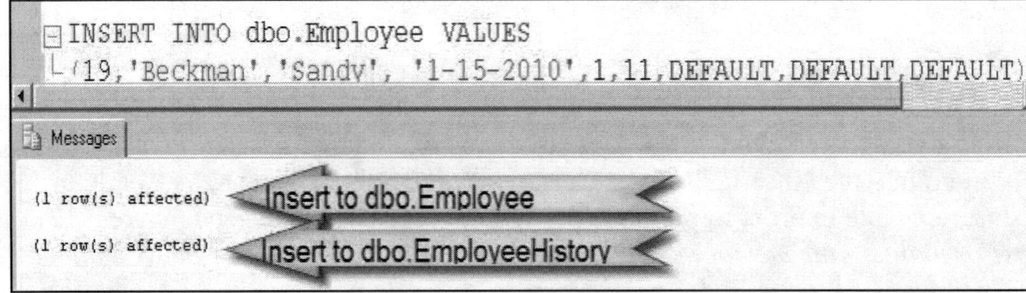

Figure 2.14 Inserting 1 record into dbo.Employee causes the trigger to fire and run another insert.

When we re-query both tables, we see that our trigger worked perfectly. When we inserted Sandy Beckman's record into the Employee table, the trigger immediately inserted a copy of her record into the EmployeeHistory table (Figure 2.15).

```
SELECT * FROM Employee
SELECT * FROM EmployeeHistory
```

Results | Messages

19	19	Beckman	Sandy	2010-01-15 00:00:00.000	1	11	Orie...	2010-09-25 16:

	EmpID	LastName	FirstName	HireDate	LocationID	ManagerID	Status	HiredOffset
2	19	Beckman	Sandy	2010-01-15 00:00:00.000	1	11	Orientation	2010-09-2

Query executed successfully. | (local) (10.0 SP1) | Joes2ProsA10\Teacher (53) | JProCo

Figure 2.15 Our trigger worked perfectly – EmpID 19 now appears in both tables.

Enabling and Disabling Triggers

To prevent a trigger from running, you can either get rid of the trigger or you can temporarily disable the trigger. If you test fictitious data which you will later delete, you must delete it from two tables (i.e., because you created an insert trigger). For example, testing an insert from a new process creates an employee called "Dummy One" with EmpID 999. This is acceptable data for our test team, but it's not data we plan to keep or use in production. In fact, once this dummy record gets into the Employee table, our test is done and we will delete the record. Unfortunately, we risk leaving this legacy data behind in dbo.EmployeeHistory, because trg_InsertEmployee is constantly monitoring the Employee table and will fire each time an INSERT statement is run against this table. We have the option of disabling the trigger (see the code in Figure 2.16). We won't need to delete test data from our history table, because the trigger simply won't fire.

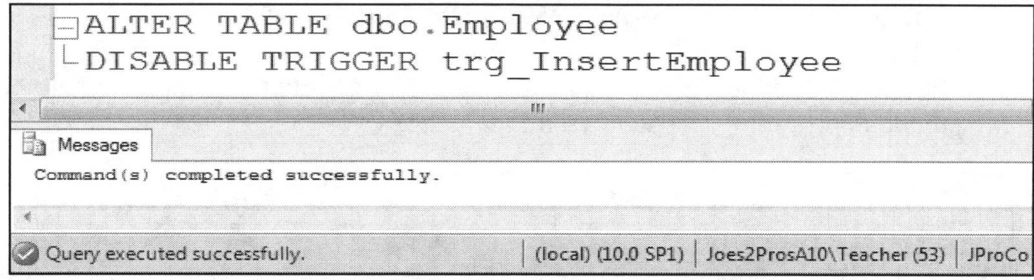
ALTER TABLE dbo.Employee
DISABLE TRIGGER trg_InsertEmployee
Messages
Command(s) completed successfully.
Query executed successfully.
(local) (10.0 SP1)
Joes2ProsA10\Teacher (53)
JProCo

Figure 2.16 You can use an ALTER TABLE statement to disable a trigger.

Now that trg_InsertEmployee is disabled, we will run a test by attempting to add some dummy data to the Employee table. If we successfully disabled the trigger, then we will expect to see just one transaction ("1 row(s) affected"), which will add one record to the Employee table and zero records to EmployeeHistory.

```
INSERT INTO Employee VALUES
(999, 'Dummy','One', '2-2-2222', 1, 11,DEFAULT,DEFAULT,DEFAULT)
```

Messages

(1 row(s) affected)

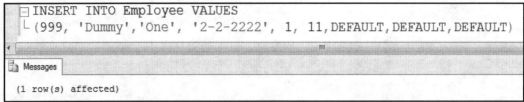

Figure 2.17 We are inserting this dummy data into dbo.Employee to confirm the trigger is disabled.

The confirmation of a single transaction (i.e., "1 row affected" shown in Figure 2.17) meets our expectations. Our insert of the dummy data affected only the Employee table. A SELECT COUNT query also confirms that the Employee table has increased to 20 records, but the EmployeeHistory table still contains just 19 records (see Figure 2.18).

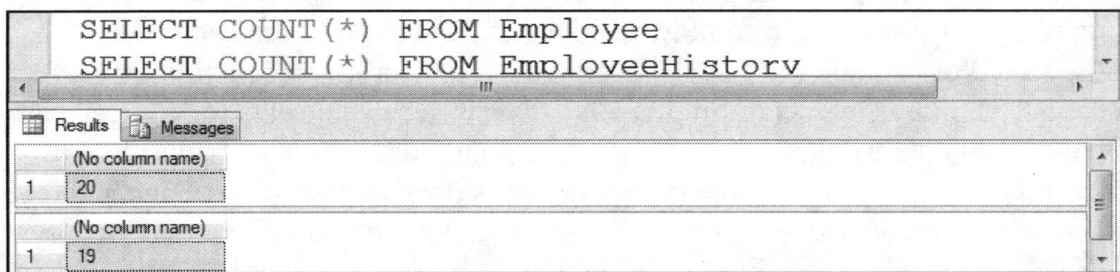

Figure 2.18 Due to the disabled insert trigger, dbo.EmployeeHistory still contains just 19 records.

It's now time to delete that one fictitious record from the Employee table. Run this DELETE statement to remove the dummy test record from your Employee table:

DELETE FROM Employee WHERE EmpID = 999

Now let's re-enable the trigger so that any data coming into dbo.Employee will be copied into dbo.EmployeeHistory (see Figure 2.19).

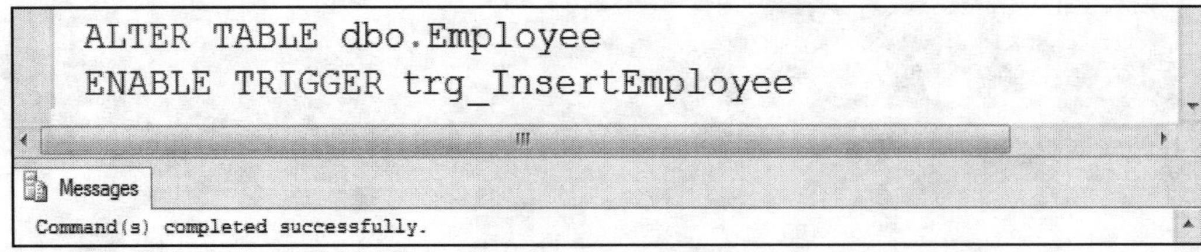

Figure 2.19 Code to re-enable the tgr_InsertEmployee trigger.

You can also disable the trigger directly. The figure below shows the alternate syntax, which will disable trg_InsertEmployee (see Figure 2.20).

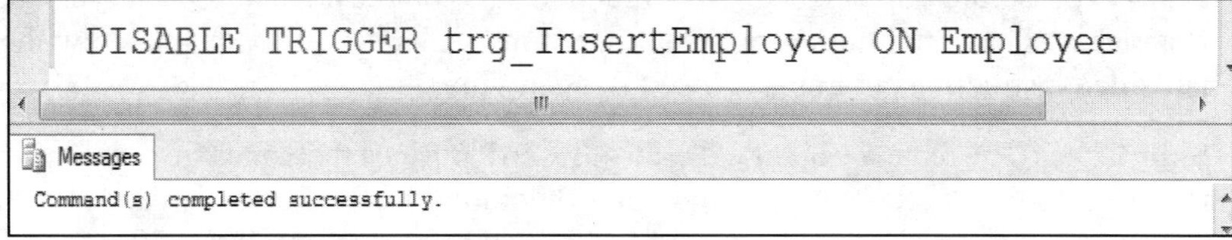

Figure 2.20 An alternate syntax for disabling our trigger.

With the trigger disabled, it won't function. Re-check the trigger in Object Explorer and notice that the trigger's icon now includes a small downward arrow, which indicates that the trigger has been disabled (see Figure 2.21).

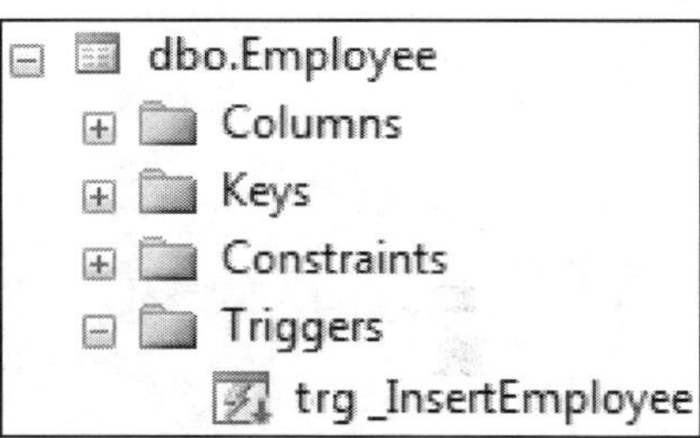

Figure 2.21 The red arrow indicates this trigger is disabled.

Now let's re-enable the trigger using the alternate code syntax (see Figure 2.22).

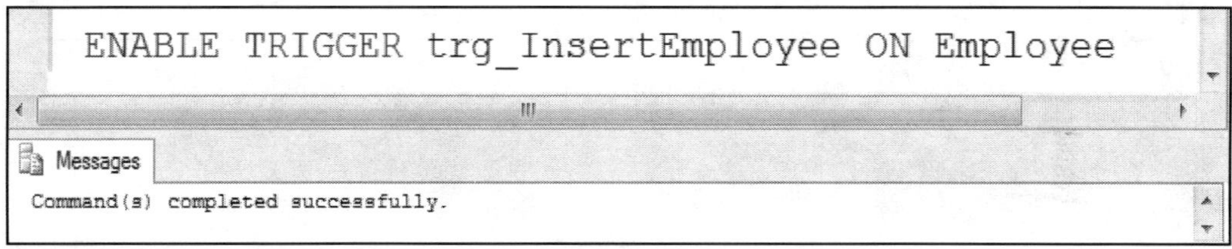

Figure 2.22 An alternate syntax for enabling a trigger.

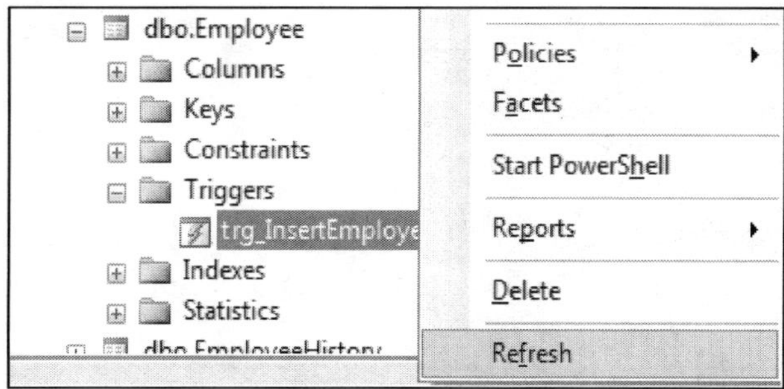

Figure 2.23 Refresh your trigger in Object Explorer to see its latest status.

Lab 2.1: Insert Triggers

Lab Prep: Before you can begin this practice lab, you must have SQL Server installed and have run the script SQLProgrammingChapter2.1Setup.sql. View the lab video instructions in Lab2.1_InsertTrigger.wmv.

Skill Check 1: Create a trigger called trg_InsertPayRates that takes inserted records into the PayRates table and copies them into the PayRatesHistory table. Test your trigger by inserting a pay of $45,000 per year for Employee 19.

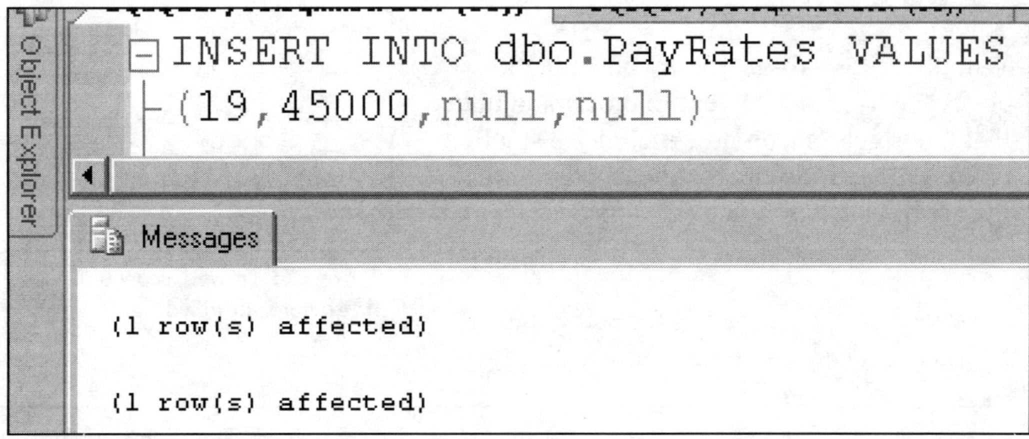

Figure 2.24 Skill Check 1

Answer Code: The T-SQL code to this practice lab can be found in the downloadable files in a file named Lab2.1_InsertTriggers.sql.

Insert Triggers - Points to Ponder

1. A trigger is a special type of stored procedure that is not called directly by a user.
2. A trigger is like a stored proc that executes when an INSERT, UPDATE, or DELETE event modifies data in a table.
3. When an insert trigger fires, it guarantees two things have occurred:
    a. You have at least one record in the Inserted table.
    b. You have at least one new record in the table that the insert trigger is on.
4. The Inserted table is a memory resident table (sometimes referred to as termed a "magic table" or a "special table") that holds a copy of the rows which have been inserted.
5. The trigger can examine the Inserted table to determine whether the trigger action(s) should be executed.
6. You can reference data from the Inserted table without having to store the data in @variables.
7. Triggers have access to the features of T-SQL and can therefore enforce complex business logic beyond constraints or rules.
8. Constraints can use system messages only for reporting errors. With triggers, you can customize error messages and mechanisms. (More information on constraints may be found in Chapter 1.)

Delete Triggers

We've learned that insert triggers run their code after an insert is made to a table. Similarly, an **after delete trigger** runs its code after a delete event occurs on a table. You will more commonly hear an (after) delete trigger simply referred to as a **delete trigger**.

Creating Delete Triggers

JProCo is a young company and thus far hasn't had anyone leave the company. We still have our original 19 employees. Since we someday may need to permanently delete a record from our Employee table, we need a history table to hold the records of employees who have left the company. In the JProCo db we have such a table, which is called dbo.FormerEmployee. Currently there are no records in the dbo.FormerEmployee table, because no one has been deleted (Figure 2.25).

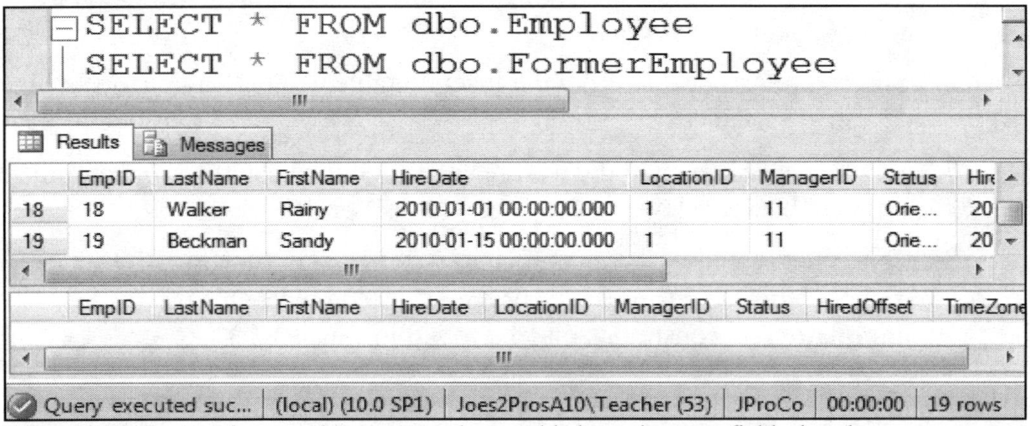

```
SELECT * FROM dbo.Employee
SELECT * FROM dbo.FormerEmployee
```

Results | Messages

	EmpID	LastName	FirstName	HireDate	LocationID	ManagerID	Status	Hire
18	18	Walker	Rainy	2010-01-01 00:00:00.000	1	11	Orie...	20
19	19	Beckman	Sandy	2010-01-15 00:00:00.000	1	11	Orie...	20

EmpID	LastName	FirstName	HireDate	LocationID	ManagerID	Status	HiredOffset	TimeZone

Query executed suc... | (local) (10.0 SP1) | Joes2ProsA10\Teacher (53) | JProCo | 00:00:00 | 19 rows

Figure 2.25 The Employee and FormerEmployee table have the same fields, but the FormerEmployee table is unpopulated since no one has left the company.

The moment a delete is made from the Employee table, we want the deleted record logged automatically into the dbo.FormerEmployee table. Figure 2.26 shows the trg_DelEmployee trigger on the Employee table which will run following a DELETE statement. This trigger will take the records from the Deleted table (which is based on what was deleted from the Employee table) and insert those records into the FormerEmployee table. A delete trigger creates the Deleted table.

(*Note:* The memory resident Inserted and Deleted tables were covered in Chapter 14, along with the OUTPUT statement in *SQL Queries Joes 2 Pros* Volume 2).

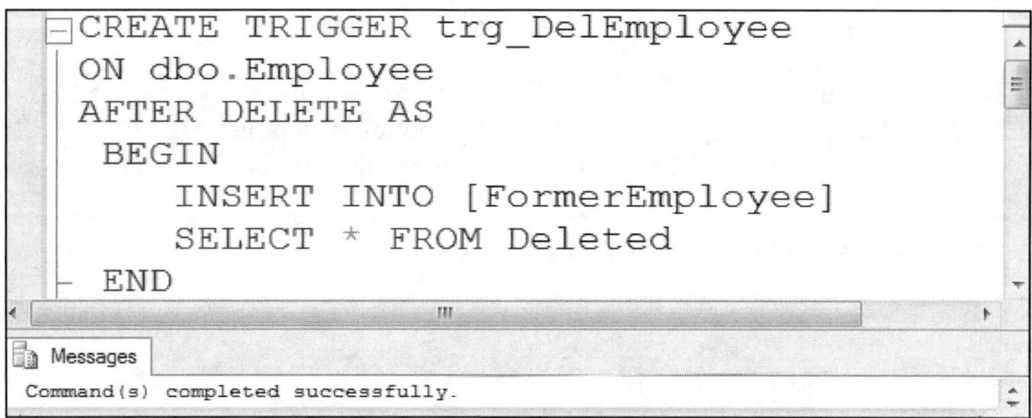

CREATE TRIGGER trg_DelEmployee
ON dbo.Employee
AFTER DELETE AS
BEGIN
INSERT INTO [FormerEmployee]
SELECT * FROM Deleted
END
Messages
Command(s) completed successfully.

Figure 2.26 Any record(s) deleted from dbo.Employee will be inserted into dbo.FormerEmployee.

After you see the "Command(s) completed successfully" confirmation, check the Object Explorer and notice that this new trigger is visible in the Triggers folder of the Employee table (see Figure 2.27). This is our second trigger on the Employee table. This first one was the trg_InsertEmployee trigger we created in the last section. Even though you can have many triggers on one table, you can only have one of each event type. The three possible event types are: *insert, update, and delete*. For example, we can't have two delete triggers on the Employee table.

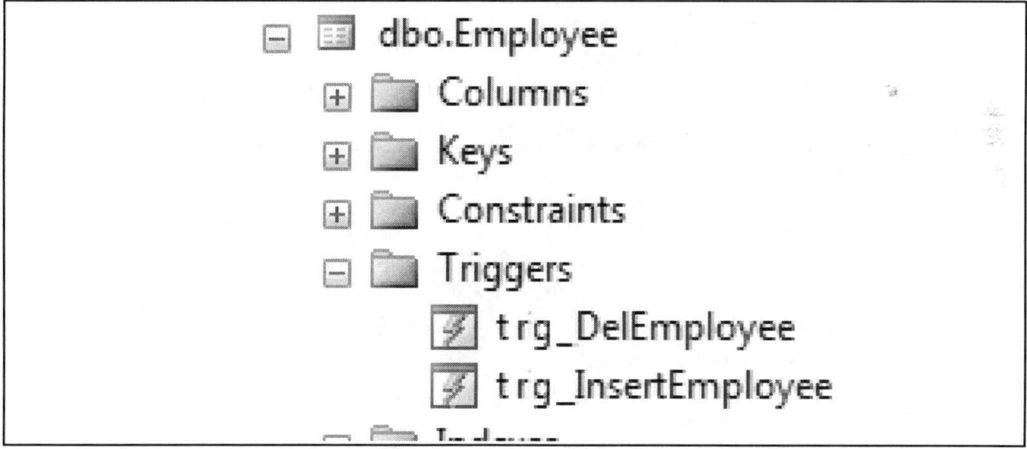

Figure 2.27 The insert and delete triggers can be seen in the Object Explorer.

Running Delete Triggers

To truly test this trigger, we should delete a record from the Employee table. Suppose that EmpID 19 (Sandy Beckman) is leaving. Running a DELETE statement should display “1 row(s) affected” twice in your messages tab.

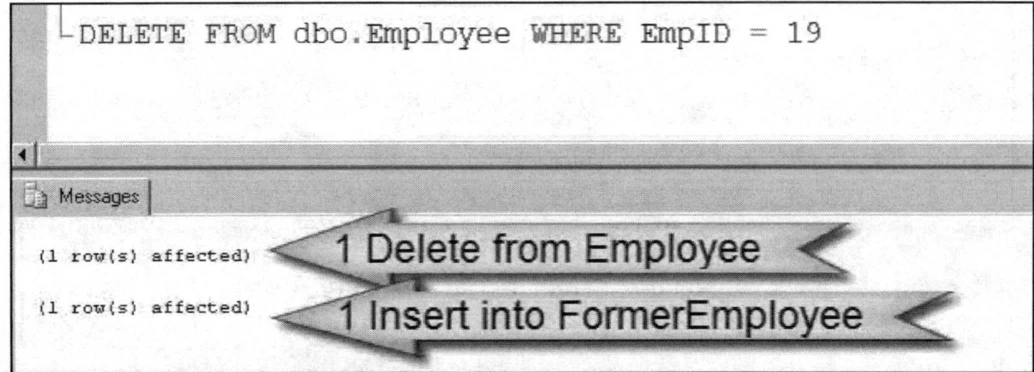

Figure 2.28 A delete from the Employee table fires the trg_DelEmployee trigger.

When you query each of the tables, you will notice that there are only 18 records in the Employee table instead of 19. The EmpID 19 row has been removed from the Employee table and now appears in the FormerEmployee table (Figure 2.29).

```
SELECT * FROM dbo.Employee
SELECT * FROM dbo.FormerEmployee
```

Results | Messages

	EmpID	LastName	FirstName	HireDate	LocationID	ManagerID	Status	Hir
17	17	Downs	Wendy	2010-09-26 10:52:22.950	1	11	Orie...	20
18	18	Walker	Rainy	2010-01-01 00:00:00.000	1	11	Orie...	20

	EmpID	LastName	FirstName	HireDate	LocationID	ManagerID	Status	Hi
1	19	Beckman	Sandy	2010-01-15 00:00:00.000	1	11	Orientation	2

Query executed suc... | (local) (10.0 SP1) | Joes2ProsA10\Teacher (54) | JProCo | 00:00:00 | 19 rows

Figure 2.29 Sandy Beckman’s record was deleted and now appears in the FormerEmployee table.

Note: In order to keep the focus on triggers, we used an extremely simplified version of a “history table” here. A historical record would also track additional datapoints, such as the employee’s departure date.

Using Triggers for Data Integrity

A common use of triggers is to protect, constrain, or add integrity to your data. To make this point more clearly, let's look at all the records from the Location table (see Figure 2.30).

```
SELECT * FROM Location
```

	LocationID	street	city	state	Latitude	Longitude	GeoLoc
1	1	545 Pike	Seattle	WA	47.455	-122.231	0xE6100000010C0A...
2	2	222 Second AVE	Boston	MA	42.372	-71.0298	0xE6100000010C56...
3	3	333 Third PL	Chicago	IL	41.953	-87.643	0xE6100000010C44...
4	4	444 Ruby ST	Spokane	WA	47.668	-117.529	0xE6100000010C2F...
5	5	1595 Main	Philadelphia	PA	39.888	-75.251	0xE6100000010C8B...
6	6	915 Wallaby Drive	Sydney	NULL	-33.876	151.315	0xE6100000010CE3...

Figure 2.30 All of the records of the Location table (JProCo.dbo.Location).

Suppose that we are decommissioning Location 3 (the Chicago office). The record containing LocationID 3 needs to be deleted from the Location table. This DELETE statement should accomplish that task (see Figure 2.31). However, take caution – if you inadvertently select and run only the first line of this DELETE statement, then you will delete every record in the Location table. If you see "6 rows affected", then you have accidentally deleted all of your records and your Location table is now unpopulated. Yikes!

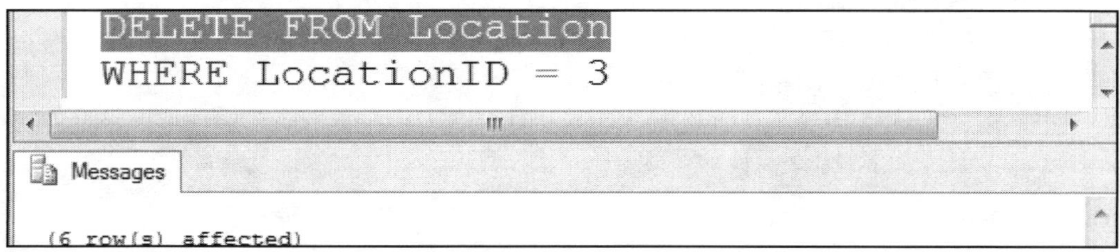
DELETE FROM Location
WHERE LocationID = 3
Messages
(6 row(s) affected)

Figure 2.31 Be careful – by selecting only part of this code, you might accidently delete all of the records from your Location table.

[*Note:* If you delete all the records from your Location table, either accidentally or because you wanted to fully demo the worst-case scenario, then please run the reset script **SQLProgrammingExtraResetLocation.sql** in order to restore the original six records to your Location table.]

To prevent this type of mishap in the future, we can add a trigger which will allow you to DELETE just one record per DML statement run against the Location table. A good name for this trigger would be trg_DelLocation. This **(after) delete trigger** will fire with each delete that takes place on the Location table. The code which you want to run when a delete occurs against dbo.Location will appear between the BEGIN and END keywords (Figure 2.32).

```
CREATE TRIGGER trg_DelLocation ON dbo.Location
AFTER DELETE AS
 BEGIN

 END
```

Figure 2.32 The trg_DelLocation trigger will run after a delete on the Location table.

What code should we place between the BEGIN and END commands? We can use an IF statement to get the count of the number of records in the Deleted table. If more than 1 record is found in the Deleted table, then we should roll back the entire transaction. Knowing this trigger runs after the DELETE statement has been called, will it be too late to undo the DELETE operation? No, because all "After Triggers" fire after the change has been made to the intermediate state records but before the transaction has been committed to storage. This means that within the trigger, you have the ability to roll back the transaction (Figure 2.33).

```
CREATE TRIGGER trg_DelLocation ON dbo.Location
AFTER DELETE AS
    BEGIN
    IF((SELECT Count(*) FROM Deleted) > 1)
    ROLLBACK TRAN
    END
```

Messages

```
Command(s) completed successfully.
```

Figure 2.33 Run all of this code to create trg_DelLocation.

Once you create the trigger (as shown in Figure 2.33), let's test our code. Attempt to delete all of the records from the Location table ("DELETE From Location"). If your trigger was created properly, then you will get the error shown in Figure 2.34.

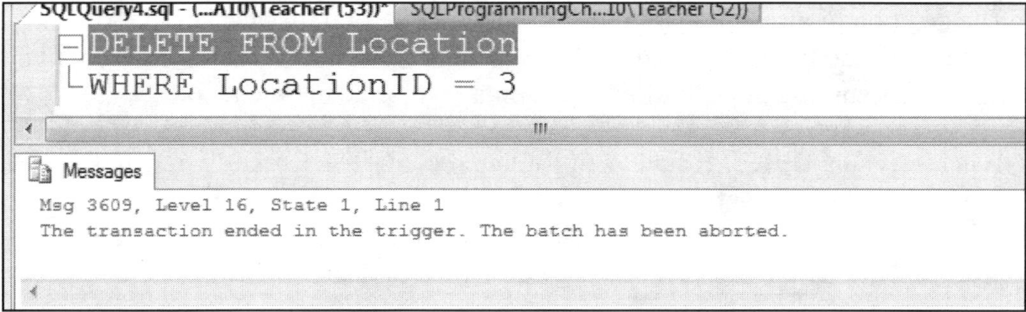

Figure 2.34 Accidently deleting more than one location at a time is rolled back by trg_DelLocation.

Now run the full DELETE statement, which removes only Location 3 (see Figure 2.35). The code in Figure 2.35 deletes one record. When you see the confirmation message "1 row(s) affected" you know that exactly one record was deleted. In order for the transaction to have completed – and therefore to have been allowed by the trigger – at most, one record could have been deleted.

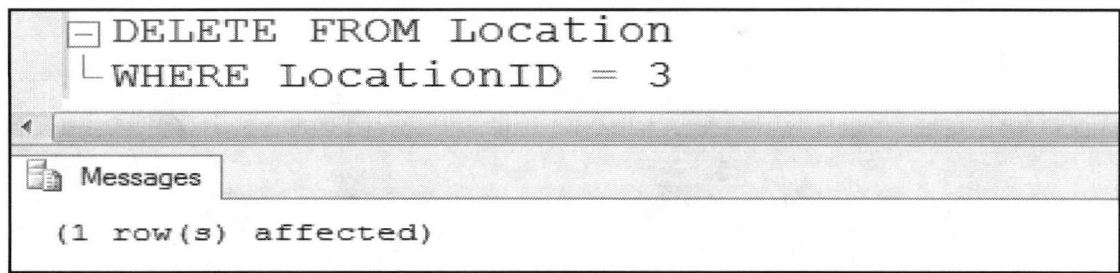

Figure 2.35 The trg_DelLocation trigger allowed the deletion of exactly one record.

Run a SELECT query and confirm Chicago is no longer in the Location table.

SQLQuery4.sql - (...A10\Teacher (53))* SQLProgrammingCh...10\Teacher (52))

```
SELECT * FROM Location
```

Results | Spatial results | Messages

	LocationID	street	city	state	Latitude	Longitude	GeoLoc
1	1	545 Pike	Seattle	WA	47.455	-122.231	0xE6100000010C0AD7A370
2	2	222 Second AVE	Boston	MA	42.372	-71.0298	0xE6100000010C560E2DB2
3	4	444 Ruby ST	Spokane	WA	47.668	-117.529	0xE6100000010C2FDD2406
4	5	1595 Main	Philade...	PA	39.888	-75.251	0xE6100000010C8B6CE7FB
5	6	915 Wallaby Dr...	Sydney	N...	-33.876	151.315	0xE6100000010CE3A59BC4

Query executed su... | (local) (10.0 SP1) | Joes2ProsA10\Teacher (53) | JProCo | 00:00:00 | 5 rows

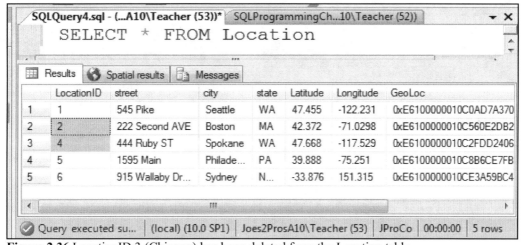

Figure 2.36 LocationID 3 (Chicago) has been deleted from the Location table.

The deletion of all the Location records at once will fail because of the trigger. Because of the trigger, any DELETE statement without a WHERE clause will not run (i.e., assuming the Location table contains more than one record).

When we ran a DELETE statement for one record, it successfully ran and committed that transaction. Therefore, we see we have Locations 1 through 6 (minus Location 3) left in our Location table. The trg_DelLocation trigger protected our data from any multi-record DELETE statement.

Lab 2.2: Delete Triggers

Lab Prep: Before you can begin this lab, you must have SQL Server installed and have run the script SQLProgrammingChapter2.2Setup.sql. It is recommended that you view the lab video instructions in Lab2.2_DeleteTriggers.wmv.

Skill Check 1: Create a trigger called trg_DeletePayRates that takes records deleted from the PayRates table and inserts them into the dbo.FormerPayRates table. Test your trigger by deleting the pay for Employee 1.

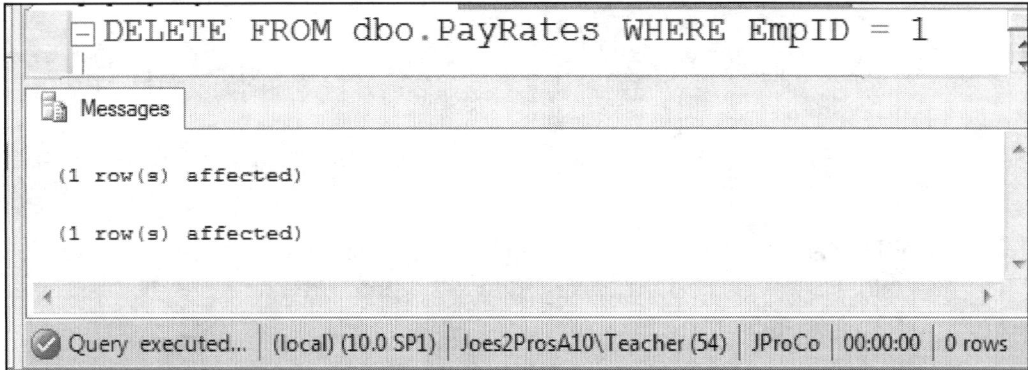

Figure 2.37 Skill Check 1.

Skill Check 2: Create a trigger called trg_DelStateList that ensures you can never delete multiple records at once from the StateList table.

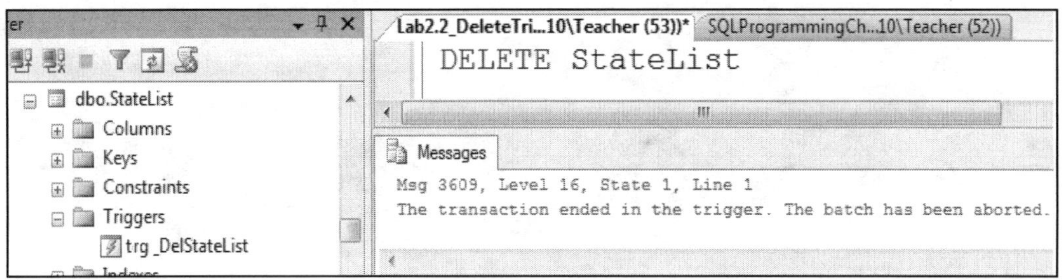

Figure 2.38 Skill Check 2.

Answer Code: The T-SQL code to this practice lab can be found in the downloadable files in a file named Lab2.2_DeleteTriggers.sql.

Delete Triggers - Points to Ponder

1. A DML trigger is a type of stored procedure that executes when the DML (Data Manipulation Language) statements UPDATE, INSERT, or DELETE run against a table or a view.
2. Much like constraints, it is possible to enforce data integrity through triggers. However, you should use constraints whenever possible.
3. A delete trigger is a stored proc that executes whenever a DELETE statement deletes data from a table.
4. When a delete trigger is fired, deleted rows from the affected table are placed in a special Deleted table.
5. When a row is appended to a Deleted table, it no longer exists in the table that fired the trigger.
6. A TRUNCATE TABLE statement run against a table will unpopulate that table. However, no DML triggers will be fired off since TRUNCATE is a DDL statement.
7. An “After Delete Trigger” fires after the change has been made to the intermediate state of the records. Records still in the intermediate state allow you the ability to roll back the transaction, if needed.

Update Triggers

We've learned that insert triggers create an Inserted table and delete triggers create a Deleted table. You can also create an **(after) update trigger,** which is more commonly referred to as an **update trigger.** This is the only trigger which creates both of these memory resident tables, since an update is really just a delete and an insert which occur in the same transaction.

Creating Update Triggers

The trg_InsertEmployee trigger does a fine job of keeping all the inserts to dbo.Employee in sync with dbo.EmployeeHistory. However, it won't work with an UPDATE statement run against the Employee table. *Insert triggers ignore updates.*

Let's look at one particular employee example. Employee 11 is "Sally Smith." She appears as EmpID 11 in the Employee table, as well as in the EmployeeHistory table. We have learned she will soon be married and her last name will become "Bowler." The JProCo database must be updated accordingly.

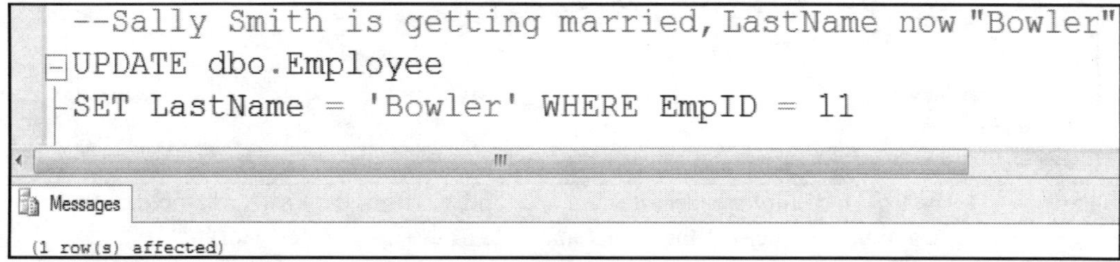

```
--Sally Smith is getting married,LastName now "Bowler"
UPDATE dbo.Employee
SET LastName = 'Bowler' WHERE EmpID = 11
```


Figure 2.39 EmpID 11's LastName has been updated to "Bowler."

Her name now appears as "Bowler" in the Employee table. But her name is still "Smith" in the EmployeeHistory table (see Figure 2.40).

```
SELECT * FROM dbo.Employee WHERE EmpID = 11
SELECT * FROM dbo.EmployeeHistory WHERE EmpID = 11
```


	EmpID	LastName	FirstName	HireDate	LocationID	ManagerID	Status	HiredOffset	Time.
1	11	Bowler	Sally	1989-04-01 00:00:00.000	1	NULL	Active	1989-04-01 00:00:00.0000000 -08:00	-08:0

	EmpID	LastName	FirstName	HireDate	LocationID	ManagerID	Status	HiredOffset	Time.
1	11	Smith	Sally	1989-04-01 00:00:00.000	1	NULL	Active	1989-04-01 00:00:00.0000000 -08:00	-08:0

Figure 2.40 The LastName "Bowler" was updated in dbo.Employee but not in EmployeeHistory.

This update to the Employee table was not reflected in the EmployeeHistory table because the insert trigger ignores UPDATE statements. We want to keep the

Employee and EmployeeHistory tables in tandem. An update trigger on the Employee table can help us accomplish this.

The code in Figure 2.41 shows the new trg_UpdEmployee trigger will take the latest LastName from the Inserted table and write that last name to the EmployeeHistory table. The trg_UpdEmployee will generate two memory resident tables, each having the same number of records but different values. The Deleted table will have one record containing the data you just replaced (Smith). The Inserted table will have one record showing the new data introduced by the UPDATE statement (Bowler). Since we want the new record "Bowler" to be in the EmployeeHistory table, this data must come from the Inserted table.

```
CREATE TRIGGER trg_UpdEmployee ON dbo.Employee
AFTER UPDATE AS
 BEGIN
    UPDATE dbo.EmployeeHistory
    SET lastname = E.LastName
    FROM dbo.EmployeeHistory EH
    INNER JOIN Inserted E
    ON EH.EmpID = E.EmpID
 END
```

Messages

Command(s) completed successfully.

Figure 2.41 The trg_UpdEmployee trigger will take updates from the LastName field of the Employee table and update them to the LastName field of the EmployeeHistory table.

Running Update Triggers

After successfully creating trg_UpdEmployee (as shown in Figure 2.41), we will test it with another update to the Employee table. There was some confusion about Sally's name, which actually should have been changed to "Zander", not "Bowler" (see Figure 2.42).

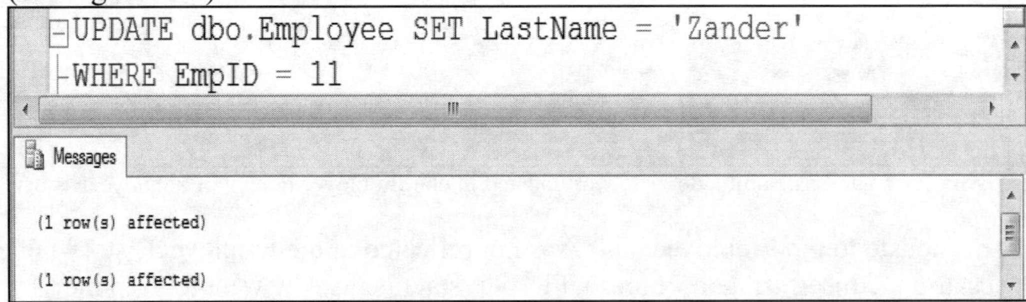
UPDATE dbo.Employee SET LastName = 'Zander'
WHERE EmpID = 11
Messages
(1 row(s) affected)
(1 row(s) affected)

Figure 2.42 An UPDATE to the Employee table will now also update the EmployeeHistory table.

Let's rerun our two SELECT statements to confirm that Sally's LastName value has been successfully updated to "Zander" in both tables (Figure 2.43).

```
SELECT * FROM dbo.Employee WHERE EmpID = 11
SELECT * FROM dbo.EmployeeHistory WHERE EmpID = 11
```

	EmpID	LastName	FirstName	HireDate	LocationID	ManagerID	Status	HiredOffset	Time
1	11	Zander	Sally	1989-04-01 00:00:00.000	1	NULL	Active	1989-04-01 00:00:00.0000000 -08:00	-08:(

	EmpID	LastName	FirstName	HireDate	LocationID	ManagerID	Status	HiredOffset	Time
1	11	Zander	Sally	1989-04-01 00:00:00.000	1	NULL	Active	1989-04-01 00:00:00.0000000 -08:00	-08:(

Figure 2.43 The LastName value of "Zander" for EmpID 11 appears in both the Employee and EmployeeHistory tables.

Update Triggers and Data Integrity

You saw how an update trigger is useful for keeping two tables updated in tandem. You might be wondering just how an update trigger is useful for data integrity.

Take the example of the StateList table. Changes to this table will be extremely rare – the U.S. hasn't added a new state since 1959, and LandMass changes would also be rare. Therefore, the data in the StateList table is very stable. Let's imagine the U.S. entered into a contract whereby Russia will sell us 50 square miles of an island which it is not using and which will be useful for our fishing business. This new island will be added to the Aleutian Island Chain in Alaska. As a result, Alaska will increase in size by 50 square miles.

```
SELECT * FROM StateList
```

	StateID	StateName	RegionName	LandMass
1	AK	Alaska	USA	656425
2	AL	Alabama	USA-Continental	52423
3	AR	Arkansas	USA-Continental	53182
4	AZ	Arizona	USA-Continental	114006
5	CA	California	USA-Continental	163707
6	CO	Colorado	USA-Continental	104100
7	CT	Connecticut	USA-Continental	5544
8	DC	District of Columbia	USA-Continental	68
9	DE	Delaware	USA-Continental	2489
10	FL	Florida	USA-Continental	65758

Figure 2.44 The StateList table.

The LandMass for Alaska will go from 656,425 to 656,475. The UPDATE statement (shown in Figure 2.45) will make this change to our StateList table.

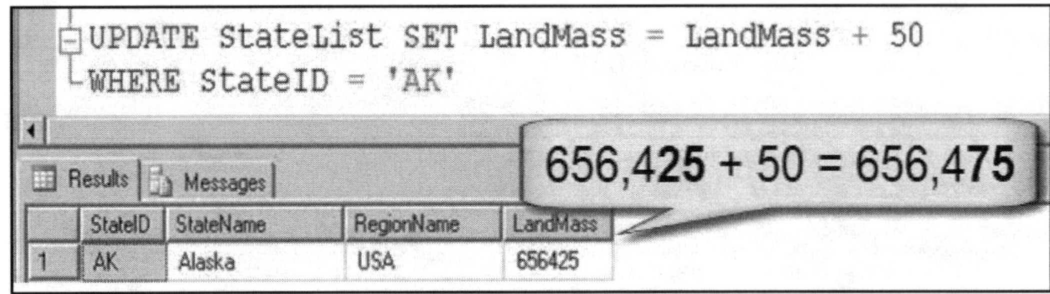

Figure 2.45 This UPDATE statement shows Alaska will gain 50 square miles of LandMass.

You could have easily and unintentionally run this UPDATE statement and forgotten your WHERE clause. Then all states would have increased by 50 square miles. Since changes to the StateList table are very uncommon, we're going to limit it so that only one state record may be updated at a time (Figure 2.46).

Changes to StateList happen to one record at a time and happen very rarely.

	StateID	StateName	RegionName	LandMass
1	AK	Alaska	USA	656425
2	AL	Alabama	[illegible]Continental	52423
3	AR	Arkansas	[illegible]Continental	53182
4	AZ	Arizona	USA-[illegible]ntinental	114006
5	CA	California	USA-Conti[illegible]ntal	163707
6	CO	Colorado	USA-Continental	104100

Figure 2.46 We want to disallow updates which affect multiple records within one statement.

Some changes should never happen. For example, once a StateID is set, it should never be changed. For example, you would want an update changing the StateID 'AK' to 'AS' to fail (Figure 2.47).

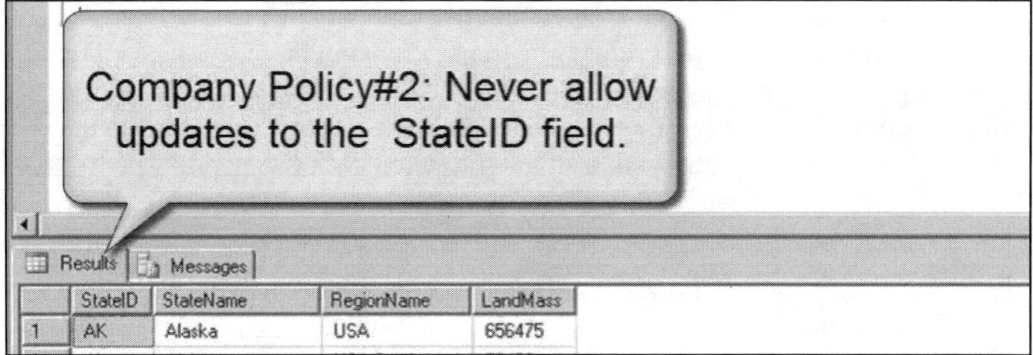

Figure 2.47 The StateID field should never be updated.

You might be tempted to create two delete triggers on the StateList table, one which prevents multiple deletes and another which prevents StateID changes. Like any other table, the StateList table can have only one delete trigger. We need to create a very complicated trigger that accomplishes two things for us: 1) ensure that you can't update more than one state at a time, and 2) never allow updates to the StateID field.

We will write the code to create the trg_UpdateStateList on the StateList table with the BEGIN and END ready to hold the code logic for our trigger. Remember, the "Update Trigger" is the only trigger which uses both the Inserted and Deleted tables (Figure 2.48).

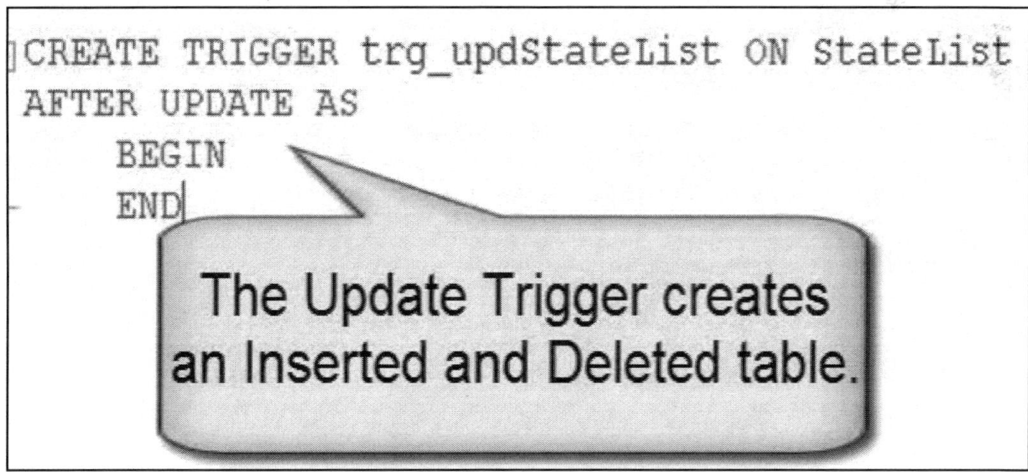

Figure 2.48 Update triggers will create two memory resident tables (Inserted and Deleted).

The code in Figure 2.49 checks for a count of more than one record that has been changed. (If such a change is found, the transaction will be rolled back.) That handles policy #1. To handle policy #2, we need another statement that says, "If we find a record where the Inserted and Deleted tables seem to have a different StateID value, then the transaction should be rolled back (Figure 2.49)."

```
CREATE TRIGGER trg_updStateList ON StateList
AFTER UPDATE AS
 BEGIN
    IF((SELECT COUNT(*) FROM Inserted )> 1)
    ROLLBACK TRAN

 END
```

Figure 2.49 The first part of the trigger will rollback transactions affecting more than one record.

To find out if two StateID fields don't match, simply run an unmatched query between the Inserted and Deleted tables. If you find null values in the StateID field of the Deleted table, then roll back the transaction (Figure 2.50).

```
CREATE TRIGGER trg_updStateList ON StateList
AFTER UPDATE AS
 BEGIN
    IF((SELECT COUNT(*) FROM Inserted )> 1)
    ROLLBACK TRAN

    IF EXISTS(SELECT * FROM Inserted
                 LEFT OUTER JOIN Deleted
                 ON Inserted.StateID = Deleted.StateID
                 WHERE Deleted.StateID IS NULL)
    ROLLBACK TRAN
 END
```

Messages

Command(s) completed successfully.

Figure 2.50 The stored procedure has a second IF statement to check for any unmatched records between the Inserted and Deleted tables.

After the trg_updStateList has been successfully created, we will do some testing. Observe that the UPDATE statement shown in Figure 2.51 would attempt to run multiple updates. However, trg_UpdateStateList blocks these updates. Because the count in the IF block is greater than one, the ROLLBACK TRAN code is executed (see Figure 2.51).

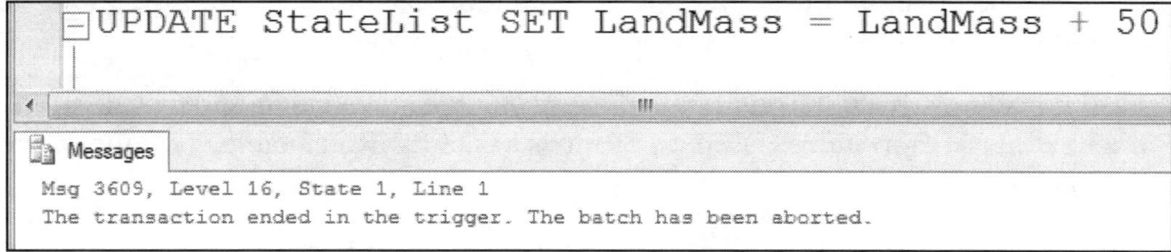
UPDATE StateList SET LandMass = LandMass + 50
Messages
Msg 3609, Level 16, State 1, Line 1
The transaction ended in the trigger. The batch has been aborted.

Figure 2.51 An update to multiple records in one transaction is disallowed by the trigger.

The UPDATE statement in Figure 2.52 would try to change a StateID field. The IF EXISTS code inside of the trigger finds an unmatched record, and thus the trigger rolls back the transaction (see Figure 2.52).

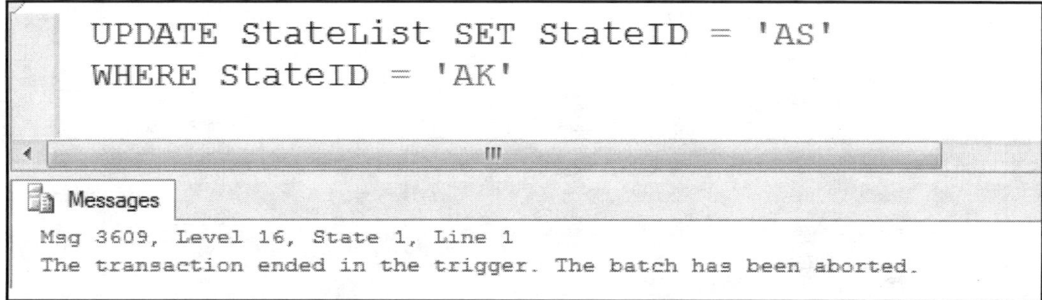
UPDATE StateList SET StateID = 'AS'
WHERE StateID = 'AK'
Messages
Msg 3609, Level 16, State 1, Line 1
The transaction ended in the trigger. The batch has been aborted.

Figure 2.52 Updating a StateID is also not allowed.

Let's attempt a change which should be allowed. The UPDATE statement in Figure 2.53 is only affecting one field and doesn't impact the StateID field. This is allowed and the transaction completes. *Success!!* The trigger allowed this change to occur and our update is successful (see Figure 2.53).

```
UPDATE StateList
SET RegionName = 'USA: Non-Continental'
WHERE StateID = 'AK'
```

Messages

```
(1 row(s) affected)
```

Figure 2.53 Updating a single record (in which the StateID field doesn't change) is allowed.

Lab 2.3: Update Triggers

Lab Prep: Before you can begin this practice lab, you must have SQL Server installed and have run the script SQLProgrammingChapter2.3Setup.sql. View the lab video instructions in Lab2.3_UpdateTriggers.wmv.

Skill Check 1: Create a trigger called trg_UpdPayRates, which updates all fields of the PayRatesHistory table based on changes to the PayRates table. Test the trigger by updating the YearlySalary of EmpID 11 to 150,000.

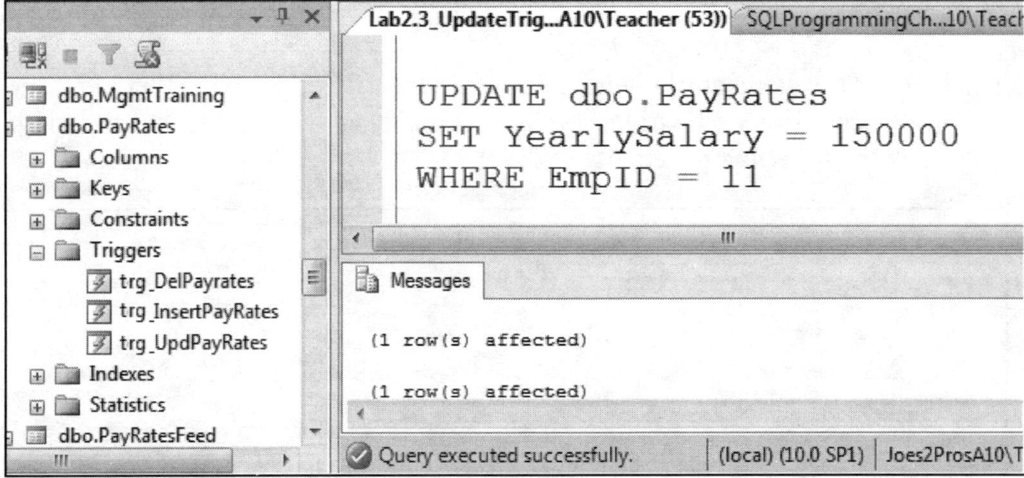

Figure 2.54 Skill Check 1 result.

Skill Check 2: Create a trigger called trg_updGrant, which will not allow you to make updates to the existing values of the GrantID field.

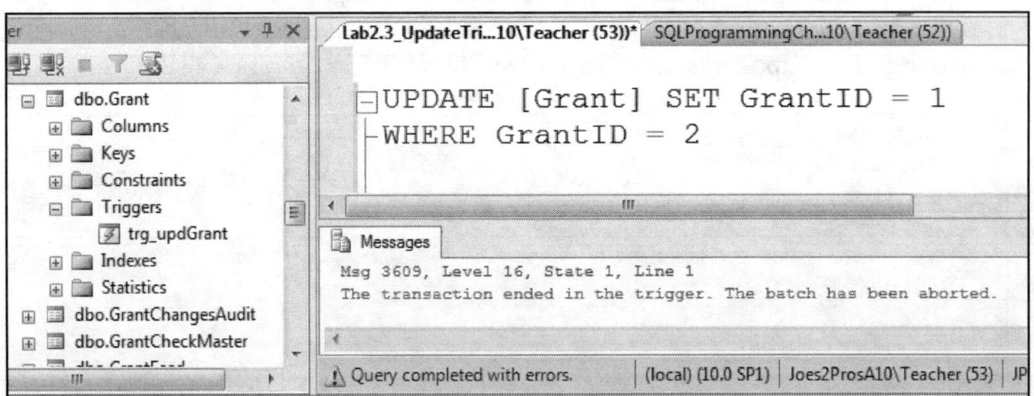

Figure 2.55 Skill Check 2 result.

Skill Check 3

Sometimes updates are made to the SalesInvoiceDetail table; these updates represent a new OrderDate for an existing SalesInvoice. After a change is made to the SalesInvoiceDetail table, you need to update the SalesInvoice.UpdatedDate field to reflect the current date and time. Write a trigger named upd_SalesInvoiceDetail to achieve this goal. Test your trigger by updating InvoiceID 1 to have a 0.05 Unit Discount (upper Figure 2.56). Check to see that the SalesInvoice table has the newer timestamp (lower Figure 2.56).

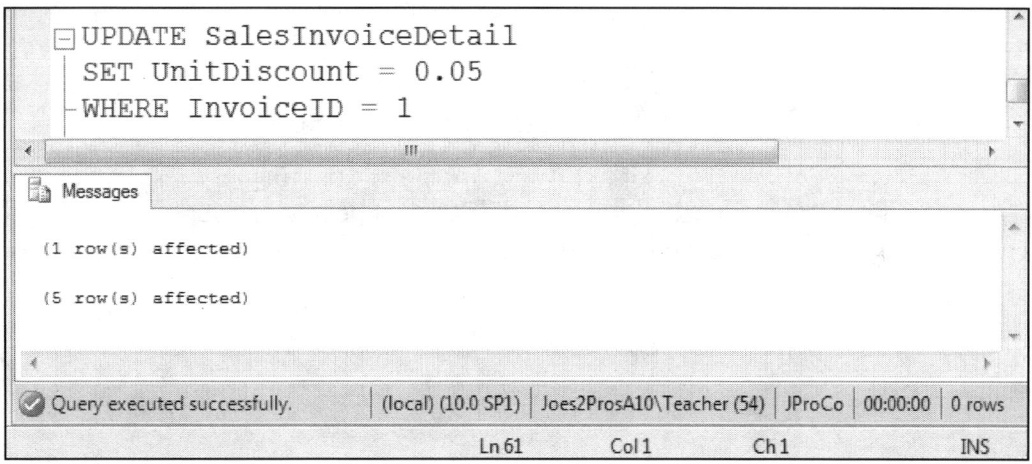

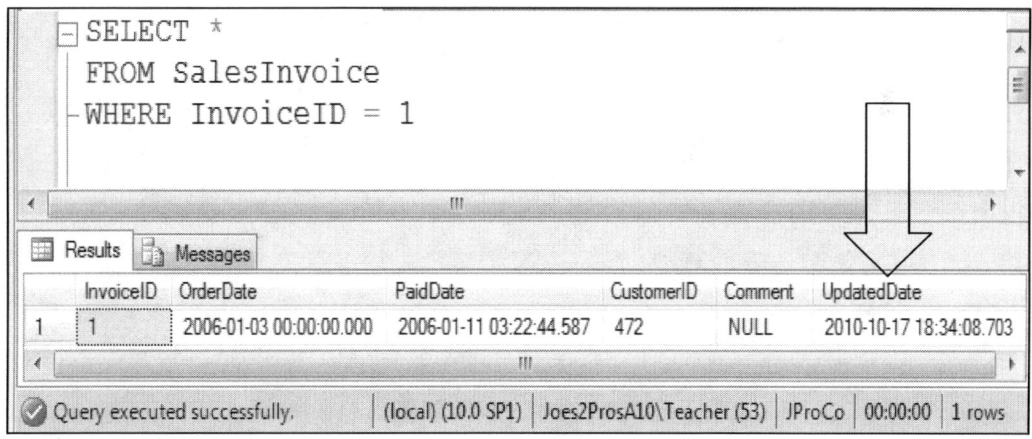

Figure 2.56 Skill Check 3.

Answer Code: The T-SQL code to this lab can be found in the downloadable files in a file named Lab2.3_UpdateTriggers.sql.

Update Triggers - Points to Ponder

1. An update trigger is a trigger that executes whenever an UPDATE statement changes data in a table or view on which the trigger is configured.
2. An update operation is really comprised of two steps: a delete and an insert.
3. The update trigger actually creates two cached tables (Deleted and Inserted).
4. If you don't want a trigger to run, there are three ways to disable the trigger:
    a. Right-click the trigger and select Disable.
    b. Execute the DISABLE TRIGGER T-SQL command.
    c. Execute the ALTER TABLE T-SQL command
5. INTERVIEW QUESTION: What are the special memory resident tables available when dealing with triggers? Most people answer "Inserted, Updated, and Deleted." However, there are only two tables: Inserted and Deleted.

Chapter Glossary

After trigger: a stored procedure that executed after the action specified has taken place.

CREATE TRIGGER: the DDL statement used to create all types of triggers.

DDL: Data Definition Language. Statements that define data structures. The most common are CREATE, ALTER, and DROP.

DELETE TABLE: a DML statement that removes records from your table and logs the action.

Delete trigger: also called an "after delete trigger." A trigger that fires after a DELETE statement has taken place on the table containing the trigger.

DML: Data Manipulation Language. Statements which manipulate or retrieve data. The most common are SELECT, INSERT, UPDATE, and DELETE.

Insert trigger: a trigger that executes after, or instead of, an insert operation.

Magic tables: see *Memory resident tables.*

Memory resident tables: Conceptual tables (Inserted and Deleted) that have the same structure as the table containing the trigger. These work behind the scenes of every INSERT, UPDATE, and DELETE operation. Several techniques make use of DML statements run against these memory resident tables (e.g., triggers, the OUTPUT clause, the MERGE statement, Change Tracking). The Inserted and Deleted tables can only be accessed within the execution (trigger) context. As of this book's publication, there is no uniformly recognized term for the Inserted and Deleted tables; you may hear SQL pros refer to them as "magic tables", "special tables", or "pseudo tables."

SELECT INTO: selects data from one table and inserts it into another table.

Special tables: see *Memory resident tables.*

Transaction: the process SQL performs to take a DML request to get committed to permanent storage.

Trigger: a stored procedure that automatically fires based on an event.

TRUNCATE TABLE: a DDL statement which removes all records from a table and does not perform any logging of the action.

Update trigger: a trigger that fires after an UPDATE statement has taken place on the table containing the trigger.

Chapter Two - Review Quiz

1.) What is the only DML statement that will never fire off an after trigger?

O a. SELECT
O b. INSERT
O c. UPDATE
O d. DELETE

2.) Which of the following are memory resident tables created by an update trigger? (Choose two)

□ a. INSERTED
□ b. UPDATED
□ c. DELETED

3.) You want to perform a test insert against your dbo.Employee table which has an insert trigger on it. You are not allowed to delete the trigger but want to perform this insert without the trigger firing. How can you do this?

O a. You can't.
O b. Downgrade the trigger before your test and then upgrade afterwards.
O c. Move the trigger to a new table then move back after your test.
O d. Disable the trigger before the test and then enable it afterwards.
O e. Enable the trigger before the test and then disable it afterwards.

4: You have a trigger named trg_InsertEmployee which fires whenever a new employee is inserted into the Employee table. You are getting ready to test a new process to import employees from an external feed. As your first test you are going to insert five fictitious employees named Dummy1 through Dummy5. If the test succeeds, then you will later delete these employees. You never want these employees to appear in the EmployeeHistory table. Your boss tells you she likes your existing triggers, so you can't delete them. To disable your trigger during testing, which two T-SQL statements could you run? (Choose two)

□ a. ALTER TABLE Employee DISABLE TRIGGER trg_InsertEmployee
□ b. DROP TRIGGER trg_InsertEmployee
□ c. DISABLE TRIGGER trg_InsertEmployee ON Employee
□ d. ALTER TRIGGER tgr_InsertEmployee ON Employee NOT FOR REPLICATION
□ e. Sp_SetTrigger@TriggerName = 'trg_InsertEmployee'. @Order = 'none'

5.) Sometimes an after trigger will have no populated memory resident tables.

O a. True
O b. False

6.) The SalesInvoice and SalesInvoiceDetail tables relate to each other on the InvoiceID column. You require that the SalesInvoice.UpdatedDate column reflect the date when a change was made to the corresponding InvoiceID in the SalesInvoiceDetail table. You want to use a trigger to fulfill the requirement. What code should you use?

O a.
```
CREATE TRIGGER upd_SalesInvoiceDetail ON SalesInvoiceDetail
INSTEAD OF UPDATE
AS
UPDATE SalesInvoiceDetail
   SET UpdatedDate = GetDate( )
   FROM Inserted INNER JOIN SalesInvoiceDetail
   ON Inserted.InvoiceID = SalesInvoiceDetail.InvoiceID
```

O b.
```
CREATE TRIGGER upd_SalesInvoiceDetailON SalesInvoiceDetail
INSTEAD OF UPDATE
AS
UPDATE SalesInvoice
   SET UpdatedDate = GetDate( )
   FROM Inserted INNER JOIN SalesInvoice
   ON Inserted.InvoiceID = SalesInvoice.InvoiceID
```

O c.
```
CREATE TRIGGER upd_SalesInvoiceDetail ON SalesInvoiceDetail
AFTER UPDATE
AS
UPDATE SalesInvoiceDetail
   SET UpdatedDate = GetDate( )
   FROM Inserted INNER JOIN SalesInvoiceDetail
   ON Inserted.InvoiceID = SalesInvoiceDetail.InvoiceID
```

O d.
```
CREATE TRIGGER upd_SalesInvoiceDetail ON SalesInvoiceDetail
AFTER UPDATE
AS
UPDATE SalesInvoice
   SET UpdatedDate = GetDate( )
   FROM Inserted INNER JOIN SalesInvoice
   ON Inserted.InvoiceID = SalesInvoice.InvoiceID
```

Answer Key

1.) a 2.) a c 3.) d 4.) a c 5.) b 6.) d

Bug Catcher Game

To play the Bug Catcher game, run the file BugCatcher_Chapter2AfterTriggers.pps from the BugCatcher folder of the companion files located at www.Joes2Pros.com.

Chapter 3. Other Triggers

While growing up, I recall my mother asking whether I had homework to do over the weekend. She taught me well! After I would say, "Yeah, but I will do it on Sunday," she told me that instead of procrastinating, I should do it on Friday night and free my schedule for the rest of the weekend. Thus, my action of doing homework on Sunday didn't need to happen. That behavior (i.e., that old routine of Sunday homework) was superseded and replaced with a new action of doing the work on Friday night. My mom is a great teacher, and that paradigm shift has helped inform my lifelong study habits and approach to learning.

This relates to the **instead of triggers** we will see in this chapter. In the last chapter, we saw triggers which handled operations that sometimes we wanted to complete but under other conditions we wanted them halted and rolled back. After triggers watch our tables – they allow good actions and disallow the bad. However, the activities **instead of triggers** watch for are ones which we never want to happen. If there's an activity you know you're never going to allow, why even let it begin to run? When after triggers roll back disallowed transactions, that process consumes system resources (the DML statement runs, the trigger determines it must be disallowed, and then the transaction gets rolled back). **Instead of triggers** block the bad actions before they even begin.

In this chapter we will also look at nested triggers, DDL triggers, and some additional techniques for using triggers to control input and activity in our database.

READER NOTE: *In order to follow along with the examples in the first section of Chapter 3, please run the setup script SQLProgrammingChapter3.0Setup.sql. The setup scripts for this book are posted at Joes2Pros.com.*

The Instead of Trigger

The **instead of trigger** never allows the user action to run. When a statement which is disallowed by the system runs, the trigger runs and provides the user a message regarding the attempted action. This is perfect for historical tables, which shouldn't be updated. Rather than allowing the update to run, you want to display a friendly message (not an error), which will prompt your users not to update this table directly.

By way of contrast, let's review the structure and code syntax of an after delete trigger. In each example in Chapter 2, we saw the DML statement run. If a DML statement met a prohibited condition, the trigger was invoked and the transaction rolled back. The trigger trg_DelEmployeeHistory enforces the policy that historical records of the EmployeeHistory archive table may not be changed (see Figure 3.1).

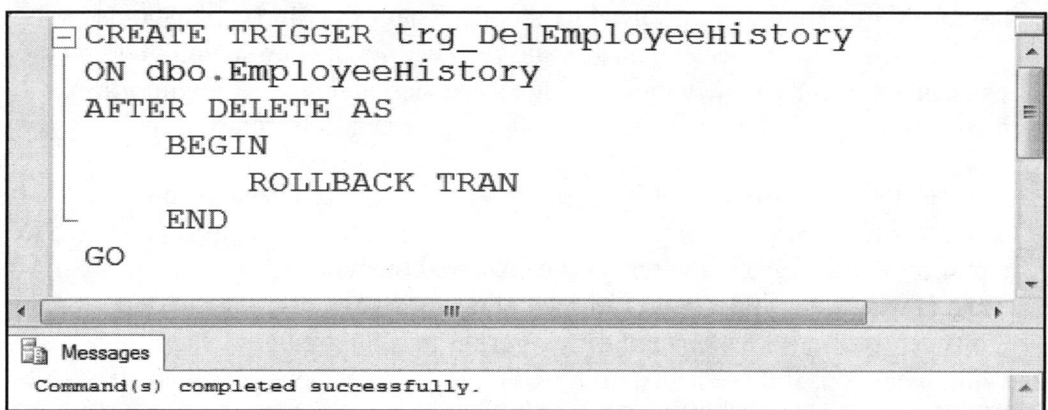
```
CREATE TRIGGER trg_DelEmployeeHistory
ON dbo.EmployeeHistory
AFTER DELETE AS
    BEGIN
        ROLLBACK TRAN
    END
GO
```
Messages
Command(s) completed successfully.

Figure 3.1 The trg_DelEmployeeHistory trigger will roll back the transaction after a delete on the EmployeeHistory table is started.

If a user attempts to delete a record from the EmployeeHistory table, they will get an error message (see Figure 3.2).

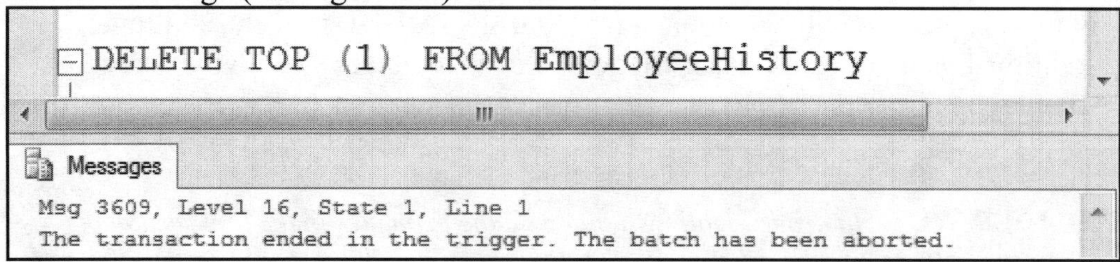
```
DELETE TOP (1) FROM EmployeeHistory
```
Messages
Msg 3609, Level 16, State 1, Line 1
The transaction ended in the trigger. The batch has been aborted.

Figure 3.2 The trigger trg_DelEmployeeHistory is rolling back all EmployeeHistory deletes.

The DELETE statement actually ran, reached the intermediate state, and then we rolled it back before the transaction could be committed.

Since all DELETE statements from the EmployeeHistory table are prohibited by policy, it would be better to have the database disallow them entirely and give your users some specific message letting them know why their operation is not allowed. As well, it would be better to not waste system resources by allowing each attempted operation to run and then be rolled back.

Let's remove the existing trg_DelEmployeeHistory trigger (see Figure 3.3) so that we can re-create it as an instead of trigger.

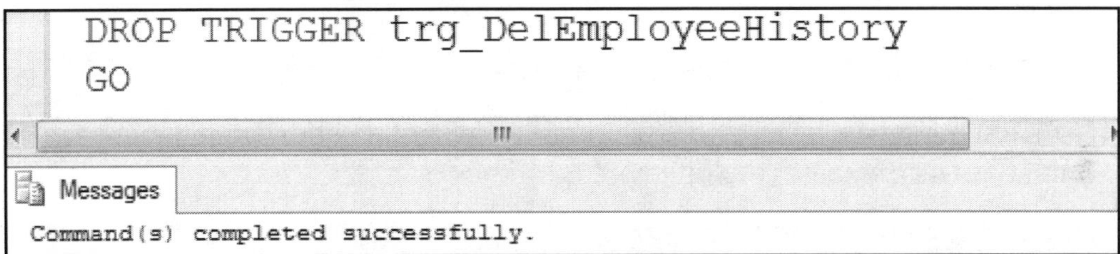
DROP TRIGGER trg_DelEmployeeHistory
GO
Messages
Command(s) completed successfully.

Figure 3.3 The trg_DelEmployeeHistory trigger is dropped so we can re-create it differently.

Creating Instead Of Triggers

Contrast this code (see Figure 3.4 below) with the after trigger we built earlier (shown in Figure 3.1). There is no ROLLBACK TRAN statement needed, since the trigger stops the DELETE statement from ever running. Observe that INSTEAD OF DELETE AS replaces AFTER DELETE AS. The code we want to run instead will appear between the BEGIN and the END commands.

```
CREATE TRIGGER trg_DelEmployeeHistory
ON dbo.EmployeeHistory
INSTEAD OF DELETE AS
    BEGIN
        --Place Code Here to run Instead of the Delete
    END
GO
```

Figure 3.4 This code builds the trg_DelEmployeeHistory instead of trigger.

We will display a print message to the user, "Historical records are never to be deleted" (see Figure 3.5).

```
CREATE TRIGGER trg_DelEmployeeHistory
ON dbo.EmployeeHistory
INSTEAD OF DELETE AS
    BEGIN
        PRINT 'Historical Records are never to be deleted'
    END
GO
```

Messages

Command(s) completed successfully.

Figure 3.5 Put what you want to run between the BEGIN and END keywords.

Running Instead Of Triggers

Let's test our new trigger by reattempting the record deletion from the EmployeeHistory table (see Figure 3.6).

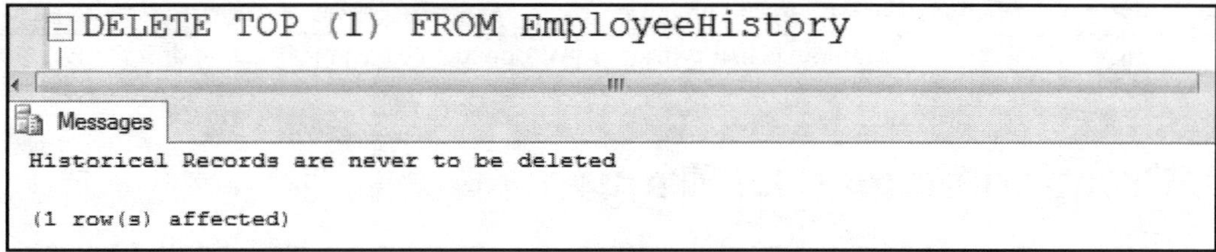
DELETE TOP (1) FROM EmployeeHistory
Messages
Historical Records are never to be deleted
(1 row(s) affected)

Figure 3.6 Testing the trigger on the EmployeeHistory table displays the print message to the user.

This transaction never takes place. The user receives the *"Historical Records are never to be deleted"* message. Notice the "1 row(s) affected" message also appears. (This will display unless your users have NOCOUNT set to ON. NOCOUNT is discussed in Chapter 13.) No row in the EmployeeHistory table is affected – this is simply a reference to the Deleted table. The memory resident tables (Inserted and Deleted) are always impacted by a delete or insert trigger, even in the case of instead of triggers.

In our next example, we'll see that this behavior can be useful and that our instead of triggers can utilize data from the memory resident tables. This example is best shown using a small dbo.Test table (created by the code in Figure 3.7) and a row of values to be inserted into it (see Figure 3.8). We need to insert just two values, since TestID is an identity field (identity fields are covered in Chapter 3 of *SQL Queries Joes 2 Pros*). Suppose that the hardcoded date value represents data from a feed – in any case, our scenario will require us to update this field.

```
CREATE TABLE Test
(
TestID INT IDENTITY(1,1),
TestName varchar(40),
CreationDate date
)
```

Messages

Command(s) completed successfully.

Figure 3.7 Create the simple table named Test, which has with three fields.

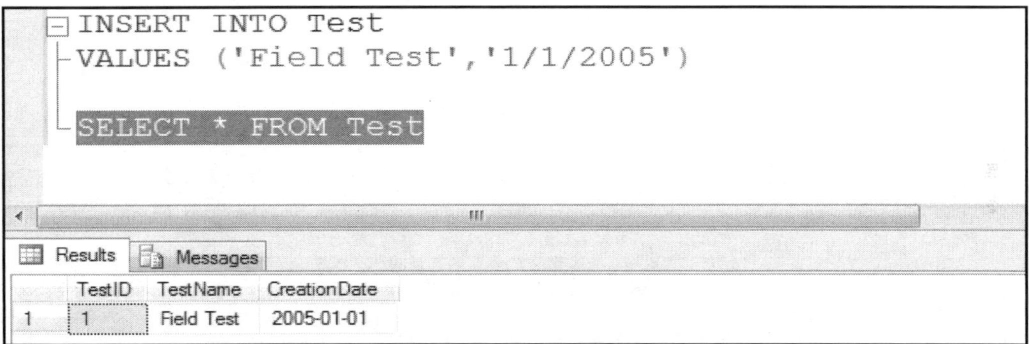
INSERT INTO Test
VALUES ('Field Test','1/1/2005')
SELECT * FROM Test
Results
Messages
TestID
TestName
CreationDate
1
1
Field Test
2005-01-01

Figure 3.8 One record has been inserted into the Test table.

We have been instructed to change any hardcoded date value to today's date. If we owned this data, we could simply include the GetDate( ) function as part of our INSERT statement. However, in this scenario we aren't the data owners of this datafeed. Someone else provided this data; we neither own the code, nor are we allowed to change it. That feed is coming from a C# (C-Sharp) calling application which we are not allowed to touch or change. Thus, whenever new data comes in, we run the UPDATE statement (see Figure 3.9).

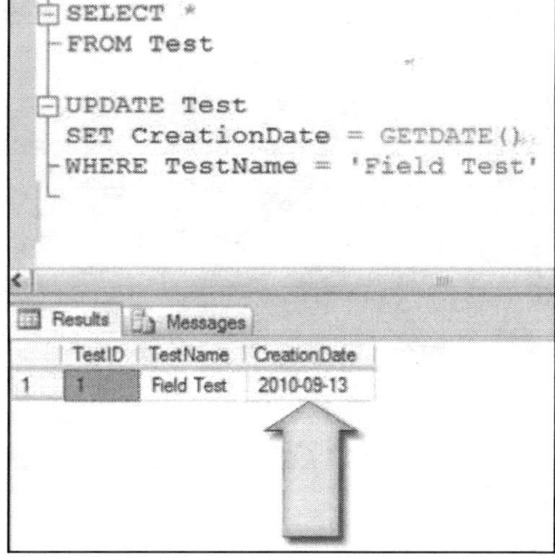
SELECT *
FROM Test
UPDATE Test
SET CreationDate = GETDATE()
WHERE TestName = 'Field Test'
Results
Messages
TestID
TestName
CreationDate
1
1
Field Test
2010-09-13

Figure 3.9 CreationDate now reflects today's date.

If we could capture the calling INSERT statement and feed the current date instead of the hardcoded values, then we could turn this into a single step with no need to update the record later. The **trg_InsertTest** instead of trigger will help us accomplish this. Study the code below (in Figure 3.10) and notice that this trigger will halt each INSERT statement and prevent it from loading data directly into the Test table. Instead, the trigger retrieves the TestName data which has been captured by the (memory resident) Inserted table, uses GetDate( ) as the CreationDate value, and then passes those datapoints into the Test table.

```
CREATE TRIGGER trg_InsertTest
ON dbo.Test
INSTEAD OF INSERT
AS
BEGIN
    INSERT INTO dbo.Test
    SELECT TestName,GetDate() FROM Inserted
END
GO
```

Messages

```
Command(s) completed successfully.
```

Query executed successfully. | (local) (10.0 SP1) | Joes2ProsA10\Teacher (54) | JProCo | 00:00:00 | 0 rows

Figure 3.10 The trigger will insert the new record with the current date into the dbo.Test table.

Let's test our new trigger by running a second insert (shown in Figure 3.11).

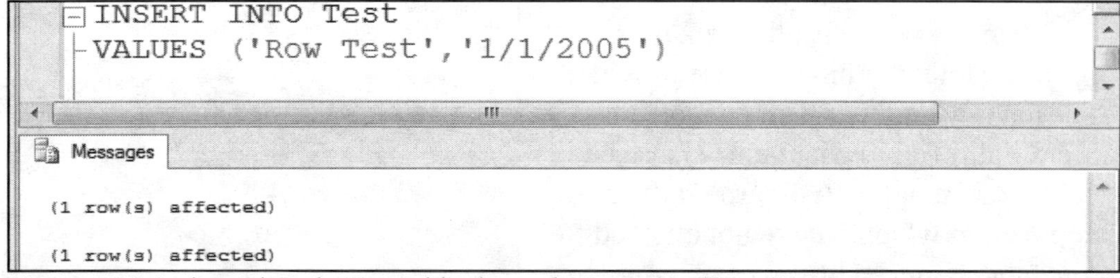
INSERT INTO Test
VALUES ('Row Test','1/1/2005')
Messages
(1 row(s) affected)
(1 row(s) affected)

Figure 3.11 An insert into the Test table shows the 1 row(s) affected message twice.

The two "1 row(s) affected" confirmations represent the Inserted table transaction and the actual record added to the Test table. Run a SELECT query to look at all the data in the Test table (see Figure 3.12). You'll notice the record was inserted as specified, except the CreationDate values reflect the current date. (*Note:* When you run this example, your CreationDate will not match Figure 3.12. It will be the current date shown by your system when you run the inserts.)

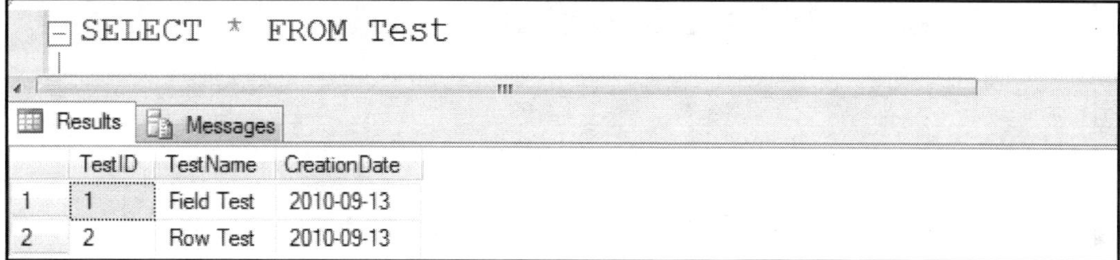

Figure 3.12 The CreationDate value for the newly inserted record is the current date.

Putting Multiple Events on One Trigger

Suppose that no changes may be made directly to the StateList table for the next month. This means no inserts, updates, or deletions will be allowed to run.

In order to solve this, you could create three separate triggers on one table (trg_InsertStateList for the inserts, trg_UpdateStateList for the updates, and trg_DelStateList for the deletions).

Alternatively, you could create one instead of trigger to look for all three events. The code below (see Figure 3.13) demonstrates the syntax for this type of a trigger.

```
CREATE TRIGGER trg_InsteadStateList
ON dbo.StateList
INSTEAD OF INSERT, DELETE, UPDATE AS
 BEGIN
        Print 'No changes are to be made to the StateList table Directly'
 END
GO
```

```
Messages
Command(s) completed successfully.
```

Figure 3.13 One trigger can look for many events (inserts, updates, and deletes).

Test this trigger by attempting to delete records contained in the StateList table. Instead of allowing any DML change to be made to StateList, this instead of trigger prints a message ("No changes are to be made to the StateList table directly").

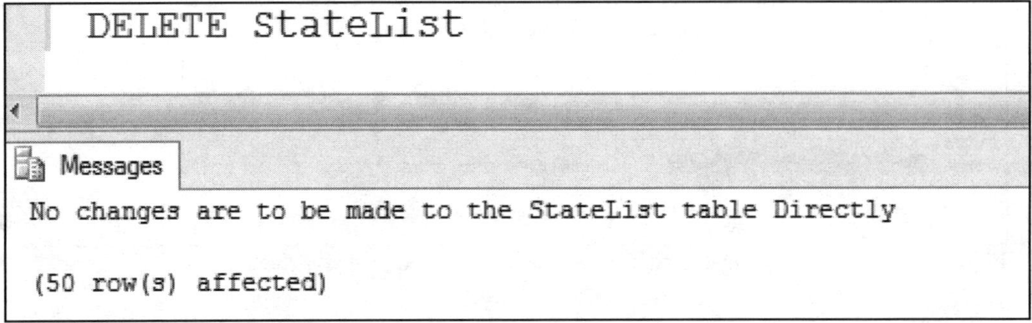
DELETE StateList
Messages
No changes are to be made to the StateList table Directly
(50 row(s) affected)

Figure 3.14 Any attempted DML change to StateList causes the trg_InsteadStateList trigger to run.

Lab 3.1: "Instead Of" Triggers

Lab Prep: Before you can begin this practice lab, you must have SQL Server installed and have run the script SQLProgrammingChapter3.1Setup.sql. View the lab video instructions in Lab3.1_InsteadOfTriggers.wmv.

Skill Check 1: Create a trigger called trg_DelPayRatesHistory on the PayRatesHistory table that shows the message "Historical records are never to be deleted" instead of performing the delete action.

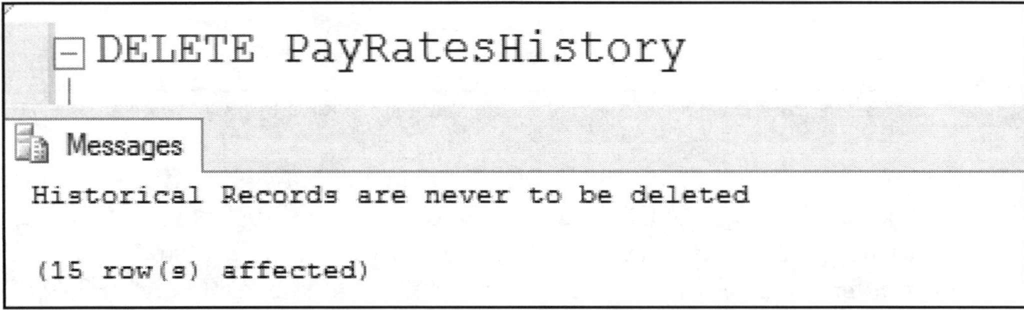

Figure 3.15 Skill Check 1.

Skill Check 2: Create a trigger called trg_InsertEmployeeHistory on the EmployeeHistory table that shows the message "Insertion of new records to the EmployeeHistory table must take place by inserting to the Employee table."

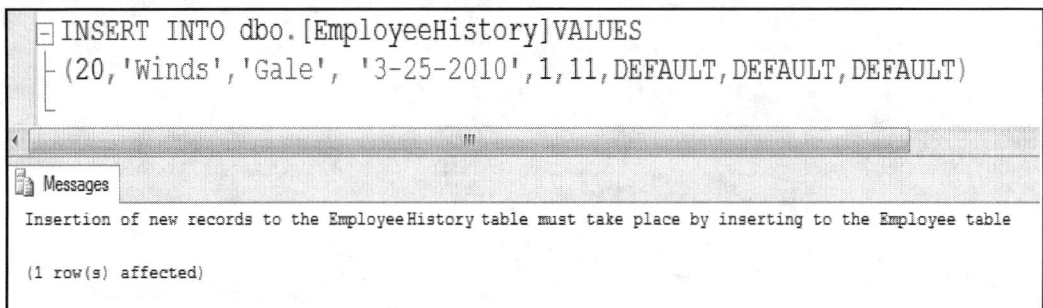

Figure 3.16 Skill Check 2.

Skill Check 3: Your MgmtTraining table has the CK_MgmtTraining_ApprovedDate constraint, which disallows dates prior to 2006. The calling application has been traced using the following code and is getting the error message you see in Figure 3.17.

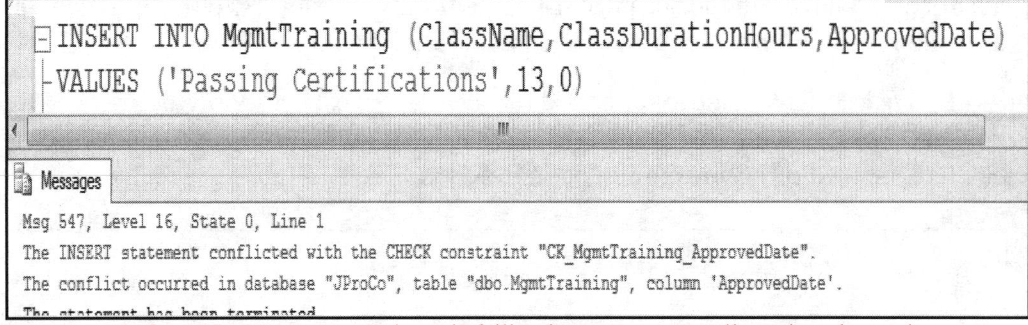

INSERT INTO MgmtTraining (ClassName,ClassDurationHours,ApprovedDate)
VALUES ('Passing Certifications',13,0)
Messages
Msg 547, Level 16, State 0, Line 1
The INSERT statement conflicted with the CHECK constraint "CK_MgmtTraining_ApprovedDate".
The conflict occurred in database "JProCo", table "dbo.MgmtTraining", column 'ApprovedDate'.

Figure 3.17 The INSERT statement above is failing but you are not allowed to change it.

You are not allowed to change the INSERT statement, but you need to insert the current time in the ApprovedDate field. Create the trg_InsertManagmentTraining trigger to use GetDate instead of zero. Run the INSERT statement and query your MgmtTraining table. When complete, your result should resemble Figure 3.18.

```
INSERT INTO MgmtTraining (ClassName,ClassDurationHours,ApprovedDate)
VALUES ('Passing Certifications',13,0)

SELECT * FROM MgmtTraining
```

Results | Messages

	ClassID	ClassName	ClassDurationHours	ApprovedDate
1	1	Embracing Diversity	12	2007-01-01 00:00:00.000
2	2	Interviewing	6	2007-01-15 00:00:00.000
3	3	Difficult Negotiations	30	2008-02-12 00:00:00.000
4	4	Empowering Others	18	2010-10-02 09:56:44.133
5	7	Passing Certifications	13	2010-10-02 10:03:44.643

Query executed successfully. | (local) (10.0 SP1) | Joes2ProsA10\Teacher (53) | JProCo

Figure 3.18 Skill Check 3 result.

Answer Code: The T-SQL code to this lab can be found in the downloadable files in a file named Lab3.1_InsteadOfTriggers.sql.

"Instead Of" Triggers - Points to Ponder

1. Triggers can intercept INSERT, UPDATE, or DELETE statements which you don't want to run.
2. There are two categories of triggers.
   a. After Triggers – executed after the INSERT, UPDATE, or DELETE is performed. You can only define these on tables. AFTER triggers can be specified for tables but not for views.
   b. Instead of Triggers – are executed in place of the usual triggering action. Unlike AFTER triggers, INSTEAD OF triggers can be specified for both tables and views.
3. An instead of trigger executes in place of the triggering action.
4. When an INSERT or DELETE trigger is associated with a table, any data inserted or deleted from the table will be written to a corresponding temporary table (also known as memory resident tables, magic tables, or special tables).
5. Each table or view is limited to one instead of trigger for each DML action. This means you may have up to one for inserts, one for updates, and/or one for deletes.
6. You cannot create an instead of trigger on views that have the WITH CHECK OPTION defined.
7. If you are not using an instead of trigger, then multiple triggers can fire off from the same event. In other words, you can have two triggers on the same table.

Nesting Triggers

A trigger which fires another trigger is known as a **nested trigger**.

Earlier in this chapter we ensured that no direct inserts could be made to the EmployeeHistory table (as we saw back in Figure 3.16). We see this rule enforced below (see Figure 3.19) where the attempted insert of EmpID 20 (Gale Winds) results in the message, "Insertion of new records to the EmployeeHistory table must take place by inserting to the Employee table." Thus, the trg_InsertEmployeeHistory trigger is still behaving as we expect it to – *we are not allowed to directly insert records into the EmployeeHistory table.*

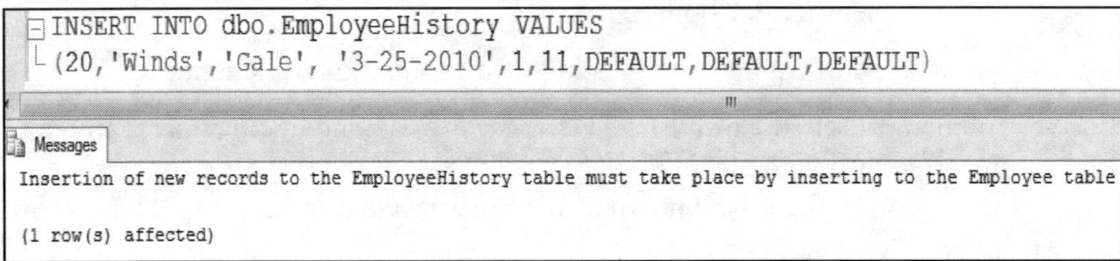

Figure 3.19 The trg_InsertEmployeeHistory trigger disallows the direct insertion of records into the EmployeeHistory table. The only row affected is the Inserted table.

Let's think back to the last chapter and recall the rules we established for the Employee table. Direct inserts are allowed to the Employee table, and each employee record must be copied into the EmployeeHistory table by the trg_InsertEmployeeHistory trigger (as last shown in Chapter 2, Figure 2.12). Only the trigger should be adding records to the EmployeeHistory table – humans should not be allowed to directly enter records into the EmployeeHistory table. Let's attempt to insert Gale's record into the Employee table and confirm our expected rules are in place (see Figure 3.20).

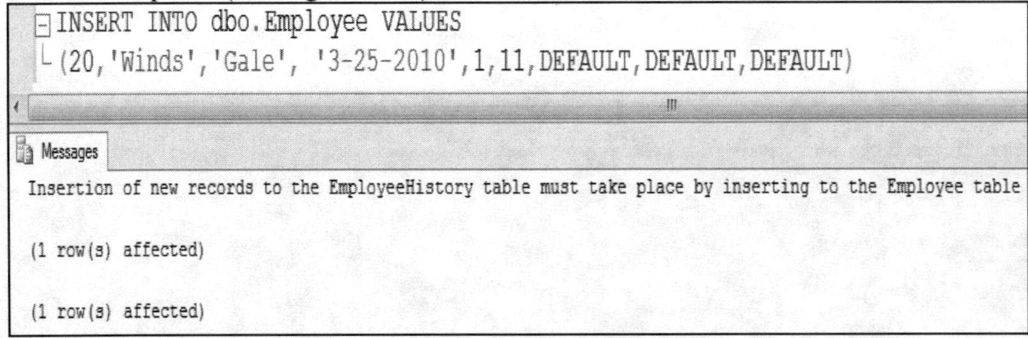

Figure 3.20 We can insert this record directly into the Employee table. However, the trigger on the EmployeeHistory table is disallowing the insert from the Employee table (tgr_insertEmployee).

We see two separate row transactions and the print message. Let's check the Employee table to see whether Gale's record was inserted successfully.

```
SELECT * FROM Employee
```

Results | Messages

	EmpID	LastName	FirstName	HireDate	LocationID	ManagerID	Status	HiredOffset	TimeZon
15	15	Jones	Tess	2011-01-17...	1	11	Orientation	2011-01-17...	-08:00
16	16	Biggs	Nancy	2011-01-17...	1	11	Orientation	2011-01-17...	-08:00
17	17	Downs	Wendy	2011-01-17...	1	11	Orientation	2011-01-17...	-08:00
18	18	Walker	Rainy	2010-01-01...	1	11	Orientation	2011-01-17...	-08:00
19	20	Winds	Gale	2010-03-25...	1	11	Orientation	2011-01-17...	-08:00

Query executed successfully. | (local) (10.0 SP1) | MoreTechA6\Student (52) | JProCo | 00:00:00 | 19 rows

Figure 3.21 Yes, the Employee table accepted our direct insertion of Gale's record.

Let's look back to the result displayed (see Figure 3.20) when we attempted to insert Gale's record directly into the Employee table. Since we know the Employee table accepted our direct insertion of Gale's record (as demonstrated by Figure 3.21), then one of the row transactions was our insert to the Employee table. Thus, it's clear the other row transaction ("1 row(s) affected") was the record temporarily captured by the Inserted table, and the printed message was produced by the EmployeeHistory table's instead of trigger (trg_InsertEmployeeHistory).

We have a problem with trg_InsertEmployeeHistory's design, because it is currently blocking all types of inserts to the EmployeeHistory table. It should allow inserts by the trigger on the Employee table but continue to disallow attempts by users to insert records directly into the Employee table. *How do you forbid just the direct inserts but allow inserts from other triggers to run?*

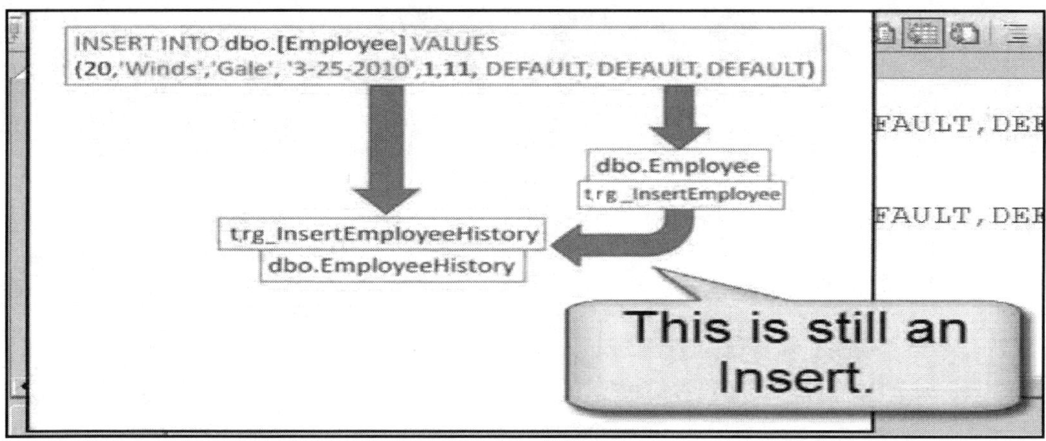

Figure 3.22 The EmployeeHistory trigger is currently preventing all types of inserts.

Using @@NESTLEVEL

Sometime people think that nesting triggers are also recursive triggers. However, **recursion** occurs when an object runs an action which, in turn, causes the action to be repeated. If the trg_InsertEmployee inserted a record into the Employee table, this would cause the trg_InsertEmployee to fire again. Notice that this is not happening here. Instead, the insert is firing another trigger, which means that these two separate triggers are nested.

The EmployeeHistory table should accept inserts which come from the Employee table's trigger (tgr_InsertEmployee). We've learned that the trigger on the EmployeeHistory table (trg_InsertEmployeeHistory) is overly restrictive and is blocking inserts from other triggers. In order to correct this situation, we need to understand how to differentiate between inserts coming from other triggers and inserts made directly to the table.

When an insert comes from a trigger and fires off another trigger, this is a **nested trigger**. Inserts from nested triggers into the EmployeeHistory table should be allowed. If an insert is called directly, the trigger will have a @@NESTLEVEL of 1. If a trigger runs a DML statement which causes another trigger to run, then the second trigger would have a @@NESTLEVEL of 2.

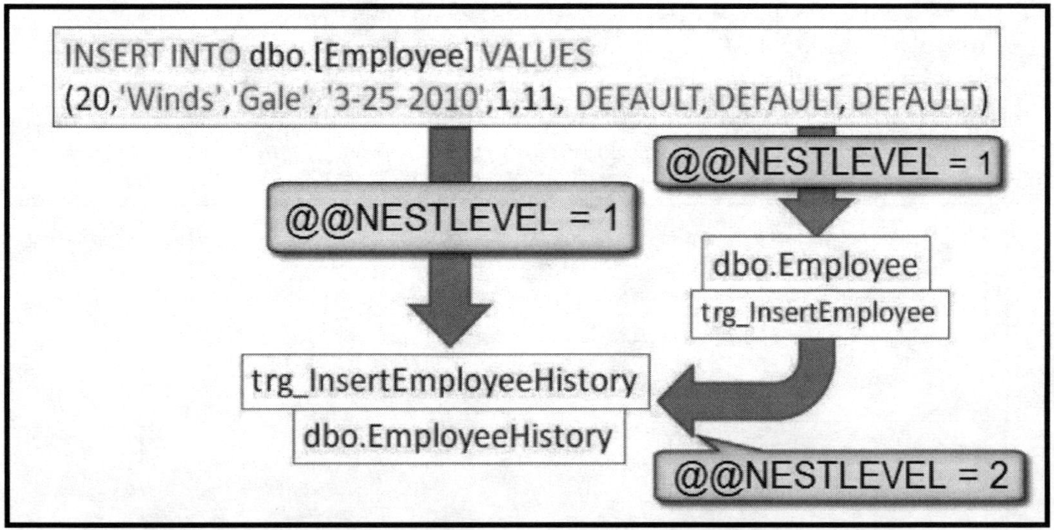

Figure 3.23 Each insert in a chain of triggers gets a higher NestLevel value.

What we need is a more discriminating trigger, one that will deny inserts at the nest level 1, but will allow inserts from other triggers at a higher nest level.

Let's reset the Employee table by deleting our last insert (EmpID 20, Gale Winds) (see Figure 3.24).

```
DELETE FROM Employee WHERE EmpID = 20
```

```
Messages
(1 row(s) affected)

(1 row(s) affected)
```

Figure 3.24 Reset the Employee table by removing our last inserted record (Gale Winds).

We must modify the trg_InsertEmployeeHistory trigger to check for the @@NESTLEVEL. Run the ALTER TRIGGER statement below (see Figure 3.25), which will block inserts where the @@NESTLEVEL is 1 and display a print message to the user. If a @@NESTLEVEL of 1 is not found, then the record will be inserted into the EmployeeTable.

```
ALTER TRIGGER dbo.trg_InsertEmployeeHistory
ON dbo.EmployeeHistory
INSTEAD OF INSERT AS
    BEGIN
        IF @@NESTLEVEL = 1
        Print 'Dont insert to EmployeeHistory directly'
        ELSE
        INSERT INTO [EmployeeHistory] SELECT * FROM Inserted
    END
GO
```

```
Messages
Command(s) completed successfully.
```

Figure 3.25 The insert is allowed if the @@NESTLEVEL is not equal to 1.

The trg_InsertEmployeeHistory trigger intercepts all inserts to the EmployeeHistory table. Inserts coming from a @@NESTLEVEL of 1 (i.e., inserts attempted directly on the EmployeeHistory table) are disallowed. If the @@NestLevel is not 1, then the record is retrieved from the Inserted table (i.e., the special memory resident table) and inserted into the EmployeeHistory table.

Let's test the revised trigger by reattempting to insert Gale's record into the Employee table (see Figure 3.26).

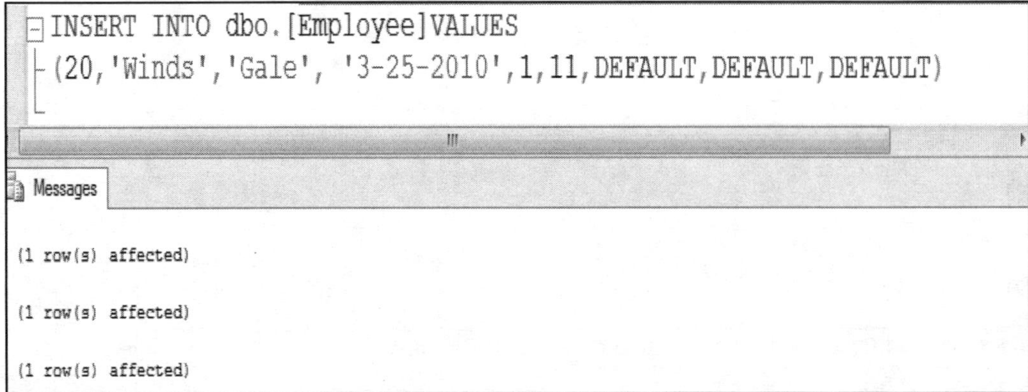

Figure 3.26 The trigger from the Employee table is able to insert into the EmployeeHistory table.

The lack of a print message, other than the three transaction confirmations ("1 row(s) affected"), is the result we expected to see. The Employee table, the Inserted table, and the EmployeeHistory table each received one record.

Let's confirm our successful result by querying the EmployeeHistory table and seeing that Gale's record (EmpID 20) has been inserted successfully by the nested trigger (see Figure 3.27).

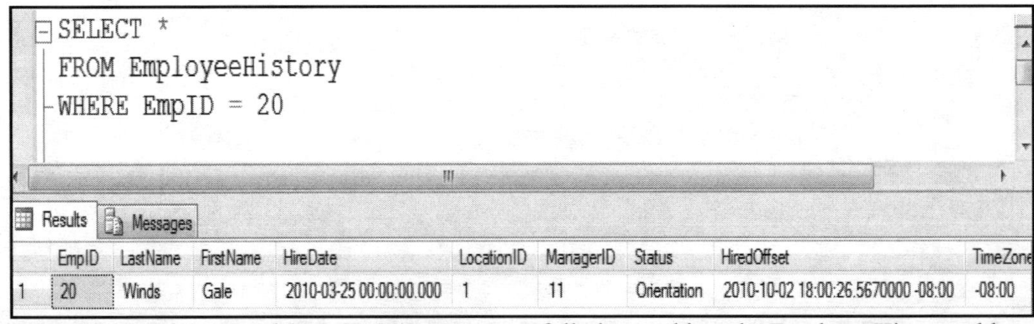

	EmpID	LastName	FirstName	HireDate	LocationID	ManagerID	Status	HiredOffset	TimeZone
1	20	Winds	Gale	2010-03-25 00:00:00.000	1	11	Orientation	2010-10-02 18:00:26.5670000 -08:00	-08:00

Figure 3.27 Gale's record (EmpID 20) was successfully inserted into the EmployeeHistory table.

Lab 3.2: Nested Triggers

Lab Prep: Before you can begin this lab, you must have SQL Server installed and have run the script SQLProgrammingChapter3.2Setup.sql. It is recommended that you view the lab video instructions in Lab3.2_NestingTriggers.wmv.

Skill Check 1: On the PayRatesHistory table, create an INSTEAD OF trigger (called trg_InsertPayRatesHistory) that will prevent direct inserts into the PayRatesHistory table but won't prevent inserts from other triggers. Test that direct inserts to PayRatesHistory fail (Figure 3.28) but inserts from other triggers will succeed (Figure 3.29).

```
INSERT INTO PayRatesHistory
VALUES (20,77000,null,null)
```

```
Messages
Dont insert to PayRates History Directly

(1 row(s) affected)
```

Figure 3.28 Skill Check 1 (part 1).

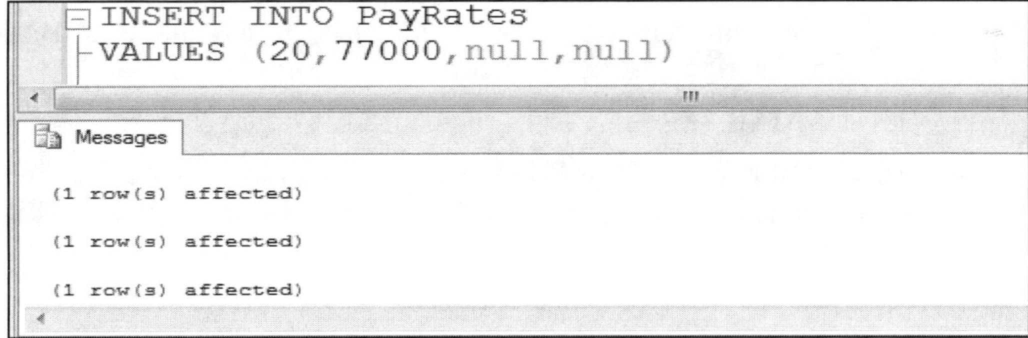
INSERT INTO PayRates
VALUES (20,77000,null,null)
Messages
(1 row(s) affected)
(1 row(s) affected)
(1 row(s) affected)

Figure 3.29 Skill Check 1 (part 2).

Answer Code: The T-SQL code to this lab can be found in the downloadable files in a file named Lab3.2_NestingTriggers.sql.

Nested Triggers - Points to Ponder

1. Nested triggers are triggers which are fired by another other trigger's DML statement(s).
2. Triggers can be linked, if necessary, to perform a series of actions in a particular situation.
3. Triggers are reactive. In other words, the action has already taken place before the trigger fires.
4. When an INSERT or DELETE trigger is associated with a table, any data inserted or deleted from the table will be written to a corresponding memory resident table (i.e., the Inserted or Deleted table).
5. A nested trigger is a trigger which executes a statement that causes an AFTER trigger to fire again.
6. There are two types of recursion:
    a. Indirect recursion occurs when the execution of the trigger causes another trigger to fire, which causes the first trigger to fire again. For example, a trigger (trig_1) fires when a table (tbl_a) is updated. The trigger executes an UPDATE statement for a second table (tbl_b). A trigger (trig_2) in tbl_b fires a trigger that executes an UPDATE statement for tbl_a. This causes trig_1 to fire again.
    b. Direct recursion occurs when the execution of a trigger causes it to fire again. For example, trig_1 fires when tbl_a is updated and code inside trig_1 also updates tbl_a, causing trig_1 to fire again.
7. Use an ALTER TRIGGER statement to modify a trigger.
8. Use ENABLE and DISABLE TRIGGER to control whether a trigger fires without dropping the trigger. For DML triggers, you can also use ALTER TABLE to enable or disable a trigger.
9. Use DROP TRIGGER to delete a trigger.
10. You should not use a trigger on a system table.
11. Constraints are checked after an INSTEAD OF trigger(s) executes. If constraints are violated, the actions executed by the INSTEAD OF trigger(s) are rolled back.
12. You cannot use INSTEAD OF DELETE/UPDATE triggers when a table has a foreign key with a cascade on DELETE/UPDATE action defined.

DDL Triggers

Thus far, our examination of triggers has focused on DML statements run against tables. As the title "DDL Triggers" implies, there are also triggers which work with DDL statements (CREATE, ALTER, or DROP). These triggers monitor your database for the attempted creation, modification, or removal of objects according to your specifications.

For example, the trigger below (see Figure 3.30) watches for any new CREATE TABLE statement appearing in your database.

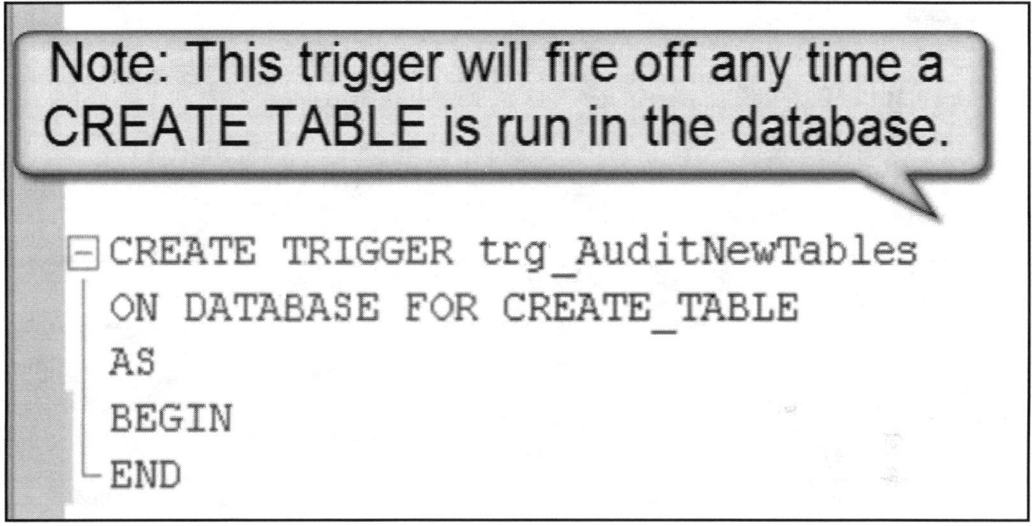

Figure 3.30 DDL triggers monitor events which take place in your database.

It's not difficult to imagine many reasons why extra scrutiny and support would be useful with respect to the creation, modification, or destruction of database objects in a production environment. Our premise for this section will be a harmless prankster who occasionally amuses himself by sneaking new tables into the database. While not a dangerous "black-hat" or a hacker, this individual's juvenile behavior actually provides a good opportunity to review and strengthen the way we enforce our database policies.

We can create DDL triggers to monitor and prompt users each time they attempt a DDL statement. We will also see examples of DDL triggers that will prohibit the creation of objects containing certain keywords.

Given our prankster's fondness for the keywords "Boss", "Slacker", and "Slax", a DDL trigger prohibiting those keywords would prevent him from creating tables whose names include those keywords.

His favorite trick is to stealthily create a dbo.BossSlax table (see Figure 3.31). In fact, this gets termed the "Slax Attack." When the boss wants to know who created the BossSlax table, the chances of the anonymous prankster confessing are low.

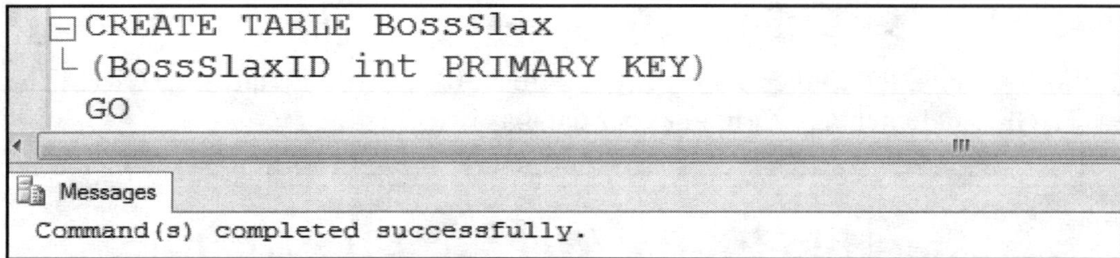
```
CREATE TABLE BossSlax
(BossSlaxID int PRIMARY KEY)
GO
```
Messages
Command(s) completed successfully.

Figure 3.31 Our prankster's favorite trick is to create a BossSlax table.

Let's drop the BossSlax table using this code (see Figure 3.32), so that we can later re-use it to test our DDL triggers.

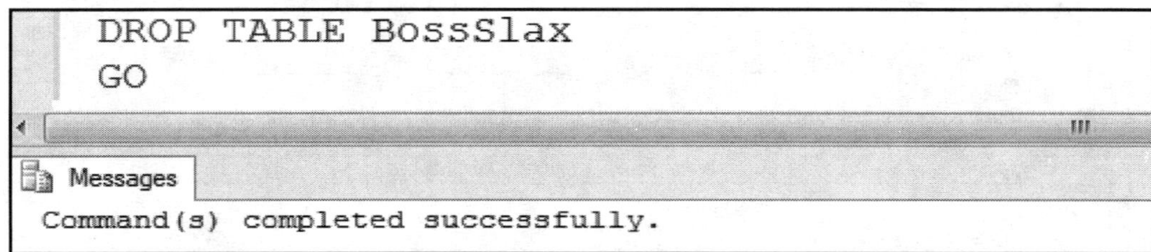
```
DROP TABLE BossSlax
GO
```
Messages
Command(s) completed successfully.

Figure 3.32 Drop the BossSlax table so that we can re-create it later to test our DDL triggers.

Creating DDL Triggers

Let's begin by creating a DDL trigger on the entire database which will fire off each time a CREATE TABLE statement is attempted. Whenever a user creates a table, we want to display the message, "Are you sure you want to do that?" (see Figure 3.33).

Make sure your context is set to the JProCo database before running this code. One way to accomplish this is to precede your CREATE TRIGGER statement with this code:

```
USE JProCo
GO
```

```
CREATE TRIGGER trg_AuditNewTables
ON DATABASE FOR CREATE_TABLE
AS
 BEGIN
    PRINT 'Are you sure you want to do that?'
 END
GO
```

Messages

```
Command(s) completed successfully.
```

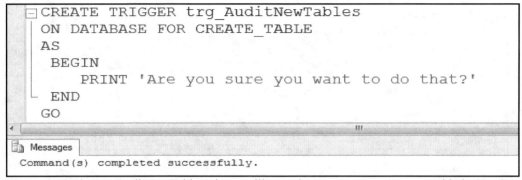

Figure 3.33 The trg_AuditNewTables trigger will run whenever you create a new table in JProCo.

Test this new trigger by executing a CREATE TABLE statement (see Figure 3.34). The message "Are you sure you want to do that?" confirms that the trigger ran when the table was created.

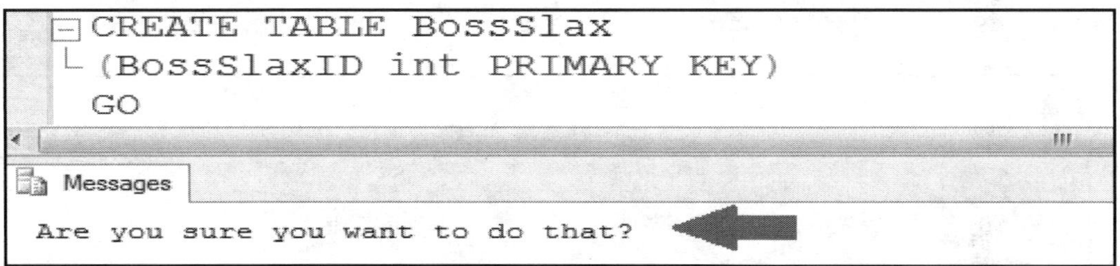

Figure 3.34 The CREATE TABLE statement caused the trigger trg_AuditNewTables to run.

Thus far, the only event we are monitoring the db for is a CREATE TABLE statement. The trg_AuditNewTables trigger only runs when you create a table in the database, but not when you alter or drop a table.

You can use DDL triggers on an entire database to look for certain CREATE, ALTER or DROP statements. Let's build a trigger which runs when you drop a table and displays a helpful message to your users (see Figure 3.36).

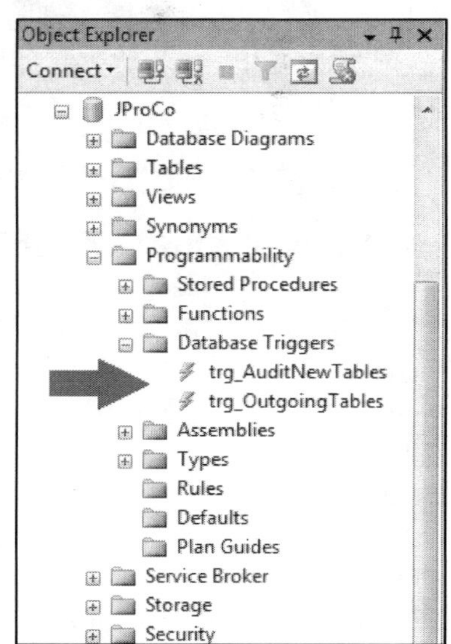

Figure 3.35 JProCo's DDL Triggers.

```
CREATE TRIGGER trg_OutgoingTables
ON DATABASE FOR DROP_TABLE
AS
 BEGIN
    PRINT 'Table going away'
 END
GO
```

Messages

```
Command(s) completed successfully.
```

Figure 3.36 The trigger trg_OutgoingTables watches for the DROP_TABLE event.

Let's test our DROP_TABLE trigger by dropping the BossSlax table (see Figure 3.37). This is the same result we will see when any JProCo table is dropped. The trg_OutgoingTables trigger fires and we see the "Table going away" message.

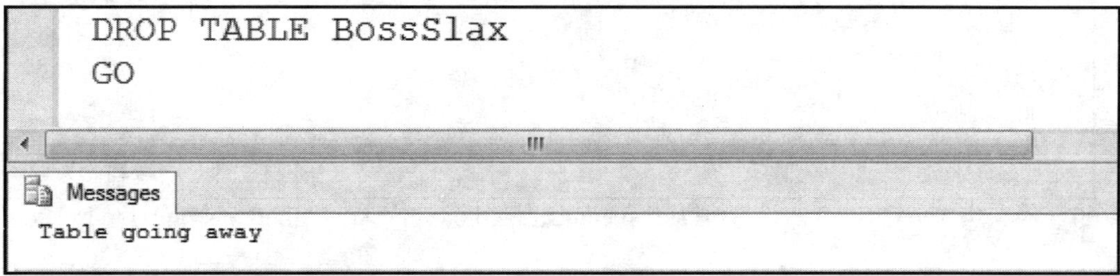
DROP TABLE BossSlax
GO
Messages
Table going away

Figure 3.37 Dropping any JProCo table will cause the trigger trg_OutgoingTables to fire.

Trigger Event Details

DDL triggers give us the ability to see event details for DDL statements.

Let's modify our trg_AuditNewTables trigger to include the EventData( ) system-supplied function in place of our user message. (*Note:* EventData( ) does not work with DML triggers.) The EventData( ) function captures data from our trigger event, which we can then view using the PRINT command.

Since the output of the EventData( ) function is an XML data type, we will get an error if we attempt to build our trigger using just this code (see Figure 3.38). We must first CAST the output using another character type, because data can't be printed from the XML data type. The PRINT statement works with all types of character data, so we can use a varchar(max) data type (see Figure 3.39).

(*Note:* The XML data type is explored in detail in Volume 5 of this series, *SQL Interoperability Joes 2 Pros*, Chapters 1-7.)

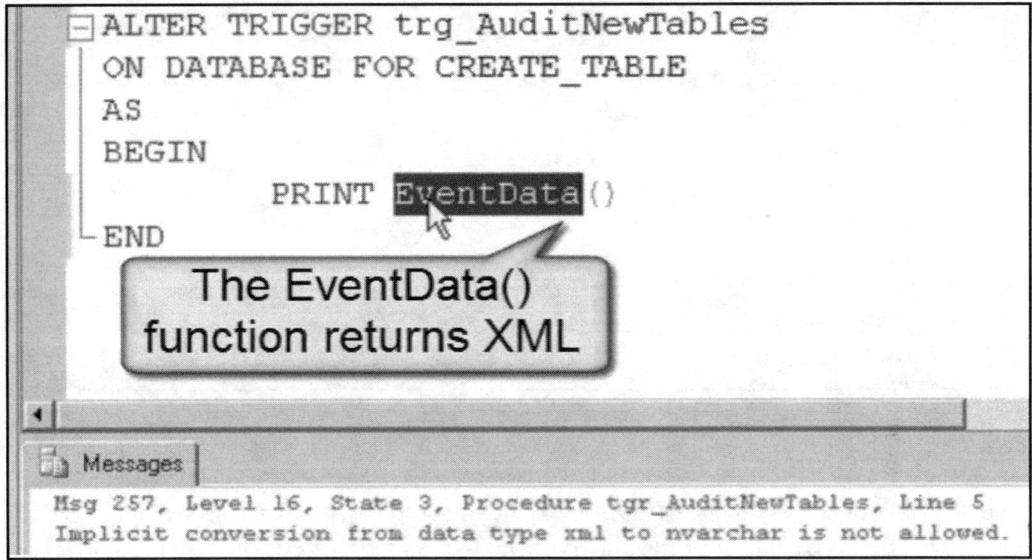

ALTER TRIGGER trg_AuditNewTables
ON DATABASE FOR CREATE_TABLE
AS
BEGIN
PRINT EventData()
END
The EventData()
function returns XML
Messages
Msg 257, Level 16, State 3, Procedure tgr_AuditNewTables, Line 5
Implicit conversion from data type xml to nvarchar is not allowed.

Figure 3.38 The EventData( ) function will only return the XML data type.

```
ALTER TRIGGER trg_AuditNewTables
ON DATABASE FOR CREATE_TABLE
AS
 BEGIN
    DECLARE @messageAction Varchar(max)
    SET  @messageAction = CAST(EventData() as varchar(max))
    PRINT @messageAction
 END
GO
```

Messages

```
Command(s) completed successfully.
```

Figure 3.39 By casting the XML data into a varchar(max), you can print the message.

Let's test this trigger by creating the BossSlax table again. Thanks to the trigger (trg_AuditNewTables), we can see the details for this "event", namely the CREATE TABLE action (Figure 3.40).

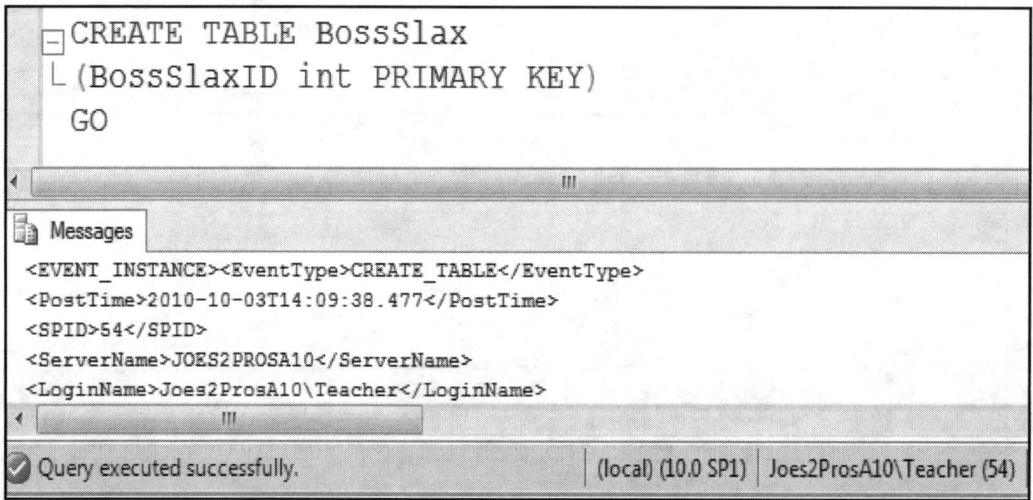

Figure 3.40 Creating a table ran the trigger that shows all the event data in your Messages tab.

Copy-Paste all of the data from the Messages tab into Notepad, so we can take a closer look at the event information. We can see the type of event (CREATE_TABLE), the time the event data was generated, the SPID (ServerProcessID), ServerName, LoginName, and UserName for the individual who ran the event. We can also see the database, schema, object name (JProCo.dbo.BossSlax table), and other details related to the event, including the full DDL statement which ran (CommandText CREATE TABLE BossSlax (BossSlaxID int PRIMARY KEY)).

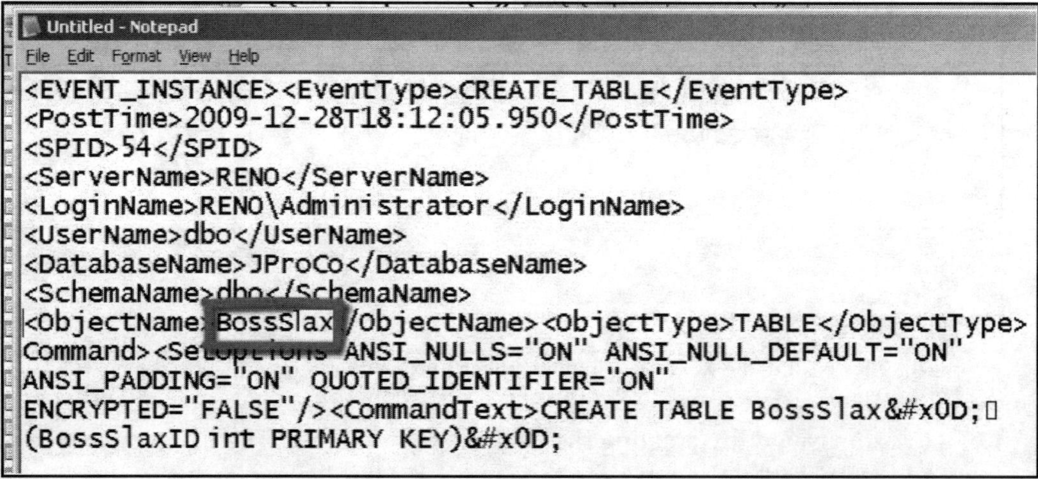

Figure 3.41 The name of the table that was created appears after the <ObjectName> XML tag.

Using Rollback

Whenever we see a table with "Slax" in the name, it's a red flag indicating that our juvenile prankster has been making trouble again. The boss gets upset, and we always have to remove the table from the database. A more efficient process would be to prevent the bogus table from being created in the first place. In other words, we would like a trigger to roll back any DDL statement with the word "Slax" in the object name.

Using what we just learned about the EventData( ) function, we can alter our trigger (trg_AuditNewTables) to search for the keyword "Slax" within the event details. In the code below (see Figure 3.42), we see a variable @messageAction which contains the event data. The CHARINDEX ("character index") function searches the contents of this variable for the word "Slax."

CHARINDEX returns a 1 or higher if a match is found and returns a 0 if nothing is found. If CHARINDEX finds 'Slax', it will return a 1 or higher. If this word is found, the trigger will ROLLBACK the transaction, and the attempted CREATE_TABLE action will not be allowed to complete.

```
ALTER TRIGGER trg_AuditNewTables
ON DATABASE FOR CREATE_TABLE
AS
 BEGIN
    DECLARE @messageAction Varchar(max)
    SET  @messageAction = CAST(EventData() as varchar(max))
    IF(CHARINDEX('Slax',@messageAction,0)>0)
    ROLLBACK
 END
GO
```

```
Messages
Command(s) completed successfully.
```

Figure 3.42 If CHARINDEX finds 'Slax', then the CREATE TABLE statement will be rolled back.

Let's test our robust trigger by dropping the BossSlax table (see Figure 3.43) and then attempting to re-create it (see Figure 3.44). Our trigger is successful! Because it found the "Slax" in the event detail, it disallowed the CREATE TABLE statement (see Figure 3.44).

```
DROP TABLE BossSlax
GO
```

Messages

```
Table going away
```

Figure 3.43 We must first DROP the BossSlax table, so that we can attempt to re-create it.

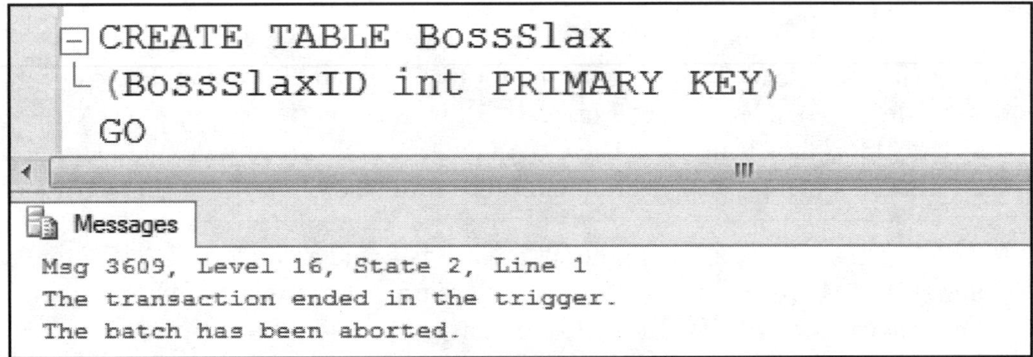
CREATE TABLE BossSlax
(BossSlaxID int PRIMARY KEY)
GO
Messages
Msg 3609, Level 16, State 2, Line 1
The transaction ended in the trigger.
The batch has been aborted.

Figure 3.44 You can't create a table with the word "Slax" in it.

You are still free to create other tables, as long as they don't have the word "Slax" in the name. In Figure 3.45 we see the creation of the BossIsCool table completed successfully.

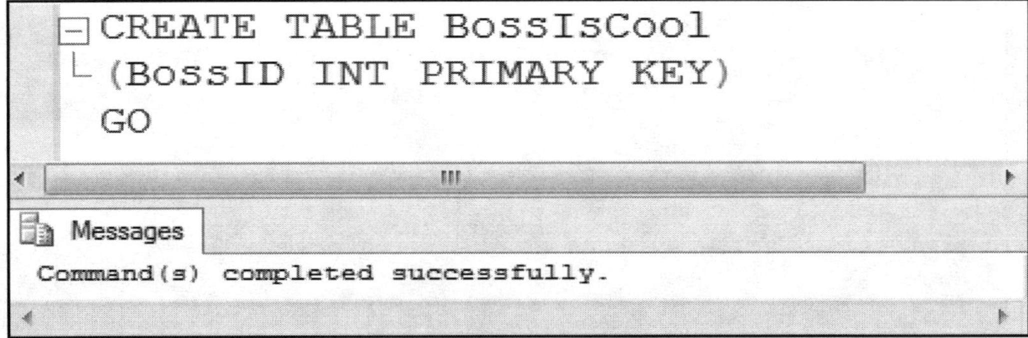
CREATE TABLE BossIsCool
(BossID INT PRIMARY KEY)
GO
Messages
Command(s) completed successfully.

Figure 3.45 DDL statements that don't have the word 'Slax' run successfully.

Such a DDL trigger could also help our business by giving us a way to prevent the creation of objects using prohibited names. *Examples:* You want to enforce the guideline that actual names of merger targets are prohibited. Similarly, in an R&D environment where the code names of projects sometimes change, a DDL trigger could help ensure an old code name isn't accidentally used.

Lab 3.3: DDL Triggers

Lab Prep: Before you can begin this lab, you must have SQL Server installed and have run the script SQLProgrammingChapter3.3Setup.sql. It is recommended that you view the lab video instructions in Lab3.3_DDLTriggers.wmv.

Skill Check 1: Create a trigger called trg_NoViewsInJanuary that will not allow anyone to create views in the JProCo database during the month of January. *Hint*: To find out if it's January, use DATEPART(month,GetDate( )) = 1 somewhere in your trigger.

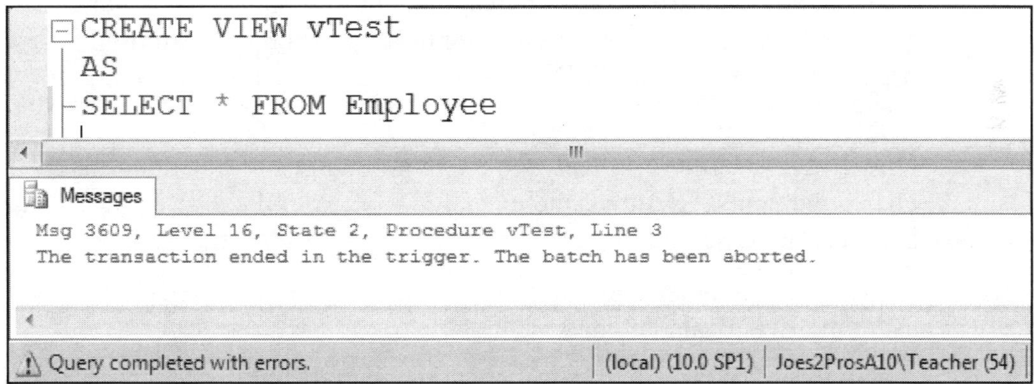
CREATE VIEW vTest
AS
SELECT * FROM Employee
Messages
Msg 3609, Level 16, State 2, Procedure vTest, Line 3
The transaction ended in the trigger. The batch has been aborted.
Query completed with errors.
(local) (10.0 SP1)
Joes2ProsA10\Teacher (54)

Figure 3.46 Skill Check 1.

Note: The easiest way to test this is to set your system clock to any date in January. After you are done with this lab example, be sure to return your system clock to your current local time.

Answer Code: The T-SQL code to this lab can be found in the downloadable files in a file named Lab3.3_DDLTriggers.sql.

DDL Triggers - Points to Ponder

1. DML stands for Data Manipulation Language and includes SELECT, INSERT, UPDATE and DELETE statements. DDL stands for Data Definition Language which includes CREATE, ALTER, and DROP statements run against database objects.
2. A DDL trigger is a type of stored procedure programmed to execute when a Data Definition Language (DDL) event occurs in the database server.
3. DDL triggers allow you to perform administrative tasks on a database as well as protect against database schema changes.
4. You can use DDL triggers to intercept database schema changes and send an error message to the user executing the code. You can also use DDL triggers to record and audit DDL statements executed on a database or server.
5. DDL triggers can be executed against more than just the standard list of DDL statements. Examples include CREATE, ALTER, DROP, GRANT, DENY, REVOKE, and UPDATE STATISTICS statements.
6. Information about an event that fires a DDL trigger may be captured by using the EventData( ) function.
7. EventData must be directly referenced inside the DDL trigger. You cannot call EventData from a routine, even a routine called by a DDL trigger.
8. DML and DDL triggers are similar in the following ways:
    a. DDL triggers are created, modified, and dropped using Transact-SQL syntax similar to that used to create DML triggers.
    b. Like DML triggers, DDL triggers can run managed code.
    c. A trigger and the statement that fires it are run within the same transaction.
    d. Like DML triggers, DDL triggers can be nested.
9. DML and DDL triggers are different in the following ways:
    a. DDL triggers run only after a Transact-SQL statement is completed.
    b. DDL triggers cannot be used as INSTEAD OF triggers.
    c. DDL triggers do not create temporary Inserted and Deleted tables.

Chapter Glossary

ADO.net: a set of software components that developers use to access data in a database.
@@NestLevel: returns the nesting level on the local server of the current stored procedure execution (if no nesting then the level is 0).
DDL: Data Definition Language. Statements which define data structures. The most common are CREATE, ALTER, and DROP.
DDL trigger: a trigger that executes based on a specified DDL event.
Direct recursion: this occurs when the execution of a trigger causes it to fire again.
DML trigger: a trigger that executes based on a specified DML event.
Identity field: a field that automatically generates its values in an incremental fashion.
Indirect recursion: this occurs when the execution of the trigger causes another trigger to fire, which causes the first trigger to fire again.
Nested trigger: a trigger that executes an event and fires another trigger.
Recursion: a programming concept where a named piece of code invokes itself.
Recursive trigger: a trigger which executes a statement that causes the same trigger to fire again.
Rollback: a process what new records in memory are discarded and never saved to permanent storage.
Transaction: the process SQL performs to take a DML request to get committed to permanent storage.
Trigger: a stored procedure that automatically fires based on an event.
Update trigger: a trigger that fires after an UPDATE statement has taken place on the table which the trigger is defined.

Chapter Three - Review Quiz

1.) What is the only DML event that does not fire off a trigger?

O a. SELECT
O b. INSERT
O c. UPDATE
O d. DELETE

2.) What are the main types of DML triggers? (Choose two)

□ a. Before Trigger
□ b. After Trigger
□ c. Instead of Trigger
□ d. In Addition to Trigger

3.) You have a trigger on the dbo.Action table that inserts records into the dbo.ActivityHistory table. The trigger in the dbo.ActivityHistory table checks for the @@NestLevel. What is the value of the @@NestLevel when the inserted records come from the trigger of the dbo.Action table?

O a. 0
O b. 1
O c. 2
O d. 3

4.) You have a trigger on the dbo.Action table that inserts records into the dbo.ActivityHistory table. The trigger in the dbo.ActivityHistory table does a check for the @@NestLevel. What is the value of the @@NestLevel when the inserted records are inserted directly by you from an INSERT INTO statement?

O a. 0
O b. 1
O c. 2
O d. 3

5.) You want a trigger to stop firing when you perform inserts. You don't want to drop and re-create the trigger. How can you temporarily stop the trigger from firing?

O a. You can't
O b. You must disable the trigger

6.) You have a foreign key which prevents the insertion of invalid LocationID values into the Employee table. You want to see the bad records which were attempted to be inserted Employee table. You create a table named dbo.BadEmployeeRecords. How do you insert records into this table?

O a. Create a DML INSTEAD OF trigger which writes the failed records to your dbo.Employee table.
O b. Create a DML AFTER trigger which writes the failed records to your dbo.Employee table.
O c. Create a DML INSTEAD OF trigger which writes the failed records to your dbo.BadEmployeeRecords table.
O d. Create a DML AFTER trigger which writes the failed records to your dbo.BadEmployeeRecords table.

7.) You have an ADO.net application that inserts data into your table. You alter the table and change two new fields to that table and make both fields non-nullable. The ADO application can no longer insert data into the table directly. You are not allowed to change the ADO code or the table. How do you insert records containing values for the new columns?

O a. Create a DDL trigger to add the new fields.
O b. Create an AFTER trigger to supply the new fields.
O c. Create an INSTEAD OF trigger to supply the new fields.

8.) You have a table named dbo.Widgets with the following fields:

- WidgetID smallint (Primary key)
- WidgetName varchar(100) NULL
- ToBeDeleted bit NULL

You do not want to allow any deletes to this table. If someone attempts to run a delete statement you want to set the ToBeDeleted flag to 1. You place the following code inside the BEGIN…END block of a trigger.

```
BEGIN
    UPDATE p SET isDeleted = 1
    FROM dbo.Widgets as P INNER JOIN DELETED as d
    ON p.WidgetID = d.WidgetID
END
```

Which SQL code would you use above this BEGIN...END block?

O a. CREATE TRIGGER del_Widget ON Widgets
AFTER DELETE AS

O b. CREATE TRIGGER del_Widget ON Widgets
INSTEAD OF DELETE AS

9.) Which statement will never fire a DDL trigger?

O a. CREATE TABLE

O b. ALTER TRIGGER

O c. DROP PROCEDURE

O d. DELETE TABLE

O e. GRANT CONTROL

10.) You want to write a trigger which will fire when someone removes a table from your database. Which DDL statement will achieve this result?

O a. CREATE TRIGGER trg_DroppedTables
ON DATABASE FOR CREATE_TABLE
AS

O b. CREATE TRIGGER trg_DroppedTables
ON DATABASE FOR CREATE_TABLE, ALTER_TABLE
AS

O c. CREATE TRIGGER trg_DroppedTables
ON DATABASE FOR DELETE_TABLE
AS

O d. CREATE TRIGGER trg_DroppedTables
ON DATABASE FOR DROP_TABLE
AS

O e. CREATE TRIGGER trg_DroppedTables
ON DATABASE FOR Remove_TABLE
AS

11.) Which system-supplied function captures and holds the details of the event that fired the DDL trigger?

O a. EventData( )
O b. EventLog( )
O c. EventDetails( )
O d. EventXML( )
O e. LogXML( )
O f. ShowXML( )

12.) You only allow DDL changes to be made to your database at the beginning of the month. Changes must take place before the 6th day of the month. You need to ensure that attempts to modify or create tables will get rolled back. Which SQL statement will achieve this result?

O a.
```
CREATE TRIGGER trg_TablesBeforeFifth
ON DATABASE FOR CREATE_TABLE
AS
  IF DATEPART(day, GetDate( ))>5
  BEGIN
   ROLLBACK
  END
GO
```

O b.
```
CREATE TRIGGER trg_TablesBeforeFifth
ON DATABASE FOR CREATE_TABLE, ALTER_TABLE
AS
  IF DATEPART(day, GetDate( ))>5
  BEGIN
   COMMIT
  END
GO
```

O c.
```
CREATE TRIGGER trg_TablesBeforeFifth
ON DATABASE FOR CREATE_TABLE, ALTER_TABLE
AS
  IF DATEPART(day, GetDate( ))>5
  BEGIN
   ROLLBACK
  END
GO
```

O d.
```
CREATE TRIGGER trg_TablesBeforeFifth
ON DATABASE FOR ALTER_TABLE
AS
  IF DATEPART(day, GetDate( ))>5
  BEGIN
   ROLLBACK
  END
GO
```

13.) Your have a function named Verify that returns a 1 if true and a 0 if false. If a 0 is returned, then SQL should generate an error and the event should not be allowed to commit. Which SQL statement will achieve this result?

O a.
```
CREATE TRIGGER trg_TEST
FOR CREATE_TABLE, ALTER_TABLE AS
IF Verify( )=0
  BEGIN
   RAISERROR ('Must wait until next month.', 16, 5)
  END
GO
```

O b.
```
CREATE TRIGGER trg_TEST ON DATABASE
FOR CREATE_TABLE,ALTER_TABLE
AS
  IF Verify( )=0
  BEGIN
   ROLLBACK
   RAISERROR ('Must wait until next month.', 16, 5)
  END
GO
```

O c.
```
CREATE TRIGGER trg_TEST
FOR CREATE_TABLE, ALTER_TABLE
AS
  IF Verify( )=1
  BEGIN
   RAISERROR ('Must wait until next month.', 16, 5)
  END
GO
```

O d.
```
CREATE TRIGGER trg_TEST ON DATABASE
FOR CREATE_TABLE, ALTER_TABLE
AS
  IF Verify( )=1
  BEGIN
   ROLLBACK
   RAISERROR ('Must wait until next month.', 16, 5)
  END
GO
```

14.) You have a Parent table and a Child table for a local school. Since the relationship between Parent and Child is a Many-to-Many relationship, you have created a ParentChild table. Your company got into legal trouble when a child's records were accidentally deleted from the Child table and the parent needed transcript records. You are not allowed to delete a child's record from the Child table if it has at least one corresponding active parent listed in the Parent table. If someone tries to delete a child, the record should remain in the table but the ISDeleted column for the child's row will be set to 1. You have proposed putting the following 2 DML statements in your trigger.

```
--Statement 1
UPDATE c SET IsDeleted = 1
FROM ParentChild pc
INNER JOIN deleted d ON pc.ChildID = d.ChildID
INNER JOIN Child c ON pc.ChildID = c.ChildID

--Statement 2
DELETE  p
FROM Child c
INNER JOIN deleted d ON c.ChildID = d.ChildID
LEFT OUTER JOIN ParentChild pc ON c.ChildID = pc.ChildID
WHERE pc.ParentID IS NULL
```

You are not allowed to use any rollback statement in your trigger but want to prevent delete changes that would cause a child record to disappear. Which trigger syntax should you use?

O a. CREATE TRIGGER trg_Child_d ON Child
AFTER DELETE
AS

O b. CREATE TRIGGER trg_Child_d ON Child
INSTEAD OF DELETE
AS

O c. CREATE TRIGGER trg_ParentChild_d ON ParentChild
AFTER DELETE
AS

O d. CREATE TRIGGER trg_ParentChild_d ON ParentChild
INSTEAD OF DELETE
AS

15.) Your database contains two tables named Order and OrderDetails that store order information. They relate to each other using the OrderID column in each table. Your business requires that the LastModifiedDate column in the Order table must reflect the date and time when a change is made in the OrderDetails table for the related order. You need to create a trigger to implement this business requirement. Which T-SQL statement should you use?

O a.
```
CREATE TRIGGER [uModDate] ON [Order]
INSTEAD OF UPDATE
AS
   UPDATE [Order]
   SET [LastModifiedDate] = GETDATE( )
   FROM Inserted
   WHERE Inserted.[OrderID] = [Order].[OrderID];
GO
```

O b.
```
CREATE TRIGGER [uModDate] ON [OrderDetails]
AFTER UPDATE
AS
   UPDATE [Order]
   SET [LastModifiedDate] = GETDATE()
   FROM Inserted
   WHERE Inserted.[OrderID] = [Order].[OrderID];
GO
```

16.) You need to ensure that tables are not dropped from your database. What should you do?

O a. Create a DDL trigger that contains COMMIT.

O b. Create a DML trigger that contains COMMIT.

O c. Create a DDL trigger that contains ROLLBACK.

O d. Create a DML trigger that contains ROLLBACK.

O e. GRANT CONTROL

Answer Key

1.) a 2.) b, c 3.) c 4.) b 5.) b 6.) c 7.) c 8.) b 9.) d 10.) d 11.) a
12.) c 13) b 14) b 15) b 16) c

Bug Catcher Game

To play the Bug Catcher game, run the file BugCatcher_Chapter3OtherTriggers.pps from the BugCatcher folder of the companion files located at www.Joes2Pros.com.

Chapter 4. Views

A great memory from my early teens is the time my science class visited a space telescope. The telescope had been preset for us to see the rings of Saturn. We all lined up and took turns looking into the telescope. That predefined view showed us the array of different orange, gold, and silver hues comprising the stunning rings around the sixth planet from our sun. If Saturn had blue and green rings, then that is what we would have seen that day. The telescope was preset to show our class precisely the information we wanted to see.

Views in SQL Server play a similar role. They provide a preset way to view data from one or more tables. They may also include aggregate fields (e.g., COUNT, SUM). Views allow your users to query a single object which behaves like a table and contains the needed joins and fields you have specified. In this way, a simple query (SELECT * FROM *ViewName*) can produce a more refined result which can serve as a report and answer business questions.

In addition to the benefit of reusable code, views offer the DBA a way to allow users to run queries without directly interacting with the production tables. We will see some **encryption** examples where users querying a view aren't even allowed to see the code which built the view.

READER NOTE: *In order to follow along with the examples in the first section of Chapter 4, please run the setup script SQLProgrammingChapter4.0Setup.sql. The setup scripts for this book are posted at Joes2Pros.com.*

Using Views

A **view** is a virtual table whose contents are defined by a query. Views can be based on one or more tables. In fact, a view can be comprised of any tabular datasource, such as a function(s) or even another view(s). You might choose to create a view because you want to expose a limited set of fields from a table(s) to certain users. By giving users permissions to a view, you allow them to see the data they need without having to grant them access to the underlying table(s). At other times, you might use a view in order to see a complex report consisting of many tables and joins, but you want to be able to obtain or refresh your report using a single object (i.e., the view).

Since we will base our first view on the Employee table, let's look at a query showing all of the records and all nine fields of this table (see Figure 4.1).

```
SELECT * FROM Employee
```

Results | Messages

	EmpID	LastName	FirstName	HireDate	LocationID	ManagerID	Status	HiredOffset	TimeZone
1	1	Adams	Alex	2001-01-01...	1	11	Active	2001-01-01 ...	-08:00
2	2	Brown	Barry	2002-08-12...	1	11	Active	2002-08-12 ...	-08:00
3	3	Osako	Lee	1999-09-01...	2	11	Active	1999-09-01 ...	-05:00
4	4	Kennson	David	1996-03-16...	1	11	Has Tenure	1996-03-16 ...	-08:00
5	5	Bender	Eric	2007-05-17...	1	11	Active	2007-05-17 ...	-08:00
6	6	Kendall	Lisa	2001-11-15...	4	4	Active	2001-11-15 ...	-08:00
7	7	Lonning	David	2000-01-01...	1	11	On Leave	2000-01-01 ...	-08:00
8	8	Marshbank	John	2001-11-15...	NULL	4	Active	2001-11-15 ...	-06:00
9	9	Newton	James	2003-09-30...	2	3	Active	2003-09-30 ...	-05:00
10	10	O'Haire	Terry	2004-10-04...	2	3	Active	2004-10-04 ...	-05:00

Query executed successfully. | (local) (10.0 SP1) | MoreTechA6\Student (51) | JProCo | 00:00:00 | 18 rows

Figure 4.1 This SELECT query displays all nine fields of the Employee table.

Tables in a production environment typically contain more fields than you wish to see in a report. A simple query (SELECT * FROM *Table*) can return an unwieldy amount of information and make reviewing your table data a challenge.

Suppose the Employee table query we use most often contains just the first seven fields of this table. Let's itemize our field list accordingly (see Figure 4.2).

```
SELECT EmpID, LastName, FirstName,
HireDate, LocationID, ManagerID, [Status]
FROM Employee
```

Results | Messages

	EmpID	LastName	FirstName	HireDate	LocationID	ManagerID	Status
1	1	Adams	Alex	2001-01-01...	1	11	Active
2	2	Brown	Barry	2002-08-12...	1	11	Active
3	3	Osako	Lee	1999-09-01...	2	11	Active
4	4	Kennson	David	1996-03-16...	1	11	Has Tenure
5	5	Bender	Eric	2007-05-17...	1	11	Active
6	6	Kendall	Lisa	2001-11-15...	4	4	Active
7	7	Lonning	David	2000-01-01...	1	11	On Leave
8	8	Marshbank	John	2001-11-15...	NULL	4	Active
9	9	Newton	James	2003-09-30...	2	3	Active
10	10	O'Haire	Terry	2004-10-04...	2	3	Active

Query executed successfully. | (local) (10.0 SP1) | MoreTechA6\Student (51) | JProCo | 00:00:00 | 18 rows

Figure 4.2 This query shows every record but only a subset of fields from the Employee table.

Creating Views With Management Studio

We want to create a view named vEmployee based on our query (shown in Figure 4.2).

We will use SQL Server Management Studio (SSMS) to create vEmployee. In the Databases folder of Object Explorer, expand the JProCo database, right-click on the Views folder, and click New View (see Figure 4.3).

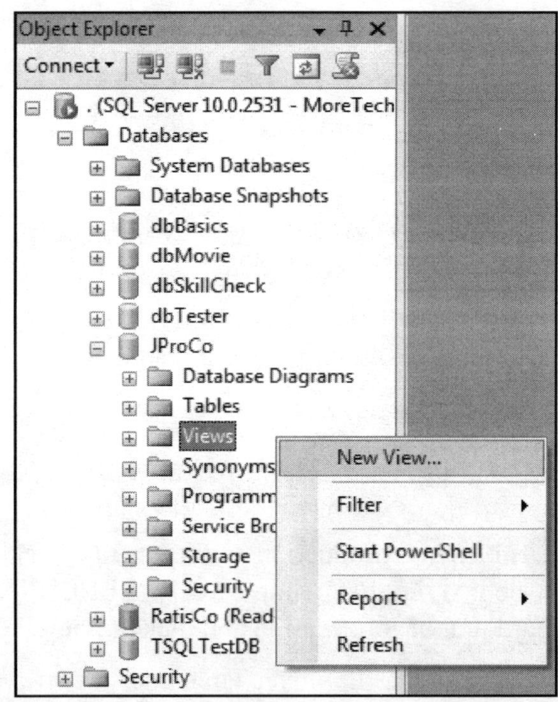

Figure 4.3 Right-click Views and select New View.

A view designer window appears behind a dialog listing the objects (tables, views, functions) we may use to build our view. Since we know our view will be based on the Employee table, click "Employee" and then click the "Add" button (Figure 4.4). Then click the Close button to exit the dialog.

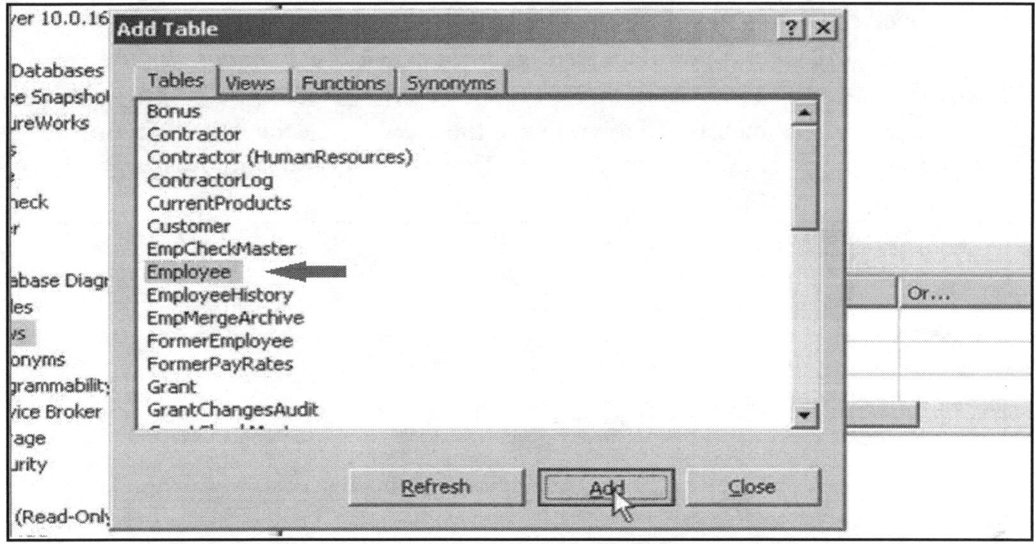

Figure 4.4 In the Add Table dialog, select and add the Employee table. Then click "Close."

Once the Add Table dialog closes, your View Designer window opens a Diagram Pane displaying a list box for each table you selected. When you check each field you need, you will see it appear in the other panes (the Criteria and SQL Panes).

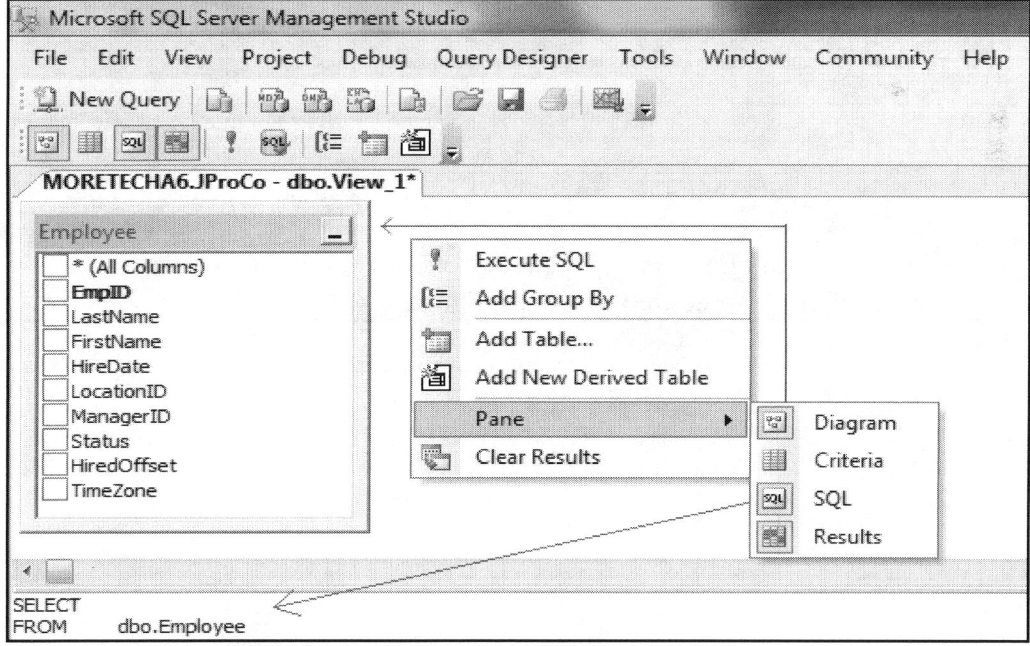

Figure 4.5 The Employee table appears in the Diagram Pane and SQL Pane of the View Designer. To see the Pane options (Diagram, Criteria, SQL, Results), right-click on Pane.

Let's check the boxes next to EmpID, FirstName, LastName, HireDate, LocationID, Manager, and Status. *(Be certain to check FirstName before you click LastName.* As you check each box, you will see the selected field appear in the Criteria and SQL Panes.) When you save the view (click the save icon or File > Save), the Choose Name dialog appears. Enter the name vEmployee and click OK to create this view (Figure 4.6).

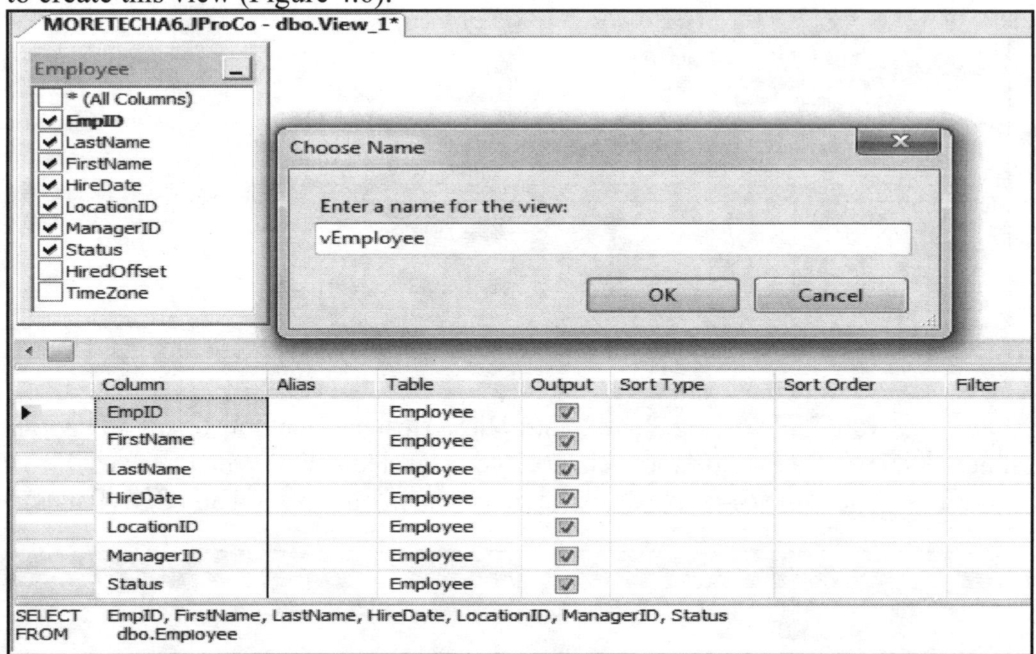

Figure 4.6 Select check boxes for the fields you want, name your view "vEmployee", and click OK.

We have successfully built the vEmployee view and can now query it. This simplified query achieves nearly the same result produced in Figure 4.2. Our result set looks like the Employee table, except it contains just the seven fields we specified – and in our specified order (see Figure 4.7).

```
SELECT * FROM vEmployee
```

Results | Messages

	EmpID	FirstName	LastName	HireDate	LocationID	ManagerID	Status
1	1	Alex	Adams	2001-01-01 ...	1	11	Active
2	2	Barry	Brown	2002-08-12 ...	1	11	Active
3	3	Lee	Osako	1999-09-01 ...	2	11	Active
4	4	David	Kennson	1996-03-16 ...	1	11	Has Tenure
5	5	Eric	Bender	2007-05-17 ...	1	11	Active
6	6	Lisa	Kendall	2001-11-15 ...	4	4	Active
7	7	David	Lonning	2000-01-01 ...	1	11	On Leave

Query executed successfully. | (local) (10.0 SP1) | MoreTechA6\Student (52) | JProCo | 00:00:00 | 18 rows

Figure 4.7 A query of our new view, vEmployee.

Creating Views Using T-SQL Code

Our last example provided an overview of the toolset which SQL Server Management Studio (SSMS) offers for creating views. However, the most robust and repeatable way of creating and maintaining your views is with T-SQL code.

A view is a great solution for reports or queries you run frequently, because you write the join logic once and then use it many times. One of our common JProCo tasks is to build a query showing all of the JProCo employees and their locations. This means we often join the Employee table to the Location table on LocationID. Suppose the key fields we always want are FirstName, LastName, City, and State. The view we will build is vEmployeeLocations and it will be based on the query shown here (Figure 4.8). Note that we want to exclude any employee without a location. Therefore, this is an inner join query, which excludes John Marshbank.

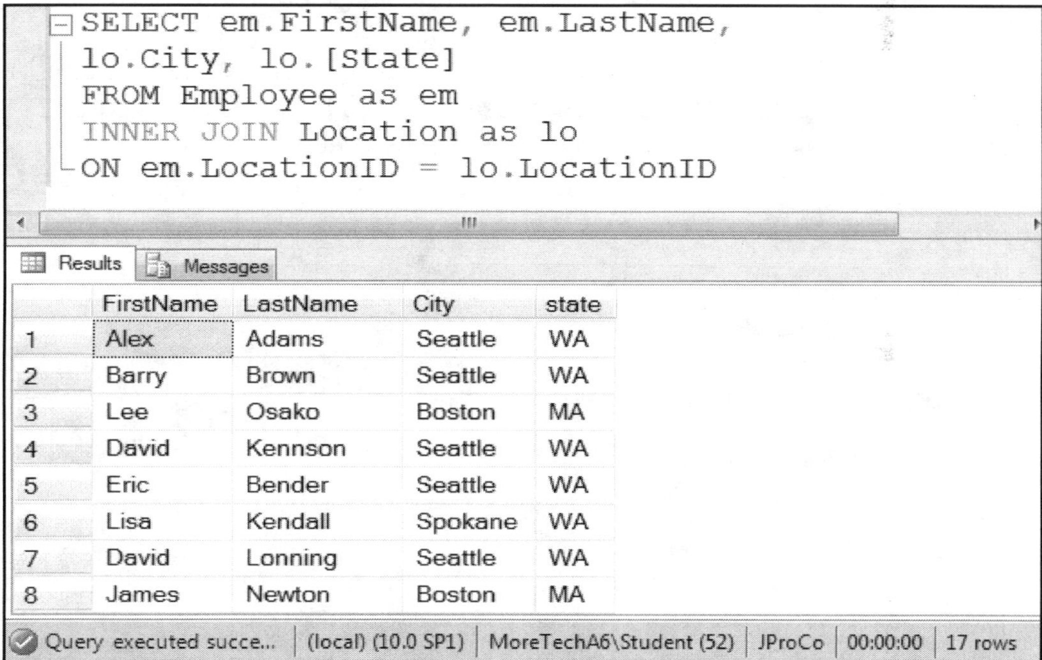

```
SELECT em.FirstName, em.LastName,
lo.City, lo.[State]
FROM Employee as em
INNER JOIN Location as lo
ON em.LocationID = lo.LocationID
```

	FirstName	LastName	City	state
1	Alex	Adams	Seattle	WA
2	Barry	Brown	Seattle	WA
3	Lee	Osako	Boston	MA
4	David	Kennson	Seattle	WA
5	Eric	Bender	Seattle	WA
6	Lisa	Kendall	Spokane	WA
7	David	Lonning	Seattle	WA
8	James	Newton	Boston	MA

Figure 4.8 This join of the Employee and Location tables containing these 4 fields is the query we run most frequently.

Let's add the needed code to this statement in order to turn our employee location report query into a view (see Figure 4.9). Notice we simply need to place a CREATE VIEW *ViewName* AS statement before our existing query.

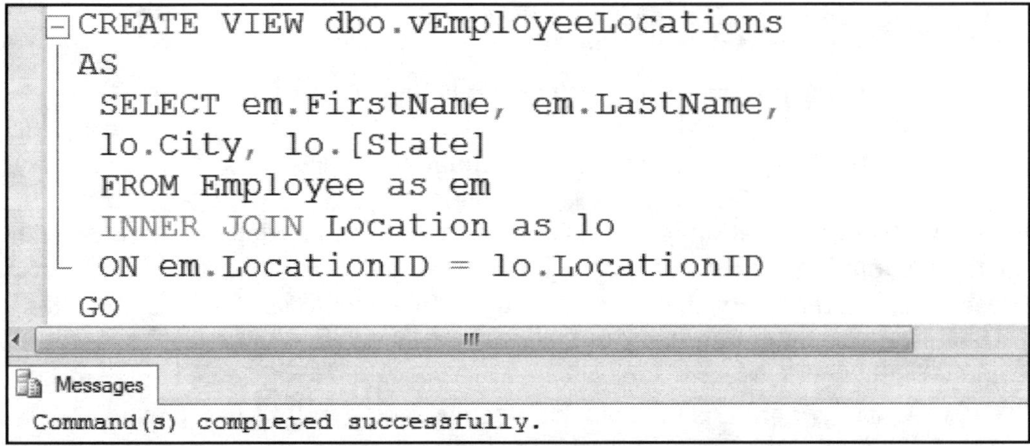

Figure 4.9 The query from our employee location report has been turned into a view.

Let's check Object Explorer and find our newly created object. Within the Databases folder, expand the Views folder inside of JProCo (see Figure 4.10). Remember that you may need to refresh the folder (right-click Views > Refresh), if you don't immediately see vEmployeeLocations. The Object Explorer doesn't spend system resources dynamically refreshing itself in real time.

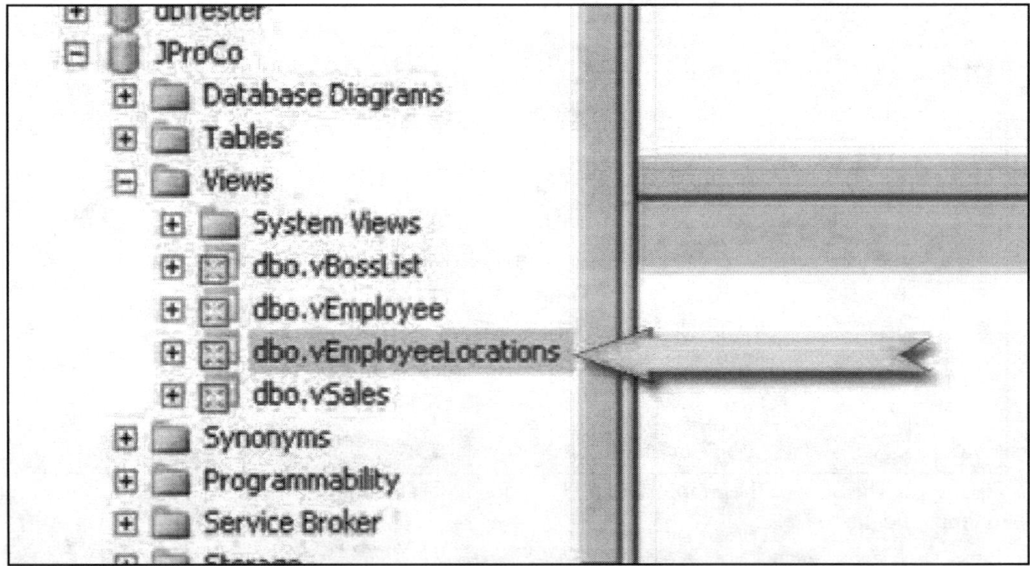

Figure 4.10 We can see our newly created view, vEmployeeLocations, in Object Explorer.

Let's query the view (see Figure 4.11). Notice that our result is identical to that which was produced by the underlying query (shown earlier in Figure 4.8).

```
SELECT * FROM vEmployeeLocations
```

Results | Messages

	FirstName	LastName	City	State
1	Alex	Adams	Seattle	WA
2	Barry	Brown	Seattle	WA
3	Lee	Osako	Boston	MA
4	David	Kennson	Seattle	WA
5	Eric	Bender	Seattle	WA
6	Lisa	Kendall	Spokane	WA
7	David	Lonning	Seattle	WA
8	James	Newton	Boston	MA
9	Terry	O'Haire	Boston	MA

Query executed successfully. | (local) (10.0 SP1) | MoreTechA6\Student (52) | JProCo | 00:00:00 | 17 rows

Figure 4.11 This view produces the same result that we saw when running the query (Figure 4.8).

Analyzing Existing Views

Suppose you have a view and you want to see its underlying code. We will look at a few techniques for accomplishing that.

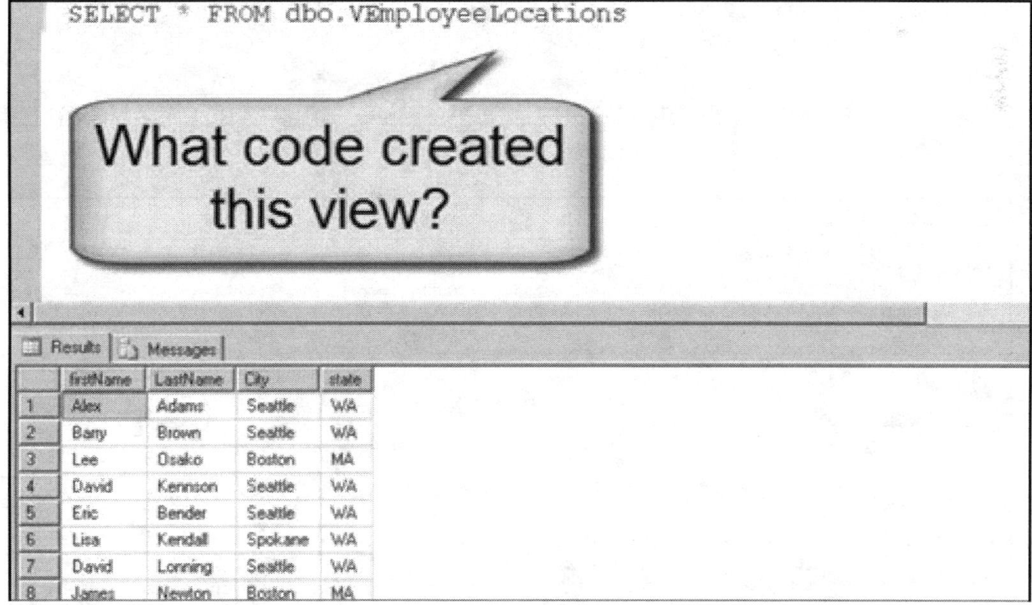

	firstName	LastName	City	state
1	Alex	Adams	Seattle	WA
2	Barry	Brown	Seattle	WA
3	Lee	Osako	Boston	MA
4	David	Kennson	Seattle	WA
5	Eric	Bender	Seattle	WA
6	Lisa	Kendall	Spokane	WA
7	David	Lonning	Seattle	WA
8	James	Newton	Boston	MA

Figure 4.12 When using a view, you may want to see the underlying code which created the view.

One way of generating the underlying code for an object is to right-click it in Object Explorer and use the "Script View as" option (see Figure 4.13).

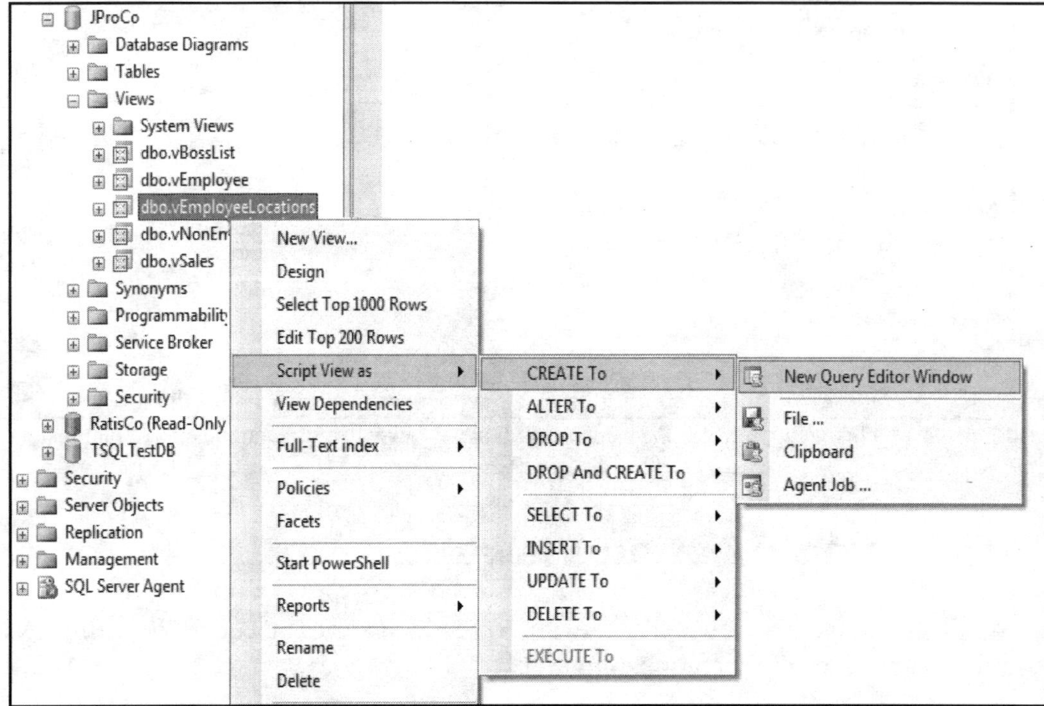

Figure 4.13 When using a view, you may want to see the underlying code which created the view.

Another handy way to see the code for any SQL Server object is to use the system stored procedure, sp_HelpText (see Figure 4.14).

```
sp_helptext 'dbo.vEmployeeLocations'
```

Results | Messages

	Text
1	CREATE VIEW dbo.vEmployeeLocations
2	AS
3	SELECT em.FirstName, em.LastName,
4	lo.City, lo.[State]
5	FROM Employee as em
6	INNER JOIN Location as lo
7	ON em.LocationID = lo.LocationID

Figure 4.14 The sp_helptext system stored procedure can show the code that created an object.

Click the field header ("Text") to select all of the code. Then Ctrl+C (or right-click the field header and choose "Copy") and Ctrl+V to paste the code into a new query window (see Figure 4.15).

```
CREATE VIEW dbo.vEmployeeLocations
AS
 SELECT em.FirstName, em.LastName,
 lo.City, lo.[State]
 FROM Employee as em
 INNER JOIN Location as lo
 ON em.LocationID = lo.LocationID
```

Figure 4.15 The results of your sp_helptext query pasted into a new window.

Yet another way to get the code for the objects in a database is by querying the database's **sys.SysComments** catalog view (see Figure 4.16).

```
USE JProCo
GO

SELECT * FROM sys.SysComments
```

Results | Messages

	id	number	colid	stat...	ctext	texttype	la...	encr...	co...	text
1	18099105	0	1	0	0x0D0...	2	0	0	0	CREATE TRIGGER tgr_InsertPayRates ON dbo.PayRates AF...
2	66099276	0	1	0	0x0D0...	2	0	0	0	CREATE TRIGGER tgr_DelEmployee ON dbo.Employee AFTE...
3	82099333	0	1	0	0x0D0...	2	0	0	0	CREATE TRIGGER tgr_DelPayrates ON dbo.PayRates AFTER...
4	98099390	0	1	0	0x0D0...	2	0	0	0	CREATE TRIGGER tgr_DelLocation ON dbo.Location AFTER ...
5	114099447	0	1	0	0x0900...	2	0	0	0	CREATE TRIGGER tgr_DelStateList ON dbo.StateList AFTE...
6	130099504	0	1	0	0x0D0...	2	0	0	0	---------Chapter 2.3 Starts here CREATE TRIGGER tgr_UpdE...
7	146099561	0	1	0	0x0D0...	2	0	0	0	CREATE TRIGGER trg_updStateList ON StateList AFTER UP...
8	162099618	0	1	0	0x0D0...	2	0	0	0	CREATE TRIGGER tgr_UpdPayRates ON dbo.PayRates...
9	178099675	0	1	0	0x0D0...	2	0	0	0	CREATE TRIGGER trg_updGrant ON [Grant] AFTER UPDATE...

Query executed successfully. | (local) (10.0 SP1) | MoreTechA6\Student (56) | JProCo | 00:00:00 | 49 rows

Figure 4.16 The **sys.SysComments** catalog view shows metadata for your database objects.

The OBJECT_ID function (Figure 4.17) is one way of getting the object's ID, which you can use to filter your **sys.SysComments** query (shown in Figure 4.16).

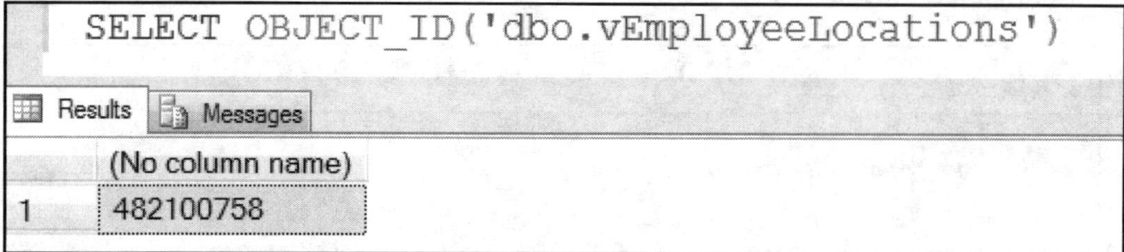

Figure 4.17 The OBJECT_ID function can be used to get an object's ID.

Alternatively, you can use the OBJECT_ID function in your WHERE clause and thus filter your query for the object you want (see Figure 4.18). From here, you can simply copy the value from the text field into a new query window.

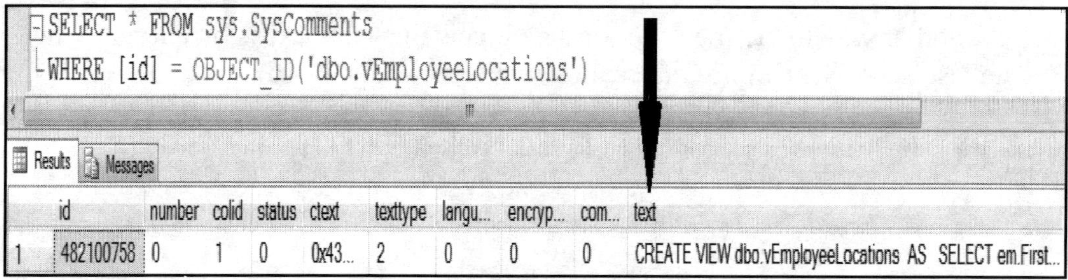

Figure 4.18 An alternate way to get the code for an object is to query the **sys.SysComments** catalog view and copy from the [text] field.

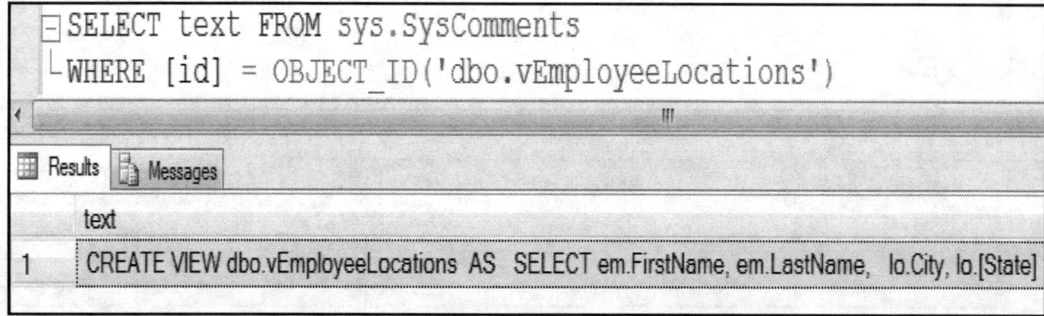

Figure 4.19 We've narrowed our select list to display just the [text] field.

Lab 4.1: Creating Views

Lab Prep: Before you can begin the lab, you must have SQL Server installed and have run the script SQLProgrammingChapter4.1Setup.sql. View the lab video instructions in Lab4.1_CreatingViews.wmv.

Skill Check 1: Create a view named vEmployeeGrants that shows the FirstName, LastName, GrantName, and Amount from an inner join of the Employee and Grant tables. Your result should match this figure below (see Figure 4.20).

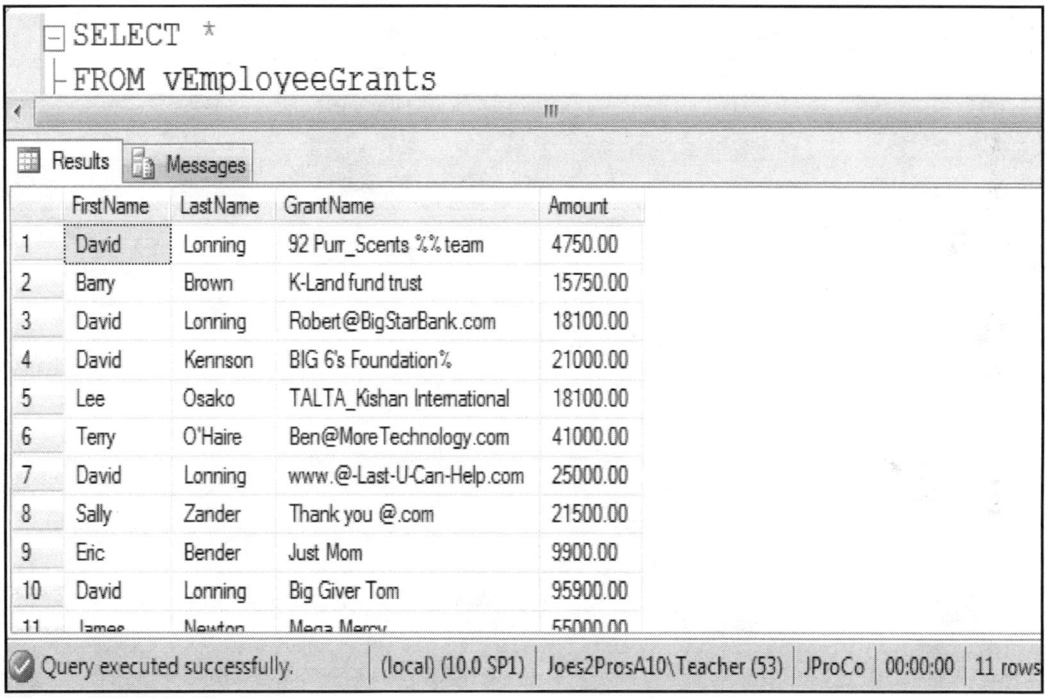

```
SELECT *
FROM vEmployeeGrants
```

Results | Messages

	FirstName	LastName	GrantName	Amount
1	David	Lonning	92 Purr_Scents %% team	4750.00
2	Barry	Brown	K-Land fund trust	15750.00
3	David	Lonning	Robert@BigStarBank.com	18100.00
4	David	Kennson	BIG 6's Foundation%	21000.00
5	Lee	Osako	TALTA_Kishan International	18100.00
6	Terry	O'Haire	Ben@MoreTechnology.com	41000.00
7	David	Lonning	www.@-Last-U-Can-Help.com	25000.00
8	Sally	Zander	Thank you @.com	21500.00
9	Eric	Bender	Just Mom	9900.00
10	David	Lonning	Big Giver Tom	95900.00
11	James	Newton	Mega Mercy	55000.00

Query executed successfully. | (local) (10.0 SP1) | Joes2ProsA10\Teacher (53) | JProCo | 00:00:00 | 11 rows

Figure 4.20 Skill Check 1.

Skill Check 2: Create a view named vEmployeePayRates which shows every employee's FirstName & LastName from the Employee table, along with all fields from the PayRates table. Be sure to show every employee, even ones who don't yet have a PayRate. Your result should resemble Figure 4.21.

```
SELECT *
FROM vEmployeePayRates
```

Results | Messages

	FirstName	LastName	EmpID	YearlySal...	MonthlySal...	HourlyRate
1	Alex	Adams	1	99000.00	NULL	NULL
2	Barry	Brown	2	87000.00	NULL	NULL
3	Lee	Osako	3	NULL	NULL	45.00
4	David	Kennson	4	NULL	6500.00	NULL
5	Eric	Bender	5	NULL	5800.00	NULL
6	Lisa	Kendall	6	53500.00	NULL	NULL
7	David	Lonning	7	NULL	6100.00	NULL
8	John	Marshbank	8	NULL	NULL	32.00
9	James	Newton	9	NULL	NULL	18.00
10	Terry	O'Haire	10	NULL	NULL	17.00

Query executed successfully. | (local) (10.0 SP1) | MoreTechA6\Student (52) | JProCo | 00:00:00 | 18 rows

Figure 4.21 Skill Check 2.

Skill Check 3:
The vSales view shows JProCo's customers and the products they ordered. Show the code which was used to create this view (vSales).

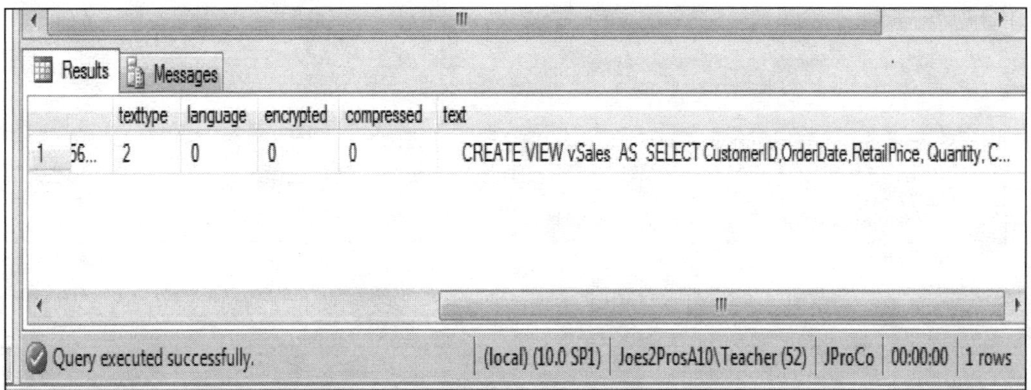

		texttype	language	encrypted	compressed	text
1	56...	2	0	0	0	CREATE VIEW vSales AS SELECT CustomerID,OrderDate,RetailPrice, Quantity, C...

Figure 4.22 Skill Check 3.

Answer Code: The T-SQL code to this lab can be found in the downloadable files in a file named Lab4.1_CreatingViews.sql.

Creating Views - Points to Ponder

1. A view is a virtual table whose contents are defined by a query.
2. Views are database objects and are stored in your database, similar to tables, stored procedures, and functions.
3. A view is a stored SELECT statement that works like a virtual table.
4. Views are a convenient way to provide access to data through a predefined query.
5. To create a view using SQL Server Management Studio, expand your database, right-click the Views folder, and choose New View.
6. A view can contain up to 1024 columns.
7. You need to have SELECT permissions on the base tables before you can create the view.
8. Views can combine data from multiple tables, columns, or sources into what looks like a single table.
9. Views can aggregate data. For example, they can show the sum of a column rather than individual values in the column.
10. The code syntax to make a new view is CREATE VIEW *ViewName* AS.
11. The tables that make up a view are called "base tables."
12. The **sys.SysComments** catalog view contains the definitions for views and stored procedures.

Altering Views

Now that we know how to create views, we want to examine the steps for modifying an existing view. We will continue working with the view we created in the last section, vEmployeeLocations. The left panel of the figure below (Figure 4.23) shows the four fields currently contained in vEmployeeLocations. The right pane shows our new goal, which will be to add the EmpID field.

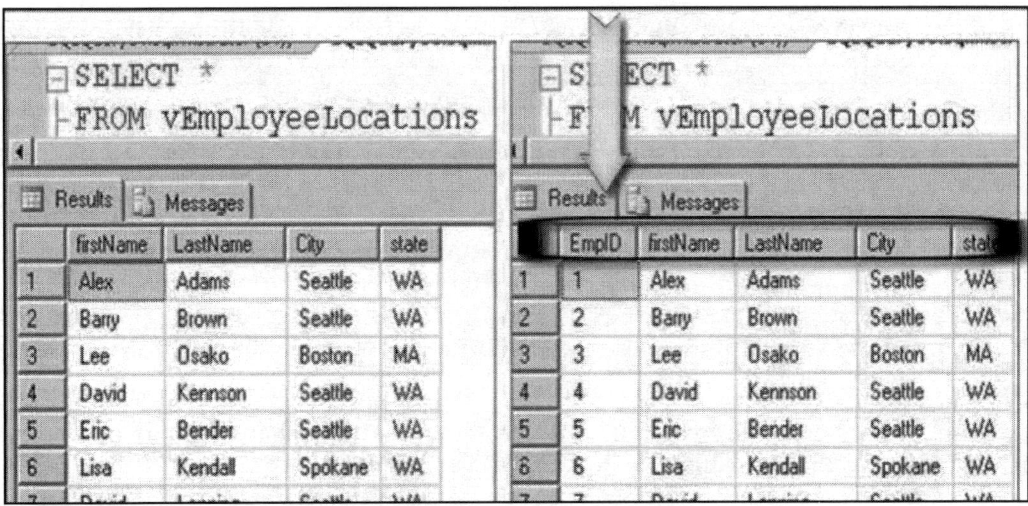

Figure 4.23 We need to add the EmpID field to the vEmployeeLocations view.

To obtain the code that created vEmployeeLocations, run sp_HelpText and pass in the object name (see Figure 4.24). Paste this code into a new query window.

```
sp_helptext 'dbo.vEmployeeLocations'
```

Results | Messages

	Text
1	CREATE VIEW dbo.vEmployeeLocations
2	AS
3	SELECT em.FirstName, em.LastName,
4	lo.City, lo.[State]
5	FROM Employee as em
6	INNER JOIN Location as lo
7	ON em.LocationID = lo.LocationID

Figure 4.24 The system sproc sp_helptext shows the source code which built the object.

As is the case with most other database objects we've encountered (tables, triggers, sprocs, etc.), we can use an ALTER statement to modify our view.

We've pasted the code we obtained from sp_HelpText (see Figure 4.24) into a new window. Change the CREATE keyword to ALTER, and add the EmpID field to achieve our goal (see Figure 4.25).

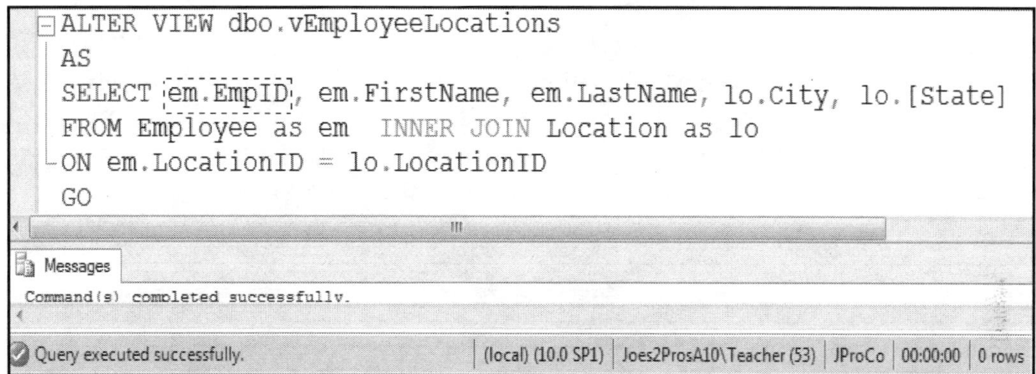

```
ALTER VIEW dbo.vEmployeeLocations
AS
SELECT em.EmpID, em.FirstName, em.LastName, lo.City, lo.[State]
FROM Employee as em  INNER JOIN Location as lo
ON em.LocationID = lo.LocationID
GO
```

Messages

Command(s) completed successfully.

Query executed successfully. | (local) (10.0 SP1) | Joes2ProsA10\Teacher (53) | JProCo | 00:00:00 | 0 rows

Figure 4.25 The ALTER VIEW statement modifies an existing view.

Query the newly modified view. Notice that the result set below (Figure 4.26) now contains the EmpID field and matches our goal data (shown earlier in the right pane of Figure 4.23).

```
SELECT * FROM dbo.vEmployeeLocations
```

Results | Messages

	EmpID	FirstName	LastName	City	State
1	1	Alex	Adams	Seattle	WA
2	2	Barry	Brown	Seattle	WA
3	3	Lee	Osako	Boston	MA
4	4	David	Kennson	Seattle	WA
5	5	Eric	Bender	Seattle	WA
6	6	Lisa	Kendall	Spokane	WA
7	7	David	Lonning	Seattle	WA

Query executed successfully. | (local) (10.0 SP1) | MoreTechA6\Student (53) | JProCo | 00:00:00 | 17 rows

Figure 4.26 Our view, vEmployeeLocations, now includes the EmpID field.

Nesting Views

You will find that working with views is very similar to working with tables in your DML programming. Our next demonstration will illustrate joining a table to a view. Now that we have added EmpID to vEmployeeLocations, it will be easier to join this view to other objects.

The Grant table is one of the JProCo objects which contain the EmpID field. We would like to run a query which will add all fields of the Grant table to our employee locations report. The focus of this report will be JProCo's Grants (currently there are 11, as shown in Figure 4.28). For each Grant, we want to see the associated employee information, including the employee's location.

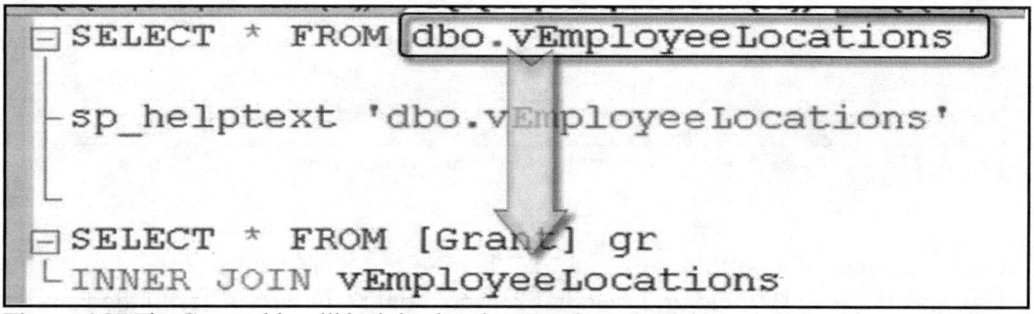

```
SELECT * FROM dbo.vEmployeeLocations

sp_helptext 'dbo.vEmployeeLocations'


SELECT * FROM [Grant] gr
INNER JOIN vEmployeeLocations
```

Figure 4.27 The Grant table will be joined to the vEmployeeLocations view to make one result set.

Since all 11 current Grant records contain an EmpID, we expect to see all 11 grants appear in the result. The one JProCo employee not appearing in the view (John Marshbank, EmpID 8) hasn't found any grants, so there's no problem with him being omitted from the dataset.

The syntax for joining the Grant table to the vEmployeeLocations view is precisely the same as the syntax we use to join two tables (see next page, Figure 4.29).

```
SELECT * FROM [Grant]
```

Results | Messages

	GrantID	GrantName	EmpID	Amount
1	001	92 Purr_Scents %% team	7	4750.00
2	002	K-Land fund trust	2	15750.00
3	003	Robert@BigStarBank.com	7	18100.00
4	005	BIG 6's Foundation%	4	21000.00
5	006	TALTA_Kishan International	3	18100.00
6	007	Ben@MoreTechnology.com	10	41000.00
7	008	www.@-Last-U-Can-Help.com	7	25000.00
8	009	Thank you @.com	11	21500.00
9	010	Just Mom	5	9900.00
10	011	Big Giver Tom	7	95900.00
11	012	Mega Mercy	9	55000.00

Query executed s... | (local) (10.0 SP1) | MoreTechA6\Student (54) | JProCo | 00:00:00 | 11 rows

Figure 4.28 JProCo currently has 11 grants.

```
SELECT * FROM [Grant] gr
INNER JOIN vEmployeeLocations vel
ON vel.EmpID = gr.EmpID
```

Results | Messages

	GrantID	GrantName	EmpID	Amount	EmpID	FirstName	LastName	City	State
1	001	92 Purr_Scents %% team	7	4750.00	7	David	Lonning	Seattle	WA
2	002	K-Land fund trust	2	15750.00	2	Barry	Brown	Seattle	WA
3	003	Robert@BigStarBank.com	7	18100.00	7	David	Lonning	Seattle	WA
4	005	BIG 6's Foundation%	4	21000.00	4	David	Kennson	Seattle	WA
5	006	TALTA_Kishan International	3	18100.00	3	Lee	Osako	Boston	MA
6	007	Ben@MoreTechnology.com	10	41000.00	10	Terry	O'Haire	Boston	MA
7	008	www.@-Last-U-Can-Help.com	7	25000.00	7	David	Lonning	Seattle	WA
8	009	Thank you @.com	11	21500.00	11	Sally	Zander	Seattle	WA
9	010	Just Mom	5	9900.00	5	Eric	Bender	Seattle	WA
10	011	Big Giver Tom	7	95900.00	7	David	Lonning	Seattle	WA
11	012	Mega Mercy	9	55000.00	9	James	Newton	Boston	MA

Query executed successfully. | (local) (10.0 SP1) | MoreTechA6\Student (55) | JProCo | 00:00:00 | 11 rows

Figure 4.29 The result set from joining the Grant table to the vEmployeeLocations view.

Let's refine our report to omit the employee names and the extra instance of the EmpID field. We will narrow the field selection list to include all fields from the Grant table and only City and State from vEmployeeLocations (see Figure 4.30).

```
SELECT gr.*, vel.City, vel.[State]
FROM [Grant] gr
INNER JOIN vEmployeeLocations vel
ON vel.EmpID = gr.EmpID
```

Results | Messages

	GrantID	GrantName	EmpID	Amount	City	State
1	001	92 Purr_Scents %% team	7	4750.00	Seattle	WA
2	002	K-Land fund trust	2	15750.00	Seattle	WA
3	003	Robert@BigStarBank.com	7	18100.00	Seattle	WA
4	005	BIG 6's Foundation%	4	21000.00	Seattle	WA
5	006	TALTA_Kishan International	3	18100.00	Boston	MA
6	007	Ben@MoreTechnology.com	10	41000.00	Boston	MA
7	008	www.@-Last-U-Can-Help.com	7	25000.00	Seattle	WA
8	009	Thank you @.com	11	21500.00	Seattle	WA
9	010	Just Mom	5	9900.00	Seattle	WA
10	011	Big Giver Tom	7	95900.00	Seattle	WA
11	012	Mega Mercy	9	55000.00	Boston	MA

Query executed successfully. | (local) (10.0 SP1) | MoreTechA6\Student (55) | JProCo | 00:00:00 | 11 rows

Figure 4.30 The field selection list has been limited to the Grant table fields plus City and State.

Suppose JProCo's Grant office says this report is perfect and they would like it in the form of a view, so they won't need to ask the IT team to re-write the code each time they want to run it.

Basing a view on another view is known as **nesting views**. The GrantLocations view is based on the [Grant] table and the vEmployeeLocations view (Figure 4.31).

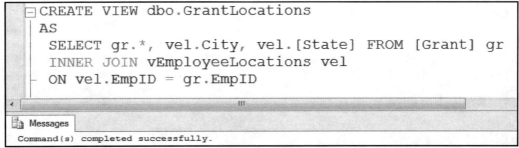

```
CREATE VIEW dbo.GrantLocations
AS
 SELECT gr.*, vel.City, vel.[State] FROM [Grant] gr
 INNER JOIN vEmployeeLocations vel
 ON vel.EmpID = gr.EmpID
```

Messages

Command(s) completed successfully.

Figure 4.31 One of the base tables of the GrantLocations view is a view (vEmployeeLocations).

Notice that SQL Server allowed us to create the view using the name "GrantLocations." While a best practice is to prefix objects (e.g., v for views, trg for triggers) so that you can easily differentiate them from tables in your code, SQL Server doesn't enforce naming conventions for database objects.

Let's query our new view to confirm it gives us the expected result. If we created the GrantLocations view correctly, it should resemble the base query (shown earlier in Figure 4.30). Success! Both queries produce the same result set.

```
SELECT * FROM GrantLocations
```

Results | Messages

	GrantID	GrantName	EmpID	Amount	City	State
1	001	92 Purr_Scents %% team	7	4750.00	Seattle	WA
2	002	K-Land fund trust	2	15750.00	Seattle	WA
3	003	Robert@BigStarBank.com	7	18100.00	Seattle	WA
4	005	BIG 6's Foundation%	4	21000.00	Seattle	WA
5	006	TALTA_Kishan Internati...	3	18100.00	Boston	MA
6	007	Ben@MoreTechnology....	10	41000.00	Boston	MA
7	008	www.@-Last-U-Can-Hel...	7	25000.00	Seattle	WA
8	009	Thank you @.com	11	21500.00	Seattle	WA
9	010	Just Mom	5	9900.00	Seattle	WA
10	011	Big Giver Tom	7	95900.00	Seattle	WA
11	012	Mega Mercy	9	55000.00	Boston	MA

Query executed successfully. | (local) (10.0 SP1) | Joes2ProsA10\Teacher (54) | JProCo | 00:00:00 | 11 rows

Figure 4.32 Result set from querying the GrantLocations view.

Lab 4.2: Altering Views

Lab Prep: Before you can begin the lab, you must have SQL Server installed and have run the script SQLProgrammingChapter4.2Setup.sql. View the lab video instructions in Lab4.2_AlteringViews.wmv.

Skill Check 1: Alter the vEmployeeGrants view to include EmpID as the first field of the view.

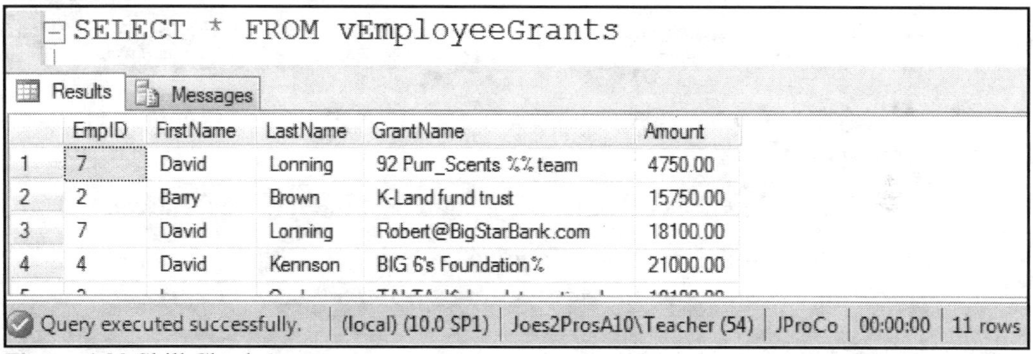

```
SELECT * FROM vEmployeeGrants
```

	EmpID	FirstName	LastName	GrantName	Amount
1	7	David	Lonning	92 Purr_Scents %% team	4750.00
2	2	Barry	Brown	K-Land fund trust	15750.00
3	7	David	Lonning	Robert@BigStarBank.com	18100.00
4	4	David	Kennson	BIG 6's Foundation%	21000.00

Query executed successfully. | (local) (10.0 SP1) | Joes2ProsA10\Teacher (54) | JProCo | 00:00:00 | 11 rows

Figure 4.33 Skill Check 1.

Skill Check 2: Alter the vEmployeePayRates view to be based on a join of the vEmployeeLocations view and the PayRates table. Include City as a field in the select list.

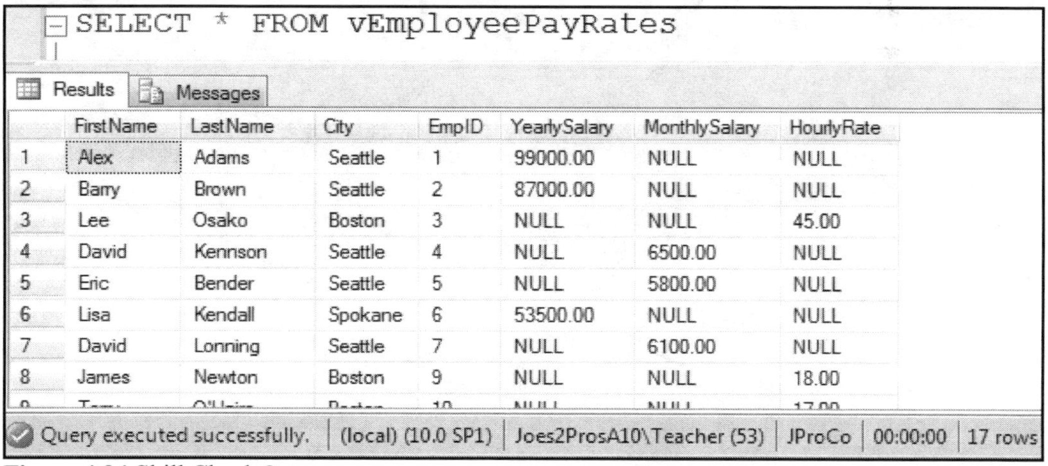

```
SELECT * FROM vEmployeePayRates
```

	FirstName	LastName	City	EmpID	YearlySalary	MonthlySalary	HourlyRate
1	Alex	Adams	Seattle	1	99000.00	NULL	NULL
2	Barry	Brown	Seattle	2	87000.00	NULL	NULL
3	Lee	Osako	Boston	3	NULL	NULL	45.00
4	David	Kennson	Seattle	4	NULL	6500.00	NULL
5	Eric	Bender	Seattle	5	NULL	5800.00	NULL
6	Lisa	Kendall	Spokane	6	53500.00	NULL	NULL
7	David	Lonning	Seattle	7	NULL	6100.00	NULL
8	James	Newton	Boston	9	NULL	NULL	18.00

Query executed successfully. | (local) (10.0 SP1) | Joes2ProsA10\Teacher (53) | JProCo | 00:00:00 | 17 rows

Figure 4.34 Skill Check 2.

Answer Code: The T-SQL code to this lab can be found in the downloadable files in a file named Lab4.2_AlteringViews.sql.

Altering Views - Points to Ponder

1. The tables that make up a view are called “base tables.”
2. The data available through the view continues to reside in the base table (or tables).
3. You can’t create a view from temporary tables.
4. Views can reference data in multiple tables and across multiple databases on the same or even remote servers. In addition, views can reference other views. (Please note: the topic of remote servers is outside the scope of this book.)
5. The **sys.SysComments** catalog view contains the definitions for views and stored procedures.
6. You can build views on other views and nest them up to 32 levels.
7. You can see the definition of a view with the sp_HelpText stored procedure, as long as the view is not encrypted (see next lab).

View Options

Not every query may be turned into a view. Not unlike tables, there are rules which must be followed before your queries may be turned into views.

For example, you must give each field in your table a name – you cannot create a table with a nameless field. This same rule applies to fields in your views.

In this section, we will also examine options for encrypting and schemabinding your views.

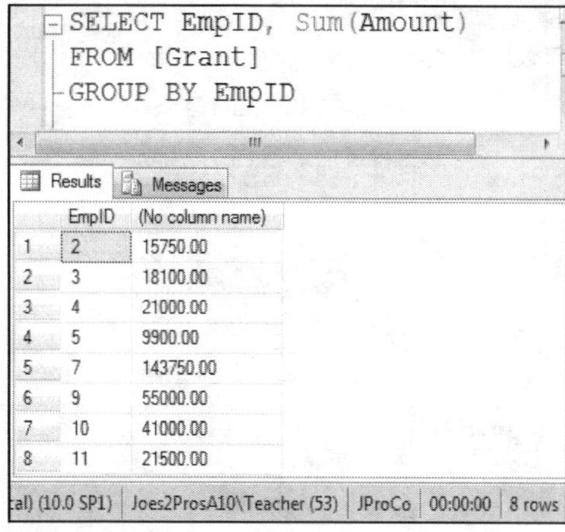

Figure 4.35 A simple aggregation query.

View Rules

This query (Figure 4.35) includes a simple aggregation which totals the grant amounts according to EmpID. It's a handy report, but we can't turn it into a view. The error message shown below (see Figure 4.36) displays when you attempt to run this code and create the view. Notice that it says "…no column name was specified for column 2."

We must first make certain this expression field column has a name before we can create this view.

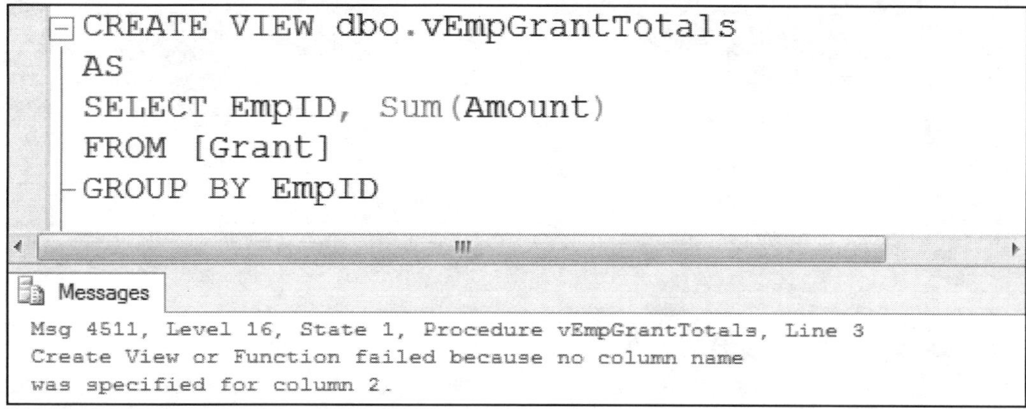

Figure 4.36 A query with unnamed fields cannot become a view.

Alias the expression field as "TotalAmount" and then run this CREATE VIEW statement for vEmpGrantTotals (see Figure 4.37).

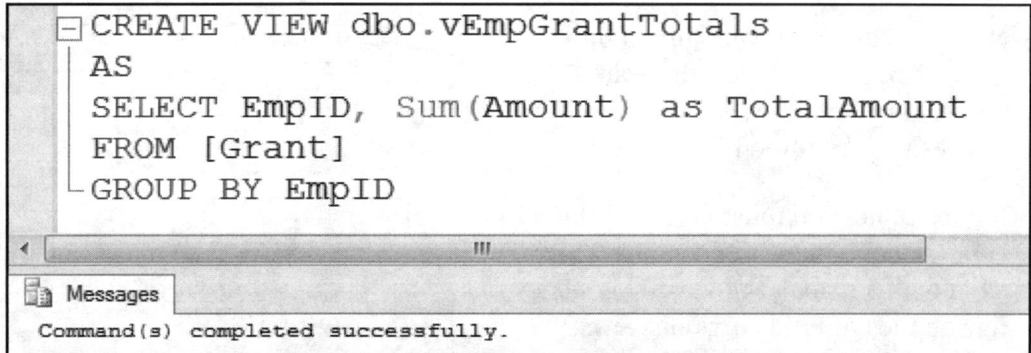
CREATE VIEW dbo.vEmpGrantTotals
AS
SELECT EmpID, Sum(Amount) as TotalAmount
FROM [Grant]
GROUP BY EmpID
Messages
Command(s) completed successfully.

Figure 4.37 Aliasing your expression field to have a name allows the view to be created.

Query the newly created view, vEmpGrantTotals, and look at its data (see Figure 4.38). We see eight records, and the amounts are the same as we saw produced by the base query (shown earlier in Figure 4.35).

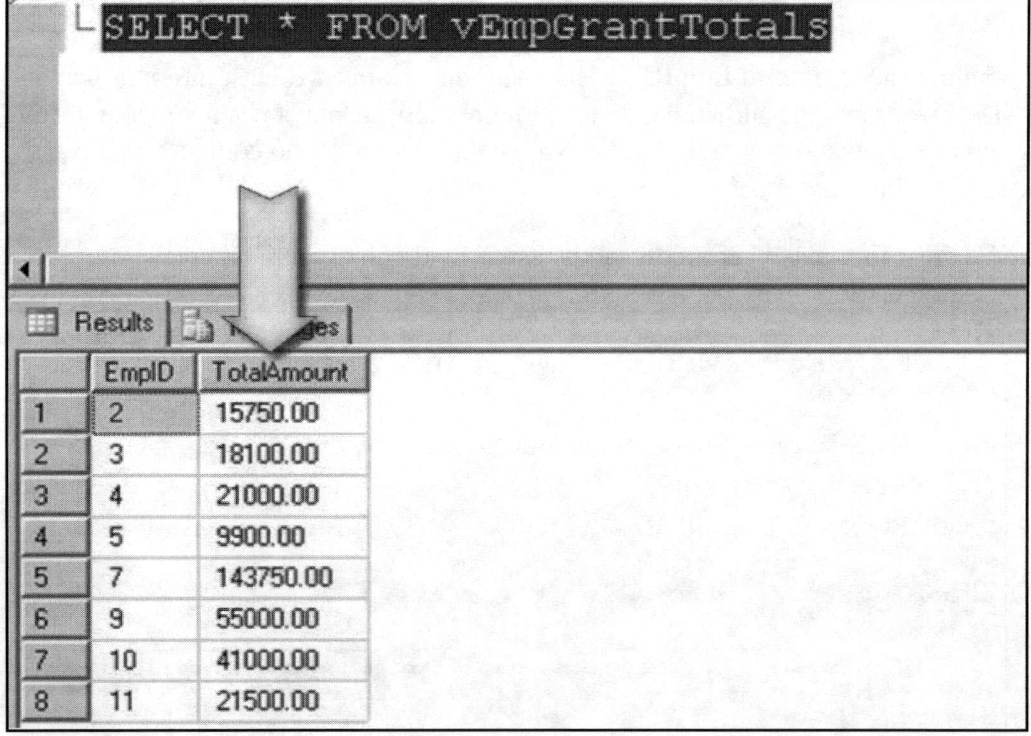
SELECT * FROM vEmpGrantTotals
Results

	EmpID	TotalAmount
1	2	15750.00
2	3	18100.00
3	4	21000.00
4	5	9900.00
5	7	143750.00
6	9	55000.00
7	10	41000.00
8	11	21500.00

Figure 4.38 The vEmpGrantTotals view shows eight records and both fields have their own name.

Encrypting Views

Suppose you want to make sure that people can utilize this view to run reports, but you don't want them to be capable of seeing or recreating the underlying code. As we saw earlier in this chapter, the sp_HelpText system stored procedure reveals the code which created an object (as illustrated below, Figure 4.39).

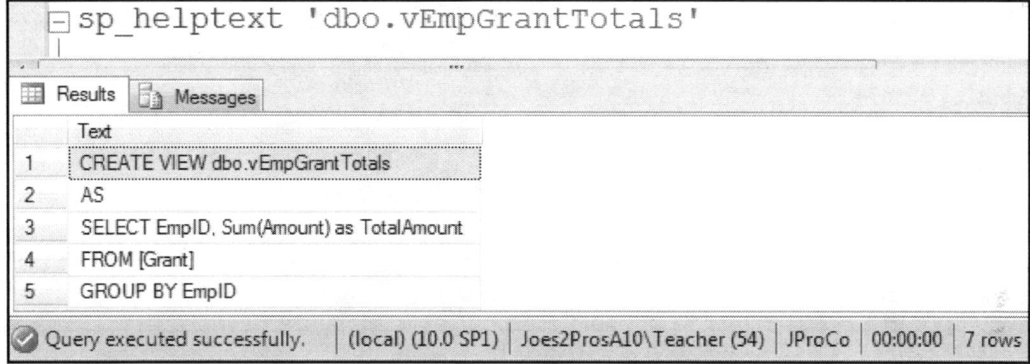

sp_helptext 'dbo.vEmpGrantTotals'
Results
Messages
Text
1 CREATE VIEW dbo.vEmpGrantTotals
2 AS
3 SELECT EmpID, Sum(Amount) as TotalAmount
4 FROM [Grant]
5 GROUP BY EmpID
Query executed successfully. | (local) (10.0 SP1) | Joes2ProsA10\Teacher (54) | JProCo | 00:00:00 | 7 rows

Figure 4.39 sp_helptext shows the code that created the vEmpGrantTotals view.

We want to alter this view so that the source code is encrypted. Two modifications to the code for vEmpGrantTotals (Figures 4.37 and 4.39) will make this change:

1) Change CREATE VIEW to ALTER VIEW.

2) Add WITH ENCRYPTION before the AS keyword.

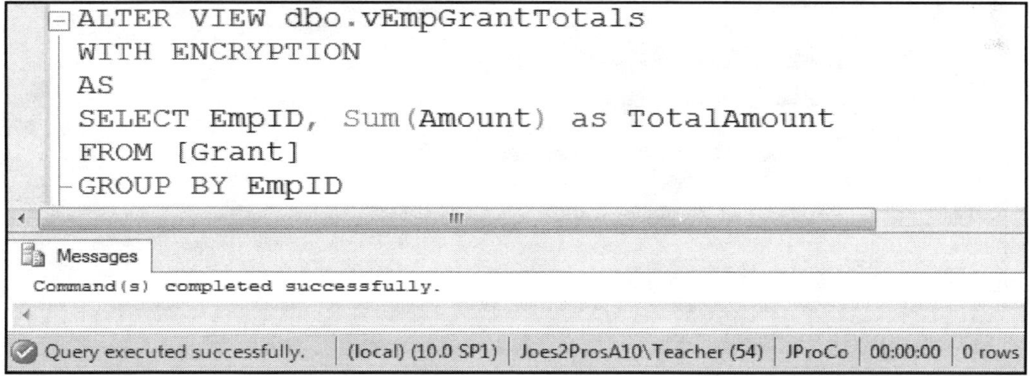

Figure 4.40 This code encrypts the vEmpGrantTotals view.

The best practice after we create or alter an object is to run a SELECT statement to confirm that it produces the expected result. When we do this with our newly encrypted view, vEmpGrantTotals, we see that the data appears correctly (see Figure 4.41). This matches the result we saw before we encrypted the view (shown earlier in Figure 4.38). But look at Object Explorer and notice that a small padlock now appears on the icon for vEmpGrantTotals (see the left panel of Figure 4.41).

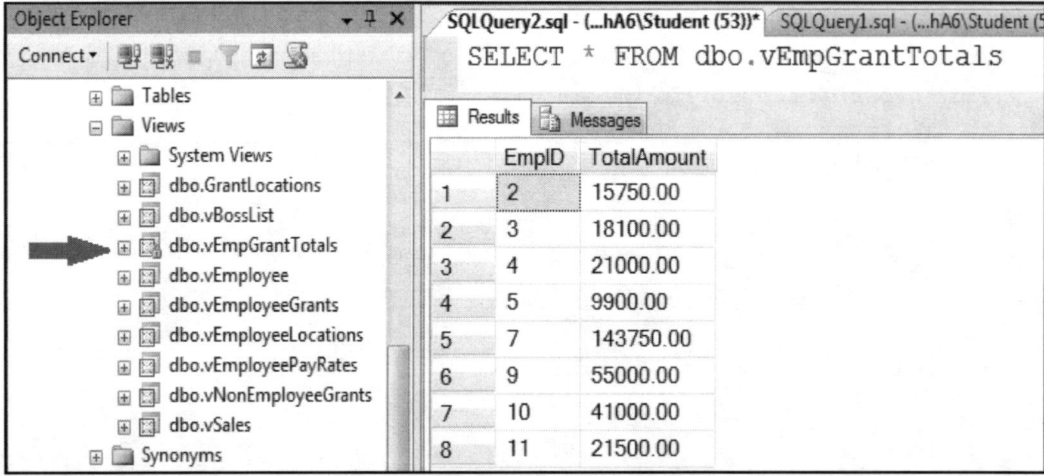

	EmpID	TotalAmount
1	2	15750.00
2	3	18100.00
3	4	21000.00
4	5	9900.00
5	7	143750.00
6	9	55000.00
7	10	41000.00
8	11	21500.00

Figure 4.41 The result set for vEmpGrantTotals is the same after we encrypted the view.

Earlier in this chapter, we were able to right-click a view in Object Explorer and choose "Script View as" to see the code for the view (shown earlier in Figure 4.13). Now when we attempt that maneuver for our encrypted view, SSMS gives us a message saying that the text is encrypted and we can't script this view.

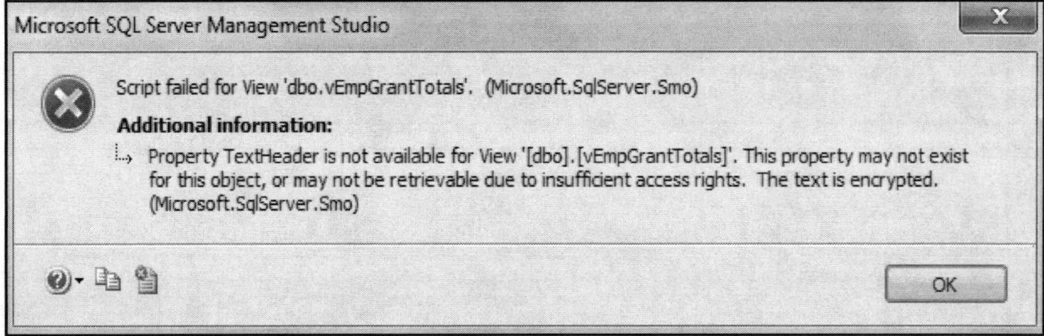

Figure 4.42 Management Studio (SSMS) will not allow us to generate code for the encrypted view.

The properties dialog for vEmpGrantTotals also tells us that the view is now encrypted (see Figure 4.43, Encrypted = True).

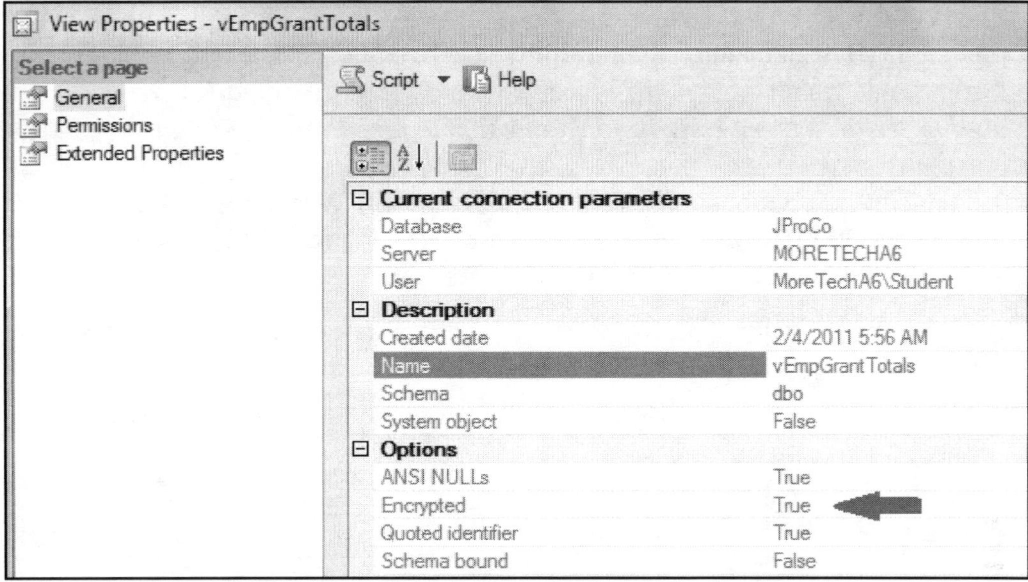

Figure 4.43 Right-click vEmpGrantTotals in Object Explorer to see its Properties.

Attempt to run the sp_HelpText sproc and notice the message, "The text for object 'dbo.vEmpGrantTotals' is encrypted." (see Figure 4.44)

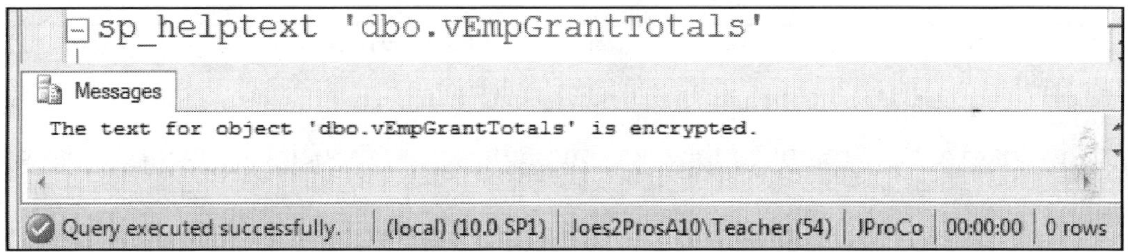

Figure 4.44 You can't use sp_helptext to see the code for an encrypted view.

The catalog views also will not reveal source code for an encrypted object.

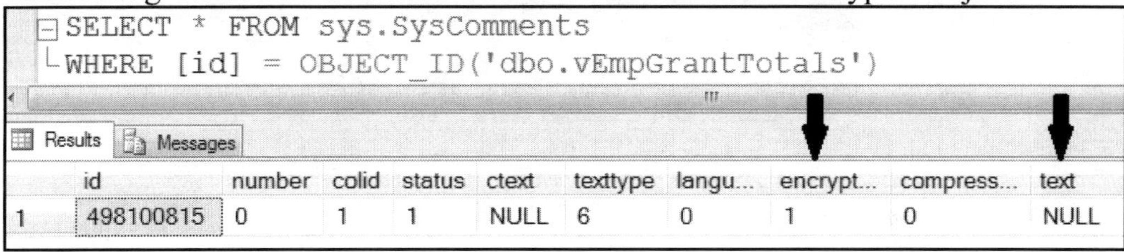

	id	number	colid	status	ctext	texttype	langu...	encrypt...	compress...	text
1	498100815	0	1	1	NULL	6	0	1	0	NULL

Figure 4.45 sys.SysComments says vEmpGrantTotals is encrypted and won't reveal the code.

The WITH ENCRYPTION option allows the view to run properly with respect to running DML statements (e.g., returning data to a query). The only difference is that the code which created the object cannot be seen. ***Every utility we previously used to see the source code is now unavailable for vEmpGrantTotals.***

To remove encryption, simply rerun the ALTER VIEW statement without the "WITH ENCRYPTION" clause (see Figure 4.46). Refresh JProCo's Views folder and notice the padlock icon disappears from the view.

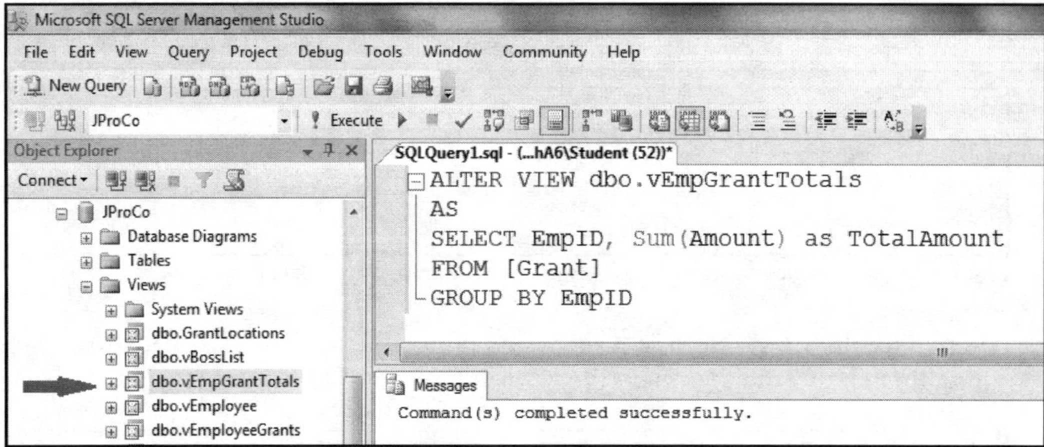

Figure 4.46 Remove the encryption by rerunning the ALTER VIEW statement without the "WITH ENCRYPTION" syntax.

Now that we have removed the encryption, the sproc sp_helptext again displays the source code for vEmpGrantTotals (see Figure 4.47). The same is true for all of the other utilities (e.g., "Script View as" in Object Explorer, sys.SysViews query).

```
sp_helptext 'dbo.vEmpGrantTotals'
```

Results | Messages

	Text
1	CREATE VIEW dbo.vEmpGrantTotals
2	AS
3	SELECT EmpID, Sum(Amount) as TotalAmount
4	FROM [Grant]
5	GROUP BY EmpID

Figure 4.47 Since we removed the encryption on vEmpGrantTotals, sp_HelpText now shows us the source code.

Schemabinding Views

Let's look at a view with multiple sources of data – in other words, a view which has two or more base tables. Run the sp_HelpText sproc on vEmployeeGrants to obtain the code which created this view (see Figure 4.48).

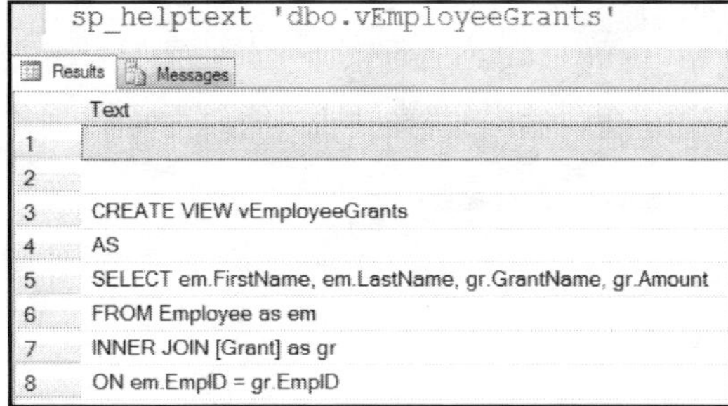

Figure 4.48 Run the sp_helptext sproc.

The vEmployeeGrants view has two sources of data (i.e., two base tables): the Employee table and the Grant table.

```
CREATE VIEW vEmployeeGrants
AS
SELECT em.EmpID, em.FirstName, em.LastName, gr.Gra
FROM Employee as em
INNER JOIN [Grant] as gr
ON em.empID = gr.EmpID
```

Figure 4.49 The two base tables of vEmployeeGrants are Employee and Grant.

Every view depends on its base table(s) in order to properly run and display its data. A change to the base table data can change what the view displays. Dropping a base table would break any view which depends on that table.

To learn more about specific views and their base tables (i.e., their sources of data), we will look at a few system catalog views. The **sys.Views** catalog view shows us the names of all of the views in our database. The **sys.Sql_Dependencies** catalog view keeps track of objects which depend on other objects in your database.

We will join both of these catalog views on Object_ID to show our list of views. Since we are only interested in the base tables of vEmployeeGrants, this query will filter on the [name] field (name = 'vEmployeeGrants', as shown in Figure 4.50).

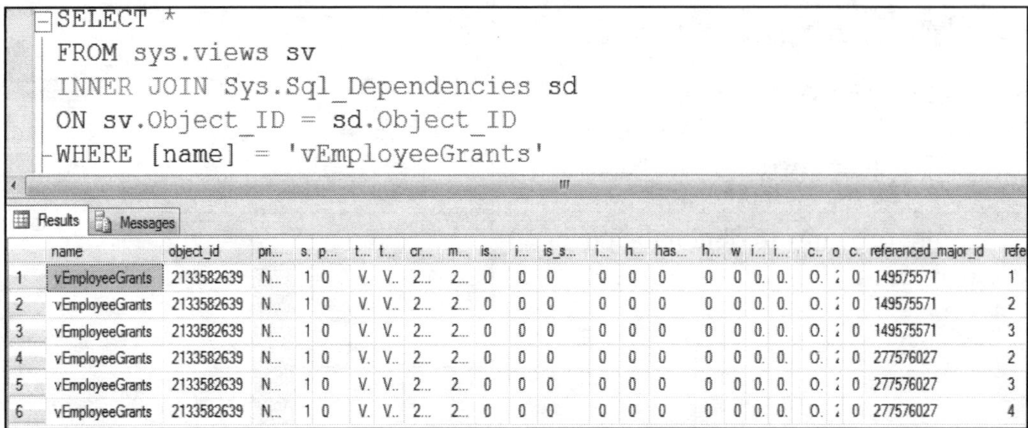

```
SELECT *
FROM sys.views sv
INNER JOIN Sys.Sql_Dependencies sd
ON sv.Object_ID = sd.Object_ID
WHERE [name] = 'vEmployeeGrants'
```

	name	object_id	pri...	s.	p...	t...	t...	cr...	m...	is...	i...	is_s...	i...	h...	has...	h...	w	i...	i...	c..	o	c.	referenced_major_id	refe
1	vEmployeeGrants	2133582639	N...	1	0	V.	V..	2...	2...	0	0	0	0	0	0	0	0	0.	0.	O.	:	0	149575571	1
2	vEmployeeGrants	2133582639	N...	1	0	V.	V..	2...	2...	0	0	0	0	0	0	0	0	0.	0.	O.	:	0	149575571	2
3	vEmployeeGrants	2133582639	N...	1	0	V.	V..	2...	2...	0	0	0	0	0	0	0	0	0.	0.	O.	:	0	149575571	3
4	vEmployeeGrants	2133582639	N...	1	0	V.	V..	2...	2...	0	0	0	0	0	0	0	0	0.	0.	O.	:	0	277576027	2
5	vEmployeeGrants	2133582639	N...	1	0	V.	V..	2...	2...	0	0	0	0	0	0	0	0	0.	0.	O.	:	0	277576027	3
6	vEmployeeGrants	2133582639	N...	1	0	V.	V..	2...	2...	0	0	0	0	0	0	0	0	0.	0.	O.	:	0	277576027	4

Figure 4.50 Join **sys.views** to **sys.Sql_Dependencies** to see the Object_ID values which your view depends upon.

Our query joining **sys.views** and **sys.Sql_Dependencies** (Figure 4.50) needs one improvement in order for us to see the actual names of the base tables. The Object_ID for each base table appears in the field, referenced_major_id. In order to find the names of these objects, we will use the OBJECT_NAME( ) function and pass in the referenced_major_id values (see first line of code, Figure 4.51).

```
SELECT OBJECT_NAME(referenced_major_id) as BaseTable, *
FROM sys.views sv
INNER JOIN Sys.Sql_Dependencies sd
ON sv.Object_ID = sd.Object_ID
WHERE [name] = 'vEmployeeGrants'
```

	BaseTable	name	object_id	principal_id	schema_id	parent_object_id	type	type_desc	create_date	modify_date
1	Employee	vEmployeeGrants	2133582639	NULL	1	0	V	VIEW	2010-10-08 14:14:44.380	2010-10-08 14:14:44.423
2	Employee	vEmployeeGrants	2133582639	NULL	1	0	V	VIEW	2010-10-08 14:14:44.380	2010-10-08 14:14:44.423
3	Employee	vEmployeeGrants	2133582639	NULL	1	0	V	VIEW	2010-10-08 14:14:44.380	2010-10-08 14:14:44.423
4	Grant	vEmployeeGrants	2133582639	NULL	1	0	V	VIEW	2010-10-08 14:14:44.380	2010-10-08 14:14:44.423
5	Grant	vEmployeeGrants	2133582639	NULL	1	0	V	VIEW	2010-10-08 14:14:44.380	2010-10-08 14:14:44.423
6	Grant	vEmployeeGrants	2133582639	NULL	1	0	V	VIEW	2010-10-08 14:14:44.380	2010-10-08 14:14:44.423

Figure 4.51 By using the OBJECT_NAME( ) function, you can get the names of the base tables.

We now see that vEmployeeGrants depends on the Employee table and the Grant table as its base tables. Next we will drop the Grant table (see Figure 4.52). Notice that we are only dropping the Grant table - we are *not* dropping vEmployeeGrants.

```
DROP TABLE [Grant]
```

Messages

Command(s) completed successfully.

Figure 4.52 The Grant table has been dropped.

Recognize that we have just dropped one of this view's (vEmployeeGrants) base tables. (For the moment, we won't consider the many other JProCo views, functions, or sprocs which rely upon the Grant table. We will restrict our focus to this **dependent object,** vEmployeeGrants, and its **dependency**, the Grant table.)

Query the view and notice we get an "Invalid object name 'Grant'" error message (see Figure 4.53). ***When you drop a dependency, you break all of the objects that depend on it.***

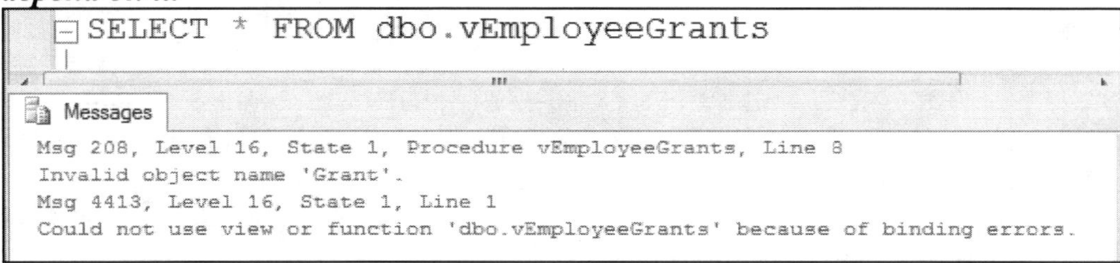

SELECT * FROM dbo.vEmployeeGrants
Messages
Msg 208, Level 16, State 1, Procedure vEmployeeGrants, Line 8
Invalid object name 'Grant'.
Msg 4413, Level 16, State 1, Line 1
Could not use view or function 'dbo.vEmployeeGrants' because of binding errors.

Figure 4.53 With the Grant table gone, the vEmployeeGrants view no longer works.

Note: If you just dropped your Grant table, please replace it by running the latest setup script (SQLProgrammingChapter4.2Setup.sql).

Finding Dependencies

We know that dropping the Grant table would cause serious problems for the view, vEmployeeGrants. Let's now think about the many JProCo objects which depend on the Grant table. In case the Grant table were ever accidentally dropped, or a design change was contemplated which would remove the Grant table, we would need a utility to show us all the objects which depend on the Grant table.

There is a system-supplied stored procedure, sp_depends, which will list all dependent objects for the object name you pass in. In this case, we want to find out every object that depends on the Grant table (see Figure 4.54).

```
sp_depends 'dbo.[Grant]'
```

Results | Messages

	name	type
1	dbo.GrantLocations	view
2	dbo.ResetGrantTables	stored procedure
3	dbo.UpdateGrant	stored procedure
4	dbo.UpsertGrant	stored procedure
5	dbo.vEmployeeGrants	view
6	dbo.vNonEmployeeGrants	view

Figure 4.54 These six objects will break if the Grant table is dropped.

Knowing the objects which use the Grant table might be very useful. Perhaps company policy can be built around which tables will need extra care before you change them. You might even create a DDL trigger which will roll back if someone tries to drop the Grant table.

Losing the Grant table is just one way to break our vEmployeeGrants view. If the Employee table were dropped, that would also cripple vEmployeeGrants. Therefore, our next goal is to ensure that vEmployeeGrants never loses a dependency.

Add "ALTER VIEW" and "WITH SCHEMABINDING" to your code which creates vEmployeeGrants (shown earlier in Figure 4.48). The syntax WITH SCHEMABINDING will prevent dependencies of this view from being dropped. Notice that in order to use SCHEMABINDING, we must use two-part naming for our tables (dbo.Employee, dbo.[Grant]) see Figure 4.55).

```
ALTER VIEW vEmployeeGrants
WITH SCHEMABINDING
AS
SELECT em.EmpID, em.FirstName, em.LastName, g
FROM dbo.Employee as em
INNER JOIN dbo.[Grant] as gr
ON em.empID = gr.EmpID
```

Figure 4.55 To successfully add the SCHEMABINDING option, you must use at least two-part naming for the base tables. Run the code you see here in order to schema bind both of these tables.

To confirm that our schemabinding is now protecting the base tables, let's try dropping one of them. Success! When we attempt to drop the Grant table, we get an error message informing us that we cannot drop the Grant table because it is being referenced by the object vEmployeeGrants (see Figure 4.56).

```
DROP TABLE [Grant]
```

Messages

```
Msg 3729, Level 16, State 1, Line 1
Cannot DROP TABLE 'Grant' because it is being referenced
by object 'vEmployeeGrants'.
```

Figure 4.56 The Grant table can't be dropped as long as one of its dependencies is schema bound.

When you use the WITH SCHEMABINDING option on an object, it prevents any of the dependencies of the object from being deleted. If you wanted to drop the Grant table, you would first need to either drop the vEmployeeGrants view or remove the schemabinding.

If we wanted to add both schemabinding and encryption to vEmployeeGrants, we would need to use this syntax (see Figure 4.57). You must include both in the same WITH clause, because a DDL statement may have only one WITH clause.

After we run the code below (Figure 4.57), vEmployeeGrants is both schema bound and encrypted. This means that neither of the base tables (Grant, Employee) of vEmployeeGrants may be deleted, and no one will be able to see the code which created the view.

```
ALTER VIEW vEmployeeGrants
WITH SCHEMABINDING,ENCRYPTION
AS
SELECT em.EmpID, em.FirstName, em.LastName, gr.GrantName, gr.Amount
FROM dbo.Employee as em
INNER JOIN dbo.[Grant] as gr
ON em.empID = gr.EmpID
GO
```

Messages

```
Command(s) completed successfully.
```

Figure 4.57 The vEmployeeGrants view is now encrypted and schema bound.

The process to remove schemabinding is the same process we used to remove encryption (shown in Figures 4.46 and 4.47). Simply rerun the ALTER VIEW statement without the "WITH SCHEMABINDING" clause.

```
ALTER VIEW vEmployeeGrants
AS
SELECT em.EmpID, em.FirstName, em.LastName, gr.GrantName, gr.Amount
FROM dbo.Employee as em
INNER JOIN dbo.[Grant] as gr
ON em.empID = gr.EmpID
GO
```

Messages

```
Command(s) completed successfully.
```

Figure 4.58 This view has been modified to remove the encryption and schema bound.

With the schemabinding protection removed, we again are able to make the blunder of dropping our Grant table.

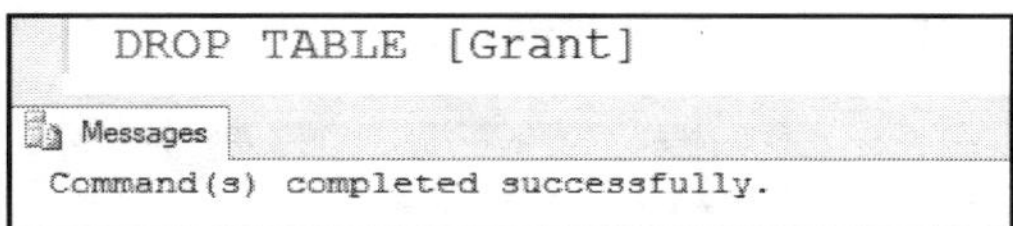

```
DROP TABLE [Grant]
```

Messages

```
Command(s) completed successfully.
```

Figure 4.59 The DROP TABLE now succeeds.

Lab 4.3: View Options

Lab Prep: Before you can begin the lab, you must have SQL Server installed and have run the script SQLProgrammingChapter4.3Setup.sql. View the lab video instructions in Lab4.3_ViewOptions.wmv.

Skill Check 1: Create an aggregate view called vCustomerQuantity based on the vSales view that shows each CustomerID and the total quantity they have ordered. The expression field should be called TotalQty.

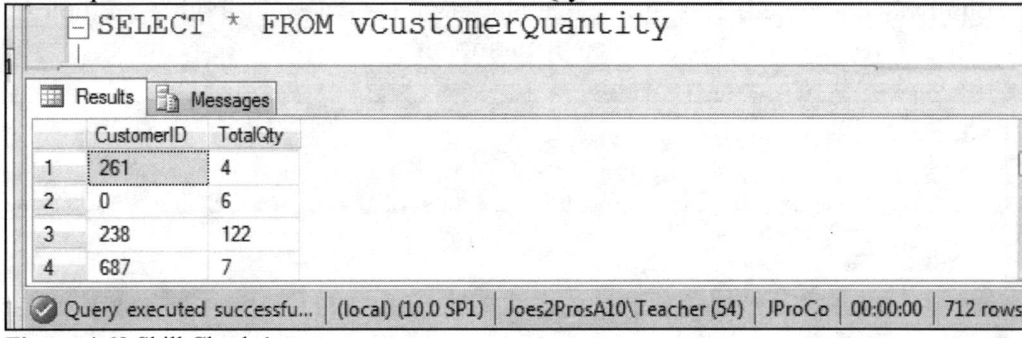

Figure 4.60 Skill Check 1.

Skill Check 2: Take the vCustomerQuantity view and encrypt it so that nobody can read the code used to create the view.

Figure 4.61 Skill Check 2.

Skill Check 3
Find out how many objects depend on the dbo.Employee table. (*Note:* If you don't run the current setup script, SQLProgrammingChapter4.3Setup.sql, you may see an eighth record in your result.

1	dbo.GetLocationCount	stored procedure
2	dbo.ResetEmployeeTables	stored procedure
3	dbo.spGetEmployeeLastAndState	stored procedure
4	dbo.vBossList	view
5	dbo.vEmployee	view
6	dbo.vEmployeeGrants	view
7	dbo.vEmployeeLocations	view

Figure 4.62 Skill Check 3.

Skill Check 4
Ensure that all dependencies of the vSales view cannot be deleted.

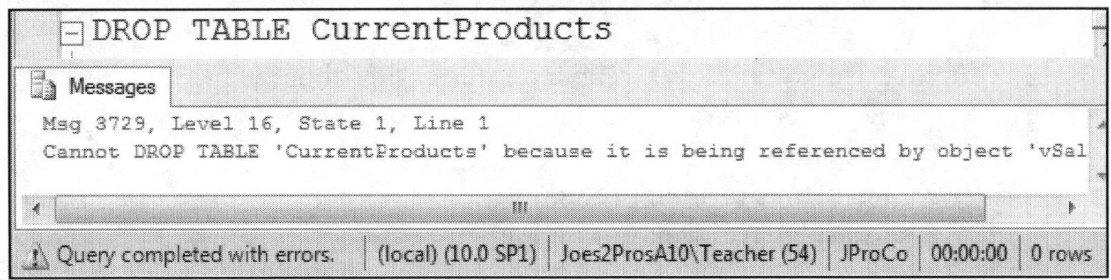
DROP TABLE CurrentProducts
Messages
Msg 3729, Level 16, State 1, Line 1
Cannot DROP TABLE 'CurrentProducts' because it is being referenced by object 'vSal
Query completed with errors.
(local) (10.0 SP1)
Joes2ProsA10\Teacher (54)
JProCo
00:00:00
0 rows

Figure 4.63 Skill Check 4.

Answer Code: The T-SQL code to this lab can be found in the downloadable files in a file named Lab4.3_ViewOptions.sql.

Altering Views - Points to Ponder

1. There are four main ways to obtain information about views.
    a. SQL Server Management Studio (SSMS)
    b. sys.views catalog view
    c. sp_helptext stored procedure
    d. sys.sql_dependencies catalog view
2. Views can aggregate data. For example, they can show the sum of a column rather than individual values in the column.
3. In views you must specify column names for:
    a. Columns derived from mathematical expressions, functions, or constants.
    b. Columns in the tables (usually from a join) that share the same name.
4. If you specify the WITH ENCRYPTION option, no one (including you) will be able to read your view's description in the sys.SysComments catalog view or the sp_HelpText stored procedure.
5. To remove WITH ENCRYPTION from a view, simply remove the WITH ENCRYPTION syntax and run the ALTER VIEW statement.
6. Altering a view has an advantage over dropping and re-creating the view, since the original permissions are retained.
7. If you need to change a view, you can modify it by either using the UI or an ALTER VIEW statement.
8. Modifying a view does not change the permissions of the view. If you drop a view, however, the permissions must be reassigned.
9. Dropping a base table will cause the dependent view to break.
10. Before you drop any table or view, you should check to see if any view depends on it.
11. If you no longer need a view, you can remove its definition from the database by either the using the UI or running a DROP VIEW statement.
12. The T-SQL syntax to drop a view is DROP VIEW *ViewName.*
13. Views cannot use ORDER BY unless a TOP *n,* or a FOR XML, clause is included. (The latter point is discussed in Volume 5, *SQL Interoperability.*)

Chapter Glossary

ALTER VIEW: a DDL statement to change the definition of an existing view.
Catalog views: a predefined view you can query from to see your database metadata.
CREATE VIEW: DDL statement to create the definition of a new view.
Dependencies: references that are used in SQL code that make one object rely upon another object.
Dependent object: a database object (e.g., a view) which references – in other words, depends upon – another database object(s).
Encrypt(ion): a way to scramble data so it can't be read by others.
SCHEMABINDING: objects that are schema-bound can have their definition changed, but objects that are referenced by schema bound objects cannot have their definition changed.
sp_helptext: system-supplied stored procedure that reports information about a database object.
sys.sql_dependencies: a catalog view that contains a row for each dependency of a referencing object.
sys.syscomments: a catalog view which contains the code that created each SQL object created within a database.
sys.SysObjects: contains one row for each object created in a database.
sys.Views: contains one row for each View created in a database.
Temporary table: a table prefixed with a # ("pound sign") and that is only visible within one session of SQL Server.
TOP *n*: a row limiting clause that takes the top number of rows that you specify.
Two-part naming: a combination of schema and table name separated by a dot (example: Sales.Campaigns, dbo.Employee).
Indexed view: a virtual table created when you place a clustered index on a view.
View Designer: a graphical design tool that will construct the create view statement for you.
WITH ENCRYPTION: the code option which will encrypt the definition of an object.
WITH SCHEMABINDING: the code option which will schema bind an object.

Chapter Four - Review Quiz

1.) You have a view that joins the Employee table to the Location table. These two tables in this view are called what?

O a. View Table(s)
O b. Base Table(s)
O c. Dependent Table(s)
O d. Source Table(s)

2.) You can base a view on another view. (True/False)

O a. True
O b. False

3.) The following query cannot be made into a view

```
CREATE VIEW Sales.vTravelTripsLocationRating
AS
SELECT LocationID, AVG(Rating)
FROM Sales.TravelTrip
GROUP BY LocationID
```

What must you do in order for this view to be created?

O a. Change the word CREATE to ALTER.
O b. Add the words ORDER BY after Group By.
O c. Alias all expression fields with an identifier.
O d. Remove the schema name from the base table.

4.) What are two ways to see the code that created a view? (Choose two)

□ a. WITH SCHEMABINDING
□ b. WITH ENCRYPTION
□ c. Sp_helptext
□ d. Sp_Depends
□ e. Sys.Syscomments

5.) What does the WITH ENCRYPTION option achieve?

O a. It prevents other users from seeing the code that created the view.
O b. It prevents the deletion of base tables being used by the view.
O c. It hides the information in the Sys.SQL_Dependencies.
O d. It prevents the view from ever being altered again.

6.) What happens to a view if the underlying table is dropped?
O a. The view no longer works.
O b. The view uses the latest cached data until the table is restored.
O c. The view uses the default or fallback table.

7.) What is a requirement that must be in place in order for you to use WITH SCHEMABINDING?

O a. All base tables must be tables and can't be views.
O b. All base tables must be referenced by the schema name.
O c. It prevents the deletion of base tables being used by the view
O d. It hides the information in the Sys.SQL_Dependencies.
O e. It prevents the view from ever being altered again.

8.) What is one reason why **sp_helptext** won't allow you to see the code used to build a view?
O a. The view is set to read only.
O b. The table behind the view is set to read only.
O c. The view is set to encryption.
O d. The view is built with compression.

9.) You have a table named Sales.TravelTrip and a developer has given you some suggested code for building a view. The code for the view is as follows:
CREATE VIEW vTravelSelect AS SELECT * FROM TravelTrip
The code errors out. What must you do?
O a. Change the column type so there are no text fields.
O b. Include the Sales schema name with the table in the statement.
O c. Change the column count so it does not use the * notation.

Answer Key

1.) b 2.) a 3.) c 4.) c, e 5.) a 6.) a 7.) b 8.) c 9) b

Bug Catcher Game

To play the Bug Catcher game, run the file BugCatcher_Chapter4CreatingViews.pps from the BugCatcher folder of the companion files located at www.Joes2Pros.com.

Chapter 5. Updating and Maintaining Views

As we saw in the previous chapter, views are great tools for narrowing the focus of your data. Like a spotlight in a theatrical stage production, a view can provide a laser-like focus on just the portion of data that you need and can help reduce complexity by tuning out data which you don't need to see.

This chapter expands our work with views to include all of the DML statements (SELECT, INSERT, UPDATE, DELETE). Much the same way views allow DBAs and their users to see just the needed data, views also offer a more controlled and surgical approach to updating table data. DBAs can also use tools, such as CHECK OPTION, in combination with views to limit the updates that users are allowed to make to base tables. We will also see an example where a view with CHECK OPTION does a better job of controlling user input than would a trigger.

The strategy of utilizing views with data is similar to the mission and goal of the *Joes 2 Pros* method. For a beginner contemplating the journey to master a toolset as vast and powerful as SQL Server, the outlook can be daunting. By spotlighting one new tool at a time and scaling down examples to be manageable, *Joes 2 Pros* aims to let students wade into deeper waters at their own pace and gain proficiency without fear of drowning.

In this chapter we will also look at **indexed views**. These are a departure from "regular" views, because placing an index on a view causes the view to be materialized persistently – that is, not just at runtime – and it retains a copy of the data.

READER NOTE: *In order to follow along with the examples in the first section of Chapter 5, please run the setup script SQLProgrammingChapter5.0Setup.sql. The setup scripts for this book are posted at Joes2Pros.com. An additional script, SQLProgrammingExtraResetGrant.sql, will be used throughout this chapter.*

Manipulating Data Through Views

As we learned in the previous chapter, a view is a stored query against one or more database tables. Views are also known as "virtual tables." The data and query results made available by views are not stored physically. While the Object Explorer keeps track of the views you create, views don't occupy any permanent memory storage the way database tables do.

Views behave much like tables when it comes to writing SELECT statements against them. In this section, we will see how views work with other DML statements like INSERT, UPDATE, and DELETE.

Views do NOT contain data, but updates to views affect the data in the base tables. This portion of the chapter is called manipulating data "through views" to help emphasize that point. Views do not maintain separate copies of data. Instead, they give you another way to interact with the data residing in your base tables.

Selecting Data Through Views

Selecting data through a view works and looks just the same as selecting data from a table. In the example we'll see here, the Employee table is the base table (20 records, 9 fields). If we look at the records from the vEmployee view, it appears to be nearly the same with 20 records and 7 fields (Figure 5.1).

```
SELECT * FROM Employee ORDER BY EmpID
SELECT * FROM vEmployee ORDER BY EmpID
```

Results | Messages

	EmpID	LastName	FirstName	HireDate	LocationID	ManagerID	Status	HiredOffset	TimeZon
15	15	Jones	Tess	2010-10-19 16:59:37.940	1	11	Orientation	2010-10-19 16:59:37.9400000 -08:00	-08:00
16	16	Biggs	Nancy	2010-10-19 16:59:37.947	1	11	Orientation	2010-10-19 16:59:37.9470000 -08:00	-08:00
17	17	Downs	Wendy	2010-10-19 16:59:37.950	1	11	Orientation	2010-10-19 16:59:37.9500000 -08:00	-08:00
18	18	Walker	Rainy	2010-01-01 00:00:00.000	1	11	Orientation	2010-10-19 16:59:38.0470000 -08:00	-08:00
19	19	Beckman	Sandy	2010-01-15 00:00:00.000	1	11	Orientation	2010-10-19 16:59:38.0500000 -08:00	-08:00
20	20	Winds	Gale	2010-03-25 00:00:00.000	1	11	Orientation	2010-10-19 16:59:38.1970000 -08:00	-08:00

	EmpID	FirstName	LastName	HireDate	LocationID	ManagerID	Status
15	15	Tess	Jones	2010-10-19 16:59:37.940	1	11	Orie...
16	16	Nancy	Biggs	2010-10-19 16:59:37.947	1	11	Orie...
17	17	Wendy	Downs	2010-10-19 16:59:37.950	1	11	Orie...
18	18	Rainy	Walker	2010-01-01 00:00:00.000	1	11	Orie...
19	19	Sandy	Beckman	2010-01-15 00:00:00.000	1	11	Orie...
20	20	Gale	Winds	2010-03-25 00:00:00.000	1	11	Orie...

Query executed successfully. | (local) (10.0 SP1) | Joes2ProsA10\Teacher (53) | JProCo

Figure 5.1 The Employee table and the vEmployee view show the same 20 records.

Views are useful for showing just the relevant data. The vEmployee view contains the same records as the table, but most of our reports don't need the timezone data. This view has simply omitted a few fields and we've chosen to show just the key fields we need to see.

Updating Records Through Views

Most of the time DML statements (inserts, updates, and deletes) against views work the same as they do against tables. Let's take a look at Alex Adams who is EmpID 1 and currently works for ManagerID 11 (Sally Zander). If we were to make a change to Alex Adams in the Employee table, that change would also be reflected in the view. Let's change Alex to report to ManagerID 4 (David Kennson) with the following code:

```
UPDATE Employee SET ManagerID = 4
WHERE EmpID = 1
```

After you've successfully run the code, check the records of the Employee table. We can see Alex's new manager reflected in the Employee table (Figure 5.2). If you query the vEmployee view, you can see the new data there, too (Figure 5.3).

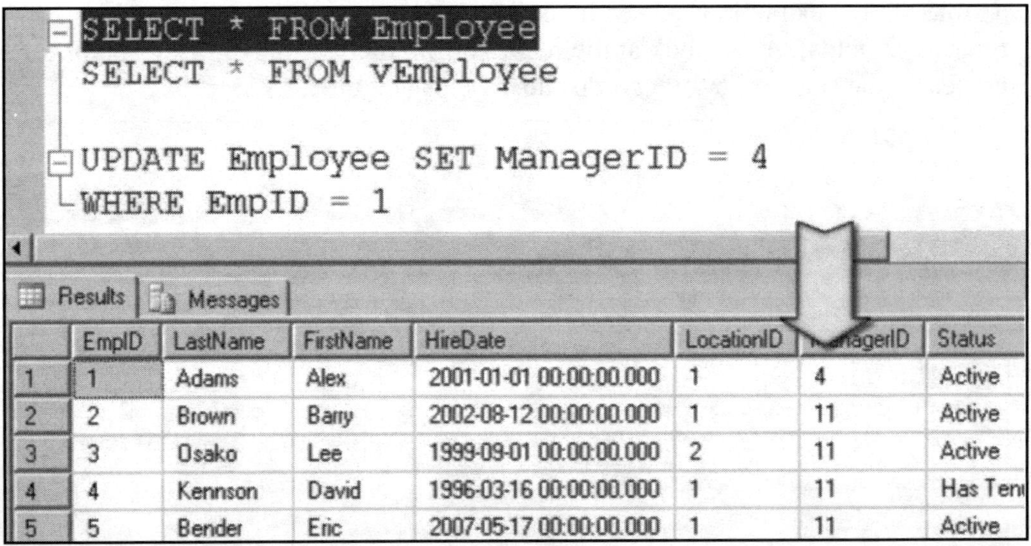
SELECT * FROM Employee
SELECT * FROM vEmployee
UPDATE Employee SET ManagerID = 4
WHERE EmpID = 1
Results
Messages

	EmpID	LastName	FirstName	HireDate	LocationID	agerID	Status
1	1	Adams	Alex	2001-01-01 00:00:00.000	1	4	Active
2	2	Brown	Barry	2002-08-12 00:00:00.000	1	11	Active
3	3	Osako	Lee	1999-09-01 00:00:00.000	2	11	Active
4	4	Kennson	David	1996-03-16 00:00:00.000	1	11	Has Ten
5	5	Bender	Eric	2007-05-17 00:00:00.000	1	11	Active

Figure 5.2 The Employee table and the vEmployee view both reflect Alex's new manager.

Currently the Employee table shows us 20 records, and the vEmployee view based on the Employee table also shows us the same 20 records. Notice in Figure 5.3 that both result sets show Alex Adams' record with the new ManagerID of 4.

```
SELECT * FROM Employee WHERE EmpID = 1
SELECT * FROM vEmployee WHERE EmpID = 1
```

Results | Messages

	EmpID	LastName	FirstName	HireDate	LocationID	ManagerID	Status	HiredOffset	TimeZone
1	1	Adams	Alex	2001-01-01 00:00:00.000	1	4	Active	2001-01-01 00:00:00.0000000 -08:00	-08:00

	EmpID	FirstName	LastName	HireDate	LocationID	ManagerID	Status
1	1	Alex	Adams	2001-01-01 00:00:00.000	1	4	Active

Figure 5.3 After the table update, the Employee table and the vEmployee view are still in sync and showing the same records.

Inserting Records Through Views

Since the vEmployee view was built without criteria, it will always show the same number of records as the base table. This view contains a SELECT statement (see Figure 5.4) whose purpose is simply to narrow the field list down to our seven key fields. Therefore, vEmployee will always be in sync with the Employee table.

```
sp_helptext vEmployee
```

Results | Messages

Text
CREATE VIEW dbo.vEmployee
AS
SELECT EmpID, FirstName, LastName, HireDate, LocationID, ManagerID, [Status]
FROM Employee

Figure 5.4 The vEmployee view was designed to constantly be in sync with the Employee table.

This means that if we insert a 21st record into the Employee table, then we will also see the 21st record in the view.

But what if we were to insert a record into the view – *would it also show up in the Employee table?* Let's test that out (see below, Figure 5.5).

```
INSERT INTO vEmployee VALUES
(21,'Sue','Fines',GetDate(),1,4,Default)
```

Messages

```
(1 row(s) affected)
```

Figure 5.5 Inserting a row into the view has affected 1 row in a single object.

The "1 row(s) affected" confirmation tells us that our insert of one record (Sue Fines) has impacted one object, namely the Employee table.

We now see 21 records in the Employee table, including the new record for Sue Fines (see Figure 5.6). So the answer is yes – the record inserted through the view was successfully inserted into the Employee table.

```
SELECT * FROM Employee
```

	EmpID	LastName	FirstName	HireDate	LocationID	ManagerID	Status	HiredOffset
20	20	Winds	Gale	2010-03-25 00:00:00.000	1	11	Orientation	2010-10-19
21	21	Fines	Sue	2010-10-19 17:10:37.817	1	4	Orientation	2010-10-19

Query executed successfully. | (local) (10.0 SP1) | Joes2ProsA10\Teacher (53) | JProCo | 00:00:00 | 21 rows

Figure 5.6 We are delighted to see 21 records showing in the Employee table.

Following the insert, we see all 21 records from the Employee table showing in the vEmployee view (see Figure 5.7).

```
SELECT * FROM vEmployee
```

	EmpID	FirstName	LastName	HireDate	LocationID	ManagerID	Status
18	18	Rainy	Walker	2010-01-01 00:00:00.000	1	11	Orientation
19	19	Sandy	Beckman	2010-01-15 00:00:00.000	1	11	Orientation
20	20	Gale	Winds	2010-03-25 00:00:00.000	1	11	Orientation
21	21	Sue	Fines	2010-10-19 17:10:37.817	1	4	Orientation

Query executed succe... | (local) (10.0 SP1) | Joes2ProsA10\Teacher (53) | JProCo | 00:00:00 | 21 rows

Figure 5.7 As expected, all 21 records from the Employee table appear in the view, vEmployee.

You can run DML statements against base tables through views. *But let's recall that views don't actually contain data. Most views are dynamic, unmaterialized objects which do not contain data.* (The exception case is an indexed view, since the index contains a copy of the data.) So when we inserted the 21st record (shown earlier in Figure 5.5), the view simply passed the record into the Employee table.

In the last example we changed a single record through the view, which changed the same record in the base table. We're now going to update many records at once through a view. Before we get started, let's look at all of the records in the Grant table (Figure 5.8).

```
SELECT * FROM [Grant]
```

	GrantID	GrantName	EmpID	Amount
1	001	92 Purr_Scents %% team	7	4750.00
2	002	K-Land fund trust	2	15750.00
3	003	Robert@BigStarBank.com	7	18100.00
4	005	BIG 6's Foundation%	4	21000.00
5	006	TALTA_Kishan International	3	18100.00
6	007	Ben@MoreTechnology.com	10	41000.00
7	008	www.@-Last-U-Can-Help.com	7	25000.00
8	009	Thank you @.com	11	21500.00
9	010	Just Mom	5	9900.00
10	011	Big Giver Tom	7	95900.00
11	012	Mega Mercy	9	55000.00

Query executed successfully. | (local) (10.0 SP1) | MoreTechA6\Student (55) | JProCo | 00:00:00 | 11 rows

Figure 5.8 In preparation for the next example, we look at the records and data in the Grant table.

We see 11 records in the Grant table, which includes some small grants and some larger ones. Let's call grants with an amount greater than $20,000 "large grants." We will use the following code to build a view showing just these large grants:

```
CREATE VIEW vHighValueGrants
AS
SELECT GrantName, EmpID, Amount
FROM [Grant]
WHERE Amount > 20000
```

Let's run this code and then look at our newly created view. Recall this won't show us all the grants, just the ones with amounts exceeding 20,000 (Figure 5.9).

```
SELECT * FROM vHighValueGrants
```

	GrantName	EmpID	Amount
1	BIG 6's Foundation%	4	21000.00
2	Ben@MoreTechnology.com	10	41000.00
3	www.@-Last-U-Can-Help.com	7	25000.00
4	Thank you @.com	11	21500.00
5	Big Giver Tom	7	95900.00
6	Mega Mercy	9	55000.00

Query executed successfully. | (local) (10.0 SP1) | MoreTechA6\Student (52) | JProCo | 00:00:00 | 6 rows

Figure 5.9 Our newly created view, vHighValueGrants, shows that we have six large grants.

There are six large grants. Now let's make an update to all the large grants. Suppose the company plans to match an additional $1,000 for each grant over $20,000. In other words, the Amount of the $21,000 grant will become $22,000. The $41,000 grant will become $42,000, and so forth. The data changes we expect to see are penciled in below (see Figure 5.10).

```
SELECT * FROM vHighValueGrants
```

	GrantName	EmpID	Amount	
1	BIG 6's Foundation%	4	21000.00	22,000
2	Ben@MoreTechnology.com	10	41000.00	42,000
3	www.@-Last-U-Can-Help.com	7	25000.00	26,000
4	Thank you @.com	11	21500.00	22,500
5	Big Giver Tom	7	95900.00	96,900
6	Mega Mercy	9	55000.00	56,000

Query exec... | (local) (10.0 SP1) | Joes2ProsA10\Teacher (53) | JProCo | 00:00:00 | 6 rows

Figure 5.10 JProCo plans to match an additional $1,000 for each grant greater than $20,000.

Let's write the UPDATE statement to implement this change and increment each record appearing in vHighValueGrants by 1,000. Notice that the UPDATE statement for a view uses the same syntax as we use when updating a table (see Figure 5.11).

```
UPDATE vHighValueGrants
SET Amount = Amount + 1000
```

Messages

(6 row(s) affected)

Figure 5.11 JProCo plans to match an additional $1,000 for each grant greater than $20,000.

Let's query vHighValueGrants and see the effect of the UDPATE statement (see Figure 5.12).

```
SELECT * FROM vHighValueGrants
```

	GrantName	EmpID	Amount
1	BIG 6's Foundation%	4	22000.00
2	Ben@MoreTechnol...	10	42000.00
3	www.@-Last-U-Can...	7	26000.00
4	Thank you @.com	11	22500.00
5	Big Giver Tom	7	96900.00
6	Mega Mercy	9	56000.00

Query executed successfully. | (local) (10.0 SP1) | MoreTechA6\Student (52) | JProCo | 00:00:00 | 6 rows

Figure 5.12 Our update statement increases each Amount, as expected (see Figure 5.10).

Following the UPDATE statement, we see each Amount has increased by 1,000 and matches the values we expected to see. Now let's check the Grant table and confirm the view passed the six new amounts to the base table (see Figure 5.13).

```
SELECT * FROM [Grant]
```

Results | Messages

	GrantID	GrantName	EmpID	Amount
1	001	92 Purr_Scents %% team	7	4750.00
2	002	K-Land fund trust	2	15750.00
3	003	Robert@BigStarBank.com	7	18100.00
4	005	BIG 6's Foundation%	4	22000.00
5	006	TALTA_Kishan International	3	18100.00
6	007	Ben@MoreTechnology.com	10	42000.00
7	008	www.@-Last-U-Can-Help.com	7	26000.00
8	009	Thank you @.com	11	22500.00
9	010	Just Mom	5	9900.00
10	011	Big Giver Tom	7	96900.00
11	012	Mega Mercy	9	56000.00

Query executed successfully. | (local) (10.0 SP1) | MoreTechA6\Student (52) | JProCo | 00:00:00 | 11 rows

Figure 5.13 The vHighValueGrants view successfully passed the new amounts to the Grant table.

We see that the six records affected by the UPDATE statement were stored in the Grant table, and we can see the changes there. Keep in mind that not all grants were updated. For example, the amount of GrantID 001 was $4,750 before the update and remains the same afterward. ***Only the records returned by a view may be updated through the view.***

Compare this rule and the vHighValueGrants scenario to the first example we saw in this chapter (Figures 5.1 thru 5.7). Since the vEmployee view was created without criteria, it is able to write to every record in the Employee table. However, we created the vHighValueGrants view with a scope of just the records having an amount >$20,000. It is only permitted to SELECT, INSERT, UPDATE, or DELETE records which are >$20,000 in the base table.

Lab 5.1: Manipulating Data Through Views

Lab Prep: Before you can begin this lab, you must have SQL Server installed and have run the script SQLProgrammingChapter5.1Setup.sql.

Skill Check 1: Create a view called vSeattleEmployee which shows the 15 employees from LocationID 1. Show the EmpID, FirstName, LastName, LocationID, and Status fields.

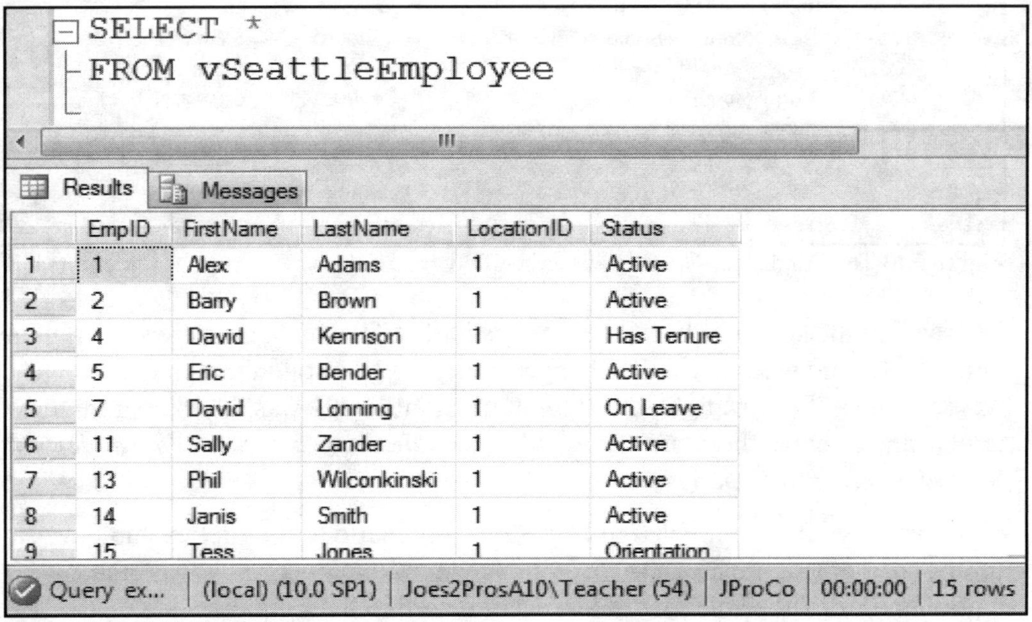

```
SELECT *
FROM vSeattleEmployee
```

	EmpID	FirstName	LastName	LocationID	Status
1	1	Alex	Adams	1	Active
2	2	Barry	Brown	1	Active
3	4	David	Kennson	1	Has Tenure
4	5	Eric	Bender	1	Active
5	7	David	Lonning	1	On Leave
6	11	Sally	Zander	1	Active
7	13	Phil	Wilconkinski	1	Active
8	14	Janis	Smith	1	Active
9	15	Tess	Jones	1	Orientation

Query ex... | (local) (10.0 SP1) | Joes2ProsA10\Teacher (54) | JProCo | 00:00:00 | 15 rows

Figure 5.14 Skill Check 1.

Skill Check 2: Write an UPDATE statement against the vSeattleEmployee view to change employees currently showing a Status of 'Orientation' to a Status of 'Active'.

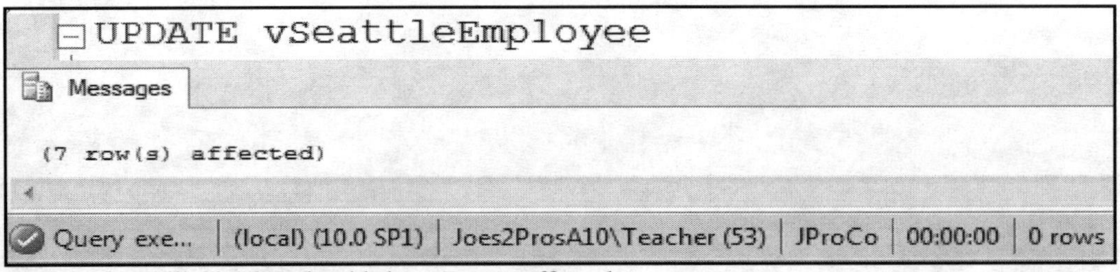

```
UPDATE vSeattleEmployee
```

```
(7 row(s) affected)
```

Query exe... | (local) (10.0 SP1) | Joes2ProsA10\Teacher (53) | JProCo | 00:00:00 | 0 rows

Figure 5.15 Skill Check 2 should show 7 rows affected.

Skill Check 3: Write an UPDATE statement against the vEmployee view to change James Newton (EmpID = 9) to work in Seattle (LocationID = 1). When that is done, check to confirm that James now appears in the vSeattleEmployee view. You should have 16 Seattle employee records in your view instead of 15.

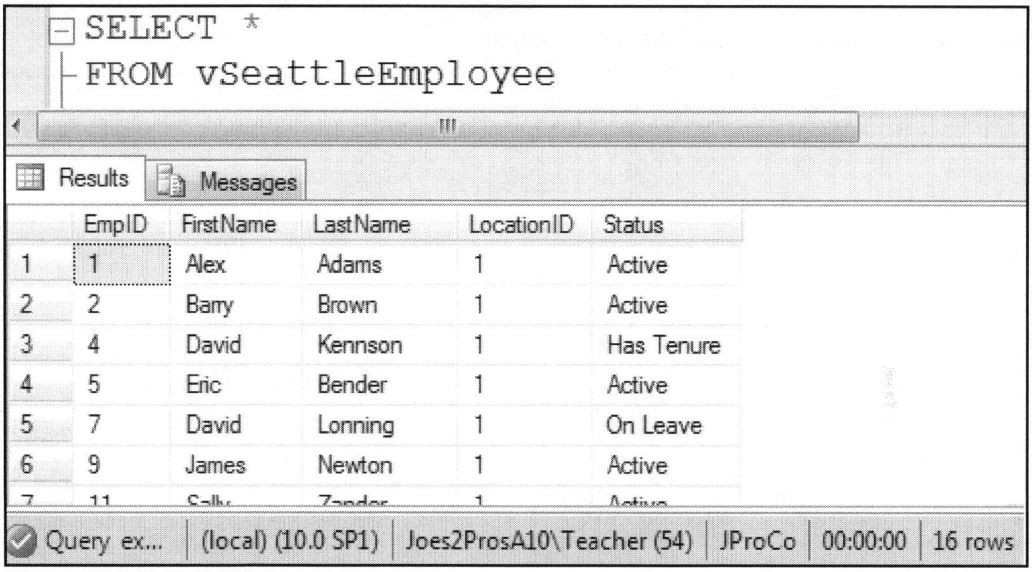

```
SELECT *
FROM vSeattleEmployee
```

Results | Messages

	EmpID	FirstName	LastName	LocationID	Status
1	1	Alex	Adams	1	Active
2	2	Barry	Brown	1	Active
3	4	David	Kennson	1	Has Tenure
4	5	Eric	Bender	1	Active
5	7	David	Lonning	1	On Leave
6	9	James	Newton	1	Active

Query ex... | (local) (10.0 SP1) | Joes2ProsA10\Teacher (54) | JProCo | 00:00:00 | 16 rows

Figure 5.16 Skill Check 3 result.

Answer Code: The T-SQL code to this lab can be found in the downloadable files in a file named Lab5.1_DataManipulationThroughViews.sql.

Manipulating Data Through Views - Points to Ponder

1. Views do not maintain separate copies of data. Therefore, when you are modifying records in a view, you are really modifying the records in the underlying base table.
2. Any DML changes made to a table through a view can SET columns to just one base table at a time.

View Modification Restrictions

In this section, we will learn a few restrictions and some pitfalls to avoid when using view to modify your data. After seeing some tricky scenarios involving INSERT, UPDATE, and DELETE statements against views, we will explore the use of CHECK OPTION to prevent unintended changes to our data.

Inserting Data Through Views

When inserting records into a table, you must supply values for all required fields. *The same rule holds true for views.*

Our first example involves the Grant table and the vHighValueGrants view. Query the Grant table and notice that it currently has 4 fields and 11 records (Figure 5.17).

```
SELECT * FROM [Grant]
```

Results | Messages

	GrantID	GrantName	EmpID	Amount
1	001	92 Purr_Scents %% team	7	4750.00
2	002	K-Land fund trust	2	15750.00
3	003	Robert@BigStarBank.com	7	18100.00
4	005	BIG 6's Foundation%	4	22000.00
5	006	TALTA_Kishan International	3	18100.00
6	007	Ben@MoreTechnology.com	10	42000.00
7	008	www.@-Last-U-Can-Help.com	7	26000.00
8	009	Thank you @.com	11	22500.00
9	010	Just Mom	5	9900.00
10	011	Big Giver Tom	7	96900.00
11	012	Mega Mercy	9	56000.00

Query executed succ... | (local) (10.0 SP1) | Joes2ProsA10\Teacher (53) | JProCo | 00:00:00 | 11 rows

Figure 5.17 The Grant table contains 4 fields and 11 records.

The vHighValueGrants view shows the large grants (defined as >$20k) from the Grant table. It currently includes three fields and six records (see Figure 5.18).

```
SELECT * FROM vHighValueGrants
```

	GrantName	EmpID	Amount
1	BIG 6's Foundation%	4	22000.00
2	Ben@MoreTechnology.com	10	42000.00
3	www.@-Last-U-Can-Help.com	7	26000.00
4	Thank you @.com	11	22500.00
5	Big Giver Tom	7	96900.00
6	Mega Mercy	9	56000.00

Query executed succe... | (local) (10.0 SP1) | Joes2ProsA10\Teacher (53) | JProCo | 00:00:00 | 6 rows

Figure 5.18 The vHighValueGrants view currently includes 3 fields and 6 records.

Let's attempt to add this new record (see Figure 5.19) to the Grant table through the vHighValueGrants view. Note that the INSERT statement fails, and the error message indicates that we attempted to insert a null value into the GrantID column.

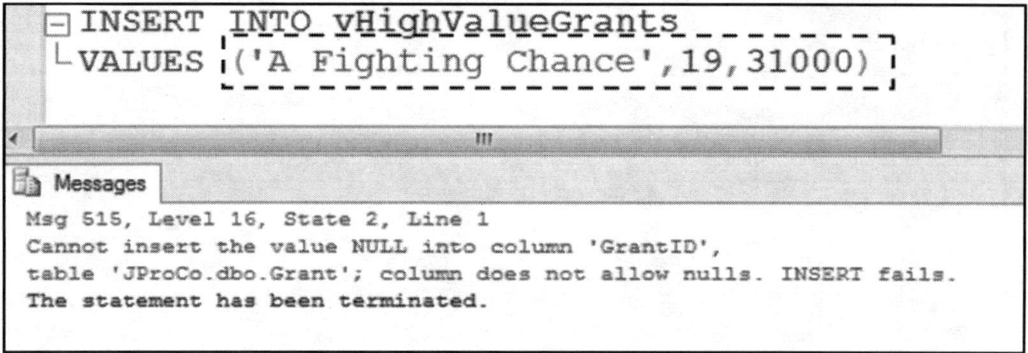

INSERT INTO vHighValueGrants
VALUES ('A Fighting Chance',19,31000)
Messages
Msg 515, Level 16, State 2, Line 1
Cannot insert the value NULL into column 'GrantID',
table 'JProCo.dbo.Grant'; column does not allow nulls. INSERT fails.
The statement has been terminated.

Figure 5.19 Our attempt to update the Grant table through vHighValueGrants is unsuccessful.

GrantID is a non-nullable, primary key field. This means that every record added to the Grant table must include a unique GrantID value.

The root problem is that the GrantID field isn't included in the view. Therefore, vHighValueGrants cannot "see" or manipulate the GrantID field. As long as vHighValueGrants doesn't include the GrantID field, you won't be able use this view to manipulate the Grant table as currently structured.

You can't place a null value in a non-nullable field. If a DML statement through a view would place a null value in a non-nullable field, then the change will be disallowed.

Deleting Data Through Views

The syntax for deleting records through views is the same syntax used to delete records from tables. This DELETE statement against vHighValueGrants (see below, Figure 5.20) will remove all of the large grants from the Grant table.

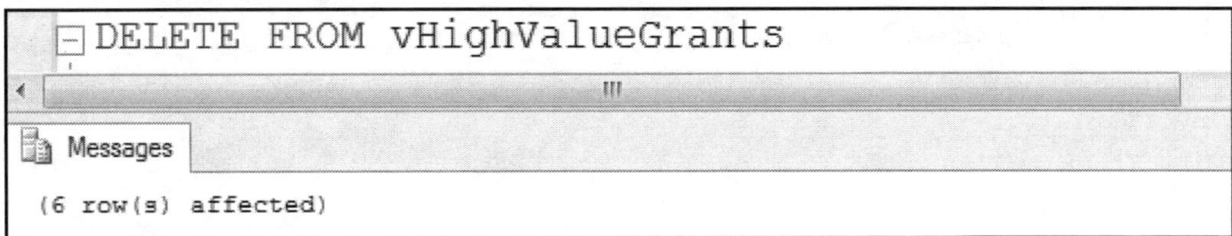
DELETE FROM vHighValueGrants
Messages
(6 row(s) affected)

Figure 5.20 You can delete records from the Grant table through the vHighValueGrants view.

Following the deletion, there are now five records remaining in the Grant table.

```
SELECT *
FROM [Grant]
```

Results | Messages

	GrantID	GrantName	EmpID	Amount
1	001	92 Purr_Scents %% team	7	4750.00
2	002	K-Land fund trust	2	15750.00
3	003	Robert@BigStarBank.com	7	18100.00
4	006	TALTA_Kishan International	3	18100.00
5	010	Just Mom	5	9900.00

Figure 5.21 The Grant table now contains five records. It previously contained 11 (see Figure 5.18).

You cannot use a view to run DELETE statements affecting more than one base table. The previous deletion (Figure 5.20) was successful because it involved a single base table. This DELETE statement against the GrantLocations view fails, because it would affect multiple base tables (see Figure 5.22).

```
DELETE FROM GrantLocations
```

Messages

```
Msg 4405, Level 16, State 1, Line 1
View or function 'GrantLocations' is not updatable
because the modification affects multiple base tables.
```

Figure 5.22 The GrantLocations view may not be used to remove records, because this would affect multiple base tables. As mentioned in Chapter 4 (Figures 4.31-4.32), SQL Server doesn't enforce naming conventions for views. SQL pros tend to prefix a view with "v" or "vw" (vGrantLocations versus GrantLocations), but this is simply a best practice and not a requirement.

Note: We've just performed some destructive examples impacting our Grant data. To continue our demonstration using the views which we've built, we must reset the Grant table and vHighValueGrants to again display the values shown in Figures 5.17 and 5.18. Run the script SQLProgrammingExtraResetGrant.sql (Figure 5.23).

```
--SQLProgrammingExtraResetGrant.sql
USE JProCo
GO

IF NOT EXISTS(SELECT * FROM sys.tables WHERE [name] = 'Grant')
CREATE TABLE [Grant]
(
```

Figure 5.23 The script SQLProgrammingExtraResetGrant.sql may be found at *Joes2Pros.com*.

Updating Data Through Views

In the last section, we used an UPDATE statement to increment a single field in a view having a single base table (shown in Figures 5.11-5.12). Just like with DELETE statements against views, SQL Server will not allow an UPDATE statement to affect multiple base tables. However, we must be cautious when using a view to modify data.

Let's return to the vEmployeeLocations view. This view includes data from multiple base tables. Three of its fields (EmpID, FirstName, LastName) come from dbo.Employee, and the other two fields (City, State) come from dbo.Location.

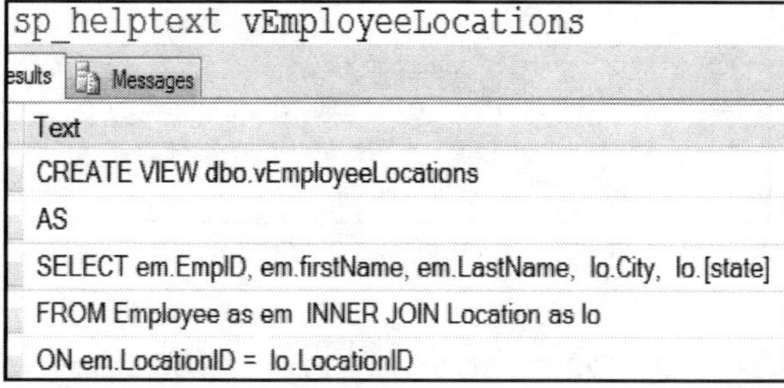

Figure 5.24 The source code for vEmployeeLocations.

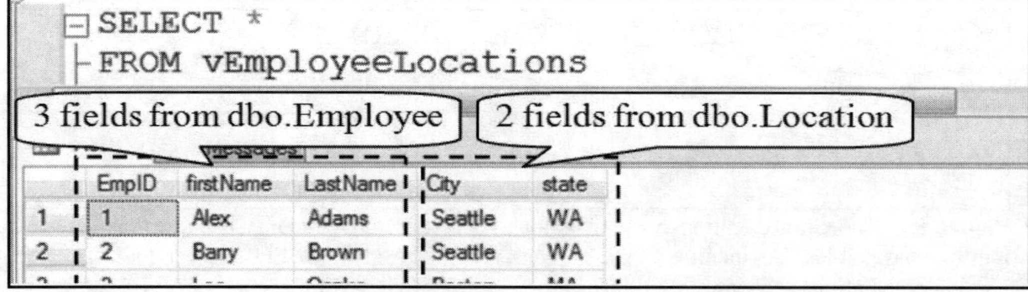

Figure 5.25 The vEmployeeLocations view pulls data from multiple base tables.

A view can make an update to one or more fields in a single base table. The following two updates affect data in the Employee table. After you successfully run each UPDATE statement (and you see "1 row(s) affected" for each), run the SELECT statement against the view in order to see the changed data.

The first statement will change Employee 11's last name from Zander back to Smith. Apparently the record changes for JProCo's internal systems and her external professional associations were too numerous, so Sally is choosing to postpone her official name change for awhile (see Figure 5.26).

```
SELECT *
FROM vEmployeeLocations

UPDATE vEmployeeLocations
SET LastName = 'Smith'
WHERE EmpID = 11
```

Results | Messages

	EmpID	firstName	LastName	City	state
8	9	James	Newton	Seattle	WA
9	10	Terry	O'Haire	Boston	MA
10	11	Sally	Smith	Seattle	WA

Figure 5.26 EmpID 11's LastName value is successfully changed from Zander to Smith.

Another change is needed for David Kennson, whose name is incorrect in the database. His name should appear as "Dave Kinnison." SQL Server will allow this change to multiple fields, because both fields are in the same base table. After we run the UPDATE statement, we see the change appears in the view (Figure 5.27).

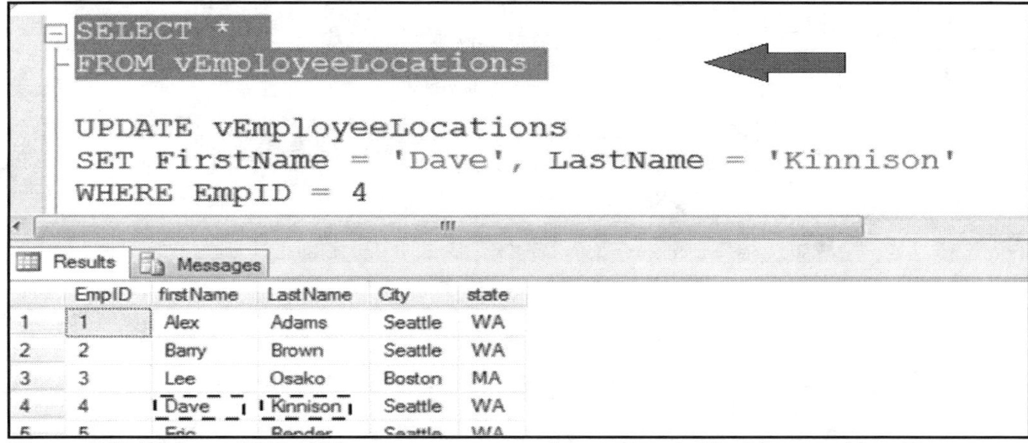

Figure 5.27 With one UPDATE statement, we can change Dave's FirstName and LastName.

Now let's look at a change that may seem as straightforward as our last two updates but is actually problematic. We will run the UPDATE statement in order to demonstrate a pitfall to watch for when updating your table data through a view that has multiple base tables.

We need to make another update to Employee 4. He has been working in the Seattle office, but next week he will begin working in Tacoma. Notice that the UPDATE statement reflecting Dave's new City would change the value of a field in the Location table, yet it predicates on the Employee table (see Figure 5.28). Our previous two UPDATE operations changed values in the Employee table and predicated on the Employee table (as shown in Figures 5.26 and 5.27).

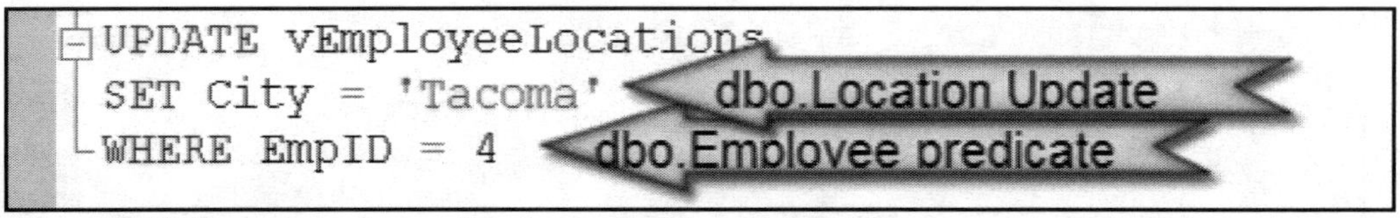

```
UPDATE vEmployeeLocations
SET City = 'Tacoma'      dbo.Location Update
WHERE EmpID = 4     dbo.Employee predicate
```

Figure 5.28 We want to change Employee 4's City value to Tacoma.

Let's see what happens when we run this query (see Figure 5.29). Then let's query the view and see the change reflected by the data (see Figure 5.30).

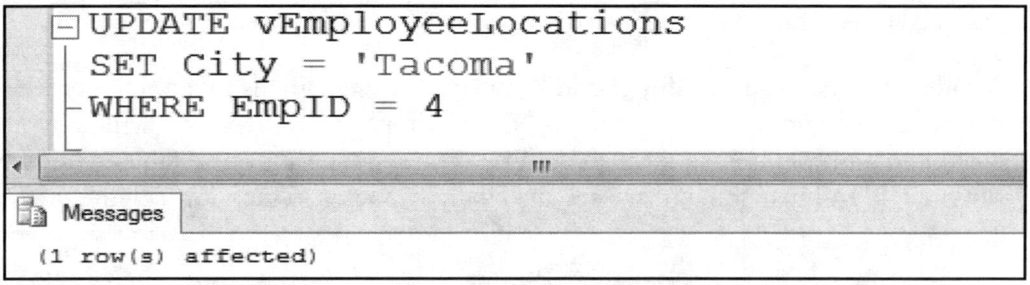

```
UPDATE vEmployeeLocations
SET City = 'Tacoma'
WHERE EmpID = 4
```

Messages

```
(1 row(s) affected)
```

Figure 5.29 We want this change to affect only Employee 4.

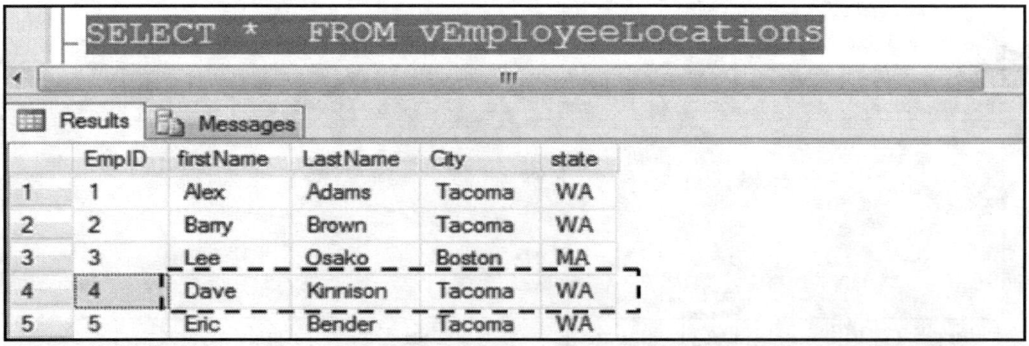

```
SELECT * FROM vEmployeeLocations
```

Results | Messages

	EmpID	firstName	LastName	City	state
1	1	Alex	Adams	Tacoma	WA
2	2	Barry	Brown	Tacoma	WA
3	3	Lee	Osako	Boston	MA
4	4	Dave	Kinnison	Tacoma	WA
5	5	Eric	Bender	Tacoma	WA

Figure 5.30 The Tacoma change has been made for other employees, not just Dave Kinnison.

While the "1 row(s) affected" confirmation initially looks encouraging, our query of the view reveals that all employees working at the Seattle location now have a City value of "Tacoma" (see Figure 5.30).

A query of the Location table will help clarify the issue. The UPDATE statement we ran (shown in Figure 5.29) changed the City value for LocationID 1 to Tacoma (see Figure 5.31). This is the change signified by the "1 row(s) affected" confirmation shown in Figure 5.29!! Dave's LocationID is 1. The UPDATE statement changed the City value for LocationID 1 to Tacoma. Our update was intended for Dave's record, but it affected all employees with a LocationID of 1.

```
SELECT *
FROM Location
```

Results | Spatial results | Messages

	LocationID	street	city	state	Latitude	Longitude	GeoLoc
1	1	545 Pike	Tacoma	WA	47.455	-122.231	0xE6100000010(
2	2	222 Second AVE	Boston	MA	42.372	-71.0298	0xE6100000010(
3	4	444 Ruby ST	Spokane	WA	47.668	-117.529	0xE6100000010(
4	5	1595 Main	Philade...	PA	39.888	-75.251	0xE6100000010(
5	6	915 Wallaby Dr...	Sydney	N...	-33.876	151.315	0xE6100000010(

Figure 5.31 LocationID 1 now reflects the City of Tacoma.

To understand how this happened, let's take a look behind the scenes at the underlying tables and fields of vEmployeeLocations. The City and State fields are normalized data being supplied by the lookup table, Location. In other words, these values aren't part of a denormalized table where each employee record would contain its own City field. (Had that been the case, then our UPDATE statement would have only changed Dave Kinnison's city to Tacoma, and the other employee records wouldn't have been impacted.)

So this is one pitfall to be cautious of. ***When updating a base table, be careful – it might be representative of other records in related tables.*** We've just seen an example where SQL Server was overly permissive and allowed us to change many more records than we intended. If you have a doubt, it may be safest to run the UPDATE directly against the base table instead of against the view.

One way of correcting our mistake is to run another UPDATE statement through the view to revert Location 1 back to Seattle (see Figure 5.32).

```
UPDATE vEmployeeLocations
SET City = 'Seattle'
WHERE EmpID = 4
```

Messages

(1 row(s) affected)

Figure 5.32 This UPDATE statement corrects our mistake and changes Location 1 back to Seattle.

When we re-query vEmployeeLocations, we see that all Seattle employees (including Dave Kinnison) again show Seattle as their City (see Figure 5.33).

```
SELECT * FROM vEmployeeLocations
```

Results | Messages

	EmpID	firstName	LastName	City	state
1	1	Alex	Adams	Seattle	WA
2	2	Barry	Brown	Seattle	WA
3	3	Lee	Osako	Boston	MA
4	4	Dave	Kinnison	Seattle	WA
5	5	Eric	Bender	Seattle	WA
6	6	Lisa	Kendall	Spok...	WA
7	7	David	Lonning	Seattle	WA
8	9	James	Newton	Seattle	WA

Figure 5.33 This update statement corrects our mistake and changes Location 1 back to Seattle.

Another way to change the LocationID 1 from Tacoma back to Seattle would be to directly update the Location table, as shown below (see Figure 5.34).

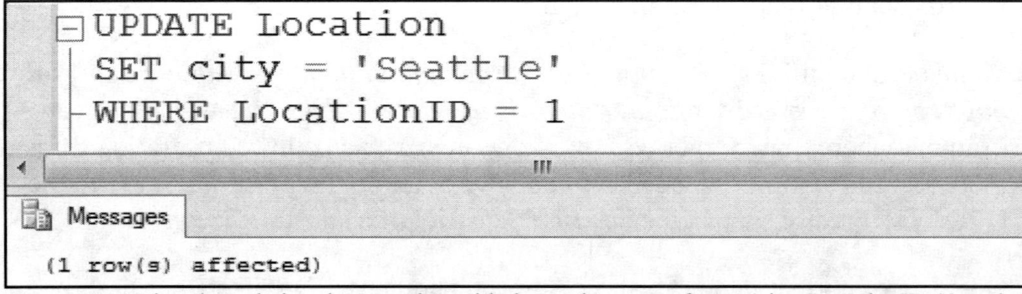
UPDATE Location
SET city = 'Seattle'
WHERE LocationID = 1
Messages
(1 row(s) affected)

Figure 5.34 Directly updating the Location table is another way of correcting LocationID 1's value.

Finally, let's attempt a query to illustrate the rule that ***SQL Server will not allow an UPDATE statement to affect multiple base tables.***

The UPDATE statement here attempts to change a field in one base table (the LastName field in the Employee table) at the same time it changes a field in another base table (the City field in the Location table) (see Figure 5.35).

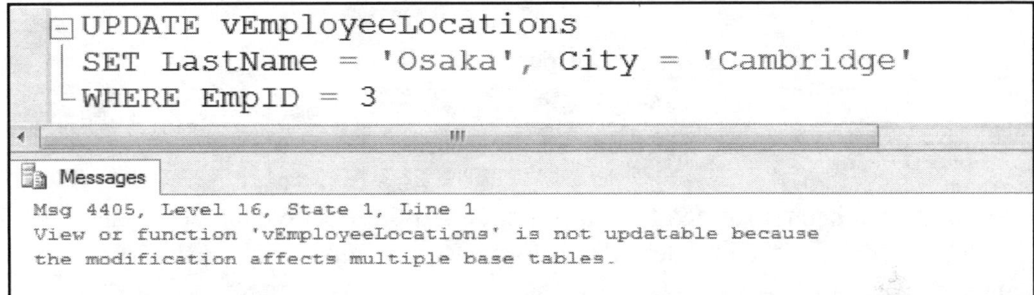
```
UPDATE vEmployeeLocations
SET LastName = 'Osaka', City = 'Cambridge'
WHERE EmpID = 3
```

Messages

```
Msg 4405, Level 16, State 1, Line 1
View or function 'vEmployeeLocations' is not updatable because
the modification affects multiple base tables.
```

Figure 5.35 This UPDATE statement affecting LastName in the Employee table and City in the Location table is disallowed by SQL Server, since it would affect multiple base tables.

If the JProCo DBA needs to make these changes, he would need to accomplish them in another way. The City value change would need to be made directly to the Location table. The LastName value could be done either through the view or directly to the Employee table.

Using Check Option

CHECK OPTION is a very handy tool we can use with our views. Each time a DML statement is run against the view, CHECK OPTION validates that the resulting record set will be true to the SELECT statement which built the view. If a modification would remove a record defined by the view, then CHECK OPTION prevents the transaction from being committed.

Our demonstration of CHECK OPTION will utilize the vHighValueGrants view. If you have already run the Grant reset script SQLProgrammingExtraResetGrant.sql, then your vHighValueGrants to be reset to the values shown in Figure 5.36 (and identical to Figure 5.18, before we performed the destructive examples).

Recall that, in order to incentivize large grants, JProCo planned to offer a $1,000 match for each grant larger than $20,000. The $1,000 match is currently included in our vHighValueGrants amounts (see Figure 5.36).

```
SELECT * FROM vHighValueGrants
```

Results | Messages

	GrantName	EmpID	Amount
1	BIG 6's Foundation%	4	22000.00
2	Ben@MoreTechnol...	10	42000.00
3	www.@-Last-U-Can...	7	26000.00
4	Thank you @.com	11	22500.00
5	Big Giver Tom	7	96900.00
6	Mega Mercy	9	56000.00

Query executed successfully. | (local) (10.0 SP1) | MoreTechA6\Student (52) | JProCo | 00:00:00 | 6 rows

Figure 5.36 Each large grant Amount value has been increased by $1,000.

We have just been informed that the campaign didn't receive the necessary approval from the stakeholders. Therefore, we must remove all of the $1,000 matching amounts.

After we run this UPDATE statement (see Figure 5.37), the grants will all be returned to their baseline values (shown in Figure 5.38).

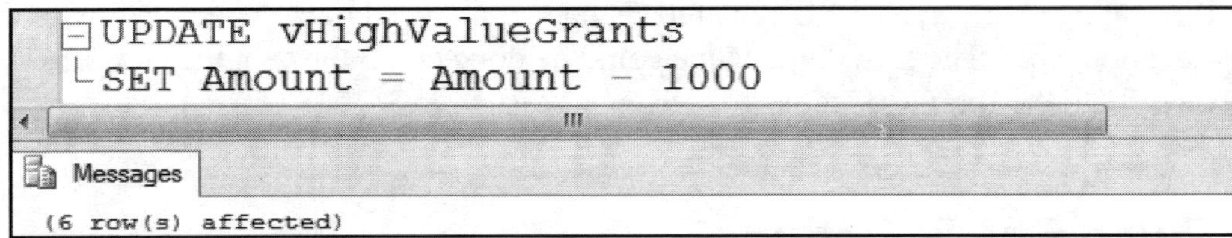

```
UPDATE vHighValueGrants
SET Amount = Amount - 1000
```

Messages

(6 row(s) affected)

Figure 5.37 This UPDATE statement decrements each record in vHighValueGrants by $1000.

The $1000 increase has been removed (see Figure 5.38).

```
SELECT * FROM vHighValueGrants
```

Results | Messages

	GrantName	EmpID	Amount
1	BIG 6's Foundation%	4	21000.00
2	Ben@MoreTechnology.com	10	41000.00
3	www.@-Last-U-Can-Help.com	7	25000.00
4	Thank you @.com	11	21500.00
5	Big Giver Tom	7	95900.00
6	Mega Mercy	9	55000.00

Query executed succ... | (local) (10.0 SP1) | Joes2ProsA10\Teacher (53) | JProCo | 00:00:00 | 6 rows

Figure 5.38 The large grants are decremented by $1,000 and thus returned to their baseline values.

Suppose you accidentally ran the decrement step (shown in Figure 5.37) twice. Before we "accidentally" run the UPDATE statement again in order to create this scenario, let's consider the amounts currently shown by the view (see Figure 5.38).

The smallest grant in the vHighValueGrants view is $21,000. If we rerun the UPDATE statement, this grant will become $20,000. *Recall that each grant must be greater than $20,000 in order to appear in the view.*

Run the UPDATE statement again and then run a SELECT statement to see all of the records in the vHighValueGrants view (see Figure 5.39). The $21,000 grant (contributed by Big 6's Foundation %) was reduced to $20,000 and thus has fallen out of the view. Now that this grant has fallen outside the criteria of vHighValueGrants, the view no longer has the ability to "see" or manipulate this record using DML statements. For the five remaining grants, you can correct their amounts and reverse the "accidental" run of the UPDATE statement by incrementing each grant by $1000. However, the only way to correct the amount of the missing grant is by running an UPDATE statement directly against the Grant table.

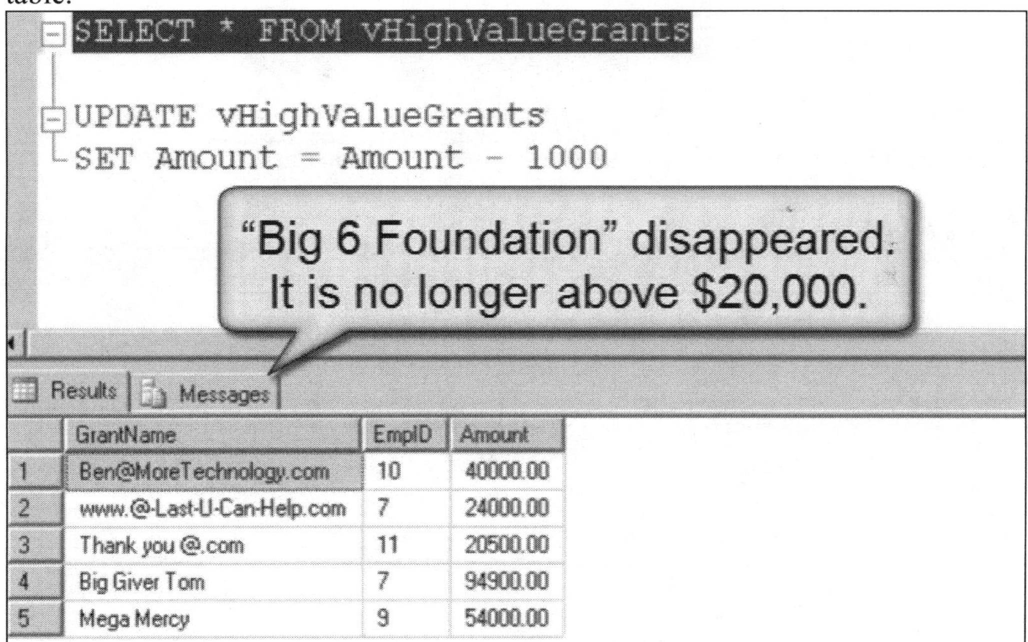

	GrantName	EmpID	Amount
1	Ben@MoreTechnology.com	10	40000.00
2	www.@-Last-U-Can-Help.com	7	24000.00
3	Thank you @.com	11	20500.00
4	Big Giver Tom	7	94900.00
5	Mega Mercy	9	54000.00

Figure 5.39 There are only 5 large grants remaining in the view after the second $1000 decrement.

This action was clearly a mistake. We didn't intend to remove a record from the view, but as it is currently configured, vHighValueGrants isn't protected against these kinds of mistakes. In order to prevent data updates which would cause records to disappear from our view, we can either place a trigger on the Grant table, or we can use CHECK OPTION.

Before proceeding, let's reset the amounts for all of the large grants by running this UPDATE statement and then a SELECT statement to verify the amounts (see Figure 5.40 – these amounts are the same as seen in Figures 5.38).

```
UPDATE [Grant]
SET Amount = Amount + 1000
WHERE Amount >= 20000

SELECT * FROM vHighValueGrants
```

Results | Messages

	GrantName	EmpID	Amount
1	BIG 6's Foundation%	4	21000.00
2	Ben@MoreTechnology.com	10	41000.00
3	www.@-Last-U-Can-Help.com	7	25000.00
4	Thank you @.com	11	21500.00
5	Big Giver Tom	7	95900.00
6	Mega Mercy	9	55000.00

Figure 5.40 This SELECT statement shows our large grant amounts have all been restored.

Let's examine the trigger approach (see Figure 5.41).

```
CREATE TRIGGER trg_UpdateGrant
ON dbo.[Grant]
AFTER UPDATE
AS
BEGIN
    IF EXISTS( SELECT * FROM Inserted ins
        INNER JOIN Deleted del
        ON ins.GrantName = del.GrantName
        WHERE del.Amount > 20000
        AND ins.Amount <= 20000)
    ROLLBACK TRAN
END
```

Messages

```
Command(s) completed successfully.
```

Figure 5.41 This trigger will prevent large grants (>$20,000) from falling to, or below, $20,000.

If you create the trigger and then attempt to decrement the vHighValueGrants view, you'll find that the trigger will not allow the transaction. (The decrement would cause a grant (the one contributed by Big 6's Foundation %) to fall to $20,000 and thus it won't meet the criteria of the vHighValueGrants view.)

```
UPDATE vHighValueGrants
SET Amount = Amount - 1000

Messages
Msg 3609, Level 16, State 1, Line 1
The transaction ended in the trigger. The batch has been aborted.
```

Figure 5.42 trg_UpdateGrant will not allow vHighValueGrants to fall to, or below, $20,000.

The trigger has protected our view. The transaction which attempted to reduce a large grant from $21,000 to $20,000 was forbidden and ended in the trigger (see Figure 5.42).

But let's recognize that the trigger would also prevent any existing grant from ever being changed to an amount $20,000, or lower. In other words, the trigger is so restrictive that even a DBA would be disallowed from directly updating the Grant table if the change would reduce an existing grant amount to become $20,000 or lower (see Figure 5.43).

```
UPDATE [Grant]
SET Amount = Amount - 1000
WHERE Amount >= 20000

Messages
Msg 3609, Level 16, State 1, Line 1
The transaction ended in the trigger. The batch has been aborted.
```

Figure 5.43 trg_UpdateGrant prevents certain updates made directly to the Grant table.

The trigger is more restrictive than we intended. Our goal was simply to restrict users from making an accidental data change through the view which would result in a grant being removed from the view.

Let's reattempt our goal by using CHECK OPTION. First we will remove the trigger, since it is an "overkill" approach and constrains more activities than we intended.

In Object Explorer, right-click the trigger to delete it (see Figure 5.44).

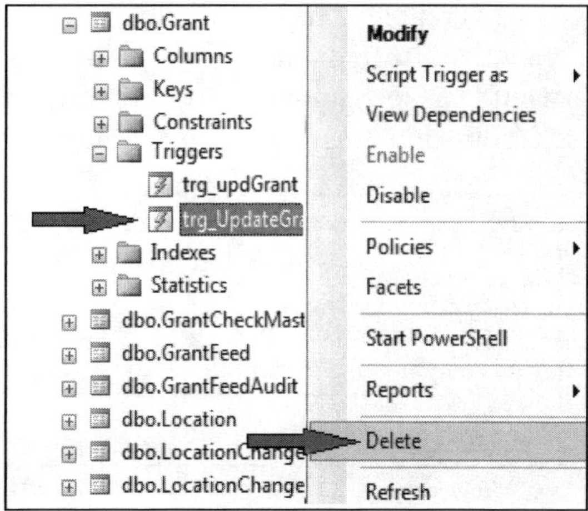

Figure 5.44 Right-click to delete trg_UpdateGrant.

Let's rebuild the vHighValueGrants view to include CHECK OPTION. This tells the view to disallow data changes through the view which would cause any record to fall outside of the criteria of the view (see Figure 5.45).

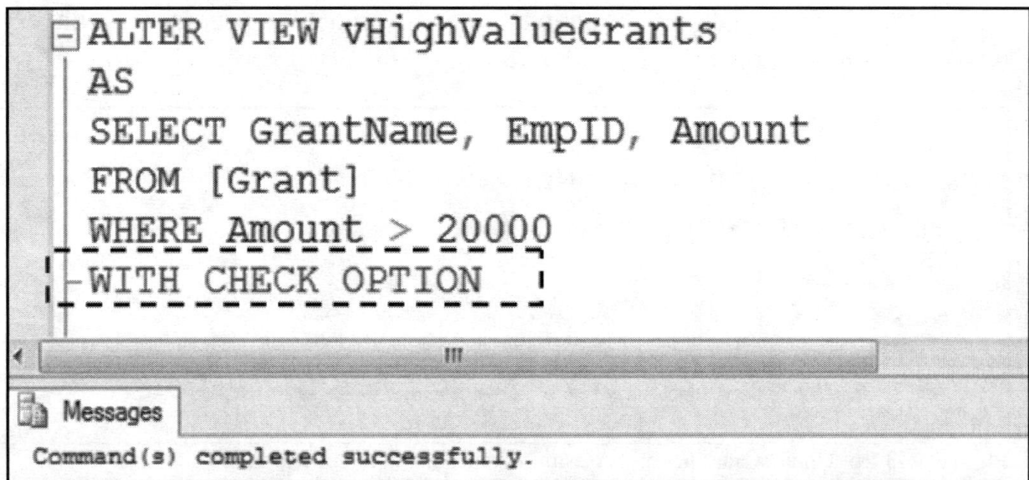

ALTER VIEW vHighValueGrants
AS
SELECT GrantName, EmpID, Amount
FROM [Grant]
WHERE Amount > 20000
WITH CHECK OPTION
Messages
Command(s) completed successfully.

Figure 5.45 The vHighValueGrants view is rebuilt to include WITH CHECK OPTION.

Let's test CHECK OPTION by reattempting the decrement step through the vHighValueGrants view (see Figure 5.46). The error message shows that CHECK OPTION causes the UPDATE statement to fail, because it would cause a row (i.e., the Big 6's Foundation % grant) to fall out of the view.

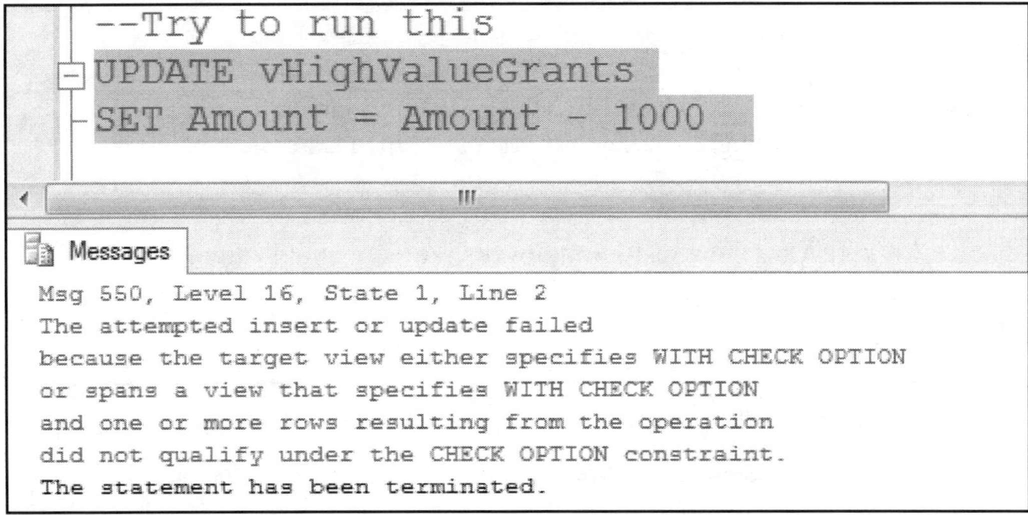

```
--Try to run this
UPDATE vHighValueGrants
SET Amount = Amount - 1000
```

Messages

```
Msg 550, Level 16, State 1, Line 2
The attempted insert or update failed
because the target view either specifies WITH CHECK OPTION
or spans a view that specifies WITH CHECK OPTION
and one or more rows resulting from the operation
did not qualify under the CHECK OPTION constraint.
The statement has been terminated.
```

Figure 5.46 This decrement was prevented by the CHECK OPTION on the view.

While CHECK OPTION is protecting our grant data from unintended changes made through the view, it doesn't interfere with our ability to make changes directly against the Grant table.

To prove this point, let's run this decrement (see Figure 5.47) which we know will bring a large grant amount down to $20,000 – a value which puts it outside the criteria underlying the vHighValueGrants view. CHECK OPTION does not stop us from making this change.

```
UPDATE [Grant]
SET Amount = Amount - 1000
WHERE Amount >= 20000
```

Messages

```
(6 row(s) affected)
```

Figure 5.47 This UPDATE statement to the Grant table is allowed. CHECK OPTION only serves to protect a view – it doesn't restrict your ability to directly update a base table.

Lab 5.2: View Modification Restrictions

Lab Prep: Before you can begin the lab, you must have SQL Server installed and have run the script SQLProgrammingChapter5.2Setup.sql.

Skill Check 1: Query the vBossList view. Attempt to update Sally's last name back to 'Zander' through the view. If you can't, then state the reason why.

Skill Check 2: Alter the vSeattleEmployee view so that any attempted change through the view will not allow updates which would cause records to disappear from the view.

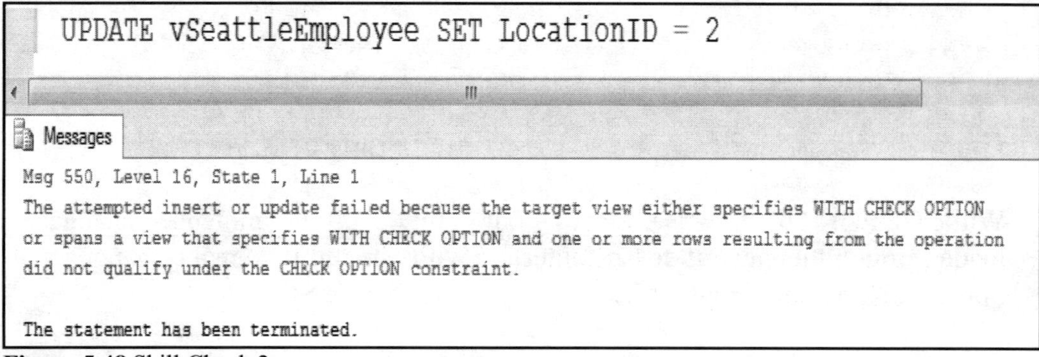
UPDATE vSeattleEmployee SET LocationID = 2
Messages
Msg 550, Level 16, State 1, Line 1
The attempted insert or update failed because the target view either specifies WITH CHECK OPTION or spans a view that specifies WITH CHECK OPTION and one or more rows resulting from the operation did not qualify under the CHECK OPTION constraint.
The statement has been terminated.

Figure 5.48 Skill Check 2.

Skill Check 3: Run an update statement against the GrantLocations view to change the amount of Grant 011 to be exactly 19000.

Answer Code: The T-SQL code to this lab can be found in the downloadable files in a file named Lab5.2_ViewModificationRestrictions.sql.

View Modifications - Points to Ponder

1. The query defining by a view can include another view.
2. You cannot make updates to fields through a view, if they are part of an expression or aggregated field.
3. You cannot make updates through a view if the records were summarized with a SELECT DISTINCT clause.
4. Two ways to restrict users from being able to update through a view:
   a) use WITH CHECK OPTION.
   b) use an INSTEAD OF trigger.
5. If a view has an INSTEAD OF UPDATE trigger defined on it, then the view is considered to be not at all updatable.
6. A view's underlying data cannot be changed by an UPDATE statement which would affect more than one of the view's base tables.

Indexed Views Overview

In *SQL Architecture Basics Joes 2 Pros* (Chapters 9-11), we learned how to create a covering index so the fields in your query's WHERE and ON clauses require less processing time. When you use the same optimally-tuned query to build a view, your view will benefit from the covering indexes on the base tables.

Suppose you have a view with three base tables, and you've done a good job setting up indexes on the tables. The view benefits from the table indexes and consequently your queries against the view will have good performance. For example, a query from the view producing one record will use three seeks rather than three scans. If you took the additional step of indexing the view, then that same query would instead run a single seek and thus return your result faster.

Creating an Index on a View

Let's create another view, and later we will observe how indexing can increase the performance of the view. The query below joins the SalesInvoice table to the Customer table (see Figure 5.49). Since we don't want all fields, we will select InvoiceID and OrderDate from the SalesInvoice table. From the Customer table we will get the CustomerID, FirstName, and LastName fields. This query produces a good report of customers, their InvoiceIDs, and dates they placed their orders (see next page – Figure 5.50).

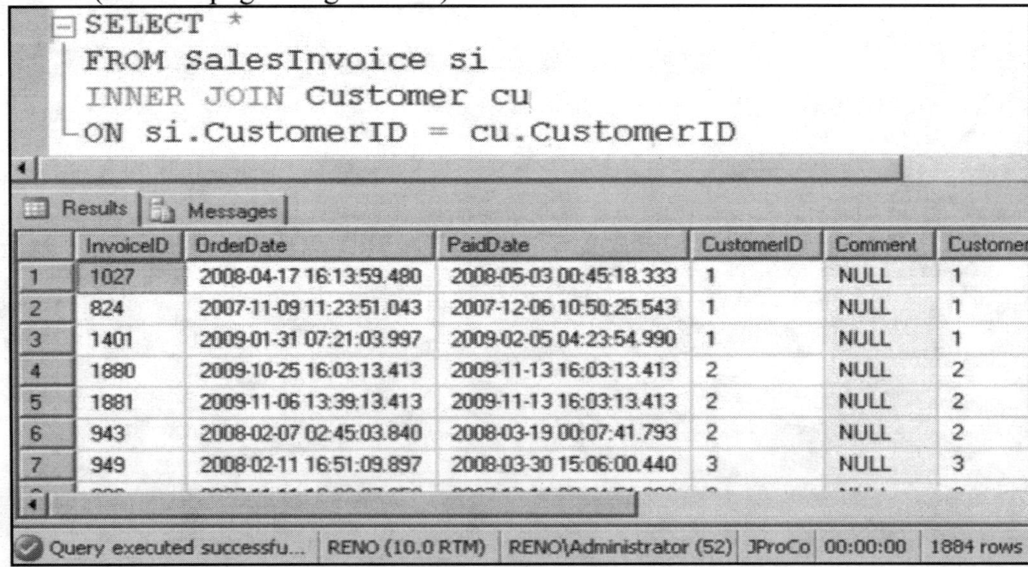

```
SELECT *
FROM SalesInvoice si
INNER JOIN Customer cu
ON si.CustomerID = cu.CustomerID
```

	InvoiceID	OrderDate	PaidDate	CustomerID	Comment	Customer
1	1027	2008-04-17 16:13:59.480	2008-05-03 00:45:18.333	1	NULL	1
2	824	2007-11-09 11:23:51.043	2007-12-06 10:50:25.543	1	NULL	1
3	1401	2009-01-31 07:21:03.997	2009-02-05 04:23:54.990	1	NULL	1
4	1880	2009-10-25 16:03:13.413	2009-11-13 16:03:13.413	2	NULL	2
5	1881	2009-11-06 13:39:13.413	2009-11-13 16:03:13.413	2	NULL	2
6	943	2008-02-07 02:45:03.840	2008-03-19 00:07:41.793	2	NULL	2
7	949	2008-02-11 16:51:09.897	2008-03-30 15:06:00.440	3	NULL	3

Figure 5.49 This query joins the SalesInvoice and Customer tables.

```
SELECT si.InvoiceID,
si.OrderDate, cu.CustomerID,
cu.FirstName, Cu.LastName
FROM SalesInvoice si
INNER JOIN Customer cu
ON si.CustomerID = cu.CustomerID
```

Results | Messages

	InvoiceID	OrderDate	CustomerID	FirstName	LastName
1	1027	2008-04-17 16:13:59.480	1	Mark	Williams
2	824	2007-11-09 11:23:51.043	1	Mark	Williams
3	1401	2009-01-31 07:21:03.997	1	Mark	Williams
4	1880	2009-10-25 16:03:13.413	2	Lee	Young
5	1881	2009-11-06 13:39:13.413	2	Lee	Young
6	943	2008-02-07 02:45:03.840	2	Lee	Young
7	949	2008-02-11 16:51:09.897	3	Patricia	Martin
8	828	2007-11-11 16:26:37.253	3	Patricia	Martin

Query executed successfu... | RENO\Administrator (52) | JProCo | 00:00:00 | 1884 rows

Figure 5.50 This query shows sales invoices and the customers who placed these orders.

Let's turn this query into a view named vCustomerSales (see Figure 5.51).

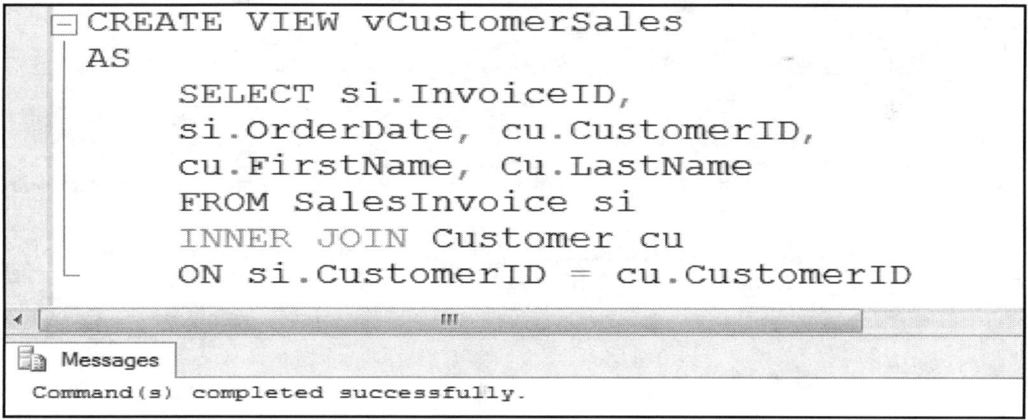
CREATE VIEW vCustomerSales
AS
SELECT si.InvoiceID,
si.OrderDate, cu.CustomerID,
cu.FirstName, Cu.LastName
FROM SalesInvoice si
INNER JOIN Customer cu
ON si.CustomerID = cu.CustomerID
Messages
Command(s) completed successfully.

Figure 5.51 Our current query (see Figure 5.53) is used to create the vCustomerSales view.

Let's query our new view, vCustomerSales, and notice that the result set (see next page, Figure 5.52) is the same as the result produced by the query used to create the view (see Figure 5.50).

```
SELECT * FROM vCustomerSales
```

	InvoiceID	OrderDate	CustomerID	FirstName	LastName
1	1027	2008-04-17 16:13:59.480	1	Mark	Williams
2	824	2007-11-09 11:23:51.043	1	Mark	Williams
3	1401	2009-01-31 07:21:03.997	1	Mark	Williams

Query... | (local) (10.0 SP1) | Joes2ProsA10\Teacher (51) | JProCo | 00:00:00 | 1884 rows

Figure 5.52 A query of the vCustomerSales view.

Examining the execution plan for this query, it appears to perform two scans. It takes approximately 0.07 seconds to run (see Figure 5.53).

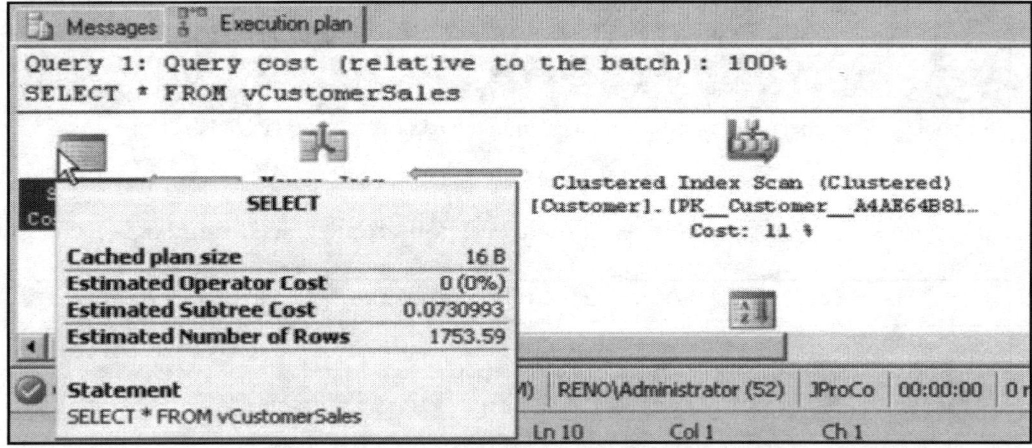

Figure 5.53 Our query of the vCustomerSales view is not very selective and runs in 0.07 seconds.

Now let's attempt a more selective query (Figure 5.54) and then examine its execution details (see next page - Figure 5.55).

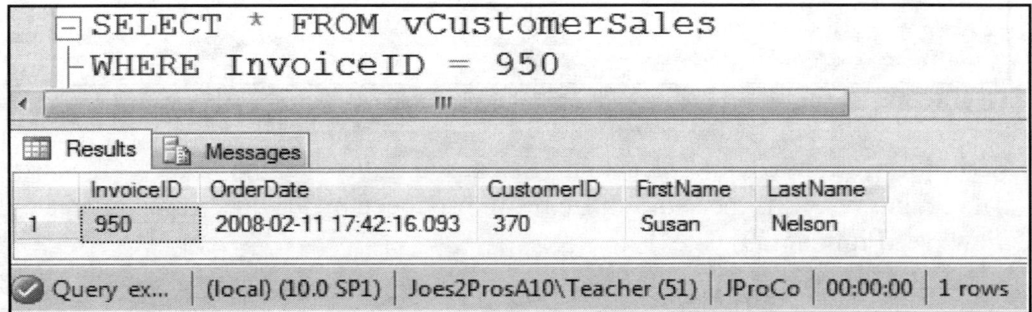

```
SELECT * FROM vCustomerSales
WHERE InvoiceID = 950
```

	InvoiceID	OrderDate	CustomerID	FirstName	LastName
1	950	2008-02-11 17:42:16.093	370	Susan	Nelson

Query ex... | (local) (10.0 SP1) | Joes2ProsA10\Teacher (51) | JProCo | 00:00:00 | 1 rows

Figure 5.54 This query is much more selective and returns just one record.

The query execution plan indicates that it run two seeks – one for the clustered index on the primary key field of the SalesInvoice table and one for the clustered index on the primary key field of the Customer table (see Figure 5.55). Because index seeks are performed for this query, we know there must be a covering index on the InvoiceID field.

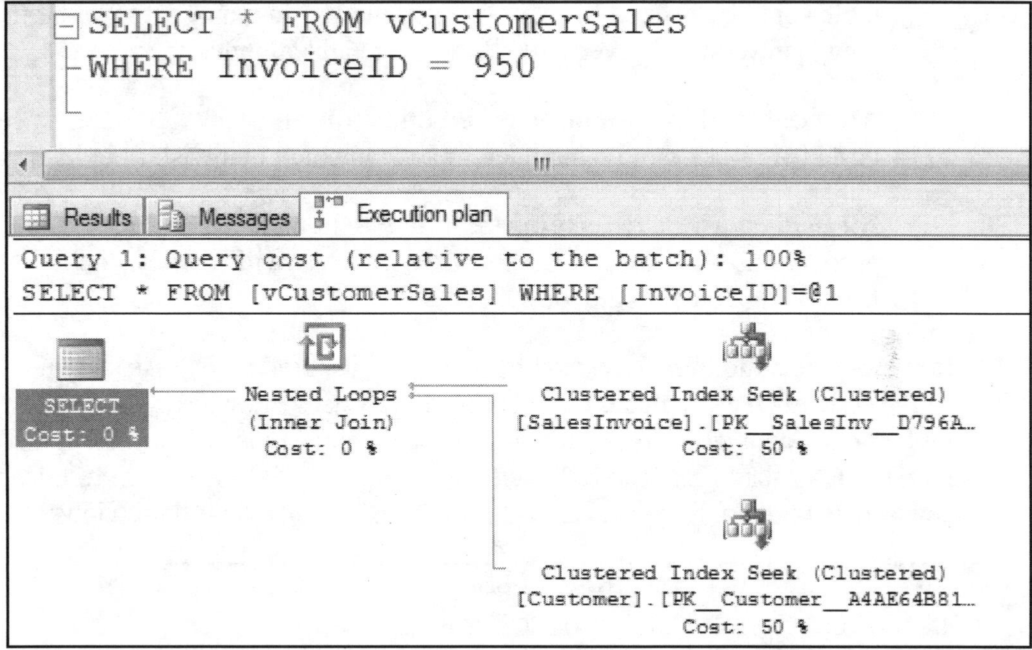

Figure 5.55 Two clustered seeks are run for this selective query against the vCustomerSales view.

The cost of this query is just over 0.006 seconds (see Figure 5.56).

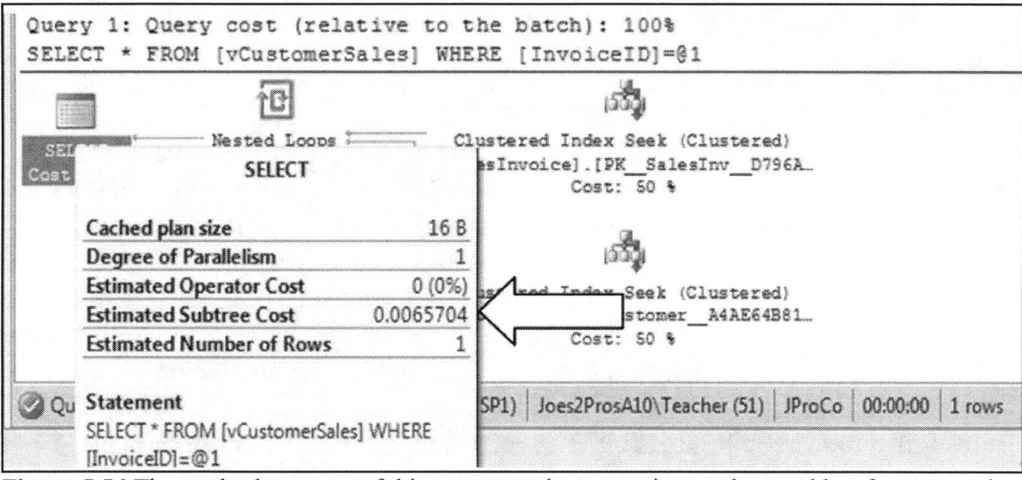

Figure 5.56 The total subtree cost of this query was just over six one-thousandths of one second.

The performance of this query can be further enhanced, if we add an index directly on the view. Our demonstration will focus on three key requirements for creating indexed views, all of which are enforced by SQL Server:

1) **The view must be schema bound.** Since you must ensure that no base table could be deleted from an indexed view, you must schema bind the view before SQL Server will allow you to add an index to it.

2) **An indexed view cannot be based upon another view.** In other words, nested views cannot be included in a view which you wish to index.

3) **All fields must be deterministic.** If any field included in the view produces non-deterministic values, SQL Server will disallow the index from being added to the view.

The first index you add to a view must be a unique clustered index. As shown below, the code to create a clustered index on a view uses the same syntax as putting the index on a table. This code will place a unique clustered index on the InvoiceID field of the vCustomerSales view (see Figure 5.57). If we fail to make the view schema bound, SQL Server will prompt us to schema bind the view.

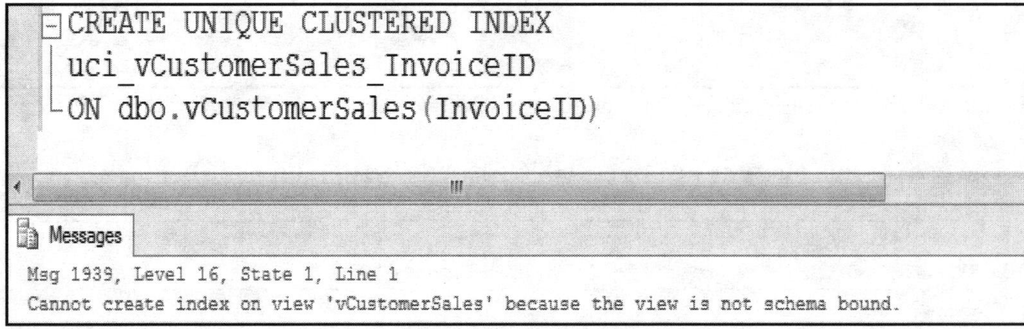

CREATE UNIQUE CLUSTERED INDEX
uci_vCustomerSales_InvoiceID
ON dbo.vCustomerSales(InvoiceID)
Messages
Msg 1939, Level 16, State 1, Line 1
Cannot create index on view 'vCustomerSales' because the view is not schema bound.

Figure 5.57 The index creation attempt on this view fails because the view is not schema bound.

Let's alter the vCustomerSales view and add the WITH SCHEMABINDING clause (see Figure 5.58, next page). *(Note: The code to create the vCustomerSales view comes from Figure 5.54.)*

Recall that SCHEMABINDING requires that we must use two-part naming for the base tables. In order to qualify the base table names, SalesInvoice becomes dbo.SalesInvoice, and Customer becomes dbo.Customer (the SQL Server error messaging appears in Figure 5.58; the corrected ALTER VIEW statement including the two-part table names appears in Figure 5.59).

```
ALTER VIEW vCustomerSales
WITH SCHEMABINDING
AS
    SELECT si.InvoiceID,
    si.OrderDate, cu.CustomerID,
    cu.FirstName, Cu.LastName
    FROM SalesInvoice si
    INNER JOIN Customer cu
    ON si.CustomerID = cu.CustomerID
```

Messages

```
Msg 4512, Level 16, State 3, Procedure vCustomerSales, Line 4
Cannot schema bind view 'vCustomerSales' because name 'SalesInvoice' is invalid for schema binding.
Names must be in two-part format and an object cannot reference itself.
```

Figure 5.58 SQL Server requires us to use two-part naming when adding SCHEMABINDING.

```
ALTER VIEW vCustomerSales
WITH SCHEMABINDING
AS
    SELECT si.InvoiceID,
    si.OrderDate, cu.CustomerID,
    cu.FirstName, Cu.LastName
    FROM dbo.SalesInvoice si
    INNER JOIN dbo.Customer cu
    ON si.CustomerID = cu.CustomerID
```

Messages

```
Command(s) completed successfully.
```

Figure 5.59 The code runs if you prefix the base tables with the correct schema name.

The ALTER VIEW statement completes successfully, so we know our view is now schema bound. We now may reattempt to create the index on the view.

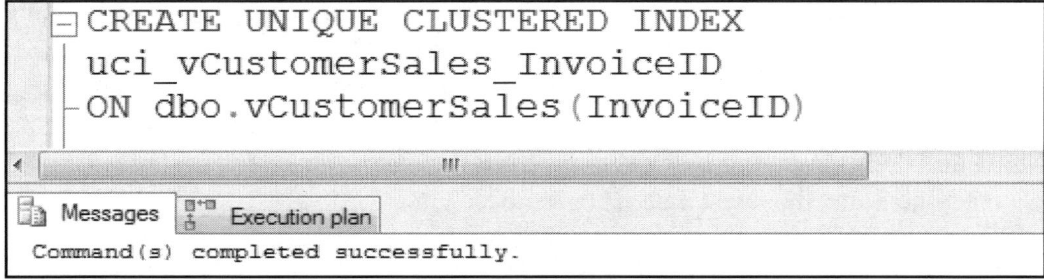
CREATE UNIQUE CLUSTERED INDEX
uci_vCustomerSales_InvoiceID
ON dbo.vCustomerSales(InvoiceID)
Messages
Execution plan
Command(s) completed successfully.

Figure 5.60 Now that the view is schema bound, the index is successfully created.

With the unique clustered index successfully added to the vCustomerSales view, let's reattempt our selective query for InvoiceID 950 (see Figure 5.61). The execution plan tells us that the index we added to this view has improved performance considerably. The query now performs just one clustered index seek and runs in half the time or in roughly 0.003 seconds (see Figure 5.61 versus the original 0.006 cost shown in Figure 5.56).

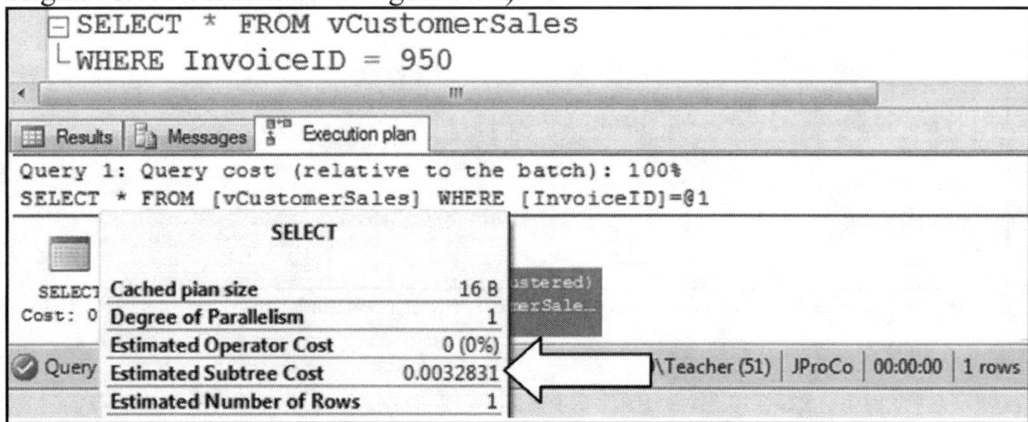

Figure 5.61 The new query execution plan shows the reduced cost of just over three one-thousandths of one second.

Materialized Views

In our extensive study of indexes in *SQL Architecture Basics Joes 2 Pros (Volume 3),* we learned that a clustered index dictates the physical ordering of the data in a table. The same is true for indexed views. And since the first index you add to a view must be a unique clustered index, all indexed views have a clustered index to physically order the data contained in the view.

Indexing a view causes the view to be persistently **materialized** and stored in the database. In other words, the view contains a physical copy of the view data (including computations associated with joins, aggregate queries, etc.) for quicker retrieval. This is a departure from regular views (i.e., non-indexed views) which do not contain any data. Normally a view pulls data from its base table(s) and performs the needed computations at query runtime. However, queries against an indexed view run more rapidly because the view can leverage the pre-computed data and doesn't need to pull anything from the base tables – the materialized view already contains the latest data from the base tables.

Another benefit of indexed views is that their persistent data and computations are available for use by other processes or queries. In our study of SQL Server's Query Optimizer (Chapters 10-12, *SQL Architecture Basics Joes 2 Pros*), we learned that it explores all available statistics in order to decide which objects will best accomplish a task. Therefore, all data from indexed views is available for Query Optimizer to utilize.

Other than the improved performance and visibility of the new clustered index in Object Explorer (see Figure 5.62), there is no noticeable difference in the behavior of an indexed view versus a non-indexed view. There are no special steps you need to take to maintain a view once you have added an index to it.

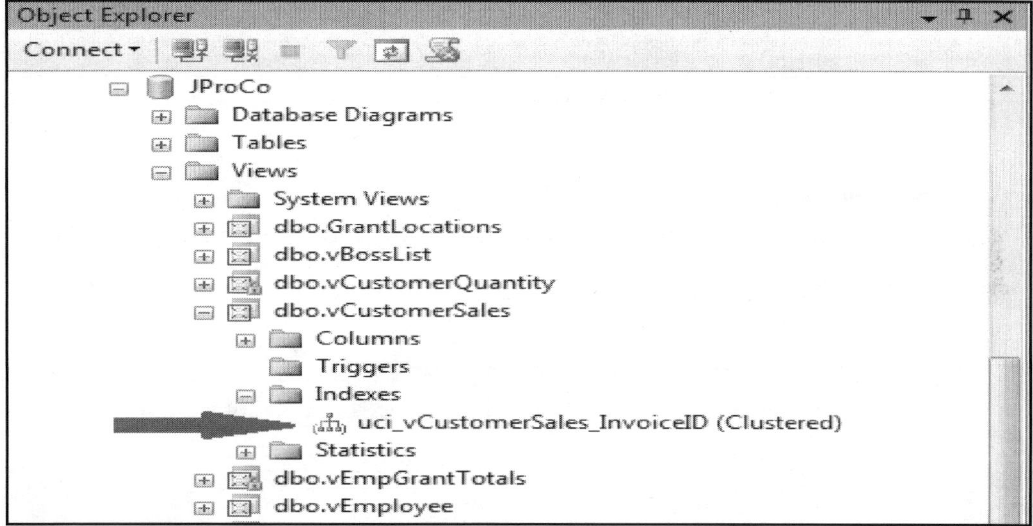

Figure 5.62 The unique clustered index we added to vCustomerSales is visible in Object Explorer.

Our next example involves the GrantLocations view, which shows the data for each grant, as well as the EmpID and location of the employee who obtained the grant (see Figure 5.63). This view does not yet have an index.

```
SELECT * FROM dbo.GrantLocations
```

Results | Messages | Execution plan

	GrantID	GrantName	EmpID	Amount	City	State
1	001	92 Purr_Scents %% team	7	4750.00	Seattle	WA
2	002	K-Land fund trust	2	15750.00	Seattle	WA
3	003	Robert@BigStarBank.com	7	18100.00	Seattle	WA
4	005	BIG 6's Foundation%	4	21000.00	Seattle	WA
5	006	TALTA_Kishan Internati...	3	18100.00	Boston	MA
6	007	Ben@MoreTechnology....	10	41000.00	Boston	MA

Query executed successfully. | (local) (10.0 SP1) | Joes2ProsA10\Teacher (51) | JProCo | 00:00:00 | 11 rows

Figure 5.63 The GrantLocations view does not yet have an index.

We can use sp_helptext to obtain the source code for the GrantLocations view.

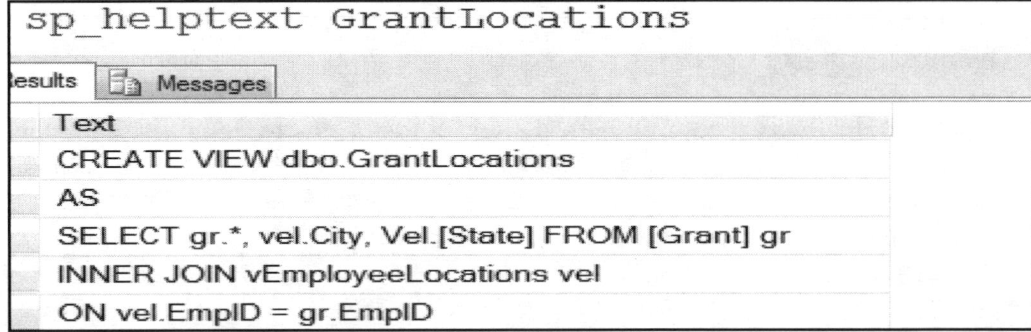

```
sp_helptext GrantLocations
```

Text
CREATE VIEW dbo.GrantLocations
AS
SELECT gr.*, vel.City, Vel.[State] FROM [Grant] gr
INNER JOIN vEmployeeLocations vel
ON vel.EmpID = gr.EmpID

Figure 5.64 The source code for the GrantLocations view.

Suppose we want to enhance our GrantLocations report by adding a ReportTime field using the GetDate( ) function. Run the following code to rebuild the view with this new field (see Figure 5.65) and then query the view (see Figure 5.66).

```
ALTER VIEW dbo.GrantLocations
AS
    SELECT gr.*, vel.City, Vel.[State]
    ,GetDate() as ReportTime --New Field
    FROM [Grant] gr
    INNER JOIN vEmployeeLocations vel
    ON vel.EmpID = gr.EmpID
```

Command(s) completed successfully.

Figure 5.65 We are adding an expression field called ReportTime to the GrantLocations view.

Observe that the ReportTime field shows us the time that the view was run. Run this query a few times and notice that you get a new ReportTime value each time.

```
SELECT * FROM dbo.GrantLocations
```

	GrantID	GrantName	EmpID	Amount	City	State	ReportTime
1	001	92 Purr_Scents %% team	7	4750.00	Seattle	WA	2009-1[illegible]-05 16:46:41.227
2	002	K-Land fund trust	2	15750.00	Seattle	WA	2009-12-05 16:46:41.227
3	003	Robert@BigStarBank.com	7	18100.00	Seattle	WA	2009-12-05 16:46:41.227

Figure 5.66 A query of the GrantLocations view shows the new ReportTime field.

Indexed View Requirements

Now that our GrantLocations view includes a seventh field (ReportTime), this gives us an opportunity to see all of the key requirements in action as we attempt to add an index to this view.

The first six fields of the GrantLocations view are **deterministic**. In other words, we can predict the result produced by a query of these fields. GrantID, GrantName, EmpID, Amount, City, and State will each produce the same values as they have in the base tables (the Grant table and the vEmployeeLocations view).

Deterministic Fields

Results | Messages

	GrantID	GrantName	EmpID	Amount	City	State	ReportTime
1	001	92 Purr_Scents %% team	7	4750.00	Seattle	WA	2009-12-05 16:46:51.250
2	002	K-Land fund trust	2	15750.00	Seattle	WA	2009-12-05 16:46:51.250
3	003	Robert@BigStarBank.com	7	18100.00	Seattle	WA	2009-12-05 16:46:51.250
4	005	BIG 6's Foundation%	4	22000.00	Seattle	WA	2009-12-05 16:46:51.250
5	006	TALTA_Kishan International	3	18100.00	Boston	MA	2009-12-05 16:46:51.250
6	007	Ben@MoreTechnology.com	10	42000.00	Boston	MA	2009-12-05 16:46:51.250
7	008	www.@-Last-U-Can-Help.com	7	26000.00	Seattle	WA	2009-12-05 16:46:51.250

Figure 5.67 The first six fields of the GrantLocations view are deterministic.

As we saw earlier, the value of the ReportTime field cannot be determined prior to runtime. In other words, the ReportTime field is **non-deterministic**.

Non-Deterministic Field

Results | Messages

	GrantID	GrantName	EmpID	Amount	City	State	ReportTime
1	001	92 Purr_Scents %% team	7	4750.00	Seattle	WA	2009-12-05 16:47:07.443
2	002	K-Land fund trust	2	15750.00	Seattle	WA	2009-12-05 16:47:07.443
3	003	Robert@BigStarBank.com	7	18100.00	Seattle	WA	2009-12-05 16:47:07.443
4	005	BIG 6's Foundation%	4	22000.00	Seattle	WA	2009-12-05 16:47:07.443
5	006	TALTA_Kishan International	3	18100.00	Boston	MA	2009-12-05 16:47:07.443
6	007	Ben@MoreTechnology.com	10	42000.00	Boston	MA	2009-12-05 16:47:07.443
7	008	www.@-Last-U-Can-Help.com	7	26000.00	Seattle	WA	2009-12-05 16:47:07.443

Figure 5.68 The last field of this view comes from the non-deterministic function called GetDate( ).

We want to increase the performance of the GrantLocations view by adding an index. Since this is the first index being added to this view, we know it must be a unique clustered index (see Figure 5.69).

We happen to know that the GrantLocations view doesn't already contain an index. One hint telling us this is that the source code we just saw doesn't include schema binding (see Figures 5.64-5.65). Another way to confirm whether a view is already indexed is to check the view in Object Explorer (as shown in Figure 5.62).

Since the GrantLocations view isn't yet schema bound, we know there is at least one factor preventing an index from being added to it. However, we will run this code to attempt the index creation and let SQL Server's messages guide us as we step through the process of adding a unique clustered index to this view.

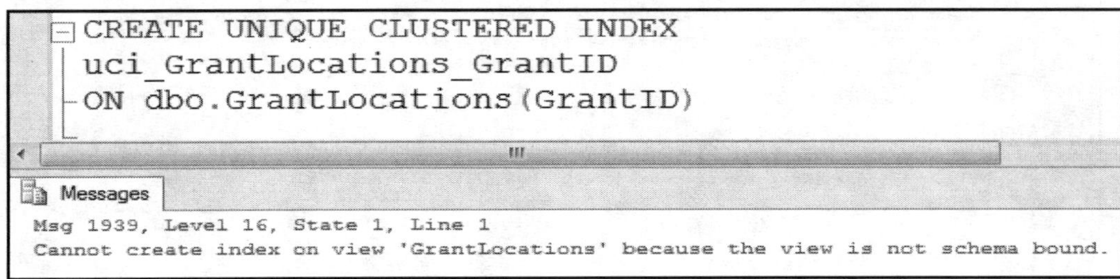

CREATE UNIQUE CLUSTERED INDEX
uci_GrantLocations_GrantID
ON dbo.GrantLocations(GrantID)
Messages
Msg 1939, Level 16, State 1, Line 1
Cannot create index on view 'GrantLocations' because the view is not schema bound.

Figure 5.69 An index cannot be created on a view if the view is not schema bound.

The first error message prompts us to schema bind the GrantLocations view. We will add the WITH SCHEMABINDING clause and make sure that all objects use two-part naming (see Figure 5.70). SQL Server now tells us we can't use the * (asterisk) syntax. Therefore, we must itemize each field in the SELECT list.

```
ALTER VIEW dbo.GrantLocations
WITH SCHEMABINDING
AS
SELECT gr.*,
vel.City, Vel.[State]
,GetDate() as ReportTime
FROM dbo.[Grant] gr
INNER JOIN dbo.vEmployeeLocations vel
ON vel.EmpID = gr.EmpID
```

```
Messages
Msg 1054, Level 15, State 7, Procedure GrantLocations, Line 4
Syntax '*' is not allowed in schema-bound objects.
```

Figure 5.70 You can't create an index on a view that uses the * in its field select list.

We have removed the asterisk (SELECT *) and have itemized all fields in the GrantLocations view and explicitly prefixed them according to which base table they come from (gr for the four fields coming from the Grant table, vel for the two fields coming from the vEmployeeLocations view - see Figure 5.71). SQL Server now tells us that we must first schema bind the vEmployeeLocations view.

```
ALTER VIEW dbo.GrantLocations
WITH SCHEMABINDING
AS
SELECT gr.GrantID, gr.GrantName, gr.EmpID, gr.Amount,
vel.City, Vel.[State]
,GetDate() as ReportTime
FROM dbo.[Grant] gr
INNER JOIN dbo.vEmployeeLocations vel
ON vel.EmpID = gr.EmpID
```

Messages

```
Msg 4513, Level 16, State 2, Procedure GrantLocations, Line 4
Cannot schema bind view 'dbo.GrantLocations'. 'dbo.vEmployeeLocations' is not schema bound.
```

Figure 5.71 The gr.* has been replaced by an itemized field list.

Run sp_helptext to obtain the source code of the needed view (see Figure 5.72). Then add the WITH SCHEMABINDING syntax and ensure all tables use two-part naming.

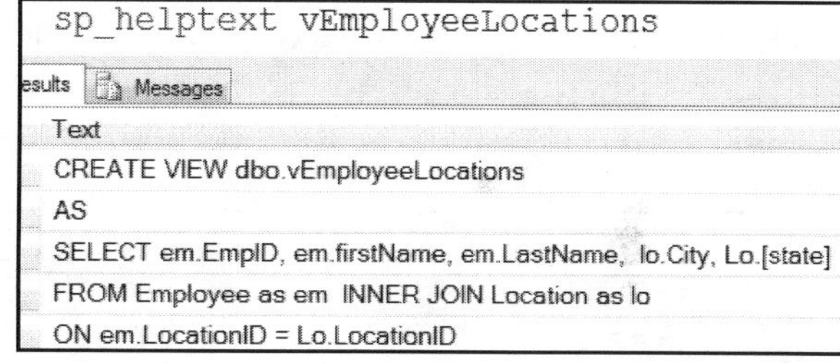

```
sp_helptext vEmployeeLocations
```

Text
CREATE VIEW dbo.vEmployeeLocations
AS
SELECT em.EmpID, em.firstName, em.LastName, lo.City, Lo.[state]
FROM Employee as em INNER JOIN Location as lo
ON em.LocationID = Lo.LocationID

Figure 5.72 The source code for vEmployeeLocations.

Run this code to schema bind the vEmployeeLocations view (see Figure 5.73).

```
ALTER VIEW dbo.vEmployeeLocations
WITH SCHEMABINDING
AS
SELECT em.EmpID, em.firstName, em.LastName,  lo.City, Lo.[state]
FROM dbo.Employee as em
INNER JOIN dbo.Location as lo
ON em.LocationID = Lo.LocationID
```

Messages

```
Command(s) completed successfully.
```

Figure 5.73 The vEmployeeLocations view is now schema bound.

With the vEmployeeLocations view now schema bound, we have handled the most recent SQL Server error message (which we saw in Figure 5.71). SQL Server now allows us to successfully schema bind the GrantLocations view (see Figure 5.74).

```
ALTER VIEW dbo.GrantLocations
WITH SCHEMABINDING
AS
    SELECT gr.GrantID, gr.GrantName, gr.EmpID, gr.Amount,
    vel.City, Vel.[State]
    ,GetDate() as ReportTime
    FROM dbo.[Grant] gr
    INNER JOIN dbo.vEmployeeLocations vel
    ON vel.EmpID = gr.EmpID
```

```
Messages
Command(s) completed successfully.
```

Figure 5.74 The GrantLocations view is now schema bound.

Let's reattempt the code to create the unique clustered index (see Figure 5.75). This error message from SQL Server reminds us that fields producing non-deterministic results cannot be included in an indexed view. Our use of the GetDate( ) function in the ReportTime field is problematic.

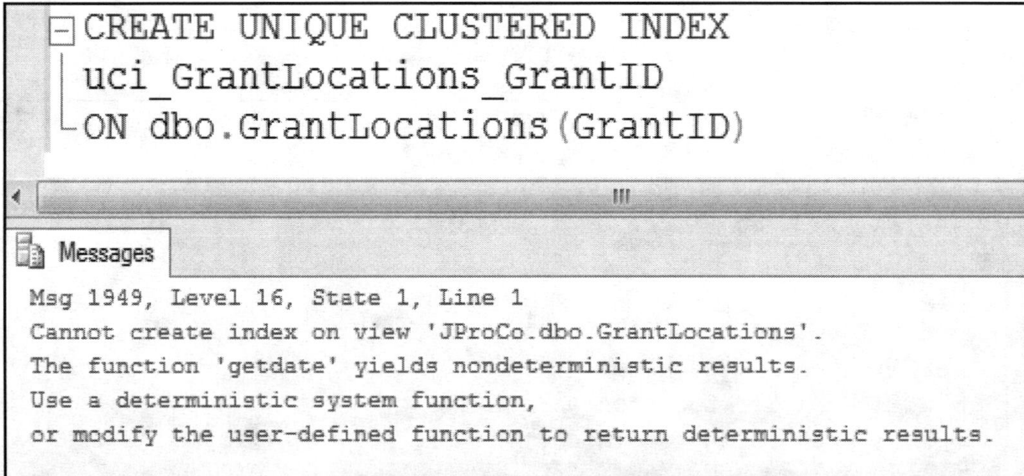

CREATE UNIQUE CLUSTERED INDEX
uci_GrantLocations_GrantID
ON dbo.GrantLocations(GrantID)
Messages
Msg 1949, Level 16, State 1, Line 1
Cannot create index on view 'JProCo.dbo.GrantLocations'.
The function 'getdate' yields nondeterministic results.
Use a deterministic system function,
or modify the user-defined function to return deterministic results.

Figure 5.75 You can't place an index on a view that uses a non-deterministic field.

Let's rerun the statement which builds the GrantLocations view and exclude the ReportTime field. Here we comment out the ReportTime field, so that it's not part of the view (see Figure 5.76).

```
ALTER VIEW dbo.GrantLocations
WITH SCHEMABINDING
AS
    SELECT gr.GrantID, gr.GrantName, gr.EmpID, gr.Amount,
    vel.City, Vel.[State]
    --,GetDate() as ReportTime
    FROM dbo.[Grant] gr
    INNER JOIN dbo.vEmployeeLocations vel
    ON vel.EmpID = gr.EmpID
```

Messages

Command(s) completed successfully.

Figure 5.76 The non-deterministic field has been removed from the GrantLocations view.

Let's rerun the statement to create the index (see Figure 5.77). SQL Server reminds us that an indexed view cannot be based upon another view. We will need to revise the GrantLocations view so that it pulls all needed fields directly from base tables, instead of from a view.

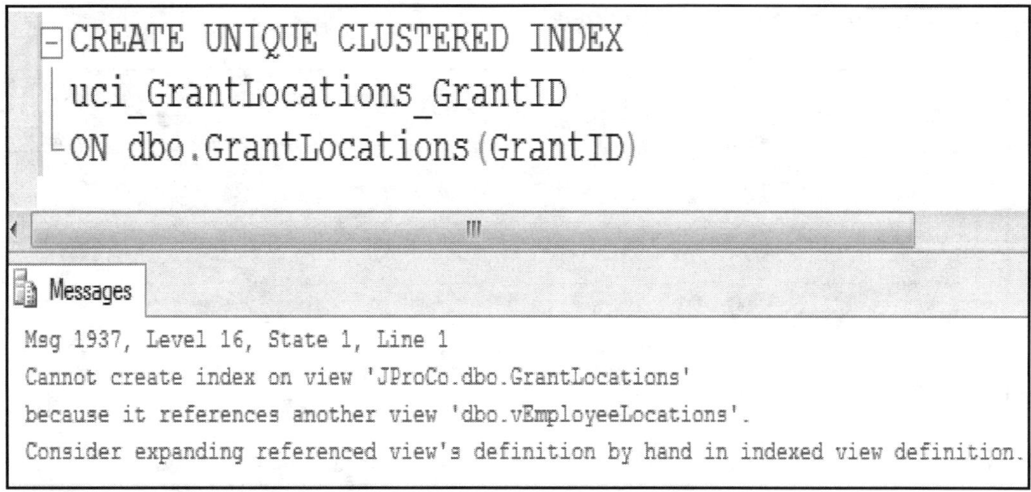
CREATE UNIQUE CLUSTERED INDEX
uci_GrantLocations_GrantID
ON dbo.GrantLocations(GrantID)
Messages
Msg 1937, Level 16, State 1, Line 1
Cannot create index on view 'JProCo.dbo.GrantLocations'
because it references another view 'dbo.vEmployeeLocations'.
Consider expanding referenced view's definition by hand in indexed view definition.

Figure 5.77 An indexed view cannot be based upon another view.

The vEmployeeLocations view is based on two tables (Employee and Location). Let's run this code (see Figure 5.78) to pull the City and State fields directly from a join of the Employee and Location tables instead of from the vEmployeeLocations view.

```
ALTER VIEW dbo.GrantLocations
WITH SCHEMABINDING
AS
    SELECT gr.GrantID, gr.GrantName, gr.EmpID, gr.Amount,
    vel.City, Vel.[State]
    FROM dbo.[Grant] gr
    INNER JOIN dbo.Employee em
    ON gr.EmpID = em.EmpID
    INNER JOIN dbo.Location vel
    ON vel.LocationID = em.LocationID
```

Messages

Command(s) completed successfully.

Figure 5.78 The GrantLocations view is no longer using any views for any of its base tables.

We have met all of SQL Server's requirements and are finally able to add a unique clustered index to the GrantID field of the GrantLocations view (see Figure 5.79). The index will create its own copy of the GrantLocations data and physically order the view's records according to GrantID.

Any query against the view which predicates on the GrantID field should see a marked improvement in performance.

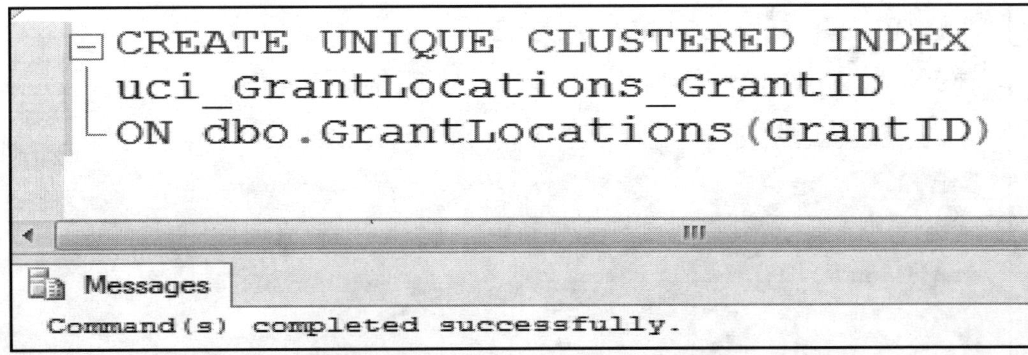
CREATE UNIQUE CLUSTERED INDEX
uci_GrantLocations_GrantID
ON dbo.GrantLocations(GrantID)
Messages
Command(s) completed successfully.

Figure 5.79 The GrantLocations view can now have indexes created on it.

We've successfully created the indexed view and have completed the main portion of our demonstration. But let's spend a moment considering SQL Server's error message which alerted us to the non-deterministic field we had to address before the index could be created (originally shown in Figure 5.75 and reproduced here as Figure 5.80).

```
Messages
Msg 1949, Level 16, State 1, Line 1
Cannot create index on view 'JProCo.dbo.GrantLocations'.
The function 'getdate' yields nondeterministic results.
Use a deterministic system function,
or modify the user-defined function to return deterministic results.
```

Figure 5.80 The GetDate( ) function is problematic, but some functions can produce deterministic results.

Notice that the error message points specifically to the GetDate( ) function as being problematic, because it produces non-deterministic values. However, SQL Server gives us the hint that we can use a deterministic system function, or we can use a user-defined function which returns deterministic results. Thus, it isn't simply that all functions will block your creation of indexed views, just the non-deterministic functions.

Let's briefly look at an example which includes a deterministic function. Here we take our current code (from Figure 5.78) which builds the GrantLocations view. Use the code shown here to rebuild the view with the L3Name field produced by the LEFT function. Rerun this code to alter the GrantLocations view (Figure 5.81).

```
ALTER VIEW dbo.GrantLocations
WITH SCHEMABINDING
AS
SELECT gr.GrantID, gr.GrantName, gr.EmpID, gr.Amount,
vel.City, Vel.[State],
LEFT(GrantName,3) as L3Name--This is deterministic
FROM dbo.[Grant] gr
INNER JOIN dbo.Employee em
ON gr.EmpID = em.EmpID
INNER JOIN dbo.Location vel
ON vel.LocationID = em.LocationID
GO
```

```
Messages
Command(s) completed successfully.
```

Figure 5.81 The L3Name expression field is based on the LEFT( ) function, which is deterministic.

The L3Name field displays the first three letters of the GrantName field. In other words, the values of L3Name are determined by the values in the GrantName field. A SELECT query will always produce the GrantName values which currently appear in the base table. Therefore, the GrantName field is deterministic and will not be changed by a SELECT query. The same is true for the L3Name field. Therefore, L3Name is deterministic (see Figure 5.82).

```
SELECT *
FROM GrantLocations
```

Results | Messages

	GrantID	GrantName	EmpID	Amount	City	State	L3Name
1	001	92 Purr_Scents %% team	7	4750.00	Seattle	WA	92
2	002	K-Land fund trust	2	15750.00	Seattle	WA	K-L
3	003	Robert@BigStarBank.com	7	18100.00	Seattle	WA	Rob

Figure 5.82 L3Name is determined by the values in the GrantName field.

Since the L3Name field is deterministic, SQL Server will allow you to successfully create a unique clustered index on the GrantLocations view (see Figure 5.83).

Note: If you wish to test this yourself, be sure to first drop the existing index before running the code which will create it again. This code drops the index:

```
DROP INDEX uci_GrantLocations_GrantID
ON dbo.GrantLocations
```

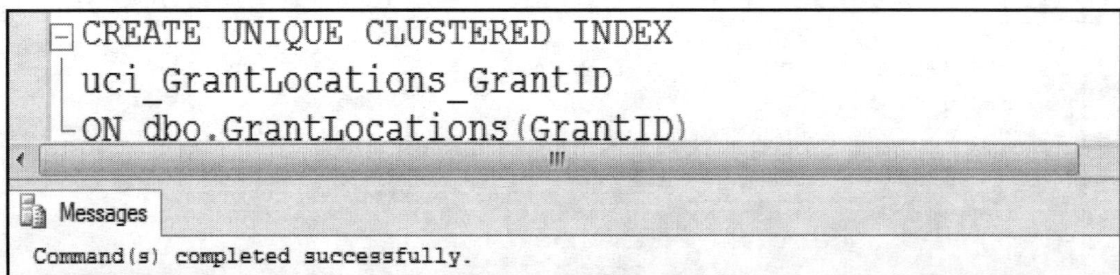
CREATE UNIQUE CLUSTERED INDEX
uci_GrantLocations_GrantID
ON dbo.GrantLocations(GrantID)
Messages
Command(s) completed successfully.

Figure 5.83 You can create an index on a view which includes a function(s), as long as the function(s) is deterministic.

Note: Deterministic functions will be further examined in Chapter 8.

Space Used By Indexed Views

So far we have accepted 'on faith' that views do not store their own data unless they are indexed. In this section, we will examine the data storage requirements of a view before and after an index is added to it:

Let's build a view based on the SalesInvoice and Customer tables:

```
CREATE VIEW vCustomerOrderDates
WITH SCHEMABINDING
AS
    SELECT si.OrderDate, cu.FirstName, cu.LastName
    FROM dbo.SalesInvoice AS si
    INNER JOIN dbo.Customer as cu
    ON si.CustomerID = cu.CustomerID
GO
```

Messages

Command(s) completed successfully.

Query executed successfully. | JOES2PROSA10 (10.50 RTM) | Joes2ProsA10\Teacher (54) | JProCo | 00:00:00 | 0 rows

Figure 5.84 We will build a new view based on the SalesInvoice and Customer tables.

When we query our new view, we see 1884 records displayed:

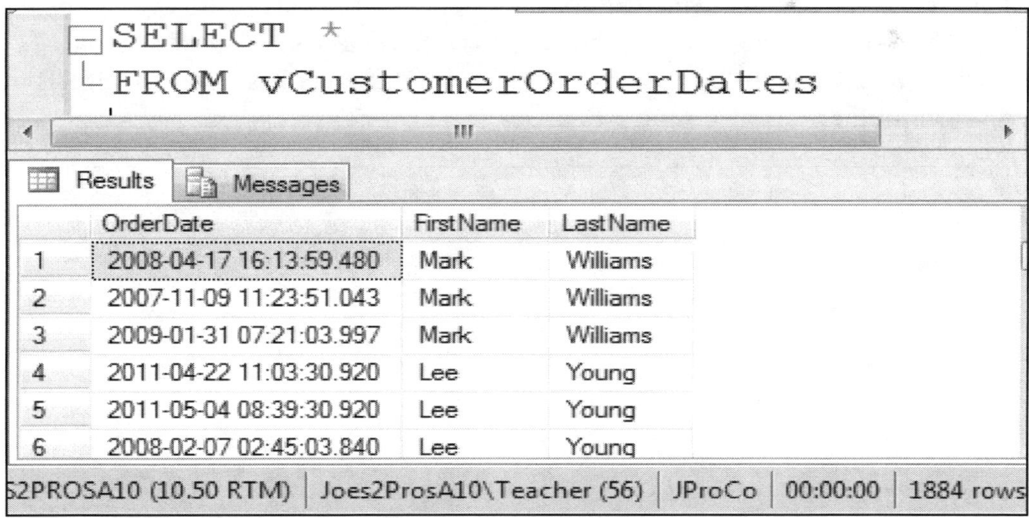

Figure 5.85 Query the view and confirm that you see 1884 rows.

The sp_spaceused utility confirms that this view takes up no space:

```
sp_spaceused vCustomerOrderDates
```

Results | Messages

	name	rows	reserved	data	index_size	unused
1	vCustomerOrderDates	NULL	NULL	NULL	0 KB	0 KB

... | JOES2PROSA10 (10.50 RTM) | Joes2ProsA10\Teacher (56) | JProCo | 00:00:00 | 1 rows

Figure 5.86 This non-indexed view occupies no storage space.

Now let's create an index on the view:

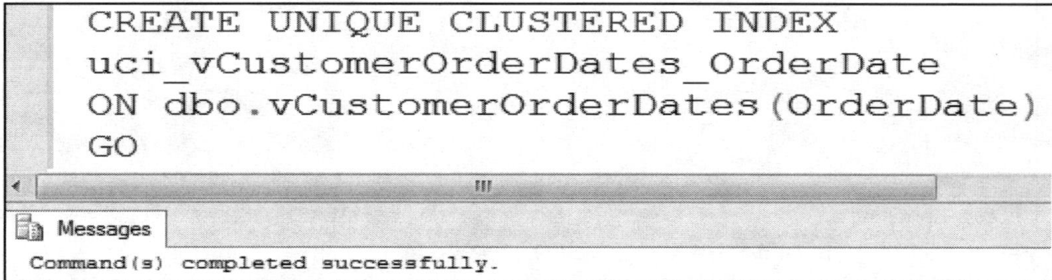
CREATE UNIQUE CLUSTERED INDEX
uci_vCustomerOrderDates_OrderDate
ON dbo.vCustomerOrderDates(OrderDate)
GO
Messages
Command(s) completed successfully.

Figure 5.87 Add a unique clustered index on the OrderDate field of vCustomerOrderDates.

Once we add the index, which permanently materializes this view, we can see that the view now occupies space in the database. This view's data now occupies 88KB with another 16KB used by the index. SQL Server has reserved 136KB in JProCo for the view vCustomerOrderDates:

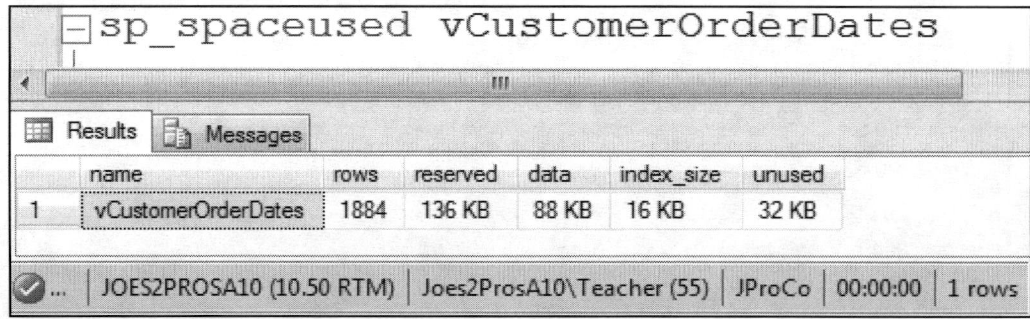

```
sp_spaceused vCustomerOrderDates
```

Results | Messages

	name	rows	reserved	data	index_size	unused
1	vCustomerOrderDates	1884	136 KB	88 KB	16 KB	32 KB

... | JOES2PROSA10 (10.50 RTM) | Joes2ProsA10\Teacher (55) | JProCo | 00:00:00 | 1 rows

Figure 5.88 After the view is indexed, a copy of the data is stored in the index and thus the view now occupies space in the JProCo database.

Note: **sp_spaceused** will be utilized again in Chapter 13.

Lab 5.3: Indexed Views

Lab Prep: Before you can begin the lab, you must have SQL Server installed and have run the SQLProgrammingChapter5.3Setup.sql script.

Skill Check 1: Alter the vSales view to include the InvoiceID and InvoiceDetailID right after the CustomerID. Make certain the view remains schema bound.

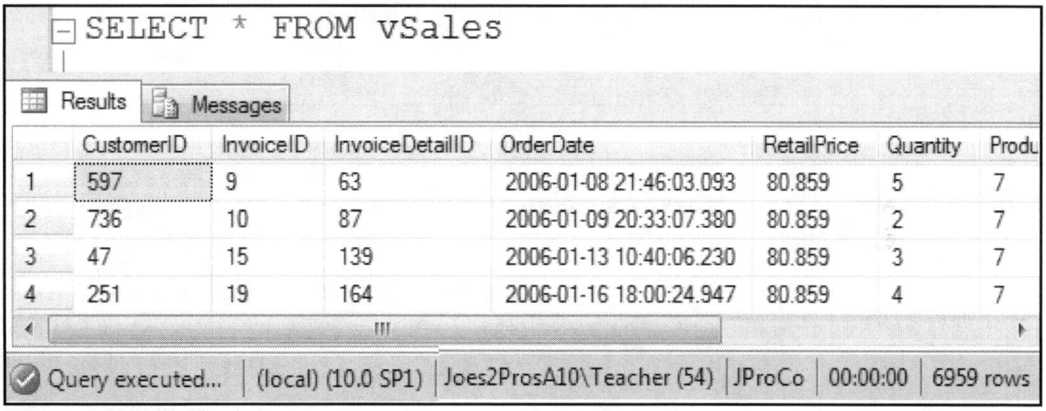

```
SELECT * FROM vSales
```

Results | Messages

	CustomerID	InvoiceID	InvoiceDetailID	OrderDate	RetailPrice	Quantity	Produ
1	597	9	63	2006-01-08 21:46:03.093	80.859	5	7
2	736	10	87	2006-01-09 20:33:07.380	80.859	2	7
3	47	15	139	2006-01-13 10:40:06.230	80.859	3	7
4	251	19	164	2006-01-16 18:00:24.947	80.859	4	7

Query executed... | (local) (10.0 SP1) | Joes2ProsA10\Teacher (54) | JProCo | 00:00:00 | 6959 rows

Figure 5.89 Skill Check 1.

Skill Check 2: Create the uci_vSales_InvoiceDetailID unique clustered index on the vSales view's InvoiceDetailID field.

Answer Code: The T-SQL code to this lab can be found in the downloadable files in a file named Lab5.3_IndexedViews.sql.

Indexed Views - Points to Ponder

1. Summary of rules for indexed views:
   a. The first index must be a unique clustered index.
   b. The view must be defined using the SCHEMABINDING option.
   c. The view cannot have a nested view (it can only reference base tables).
   d. All base tables must have the same schema as the view.
   e. All base tables must be in the same database as the view.
   f. All references must utilize two-part names.
   g. Cannot use non-deterministic fields.
2. All indexed views contain a unique clustered index.
3. Use indexes for views which include many JOIN statements.
4. Indexed views are only supported by the Enterprise or Developer editions of SQL Server.
5. Indexed views store their own data instead of just being instructions for retrieving data from a base table(s).
6. In SQL Server there are three types of views:
   a. Standard – Combines data from one or more base tables.
   b. Indexed – A view with an index that has been computed and stored.
   c. Partitioned – Has base tables from one or more servers.
7. You can create indexes on a view or calculated column only if you use deterministic functions. A deterministic function always returns the same result every time it is called. The result for a non-deterministic function may vary each time it is run.
8. For user-defined functions, SQL Server analyzes the functions and assesses whether they are deterministic or non-deterministic.
9. Views do not exist as a stored set of data values *unless* they are indexed.
10. Because of the system load imposed in maintaining indexes for views, you should limit their use to views that reference columns that change infrequently. Do not index views where the data receives many writes or updates (e.g., OLTP systems like CRM or order-processing systems).

Chapter Glossary

Deterministic function: a function which always returns the same result each time it is called.

Indexed view: a view with an index that has been computed and stored.

Materialized view: indexing a view causes the view to be persistently materialized and stored in the database. In other words, the view contains a physical copy of the view data (including computations associated with joins, aggregate queries, etc.) for quicker retrieval.

Non-deterministic function: a function whose result can vary each time it is called.

Partitioned view: a view which has base tables from one or more servers.

sp_helptext: system-supplied stored procedure that reports information about a database object.

sp_spaceused: a system stored-procedure system stored procedure which obtains space statistics for a table.

Standard view: combines data from one or more base tables.

Chapter Five - Review Quiz

1.) You are attempting to insert records into a table by performing these inserts through a view. You have verified you are updating only one base table and the insert syntax is correct. Your insert appears to run with no errors but the number of records in the table does not change. What are two possible reasons?

- □ a. The table is set to read only.
- □ b. The security context you are using does not have the proper permissions.
- □ c. The database is being backed up.
- □ d. The table has an instead of insert trigger.
- □ e. The table has an insert trigger with a rollback statement.

2.) Your SQL Server has a table named dbo.Employee. You need to create a view for each LocationID (named vSeattleEmployee, vBostonEmployee, vSpokaneEmployee, and vChicagoEmployee). You are getting ready to create the vSeattleEmployee view for LocationID 1. You need to make sure that you can update, insert, and delete against this view without changing the LocationID value for another location. Which code would you use?

O a. CREATE VIEW vSeattleEmployee AS
SELECT * FROM dbo.Employee WHERE LocationID = 1
WITH ENCRYPTION

O b. CREATE VIEW vSeattleEmployee AS
SELECT * FROM dbo.Employee WHERE LocationID = 1
WITH SCHEMABINDING

O c. CREATE VIEW WITH SCHEMABINDING, CHECK OPTION
vSeattleEmployee AS
SELECT * FROM dbo.Employee WHERE LocationID = 1

O d. CREATE VIEW vSeattleEmployee AS
SELECT * FROM dbo.Employee WHERE LocationID = 1
WITH CHECK OPTION

3.) Which is the only true statement about updating data through a view?
O a. You can make updates to one base table while predicating on another.
O b. You can make updates to two based tables if you only predicate on one.
O c. You can make updates to two based tables if you don't use a predicate.

4.) Your company uses SQL Server 2008. You are implementing a series of views that are used in ad hoc queries. Some of these views perform slowly. You create indexes on those views to increase performance, while still maintaining the company's security policy. One of the views returns the current date by using the GETDATE( ) function. This view does not allow you to create an index. You need to create an index on the view. Which two actions should you perform? (Choose two).

□ a. Remove all deterministic calls from within the view.
□ b. Remove all non-deterministic calls from within the view.
□ c. Schema bind the view.
□ d. Create the view and specify WITH CHECK OPTION.
□ e. Base this view on another view instead of a base table.

5.) You are responsible for maintaining a SQL Server 2008 database. A business analyst in the company routinely uses a view named vCustomerSales, which joins the Customers and Sales tables in the database. You need to increase the performance of the view. What should you do?

O a. Update the view to use an outer join between the Customers and Sales tables.
O b. Create a clustered index on the vCustomerSales view.
O c. Create two non clustered indexes on the same field in the view.
O d. Create two separate views that do not contain any joins – one view named vCustomers for the Customers table and another one names vSales for the Sales table.

6.) Which is the only untrue statement about indexed views?

O a. The first index on a view must be a unique clustered index.
O b. Indexed views store a copy of the data from the base tables.
O c. Indexed views require all fields to be deterministic.
O d. Indexed views require the view to be schema bound.
O e. Indexed views require the view to use Check Option.
O f. Indexed views can't be based on other non-schema bound views.

7.) You have a table named Employee and want to create several views from that table for various insert, update, and delete statements. One view will be called vSeattleEmployees and another will be called vBostonEmployees. Each regional office will use its own view. You want to make sure that updates made from Seattle do not change the other employees' locations. The same is true for Boston and all other views based on the Employee table. Seattle is LocationID 1. How do you create the vSeattleEmployees view?

O a. CREATE VIEW dbo.vSeattleEmployees
AS
SELECT EmpID, FirstName, LastName, LocationID
FROM dbo.Employee
WHERE LocationID = 1

O b. CREATE VIEW dbo.vSeattleEmployees
AS
SELECT EmpID, FirstName, LastName, LocationID
FROM dbo.Employee
WHERE LocationID = 1
WITH CHECK OPTION

O c. CREATE VIEW dbo.vSeattleEmployees
AS
SELECT EmpID, FirstName, LastName, LocationID
FROM dbo.Employee
WHERE LocationID = 1
WITH SCHEMABINDING

O d. CREATE VIEW dbo.vSeattleEmployees
WITH SCHEMABINDING
AS
SELECT EmpID, FirstName, LastName, LocationID
FROM dbo.Employee
WHERE LocationID = 1

8) You are creating a view that queries your Employee table. You need to prevent the Employee table from being dropped as long as your view exists. Which option should you use when you create the view?

O a. WITH ENCRYPTION
O b. WITH NOCHECK
O c. WITH SCHEMABINDING
O d. WITH OPENXML

9.) You have a table named dbo.Sales. You need to create three views from the sales table.

vSalesSeattle
vSalesBoston
vSalesSpokane

Each view will be used by each region to make changes to their rows. One day a Seattle sales manager updated his sales data to have a new LocationID and the record showed up on the vSalesBoston view. Changes made to the vSalesSeattle view must not be made in a way that the record falls outside of the scope of the view. Which view should you create for Region1?

O a.
```
CREATE VIEW dbo.vSalesSeattle
AS
SELECT SalesID, OrderQty, SalespersonID, RegionID
FROM dbo.Sales
WHERE RegionID = 1
WITH DIFFERENTIAL
```

O b.
```
CREATE VIEW dbo.vSalesSeattle
AS
SELECT SalesID, OrderQty, SalespersonID, RegionID
FROM dbo.Sales
WHERE RegionID = 1
WITH CHECK OPTION
```

O c.
```
CREATE VIEW dbo.vSalesSeattle
WITH SCHEMABINDING
AS
SELECT SalesID,OrderQty,SalespersonID, RegionID
FROM dbo.Sales
WHERE RegionID = 1
```

O d.
```
CREATE VIEW dbo.vSalesSeattle
WITH NOCHECK
AS
SELECT SalesID, OrderQty, SalespersonID, RegionID
FROM dbo.Sales
WHERE RegionID = 1
```

Answer Key

1.) d, e 2.) d 3.)a 4.) b, c 5.) b 6.) e 7.) b 8.) c 9.) b

Bug Catcher Game

To play the Bug Catcher game, run BugCatcher_Chapter5_UpdatingViews.pps from the BugCatcher folder of the companion files located at www.Joes2Pros.com.

Chapter 6. Stored Procedures

When my brother found out that he and his wife were expecting the first addition to their family, he really got busy getting the house ready for the new baby. In addition to finding baby toys, baby furniture, and other needed items, he started remodeling the bathroom that was next to their bedroom. It was a bigger task than one person could do within the necessary timeframe, so help was needed from our dad, me, and many friends. My brother knew I had no plumbing or electrical skills, but when it came to drywall and paint, he could simply provide me the tools and materials and I would get the work done. My father loves woodwork and shelving, so when that stage of the job came my brother gave Dad a call. For tiling work, our friend, Rhonda came to help and as long as the materials were ready, she knew what to do and carried out the task.

Stored procedures are objects that do the work they are designed to do when you call upon them. You need to make sure they have what they need (the right values and parameters), and they will perform their important tasks. Stored procedures can act like views and select data, but they can also make updates, create objects, or even be set up to backup a database or perform other maintenance tasks.

This chapter will be a refresher from previous books and will also add a few new commonly used tricks, such as returning one or more values from a stored procedure. The next chapter will explore additional techniques using stored procedures.

READER NOTE: *In order to follow along with the examples in the first section of Chapter 6, please run the setup script SQLProgrammingChapter6.0Setup.sql. The setup scripts for this book are posted at Joes2Pros.com.*

Stored Procedures Recap

Stored procedures may contain DML, DDL, TCL, or DCL statements. Our work in Volume 1 *(Beginning SQL Joes 2 Pros)* introduced us to stored procedures (commonly referred to as "sprocs"), as well as to the four T-SQL statement types.

Our subsequent performance tuning work in Volume 3 *(SQL Architecture Basics Joes 2 Pros)* gave us an appreciation stored procedures from a more sophisticated perspective. For example, a stored procedure has the advantage of caching its execution plan. In other words, SQL Server does not have to wait until runtime to evaluate a sproc's indexes, statistics, and query selectivity. For this reason, executing a sproc often runs faster than if you were to drop the code it contains into a new query window and run it.

Basic Stored Procedures

Let's begin with a query retrieving all the employees from Location 1.

```
SELECT * FROM Employee
WHERE LocationID = 1
```

Results | Messages

	EmpID	LastName	FirstName	HireDate	LocationID	ManagerID	Status	HiredOffset	TimeZone
1	1	Adams	Alex	2001-01-01 00:00:00.000	1	3	Active	2001-01-01 00:00:00.0000000 -08:00	-08:00
2	2	Brown	Barry	2002-08-12 00:00:00.000	1	11	Active	2002-08-12 00:00:00.0000000 -08:00	-08:00
3	4	Kinnison	Dave	1996-03-16 00:00:00.000	1	11	Has Tenure	1996-03-16 00:00:00.0000000 -08:00	-08:00
4	5	Bender	Eric	2007-05-17 00:00:00.000	1	11	Active	2007-05-17 00:00:00.0000000 -08:00	-08:00
5	7	Lonning	David	2000-01-01 00:00:00.000	1	11	On Leave	2000-01-01 00:00:00.0000000 -08:00	-08:00
6	9	Newton	James	2003-09-30 00:00:00.000	1	3	Active	2003-09-30 00:00:00.0000000 -05:00	-05:00
7	11	Smith	Sally	1989-04-01 00:00:00.000	1	NULL	Active	1989-04-01 00:00:00.0000000 -08:00	-08:00
8	13	Wilconkinski	Phil	2009-06-11 00:00:00.000	1	11	Active	2009-06-11 00:00:00.0000000 -08:00	-08:00
9	14	Smith	Janis	2009-10-18 00:00:00.000	1	4	Active	2009-10-18 00:00:00.0000000 -08:00	-08:00
10	15	Jones	Tess	2010-10-21 10:38:45.497	1	11	Active	2010-10-21 10:38:45.4970000 -08:00	-08:00
11	16	Biggs	Nancy	2010-10-21 10:38:45.503	1	11	Active	2010-10-21 10:38:45.5030000 -08:00	-08:00
12	17	Downs	Wendy	2010-10-21 10:38:45.510	1	11	Active	2010-10-21 10:38:45.5100000 -08:00	-08:00
13	18	Walker	Rainy	2010-01-01 00:00:00.000	1	11	Active	2010-10-21 10:38:45.5270000 -08:00	-08:00
14	19	Beckman	Sandy	2010-01-15 00:00:00.000	1	11	Active	2010-10-21 10:38:45.5300000 -08:00	-08:00
15	20	Winds	Gale	2010-03-25 00:00:00.000	1	11	Active	2010-10-21 10:38:45.6670000 -08:00	-08:00
16	21	Fines	Sue	2010-10-21 10:38:45.677	1	4	Active	2010-10-21 10:38:45.6770000 -08:00	-08:00

Query executed successfully. | (local) (10.0 SP1) | Joes2ProsA10\Teacher (54) | JProCo | 00:00:00 | 16 rows

Figure 6.1 Records for all the JProCo employees working in Location 1.

Suppose this is a query we run frequently, perhaps several times daily. It would be smarter for us to create a stored procedure rather than manually type out the query each time we need to retrieve the data. Not only will our query benefit from a cached execution plan and statistics, but the sproc will be a database object available for reuse by your team. For example, a fellow analyst or DBA can use this sproc to run this query that your team needs several times daily. Your dev team can also call upon your sproc from within another code routine or automated process they may be developing.

While in the JProCo database context, run the following code to include our query in a newly created sproc called GetSeattleEmployees (see Figure 6.2). Notice that this code simply creates the object (i.e., the stored procedure). We need to write a separate statement to invoke the sproc (see Figure 6.3).

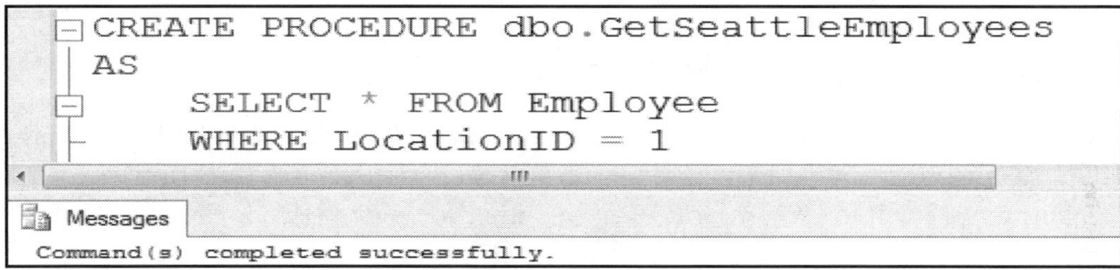

CREATE PROCEDURE dbo.GetSeattleEmployees
AS
SELECT * FROM Employee
WHERE LocationID = 1
Messages
Command(s) completed successfully.

Figure 6.2 This code creates the stored procedure GetSeattleEmployees.

An EXECUTE statement is what we need to actually run our newly created sproc. You can either choose to spell out the full keyword EXECUTE or use the shortened form EXEC, as shown here (see Figure 6.3). Notice that the result set is identical to that produced by the original query (shown earlier in Figure 6.1).

```
EXEC GetSeattleEmployees
```

Results | Messages

	EmpID	LastName	FirstName	HireDate	LocationID	ManagerID	Status	HiredOffset	TimeZone
1	1	Adams	Alex	2001-01-01 00:00:00.000	1	3	Active	2001-01-01 00:00:00.0000000 -08:00	-08:00
2	2	Brown	Barry	2002-08-12 00:00:00.000	1	11	Active	2002-08-12 00:00:00.0000000 -08:00	-08:00
3	4	Kinnison	Dave	1996-03-16 00:00:00.000	1	11	Has Tenure	1996-03-16 00:00:00.0000000 -08:00	-08:00
4	5	Bender	Eric	2007-05-17 00:00:00.000	1	11	Active	2007-05-17 00:00:00.0000000 -08:00	-08:00
5	7	Lonning	David	2000-01-01 00:00:00.000	1	11	On Leave	2000-01-01 00:00:00.0000000 -08:00	-08:00
6	9	Newton	James	2003-09-30 00:00:00.000	1	3	Active	2003-09-30 00:00:00.0000000 -05:00	-05:00
7	11	Smith	Sally	1989-04-01 00:00:00.000	1	NULL	Active	1989-04-01 00:00:00.0000000 -08:00	-08:00
8	13	Wilconkinski	Phil	2009-06-11 00:00:00.000	1	11	Active	2009-06-11 00:00:00.0000000 -08:00	-08:00
9	14	Smith	Janis	2009-10-18 00:00:00.000	1	4	Active	2009-10-18 00:00:00.0000000 -08:00	-08:00
10	15	Jones	Tess	2010-10-21 10:38:45.497	1	11	Active	2010-10-21 10:38:45.4970000 -08:00	-08:00
11	16	Biggs	Nancy	2010-10-21 10:38:45.503	1	11	Active	2010-10-21 10:38:45.5030000 -08:00	-08:00
12	17	Downs	Wendy	2010-10-21 10:38:45.510	1	11	Active	2010-10-21 10:38:45.5100000 -08:00	-08:00
13	18	Walker	Rainy	2010-01-01 00:00:00.000	1	11	Active	2010-10-21 10:38:45.5270000 -08:00	-08:00
14	19	Beckman	Sandy	2010-01-15 00:00:00.000	1	11	Active	2010-10-21 10:38:45.5300000 -08:00	-08:00
15	20	Winds	Gale	2010-03-25 00:00:00.000	1	11	Active	2010-10-21 10:38:45.6670000 -08:00	-08:00
16	21	Fines	Sue	2010-10-21 10:38:45.677	1	4	Active	2010-10-21 10:38:45.6770000 -08:00	-08:00

Query executed successfully. | (local) (10.0 SP1) | Joes2ProsA10\Teacher (54) | JProCo | 00:00:00 | 16 rows

Figure 6.3 This code calls the stored procedure GetSeattleEmployees.

You may have noticed we were able to successfully call the sproc without including "dbo" in the EXEC statement. Specifying the schema name (e.g., dbo) is usually optional when creating or invoking an object. (Chapter 13 will show performance related reasons for always using a two-part name with sprocs.) In this case we could have created the sproc with the name "GetSeattleEmployees." Since dbo is the default schema for the JProCo database, SQL Server will implicitly read the object name "GetSeattleEmployees" as "dbo.GetSeattleEmployees." In most cases, you are safe using two-part naming. You are nearly as safe using just the object name. SQL Server's error messaging will prompt you whenever a different naming format is needed.

Stored Procedure Parameters

The EXEC(UTE) command runs the code contained within the stored procedure. Our result was what we expected to see – all the employees at LocationID 1. Suppose we want to see employees at the other locations (Boston, Spokane, etc.). Should we create a separate sproc for each office?

Stored procedures offer a more flexible option for achieving our goal. We can modify our stored procedure so that it will allow us to specify a location each time we execute the sproc. Readers of Volume 1 *(Beginning SQL Joes 2 Pros)* will likely recall a similar example we utilized (Chapter 8, Parameterized Stored Procedures). Rather than hardcoding the LocationID, we will let it be defined by a variable. Each time someone runs the sproc, they will need to supply a value for their desired LocationID. Values that you pass into a sproc at runtime are called ***parameters***.

The code shown in Figure 6.6 (see next page) will build the flexible sproc designed to show us the employee records for any JProCo location. Our current query will still be the basis of the sproc. While it may be easy to recognize the variable taking the place of the hardcoded value in our current query, let's examine all of the code syntax changes the new sproc will encompass (see Figures 6.4 and 6.5).

```
--This syntax declares the variable @LocationID, which is an integer.
--The variable is currently set to 1.
DECLARE @LocationID INT = 1

SELECT * FROM Employee   --Our current query with hardcoded LocationID.
WHERE LocationID = 1     --In order to make use of the declared variable,
                         --our query would need to call upon the variable.

--The variable now replaces the hardcoded value in our query.
--If you change the 1 to another LocationID (e.g., 2, 3, 4, etc.),
--then the query will return the records for your chosen location.
DECLARE @LocationID INT = 1
SELECT * FROM Employee
WHERE LocationID = @LocationID
```

Figure 6.4 The code syntax for declaring a variable and calling upon a variable are shown here.

When we substitute the variable @LocationID for the hardcoded value in our query, it will return the records for the location which we specify (see Figure 6.5).

```
DECLARE @LocationID INT = 2
SELECT * FROM Employee
WHERE LocationID = @LocationID
```

Results | Messages

	EmpID	LastName	FirstName	HireDate	LocationID	ManagerID	Status	HiredOffset	TimeZon
1	3	Osako	Lee	1999-09-...	2	11	Active	1999-09-0...	-05:00
2	10	O'Haire	Terry	2004-10-...	2	3	Active	2004-10-0...	-05:00

Figure 6.5 The location you specify populates the variable; our query now includes the variable.

Now let's turn to the code which creates GetEmployeeByLocationID, our new sproc (see Figure 6.6). The base query is the same (compare the last 2 lines of code in Figures 6.5 and 6.6). The CREATE PROCEDURE statement declares the variable. Since we want the flexibility to choose the location at runtime, our code doesn't include any LocationID value. Run this code to create the stored procedure.

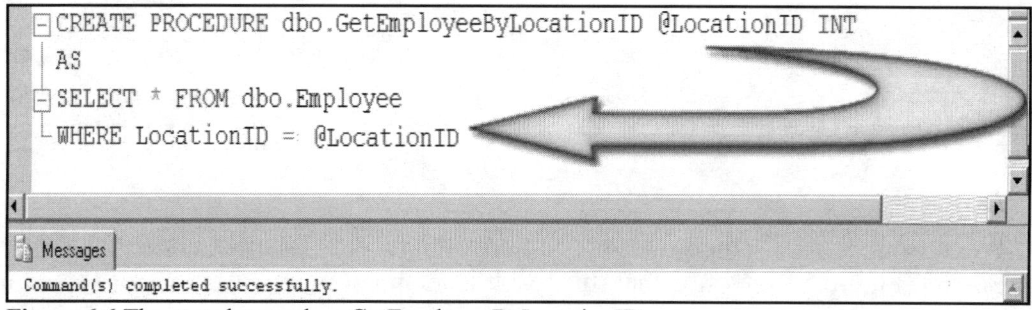
CREATE PROCEDURE dbo.GetEmployeeByLocationID @LocationID INT
AS
SELECT * FROM dbo.Employee
WHERE LocationID = @LocationID
Messages
Command(s) completed successfully.

Figure 6.6 The stored procedure GetEmployeeByLocationID.

We need to supply the LocationID value when we run the sproc. If we attempt to execute this sproc without telling it which location we want, we'll get an error message from SQL Server telling us that this procedure expects a parameter and that one wasn't supplied (see Figure 6.7).

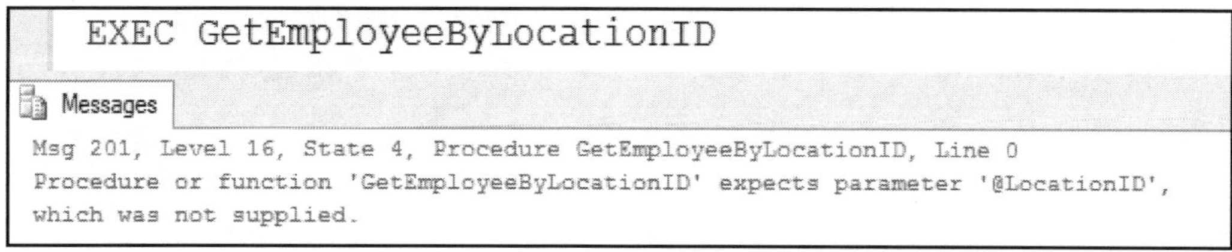
EXEC GetEmployeeByLocationID
Messages
Msg 201, Level 16, State 4, Procedure GetEmployeeByLocationID, Line 0
Procedure or function 'GetEmployeeByLocationID' expects parameter '@LocationID',
which was not supplied.

Figure 6.7 If no parameter is supplied, the GetEm ployeeByLocationID sproc cannot run.

Let's reattempt to call on GetEmployeeByLocationID and request the records for Location 1. When we pass the value 1 to the variable, we see all the Seattle employee record (see Figure 6.8).

```
EXEC GetEmployeeByLocationID 1
```

Results | Messages

	EmpID	LastName	FirstName	HireDate	LocationID	ManagerID	Status	HiredOffset	TimeZone
1	1	Adams	Alex	2001-01-01 00:00:00.000	1	3	Active	2001-01-01 00:00:00.0000000 -08:00	-08:00
2	2	Brown	Barry	2002-08-12 00:00:00.000	1	11	Active	2002-08-12 00:00:00.0000000 -08:00	-08:00
3	4	Kinnison	Dave	1996-03-16 00:00:00.000	1	11	Has Tenure	1996-03-16 00:00:00.0000000 -08:00	-08:00
4	5	Bender	Eric	2007-05-17 00:00:00.000	1	11	Active	2007-05-17 00:00:00.0000000 -08:00	-08:00
5	7	Lonning	David	2000-01-01 00:00:00.000	1	11	On Leave	2000-01-01 00:00:00.0000000 -08:00	-08:00
6	9	Newton	James	2003-09-30 00:00:00.000	1	3	Active	2003-09-30 00:00:00.0000000 -05:00	-05:00
7	11	Smith	Sally	1989-04-01 00:00:00.000	1	NULL	Active	1989-04-01 00:00:00.0000000 -08:00	-08:00
8	13	Wilconkinski	Phil	2009-06-11 00:00:00.000	1	11	Active	2009-06-11 00:00:00.0000000 -08:00	-08:00
9	14	Smith	Janis	2009-10-18 00:00:00.000	1	4	Active	2009-10-18 00:00:00.0000000 -08:00	-08:00
10	15	Jones	Tess	2010-10-21 10:47:19.033	1	11	Active	2010-10-21 10:47:19.0330000 -08:00	-08:00
11	16	Biggs	Nancy	2010-10-21 10:47:19.040	1	11	Active	2010-10-21 10:47:19.0400000 -08:00	-08:00
12	17	Downs	Wendy	2010-10-21 10:47:19.047	1	11	Active	2010-10-21 10:47:19.0470000 -08:00	-08:00
13	18	Walker	Rainy	2010-01-01 00:00:00.000	1	11	Active	2010-10-21 10:47:19.0630000 -08:00	-08:00
14	19	Beckman	Sandy	2010-01-15 00:00:00.000	1	11	Active	2010-10-21 10:47:19.0670000 -08:00	-08:00
15	20	Winds	Gale	2010-03-25 00:00:00.000	1	11	Active	2010-10-21 10:47:19.2070000 -08:00	-08:00
16	21	Fines	Sue	2010-10-21 10:47:19.217	1	4	Active	2010-10-21 10:47:19.2170000 -08:00	-08:00

Figure 6.8 This parameter specifies that we want the records for Location 1 (Seattle).

When we pass in a 2, the same sproc returns the records for Location 2, which is Boston (Figure 6.9). Notice that this result is identical to the query result shown in Figure 6.5.

```
EXEC GetEmployeeByLocationID 2
```

Results | Messages

	EmpID	LastName	FirstName	HireDate	LocationID	ManagerID	Status	HiredOffset	TimeZone
1	3	Osako	Lee	1999-09-01 00:00:00.000	2	11	Active	1999-09-01 00:00:00.0000000 -05:00	-05:00
2	10	O'Haire	Terry	2004-10-04 00:00:00.000	2	3	Active	2004-10-04 00:00:00.0000000 -05:00	-05:00

Figure 6.9 This parameter specifies that we want the records from Location 2 (Boston).

Let's create another stored procedure called GetBigGrants. This stored procedure should find grants at, or above, a specified amount. Run this code to create the stored procedure (see Figure 6.10).

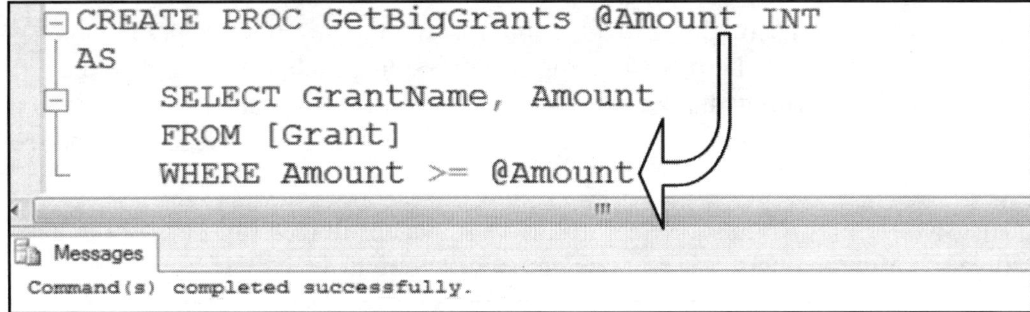

```
CREATE PROC GetBigGrants @Amount INT
AS
    SELECT GrantName, Amount
    FROM [Grant]
    WHERE Amount >= @Amount
```

Messages

Command(s) completed successfully.

Figure 6.10 This code creates the GetBigGrants procedure that requires a parameter.

Let's call the GetBigGrants sproc and specify that we want to see all the grants at, or above, $40,000 (see Figure 6.11 where we pass in the value 40000).

```
EXEC GetBigGrants 40000
```

Results | Messages

	GrantName	Amount
1	Ben@MoreTechnology.com	41000.00
2	Mega Mercy	55000.00

Figure 6.11 Two grants have an amount greater than, or equal to, $40,000.

Let's change our code to pass in 25000 (see Figure 6.12). There are three grants that are at or over the amount of $25,000 in our result set.

```
EXEC GetBigGrants 25000
```

Results | Messages

	GrantName	Amount
1	Ben@MoreTechnology.com	41000.00
2	www.@-Last-U-Can-Help.com	25000.00
3	Mega Mercy	55000.00

Figure 6.12 Three grants have an amount greater than, or equal to, $25,000.

Scalar Result Sets

A **scalar** result consists of a single value. We need to be aware of scalar data, because we will encounter scenarios in SQL Server which require a scalar value as an input and objects (e.g., scalar functions) which only produce scalar results. Scalar values can be the result of simple expressions, such as the employee data expressions we will evaluate in this section. A scalar value can also result from a complex expression, such as the many calculations and inputs needed to produce a FICO score.

Here we see a query designed to produce a scalar result (see Figure 6.13). Each time you run the query, exactly one value will be returned.

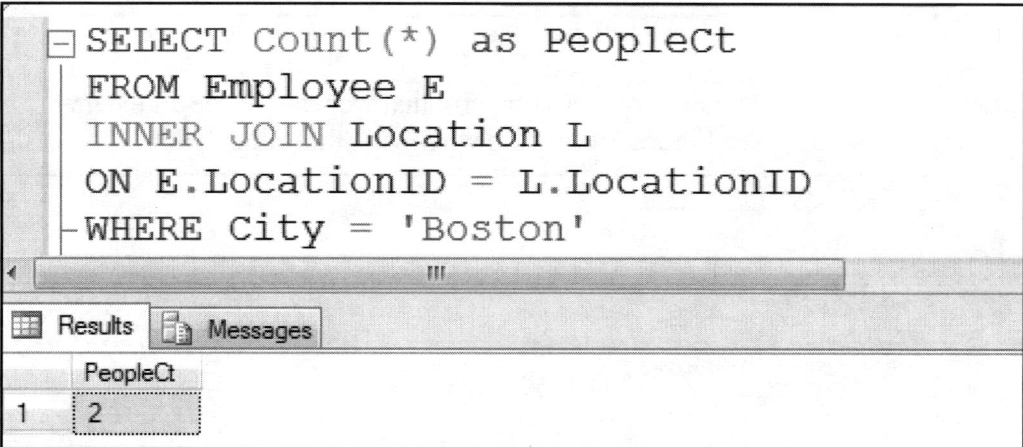

Figure 6.13 This query returns the count of employees working in Boston.

When we change the criteria to get the Seattle employees, we get the scalar value 16 (see Figure 6.14).

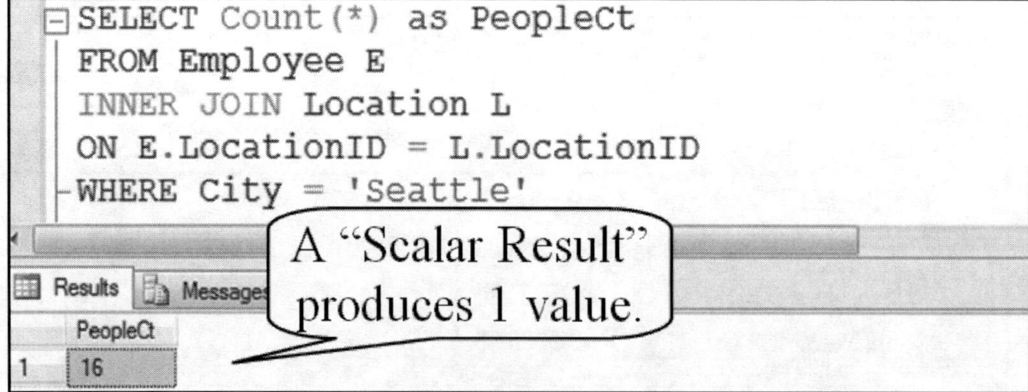

Figure 6.14 A scalar result consists of exactly one value.

Let's create a scalar stored procedure GetCityCount, which will return a single value, no matter what parameter we pass in (see Figure 6.15).

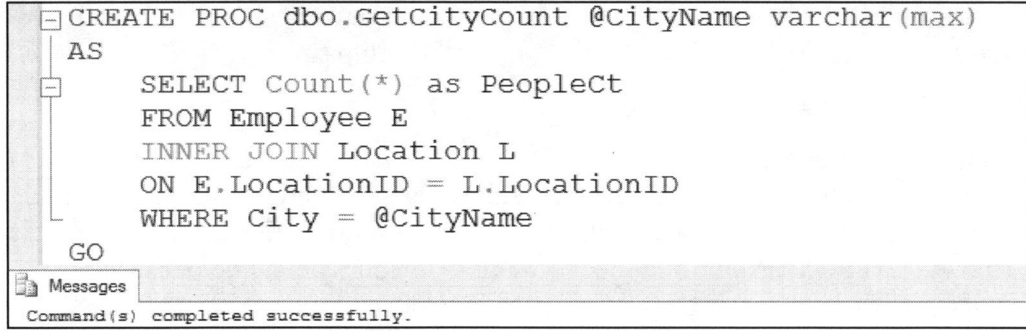

CREATE PROC dbo.GetCityCount @CityName varchar(max)
AS
SELECT Count(*) as PeopleCt
FROM Employee E
INNER JOIN Location L
ON E.LocationID = L.LocationID
WHERE City = @CityName
GO
Messages
Command(s) completed successfully.

Figure 6.15 This code creates the scalar stored procedure GetCityCount.

Let's test our stored procedure and pass in Spokane for the parameter value.

```
EXEC GetCityCount 'Spokane'
```

Results | Messages

	PeopleCt
1	2

Query executed successfu... | (local) (10.0 SP1) | Joes2ProsA10\Teacher (54) | JProCo | 00:00:00 | 1 rows

Figure 6.16 This code calls the stored procedure GetCityCount for Spokane.

The same stored procedure shows us the total of 16 when we pass in Seattle.

```
EXEC GetCityCount 'Seattle'
```

Results | Messages

	PeopleCt
1	16

Query executed successfu... | (local) (10.0 SP1) | Joes2ProsA10\Teacher (54) | JProCo | 00:00:00 | 1 rows

Figure 6.17 This code calls the stored procedure GetCityCount for Seattle.

The scalar result 0 (i.e., zero employees) is returned for Chicago (Figure 6.18).

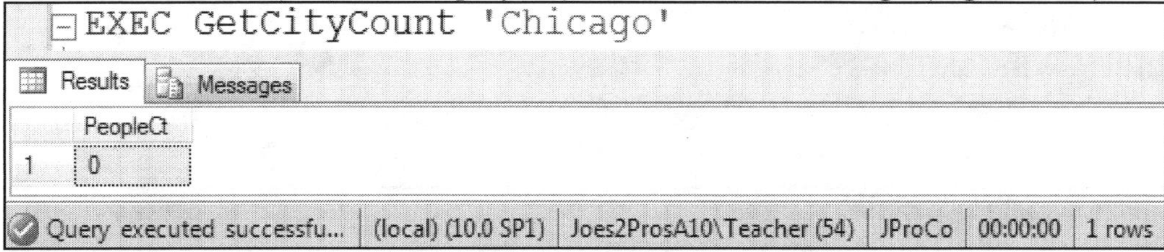

Figure 6.18 There are currently zero employees at the Chicago location.

Lab 6.1: Stored Procedures Recap

Lab Prep: Before you can begin the lab, you must have SQL Server installed and have run the script SQLProgrammingChapter6.1Setup.sql.

Skill Check 1: Create a Stored Procedure called GetLongClasses which takes an INT (integer) parameter and shows a result set of all MgmtTraining classes with a duration greater than or equal to the number of hours specified by the parameter. Show just the ClassName and the ClassDurationHours fields in your result. Run and test your stored proc by passing in 18 hours (see Figure 6.19).

```
EXEC GetLongClasses 18
```

Results | Messages

	ClassName	ClassDurationHours
1	Difficult Negotiations	30
2	Empowering Others	18

Figure 6.19 Skill Check 1 result.

Skill Check 2: Create a stored procedure that shows the number of products from the CurrentProducts table which are below a certain price. The variable should be called @Price and should have the data type of float. Call on the stored procedure by passing in the value of 35. When you are done, your result will resemble the figure you see here (see Figure 6.20).

```
EXEC ShowProductsBelowPrice 35
```

Results | Messages

	ProductName	RetailPrice
1	Ocean Cruise Tour 1 Day Mexico	32.601
2	Mountain Lodge 1 Day Scandinavia	32.574
3	Winter Tour 1 Day Scandinavia	34.506
4	Cherry Festival Tour 1 Day Mexico	31.909
5	Cherry Festival Tour 1 Day Canada	34.944

Figure 6.20 Skill Check 2 results.

Answer Code: The T-SQL code to this lab can be found in the downloadable files in a file named Lab6.1_StoredProcedureRecap.sql.

Stored Procedure Recap - Points to Ponder

1. A stored procedure is a named database object consisting of one or more T-SQL statements run together in a single execution.
2. A stored procedure is precompiled code that can be reused. You can also define your own custom stored procedures.
3. To run a stored procedure, use the EXECUTE PROCEDURE (or EXEC PROC) command.
4. With stored procedures, single execution plans are stored on the server and therefore run faster than the same statements run individually.
5. The syntax for creating a new stored procedure is CREATE PROCEDURE *procname* AS. (The keyword PROCEDURE may be shortened to PROC.)
6. Avoid naming your stored procs with the "sp_" prefix, since you could confuse those with the built-in procs. Since SQL Server first searches for any sp_name in the master db, this initial search will slow down your execution of any sproc you misname as *sp_name*.
7. To modify an existing stored procedure, use the ALTER PROC statement.
8. If you want to alter an encrypted procedure, you must include the WITH ENCRYPTION statement when you run the ALTER PROC statement.
9. Use DROP PROCEDURE *procname* when dropping a stored proc.
10. Before you drop a stored procedure, run sp_depends to see if other objects depend on it.
11. To locate a stored procedure in Object Explorer, navigate to the "Programmability" folder of your database. You will find a "Stored Procedures" folder within the "Programmability" folder.
12. See Chapter 13 for additional tips related to improving the performance of stored procedures. For example, using the 2-part name (SchemaName.SprocName) whenever invoking a sproc will improve the performance of your code.

Stored Procedure Return Values

Up to this point in our programming journey, whenever we've performed an action we've seen SQL Server return some form of output to one of the tabs in our query window (the data results tab, the message tab, or the spatial results tab).

After your stored procedure runs, oftentimes you will need to capture the output as a value or summary number to be supplied to your front-end application. Parameters returned by your procedure can drive application display elements (e.g., an update confirmation or a message produced by the PRINT command) and can even capture data for use by a web page.

Creating Return Values

Let's begin an example showing return values in action. Our SELECT statement shows that Alex Adams is EmpID 1 and works for ManagerID 3 (see Figure 6.21).

```
SELECT * FROM Employee WHERE EmpID = 1
```

Results | Messages

	EmpID	LastName	FirstName	HireDate	LocationID	ManagerID	Status	H
1	1	Adams	Alex	2001-01-01 00:00:00.000	1	3	Active	2

Figure 6.21 Alex Adams is EmpID 1 and he works for ManagerID 3.

Suppose that we want all management updates to be performed through a new stored procedure, UpdateEmployeeToNewManager. In order to update an existing employee record, this sproc requires two parameters (one for EmpID and one for ManagerID). Run this code to create the new sproc (Figure 6.22).

```
CREATE PROC UpdateEmployeeToNewManager @EmpID INT, @ManagerID INT
AS
    UPDATE Employee SET ManagerID = @ManagerID
    WHERE EmpID = @EmpID
GO
```

Messages

Command(s) completed successfully.

Figure 6.22 The UpdateEmployeeToNewManager sproc updates an existing EmpID's ManagerID.

We want to update Alex Adams to work for ManagerID 4. We need to pass in a 1 to confirm his EmpID and a 4 to specify the new ManagerID 4 (see Figure 6.23).

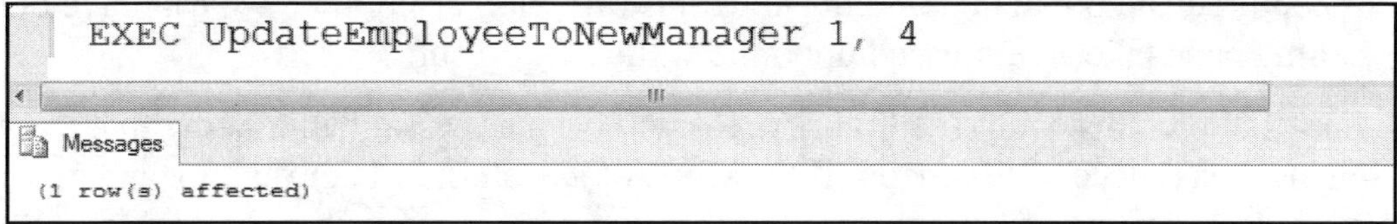

Figure 6.23 This call to the sproc should update Alex Adams to have a ManagerID of 4.

(*Note:* If you see more than one transaction confirmed ("1 row(s) affected") when you run UpdateEmployeeToNewManager, then you likely haven't run the latest setup script which disables the trigger trg_UpdEmployee.)

When we check to confirm the expected change was made, we see that yes, the Employee table now reflects Alex as working for ManagerID 4 (see Figure 6.24).

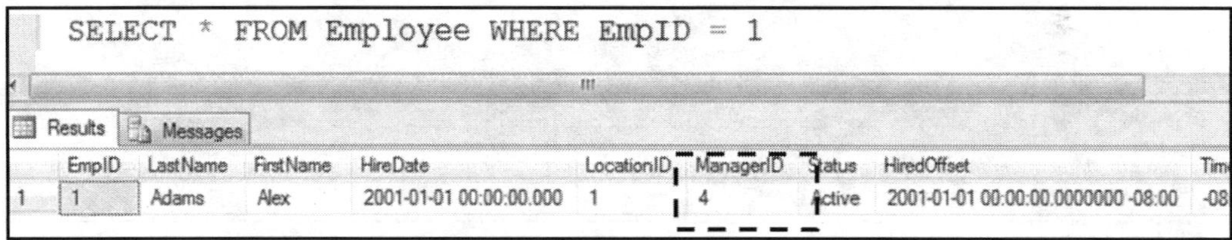

Figure 6.24 This SELECT statement confirms that Alex has a new manager.

We now want to modify our sproc to have it return the completion status with each run of the sproc. The additional code declares a new variable which is set to -1 unless a successful update occurs. The RETURN value will be -1 if no records are updated, and a 1 will indicate that at least one record is updated (Figure 6.25).

```
ALTER PROC UpdateEmployeeToNewManager @EmpID INT, @ManagerID INT
AS
    DECLARE @Status INT
    SET @Status = -1 --No Records Updated

    UPDATE Employee SET ManagerID = @ManagerID
    WHERE EmpID = @EmpID

    IF(@@ROWCOUNT) > 0
    SET @Status = 1 -- --Yes Records Updated

    RETURN @Status
GO
```

Messages

Command(s) completed successfully.

Figure 6.25 This sproc returns -1 if no records are updated and 1 if at least one record is updated.

Now we want to enhance our EXEC statement to capture the -1 or 1 value produced by the RETURN statement. The RETURN value produced by the sproc is captured and populated into the @Result variable. From there we can have our calling code take action based upon the value of @Result.

For example, this code (see Figure 6.26) will print a message indicating that a change was successfully made (if the value of @Return is 1) or that no change was made (if the value of @Return is -1).

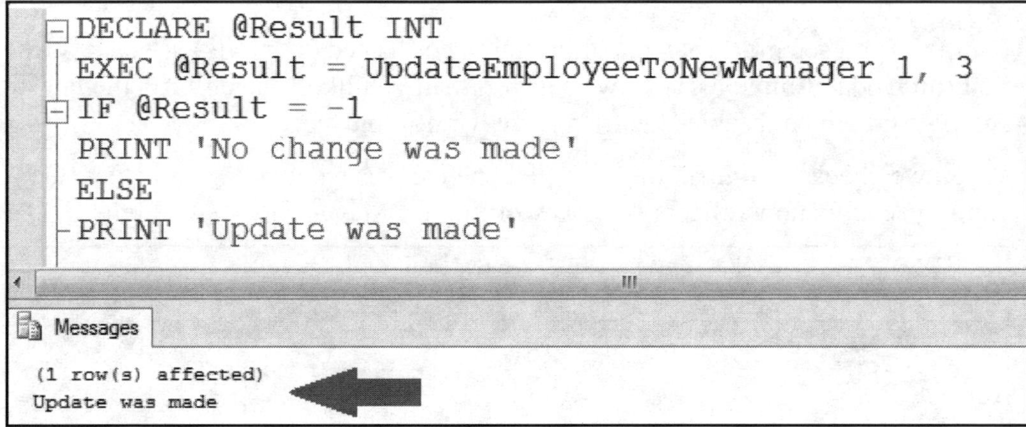

Figure 6.26 Since EmpID 1 is changed back to Manager 3, the sproc returns a 1 to the calling code.

Let's test our sproc with an employee who doesn't exist (EmpID 99). The confirmation message confirms that "No change was made", so our sproc and calling code are working as expected (see Figure 6.27).

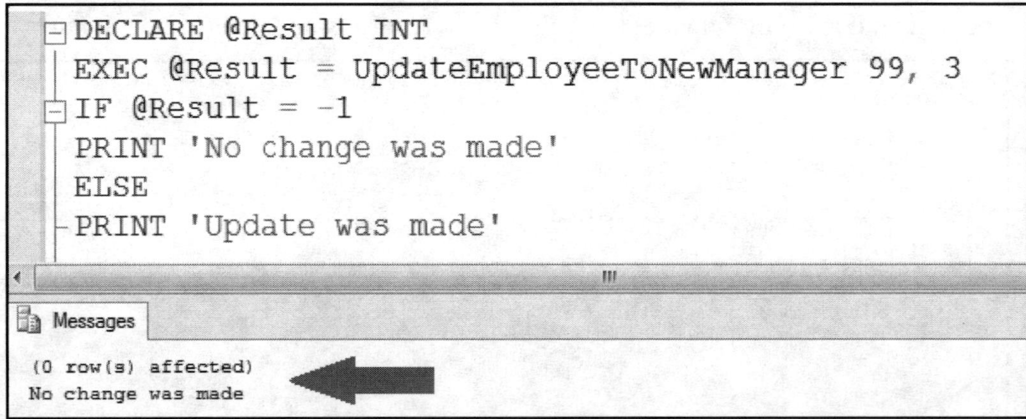

Figure 6.27 There is no EmpID 99, so no records are updated and the sproc returns a -1.

Our next example uses this simple aggregate query (see Figure 6.28) which returns a scalar result. The result shows us that it counts 16 employee records for LocationID 1.

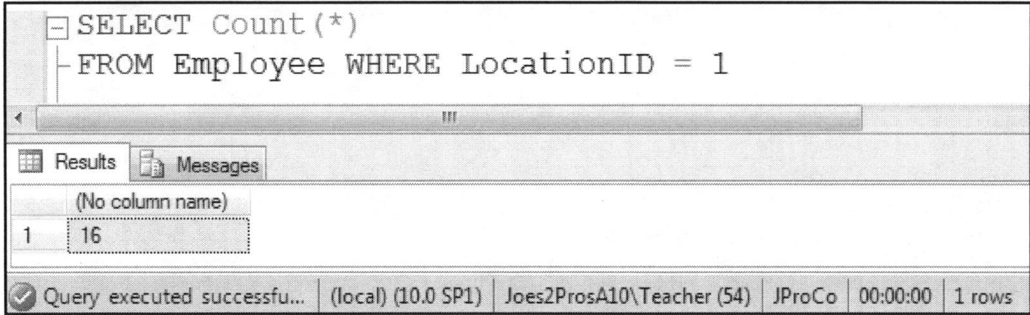

Figure 6.28 This simple aggregrated query returns a scalar result.

Let's declare a variable called @Total to capture the output from this aggregate query. Set the variable equal to the count. For example, in this case the record count is 16, so the value of the variable here would be equal to 16.

```
DECLARE @Total int
SELECT @Total = Count(*)
FROM Employee WHERE LocationID = 1
```

Messages

Command(s) completed successfully.

Figure 6.29 This code captures the value of 16 into the @Total variable.

The variable has been created and is capturing the amount from the aggregate query. However, in order to do something further with the result (e.g., print or display the result; provide the result as input to another function; etc.), we would need to add some more code.

Using Return Values

Let's put the code of our current query (from Figure 6.29) inside a new stored procedure, CountSeattleEmployees. Let's also add a RETURN statement so our calling code can capture the value of the @Total variable (see Figure 6.30 on next page).

After creating the new sproc, let's execute it (see Figure 6.31).

```
CREATE PROC CountSeattleEmployees
AS
    DECLARE @Total int
    SELECT @Total = Count(*)
    FROM Employee WHERE LocationID = 1
    RETURN @Total
GO
```

Messages

Command(s) completed successfully.

Figure 6.30 This code adds a RETURN statement to our stored procedure, CountSeattleEmployees.

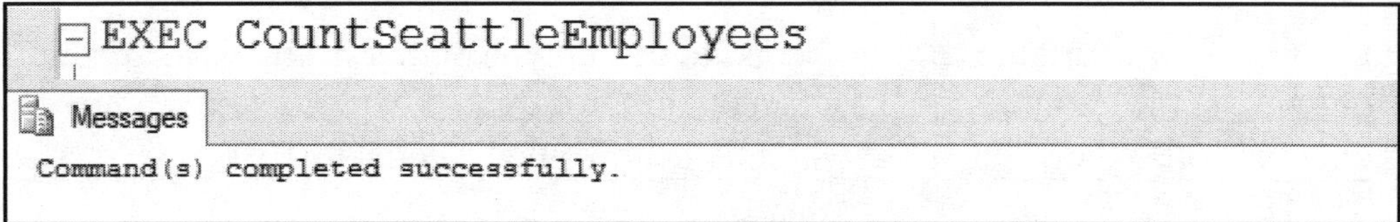
EXEC CountSeattleEmployees
Messages
Command(s) completed successfully.

Figure 6.31 This code executes our new stored procedure, CountSeattleEmployees.

Recall that the RETURN statement simply returns the result of the stored procedure to the calling code behind the scenes. Here (Figure 6.31) it captures and returns the value of @Total, but we don't see any evidence of this because the calling code doesn't include any code which utilizes the handoff.

Let's modify our calling code to employ the information provided by the RETURN statement. We will declare a new variable called @SeattleCount and have it contain the return value from the sproc (CountSeattleEmployees). At this point, there are many things we can do with this value. Let's use a SELECT statement in order to display the value to the Results tab (see Figure 6.32).

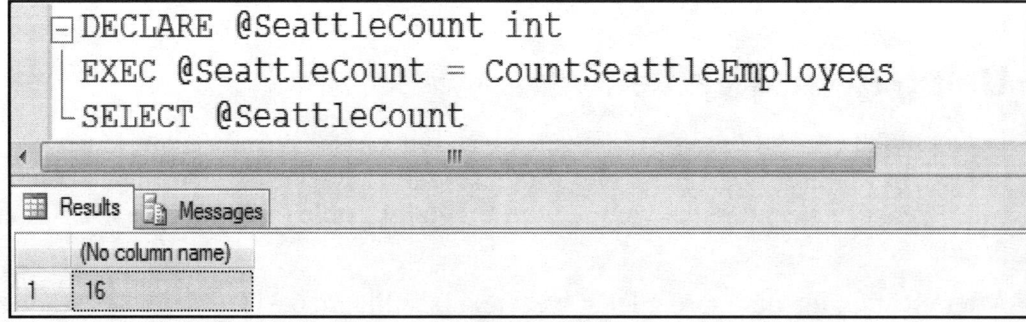
DECLARE @SeattleCount int
EXEC @SeattleCount = CountSeattleEmployees
SELECT @SeattleCount
Results
Messages
(No column name)
1
16

Figure 6.32 This code shows us the scalar value 16, which is the count of Seattle employees.

Let's turn to the query currently contained in our sproc, CountSeattleEmployees. Let's change the LocationID value to 2, in order to see the count of Boston employees. We will capture the count into the variable (@Total) and then display the result to the Messages tab using a PRINT command (see Figure 6.33).

```
DECLARE @Total int
SELECT @Total = Count(*)
FROM Employee WHERE LocationID = 2
PRINT @Total
```

Messages

2

Figure 6.33 This code shows us the scalar value 2, which is the count of Boston employees.

Notice that this query relies on a hardcoded value to determine which location's employee records to select. If we can modify this query to be more flexible, then we can parameterize our stored procedure and allow it to return records for any location we designate.

We will declare a new variable (@LocID) to store the LocationID value. By substituting the hardcoded value in the predicate with the variable, we can change the query output without having to alter the code inside the query. Observe that, since the variable @LocID is currently set to 2, identical results are seen in Figures 6.33 and 6.34.

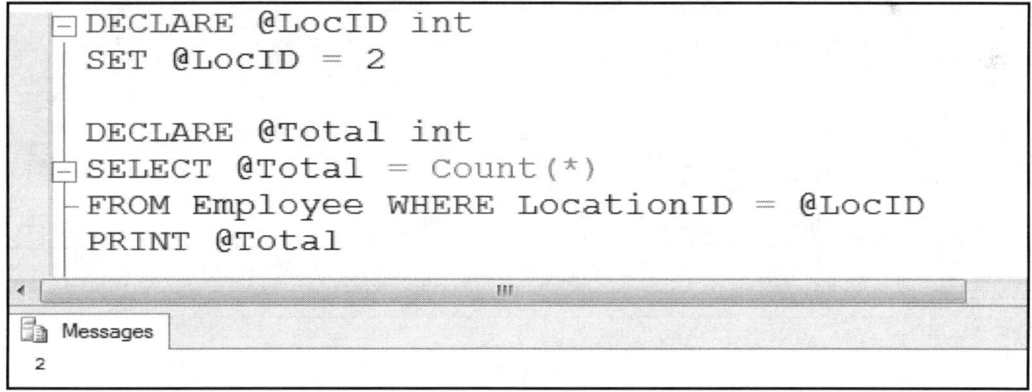

DECLARE @LocID int
SET @LocID = 2
DECLARE @Total int
SELECT @Total = Count(*)
FROM Employee WHERE LocationID = @LocID
PRINT @Total
Messages
2

Figure 6.34 This query shows the number of employees from LocationID 2 by using a variable.

Now we're ready to build a parameterized stored procedure based on this query. Our query is able to work with all current and future JProCo locations, so we will name the sproc CountEmployeesByLocation. The variable @LocationID will receive the parameter passed in by the calling code. Rather than printing the value of @Total, we will use a RETURN statement to return the result to whomever is going to execute this sproc (i.e., the calling code) (see Figure 6.35).

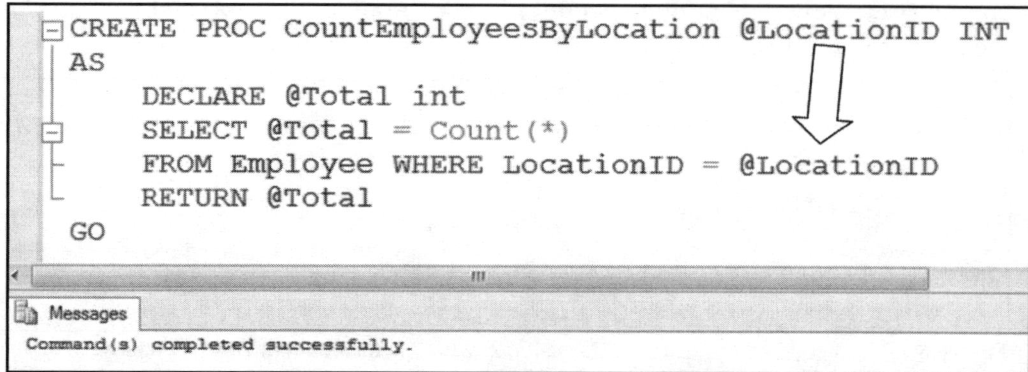
CREATE PROC CountEmployeesByLocation @LocationID INT
AS
DECLARE @Total int
SELECT @Total = Count(*)
FROM Employee WHERE LocationID = @LocationID
RETURN @Total
GO
Messages
Command(s) completed successfully.

Figure 6.35 Instead of printing the output as a message, we'll return the output to the calling code.

Let's write our calling code and test it with our new parameterized sproc, CountEmployeesByLocation. We've designed our sproc to be flexible and location neutral. Let's write our calling code from the perspective of an analyst or DBA working in one of the regional offices. Rather than handling data for all of the locations, the Spokane analyst will be reporting only Spokane data. The same is true for Boston, and so forth. The calling code will pass in the value of the LocationID as a parameter, will capture the sproc result into a variable *@CityCount*, and will use a SELECT statement to show the output (Figures 6.36).

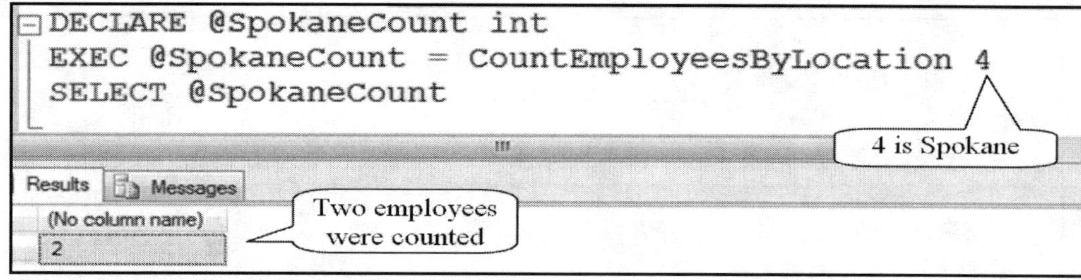
DECLARE @SpokaneCount int
EXEC @SpokaneCount = CountEmployeesByLocation 4
SELECT @SpokaneCount
4 is Spokane
Results
Messages
(No column name)
2
Two employees were counted

Figure 6.36 We are passing in the value 4, which is the LocationID for Spokane.

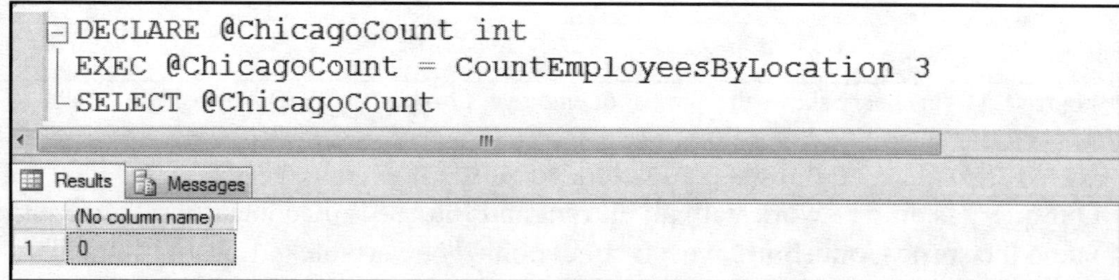
DECLARE @ChicagoCount int
EXEC @ChicagoCount = CountEmployeesByLocation 3
SELECT @ChicagoCount
Results
Messages
(No column name)
1
0

Figure 6.37 The count of employees at the Chicago location is 0.

Using Default Values

Calling this stored procedure and getting a return result works quite well, as long as we pass it the required parameter. Notice that we get an error message from SQL Server if we do not pass in a parameter (see Figure 6.38).

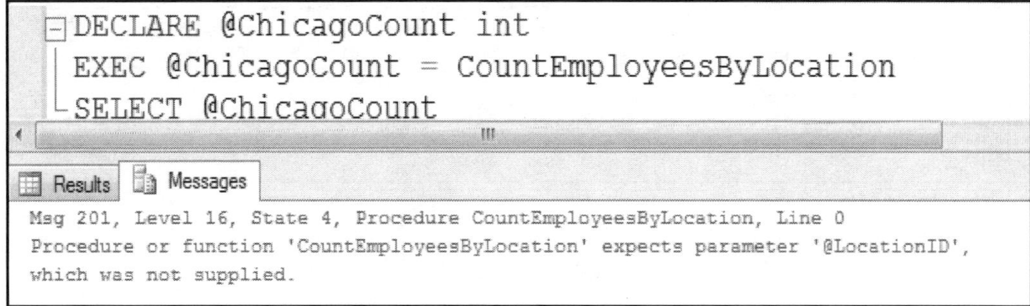

DECLARE @ChicagoCount int
EXEC @ChicagoCount = CountEmployeesByLocation
SELECT @ChicagoCount
Results
Messages
Msg 201, Level 16, State 4, Procedure CountEmployeesByLocation, Line 0
Procedure or function 'CountEmployeesByLocation' expects parameter '@LocationID',
which was not supplied.

Figure 6.38 SQL Server returns an error message if no parameter is passed to the stored procedure.

Now let's return to a more typical scenario, where we assume the role of a JProCo DBA responsible for reporting data for the entire company. While we run reports for every JProCo location, most of the time we run reports involving data for just the Seattle office. Therefore, we would like the ability to have the CountEmployeesByLocation report assume the default location should be Seattle (LocationID 1), unless we specify otherwise.

The code below shows the slight adjustment to our current sproc which will supply 1 as the default value for LocationID (see Figure 6.39). Compare this code with our current sproc (last seen in Figure 6.35) and notice that "=1" is the only additional code needed to specify the default value of 1.

```
ALTER PROC CountEmployeesByLocation @LocationID INT = 1
AS
    DECLARE @Total int
    SELECT @Total = Count(*)
    FROM Employee WHERE LocationID = @LocationID
    RETURN @Total
GO
```

Messages

```
Command(s) completed successfully.
```

Figure 6.39 The default is Location 1, which will be used if you don't pass in another parameter.

Let's call on our newly revised sproc to see the default value in action. Our calling code is essentially the same as the statement which failed earlier (see Figure 6.38), except that the city name has been genericized. When we run our calling code, we see the expected result of 16, since there are 16 employees in the default location (Seattle) (see Figure 6.40).

Figure 6.40 No parameter value was explicitly supplied so the default of 1 was used.

The default value is used when no parameter value is supplied. Providing a parameter value will override the default and run the sproc for the location you've designated. When we pass in a 4, the sproc returns the count of employees in the Spokane office (see Figure 6.41).

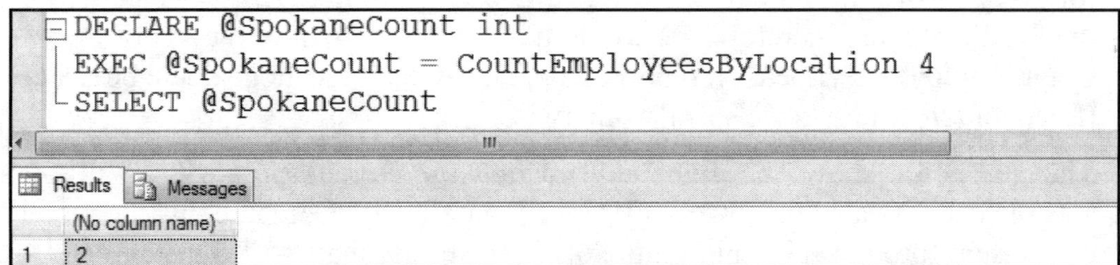

Figure 6.41 Supplying a parameter supersedes the default value and causes it to not be used.

Omitting a parameter implicitly causes the sproc to use the default value. We may also choose to use the keyword DEFAULT in our calling code. It achieves the same result, yet explicitly supplying DEFAULT makes your code more readable (see Figure 6.42).

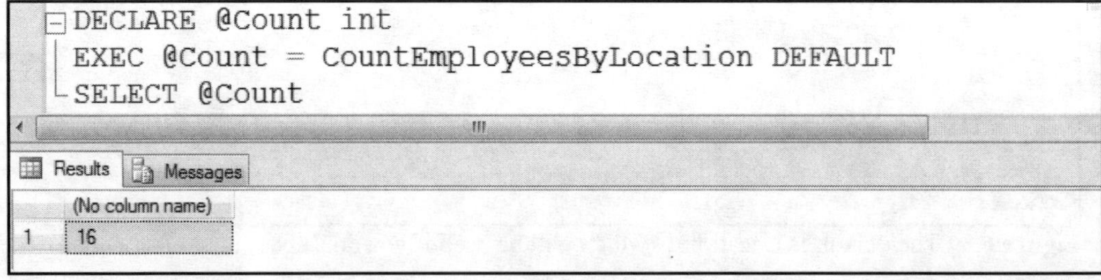

Figure 6.42 An alternate way to show the count of employees in the DEFAULT location (Seattle).

Lab 6.2: Return Values

Lab Prep: Before you can begin the lab, you must have SQL Server installed and have run the script SQLProgrammingChapter6.2Setup.sql.

Skill Check 1: Create a scalar stored procedure named CountEmployeesByCityName which returns the total count of employees based on the city name. *Hint:* You will have to join two tables to get this done. Test your stored procedure by passing in the varchar value of "Spokane."

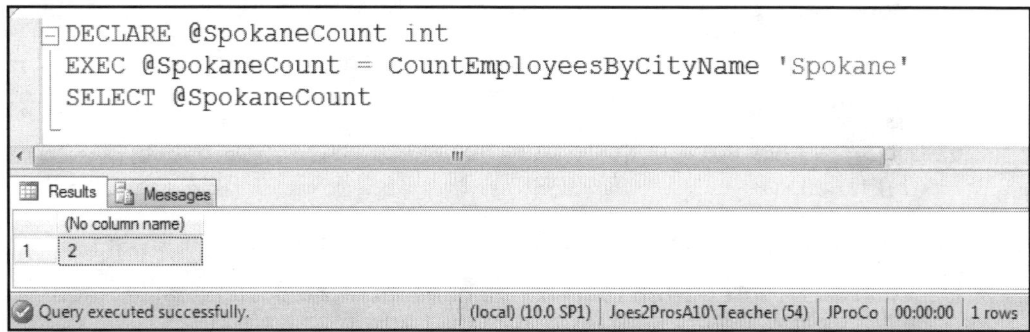

Figure 6.43 Skill Check 1.

Skill Check 2: Alter CountEmployeesByCityName so that it defaults to Seattle. Test your stored procedure by using the DEFAULT keyword.

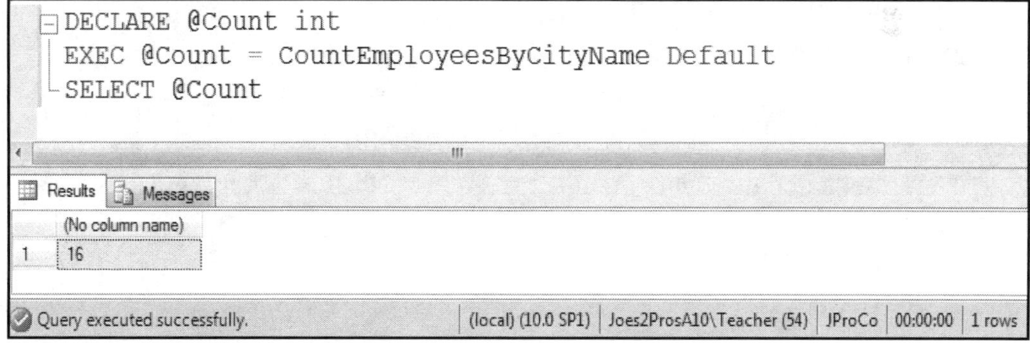

Figure 6.44 Skill Check 2 result.

Answer Code: The T-SQL code to this lab can be found in the downloadable files in a file named Lab6.2_ReturnValues.sql.

Return Values - Points to Ponder

1. Stored procedures can run code, return a value, or do both.
2. Stored procedures can invoke all types of statements including data definition language (DDL), data manipulation language (DML) statements, and even data control language (DCL) and transaction control language (TCL) statements.
3. You may return a status value to a calling procedure or batch to indicate success or failure (and the reason for failure).
4. Stored procedures can display tables, but they can return only one value.
5. Return values are optional and you do not need to capture them during execution.
6. Return values are often used to indicate a status, such as 1 if successful and 0 if failed.
7. Once a return is executed, the stored procedure is done running.
8. To define a sproc which accepts input parameters, declare one or more variables as parameters in the CREATE PROC statement.
9. If you declare a default parameter value, then supplying a parameter becomes optional. (It is not required, but you are generally free to supply a parameter if you wish. A sproc having a default value will not prevent you from supplying a parameter.)
10. There are two ways to utilize a default parameter:
    a. No value is passed in.
    b. The DEFAULT keyword is passed in.
11. To set a default value, include the syntax "= *value*" after the parameter declaration.

Output Parameters

RETURN statements are a great way to return data from stored procedure to a single variable in your calling code. However, you will encounter programming situations where you need a sproc to simultaneously return data to multiple variables. In order to accomplish this, you will need to use **output parameters**.

Below is a query which returns the count of employees from Location 1, as well as the hire date for the employee who's been at Location 1 the longest. When we run this query, we see there are 16 employees, and the first Location 1 employee was hired April 1, 1989 (see Figure 6.45).

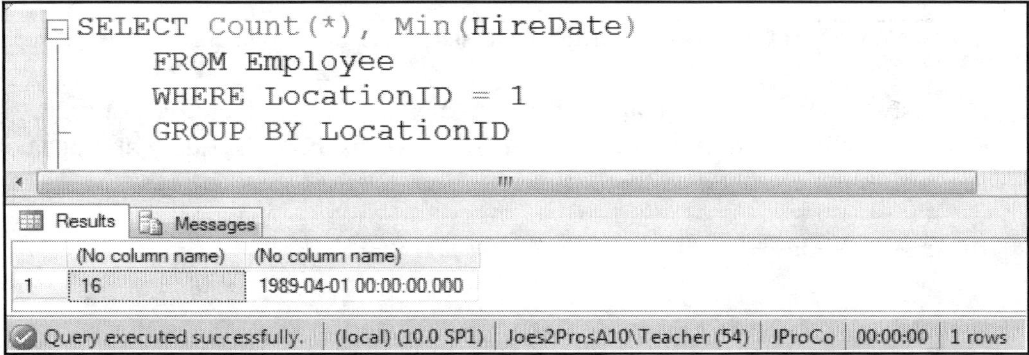

Figure 6.45 The count of Seattle employees (16) and the earliest employee's hire date (4/1/1989).

We want to build this query into a flexible stored procedure which returns data for any location you specify. We will declare a variable (@LocationID) to contain the LocationID you provide (as illustrated in Figure 6.46). You won't need to make changes to the sproc or the query – your location-specific data will be returned simply based upon the parameter value you pass into the sproc.

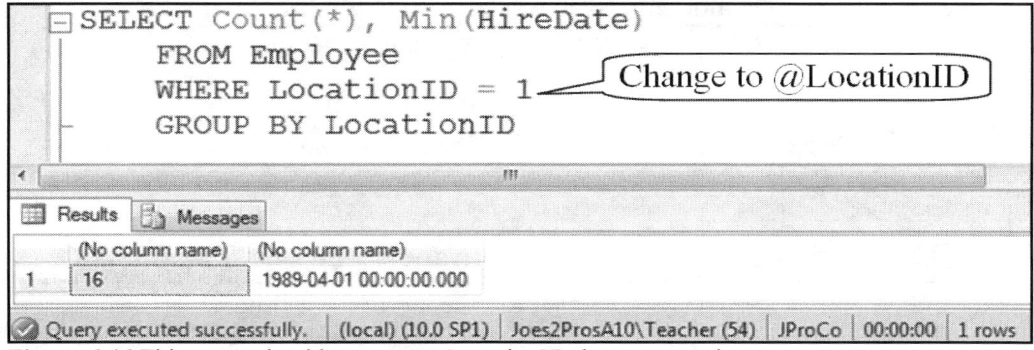

Figure 6.46 This query should accept any LocationID that you pass in.

The statement below (see Figure 6.47) builds our new parameterized sproc named GetEmployeeCountAndFirstHire. We have swapped out the hardcoded value (1) for the new variable (@LocationID).

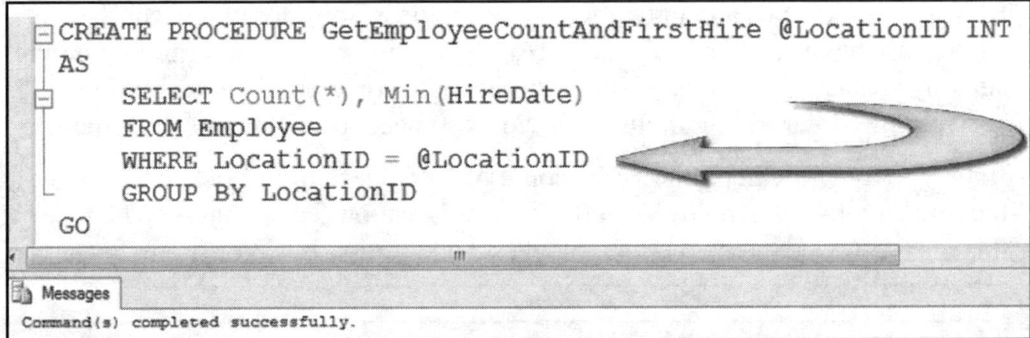

Figure 6.47 Add CREATE PROCEDURE and GO statements to turn your query into this sproc.

Let's test our new sproc by passing in the value of 1. Notice that this result is identical to that shown in Figure 6.46. In other words, both the query and our new sproc return the correct data for Location 1, Seattle (see Figure 6.48).

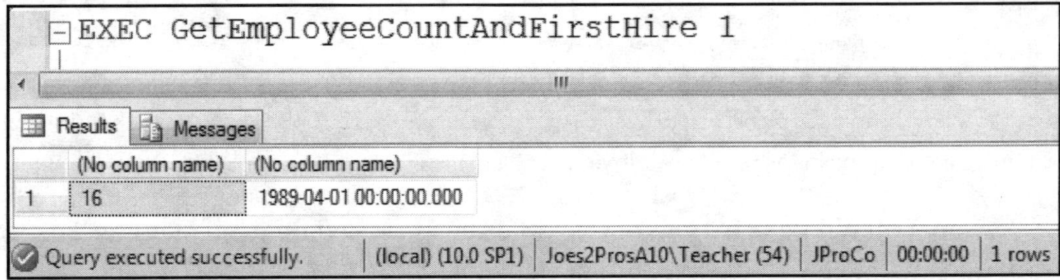

Figure 6.48 We invoke the sproc and pass in a value of 1, meaning the LocationID is 1.

Passing in a LocationID of 4 shows us there are two employees in the Spokane office, and the most senior employee was hired in 1995 (see Figure 6.49).

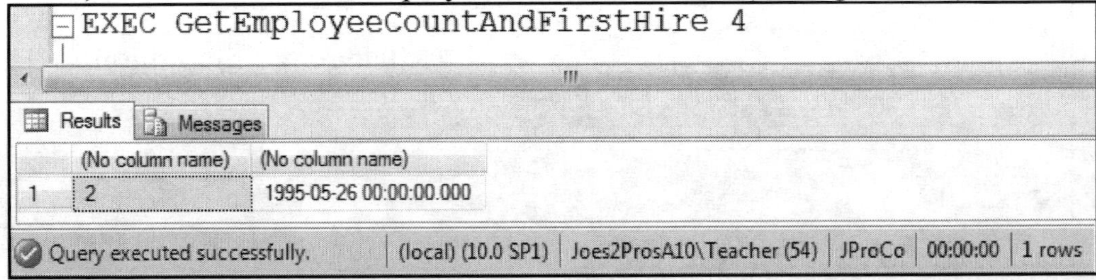

Figure 6.49 This code executes the sproc GetEmployeeCountAndFirstHire for Location 4.

Our next goal is to re-work our sproc to include output parameters. While we haven't yet seen or worked with output parameters, we know we want multiple values to be returned to the calling code by the stored procedure.

Currently our calling code consists of just an EXEC statement (Figures 6.48-6.49). We know we will need to expand our calling code. We also need two variables to capture the results from the sproc execution:

@Ct (integer) will contain the count of the employee records

@MinDate (datetime) will contain the earliest hiredate

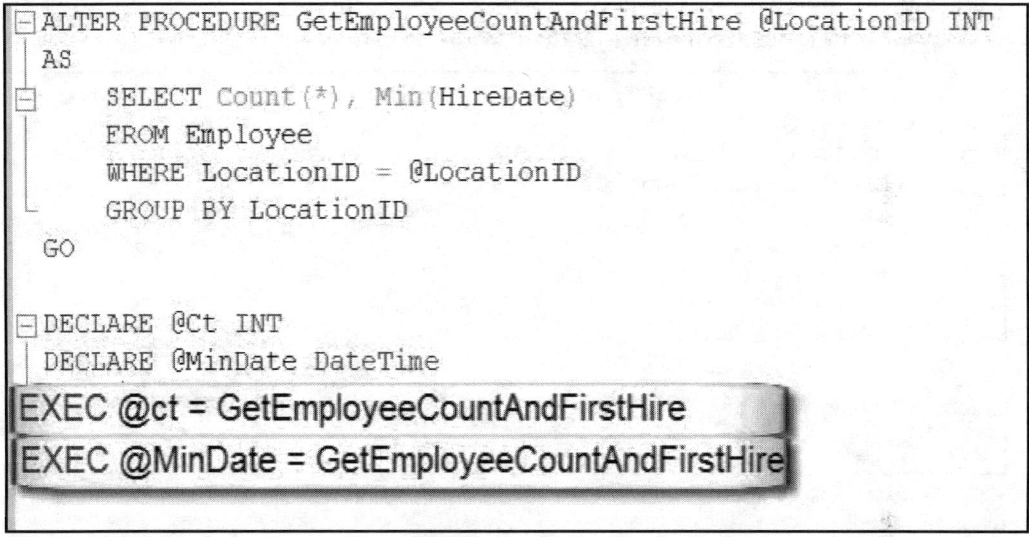

```
ALTER PROCEDURE GetEmployeeCountAndFirstHire @LocationID INT
AS
    SELECT Count(*), Min(HireDate)
    FROM Employee
    WHERE LocationID = @LocationID
    GROUP BY LocationID
GO

DECLARE @Ct INT
DECLARE @MinDate DateTime
EXEC @ct = GetEmployeeCountAndFirstHire
EXEC @MinDate = GetEmployeeCountAndFirstHire
```

Figure 6.50 A mockup of our goal: we want our calling code to receive two values from our sproc.

With a RETURN statement, we are restricted to getting back just one item at a time (either @Ct or @MinDate). But with output parameters, we can simultaneously retrieve as many values as we like.

Creating Output Parameters

With what we've learned so far, we know we can only use one return statement per stored procedure. To help illustrate this point, we've expanded our current sproc in an effort to make it produce our desired outcome. A variable has been declared for each of our required data points. However, as long as we utilize a RETURN statement, we will be limited to only capturing one value per execution of the sproc. It is not possible to use a RETURN statement within a single sproc to supply all of our needed data to our calling code (see Figure 6.51).

This code cannot achieve our goal. It will get us the @LocCount but leaves us with no way to get the result of @MinDate.

```
ALTER PROCEDURE GetEmployeeCountAndFirstHire @LocationID INT
AS
    DECLARE @MinDate DATETIME
    DECLARE @LocCount INT
    SELECT @LocCount = Count(*), @MinDate  = Min(HireDate)
    FROM Employee
    WHERE LocationID = @LocationID
    GROUP BY LocationID
    RETURN @LocCount
GO
```

```
Messages
Command(s) completed successfully.
```

Figure 6.51 This sproc cannot achieve our goal: it is only capable of returning one of our two required values.

With output parameters, you are allowed to return as many values as you need from the stored procedure. Below we have set up the calling code to capture two values from one execution of the sproc (see Figure 6.52). The OUTPUT keyword is the hint that specifies that values populating these variables will come from the stored procedure. ***Don't run this code yet since our stored procedure is not yet ready for this syntax!***

```
DECLARE @Ct INT
DECLARE @MinDate DATETIME
EXEC @Min = GetEmployeeCountAndFirstHire 1, @Ct OUTPUT, @MinDate OUTPUT
```

Figure 6.52 This is our revised calling code. Output parameters allow you to return multiple values from a stored procedure.

With our calling code perfected and ready to use (shown in Figure 6.52 – it also appears in Figure 6.54), our next task is to modify our sproc accordingly.

Notice that we have added the two parameters, their data types, and specified them as output (see Figure 6.53).

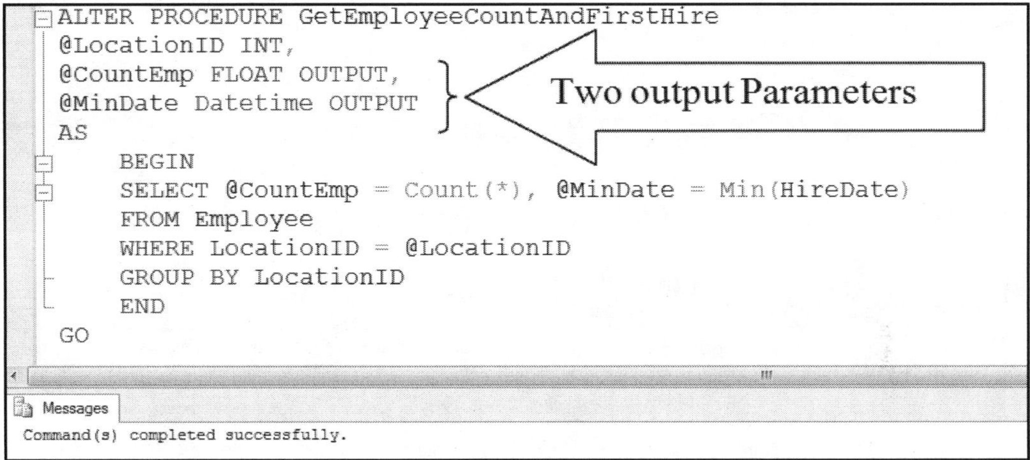
ALTER PROCEDURE GetEmployeeCountAndFirstHire
@LocationID INT,
@CountEmp FLOAT OUTPUT,
@MinDate Datetime OUTPUT
AS
BEGIN
SELECT @CountEmp = Count(*), @MinDate = Min(HireDate)
FROM Employee
WHERE LocationID = @LocationID
GROUP BY LocationID
END
GO
Two output Parameters
Messages
Command(s) completed successfully.

Figure 6.53 In order to modify our current sproc, run all of the code you see here.

Using Output Parameters

With output variables you can capture multiple values from one stored procedure.

Let's test our sproc to see whether our calling code can capture and use the expected values. Run all of the code you see here (Figure 6.54) to call the sproc and capture the output data.

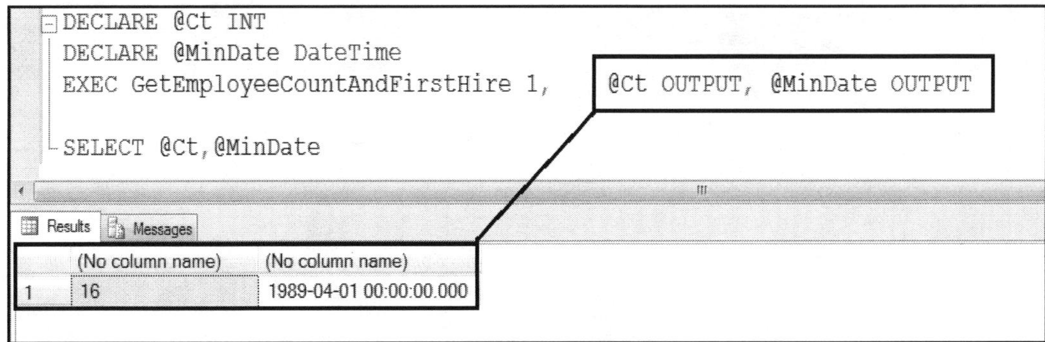
DECLARE @Ct INT
DECLARE @MinDate DateTime
EXEC GetEmployeeCountAndFirstHire 1,
@Ct OUTPUT, @MinDate OUTPUT
SELECT @Ct,@MinDate
Results
Messages
(No column name)
(No column name)
1
16
1989-04-01 00:00:00.000

Figure 6.54 We have simultaneously captured two variables from our stored procedure.

The values supplied to our calling code may be used by other applications (e.g., a front-end application, a web page, etc.). Here the values are included in expressions (see Figure 6.55).

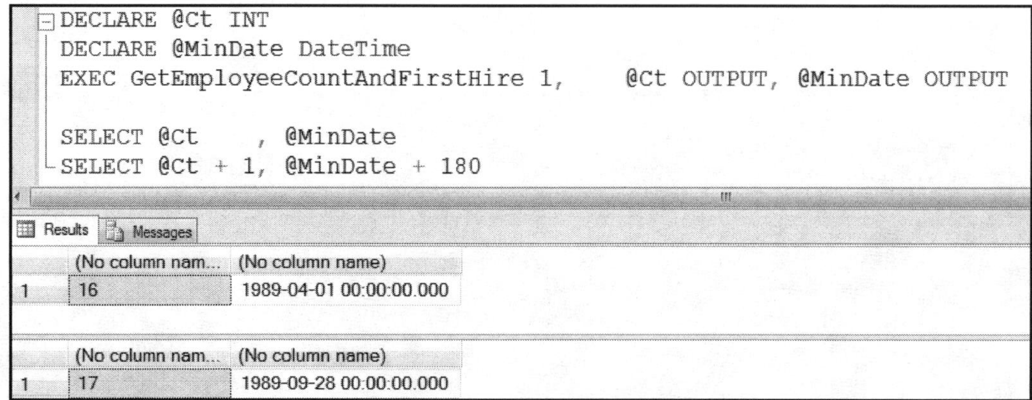
DECLARE @Ct INT
DECLARE @MinDate DateTime
EXEC GetEmployeeCountAndFirstHire 1, @Ct OUTPUT, @MinDate OUTPUT
SELECT @Ct , @MinDate
SELECT @Ct + 1, @MinDate + 180
Results
Messages
(No column nam... (No column name)
1 16 1989-04-01 00:00:00.000
(No column nam... (No column name)
1 17 1989-09-28 00:00:00.000

Figure 6.55 The values supplied to our calling application may be used in expressions or supplied to another application.

Let's modify our sproc again to add a third output parameter @MaxDate, which will capture the hire date of the newest employee (see Figure 6.56).

```
ALTER PROCEDURE GetEmployeeCountAndFirstHire
@LocationID INT,
@CountEmp FLOAT OUTPUT,
@MinDate Datetime OUTPUT,
@MaxDate Datetime OUTPUT
AS
    BEGIN
    SELECT @CountEmp = Count(*), @MinDate = Min(HireDate), @MaxDate = MAX(HireDate)
    FROM Employee
    WHERE LocationID = @LocationID
    GROUP BY LocationID
    END
GO
```

Messages

Command(s) completed successfully.

Figure 6.56 This code adds a third variable @MaxDate to capture data from our stored procedure.

Our calling code runs the sproc for LocationID 4 (Spokane). There are currently two employees in the Spokane office. The employee who has been there the longest was hired in May 1995. The most recently hired person in the Spokane office was hired in November 2001 (see Figure 6.57).

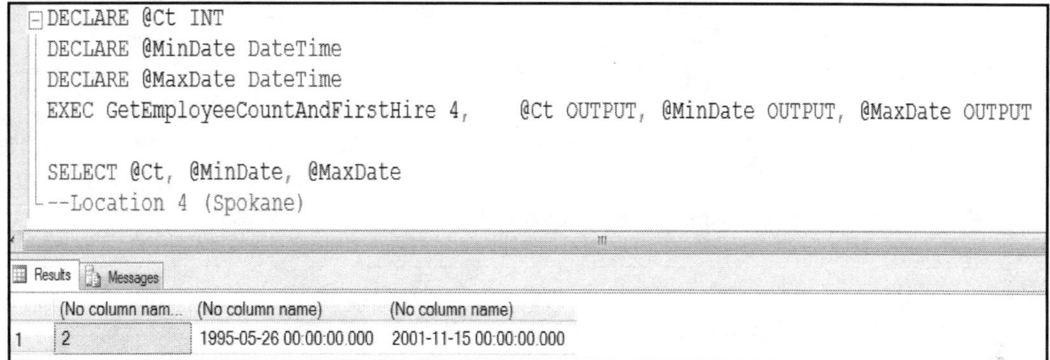

```
DECLARE @Ct INT
DECLARE @MinDate DateTime
DECLARE @MaxDate DateTime
EXEC GetEmployeeCountAndFirstHire 4,    @Ct OUTPUT, @MinDate OUTPUT, @MaxDate OUTPUT

SELECT @Ct, @MinDate, @MaxDate
--Location 4 (Spokane)
```


	(No column nam...	(No column name)	(No column name)
1	2	1995-05-26 00:00:00.000	2001-11-15 00:00:00.000

Figure 6.57 Our calling code now gets three values from our stored procedure.

Lab 6.3: Output Parameters

Lab Prep: Before you can begin the lab, you must have SQL Server installed and have run the SQLProgrammingChapter6.3Setup.sql script.

Skill Check 1: Create a stored procedure called GetProductCountAndAvgPrice that takes a varchar(100) input parameter called @CategoryID and two output parameters. One output parameter will return the count of the products. The other output parameter will return a value (Money data type) for the Average Price. Run and test your code with the code shown below (see Figure 6.58).

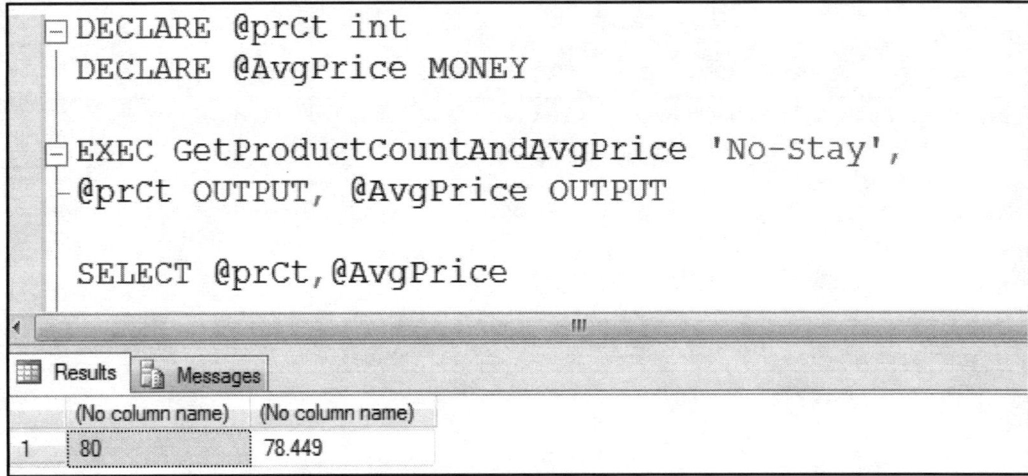

Figure 6.58 Skill Check 1 creates a stored procedure with multiple output parameters.

Answer Code: The T-SQL code to this lab can be found in the downloadable files in a file named Lab6.3_OutputParameters.sql.

Output Parameters - Points to Ponder

1. Stored procedures can use a mixture of RETURN statements and output parameters to provide data to the calling code.
2. Since they are always stored in variables, output parameters persist after procedure execution.
3. To use output parameters, you must specify the OUTPUT keyword in both the CREATE PROC and EXECUTE statements. If you don't specify a direction, then INPUT is used.
4. If the EXEC statement is missing the OUTPUT keyword, the sproc still runs but does not return the value.
5. A stored procedure may include up to 2100 parameters.
6. The RETURN statement can pass information from a sproc just like output parameters, but it is limited to one value per sproc. You can have many output parameters.
7. A stored procedure can accept parameters, produce a result set, return code, and send output parameters to the calling application.
8. SQL Server comes with many pre-defined stored procedures (called system stored procedures) for common tasks, system stored procedures begin with sp_.
9. Do not begin stored procedures that you create with "sp_." Use another unique prefix that will allow you to distinguish system stored procedures from the ones you create.
10. Common system stored procedures include:
    a. sp_helpdb returns information about databases on the server.
    b. sp_help returns a list of objects for the current database.
    c. sp_helpindex obj_name returns a list of indexes for the object.
11. You can only create a stored procedure in the current database context; therefore, you cannot include the USE *DatabaseName* statement inside a stored procedure.
12. If you execute a stored procedure that calls another stored procedure, the called stored procedure can access all objects created by the first (calling) stored procedure.
13. If you have permission to execute a stored procedure, you don't need permissions to the underlying tables that the stored procedure uses or modifies.

Chapter Glossary

Aggregate query: AVG( ), COUNT( ), MAX( ), MIN( ), SUM( ) (these are covered in Volume 2, *SQL Queries Joes 2 Pros*).
ALTER PROC(EDURE): statement used to revise an existing sproc.
CREATE PROC(EDURE): statement used to create a new sproc.
DEFAULT: optional keyword used when executing a parameterized sproc and you wish to explicitly specify that the default value will be used.
DROP PROC(EDURE): statement used to remove a sproc from the database.
EXEC(UTE) PROC(EDURE): command which runs the code contained within the stored procedure.
Materialized view: indexing a view causes the view to be persistently materialized and stored in the database. In other words, the view contains a physical copy of the view data (including computations associated with joins, aggregate queries, etc.) for quicker retrieval.
OUTPUT: keyword hint which specifies that values populating the variable(s) will come from the stored procedure.
Output parameters: allow you to return multiple values from a stored procedure. Since they are always stored in variables, output parameters persist after procedure execution.
Parameters: values which you pass into a sproc's variables at runtime.
Parameterized stored procedure: a stored procedure which requires values to be input to its variable(s) at runtime.
PRINT: a statement used to print the result of a stored procedure's execution.
RETURN: a statement used to pass to the calling code the result of a stored procedure's execution.
Scalar result: consists of a single value.
Scalar stored procedure: a sproc whose result consists of a single value.
sp_depends: a system-supplied stored procedure which returns all dependent objects for the database object specified.
sp_help: returns a list of objects for the current database.
sp_helpdb: returns information about databases on the server.
sp_helpindex obj_name: returns a list of indexes for the object.
Stored procedure: commonly referred to by the shorthand **sproc**. A reusable batch of code containing one or more statements (DML, DDL, TCL, or DCL). A sproc caches it execution plan when it is compiled, thereby providing a performance advantage.

Chapter Six - Review Quiz

1.) Which one of the following is not a way to invoke the default parameter value?
O a. EXEC @Count = CountEmployeesByLocation null.
O b. EXEC @Count = CountEmployeesByLocation.
O c. EXEC @Count = CountEmployeesByLocation default.

2.) You have permissions to execute a stored procedure called usp_A. Yesterday the SQL admin altered this stored procedure to call on usp_B. You do not have any permission on usp_B. The next time you call usp_A, what will the result be?
O a. You can call usp_A but it will always fail.
O b. You can no longer call usp_A.
O c. You can call usp_A but will only get null values back from usp_B.
O d. Usp_A will continue to work for you, just as it did before.

3.) Your stored procedure named GetEmployeeByCity has a default parameter of 'Seattle'. When you execute the stored procedure, you supply "Boston" as the parameter. What is the result of your execute statement.
O a. Seattle will be used.
O b. Boston will be used.
O c. You will get an error message.

4.) You want to create all your user-defined stored procedures with the same prefix. You want to make sure your naming convention does not impose any unnecessary performance hit. Which prefix will achieve this?
O a. Usp_*ProcName*
O b. sp_*ProcName*

5.) What is true about the type of SQL statements you can include in a stored procedure?
O a. You can put only DML statement in a stored procedure.
O b. You can put only DDL statement in a stored procedure.
O c. You can put only TCL statement in a stored procedure.
O d. You can put only DCL statement in a stored procedure.
O e. You can put any type of SQL statement in a store procedure.

Answer Key

1.) a 2.) d 3.) b 4.) a 5.) e

Bug Catcher Game

To play the Bug Catcher game, run BugCatcher_Chapter6_StoredProcedures.pps from the BugCatcher folder of the companion files located at www.Joes2Pros.com.

Chapter 7. Stored Procedure Techniques

As a child, the longest commute our family took was about 100 miles; it was to visit our grandparents in Skagit County. It seemed like a long drive and it took more preparation to get the family into the car than for a simple trip to the grocery store. As we would pull out of our driveway and onto Orchard Street, my father would point the car towards the nearest freeway entrance to start our long journey. My mother would diligently ask, "How are we doing on fuel?" My father would glance down at the fuel gauge to get an accurate answer and then reply.

Features like the steering wheel or brakes have a direct affect on the performance and handling of the car. The fuel gauge has no effect at all on how the car runs. Still it is very handy for knowing what is going on and making decisions on what to do next. There are some features in stored procedures that will have no effect on how they run but will be very handy to let you know what is happening or what has happened. This chapter will explore some of the most used options and techniques around stored procedures.

READER NOTE: *In order to follow along with the examples in the first section of Chapter 7, please run the setup script SQLProgrammingChapter7.0Setup.sql. The setup scripts for this book are posted at Joes2Pros.com.*

Stored Procedure Execution Options

SQL Server offers several types of features and built-in options which can make your stored procedures more robust. Some of these items belong inside the stored procedure code, while others help the calling code which executes the stored procedure. This chapter will explore some built-in features you can use in conjunction with stored procedures.

Capturing Stored Procedure Return Data

When using a stored procedure to insert a new record into a table, you may also need to have the sproc return a status or result to the calling code. For example, if your table contains a field with an identity counter, you may want to see what the next ID value will be. In this section, we will use the SCOPE_IDENTITY( ) function to accomplish these tasks.

SCOPE_IDENTITY( )

One dictionary definition for **scope** is "range of operation." In computer programming, the term **scope** pertains to the accessibility of items (e.g., variables) within a batch of code (or module) from other other parts of the program. Think of a scope as all the things that happen within the running of a batch of code, such as a stored procedure or a function. If two different stored procedures run simultaneously, each will have its own scope. The same stored procedure run successively (i.e., run twice in a row) will have a separate scope for each run.

Let's create a sproc to add new records to the Supplier table of the JProCo database. We only need to provide two values (SupplierName, ContactFullName), since SupplierID is an identity field and automatically generates a SupplierID value for each new record. (To learn more about setting the identity property for a field, see Volume 2 (*Beginning SQL Queries Joes 2 Pros*, Chapter 3).)

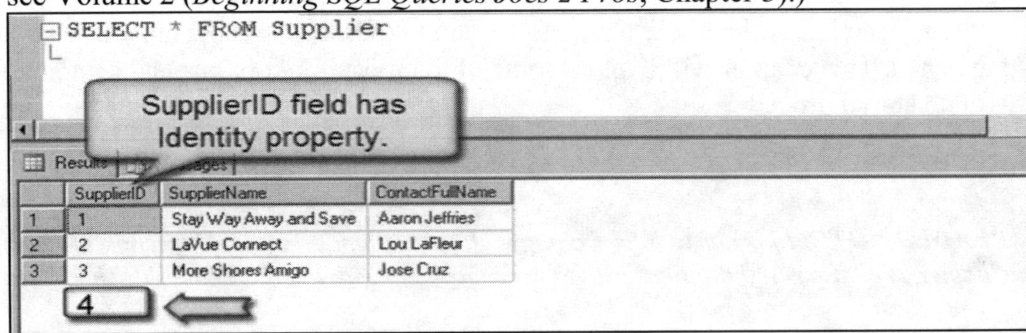

Figure 7.1 SupplierID is an identity field.

The code below creates the parameterized sproc, InsertOneSupplier. We will provide SupplierName and ContactFullName as parameter values to @sName and @sContact, respectively (see Figure 7.2).

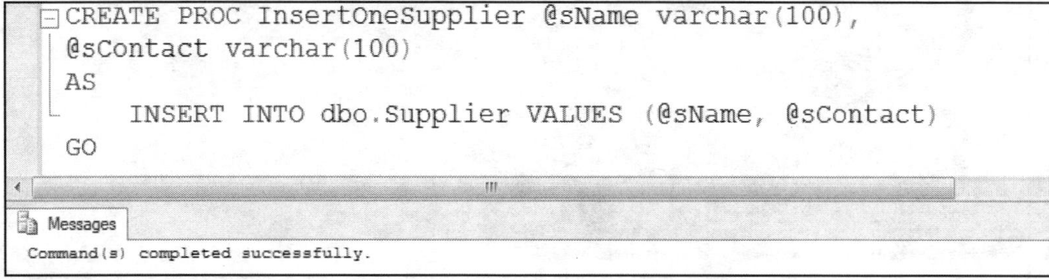

```
CREATE PROC InsertOneSupplier @sName varchar(100),
@sContact varchar(100)
AS
    INSERT INTO dbo.Supplier VALUES (@sName, @sContact)
GO
```

Messages

Command(s) completed successfully.

Figure 7.2 This code creates the InsertOneSupplier stored procedure.

Before executing our newly created sproc, let's look at our Supplier table (SELECT * FROM Supplier). It currently contains three records. When we run our sproc, we expect to create a fourth record for the supplier, White Elephant. We expect the next SupplierID value will be 4 (see Figure 7.3).

Results | Messages

	SupplierID	SupplierName	ContactFullName
1	1	Stay Way Away and Save	Aaron Jeffries
2	2	LaVue Connect	Lou LaFleur
3	3	More Shores Amigo	Jose Cruz

4 |White Elephant |Eric Gilman

Figure 7.3 We will insert "White Elephant" and expect the SupplierID value to be 4.

To insert a fourth record into this table, run the EXEC statement to call the stored procedure by using the following code:

```
EXEC InsertOneSupplier 'White Elephant', 'Eric Gilman'
```

Our sproc appears to have run successfully (see Figure7.4), but we can't know that for certain unless we check the table records (see Figure 7.5).

Figure 7.4 Calling the sproc affected 1 row and we are reasonably sure it was SupplierID 4.

Yes, our SELECT statement shows that SupplierID 4 was indeed created for our new supplier, White Elephant (see Figure 7.5).

```
EXEC InsertOneSupplier 'White Elephant', 'Eric Gilman'

SELECT * FROM Supplier
```

Results | Messages

	SupplierID	SupplierName	ContactFullName
1	1	Stay Way Away and Save	Aaron Jeffries
2	2	LaVue Connect	Lou LaFleur
3	3	More Shores Amigo	Jose Cruz
4	4	White Elephant	Eric Gilman

Figure 7.5 The "White Elephant" record has a SupplierID value of 4.

Our goal is to be able to see the SupplierID value at the time we insert our next supplier record (Fun and Far) by executing the sproc. We would like to capture this value into a variable, which we can use later in our program. *In other words, the goal is to have the sproc capture the value(s) from within its scope and return the value(s) to us.*

Before introducing SCOPE_IDENTITY( ) as a solution, let's first use what we've already learned in order to get this value to display at runtime.

We expect that Fun and Far's SupplierID will be 5 (see Figure 7.6).

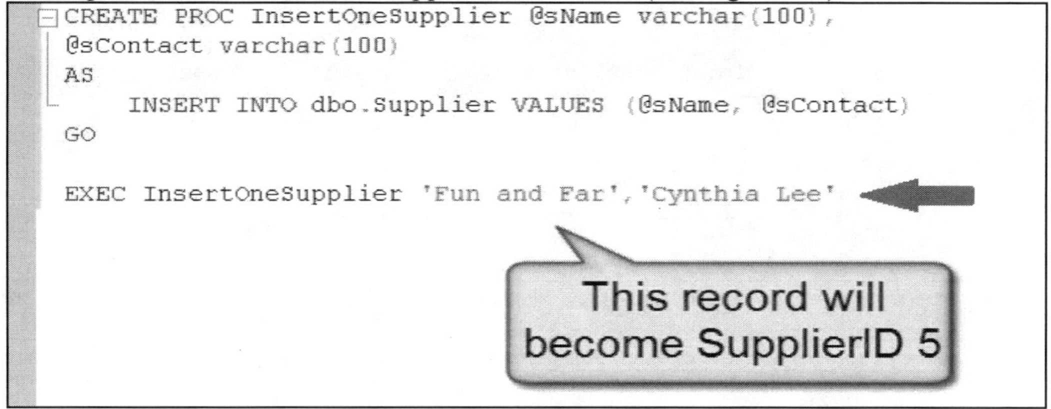
CREATE PROC InsertOneSupplier @sName varchar(100),
@sContact varchar(100)
AS
INSERT INTO dbo.Supplier VALUES (@sName, @sContact)
GO
EXEC InsertOneSupplier 'Fun and Far','Cynthia Lee'
This record will become SupplierID 5

Figure 7.6 When we add this supplier, we want the sproc to show us that it created SupplierID 5.

To accomplish our goal, we will need to add a RETURN statement to the code block of our stored procedure. Our RETURN statement uses the MAX function in order to return the highest SupplierID found in the Supplier table (see Figure 7.7).

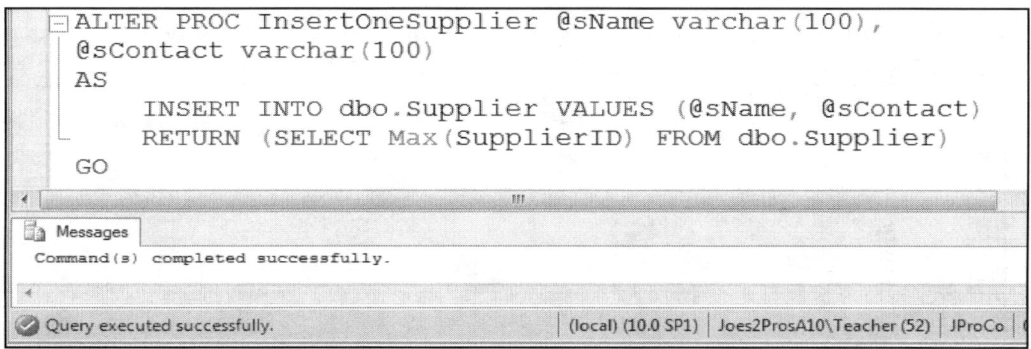
ALTER PROC InsertOneSupplier @sName varchar(100),
@sContact varchar(100)
AS
INSERT INTO dbo.Supplier VALUES (@sName, @sContact)
RETURN (SELECT Max(SupplierID) FROM dbo.Supplier)
GO
Messages
Command(s) completed successfully.
Query executed successfully.
(local) (10.0 SP1)
Joes2ProsA10\Teacher (52)
JProCo

Figure 7.7 Alter the InsertOneSupplier stored procedure to return the newest SupplierID.

After you run the ALTER PROC statement (Figure 7.7), let's run the calling code to execute InsertOneSupplier for Fun and Far (see Figure 7.8).

We need to declare a variable (@SupplierID) to contain the value captured from the stored procedure and print that value to the screen. We expect to get "5" as the result for the newly created SupplierID.

Highlight and run the DECLARE, EXEC, and PRINT statements as one batch (as shown in Figure 7.8). Success! We see the value "5" printed along with the confirmation message (1 row(s) affected) for our inserted record.

```
ALTER PROC InsertOneSupplier @sName varchar(100),
@sContact varchar(100)
AS
    INSERT INTO dbo.Supplier VALUES (@sName, @sContact)
    RETURN (SELECT Max(SupplierID) FROM dbo.Supplier)
GO

DECLARE @SupplierID int
EXEC @SupplierID = InsertOneSupplier 'Fun and Far','Cynthia Lee'
PRINT @SupplierID
```

Messages

```
(1 row(s) affected)
5
```

Figure 7.8 The Max(SupplierID) is returned by the sproc and displayed to the screen.

Let's now turn to the built-in function SCOPE_IDENTITY( ) and see how we can use it to accomplish our goal.

Run all of this code (see Figure 7.9) to change the RETURN statement to simply get the value generated by the SCOPE_IDENTITY( ) function.

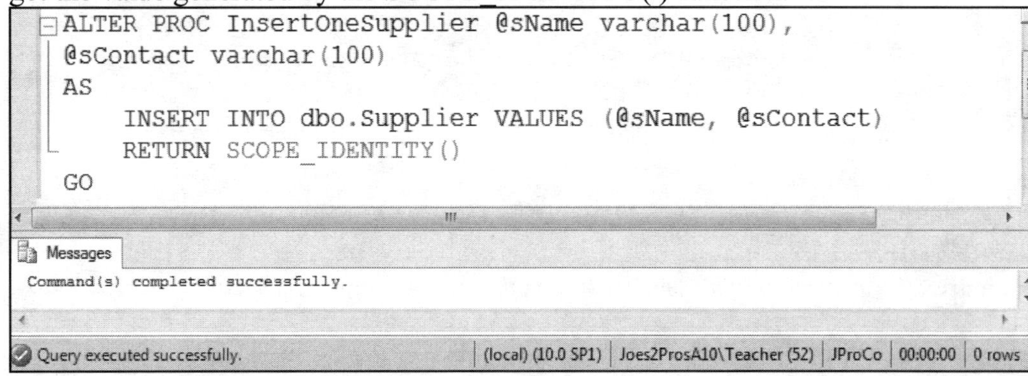
ALTER PROC InsertOneSupplier @sName varchar(100),
@sContact varchar(100)
AS
INSERT INTO dbo.Supplier VALUES (@sName, @sContact)
RETURN SCOPE_IDENTITY()
GO
Messages
Command(s) completed successfully.
Query executed successfully.
(local) (10.0 SP1)
Joes2ProsA10\Teacher (52)
JProCo
00:00:00
0 rows

Figure 7.9 The SCOPE_IDENTITY( ) function will return the value from InsertOneSupplier.

Let's test our newly revised sproc, which now utilizes the SCOPE_IDENTITY( ) function. Using the same type of DECLARE, EXEC, and PRINT statements we used for "Fun and Far", let's add a sixth supplier record for "The World and Canada" (run the highlighted code in Figure 7.10). Our new record is successfully inserted, and we see the new SupplierID value "6" displayed (Figure 7.10).

```
ALTER PROC InsertOneSupplier @sName varchar(100), @sContact varchar(100)
AS
    INSERT INTO dbo.Supplier VALUES (@sName, @sContact)
    RETURN SCOPE_IDENTITY()
GO

DECLARE @SupplierID int
EXEC @SupplierID = InsertOneSupplier 'The World and Canada','Tim McGlade'
PRINT @SupplierID
```

Messages

```
(1 row(s) affected)
6
```

Figure 7.10 Calling the InsertOneSupplier sproc shows the SupplierID which was generated during the scope of its execution.

Since our next example is going to accomplish our goal using a different SQL trick, let's be very clear that the SCOPE_IDENTITY( ) function is designed to work *inside the scope of a stored procedure*. Thus, the SCOPE_IDENTITY( ) function is included in the code which builds the stored procedure and captures the last identity generated during the scope of the sproc's execution. Not only is this coding easier but has a safety advantage. When you use the MAX function, you will get the highest number in the table. What if someone else is also inserting records at the same time as you, or even just a split second later? More numbers are coming into the table beyond what you have just inserted. If another insert took place after your insert but before the return result, you could get a higher number. However, SCOPE_IDENTITY( ) will capture just the number you inserted.

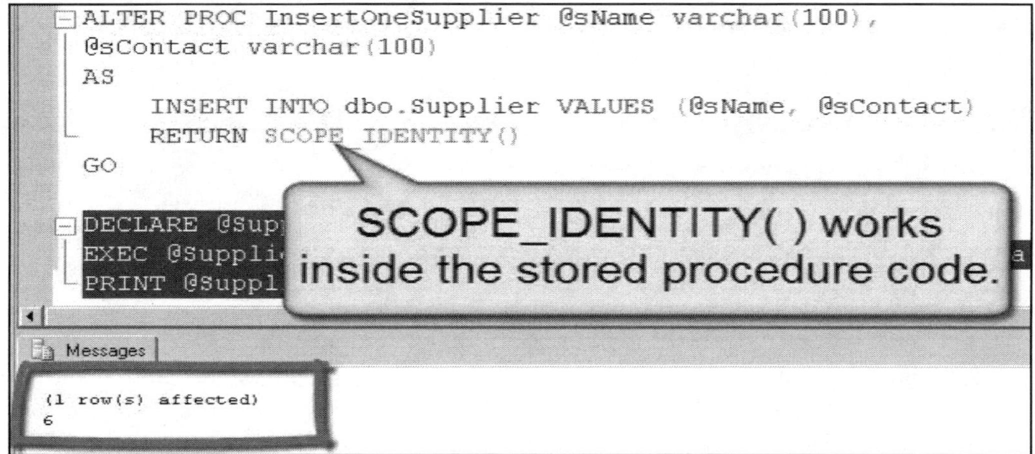
ALTER PROC InsertOneSupplier @sName varchar(100),
@sContact varchar(100)
AS
INSERT INTO dbo.Supplier VALUES (@sName, @sContact)
RETURN SCOPE_IDENTITY()
GO
SCOPE_IDENTITY( ) works
inside the stored procedure code.
Messages
(1 row(s) affected)
6

Figure 7.11 The InsertOneSupplier stored procedure returns the value found by the SCOPE_IDENTITY( ) function.

@@IDENTITY

This is the IDENTITY feature developers used before the SCOPE_IDENTITY( ) function was introduced. Prior to SQL Server 2000, @@IDENTITY was the function available to developers for retrieving identity values.

A variable beginning with the two "at" signs (@@) is called a **global variable**. The @@IDENTITY global function works anywhere (including outside the stored proc) and tells you the most recently generated ID in your current session. In Figure 7.12, we insert a seventh supplier record and use **@@IDENTITY** to return the value of this record's SupplierID.

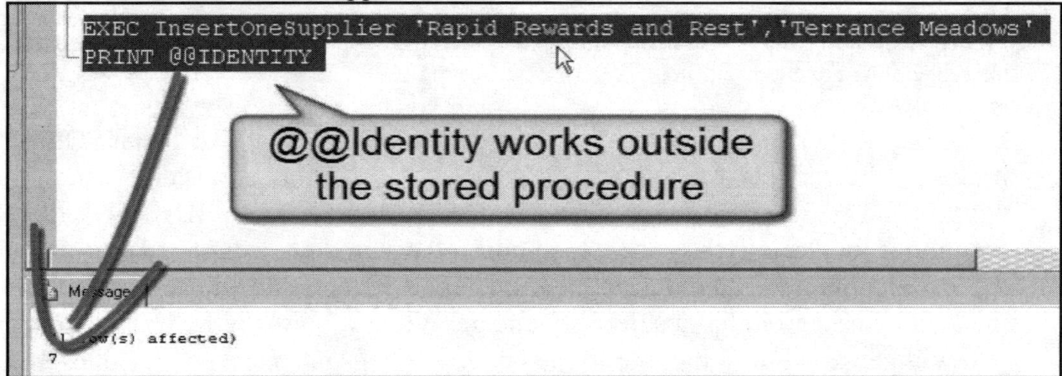

Figure 7.12 Calling on InsertOneSupplier and using @@IDENTITY to capture the return value.

The @@IDENTITY function contains the most recent value inserted into an IDENTITY column for our current connection. If there is no IDENTITY field in the current session, then our @@IDENTITY statement will return a null. If a statement inserts multiple rows, @@IDENTITY reflects the IDENTITY value for the last row inserted.

We can see that @@IDENTITY and SCOPE_IDENTITY( ) appear to do similar things for us. It is important to know when to use one of these functions versus the other. Keep in mind that these features have three points in common:

1) Both @@IDENTITY and SCOPE_IDENTITY( ) retrieve values generated within the current session. In other words, these will only work as long as IDENTITY values have been generated in the current session. If we open a new query window, neither of these features can retrieve a meaningful value.

2) We cannot specify a table with these features. (Later in this section, we will look at IDENT_CURRENT, which allows us to specify a table.)

3) If we have a trigger that performs an insert on a table with an IDENTITY column, @@IDENTITY will return the IDENTITY column from the trigger insert, while SCOPE_IDENTITY( ) will return the IDENTITY column for the insert that fired the trigger.

Let's add an eighth supplier record and see what happens when we use the SCOPE_IDENTITY( ) function (see highlighted code in Figure 7.13). The row was affected, but the identity value didn't print out. There is no result from the function and therefore the print statement finds nothing to display.

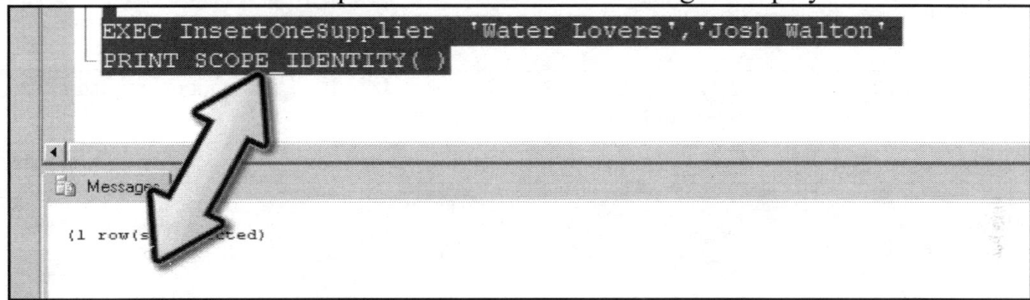

Figure 7.13 SCOPE_IDENTITY( ) will return a value if called from within this stored procedure.

Because the scope of @@IDENTITY includes everything in the current session, it is able to display the most recently assigned IDENTITY value, which is 8.

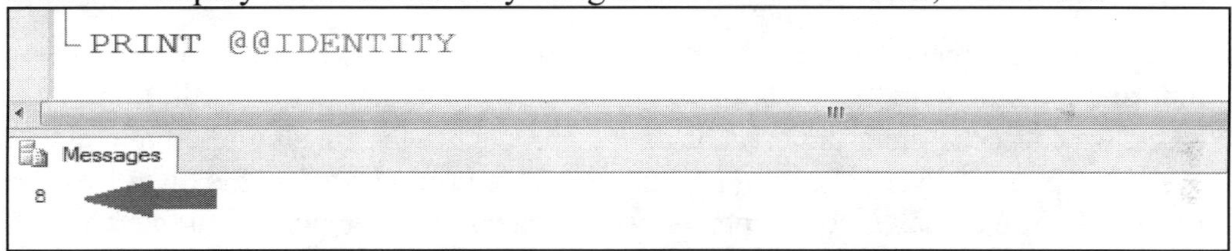

Figure 7.14 The scope of the @@IDENTITY function includes everything in your current session.

```
SELECT * FROM Supplier
```

Results | Messages

	SupplierID	SupplierName	ContactFullName
1	1	Stay Way Away and Save	Aaron Jeffries
2	2	LaVue Connect	Lou LaFleur
3	3	More Shores Amigo	Jose Cruz
4	4	White Elephant	Eric Gilman
5	5	Fun and Far	Cynthia Lee
6	6	The World and Canada	Tim McGlade
7	7	Rapid Rewards and Rest	Terrance Meadows
8	8	Water Lovers	Josh Walton

Figure 7.15 The eight records currently contained in the Supplier table.

IDENT_CURRENT( )

Another IDENTITY function introduced in SQL Server 2000 is **IDENT_CURRENT**. This function will show the highest (i.e., most recently assigned) IDENTITY value for a table. IDENT_CURRENT( ) is not limited by session or scope. To demonstrate this, let's open a new query window and show the highest IDENTITY value of the two JProCo tables which contain IDENTITY fields (see Figures 7.16 and 7.17).

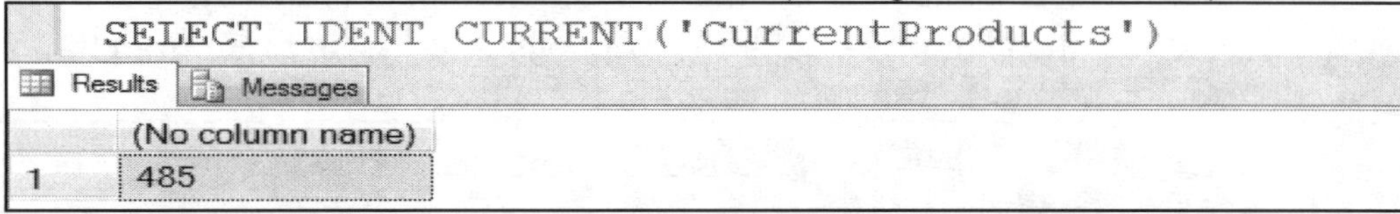

Figure 7.16 The most recently assigned ProductID value is 485. The next product inserted into the CurrentProducts table will have an IDENTITY value of 486.

```
PRINT IDENT_CURRENT('Supplier')
```

Messages

8

Figure 7.17 The most recently assigned SupplierID value is 8. The next supplier record inserted into this table will result in a SupplierID value of 9.

@@ROWCOUNT

What is the difference between the two similarly-named track and field events, the mile and the mile relay? They both end after 5280 feet (i.e., after one mile). In both cases, we cheer the final runner as he or she approaches the finish line. In the mile event, the person we are cheering has just run the entire mile all on his own. However, in the case of the relay race, the person we are cheering is the person on the relay team who is finishing the last part of the mile – they didn't run a whole mile. If the last record you affected was record 21, does that mean someone else did the first 20 records and you did just one more? Or did you manipulate all 21 records?

Sometimes you will want to know the last record you affected and sometimes you will want to return the count of records affected. The @@ROWCOUNT function will show you how many records were affected by the last DML statement. For example, this query will show 21 records in a result set:

```
SELECT * FROM Employee
```

You can't return 21 records from a stored procedure. Adding the @@ROWCOUNT will show you how many records the last run DML statement produced. In this case you get a scalar result of 21 from the code sample below:

```
SELECT * FROM Employee
SELECT @@ROWCOUNT
```

Lab 7.1: Stored Procedure Options

Lab Prep: Before you can begin the lab, you must have SQL Server installed and have run the SQLProgrammingChapter7.1Setup.sql script.

Skill Check 1: Create a stored procedure called InsertOneProduct that takes 6 parameters of @ProductName nvarchar(max), @RetailPrice money, @OrgDate datetime, @ToBeDeleted Int, @Category varchar(20), @SupplierID int and inserts these values into the CurrentProducts table. The stored procedure should return the Identity used. Test your sproc by using the following code. When you are done, your result should resemble the figure below (Figure 7.18).

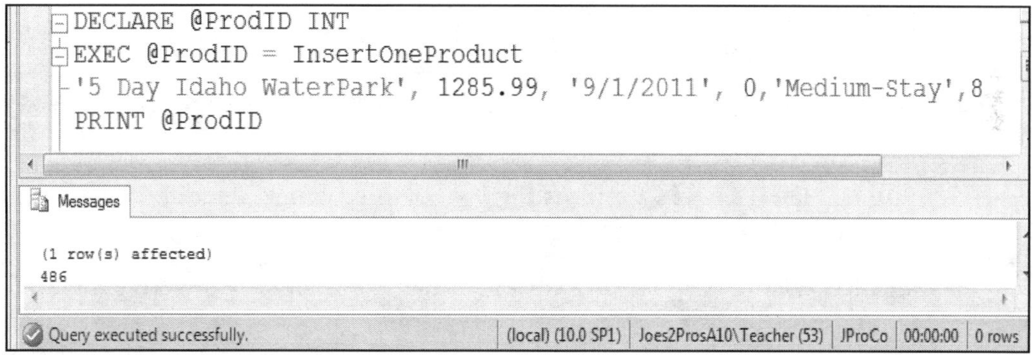

DECLARE @ProdID INT
EXEC @ProdID = InsertOneProduct
'5 Day Idaho WaterPark', 1285.99, '9/1/2011', 0,'Medium-Stay',8
PRINT @ProdID
Messages
(1 row(s) affected)
486
Query executed successfully.
(local) (10.0 SP1)
Joes2ProsA10\Teacher (53)
JProCo
00:00:00
0 rows

Figure 7.18 Skill Check 1.

Skill Check 2: Create a stored procedure called UpdateEmployeeLocation that takes two integer parameters of @EmpID and @LocationID. The stored procedure should update one record of the Employee table to the LocationID passed in to the stored procedure. ***Note:*** for the OriginationOffset field, you should supply the default value. The stored procedure should return the number of records affected. Test your code by moving EmpID 9 (James Newton) to Location #2 (Boston) and showing the return result of the stored proc using the following code:

```
DECLARE @RecordCount INT
EXEC @RecordCount = UpdateEmployeeLocation 9, 2
SELECT @RecordCount
```

Answer Code: The solutions for this lab can be found in the downloadable files in a file named Lab7.1_StoredProcedureOptions.sql.

Stored Procedure Options - Points to Ponder

1. In computer programming, the term **scope** pertains to the accessibility of variables within a batch of code (or module) from other parts of the program.
2. SCOPE_IDENTITY and @@IDENTITY return the last identity value that is generated in any table in the current session.
3. @@IDENTITY is the older technique used by developers before the SCOPE_IDENTITY( ) function was created. SCOPE_IDENTITY( ) is much better for most programming situations, because it only handles values generated within the scope of a module or programming object (sproc, function, trigger, etc.). Global functions (e.g., @@IDENTITY) are trickier to handle.
4. IDENT_CURRENT( ) and SCOPE_IDENTITY( ) were introduced in SQL Server 2000.
5. IDENT_CURRENT( ) returns the last identity value generated by a specified table.
6. @@ROWCOUNT is useful for knowing how many rows were generated by the sproc.
7. The SET QUOTED_IDENTIFIER and SET ANSI_NULLS options of a sproc have the values that the database was set to at the time of the sproc creation. Those setting of the client sessions at run time are ignored.

Table-Valued Store Procedure Parameters

Stored procedures can easily take a single parameter and use a variable to populate it. A stored procedure can readily handle two parameters in this same fashion. However, passing 1000 variables into a stored procedure would be unwieldy and would require the calling code to run 1000 times.

SQL Server 2008 now offers a way to simply pass a table into a parameterized stored procedure. That's right – you can pass a table's worth of data into a single parameter and accomplish all the needed processing with just one call.

Table Types

We are already familiar with data types like int(eger), varchar, and money. We can also create our own user-defined types. With the new **table** data type available in SQL Server 2008, we can create a user-defined data type that is based upon a table.

Our first step in preparing our table-valued parameter demonstration is to create a **table** data type. We need to consider the fields to be included in the table which we want our store procedure to accept, as well as the data types of these fields. Perhaps your table will look just like the Employee table. Perhaps the table this stored procedure will use is like no other table on your system. In the latter case, you don't have to create a new persistent table: you can define a table design without creating a table.

Using Table Types as Variables

After creating a new table type, our next step will be to declare a variable whose data type will be our new table type. In our previous examples, once we declare a variable, we can set it equal to a value or pass in a value. In the case of a **table** type, the value of that variable will be *a result set.*

Parameters will allow you to pass in any data type found in the database, including user-defined types. When you can create and declare a user-defined table type and pass that into a stored procedure, this is known as a **table-valued parameter**.

You can easily navigate Object Explorer to see the data types available for each of your databases. The Programmability folder of each database contains all of the system data types, as well as user-defined types. Within the System Data Types folder, you will find additional folders containing the numeric data types (exact and approximate), the character types, the date and time types, and so forth (Figure 7.19).

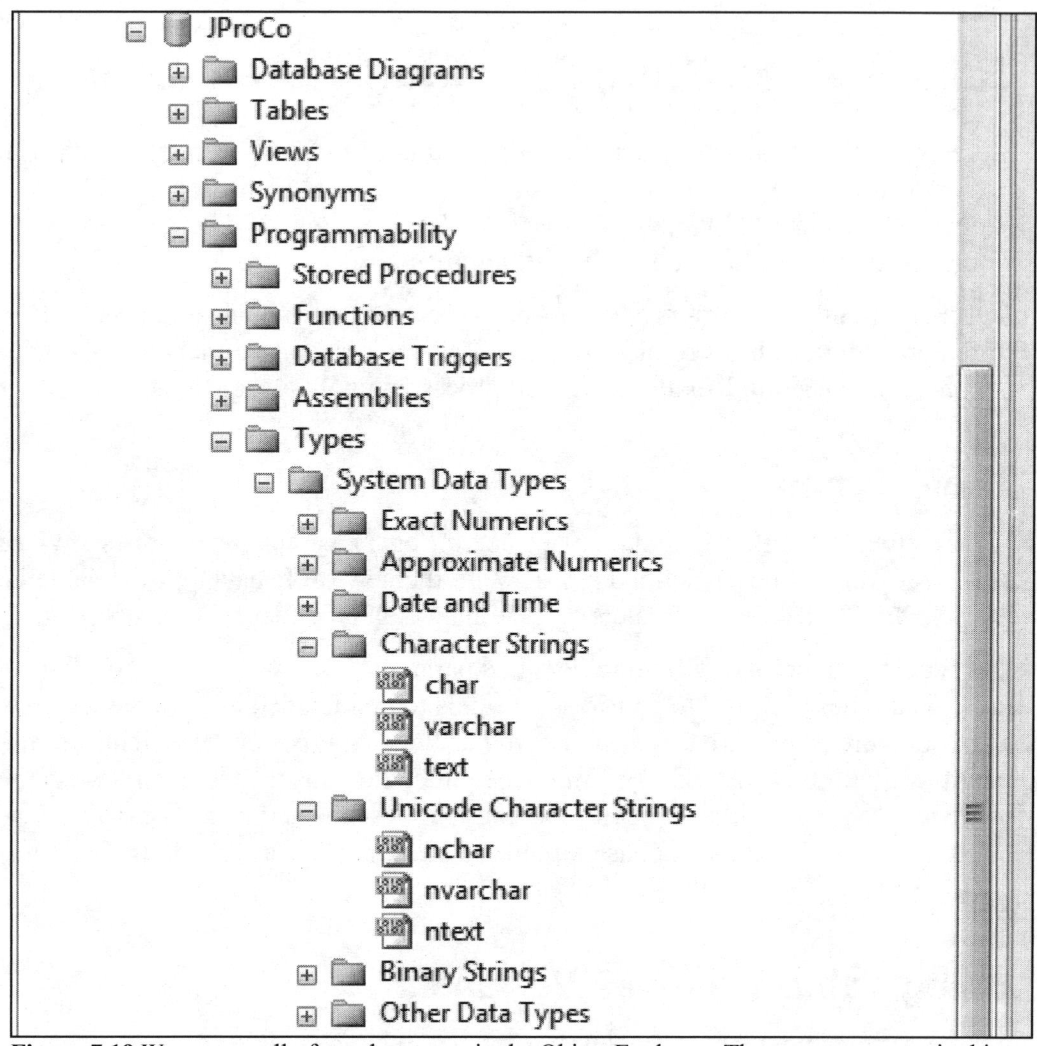

Figure 7.19 We can see all of our data types in the Object Explorer. The types we create in this section will be found in our User-Defined Table Types folder.

We will base our first example on the Grant table, which has four fields and eleven records (see Figure 7.20).

```
SELECT * FROM [Grant]
```

	GrantID	GrantName	EmpID	Amount
1	001	92 Purr_Scents %% team	7	4750.00
2	002	K-Land fund trust	2	15750.00
3	003	Robert@BigStarBank.com	7	18100.00
4	005	BIG 6's Foundation%	4	21000.00
5	006	TALTA_Kishan International	3	18100.00
6	007	Ben@MoreTechnology.com	10	41000.00
7	008	www.@-Last-U-Can-Help.com	7	25000.00
8	009	Thank you @.com	11	21500.00
9	010	Just Mom	5	9900.00
10	011	Big Giver Tom	7	19000.00
11	012	Mega Mercy	9	55000.00

Figure 7.20 The Grant table has four fields.

The first table type we will define will be called GrantTableType and it will be based upon two fields of the Grant table (GrantName and Amount). The code to accomplish this is shown here (see Figure 7.21).

```
CREATE TYPE GrantTableType AS TABLE
(GrantName varchar(50) not null,
Amount smallmoney null)
```

	GrantID	GrantName	EmpID	Amount
1	001	92 Purr_Scents %% team	7	4750.00
2	002	K-Land fund trust	2	15750.00
3	003	Robert@BigStarBank.com	7	18100.00
4	005	BIG 6's Foundation%	4	21000.00
5	006	TALTA_Kishan International	3	18100.00
6	007	Ben@MoreTechnology.com	10	41000.00
7	008	www.@-Last-U-Can-Help.com	7	25000.00
8	009	Thank you @.com	11	21500.00
9	010	Just Mom	5	9900.00
10	011	Big Giver Tom	7	19000.00
11	012	Mega Mercy	9	55000.00

Figure 7.21 The GrantTableType is created with two fields.

After you run this code and create this new type, locate GrantTableType in Object Explorer (see Figure 7.22). Traverse to JProCo > Programmability > Types > User-Defined Table Type > dbo.GrantTableType.

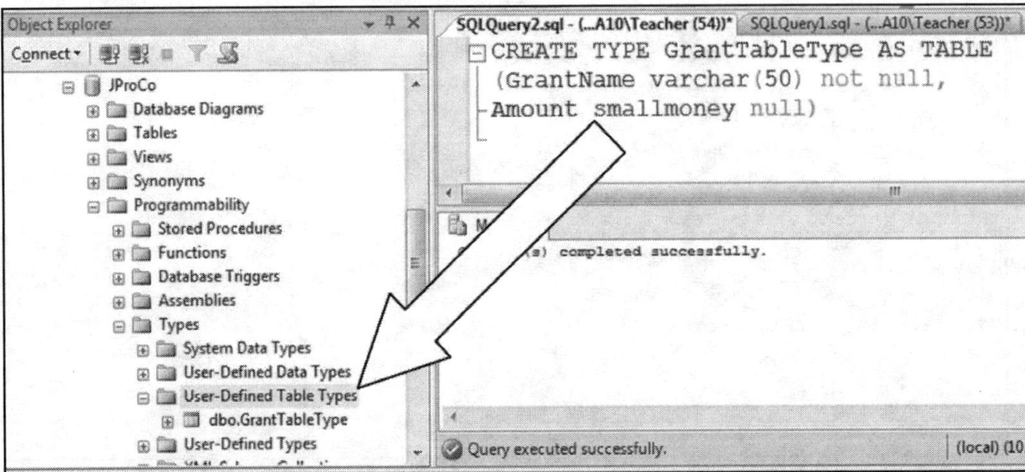

Figure 7.22 The GrantTableType can be seen in your Object Explorer.

Now let's declare a variable (@GrantTVP) whose data type is GrantTableType (i.e., our newly created table type). After we declare the variable, we will insert some data into it. Looking at the SELECT statement, we know this will bring in two fields and eleven records from the Grant table. (see Figure 7.23).

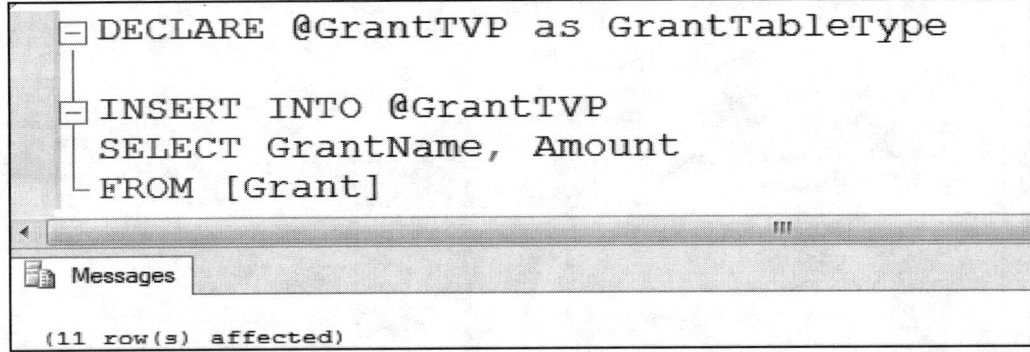

Figure 7.23 The GrantTableType variable @GrantTVP is declared and filled with 11 records from the Grant table.

The confirmation message tells us that our @GrantTVP variable has been populated with 11 rows (see Figure 7.23). Notice that we get an error message if we attempt to query from @GrantTVP (see Figure 7.24).

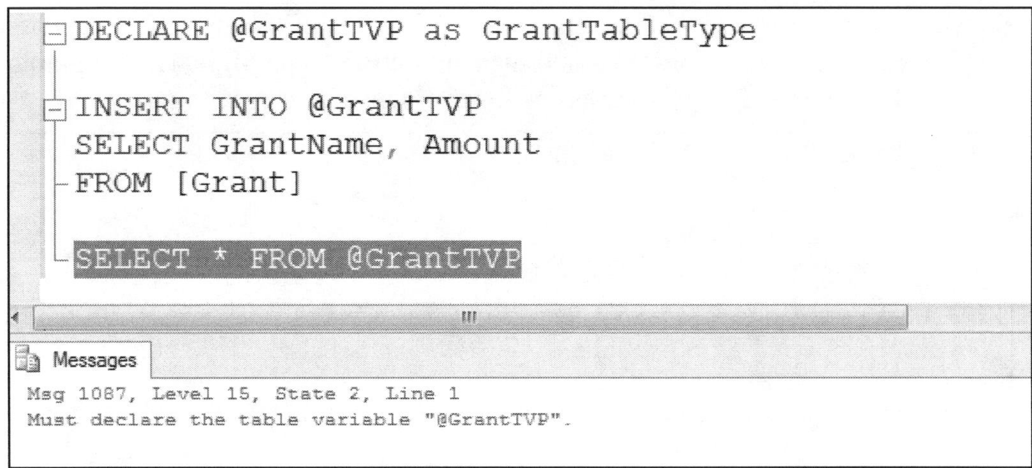

Figure 7.24 Trying to simply query from @GrantTVP throws an error message.

The error message we get from SQL Server hints that we need to declare the table variable (see Figure 7.24). In order to see our intended data, we must declare our variable, fill it with data, and select from it all at once (as shown in Figure 7.25).

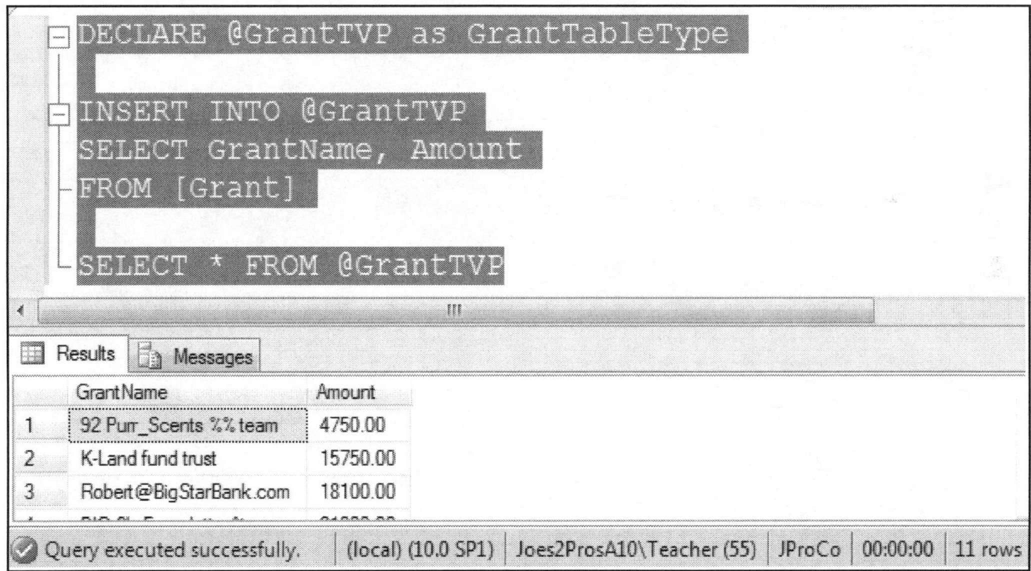

Figure 7.25 Run all of the code shown here in order to select from the table-valued parameter.

So what's the advantage of using a table type? To answer that question, let's first take a look at some familiar tables and their limitations. The MgmtTraining table, contains the approved list of classes for JProCo's managers (see Figure 7.26).

```
SELECT * FROM MgmtTraining
```

Results | Messages

	ClassID	ClassName	ClassDurationHours	ApprovedDate
1	1	Embracing Diversity	12	2007-01-01 00:00:00.000
2	2	Interviewing	6	2007-01-15 00:00:00.000
3	3	Difficult Negotiations	30	2008-02-12 00:00:00.000
4	4	Empowering Others	18	2010-10-26 17:32:57.480
5	6	Passing Certifications	13	2010-10-26 17:33:01.707

Query executed successfully. | (local) (10.0 SP1) | Joes2ProsA10\Teacher (55) | JProCo

Figure 7.26 The MgmtTraining table contains the list of approved classes.

The MgmtTrainingNew table contains the list of classes we intend to approve soon. Currently there are only two fields and two records in the MgmtTrainingNew table. (see Figure 7.27).

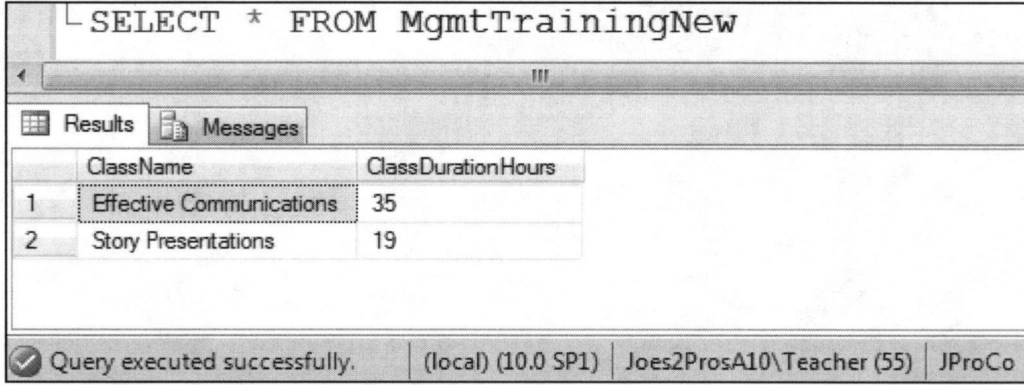

```
SELECT * FROM MgmtTrainingNew
```

Results | Messages

	ClassName	ClassDurationHours
1	Effective Communications	35
2	Story Presentations	19

Query executed successfully. | (local) (10.0 SP1) | Joes2ProsA10\Teacher (55) | JProCo

Figure 7.27 The MgmtTrainingNew table has two fields.

Table-Valued Parameters

Once a class from the MgmtTrainingNew table is approved, that class record must be placed in the MgmtTraining table. Now let's think about how we would add these two records using a stored procedure. Would we run the stored procedure twice (i.e., once for each record)? A better choice would be to pass the entire

MgmtTrainingNew table into a stored procedure and have that stored procedure populate the MgmtTraining table.

We're going to pass in a value to our parameter @TableName and then use that parameter in the logic of our stored procedure. Notice that we get an error message when we attempt this (see Figure 7.28). We cannot pass in a table, but one of the messages hints that we can pass in a type.

```
CREATE PROCEDURE AddNewTraining @TableName TABLE
AS
    INSERT INTO dbo.MgmtTraining
    (ClassName, ClassDurationHours,ApprovedDate)
    SELECT mt.ClassName,mt.ClassDurationHours,GETDATE()
    FROM @TableName as mt
GO
```

```
Messages
Msg 156, Level 15, State 1, Procedure AddNewTraining, Line 1
Incorrect syntax near the keyword 'TABLE'.
Msg 1087, Level 15, State 2, Procedure AddNewTraining, Line 6
Must declare the table variable "@TableName".
```

Figure 7.28 A table cannot be passed into a store procedure but a type can.

Let's add a statement to create a type (MgmtTrainingType). Notice that we must add the type to the code of our sproc (see Figure 7.29). When passing in a table type, you must set it to READONLY.

```
CREATE TYPE MgmtTrainingType AS TABLE
(ClassName varchar(50) not null,
ClassDurationHours int null)
GO

CREATE PROCEDURE AddNewTraining @TableName MgmtTrainingType READONLY
AS
    INSERT INTO dbo.MgmtTraining
    (ClassName, ClassDurationHours,ApprovedDate)
    SELECT mt.ClassName,mt.ClassDurationHours,GETDATE()
    FROM @TableName as mt
GO
```

```
Messages
Command(s) completed successfully.
```

Figure 7.29 When passing in a table type, you must set it to READONLY.

We will declare a variable named @ClassTVP using the table type (MgmtTrainingType) we created earlier (shown in Figure 7.29). This table-type variable (@ClassTVP) is then populated with records from the MgmtTrainingNew table. We then can call upon the stored procedure AddNewTraining and pass this variable into the table-valued parameter (see Figure 7.30).

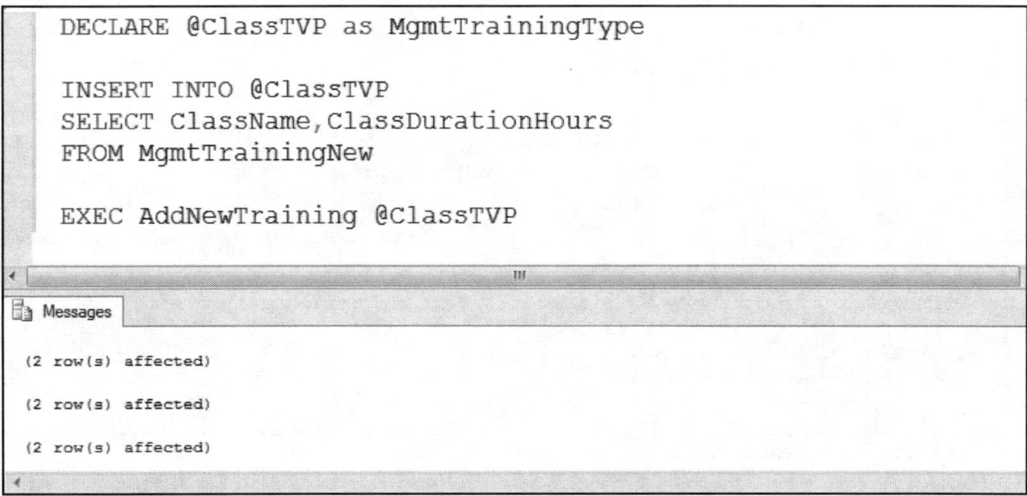
DECLARE @ClassTVP as MgmtTrainingType
INSERT INTO @ClassTVP
SELECT ClassName,ClassDurationHours
FROM MgmtTrainingNew
EXEC AddNewTraining @ClassTVP
Messages
(2 row(s) affected)
(2 row(s) affected)
(2 row(s) affected)

Figure 7.30 The @ClassTVP variable is populated and passed into the AddNewTraining stored procedure as a parameter.

Let's run a query on the MgmtTraining table and check to see whether the new class records appear. Success! Both of the new records now show up in the MgmtTraining table (see Figure 7.31).

```
SELECT * FROM MgmtTraining
```

Results | Messages

	ClassID	ClassName	ClassDurationHours	ApprovedDate
1	1	Embracing Diversity	12	2007-01-01 00:00:00.000
2	2	Interviewing	6	2007-01-15 00:00:00.000
3	3	Difficult Negotiations	30	2008-02-12 00:00:00.000
4	4	Empowering Others	18	2010-10-26 17:32:57.480
5	6	Passing Certifications	13	2010-10-26 17:33:01.707
6	7	Effective Communications	35	2010-10-26 17:52:42.937
7	8	Story Presentations	19	2010-10-26 17:52:42.937

Query executed successfully | (local) (10.0 SP1) | Joes2ProsA10\Teacher (55) | JProCo | 00:00:00 | 7 rows

Figure 7.31 Two records were successfully added to the MgmtTraining table.

Lab 7.2: Table-Valued Stored Procedure Parameters

Lab Prep: Before you can begin the lab, you must have SQL Server installed and have run the SQLProgrammingChapter7.2Setup.sql script.

Skill Check 1: Create a table type named GrantType which has an identical structure to the Grant table. Verify the new type exists in the Object Explorer. When complete, your Object Explorer tree should match that shown here (see Figure 7.32).

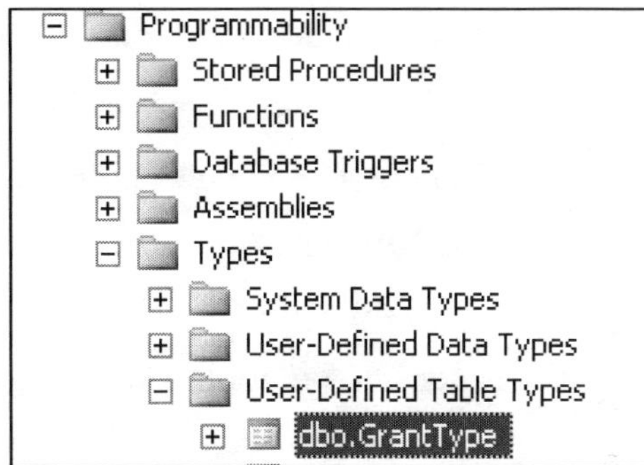

Figure 7.32 Skill Check 1.

Skill Check 2: Create a sproc called AddNewGrants, which accepts a parameter called @TVP which is of the GrantType type created in the last skill check and populates all records in the [Grant] table. Test your sproc by using the following code. Your result should resemble the figure you see here (Figure 7.33).

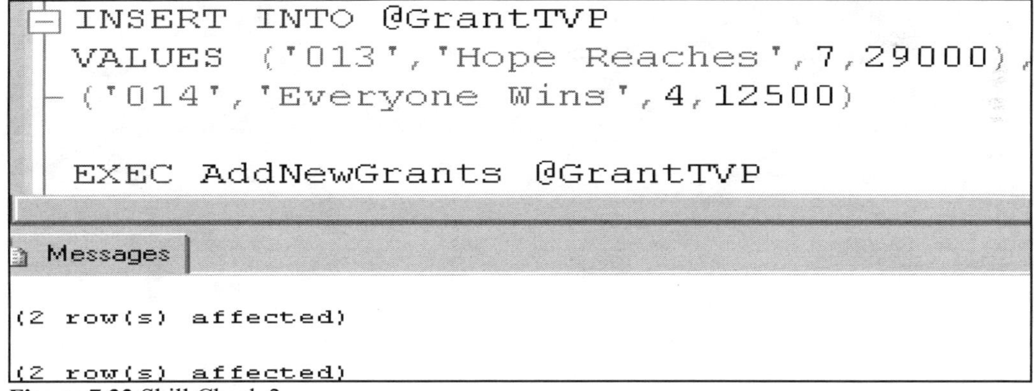

Figure 7.33 Skill Check 2.

Answer Code: The T-SQL code to this lab can be found in the downloadable files in a file named Lab7.2_TableValuedStoredProcedures.sql.

Table-Valued Stored Procedures - Points to Ponder

1. Table-valued parameters are new in SQL Server 2008.
2. Table-valued parameters are a great way to pass in multiple rows of data at once, instead of just one value at a time.
3. To declare table type variables, you must use user-defined table types.
4. You create a table as a data type and then you can create a parameter that refers to that type.
5. The type will exist in your database until you explicitly drop it.
6. After you create the table variable, you fill it with data by using an INSERT statement.
7. You must fill your table variable before passing it in as a parameter.
8. When used with stored procedures and other SQL routines, table-valued parameters must be passed in as READONLY.
9. Once the type is created, you can reuse the type with other DECLARE statements.
10. You create table-value variables as you do other local variables (i.e., create them using a DECLARE statement).

Chapter Glossary

@@IDENTITY: a global function which returns the last identity value generated within a session; used by developers prior to the inception of the newer function, SCOPE_IDENTITY( ).
@@ROWCOUNT: returns the number of rows generated by a sproc.
Global variable: a variable whose scope is global and which begins with two "at" signs (@@).
IDENT_CURRENT( ): returns the last identity value generated by a specified table.
READONLY: keyword used with stored procedures and other SQL routines; table-valued parameters must be passed in as READONLY.
Scope: "range of operation"; think of a scope as all things that happen within the running of a batch of code, such as a stored procedure or a function.
SCOPE_IDENTITY( ): function which returns the last identity value generated within a batch.
Scalar stored procedure: a sproc whose result consists of a single value.
Table-valued parameter: a variable whose data type is table.

Chapter Seven – Review Quiz

1.) What does the SCOPE_IDENTITY( ) function do?

O a. It gets the most recently generated identity value from inside the stored procedure.
O b. It gets the most recently generated identity value from code calling the stored procedure.
O c. It gets the next identity value from inside the stored procedure.
O d. It gets the next identity value from code calling the stored procedure.

2.) What is the difference between SCOPE_IDENTITY( ) and @@IDENTITY?

O a. SCOPE_IDENTITY( ) only works inside the stored procedure.
O b. SCOPE_IDENTITY( ) only works with code which calls on the stored procedure.
O c. SCOPE_IDENTITY( ) shows the most recent number, whereas @@Identity shows the next number.

3.) What are two advantages of running code inside a stored procedure versus running the same code in an ad hoc fashion? (Choose two)

□ a. Cached plans can increase SQL performance.
□ b. It's easier to call upon a stored procedure than to have to re-type or re-open a script.
□ c. Stored procedures allow you to join more tables in a single query than ad hoc code.
□ d. Running code explicitly does not allow you to mix DML and DDL statements within a single execution.

4.) Before you can create a table-valued stored procedure, what must you first do?

O a. Execute the store procedure.
O b. Qualify the table with schema or dbo.
O c. Create a persistent table.
O d. Create a table data type.
O e. Create a view.

5.) You have the following code:

```
CREATE PROC AddNewGrants @TVP GrantType
AS
        INSERT INTO dbo.[Grant]
        (GrantID, GrantName, EmpID, Amount)
        SELECT GrantID, GrantName, EmpID, Amount
        FROM @TVP
GO
```

You have verified that the GrantType was created and the fields match. What do you need to do to make the code work?

O a. Add READONLY after the GO.
O b. Add READONLY after the type.
O c. Add READONLY after the [Grant] table.
O d. Add READONLY after the FROM clause.

6.) You need to create a stored procedure which accepts a table-valued parameter named @Suppliers. What code will achieve this result?

O a. CREATE PROCEDURE AddSuppliers
@Suppliers Float READONLY

O b. CREATE PROCEDURE AddSuppliers
@Suppliers Int READONLY

O c. CREATE PROCEDURE AddSuppliers
@Suppliers Money READONLY

O d. CREATE PROCEDURE AddSuppliers
@Suppliers SupplierType READONLY

O e. CREATE PROCEDURE AddSuppliers
@Suppliers GeographyType READONLY

Answer Key

1.) a 2.) a 3.) a, b 4.) d 5.) b 6.) d

Bug Catcher Game

To play the Bug Catcher game, run BugCatcher_Chapter7_StoredProcedureOptions.pps found in the BugCatcher folder of the companion files located at www.Joes2Pros.com.

Chapter 8. User-Defined Functions

The other day someone asked me for the time. I pulled out my cell phone and pressed the button to light up my screen and said, "It's 2:35 p.m." Without realizing it, I was acting much like a function in SQL Server does.

A function is a routine which performs a task and returns a result set. In this case, my result set was comprised of the single value returned after looking at my clock. Later that same day at Jack in the Box, I ordered a Jumbo Jack which was priced at $1.29. The register ran a function on my order total and displayed $1.39 for the price after sales tax. Again, a result was returned after some calculation and lookup activity.

Functions make our lives easier by performing predictable, repetitive tasks for use over and over again and providing us the end result. In Volume 2 *(SQL Queries Joes 2 Pros)*, we examined system-supplied functions, including string functions (e.g., SUBSTRING( ), LEFT( ), RIGHT( ), UPPER( ), LOWER( )) and time functions (e.g., GETDATE( ), DATEPART( )). We passed in the requisite inputs, which these functions processed and then returned an output. In this chapter, we will examine a variety of functions and create our own user-defined functions in SQL Server. The final section of this chapter includes a callback to Chapter 5, where we introduced deterministic and non-deterministic fields and their use in indexed views. (Refer to the discussion beginning at Figure 5.70, as well as to "Indexed Views - Points to Ponder.") Once we understand how to use and build our own functions, we will explore how to include them in views and indexed views.

READER NOTE: *In order to follow along with the examples in the first section of Chapter 8, please run the setup script SQLProgrammingChapter8.0Setup.sql. The setup scripts for this book are posted at Joes2Pros.com.*

Functions versus Stored Procedures

As you might guess, my classroom students study topics in the same order they appear in this book series. When my classes reach this chapter on user-defined functions, I invariably have students ask me what differences exist between stored procedures and functions. We use similar T-SQL code to build both of these objects, and our work with parameterized stored procedures resembles passing an argument into a function and receiving a result.

A detailed list comparing stored procedures and functions appears at the end of this section (see "Scalar Functions – Points to Ponder"). In this list, you will find several noteworthy points, including the following:

1) Everything you can accomplish with a user-defined function may also be accomplished using a stored procedure.
2) DML statements are the only type of statement you can run within a function (i.e., no DDL, DCL, or TCL statements allowed in functions but they are allowed in stored procedures).
3) User-defined functions are called by a SQL statement (e.g., a SELECT statement), whereas stored procedures must be invoked by an EXECUTE (or EXEC) statement.

Scalar Functions

From our earlier work with scalar data results (Chapter 6), you can likely guess that a **scalar function** is one where each time you run it, you get exactly one answer. For example, everyone would have one answer to the question, "How much did you pay in taxes last year?" The answer is a number, and for some folks that number may be zero. Warren Buffett's answer to that question would be larger than most but it would still be a single value. Scalar functions return a single value no matter how many calculations and input go into them. Up to this point in our study, we have seen many scalar functions, like GetDate( ) which returns the current date and time according to your computer's clock.

Creating and Implementing Scalar Functions

You create scalar functions with a CREATE FUNCTION statement. You call upon a scalar function with a SELECT statement. Oftentimes functions are just calculations (like Sales Tax * Price). Our first example (see Figure 8.1) sets the variable @MyFavNum to 4 and then performs a calculation to double that amount. Notice that the doubling calculation is done *ad hoc* – in other words, it's a one-time calculation and is not part of a repeatable code module. Another variable captures the doubled amount (@MyFavNum * 2), and a SELECT statement calls and displays this amount (see Figure 8.1).

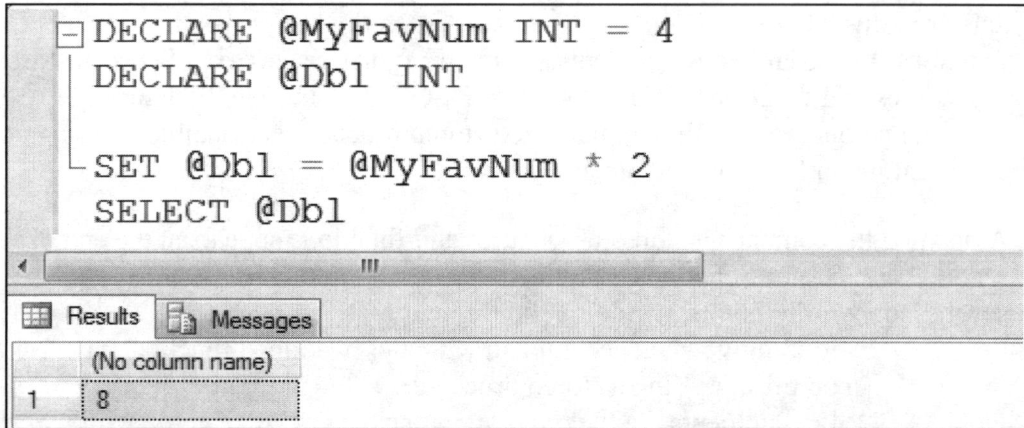
DECLARE @MyFavNum INT = 4
DECLARE @Dbl INT
SET @Dbl = @MyFavNum * 2
SELECT @Dbl
Results
Messages
(No column name)
1
8

Figure 8.1 An ad hoc calculation which doubles the value of @MyFavNum is shown here.

If doubling numbers is a task you perform frequently, you can build a function to do this for you. Let's create a function called ReturnDouble that takes an integer parameter (@Num), runs a double calculation, and stores the result in the @Dbl variable (Figure 8.2). Finally, the value of @Dbl is returned to the calling code.

```
CREATE FUNCTION ReturnDouble(@Num int)
RETURNS INT
AS
BEGIN
    DECLARE @Dbl int
    SELECT @Dbl = @Num * 2
    RETURN @Dbl
END
GO
```

Messages

```
Command(s) completed successfully.
```

Figure 8.2 The ReturnDouble function will take a parameter and return twice that value.

The most common way to call upon an existing function is via a SELECT statement. In Figure 8.3, we query the value of this function by passing in 14 and the result set is a scalar value of 28. ***Note:*** The schema name ("dbo") is optional in the CREATE FUNCTION statement; however, you must use the two-part name when calling upon your scalar functions. If you attempt to run this SELECT statement without the schema name (SELECT ReturnDouble(14)), it will not work.

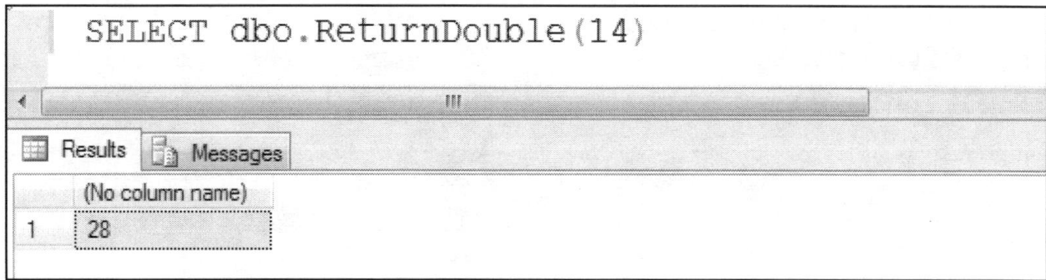

Figure 8.3 The ReturnDouble function is used in a select statement and the scalar result is shown.

You can create as many functions in your database as you need. Suppose you are taking over a database project from someone else and you want to see what functions exist on the system. All functions can be browsed as you would any other object created in SQL Server. In Figure 8.4 we can see our new function in the Object Explorer by traversing the following path:
OE > Databases > JProCo > Programmability > Functions > Scalar-valued Functions > dbo.ReturnDouble

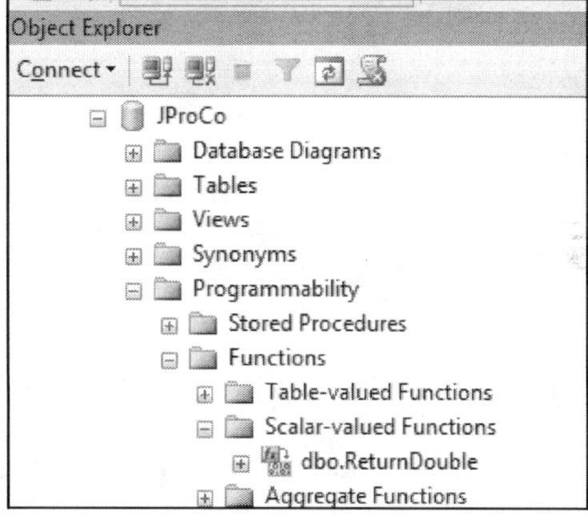

Figure 8.4 The ReturnDouble function can be found in the Object Explorer tree.

Using Functions With Queries

We just added created a function containing a query in order to return data in a repeatable way. You can also include a function as an expression field within a SELECT list. For example, we know the retail price of the first product in the CurrentProducts table is roughly $61. If you were to double that amount, it would be roughly $122. In Figure 8.5 we have two queries. The first query shows all records but just two fields of the CurrentProducts table. The second query is the same but it also includes an expression field which uses the ReturnDouble function by passing in the Retail Price. The expression field values should be double the values of the RetailPrice field. (Since the function uses integers, and the result is rounded to the nearest dollar, we don't see the pennies.) The ReturnDouble function is used with this query to make a calculation on each record. This function ran 486 times within the query and produced 486 scalar results. ***Note***: You must use the two-part name when calling upon ReturnDouble, since it's a user-defined function.

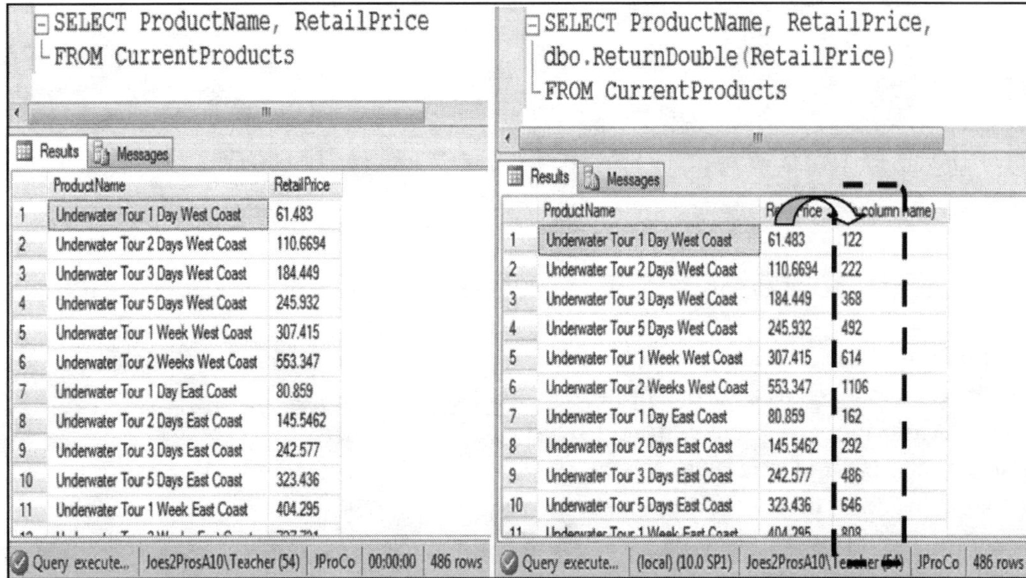

Figure 8.5 ReturnDouble function is used with a query to perform a calculation on each record.

Functions with Multiple Parameters

As you know, functions are SQL Server objects which are built using T-SQL code. Functions can accept one or more parameters and return a scalar or a table-like result set. Figure 8.6 shows the code used to build the AddTwoNumbers function which takes two integer parameters and returns the sum of the parameters.

```
CREATE FUNCTION dbo.AddTwoNumbers(@Num1 int, @Num2 int)
RETURNS INT
AS
BEGIN
    DECLARE @ttl int
    SELECT @ttl = @Num1 + @Num2
    RETURN @ttl
END
```

Messages

```
Command(s) completed successfully.
```

Figure 8.6 The AddTwoNumbers function takes two parameters and returns a scalar result.

Recall that scalar functions will always return just a single value, regardless of how many inputs are included in the function. When we pass two integers into the AddTwoNumbers function, we get just one number in our result (see Figure 8.7).

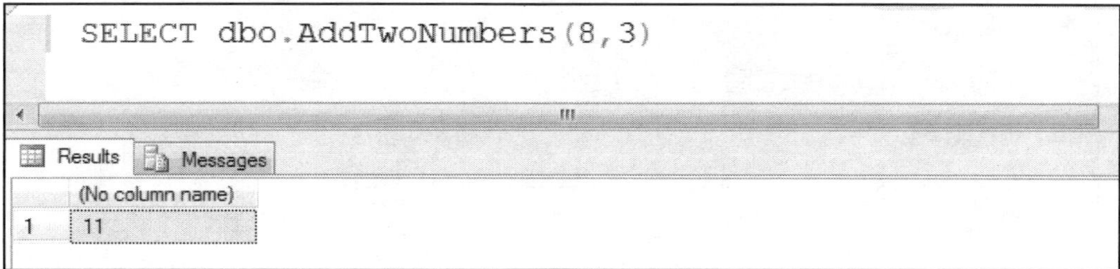
```
SELECT dbo.AddTwoNumbers(8,3)
```

	(No column name)
1	11

Figure 8.7 Passing in 8 and 3 to the AddTwoNumbers function gives us a result of 11.

Aggregate Functions Recap

Scalar functions can be used to tell a significant story in business. The quantity that your customers tend to order of a certain product is an interesting number, and one you must know in order to formulate compelling sales offerings. For example, when shopping for paint brushes online, I frequently order 10-15 brushes at a time. When using an online travel site to book a vacation, I generally order two tickets. A volume discount for 20 paint brushes would get my attention – I would definitely increase my order to 20 brushes. However, a volume discount for 20 trips to Mexico would be unlikely to alter my purchasing behavior. I'm going to purchase two tickets for my Mexican vacation no matter how attractive the 20-ticket price is.

The query in Figure 8.8 shows us the average quantity that was ordered for a given ProductID. For example, when ProductID 7 is ordered, the customer (on average) puts three of them on one invoice.

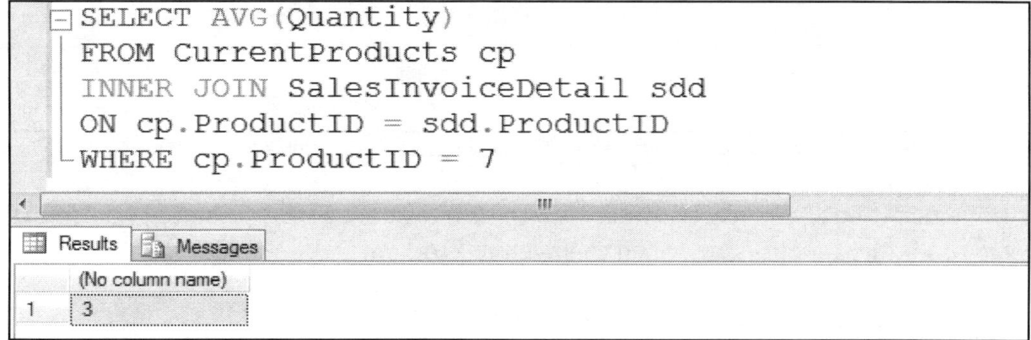
```
SELECT AVG(Quantity)
FROM CurrentProducts cp
INNER JOIN SalesInvoiceDetail sdd
ON cp.ProductID = sdd.ProductID
WHERE cp.ProductID = 7
```

	(No column name)
1	3

Figure 8.8 When ProductID 7 is ordered, customers (on average) put 3 of them on one invoice.

Notice that this query does not give us the true average. The average is really 3.63 and not 3. That rounding error occurs because Quantity is an integer. In order to see the true average for ProductID 7, we can CAST Quantity as a float (Figure 8.9).

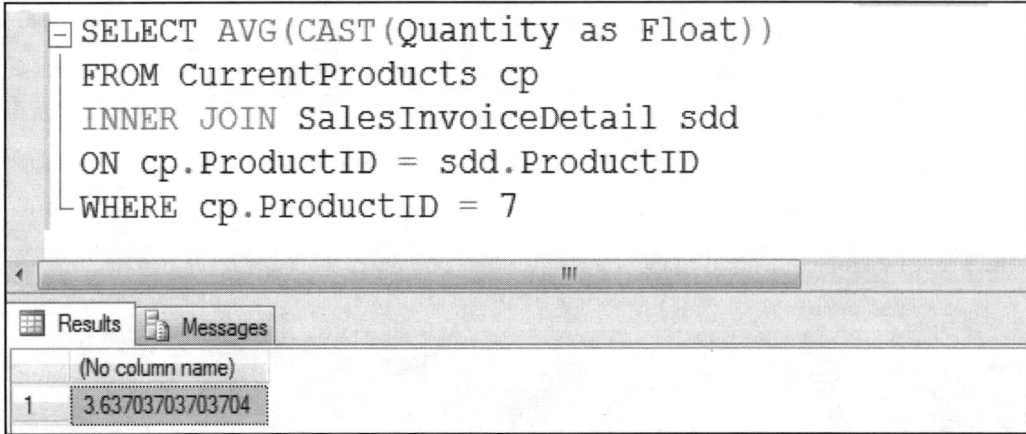
```
SELECT AVG(CAST(Quantity as Float))
FROM CurrentProducts cp
INNER JOIN SalesInvoiceDetail sdd
ON cp.ProductID = sdd.ProductID
WHERE cp.ProductID = 7
```

	(No column name)
1	3.63703703703704

Figure 8.9 By treating Quantity as a float instead of an INT, we see a more precise average.

If a product has never been ordered, then there is no way to determine an average quantity per order. In Figure 8.10 we see that, since ProductID 1 has never been ordered, the scalar result is null.

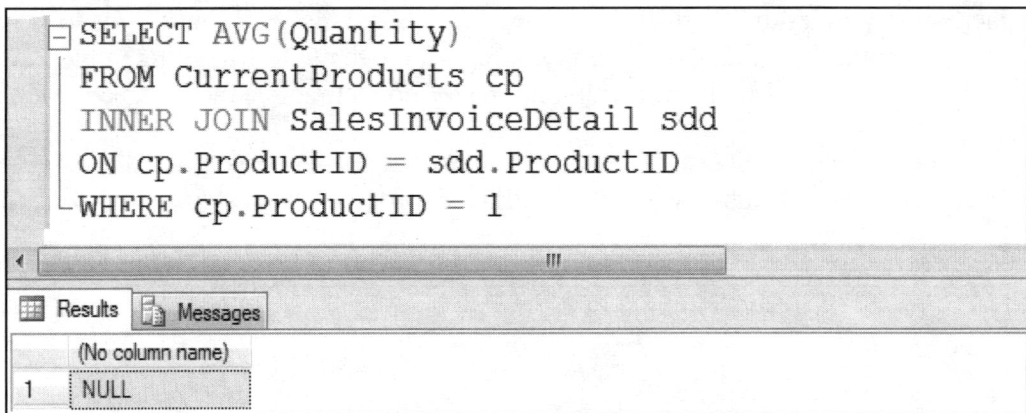
```
SELECT AVG(Quantity)
FROM CurrentProducts cp
INNER JOIN SalesInvoiceDetail sdd
ON cp.ProductID = sdd.ProductID
WHERE cp.ProductID = 1
```

	(No column name)
1	NULL

Figure 8.10 If there are no records then the AVG( ) aggregate function returns a null result.

If we plan to use this query often, we can turn it into a scalar function. Each time we run it, the function will need to have the ProductID passed in.

Let's create the function GetAverageSalesByProduct, which will accept a ProductID parameter and predicate on all invoices matching that value. The result will be aggregated to find the average quantity (see Figure 8.11).

```
CREATE FUNCTION GetAverageSalesByProduct (@ProductID int)
RETURNS float
AS
BEGIN
    DECLARE @Average float

    SELECT @Average =  AVG(CAST(Quantity as Float))
    FROM CurrentProducts cp
    INNER JOIN SalesInvoiceDetail sdd
    ON cp.ProductID = sdd.ProductID
    WHERE cp.ProductID = @ProductID

    RETURN @Average
END
```

Messages

Command(s) completed successfully.

Figure 8.11 GetAverageSalesByProduct requires an integer to be passed in to @ProductID.

Let's run our new function for ProductID 7 (see Figure 8.12).

```
SELECT dbo.GetAverageSalesByProduct(7)
```

Results | Messages

	(No column name)
1	3.63703703703704

Figure 8.12 Calling on GetAverageSalesByProduct and passing in a 7 gets you the average scalar result.

Notice that this function we've created may not always produce the type of scalar result we want. For example, if we've never sold any units of ProductID 1, then the average should be zero. However, here we see our function returns a null for ProductID 1 (see Figure 8.13). If the calling code will not accept nulls, then this function would break the calling code.

```
SELECT dbo.GetAverageSalesByProduct(1)
```

Results | Messages

	(No column name)
1	NULL

Figure 8.13 This function produces a null result since ProductID 1 has never sold.

Because nulls and zeros (0) are NOT the same thing, we need to add a little extra logic to our code. In Figure 8.14 we alter the function to check the value of the @Average variable after the aggregation. Since we were told not to return any null values, we will change those to a value of zero before the final statement runs and returns the value of the variable (@Average) to the calling code.

```
ALTER FUNCTION GetAverageSalesByProduct (@ProductID int)
RETURNS float
AS
BEGIN
    DECLARE @Average float

    SELECT @Average =  AVG(CAST(Quantity as Float))
    FROM CurrentProducts cp
    INNER JOIN SalesInvoiceDetail sdd
    ON cp.ProductID = sdd.ProductID
    WHERE cp.ProductID = @ProductID

    IF (@Average IS NULL)
    SET @Average = 0

    RETURN @Average
END
```

Messages

Command(s) completed successfully.

Figure 8.14 Null values are changed to zero before the result is returned.

GetAverageSalesByProduct is the user-defined function we just created. It is not a built-in function. The Object Explorer tree shows the three scalar functions we have created thus far in this chapter (see Figure 8.15).

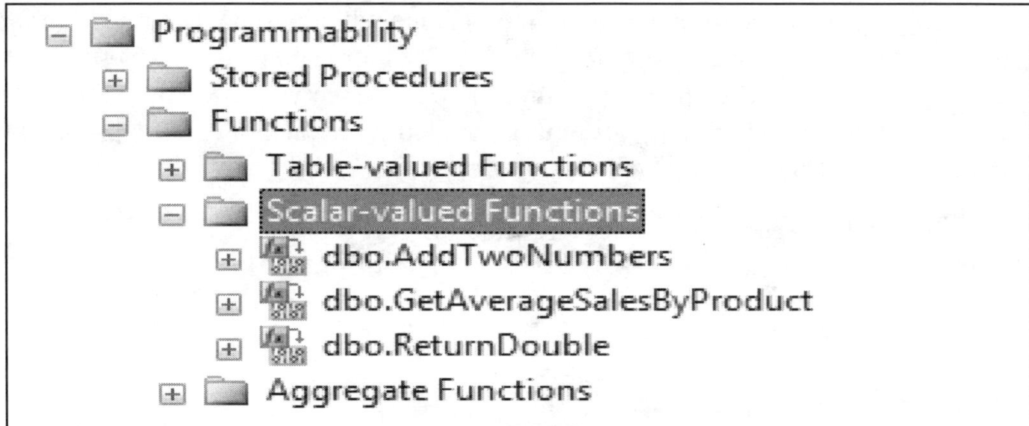

Figure 8.15 Object Explorer shows the three scalar functions we have created thus far.

With our robust scalar function, GetAverageSalesByProduct, we can query all the records of the CurrentProducts table and see the average quantity per invoice for each product. If a product has never been sold, then the average will be zero.

Let's write a statement to call upon GetAverageSalesByProduct and sort our result by ProductID. Here we've intentionally used the simple name (i.e., instead of the two-part name) in order to examine the error message that SQL Server returns (see Figure 8.16).

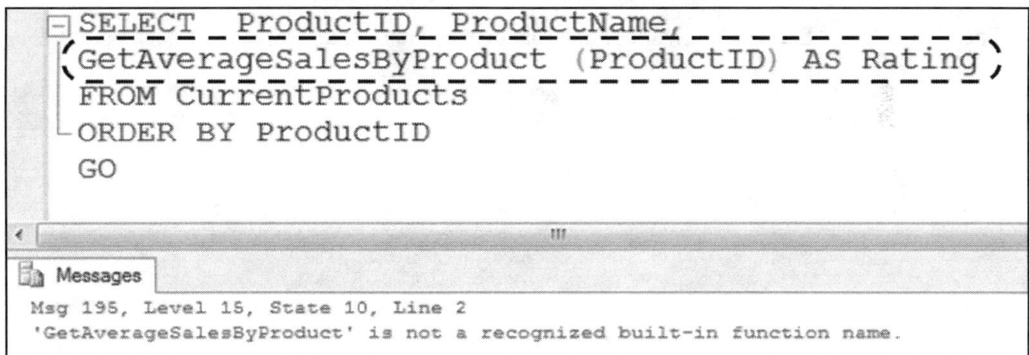

Figure 8.16 To call upon a user-defined function you cannot use the simple name.

The error message reads, "GetAverageSalesByProduct is not a recognized built-in function name." It may seem surprising to see this message, since we know GetAverageSalesByProduct is not a built-in function (i.e., it is one of the user-defined functions we've created). *SQL Server assumes that any function called by its simple name is a system-supplied function.*

Let's modify our code to prefix the function name with the schema name (dbo) and then re-attempt our code. By specifying dbo.GetAverageSalesByProduct, our query now runs successfully (see Figure 8.17). Since we've passed the ProductID argument into the function, it will return one record for each of the 486 products found in the CurrentProducts table.

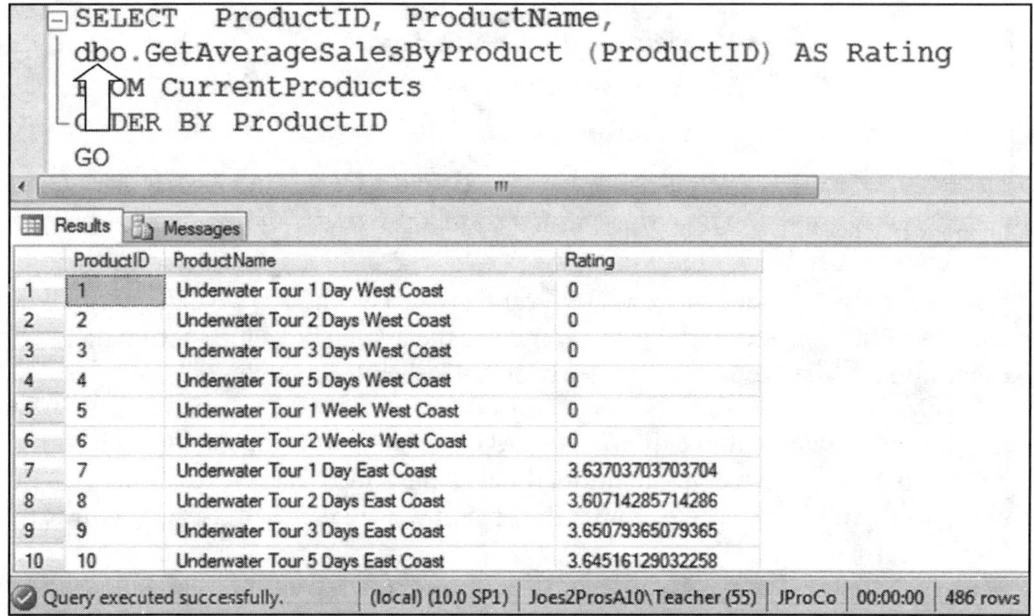
```
SELECT  ProductID, ProductName,
dbo.GetAverageSalesByProduct (ProductID) AS Rating
FROM CurrentProducts
ORDER BY ProductID
GO
```

	ProductID	ProductName	Rating
1	1	Underwater Tour 1 Day West Coast	0
2	2	Underwater Tour 2 Days West Coast	0
3	3	Underwater Tour 3 Days West Coast	0
4	4	Underwater Tour 5 Days West Coast	0
5	5	Underwater Tour 1 Week West Coast	0
6	6	Underwater Tour 2 Weeks West Coast	0
7	7	Underwater Tour 1 Day East Coast	3.63703703703704
8	8	Underwater Tour 2 Days East Coast	3.60714285714286
9	9	Underwater Tour 3 Days East Coast	3.65079365079365
10	10	Underwater Tour 5 Days East Coast	3.64516129032258

Query executed successfully. | (local) (10.0 SP1) | Joes2ProsA10\Teacher (55) | JProCo | 00:00:00 | 486 rows

Figure 8.17 Using the two-part name in the function will allow the query to run successfully.

Lab 8.1: Scalar Functions

Lab Prep: Before you can begin the lab, you must have SQL Server installed and have run the script SQLProgrammingChapter8.1Setup.sql.

Skill Check 1: Create a function called GetTotalSalesByProductID which takes a ProductID integer parameter and returns the total as the Quantity multiplied by the RetailPrice. *Hint:* use the CurrentProducts and SalesInvoiceDetail tables.

Test your function by using the code seen in the figure here.

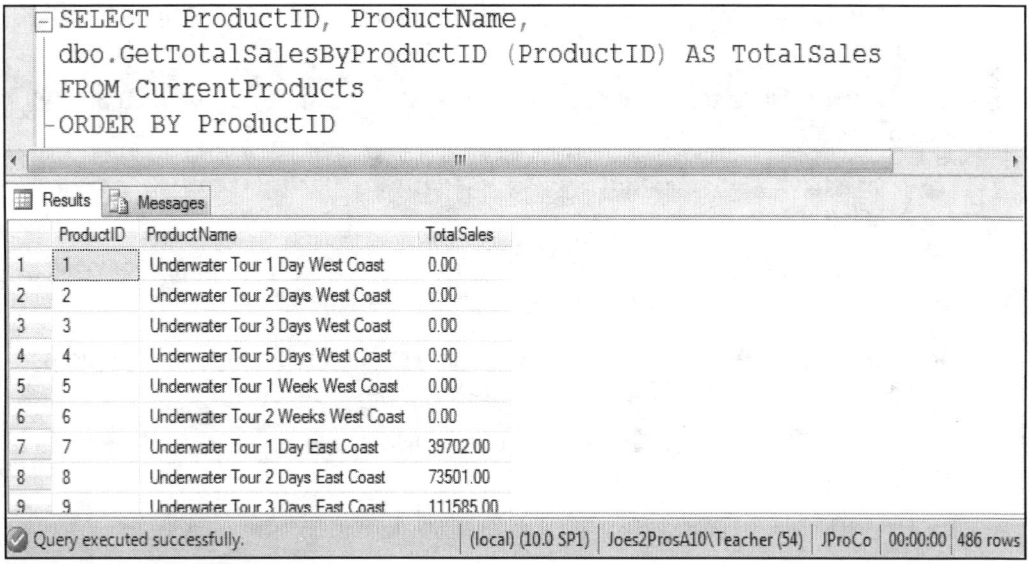

```
SELECT  ProductID, ProductName,
dbo.GetTotalSalesByProductID (ProductID) AS TotalSales
FROM CurrentProducts
ORDER BY ProductID
```

	ProductID	ProductName	TotalSales
1	1	Underwater Tour 1 Day West Coast	0.00
2	2	Underwater Tour 2 Days West Coast	0.00
3	3	Underwater Tour 3 Days West Coast	0.00
4	4	Underwater Tour 5 Days West Coast	0.00
5	5	Underwater Tour 1 Week West Coast	0.00
6	6	Underwater Tour 2 Weeks West Coast	0.00
7	7	Underwater Tour 1 Day East Coast	39702.00
8	8	Underwater Tour 2 Days East Coast	73501.00
9	9	Underwater Tour 3 Days East Coast	111585.00

Query executed successfully. | (local) (10.0 SP1) | Joes2ProsA10\Teacher (54) | JProCo | 00:00:00 | 486 rows

Figure 8.18 Skill Check 1 result.

Answer Code: The T-SQL code to this lab can be found in the downloadable files in a file named Lab8.1_ScalarFunctions.sql.

Scalar Functions - Points to Ponder

1. A function is a SQL object stored in a database and consisting of T-SQL code that accepts parameters.
2. A user-defined function is a routine that you can create to accept parameters, perform a task, and return a result set.
3. Functions are routines consisting of one or more T-SQL statements encapsulated for re-use.
4. The body of a function is defined within a BEGIN…END block.
5. There are many types of functions; scalar is just one of them. Some functions return a single value and others return a list of values.
6. A scalar function returns a single value of the type defined in the RETURNS clause.
7. If you are asked to create a function that returns a single value then always choose a scalar function.
8. Above the body the T-SQL syntax is CREATE FUNCTION *FunctionName* RETURNS *datatype* AS….
9. To alter a function you would use the ALTER FUNCTION command, to drop it you would use the DROP FUNCTION command.
10. Both User-Defined Functions (UDFs) and stored procedures allow you to combine and save SQL statements for future use.
11. You can use functions as part of an expression field in a SELECT statement. Stored procedures can't be part of a query.
12. Everything you can do in a UDF can be done with a stored procedure.
13. Not every SQL statement or operation is valid within a function. The following are not allowed in a UDF:
    a. Calling on other non-deterministic functions like GetDate( ).
    b. UPDATE, INSERT, or DELETE statements to a view or table. You can, however, update a variable (UPDATE @Num = @Num + 1).
    c. No DDL, DCL, or TCL statements allowed in a function.
    d. Functions do not support error handling (see Chapters 10 and 11).
14. UDF's have some limitations that stored procedures do not have, such as:
    a. Stored procedures are called independently with an EXEC command, whereas functions must be called by a SQL statement.
    b. Functions must always return a value, whereas stored procedures do not have this requirement.

Table-Valued Functions

In the last section, we learned that scalar-valued functions return a single value. **Table-valued functions** return tabular result sets ("tabular" meaning like a table). Table-valued functions look a lot like views because they both show us a tabular result set. Table-valued functions can be based on one or more base tables.

Creating and Implementing Table-Valued Functions

The body of a table-valued function will essentially contain a query. Let's begin with a query containing four fields and all of the records from the CurrentProducts table (Figure 8.19).

```
SELECT ProductID, ProductName, RetailPrice, Category
FROM CurrentProducts
```

Results | Messages

	ProductID	ProductName	RetailPrice	Category
1	1	Underwater Tour 1 Day West Coast	61.483	No-Stay
2	2	Underwater Tour 2 Days West Coast	110.6694	Overnight-Stay
3	3	Underwater Tour 3 Days West Coast	184.449	Medium-Stay
4	4	Underwater Tour 5 Days West Coast	245.932	Medium-Stay
5	5	Underwater Tour 1 Week West Coast	307.415	LongTerm-Stay

Query executed successfully. | (local) (10.0 SP1) | Joes2ProsA10\Teacher (53) | JProCo | 00:00:00 | 486 rows

Figure 8.19 This query contains four fields and all records of the CurrentProducts table.

This query will become the heart of a new table-valued function, GetAllProducts (see Figure 8.20). By placing the query within a set of parentheses, and after the keyword RETURN, we have the body of the function. The RETURNS TABLE keyword specifies that the table-valued function GetAllProducts must return the result in the form of a table (see Figure 8.20).

```
CREATE FUNCTION GetAllProducts( )
RETURNS TABLE
AS
RETURN
    (SELECT ProductID, ProductName, RetailPrice, Category
    FROM CurrentProducts)
GO
```

Messages

Command(s) completed successfully.

Figure 8.20 The GetAllProducts table-valued function is created and returns a tabular result set.

Just how do you query a table-valued function? The syntax is somewhat similar to how you would run a SELECT statement against a table or a view. Compare Figures 8.21 and 8.22 and notice that SQL Server requires that a set of parentheses follow the name of a table-valued function in a query.

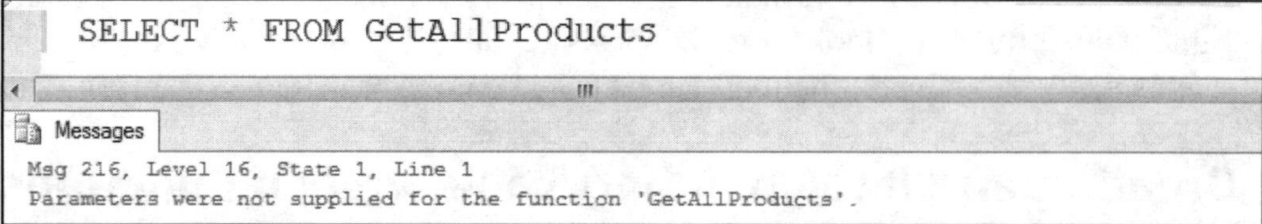

Figure 8.21 Querying a table-valued function without its parentheses results in an error message.

All functions need to be called by using a set of parentheses with all required parameters inside them. If the function has no parameters (which is currently the case with GetAllProducts), then you will simply include an empty set of parentheses (see Figure 8.22).

```
SELECT * FROM GetAllProducts()
```

Results | Messages

	ProductID	ProductName	RetailPrice	Category
1	1	Underwater Tour 1 Day West Coast	61.483	No-Stay
2	2	Underwater Tour 2 Days West Coast	110.6694	Overnight-Stay
3	3	Underwater Tour 3 Days West Coast	184.449	Medium-Stay
4	4	Underwater Tour 5 Days West Coast	245.932	Medium-Stay
5	5	Underwater Tour 1 Week West Co...	307.415	LongTerm-St...

Query executed successfully. | (local) (10.0 SP1) | Joes2ProsA10\Teacher (53) | JProCo | 00:00:00 | 486 rows

Figure 8.22 You must include parentheses when calling upon any type of function.

To view all of the table-valued functions contained in the JProCo database from within the Object Explorer tree, traverse this path:

OE > Databases > JProCo > Programmability > Functions > Table-valued Functions

In Figure 8.23, we see JProCo currently contains five table-valued functions. Notice that the GetAllProducts table-valued function which we just created is present.

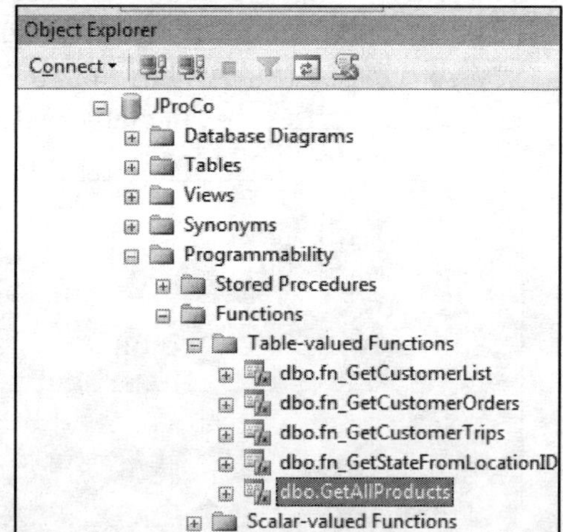

Figure 8.23 JProCo's table-valued functions.

Views versus Parameterized Table-Valued Functions

Views and table-valued functions are both useful ways to see the result set for a pre-defined query. There is no way to pass a variable into a view and change the way it runs. Views are hard-coded and their criteria do not change. A table-valued function can display different results by passing values into its parameter(s) at runtime. Let's begin by selecting all 'No-Stay' records from the CurrentProducts table (see Figure 8.24). We want to turn this query into a function and allow that function to pick the category.

```
SELECT ProductID, ProductName, RetailPrice, Category
FROM CurrentProducts
WHERE Category = 'No-Stay'
```

Results | Messages

	ProductID	ProductName	RetailPrice	Category
1	1	Underwater Tour 1 Day West Coast	61.483	No-Stay
2	7	Underwater Tour 1 Day East Coast	80.859	No-Stay
3	13	Underwater Tour 1 Day Mexico	105.059	No-Stay
4	19	Underwater Tour 1 Day Canada	85.585	No-Stay
5	25	Underwater Tour 1 Day Scandinavia	116.118	No-Stay
6	31	History Tour 1 Day West Coast	74.622	No-Stay
7	37	History Tour 1 Day East Coast	107.159	No-Stay
8	43	History Tour 1 Day Mexico	71.142	No-Stay

Query executed successfully. | (local) (10.0 SP1) | Joes2ProsA10\Teacher (54) | JProCo | 00:00:00 | 80 rows

Figure 8.24 This query shows all 'No-Stay' products from the CurrentProducts table.

We're going to enclose our query in parentheses, indent it, and then add some code to create a function. We will create the GetCategoryProducts function which takes an @Category parameter (see Figure 8.25). The query within the table-valued function will predicate on the value passed in when the function is called.

```
CREATE FUNCTION GetCategoryProducts (@Category NVARCHAR(25))
RETURNS TABLE
AS
RETURN
(
    SELECT ProductID, ProductName, RetailPrice, Category
    FROM CurrentProducts
    WHERE Category = @Category
)
GO
```

Messages

Command(s) completed successfully.

Figure 8.25 The GetCategoryProducts will return a result set predicating on the parameter value.

Now let's call upon our newly created table-valued function and specify 'No-stay' as the category. Running this query (see Figure 8.26) against GetCategoryProducts while passing in the parameter value of 'No-stay' will return a result set consisting of 80 records.

```
SELECT * FROM GetCategoryProducts('No-stay')
```

	ProductID	ProductName	RetailPrice	Category
1	1	Underwater Tour 1 Day West Coast	61.483	No-Stay
2	7	Underwater Tour 1 Day East Coast	80.859	No-Stay
3	13	Underwater Tour 1 Day Mexico	105.059	No-Stay
4	19	Underwater Tour 1 Day Canada	85.585	No-Stay
5	25	Underwater Tour 1 Day Scandinavia	116.118	No-Stay
6	31	History Tour 1 Day West Coast	74.622	No-Stay
7	37	History Tour 1 Day East Coast	107.159	No-Stay

Query executed successfully. | (local) (10.0 SP1) | Joes2ProsA10\Teacher (55) | JProCo | 00:00:00 | 80 rows

Figure 8.26 Calling on GetCategoryProducts with the 'No-Stay' Category produces 80 rows.

Change the parameter value to 'Medium-stay' and run this query. The GetCategoryProducts function now returns164 records (see Figure 8.27).

```
SELECT * FROM GetCategoryProducts('Medium-stay')
```

	ProductID	ProductName	RetailPrice	Category
1	3	Underwater Tour 3 Days West Coast	184.449	Medium-Stay
2	4	Underwater Tour 5 Days West Coast	245.932	Medium-Stay
3	9	Underwater Tour 3 Days East Coast	242.577	Medium-Stay
4	10	Underwater Tour 5 Days East Coast	323.436	Medium-Stay
5	15	Underwater Tour 3 Days Mexico	315.177	Medium-Stay
6	16	Underwater Tour 5 Days Mexico	420.236	Medium-Stay
7	21	Underwater Tour 3 Days Canada	256.755	Medium-Stay

Query executed successfully. | (local) (10.0 SP1) | Joes2ProsA10\Teacher (55) | JProCo | 00:00:00 | 164 rows

Figure 8.27 Changing the parameter value to 'Medium-stay' returns 164 rows.

Whenever you call a function, you must remember to use a set of parentheses and include the parameter(s) which the function expects. Earlier in this section, we demonstrated this by running our queries without parentheses. In the next figure (see Figure 8.28), let's demonstrate the error message which results from forgetting to include the needed parameter within the parentheses. SQL Server's error message tells us that our code doesn't match the function's parameter signature. In other words, it reminds us that we need to specify a Category.

```
SELECT * FROM GetCategoryProducts()
```

Messages

```
Msg 313, Level 16, State 3, Line 1
An insufficient number of arguments were supplied
for the procedure or function GetCategoryProducts.
```

Figure 8.28 Not supplying the right parameters to your function will generate an error message.

Lab 8.2: Table-Valued Functions

Lab Prep: Before you can begin the lab, you must have SQL Server installed and have run the script SQLProgrammingChapter8.2Setup.sql.

Skill Check 1: Create a function named GetGrants( ) that returns the GrantID, GrantName, EmpID, and Amount fields from all records of the grant table. Call on this function with a Select statement. When you're done, your result should resemble this figure (see Figure 8.29).

```
SELECT * FROM GetGrants()
```

Results | Messages

	GrantID	GrantName	EmpID	Amount
1	001	92 Purr_Scents %% team	7	4750.00
2	002	K-Land fund trust	2	15750.00
3	003	Robert@BigStarBank.com	7	18100.00
4	005	BIG 6's Foundation%	4	21000.00
5	006	TALTA_Kishan International	3	18100.00
6	007	Ben@MoreTechnology.com	10	41000.00
7	008	www.@-Last-U-Can-Help.com	7	25000.00
8	009	Thank you @.com	11	21500.00
9	010	Just Mom	5	9900.00
10	011	Big Giver Tom	7	19000.00
11	012	Mega Mercy	9	55000.00
12	013	Hope Reaches	7	29000.00
13	014	Everyone Wins	4	12500.00

(local) (10.0 SP1) | Joes2ProsA10\Teacher (54) | JProCo | 00:00:00 | 13 rows

Figure 8.29 Skill Check 1.

Skill Check 2: Create a Function named GetGrantsByCity that takes a Varchar(25) @City parameter and returns all the grants procured by employees of that city. Call on this function with a Select statement and pass in 'Seattle' to your parameter. When you're done, your result should resemble this figure (see Figure 8.30).

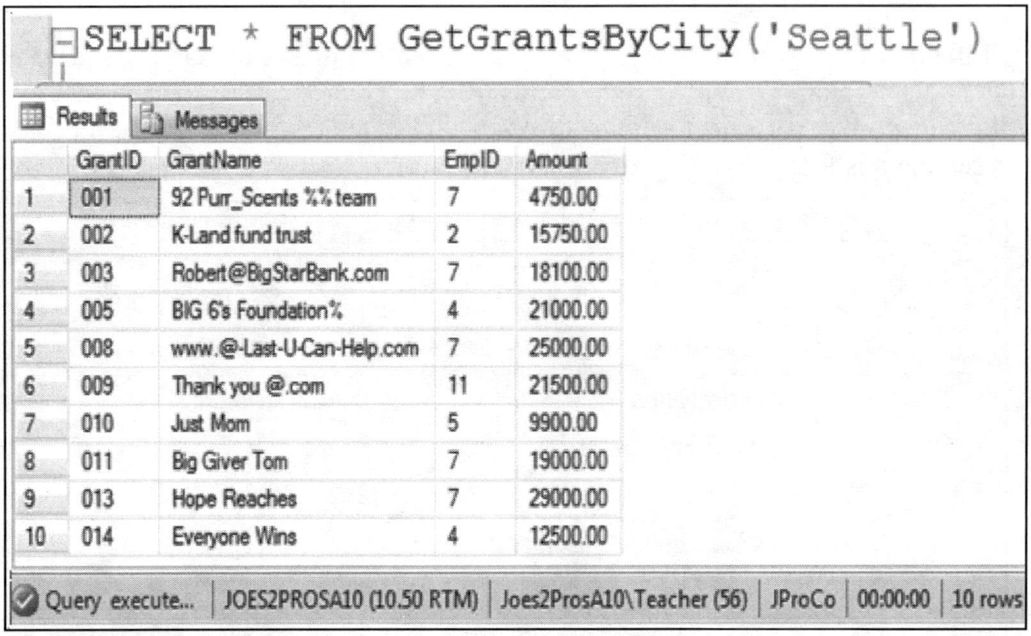

```
SELECT * FROM GetGrantsByCity('Seattle')
```

Results | Messages

	GrantID	GrantName	EmpID	Amount
1	001	92 Purr_Scents %% team	7	4750.00
2	002	K-Land fund trust	2	15750.00
3	003	Robert@BigStarBank.com	7	18100.00
4	005	BIG 6's Foundation%	4	21000.00
5	008	www.@-Last-U-Can-Help.com	7	25000.00
6	009	Thank you @.com	11	21500.00
7	010	Just Mom	5	9900.00
8	011	Big Giver Tom	7	19000.00
9	013	Hope Reaches	7	29000.00
10	014	Everyone Wins	4	12500.00

Query execute... | JOES2PROSA10 (10.50 RTM) | Joes2ProsA10\Teacher (56) | JProCo | 00:00:00 | 10 rows

Figure 8.30 Skill Check 2 result.

Answer Code: The T-SQL code to this lab can be found in the downloadable files in a file named Lab8.2_TableValuedFunctions.sql.

Table-Valued Functions - Points to Ponder

1. Functions are similar to stored procedures in the way they work, but you must call a function using a SELECT statement or a WHERE clause within a SELECT statement.
2. When functions are executed, they can return results in the form of a value or a table.
3. You can reference a table-valued function in the FROM clause of a SELECT statement just like you when querying a view or a table.
4. User-defined functions accept values through parameters, and they return a result set based on the calculations performed on them.
5. User-defined functions allow you to create code once and invoke it (i.e., call upon it) multiple times.
6. There are three types of functions:
   a. Scalar function – returns a single value like Count( ) or Max( ).
   b. Table-valued function – returns a table that is the result of a single SELECT statement, similar to a view but it can take parameters.
   c. Multi-statement table-valued function – returns a table built with one or more T-SQL statements.
7. Table functions specify TABLE as the return type (RETURNS TABLE).
8. Table functions have a great advantage over views: they allow a parameterized look at your table data.
9. The SELECT statement in the RETURN clause of a table-valued function must be enclosed in parentheses: RETURN SELECT (…). (Code samples may be found in Figures 8.20 and 8.25.)
10. When calling functions, a set of parentheses must follow the function name. Inside of these, you will include any values to be passed into the parameters of the function. If there are no parameters, leave the parentheses empty.
11. Use a table-valued function anywhere you would normally use a view. *Example:* SELECT * FROM dbo.GetEmployee(3).
12. SQL Server comes with pre-defined functions (called system functions), or you can define your own functions (user-defined functions or UDFs).

Function Determinability

Some questions always have the same answer. For example, if you ask for my initials, I will say "R.A.M." If you ask me that same question tomorrow you would get the same answer. Unless I actually change the source of the data (i.e., change my name), this answer will always be the same. This is an example of a **deterministic** operation.

If you were to ask what I am doing today, you might get an answer like "Work" on a Monday, or "Church" on a Sunday. This type of a question is a **non-deterministic** operation, because the answer is not always the same. In other words, the answer will vary depending upon conditions, such as when the question is asked, and thus cannot be answered prior to runtime. This section will explore both deterministic and non-deterministic functions.

Using Deterministic Functions

Let's begin with a query selecting four fields from the MgmtTraining table.

```
SELECT ClassID, ClassName, ClassDurationHours, ApprovedDate
FROM dbo.MgmtTraining
```

Results | Messages

	ClassID	ClassName	ClassDurationHours	ApprovedDate
1	1	Embracing Diversity	12	2007-01-01 00:00:00.000
2	2	Interviewing	6	2007-01-15 00:00:00.000
3	3	Difficult Negotiations	30	2008-02-12 00:00:00.000
4	4	Empowering Others	18	2010-10-27 15:08:19.583
5	6	Passing Certifications	13	2010-10-27 15:08:23.440
6	7	Effective Communications	35	2010-10-27 15:08:23.730
7	8	Story Presentations	19	2010-10-27 15:08:23.730

Figure 8.31 A simple query returning four fields from the MgmtTraining table.

Let's create a fifth field (ShortName) that pulls the first five letters from the ClassName field. The ShortName value for the first record would be "Embra," which are the first five letters of "Embracing Diversity."

```
SELECT ClassID, ClassName, ClassDurationHours, ApprovedDate,
LEFT(ClassName,5) as ShortName
FROM dbo.MgmtTraining
```

Results | Messages

	ClassID	ClassName	ClassDurationHours	ApprovedDate	ShortName
1	1	Embracing Diversity	12	2007-01-01 00:00:00.000	Embra
2	2	Interviewing	6	2007-01-15 00:00:00.000	Inter
3	3	Difficult Negotiations	30	2008-02-12 00:00:00.000	Diffi
4	4	Empowering Others	18	2010-10-27 15:08:19.583	Empow
5	6	Passing Certifications	13	2010-10-27 15:08:23.440	Passi
6	7	Effective Communications	35	2010-10-27 15:08:23.730	Effec
7	8	Story Presentations	19	2010-10-27 15:08:23.730	Story

Figure 8.32 The LEFT( ) deterministic function is being used as an expression field in the query.

Before we even run this query (in Figure 8.32), we know what the results will be because they come directly from the ClassName field. No change to the ShortName field is possible unless a change first happens in the ClassName field. Deterministic fields will never change their values without their source fields changing first.

Deterministic Functions in Views

You can put all types of system-supplied functions into views. In Figure 8.33 a query using the LEFT( ) function to create the ShortName expression field is placed inside the vTraining view. The view is created with SCHEMABINDING to prevent someone from deleting the dbo.MgmtTraining base table.

```
CREATE VIEW vTraining
WITH SCHEMABINDING
AS
    SELECT ClassID, ClassName,
    ClassDurationHours, ApprovedDate,
    LEFT(ClassName,5) as ShortName
    FROM dbo.MgmtTraining
GO
```

```
Messages
Command(s) completed successfully.
```

Figure 8.33 A query with a function is created inside the vTraining view.

We are able to predicate on any field contained in the vTraining view. In Figure 8.34, our query predicates on the ShortName field, which is the expression field that uses the LEFT function.

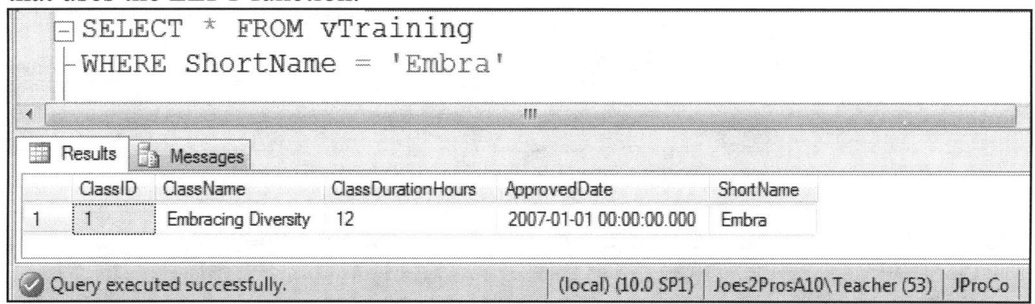

Figure 8.34 Predicating on the expression field from outside the view gets your desired result set.

Suppose your company states that this query in Figure 8.34 needs to run as fast as possible. We know we'll get better performance if we predicate on an indexed field when we query the view. Let's create an index on this view (see Figure 8.35). It runs successfully because all functions present (in this case we have just one) are *deterministic.*

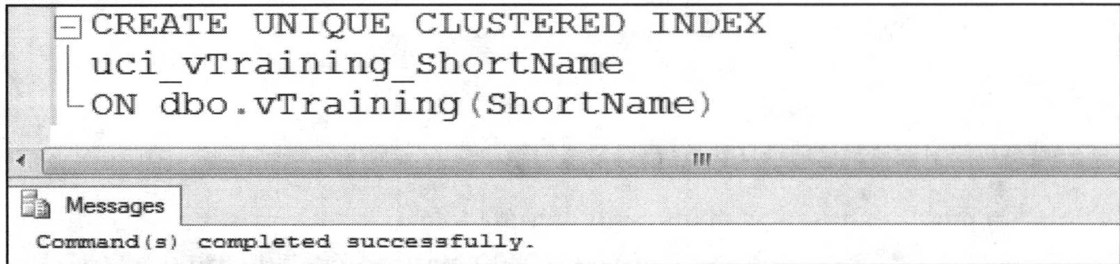
CREATE UNIQUE CLUSTERED INDEX
uci_vTraining_ShortName
ON dbo.vTraining(ShortName)
Messages
Command(s) completed successfully.

Figure 8.35 We can create an index on vTraining since all of its functions are deterministic.

Non-Deterministic Functions in Views

You can index a view containing an expression field that is created with a function if all the fields are deterministic. If even one non-deterministic field is present, then the view cannot be indexed.

Our next example will use the Customer table in the JProCo database. Let's create an expression field from the GETDATE function (see Figure 8.36).

```
SELECT CustomerID, CustomerType,
FirstName, LastName, GETDATE() as RunTime
FROM dbo.Customer
WHERE CustomerType = 'Consumer'
```

Results | Messages

	CustomerID	CustomerType	FirstName	LastName	RunTime
1	1	Consumer	Mark	Williams	2010-10-27 15:37:48.773
2	2	Consumer	Lee	Young	2010-10-27 15:37:48.773
3	3	Consumer	Patricia	Martin	2010-10-27 15:37:48.773
4	4	Consumer	Mary	Lopez	2010-10-27 15:37:48.773

Query executed successfully. | (local) (10.0 SP1) | Joes2ProsA10\Teacher (53) | JProCo

Figure 8.36 The query includes an expression field based upon a non-deterministic function.

Notice that Mark Williams appears here as Customer 1 because he's CustomerID 1 in the Customer table. CustomerID = 1 will always be Mark Williams (i.e., deterministic). However, each RunTime value returned by the GETDATE field will be different every time we run this query (i.e., non-deterministic).

We are able to successfully create a view (vCustomer) (see Figure 8.37), which includes the non-deterministic function, GETDATE( ).

```
CREATE VIEW vCustomer
WITH SCHEMABINDING
AS
    SELECT CustomerID, CustomerType,
    FirstName, LastName, GETDATE() as RunTime
    FROM dbo.Customer
    WHERE CustomerType = 'Consumer'
GO
```

Messages

Command(s) completed successfully.

Figure 8.37 The vCustomer view is created from a query using a non-deterministic function.

We are able to successfully query the vCustomer view and predicate on the CustomerID field (see Figure 8.38).

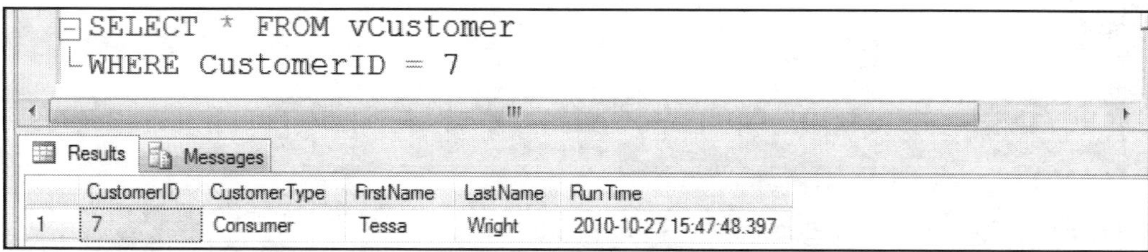

Figure 8.38 This vCustomer view is predicating on CustomerID.

Management has asked if you can get this query (from Figure 8.38) to run any faster. You attempt to create an index on this view but it fails (see Figure 8.39). The error message says you can't use non-deterministic fields.

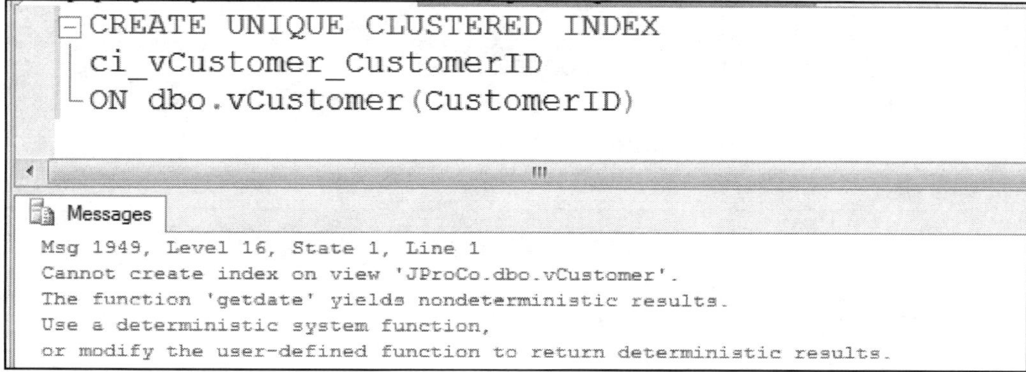

CREATE UNIQUE CLUSTERED INDEX
ci_vCustomer_CustomerID
ON dbo.vCustomer(CustomerID)
Messages
Msg 1949, Level 16, State 1, Line 1
Cannot create index on view 'JProCo.dbo.vCustomer'.
The function 'getdate' yields nondeterministic results.
Use a deterministic system function,
or modify the user-defined function to return deterministic results.

Figure 8.39 An index can't be created on a view which includes a non-deterministic function.

User-Defined Function Determinability

SQL already knows that LEFT is a deterministic function and GETDATE is non-deterministic. When you create a user-defined function, you can create either type of function. The choices you make in constructing your function affect whether the function is deterministic or non-deterministic. Since deterministic functions always return the same result for each input value(s), this function is deterministic (Figure 8.40). For example, if we pass in $100 to the @Price parameter, the value returned will always be $109.50.

```
CREATE FUNCTION dbo.CalculatePriceWithTax(@Price Money)
RETURNS Money
AS
BEGIN
    DECLARE @Total Money
    SET @Total = @Price * 1.095
    RETURN @Total
END
GO
```

Messages

```
Command(s) completed successfully.
```

Figure 8.40 The CalculatePriceWithTax function is created.

If we try to include our new function (CalculatePriceWithTax) in a new schema bound view (vProductPrices), we will get this error message (see Figure 8.41). In order to schema bind this view, the function must first be schema bound.

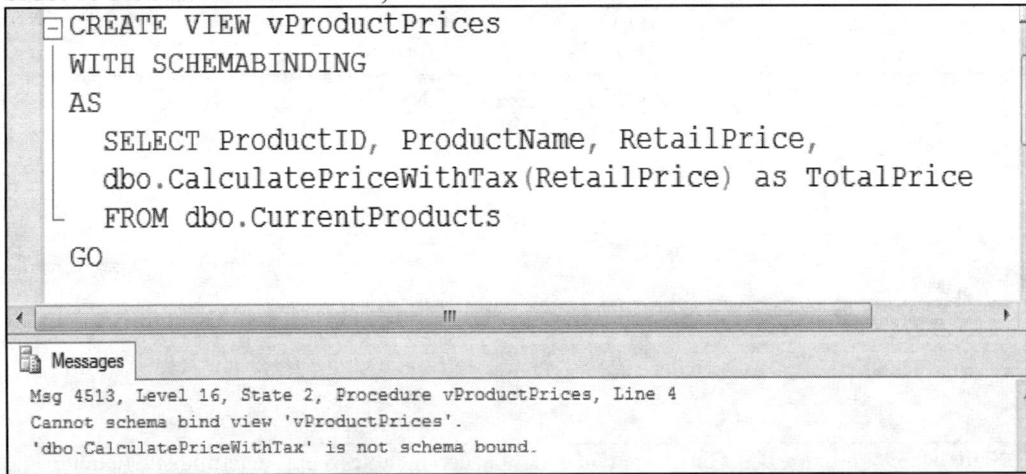

```
CREATE VIEW vProductPrices
WITH SCHEMABINDING
AS
  SELECT ProductID, ProductName, RetailPrice,
  dbo.CalculatePriceWithTax(RetailPrice) as TotalPrice
  FROM dbo.CurrentProducts
GO
```

Messages

```
Msg 4513, Level 16, State 2, Procedure vProductPrices, Line 4
Cannot schema bind view 'vProductPrices'.
'dbo.CalculatePriceWithTax' is not schema bound.
```

Figure 8.41 You can only use schema bound, user-defined functions in schema bound views.

Let's ALTER the function to make it schema bound (see Figure 8.42). SQL Server now allows us to include this user-defined function within a schema bound view.

```
ALTER FUNCTION dbo.CalculatePriceWithTax(@Price Money)
RETURNS Money
WITH SCHEMABINDING
AS
BEGIN
    DECLARE @Total Money
    SET @Total = @Price * 1.095
    RETURN @Total
END
GO
```

Messages

Command(s) completed successfully.

Figure 8.42 The CalculatePriceWithTax function is altered to use SCHEMABINDING.

We can now reattempt our code which failed earlier (shown in Figure 8.41). It now runs successfully (see Figure 8.43). The view is now schema bound and uses the dbo.CalculatePriceWithTax user-defined scalar function.

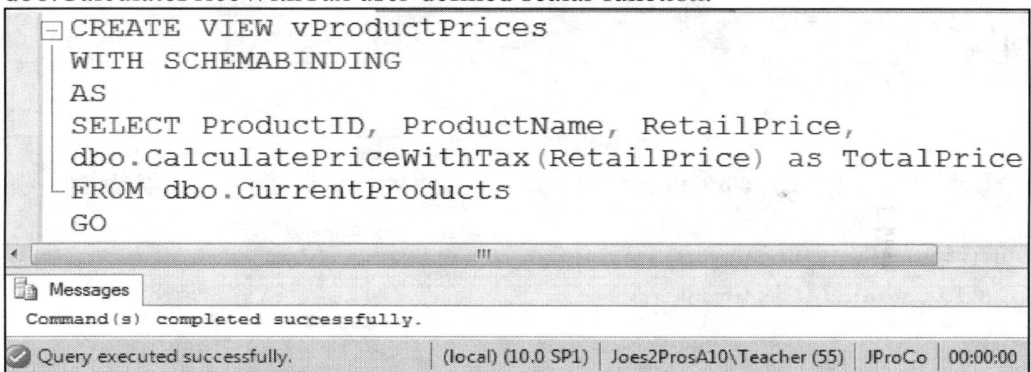

```
CREATE VIEW vProductPrices
WITH SCHEMABINDING
AS
SELECT ProductID, ProductName, RetailPrice,
dbo.CalculatePriceWithTax(RetailPrice) as TotalPrice
FROM dbo.CurrentProducts
GO
```


Figure 8.43 The vProductPrices view is created successfully and is schema bound.

Any function that is schema bound is considered by SQL Server to be deterministic. Since this view (vProductPrices) is schema bound, we know it includes only deterministic function(s). Thus, we should now be able to add an index to this view. Let's add a unique clustered index to the ProductID field of the vProductPrices view (see Figure 8.44).

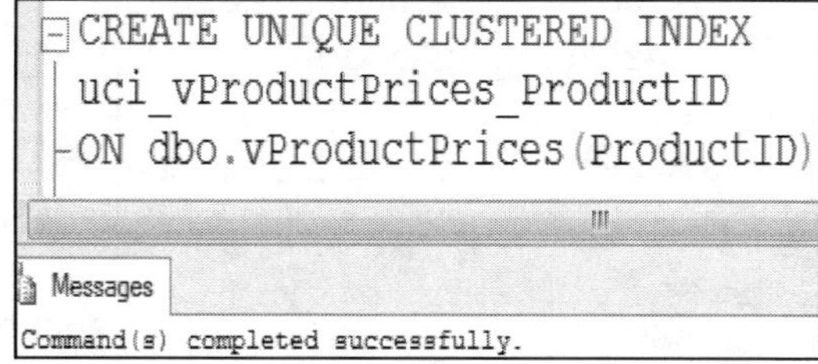

```
CREATE UNIQUE CLUSTERED INDEX
uci_vProductPrices_ProductID
ON dbo.vProductPrices(ProductID)
```


Figure 8.44 An index is added to vProductPrices.

Lab 8.3: Function Determinability

Lab Prep: Before you can begin the lab, you must have SQL Server installed and have run the SQLProgrammingChapter8.3Setup.sql script.

Skill Check 1: Create a view vLocations which selects the LocationID, Street, and City fields. Include an expression field called BigCity which uses the UPPER( ) function to capitalize every city name found in the Location table.

```
SELECT * FROM vLocations
```

Results | Messages

	LocationID	street	city	BigCity
1	1	545 Pike	Seattle	SEATTLE
2	2	222 Second AVE	Boston	BOSTON
3	4	444 Ruby ST	Spokane	SPOKANE
4	5	1595 Main	Philadelphia	PHILADELPHIA
5	6	915 Wallaby Drive	Sydney	SYDNEY

Query executed... | (local) (10.0 SP1) | Joes2ProsA10\Teacher (54

Figure 8.45 Skill Check 1 result.

Skill Check 2: Create a Unique Clustered Index called uci_vLocations_LocationID on the LocationID field of the vLocations view.

Answer Code: The T-SQL code to this lab can be found in the downloadable files in a file named Lab8.3_DeterministicFunctions.sql.

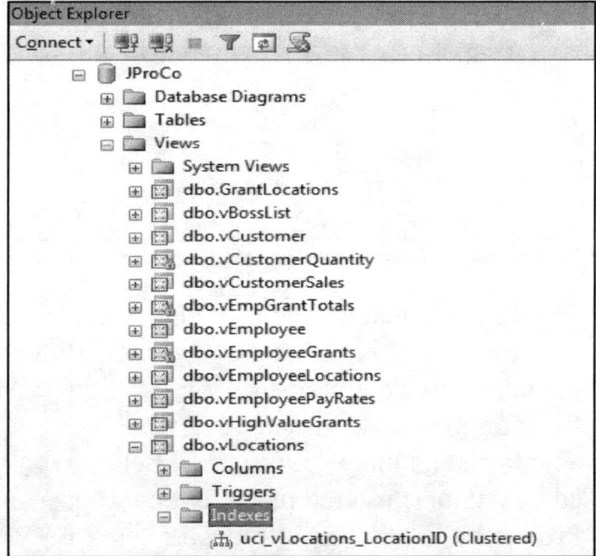

Figure 8.46 Add a unique clustered index to vLocations.

Function Determinability - Points to Ponder

1. All functions are either deterministic or non-deterministic.
2. Deterministic functions are ones that don't change their value unless the underlying data in the table changes.
3. Non-deterministic functions can return different values even when the data in the database does not change.
4. You can place both deterministic and non-deterministic functions inside of a view.
5. You can only index a view containing functions if all the functions are deterministic.
6. User-defined functions are deterministic when:
    a. The function is schema-bound.
    b. All functions it calls upon are deterministic.

Chapter Glossary

BEGIN…END block: used to enclose the body of a function.
Deterministic function: a function whose result doesn't change unless the underlying data in the table changes.
Function: a SQL object stored in a database and consisting of prewritten code that accepts parameters.
Multi-statement table-valued function: returns a table built by one or more T-SQL statements.
Non-deterministic function: a function whose result can return different values even when the data in the database does not change.
Scalar function: a function whose result consists of a single value; Count( ) and Max( ) are examples of scalar functions.
Table-valued function: a function which takes a table as an input and whose output is a result set; similar to a view but it can take parameters.
User-defined function (UDF): a routine that you can create to accept parameter values, perform a task, and return a result set.

Chapter Eight - Review Quiz

1.) You are told to create a scalar function. This means your function should:

O a. Return no values.
O b. Return a single value.
O c. Return a list of values.
O d. Return a table of values.

2.) You need to create two functions that will each return a scalar result of the number of hours each user has logged for: 1) the current day, and 2) month to date. You will pass in the user ID as a parameter value. What must you do?

□ a. Create a function that returns a list of values representing the login times for a given user.
□ b. Create a function that returns a list of values representing the people who have logged more hours than the current user has logged.
□ c. Create a function that returns a numeric value representing the number of hours that a user has logged for the current day.
□ d. Create a function that returns a number value representing the number of hours that a user has logged for the current month.

3.) You are responsible for managing a SQL Server 2008 database that stores sales information. Many values in NChar columns in the database tables contain preceding or trailing spaces. You need to implement a mechanism that selects the data from the tables but without the leading and trailing spaces. Your solution must be available for reuse in Transact-SQL statements and views. What should you do?

O a. Create DML triggers that query the Inserted and Deleted tables.
O b. Create a stored procedure that calls the LTRIM and RTRIM built-in functions.
O c. Create a Transact-SQL function that calls the LTRIM and RTRIM built-in functions.
O d. Call the TRIM built-in functions.

4.) You want to return a Boolean result that examines a date and determines whether it occurs in a leap year. What type of function will do this?

O a. Table-valued.
O b. Scalar-valued.

5.) You have a view that uses an expression field which comes from a function. You want to index this column but get the following error message:

Msg 1949, Level 16, State 1, Line 2
Cannot create index on view 'JProCo.dbo.vCustomer'.
The function 'getdate' yields nondeterministic results. Use a deterministic system function, or modify the user-defined function to return deterministic results.

You create another view using the LEFT( ) function as an expression field, and this view indexes just fine. Which ObjectProperty is allowing the LEFT( ) function to be part of an indexed view?

O a. IsDeterministic is set to true.
O b. IsDeterministic is set to false.

6.) The following query finds all reports for leap year months since 1950:

SELECT *
FROM Reports
WHERE ???????? (rMonth, rYear) = 29
AND rYear > 1950

If, for a specified year, the month of February will contain 29 days, you want the query to include the record in your query. Which object should you use in your query predicate?

O a. DML trigger
O b. Stored procedure
O c. Table-valued function
O d. Scalar function

Answer Key

1.) b 2.) c, d 3.) c 4.) b 5.) a 6.) d

Bug Catcher Game

To play the Bug Catcher game, run the file BugCatcher_Chapter8_Functions.pps from the BugCatcher folder of the companion files located at www.Joes2Pros.com.

Chapter 9. SQL Error Messages

Have you ever heard a team member or co-worker say "That's not my problem" or "That's not my job"? Often when we hear this sentiment, it's associated with someone not willing to lend a hand to solve an issue but rather presumes someone else will do the work. Until SQL Server 2005, the "that's-not-my-problem" poster pretty well described SQL Server's approach toward error handling. It would tell you when an error occurred, but it was entirely up to the calling code to deal with the error. A custom application written in another language (e.g., C#) was needed to actually handle the error.

SQL Server has improved greatly since SQL Server 2000. It still has the same ability to point out errors but has significantly enhanced its capabilities and options for handling errors. In this chapter, we will explore the ways SQL Server raises errors and the options for having SQL handle those errors for you.

READER NOTE: *In order to follow along with the examples in the first section of Chapter 9, please run the setup script SQLProgrammingChapter9.0Setup.sql. The setup scripts for this book are posted at Joes2Pros.com.*

SQL Server Error Messages

By now, most readers have likely learned that it is better to deal with problems early on while they are small. SQL Server detects and helps you identify most errors before you are even allowed to run the code. For example, if you try to run a query against a table which does not exist, SQL Server informs you via IntelliSense while you're coding the query or via an error message when you attempt to run the query. You also will get an error message if you try to insert a null value into a non-nullable field. This section will cover how SQL Server raises error messages.

Errors in SQL Statements

SQL Server will raise errors when the code you have written cannot or should not execute. For example, a table should not be created if one with the same name already exists. Also, you can't run a stored procedure if the name you are calling does not exist. Attempting to run such code will cause SQL to raise an error.

SQL Server raises an error whenever a statement cannot, or should not, complete its execution. For example, we know there is already an Employee table in the JProCo database. In Figure 9.1 we see code to create another Employee table. *If we attempt to run the code below, should SQL Server permit our longstanding Employee table to be overwritten?*

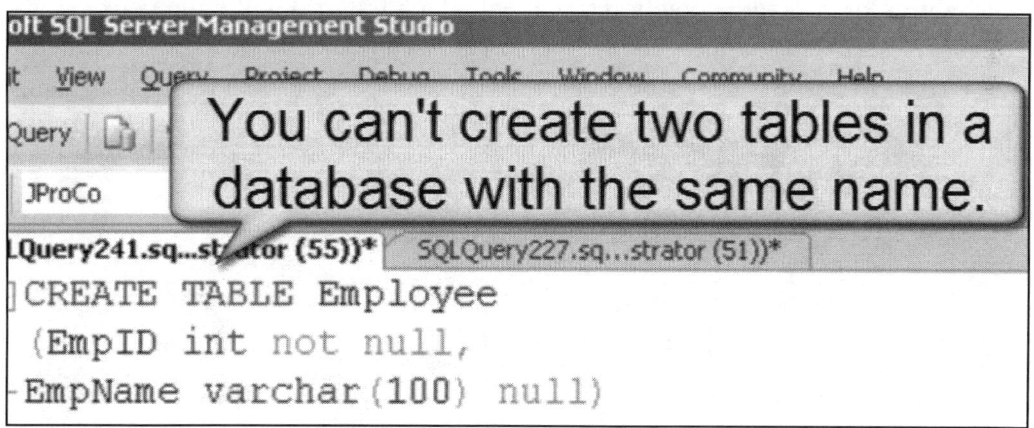

Figure 9.1 There is already an Employee table in the db, which we don't want to be overwritten.

Having a new, empty Employee table overwrite the one we are using would *not* be a good idea. In Figure 9.2 we see SQL Server prevent the accidental loss of the valuable data in the existing Employee table. When we run this, SQL Server alerts us that our code cannot be run and displays the reason in an error message.

Messages
Msg 2714, Level 16, State 6, Line 1
There is already an object named 'Employee' in the database.
Error Message (Error Text)

Figure 9.2 SQL Server alerts us that there is already an Employee table in our database.

Notice that this is error message 2714 (see Figures 9.2 and 9.3). Error severity levels range from a low of 0 to a maximum of 25, and the error severity level here is 16. We will discuss error severity later in this chapter.

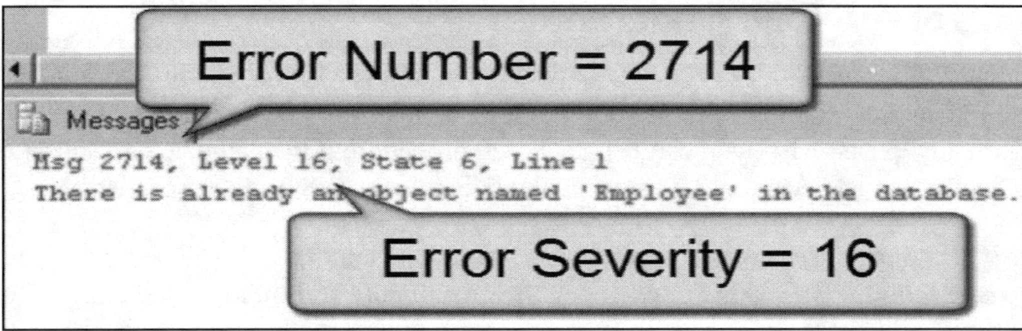
Error Number = 2714
Messages
Msg 2714, Level 16, State 6, Line 1
There is already an object named 'Employee' in the database.
Error Severity = 16

Figure 9.3 We will discuss error severity later in this chapter.

Now let's try a very similar statement, except we'll use a different name to create the table. Here is a table creation statement which will run without an error (Figure 9.4). *This is because there is no object named TempStaff in the JProCo database.*

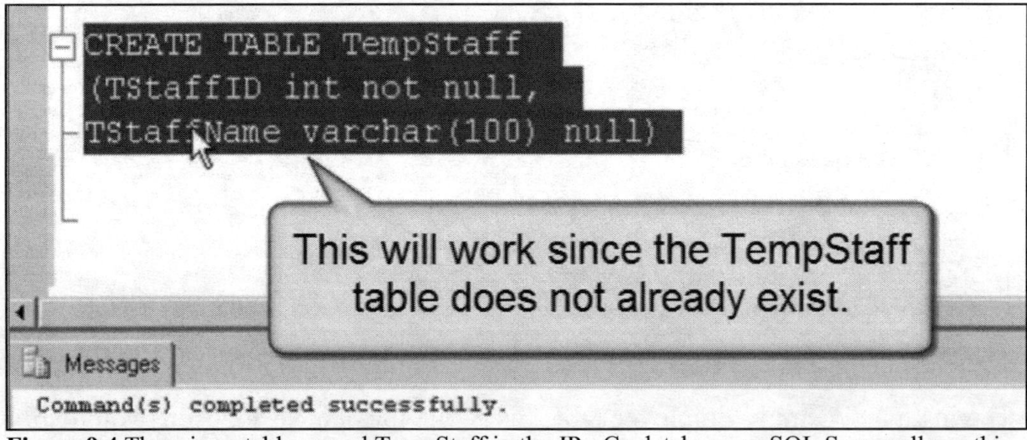
CREATE TABLE TempStaff
(TStaffID int not null,
TStaffName varchar(100) null)
This will work since the TempStaff table does not already exist.
Messages
Command(s) completed successfully.

Figure 9.4 There is no table named TempStaff in the JProCo database, so SQL Server allows this code to run and the TempStaff table to be created.

As you can see, a perfectly written table creation statement sometimes will work and under other conditions it may error out. Next we want to create a statement which will never work; it will always return an error message.

In Figure 9.5, the SometimesBad stored procedure will sometimes throw an error message. Don't run this code yet – let's first examine what it does. If SQL finds the TempStaff table, then it will attempt to run the table creation statement. Imagine the TempStaff table didn't exist. In that case, nothing would happen. The IF EXISTS condition would be false so the CREATE TABLE statement would not be attempted.

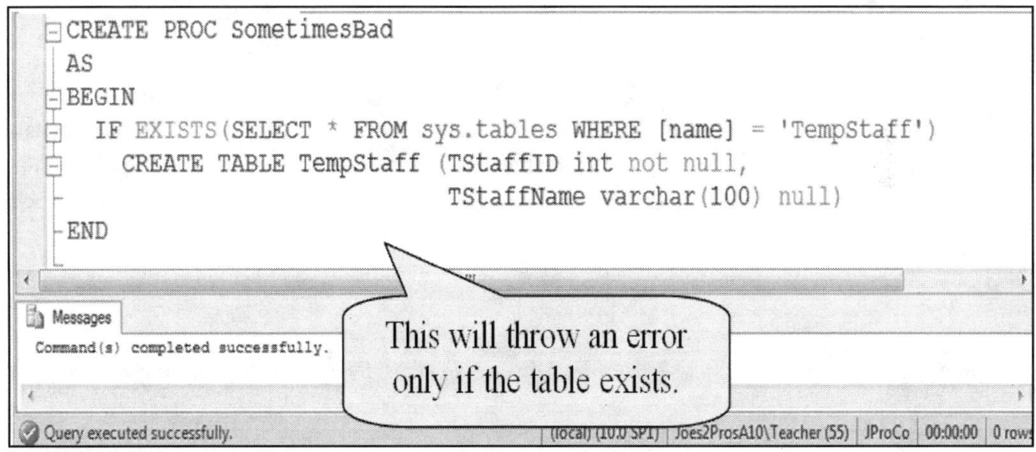

Figure 9.5 This code will throw an error only if the table exists.

We know one way to generate an error is to try creating a table which already exists. Another way is to try dropping a table which doesn't exist. If you run the SometimesBad stored procedure, it will only throw an error if the TempStaff table already exists. For testing purposes, we want a stored procedure like SometimesBad to always throw an error message. Our next step will be to add an ELSE statement which says that we want to drop the table if it is not found (Figure 9.6).

Look closely at this code and recognize that it will always throw an error (Figure 9.6). If the TempStaff table exists, then trying to execute a statement to create this table generates an error. And if the TempStaff table doesn't exist, then executing a statement which attempts to drop this table will similarly generate an error.

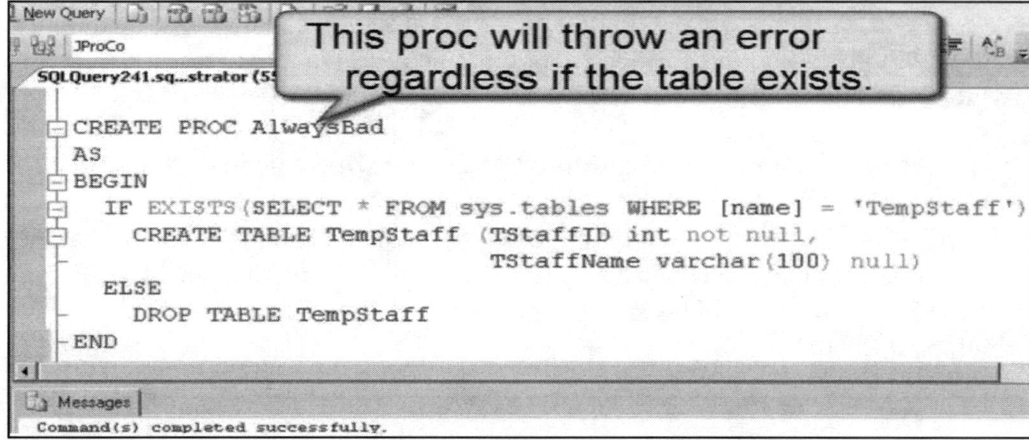

Figure 9.6 This proc will throw an error regardless of whether the table exists.

If you were to create and run the AlwaysBad sproc, you would see that attempting to execute it will <u>always</u> result in an error message (see Figures 9.7-9.8). During the sproc execution, SQL tried to create the TempStaff table which already existed.

```
EXEC AlwaysBad
```

Messages

```
Msg 2714, Level 16, State 6, Procedure AlwaysBad, Line 5
There is already an object named 'TempStaff' in the database.
```

Figure 9.7 The AlwaysBad stored procedure throws an error message if the TempStaff table exists.

If the table is not present, then the same stored procedure would still throw an error. Message 3701 indicates that you can't drop the table because it does not exist (see Figure 9.8).

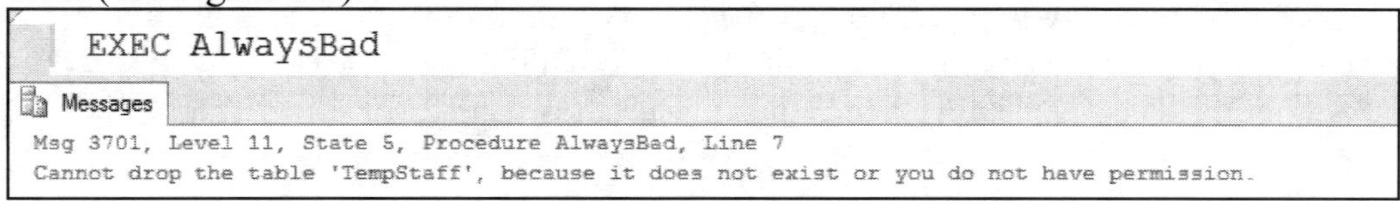

EXEC AlwaysBad
Messages
Msg 3701, Level 11, State 5, Procedure AlwaysBad, Line 7
Cannot drop the table 'TempStaff', because it does not exist or you do not have permission.

Figure 9.8 The AlwaysBad sproc will also throw an error message if the table does not exist.

Again, we know that SQL Server will raise an error whenever a statement cannot, or should not, complete its execution. It's also possible to define your own conditions where SQL Server does not encounter an error but nonetheless doesn't run due to a situation which goes against company policy. For example, updating an employee's payrate to below minimum wage is not a SQL error. However, in such a situation you would prefer that SQL Server generate an error message rather than allowing the bad code to execute.

Custom Error Messages

Suppose you have a stored procedure named UpdateOneEmployee which changes one employee record at a time. The logic of this stored procedure will allow you to potentially update two employees with the same info. Since it is against company policy to update more than one employee record a time, it's extremely unlikely that anyone would ever attempt to update multiple records at once. However, because SQL Server has no restriction against inserting or updating many records in one transaction, you want to add a layer of protection to help enforce company policy. This is a case where you don't want SQL Server to allow this update, even though SQL Server doesn't define it as an error. To accomplish the goal, you can raise your own error message based on conditions which you define.

Let's begin this example by looking at all of the fields and records of the Employee table. We see 21 records and EmpID values ranging from 1 to 21 (see Figure 9.9).

```
SELECT * FROM Employee
```

	EmpID	LastName	FirstName	HireDate	LocationID	ManagerID	Status	HiredOffset	TimeZone
19	19	Beckman	Sandy	2010-01-15 00:00:00.000	1	11	Active	2010-11-01 15:54:54.2300000 -08:00	-08:00
20	20	Winds	Gale	2010-03-25 00:00:00.000	1	11	Active	2010-11-01 15:54:54.3700000 -08:00	-08:00
21	21	Fines	Sue	2010-11-01 15:54:54.380	1	4	Active	2010-11-01 15:54:54.3800000 -08:00	-08:00

Query executed successfully. | (local) (10.0 SP1) | Joes2ProsA10\Teacher (54) | JProCo | 00:00:00 | 21 rows

Figure 9.9 Prepare for the next example by looking at the records and fields of the Employee table.

What we would like to do is create a stored procedure which changes the employee's status based on the EmpID. The update will change the value of the status field. Below (see Figure 9.10) we have a partially written stored procedure that uses the @Status parameter to set the value of the Status field in the Employee table. ***Don't run this code yet.*** Since it doesn't use criteria to filter the Employee records, this sproc would change ALL employees to the same status – *very bad!*

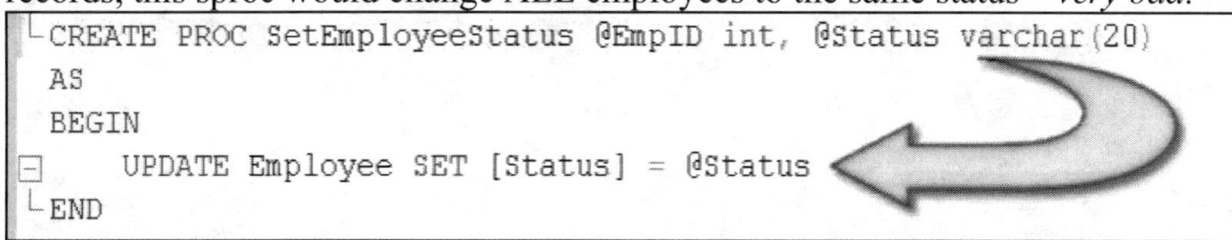

```
CREATE PROC SetEmployeeStatus @EmpID int, @Status varchar(20)
AS
BEGIN
    UPDATE Employee SET [Status] = @Status
END
```

Figure 9.10 This stored procedure will change each employee's status but does not use the EmpID parameter yet.

Let's complete the code by using the @EmpID parameter (Figure 9.11). This stored procedure will change an individual employee's status based on the EmpID.

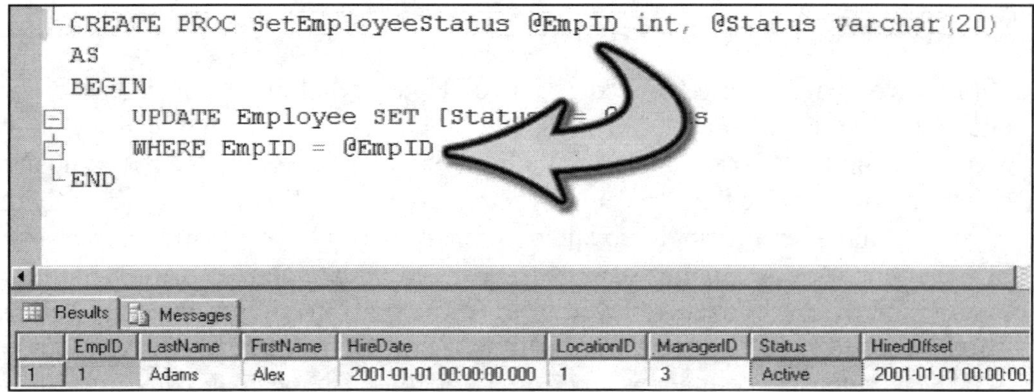

Figure 9.11 This stored procedure will change each employee's status based on the EmpID.

With the sproc created, we can test this procedure by executing it to set the record of Employee 1's status to "on leave":

EXEC **SetEmployeeStatus** 1, 'On Leave'

We can confirm the status change by querying the Employee table (see top of Figure 9.12, SELECT * FROM Employee). (Recall that Employee 1's status was Active in the previous figure.) Passing the values 1 and 'On Leave' into SetEmployeeStatus changes the Status field for Employee 1 to 'On Leave.'

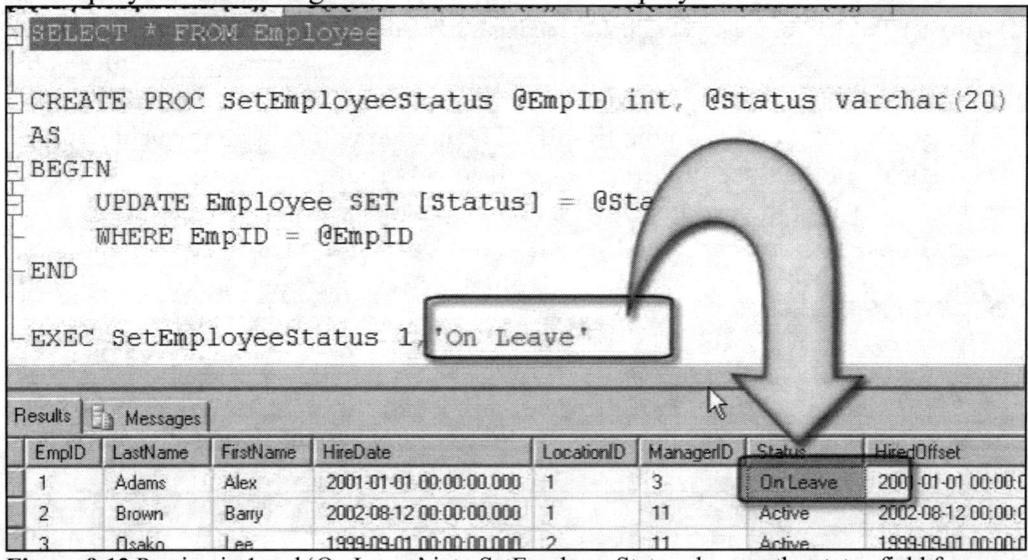

Figure 9.12 Passing in 1 and 'On Leave' into SetEmployeeStatus changes the status field for Employee 1 to 'On Leave.'

Let's execute this statement for an employee which doesn't exist (see Figure 9.13). Notice that our result is not actually an error. The statement runs alright, but no rows are affected because no records in JProCo's Employee table meet the criteria.

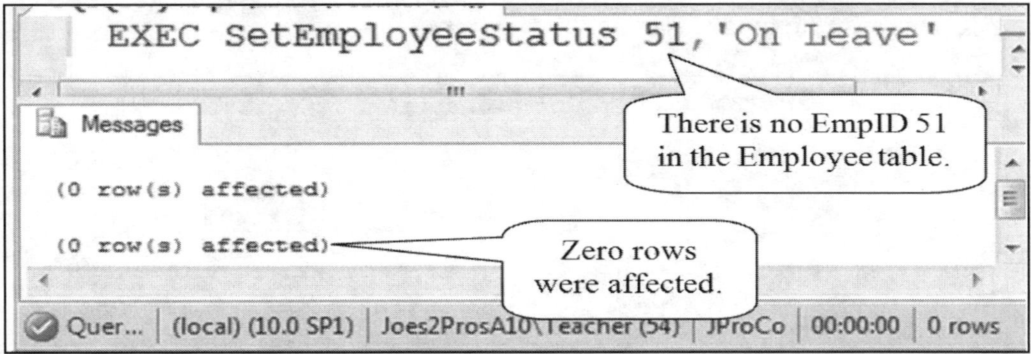
EXEC SetEmployeeStatus 51,'On Leave'
Messages
(0 row(s) affected)
(0 row(s) affected)
There is no EmpID 51 in the Employee table.
Zero rows were affected.
Quer... | (local) (10.0 SP1) | Joes2ProsA10\Teacher (54) | JProCo | 00:00:00 | 0 rows

Figure 9.13 There is no EmpID 51, so no rows are affected.

This is not a SQL Server error. But what if the 51 was a typo? What if the intent was to update the status for Employee 11 or Employee 21? In that case, it would be helpful to program your code to alert you if you accidentally attempted to run a statement for a non-existent EmpID.

Let's alter the stored procedure by adding two more statements (see Figure 9.14). If we see that no rows are affected then we will raise a level 16 error that alerts us, "Nothing was done!"

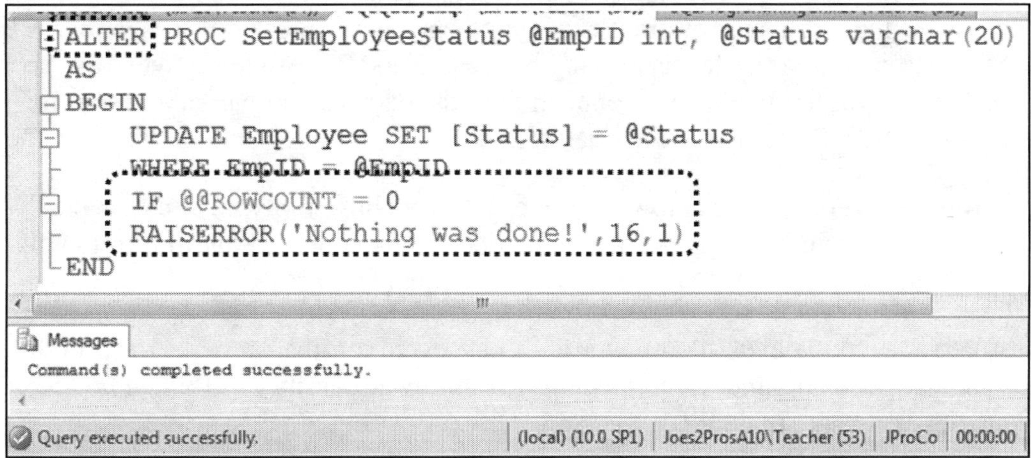
ALTER PROC SetEmployeeStatus @EmpID int, @Status varchar(20)
AS
BEGIN
UPDATE Employee SET [Status] = @Status
WHERE EmpID = @EmpID
IF @@ROWCOUNT = 0
RAISERROR('Nothing was done!',16,1)
END
Messages
Command(s) completed successfully.
Query executed successfully. | (local) (10.0 SP1) | Joes2ProsA10\Teacher (53) | JProCo | 00:00:00

Figure 9.14 The SetEmployeeStatus sproc is altered to raise an error if no records are affected.

With the sproc updated, let's run our prior EXEC statements for EmpID 1 and EmpID 51. EmpID 1 runs the same as it did previously. Here you can see that calling on the stored procedure and passing in 51 for the EmpID returns our user-defined error message (see Figure 9.15). The severity is level 16 and the message says "Nothing was done!"

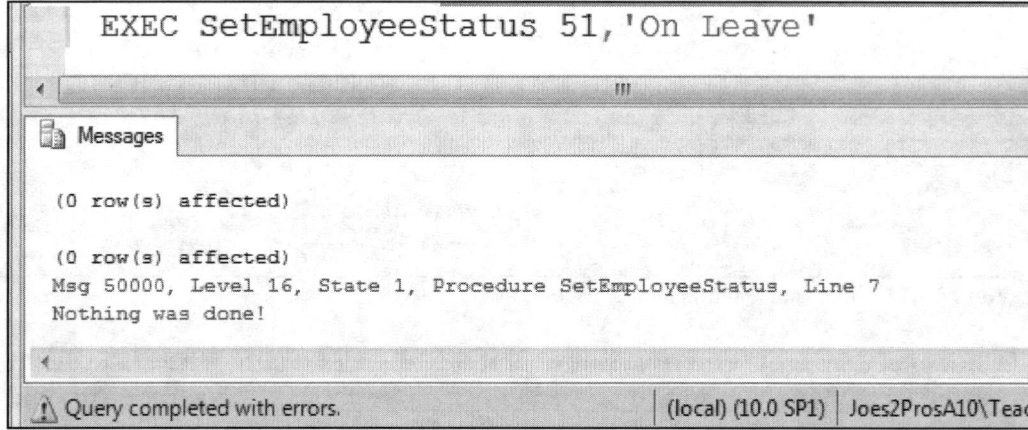
EXEC SetEmployeeStatus 51,'On Leave'
Messages
(0 row(s) affected)
(0 row(s) affected)
Msg 50000, Level 16, State 1, Procedure SetEmployeeStatus, Line 7
Nothing was done!
Query completed with errors.
(local) (10.0 SP1)
Joes2ProsA10\Tea

Figure 9.15 An error is thrown when you test the stored procedure with no affected records.

Error Severity

Most errors you will see have a severity of between 11 and 16. These are known as **user errors** and come with many options for how to deal with them. Did your error cause a simple rollback, or did it crash your system and break all connections? SQL has error severity levels ranging between 0 and 25. Anything over 20 is so bad that it will terminate your connection to the database. In fact, in order to raise errors that high, you must be a sysadmin.

Errors of severity10 and below are not even errors but simply informational notifications of events which have taken place. Any code looking for errors will ignore those with severity levels less than or equal to 10.

An error severity level of 16 seems a bit too severe for just having zero records updated. Let's alter the stored procedure to throw a severity of 11 when no records are updated (see Figure 9.16).

```
ALTER PROC SetEmployeeStatus @EmpID int, @Status varchar(20)
AS
BEGIN
    UPDATE Employee SET [Status] = @Status
    WHERE EmpID = @EmpID
    IF @@ROWCOUNT = 0
    RAISERROR('Nothing was done!',11,1)
END
```

```
Messages
Command(s) completed successfully.
Query executed successfully. | (local) (10.0 SP1) | Joes2ProsA10\Teacher (53) | JProCo | 00:00:00 | 0 rows
```

Figure 9.16 The stored procedure will throw a severity 11 error message when no records are affected.

With the stored procedure altered, we would expect to see a lower error severity when no records are affected. An error is thrown but the severity is now showing as 11 (see Figure 9.17).

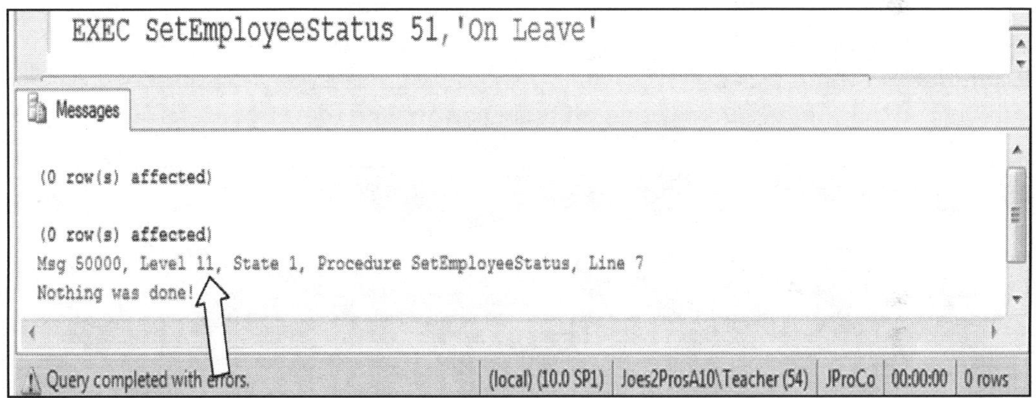
EXEC SetEmployeeStatus 51,'On Leave'
Messages
(0 row(s) affected)
(0 row(s) affected)
Msg 50000, Level 11, State 1, Procedure SetEmployeeStatus, Line 7
Nothing was done!
Query completed with errors.
(local) (10.0 SP1)
Joes2ProsA10\Teacher (54)
JProCo
00:00:00
0 rows

Figure 9.17 The error severity is now showing level 11.

A severity of 11 is still an error. The text appearing in red indicates an error. Text in black, such as the "0 the row(s) affected" is just an informational message. We can test this a little further with an ALTER PROC statement that reduces the error severity level to 10 (see Figure 9.18).

```
ALTER PROC SetEmployeeStatus @EmpID int, @Status varchar(20)
AS
BEGIN
    UPDATE Employee SET [Status] = @Status
    WHERE EmpID = @EmpID
    IF @@ROWCOUNT = 0
    RAISERROR('Nothing was done!',10,1)
END
```

Messages

Command(s) completed successfully.

Query executed successfully. | (local) (10.0 SP1) | Joes2ProsA10\Teacher (53) | JProCo | 00:00:00

Figure 9.18 The SetEmployeeStatus sproc will throw a severity level 10 message.

To test this, we will again try to update the nonexistent EmpID 51. Notice that we see no red text (Figure 9.19). There is no error displayed here but the message reads, "Nothing was Done!" Since severity levels 0-10 are not errors, the black printout "Nothing was done!" is an informational message (see Figure 9.19). Levels 11 and higher are considered raised errors and thus are printed in red font.

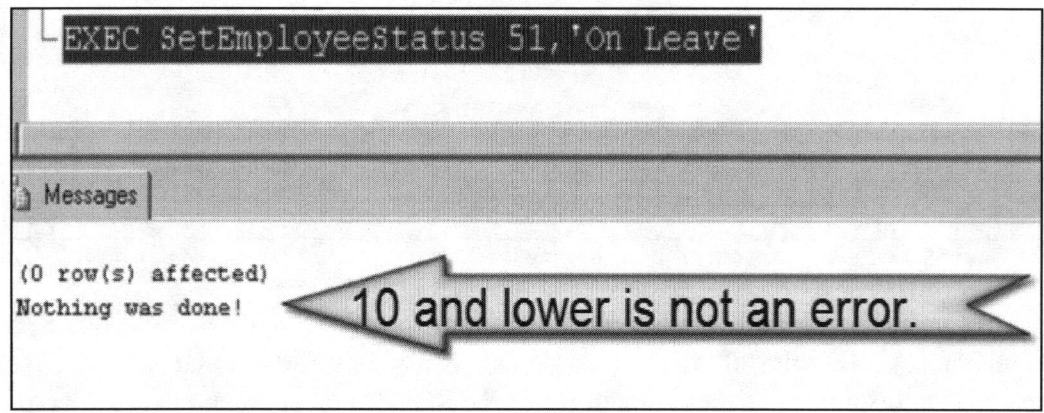
EXEC SetEmployeeStatus 51,'On Leave'
Messages
(0 row(s) affected)
Nothing was done!
10 and lower is not an error.

Figure 9.19 A severity of 10 or lower is not an error.

Using Error Message Variables

There are a few more options for programming your code to raise errors from within a stored procedure. We'll use the Grant table for our next example.

```
SELECT * FROM [Grant]
```

	GrantID	GrantName	EmpID	Amount
7	008	www.@-Last-U-Can-Help.com	7	25000.00
8	009	Thank you @.com	11	21500.00
9	010	Just Mom	5	9900.00
10	011	Big Giver Tom	7	19000.00
11	012	Mega Mercy	9	55000.00
12	013	Hope Reaches	7	29000.00
13	014	Everyone Wins	4	12500.00

Query... | (local) (10.0 SP1) | Joes2ProsA10\Teacher (53) | JProCo | 00:00:00 | 13 rows

Figure 9.20 The Grant table has 4 fields and 13 records.

Suppose we occasionally have grant donors who contact us to let us know they want to increase the amount of their grant. To illustrate this, let's write a small program called AddGrantAmount (see Figure 9.21).

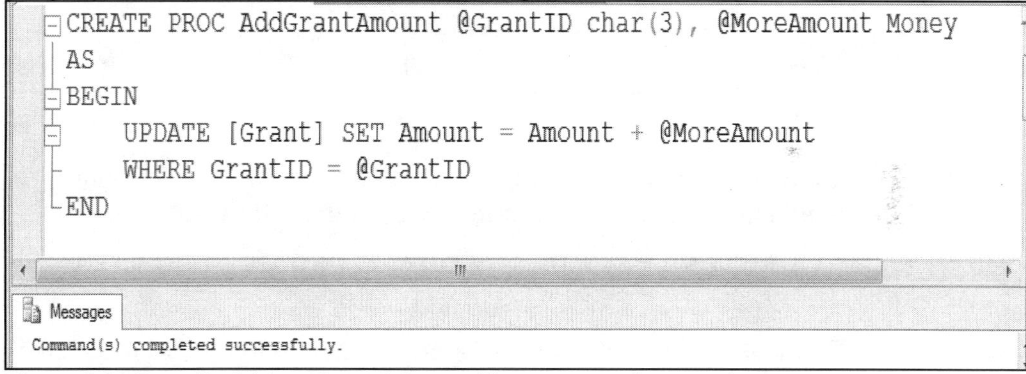

```
CREATE PROC AddGrantAmount @GrantID char(3), @MoreAmount Money
AS
BEGIN
    UPDATE [Grant] SET Amount = Amount + @MoreAmount
    WHERE GrantID = @GrantID
END
```

Messages

Command(s) completed successfully.

Figure 9.21 Run all of this code, and then we'll test our newly created sproc.

We'll test AddGrantAmount by increasing GrantID 005 by $1000. In Figure 9.22 we can see that the current amount of GrantID 005 is $21,000. If we were to add an additional $1000 the new amount would become $22,000.

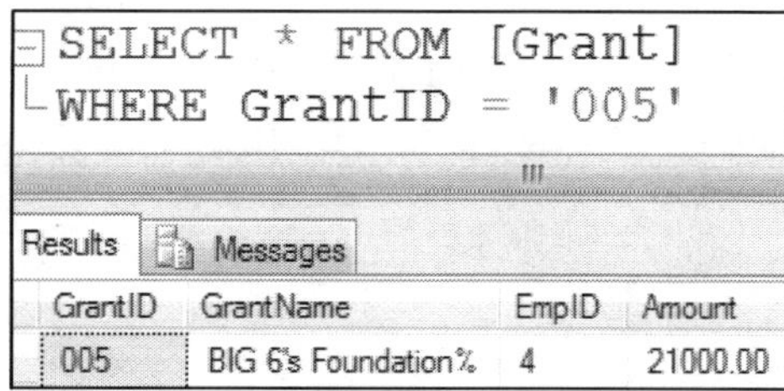

```
SELECT * FROM [Grant]
WHERE GrantID = '005'
```

GrantID	GrantName	EmpID	Amount
005	BIG 6's Foundation%	4	21000.00

Figure 9.22 The amount of GrantID 005 is $21,000.

Let's call on the AddGrantAmount stored procedure and pass in 005 for the GrantID and 1000 for the amount (see Figure 9.23).

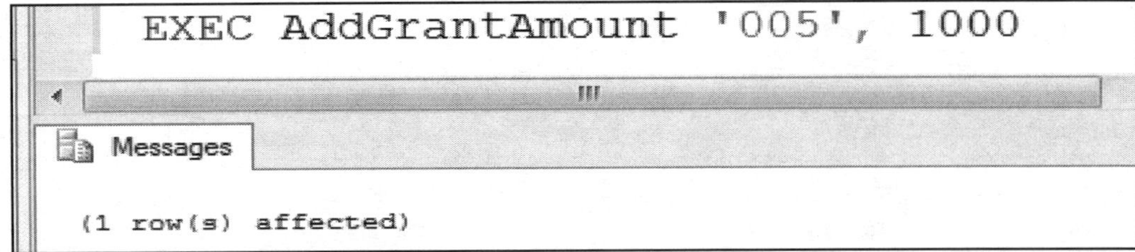

Figure 9.23 This should add 1000 to GrantID 005.

A SELECT statement confirms that the amount for GrantID 005 has increased to $22,000 (see Figure 9.24).

```
SELECT * FROM [Grant]
WHERE GrantID = '005'
```

Results | Messages

	GrantID	GrantName	EmpID	Amount
1	005	BIG 6's Foundation%	4	22000.00

Figure 9.24 The amount of GrantID 005 was increased to $22,000.

If we call on the code again, the Amount will increase further. The Amount for GrantID 005 would increase to $22,090 after you run the following code:

```
EXEC AddGrantAmount '005', 90
```

A SELECT statement confirms that the amount was increased by $90 to $22,090 (see Figure 9.25).

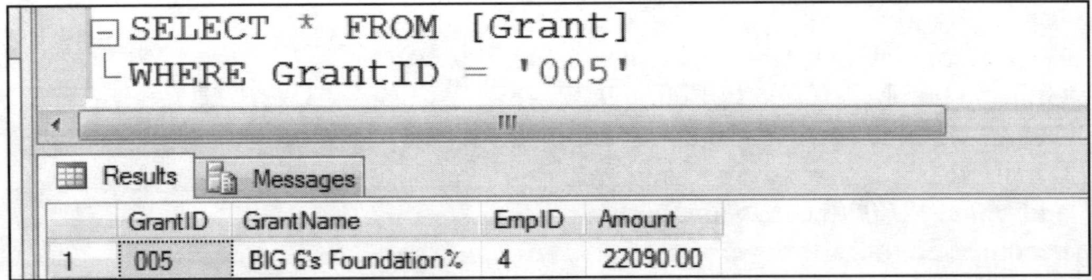

	GrantID	GrantName	EmpID	Amount
1	005	BIG 6's Foundation%	4	22090.00

Figure 9.25 The Amount of GrantID 005 is now $22,090.

Now we'd like to alter our stored procedure to print an informational message whenever we run AddGrantAmount. We would like a customized message to show us the number of grants which have been increased. The severity level will be 10, which will print a notification message each time we run the AddGrantAmount sproc. In Figure 9.26 we have partially written the statement to raise the error and have chosen 10 for the second parameter. This will set the severity level to 10, which we know indicates an informational message printed in black font.

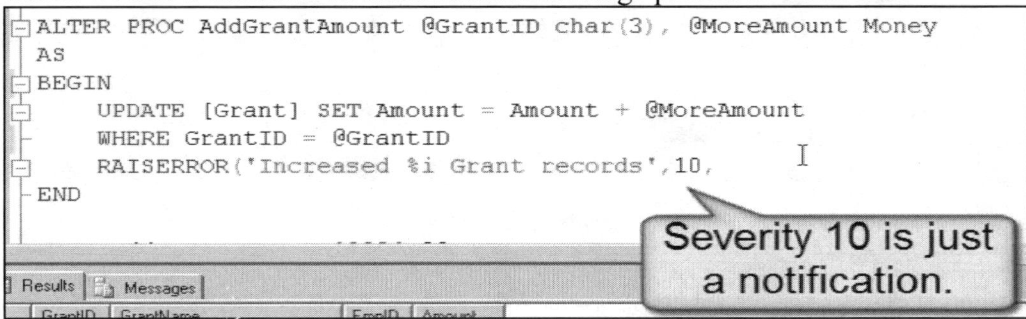
ALTER PROC AddGrantAmount @GrantID char(3), @MoreAmount Money
AS
BEGIN
UPDATE [Grant] SET Amount = Amount + @MoreAmount
WHERE GrantID = @GrantID
RAISERROR('Increased %i Grant records',10,
END
Severity 10 is just a notification.
Results
Messages

Figure 9.26 A notification message will print each time we run AddGrantAmount.

In Figure 9.27 we complete the alteration of our AddGrantAmount stored procedure. Here we'll include the global function @@ROWCOUNT to show the number of rows which have been affected by the stored procedure. The amount will be captured by the %i variable.

```
ALTER PROC AddGrantAmount @GrantID char(3), @MoreAmount Money
AS
BEGIN
    UPDATE [Grant] SET Amount = Amount + @MoreAmount
    WHERE GrantID = @GrantID
    RAISERROR('Increased %i Grant records',10,1,@@ROWCOUNT )
END
```

Figure 9.27 Including @@ROWCOUNT will show the number of rows affected by the sproc.

Run the EXEC statement and notice the confirmation "Increased 1 Grant records" prints as a message, since the severity is below 11 (see Figure 9.28).

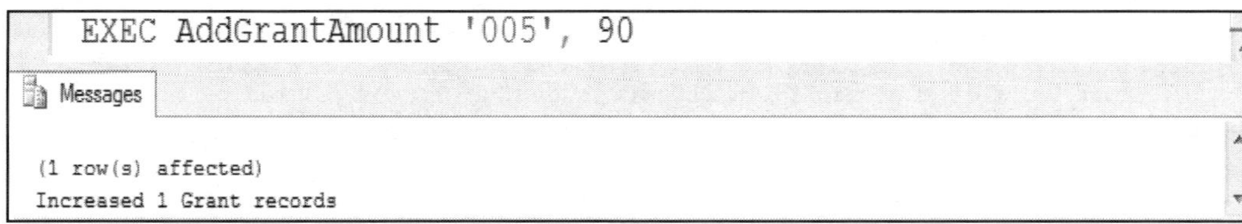
EXEC AddGrantAmount '005', 90
Messages
(1 row(s) affected)
Increased 1 Grant records

Figure 9.28 Execute the revised stored procedure in order to see the new message printed.

The %i dynamically prints a 1 to display the count of rows affected. In Figure 9.29, we see the process flow for how this message is generated and displayed.

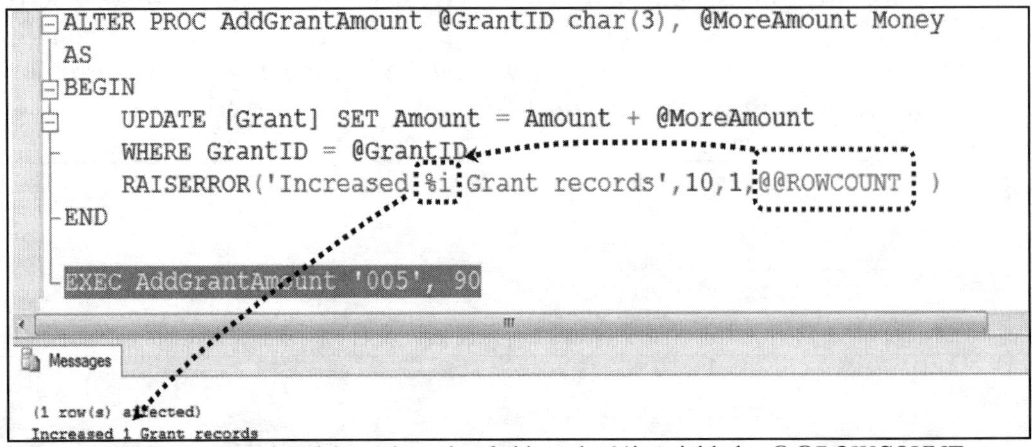
ALTER PROC AddGrantAmount @GrantID char(3), @MoreAmount Money
AS
BEGIN
UPDATE [Grant] SET Amount = Amount + @MoreAmount
WHERE GrantID = @GrantID
RAISERROR('Increased %i Grant records',10,1,@@ROWCOUNT)
END
EXEC AddGrantAmount '005', 90
Messages
(1 row(s) affected)
Increased 1 Grant records

Figure 9.29 The 1 was printed from the value fed into the %i variable by @@ROWCOUNT.

Now let's evaluate the potential for an error by our sproc when we convert the GrantID field to an INT. Remember the GrantID is passed in as a char(3) data type. We will change the predicate to utilize this integer instead of the char data as seen in Figure 9.30. Why? Because we've been given a warning that the database team is going to convert the GrantID to an integer very soon. In fact, they said it should never have been created as character data. All stored procedures which depend on this field need to be prepared to use the integer version of this field.

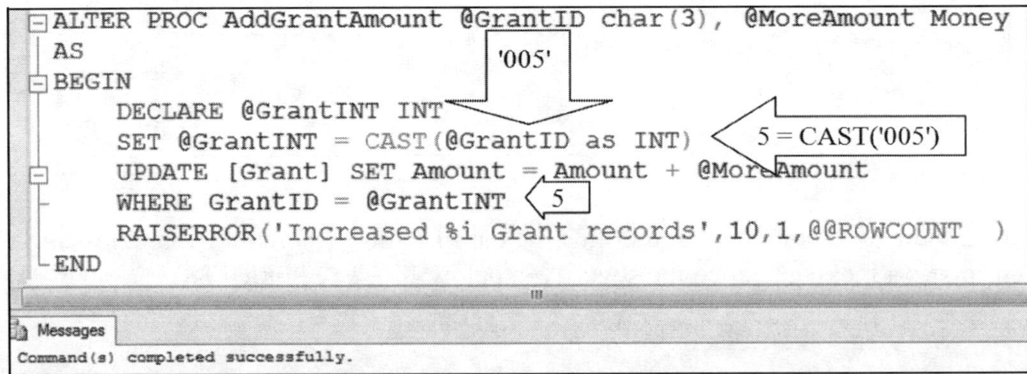
ALTER PROC AddGrantAmount @GrantID char(3), @MoreAmount Money
AS
'005'
BEGIN
DECLARE @GrantINT INT
SET @GrantINT = CAST(@GrantID as INT)
5 = CAST('005')
UPDATE [Grant] SET Amount = Amount + @MoreAmount
WHERE GrantID = @GrantINT
5
RAISERROR('Increased %i Grant records',10,1,@@ROWCOUNT)
END
Messages
Command(s) completed successfully.

Figure 9.30 We will further error proof the sproc AddGrantAmount by converting the data type of the GrantID field to an INT.

Let's run an EXEC statement for AddGrantAmount (see Figure 9.31). Notice we have the potential for an error if a user spells out "five" instead of using the numeral 5. Our CAST function will not be able to work with character data that has non-numeric values. A conversion error is generated. You can convert '005' into a 5, but the CAST function does not know how to handle 'Five'.

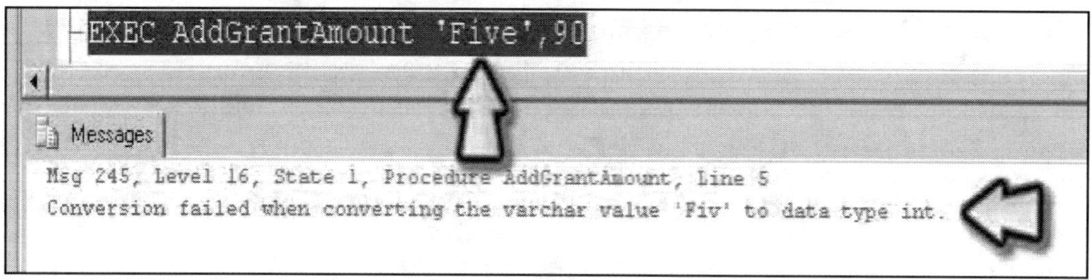

Figure 9.31 We will test out the sproc by attempting to add the GrantID "Five."

The CAST function failing with a conversion error means our RAISERROR code never gets a chance to run. The stored procedure terminates and the informational message is not displayed to the Messages tab. We see the conversion error but not the level 10 severity message, since the sproc terminates (see Figure 9.32).

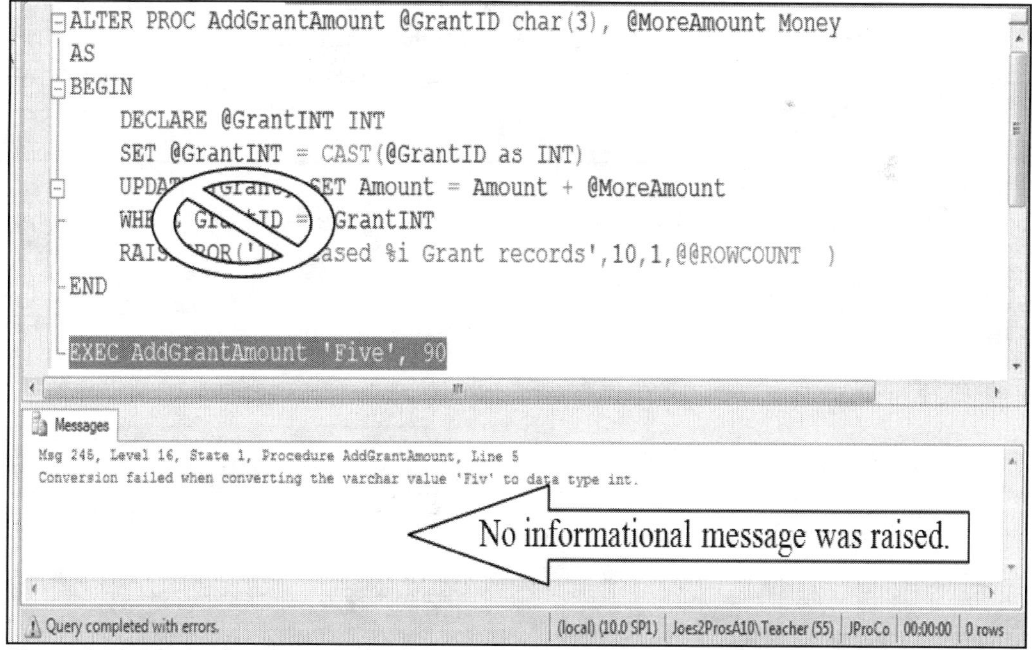

Figure 9.32 Our test input causes the CAST function to fail, and the stored procedure terminates.

Lab 9.1: SQL Server Error Messages

Lab Prep: Before you can begin the lab, you must have SQL Server installed and have run the script SQLProgrammingChapter9.1Setup.sql.

Skill Check 1: Create a stored procedure called SetGrantAmount which takes @GrantID char(3) as the first parameter and @Amount money as the second parameter. The procedure should update the Amount for the GrantID specified. The stored procedure should raise an error if no records are updated. Test this by trying to update GrantID 015. When done, your result should resemble the figure below (see Figure 9.33).

```
EXEC SetGrantAmount '015',28000
```

Messages

```
(0 row(s) affected)
Msg 50000, Level 11, State 1, Procedure SetGrantAmount, Line 7
No Grants were set!
```

Figure 9.33 Skill Check 1 creates a sproc called SetGrantAmount and raises a user-defined error.

Skill Check 2: Create a Stored Procedure called AddBonusPoint which takes an int parameter named @EmpID and increments the BonusPoints field in the PayRates table. Raise an informational message with a level 10 severity which shows how many records were updated. Test your procedure with EmpID 2.

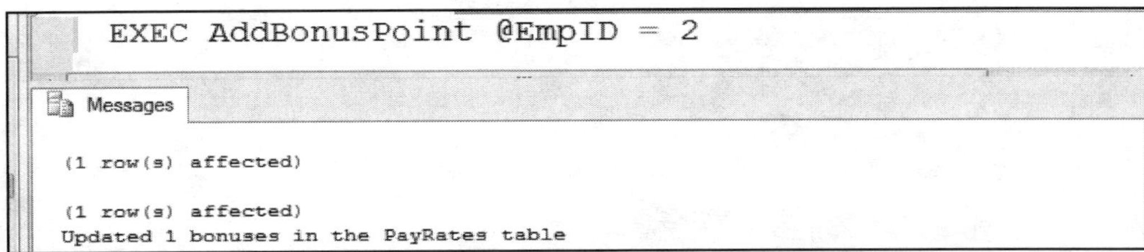
EXEC AddBonusPoint @EmpID = 2
Messages
(1 row(s) affected)
(1 row(s) affected)
Updated 1 bonuses in the PayRates table

Figure 9.34 Skill Check 2 should be executed with the code shown in this figure.

Query your PayRates table to see that Employee 2 has a bonus point. Your result should look like Figure 9.35.

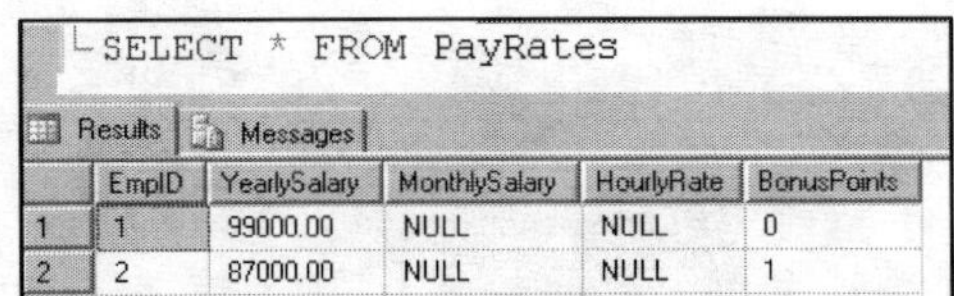
SELECT * FROM PayRates

Results | Messages

	EmpID	YearlySalary	MonthlySalary	HourlyRate	BonusPoints
1	1	99000.00	NULL	NULL	0
2	2	87000.00	NULL	NULL	1

Figure 9.35 Testing Skill Check 2.

Answer Code: The T-SQL code to this lab can be found in the downloadable files in a file named Lab9.1_SQLServerErrorMessages.sql.

SQL Server Error Messages - Points to Ponder

1. Components of the SQL Server error message are:
   a. Message Number – often referred to as Error number. This is the Message ID of the error. Message Numbers below 50,000 are system supplied errors. Message Numbers at or above 50,000 are user-defined errors.
   b. Severity Level – ranging from 0 to 25. Levels 1-10 are informative, whereas 11 and higher are actual errors.
   c. State – rarely used. If you raise the same error in several places, you can use this to mark the point at which the error was raised.
   d. Procedure – this is the name of the stored procedure, trigger, or function where the error occurred. If you are just running code in a query window then "Procedure" will be blank.
   e. Line – the line number in the procedure, function, trigger, or batch that contains the error.
   f. Message Text – the actual message of the error telling you what went wrong.
2. The Sys.Messages table in the master database contains the list of all error messages.
3. If you want your procedure to raise an error defined by your own conditions, and this is not a system error, then you can call the RAISERROR( ) function. The first parameter can be a message number, text or a local @ variable. The message number corresponds to the message_id column in the sys.messages table.
4. If you use RAISERROR and specify text without a message number, you will get a message number of 50,000.
5. If you specify the message number and not the text, then you will get the text belonging to the message as listed in the Sys.Messages table.
6. You can't manually raise errors below 13000. Those may be raised only by the system.
7. Error Severity of 10 or below is not really an error message at all. It is considered informational.
8. Errors of 20-25 result in connection termination. If you want to raise an error of 20 or higher, then you must be a sysadmin and provide the WITH LOG option.

SQL Error Actions

How does SQL Server react to an error? In other words, when SQL raises an error in one statement, should it stop or continue processing? Actually there are four different reactions SQL might take in response to an error.

Let's take the scenario in Figure 9.36 where a SQL client is going to execute a user stored procedure called usp_A. This stored procedure consists of two statements. The first statement is going to call usp_B and the second will call usp_C. Both usp_B and usp_C have three statements inside which could potentially throw an error.

Just how will SQL Server react when it encounters an error? This is known as a **SQL error action**. This section will discuss the possible reactions to errors in this hierarchy.

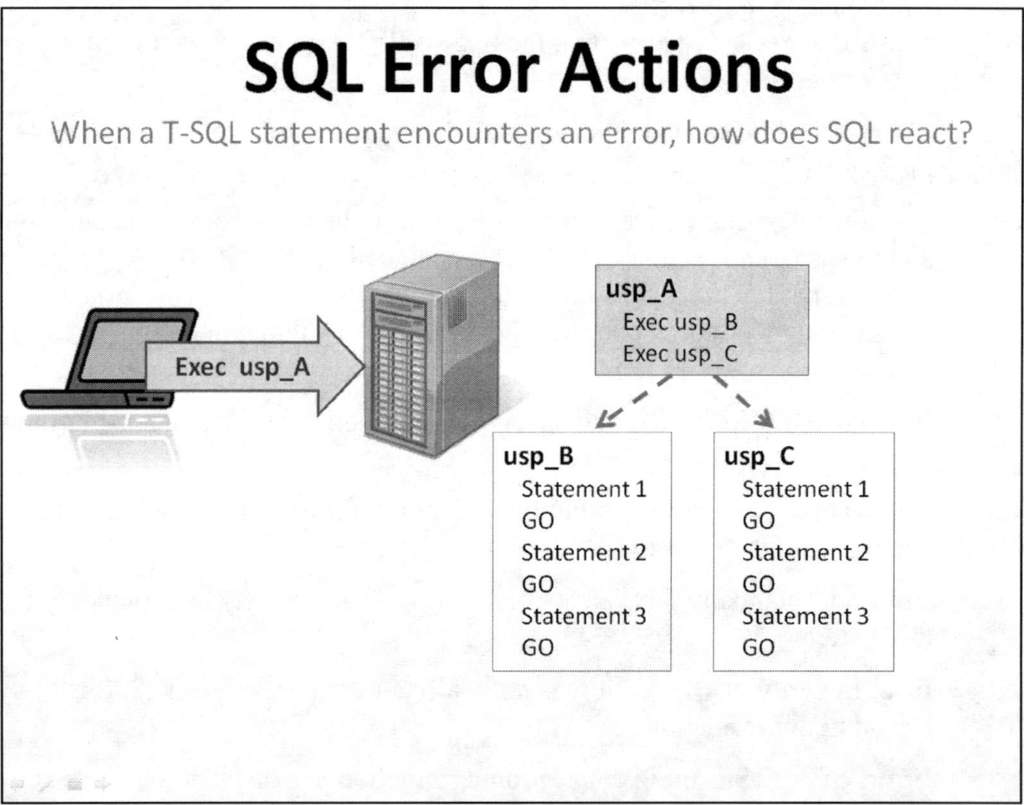

Figure 9.36 usp_A calls two stored procedures (usp_B and usp_C). Each sproc contains three statements.

Statement Termination

If an error is encountered in Statement 2 of usp_B, SQL might decide to proceed to Statement 3. This is the least disruptive reaction possible to an error; a single statement fails to run but all other statements continue operating as expected.

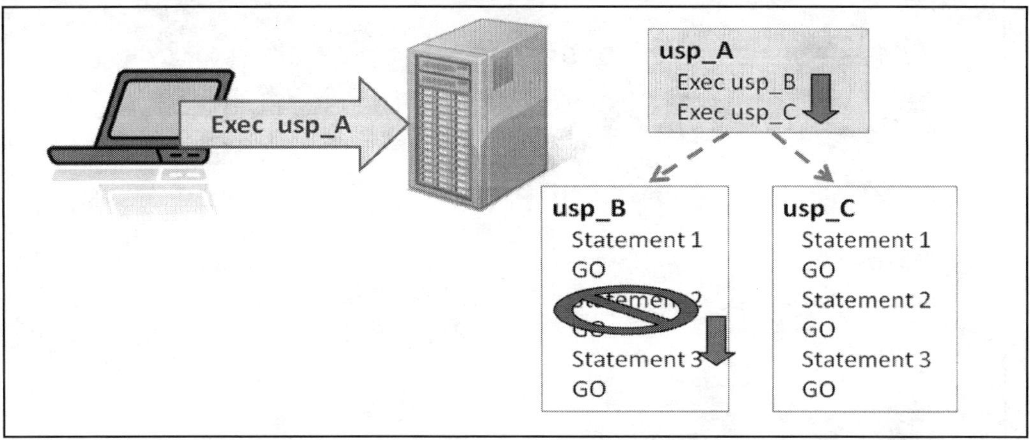

Figure 9.37 Statement Termination occurs when a single statement fails but execution of subsequent statements continues.

In Statement Termination there is no disruption to the calling code, and usp_A continues by running the rest of its code, including all the statements in usp_C.

Scope Abortion

In Scope Abortion, the failed statement causes the function or stored proc to fail. While usp_B halts after one failed statement, the execution from usp_A will continue to run by calling on usp_C (see Figure 9.38).

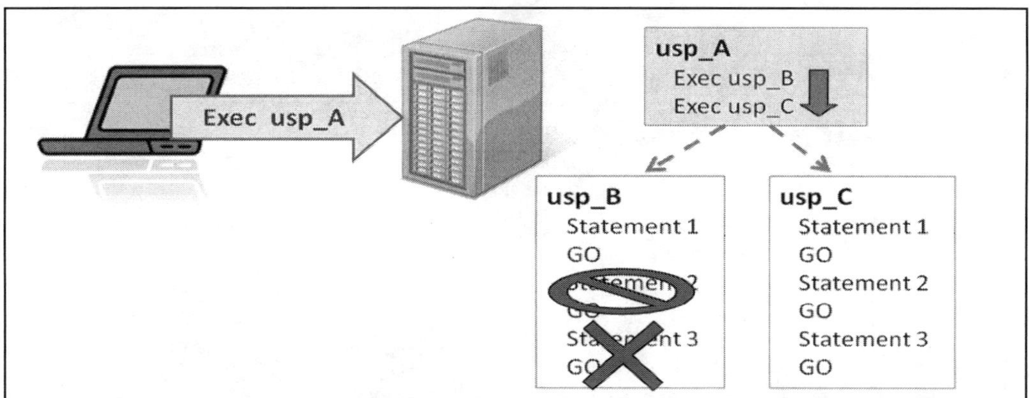

Figure 9.38 With Scope Abortion the failure of Statement 2 means Statement 3 does not get run.

Batch Abortion

With Batch Abortion, a failure in statement 2 will cause usp_B to fail and usp_A to return a failure to the calling code. The call to usp_C never takes place.

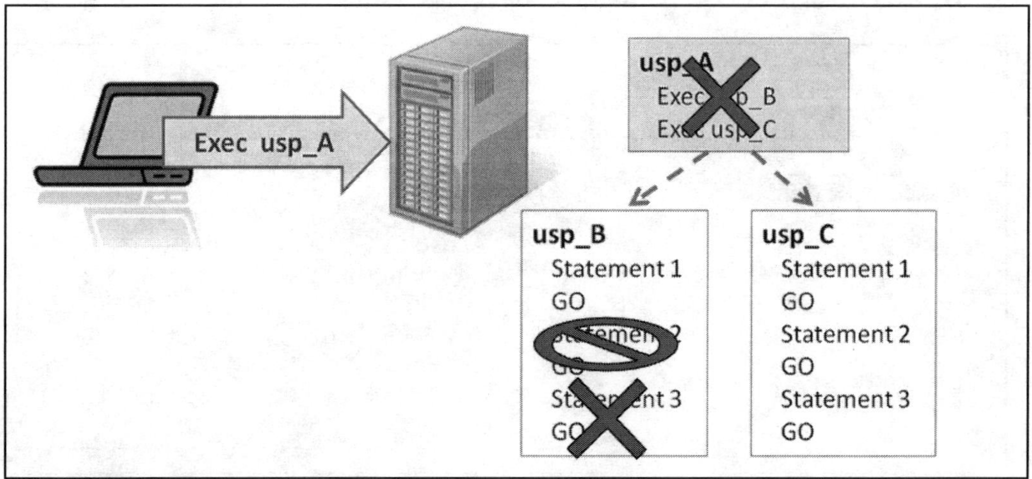

Figure 9.39 A failure in statement 2 will cause usp_B to fail and usp_A to return a failure to the calling code.

Connection Termination

In the most drastic of error scenarios, the connection from the client to the SQL Server database is severed. In Figure 9.40 we see an illustration where the connection from the client to the server is broken. This is usually due to an error with a severity greater than 20. *The typical 11-16 severity error will not cause a connection termination.*

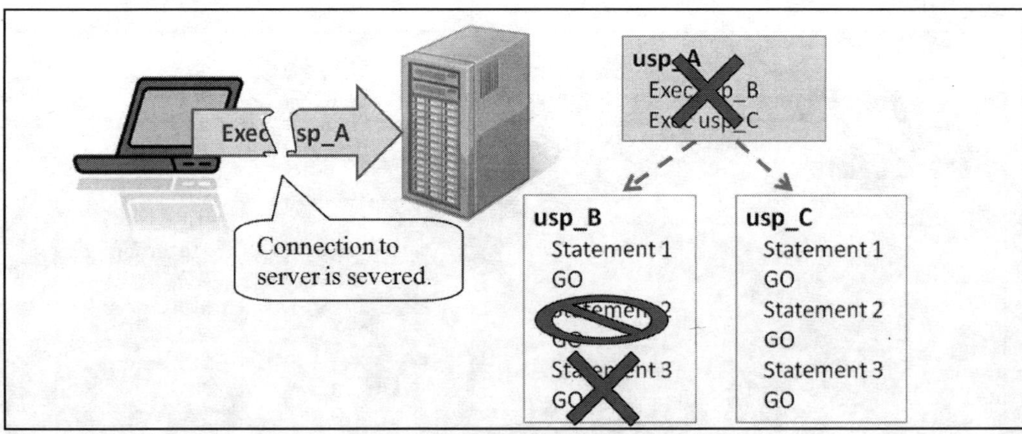

Figure 9.40 Illustration of connection termination (a drastic possibility).

If you completed the last lab (9.1), or you have run the 9.1 reset script, then you have a stored procedure called AddGrantAmount. This stored procedure takes two parameters: @GrantID and @Amount. Based on the GrantID, you will add the specified @Amount to the existing Amount value for that record. Inside the stored procedure is code which performs the update statement and then raises an informational message based on the number of grants which were updated.

You have another stored procedure called AddBonusPoint which, based on the employee ID (EmpID), will add one point to the employee's BonusPoint value contained in the PayRates table. The code for both stored procedures can be seen below (see Figure 9.41). Notice that each of these stored procedures contains a single update statement.

```
ALTER PROC AddGrantAmount @GrantID char(3), @MoreAmount Money
AS
BEGIN

    DECLARE @GrantINT INT
    SET @GrantINT = CAST(@GrantID as INT)
    UPDATE [Grant] SET Amount = Amount + @MoreAmount
    WHERE GrantID = @GrantINT
    RAISERROR('Increased %i Grant records',10,1,@@ROWCOUNT  )
END
GO

CREATE PROC AddBonusPoint @EmpID int
AS
BEGIN
    UPDATE PayRates SET BonusPoints = BonusPoints + 1
    WHERE EmpID = @EmpID
    RAISERROR('Updated %i bonuses in the PayRates table',10,1,@@RowCount)
END
GO
```

Figure 9.41 Each of these stored procedures contains just one statement.

If you look at the Employee table, you'll notice a new field LatestGrantActivity, which contains the timestamp of the latest change made to one of that employee's grants (see Figure 9.42).

```
SELECT * FROM Employee
```

	EmpID	LastName	FirstName	HireDate	LocationID	ManagerID	Status	HiredOffset	TimeZone	LatestGrantActivity
1	1	Adams	Alex	2001-01-01...	1	3	On Leave	2001-01-01 00:00:00.00...	-08:00	NULL
2	2	Brown	Barry	2002-08-12...	1	11	Active	2002-08-12 00:00:00.00...	-08:00	2002-08-12 00:00:00.000
3	3	Osako	Lee	1999-09-01...	2	11	Active	1999-09-01 00:00:00.00...	-05:00	1999-09-01 00:00:00.000
4	4	Kinnison	Dave	1996-03-16...	1	11	Has Tenure	1996-03-16 00:00:00.00...	-08:00	1996-03-16 00:00:00.000
5	5	Bender	Eric	2007-05-17...	1	11	Active	2007-05-17 00:00:00.00...	-08:00	2007-05-17 00:00:00.000

Query executed successfully. | (local) (10.0 SP1) | Joes2ProsA10\Teacher (53) | JProCo | 00:00:00 | 21 rows

Figure 9.42 A new field, LatestGrantActivity, has been added to the Employee table.

If an employee gets a new grant, or an update to an existing grant, then we want to update the LatestGrantActivity field (see Figure 9.43). Immediately after the code block inside AddGrantAmount makes a change to a grant, we want to capture the current time and update the Employee table. This stored procedure will have two update statements run against two tables (Grant and Employee) (Figure 9.44).

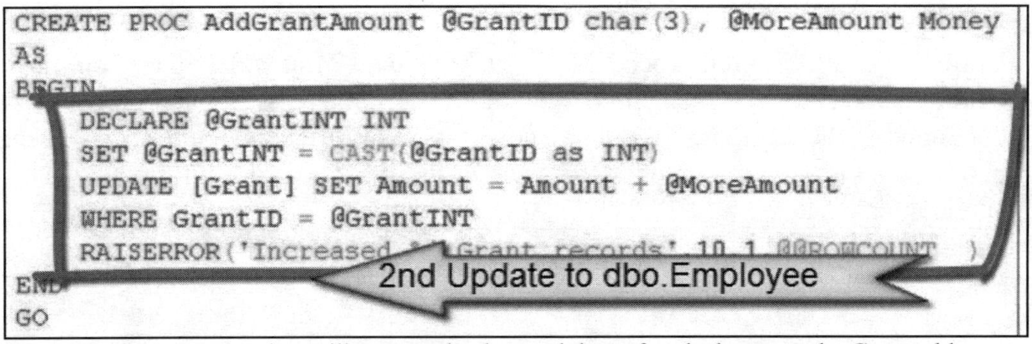

```
CREATE PROC AddGrantAmount @GrantID char(3), @MoreAmount Money
AS
BEGIN
    DECLARE @GrantINT INT
    SET @GrantINT = CAST(@GrantID as INT)
    UPDATE [Grant] SET Amount = Amount + @MoreAmount
    WHERE GrantID = @GrantINT
    RAISERROR('Increased %i Grant records',10,1,@@ROWCOUNT )
END
GO
```

2nd Update to dbo.Employee

Figure 9.43 A second update will capture the date and time of each change to the Grant table.

Here we see a second update statement which sets LatestGrantActivity to the current time for the employee who found that grant (see Figure 9.44). Notice that we'll also want to include a RAISERROR statement to raise an informational (severity 10) message showing if any of the employee records gets updated. Recall that 0 employees may be updated if one of the grants has no employee associated with it.

```
ALTER PROC AddGrantAmount @GrantID char(3), @MoreAmount Money
AS
BEGIN

    DECLARE @GrantINT INT
    SET @GrantINT = CAST(@GrantID as INT)
    UPDATE [Grant] SET Amount = Amount + @MoreAmount
    WHERE GrantID = @GrantINT
    RAISERROR('Increased %i Grant records',10,1,@@ROWCOUNT  )

    UPDATE em SET Em.LatestGrantActivity = CURRENT_TIMESTAMP
    FROM Employee as em INNER JOIN [Grant] as gr
    ON em.EmpID = gr.EmpID
    WHERE GrantID = @GrantID
    RAISERROR('Updated %i Employee records',10,1,@@ROWCOUNT )
END
GO
```

Messages

Command(s) completed successfully.

Figure 9.44 This code will make the second update described above and in Figure 9.43.

Consider the various inputs which could cause each update statement to fail. Notice how we utilize the @GrantID parameter versus the @GrantINT variable (see Figure 9.45). We want to ensure there is zero chance of a conversion error in the second update statement.

```
ALTER PROC AddGrantAmount @GrantID char(3), @MoreAmount Money
AS
BEGIN

    DECLARE @GrantINT INT
    SET @GrantINT = CAST(@GrantID as INT)      Cast to Int
    UPDATE [Grant] SET Amount = Amount + @MoreAmount
    WHERE GrantID = @GrantINT      Int
    RAISERROR('Increased %i Grant records',10,1,@@ROWCOUNT  )

    UPDATE em SET Em.LatestGrantActivity = CURRENT_TIMESTAMP
    FROM Employee as em INNER JOIN [Grant] as gr
    ON em.EmpID = gr.EmpID
    WHERE GrantID = @GrantID      Char(3)
    RAISERROR('Updated %i Employee records',10,1,@@ROWCOUNT )
END
GO
```

Figure 9.45 The second update is based on the char(3) GrantID data instead of the int GrantID.

Now let's attempt to alter just Grant 003 and increase its amount by $1000. Before we do that, let's first look at the current value of this grant's Amount.

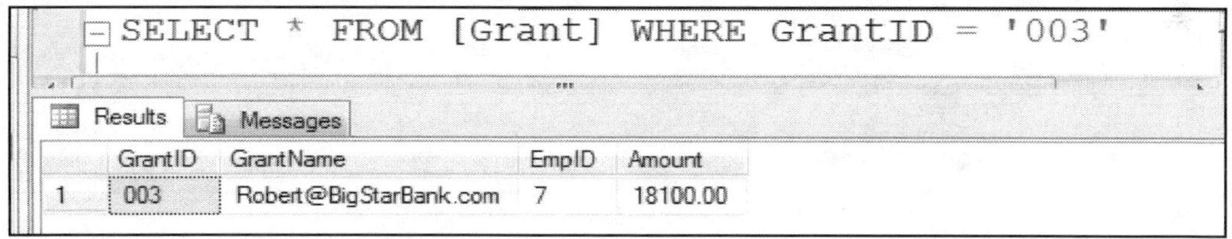

```
SELECT * FROM [Grant] WHERE GrantID = '003'
```

Results | Messages

	GrantID	GrantName	EmpID	Amount
1	003	Robert@BigStarBank.com	7	18100.00

Figure 9.46 GrantID '003' is $18,100 and was found by Employee 7 (David Lonning).

We see the record for Employee 7 (David Lonning) in the Employee table (see Figure 9.47).

```
SELECT * FROM Employee WHERE EmpID = 7
```

Results | Messages

	EmpID	LastName	FirstName	Hire...	LocationID	ManagerID	Status	HiredOffset	TimeZone	LatestGrantActivity
1	7	Lonning	David	20...	1	11	On Leave	2000-01-01 0...	-08:00	2000-01-01 00:00:00.000

Figure 9.47 David Lonning's Employee record shows Jan 1, 2000 as the latest timestamp for the LatestGrantActivity field.

David Lonning's last Grant activity was in the year 2000. If we update one of his grants, then his LatestGrantActivity field will be updated to reflect the timestamp of the change. Now let's run the code to execute the sproc and increase Grant 003 by $1000. At the same time, we expect it to also update David Lonning's Employee record (see Figure 9.48).

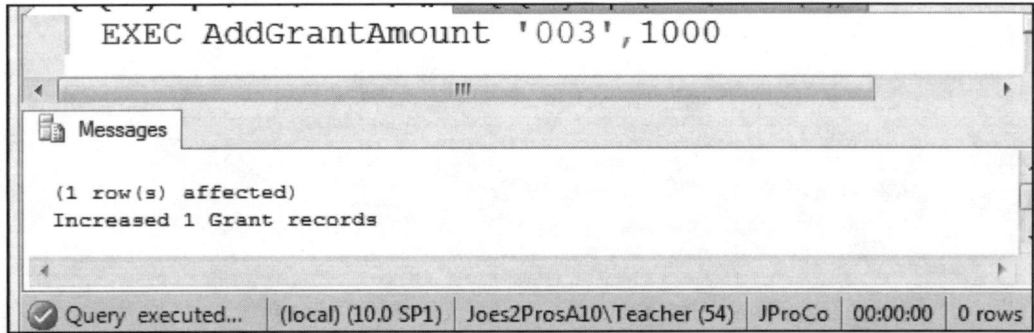
EXEC AddGrantAmount '003',1000
Messages
(1 row(s) affected)
Increased 1 Grant records
Query executed... (local) (10.0 SP1) Joes2ProsA10\Teacher (54) JProCo 00:00:00 0 rows

Figure 9.48 This code increases Grant 003 by $1000 and updates David's Employee record.

Both statements included in the AddGrantAmount stored proc (shown earlier -- see Figure 9.45) ran successfully. We can see the Amount of Grant 003 has increased by $1000 (see Figure 9.49). The revised Amount value is now $19,100.

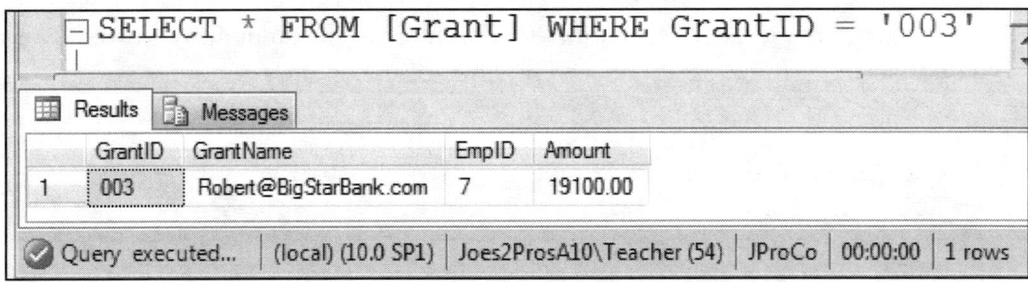
SELECT * FROM [Grant] WHERE GrantID = '003'
Results
Messages
GrantID GrantName EmpID Amount
1 003 Robert@BigStarBank.com 7 19100.00
Query executed... (local) (10.0 SP1) Joes2ProsA10\Teacher (54) JProCo 00:00:00 1 rows

Figure 9.49 Grant 003 has been increased by $1000 (from $18,100 to $19,100).

When we re-check David's record in the Employee table, we see that the LatestGrantActivity field now shows a 2010 timestamp. It successfully reflects the update we just made to David's Grant 003 (see Figures 9.48 through 9.50).

```
SELECT * FROM Employee WHERE EmpID = 7
```

	EmpID	LastName	FirstName	HireDate	LocationID	ManagerID	Status	HiredOffset	TimeZone	LatestGrantActivity
1	7	Lonning	David	2000-01-01 ...	1	11	On Leave	2000-01-01 ...	-08:00	2010-11-02 14:08:...

Figure 9.50 David's updated Employee record has an updated LatestGrantActivity field.

Now let's consider errors which these statements could encounter. As illustrated by Figure 9.51, if the Grant table update statement failed, would we want the Employee table to still be updated?

```
DECLARE @GrantINT INT
SET @GrantINT = CAST(@GrantID as INT)
UPDATE [Grant] SET Amount = Amount + @MoreAmount
WHERE GrantID = @GrantINT
RAISERROR('Increased %i Grant records',10,1,@@ROWCOUNT  )

UPDATE em SET Em.LatestGrantActivity = CURRENT_TIMESTAMP
FROM Employee as em INNER JOIN [Grant] as gr
ON em.EmpID = gr.EmpID
WHERE GrantID = @GrantID
RAISERROR('Updated %i Employee records',10,1,@@ROWCOUNT )
```

Figure 9.51 If the first statement inside the stored procedure fails will the second statement run?

As we expected, the input of 'One Thousand' as the second parameter (see Figure 9.52) produces a conversion error in the first update statement. The conversion error results in a batch abortion: the stored procedure terminates without running the rest of the statements.

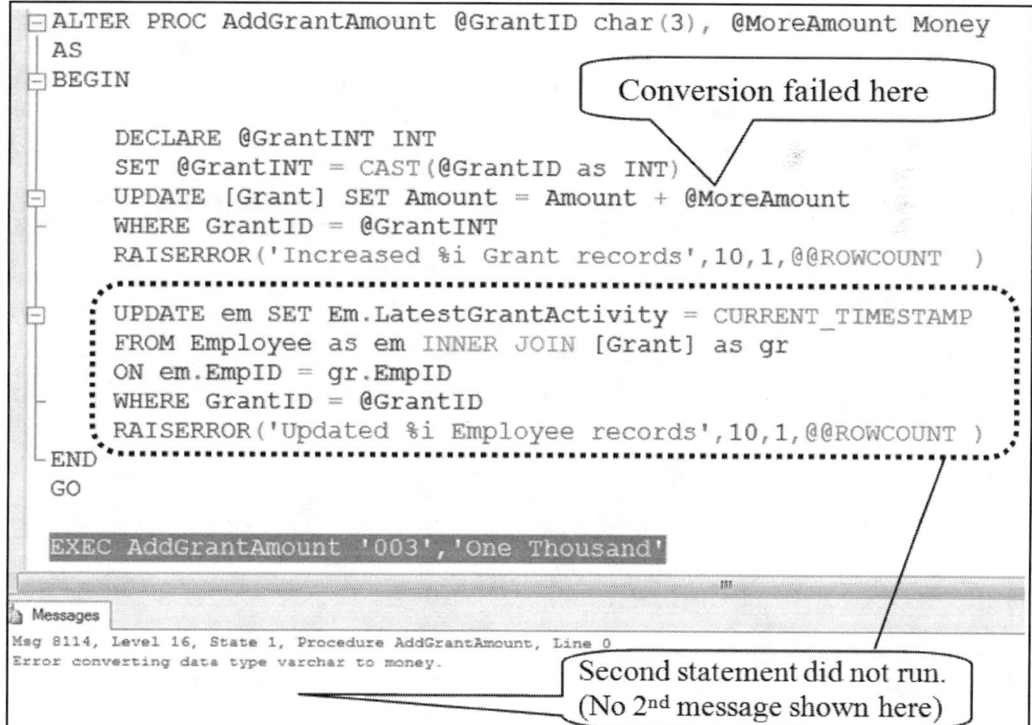

Figure 9.52 The conversion error results in a batch abortion where the stored procedure terminates without running the rest of the statements.

You can confirm that no record was updated in either the Grant table or the Employee table by using the following code:

```
SELECT * FROM [Grant] WHERE GrantID = '003'
SELECT * FROM Employee WHERE EmpID = 7
```

The results are the same as those seen in Figure 9.49 and 9.50. So we clearly see that the conversion error in the first update of the stored procedure caused a **batch abortion** action by SQL Server.

Now let's attempt to generate another error by sending in a NULL value for the Amount (see Figure 9.53). We expect this will produce an error, because the Amount field can't be NULL. We see this will cause a null conversion error on the first update statement. As expected, we get a Level 16 error saying that a NULL cannot be inserted into the Amount field. Look closely at the message pane and notice that the second statement ran and updated the Employee table. So we clearly see that a NULL inserted into a non-nullable field caused a **statement termination** action by SQL Server.

```
ALTER PROC AddGrantAmount @GrantID char(3), @MoreAmount Money
AS
BEGIN
    DECLARE @GrantINT INT
    SET @GrantINT = CAST(@GrantID as INT)
    UPDATE [Grant] SET Amount = Amount + @MoreAmount
    WHERE GrantID = @GrantINT
    RAISERROR('Increased %i Grant records',10,1,@@ROWCOUNT  )

    UPDATE em SET Em.LatestGrantActivity = CURRENT_TIMESTAMP
    FROM Employee as em INNER JOIN [Grant] as gr
    ON em.EmpID = gr.EmpID
    WHERE GrantID = @GrantID
    RAISERROR('Updated %i Employee records',10,1,@@ROWCOUNT )
END
GO

EXEC AddGrantAmount '003',Null
```

Amount field is not nullable.

Messages

```
Msg 515, Level 16, State 2, Procedure AddGrantAmount, Line 10
Cannot insert the value NULL into column 'Amount', table 'JProCo.dbo.Grant'; column does not allow nulls. UPDATE fails.
The statement has been terminated.
Increased 0 Grant records

(1 row(s) affected)

(1 row(s) affected)
Updated 1 Employee records
```

Second statement ran.
(2nd message shown here)

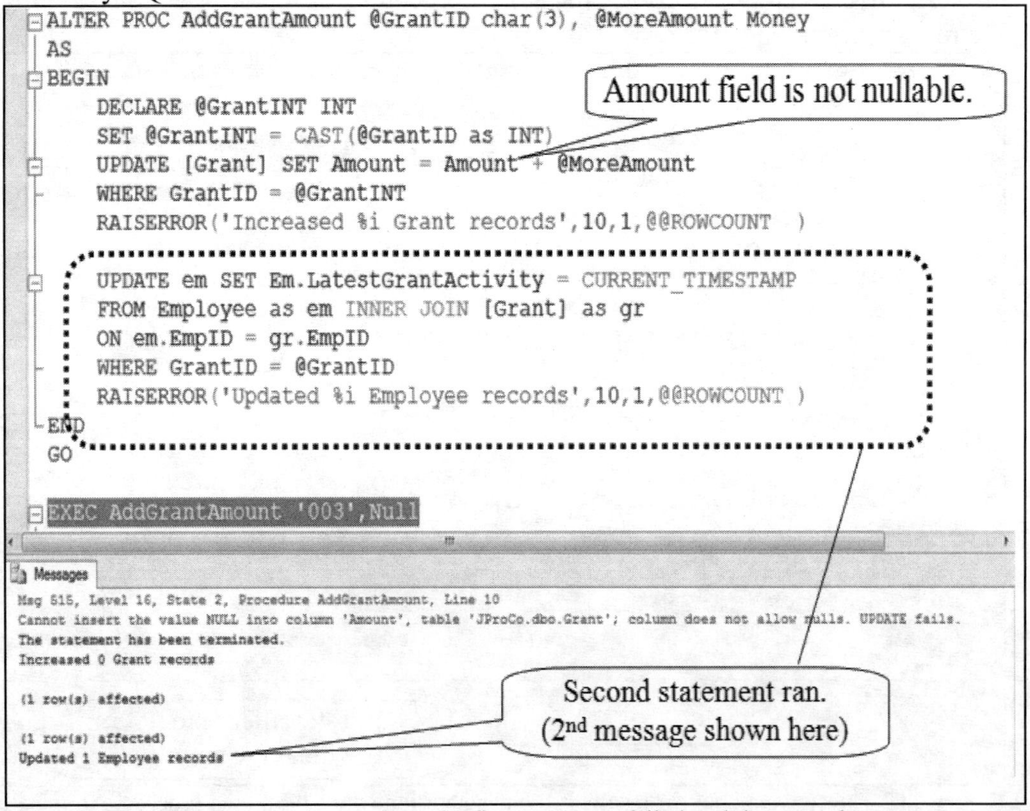

Figure 9.53 Within the stored procedure, the first statement failed and the second statement ran.

Since a null violation is considered less drastic, it generated only a single statement termination. The first statement didn't run, but the second statement did. The process flow below shows that the first statement threw an error but the stored procedure continued execution of the next statement (see Figure 9.54).

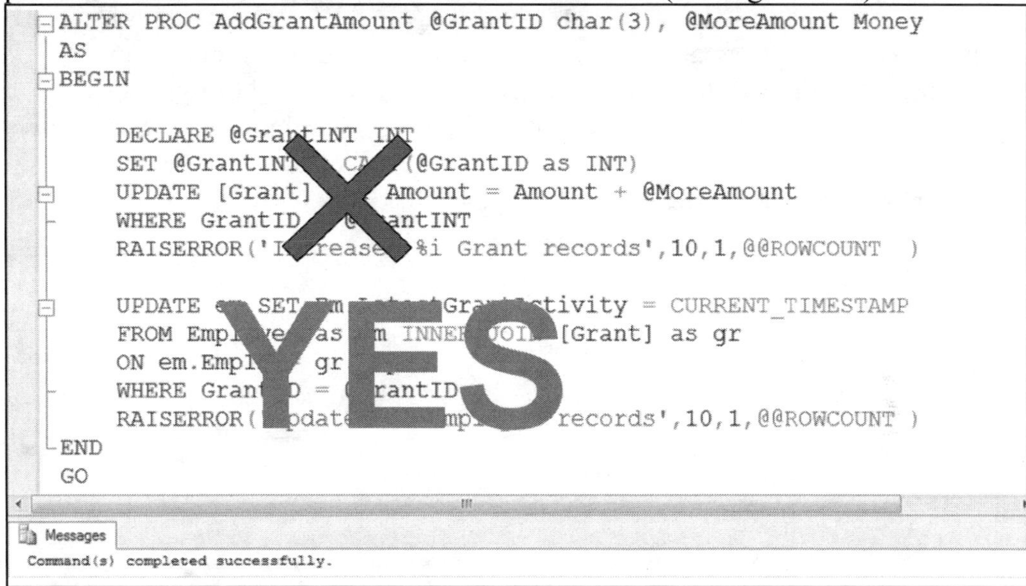

ALTER PROC AddGrantAmount @GrantID char(3), @MoreAmount Money
AS
BEGIN
DECLARE @Gra tINT I T
SET @GrantIN C (@GrantID as INT)
UPDATE [Grant] Amount = Amount + @MoreAmount
WHERE GrantID antINT
RAISERROR('I rease %i Grant records',10,1,@@ROWCOUNT)
UPDATE SET Gr ivity = CURRENT_TIMESTAMP
FROM Emp as INNE JOI [Grant] as gr
ON em.Emp gr
WHERE Gran D = rantID
RAISERROR(pdat records',10,1,@@ROWCOUNT)
END
GO
YES
Messages
Command(s) completed successfully.

Figure 9.54 The first statement didn't run, but the second statement did run (see also Figure 9.55).

When we re-check the Employee table, we see that David Lonning's LatestGrantActivity field has been updated yet again (see Figure 9.55).

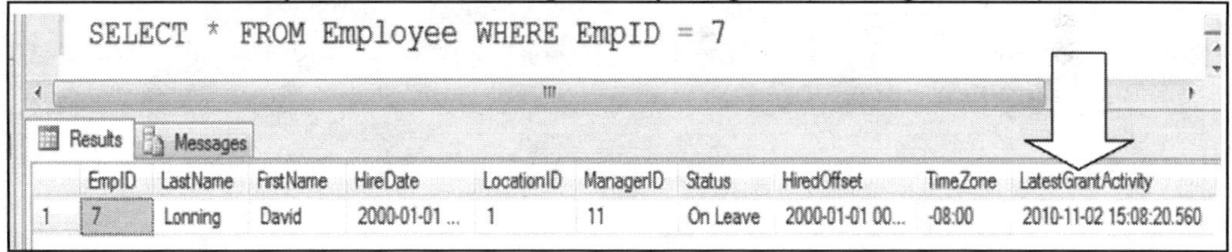

	EmpID	LastName	FirstName	HireDate	LocationID	ManagerID	Status	HiredOffset	TimeZone	LatestGrantActivity
1	7	Lonning	David	2000-01-01 ...	1	11	On Leave	2000-01-01 00...	-08:00	2010-11-02 15:08:20.560

Figure 9.55 The LatestGrantActivity from EmpID 7 was updated again (contrast with Figure 9.50).

XACT_ABORT

As introduced earlier in this section (Figures 9.36-9.40), the severity of the error dictates the action which SQL Server will take (e.g., single statement termination, batch abortion, or the most drastic step of client connection termination).

Recall our example where the Employee timestamp field (LatestGrantActivity) was updated, despite the corresponding Grant record not successfully updating. We might decide that in all cases of an error with our stored procedure it would be better to abort the entire batch. Otherwise, the timestamp field LatestGrantActivity will be out of sync with the updates which were actually made to an employee's grants.

In this case, we can use the SQL command **XACT_ABORT** ("transact abort"), which aborts the entire batch if any error is encountered (see Figure 9.56). Activating XACT_ABORT means all errors with a severity 11 or greater will result in batch abortion. Compare Figure 9.56 to Figure 9.53 and notice this is the same stored procedure call. The big difference is that the second update did not run after the first error was encountered. With the XACT_ABORT setting on, any error of severity 11 or greater will result in batch abortion.

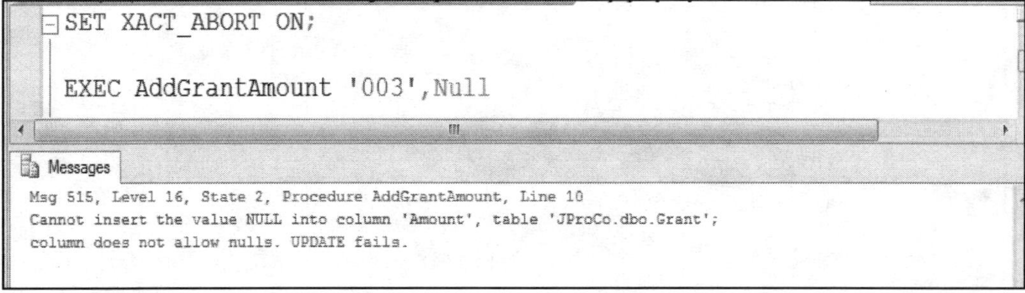
SET XACT_ABORT ON;
EXEC AddGrantAmount '003',Null
Messages
Msg 515, Level 16, State 2, Procedure AddGrantAmount, Line 10
Cannot insert the value NULL into column 'Amount', table 'JProCo.dbo.Grant';
column does not allow nulls. UPDATE fails.

Figure 9.56 Activating XACT_ABORT means all errors with a severity 11 or greater will result in batch abortion.

If you set XACT_ABORT to "OFF", then SQL will choose those errors which are drastic enough to fail an entire stored procedure (or batch). In other words, SQL Server will pick the error action based on the error which was raised. In Figure 9.57 we see the effects of setting XACT_ABORT to OFF and using the same call to the AddGrantAmount stored procedure.

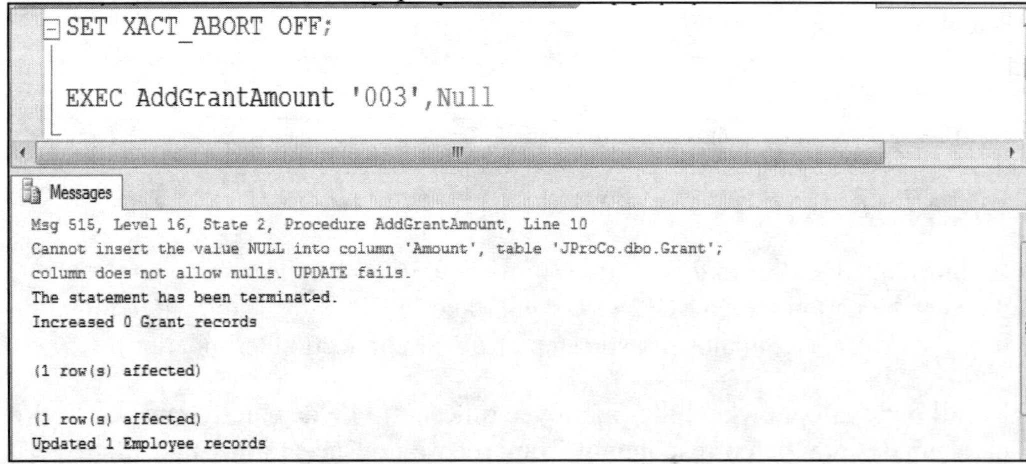
SET XACT_ABORT OFF;
EXEC AddGrantAmount '003',Null
Messages
Msg 515, Level 16, State 2, Procedure AddGrantAmount, Line 10
Cannot insert the value NULL into column 'Amount', table 'JProCo.dbo.Grant';
column does not allow nulls. UPDATE fails.
The statement has been terminated.
Increased 0 Grant records
(1 row(s) affected)
(1 row(s) affected)
Updated 1 Employee records

Figure 9.57 The syntax for deactivating XACT_ABORT.

Lab 9.2: SQL Error Actions

Lab Prep: Before you can begin the lab, you must have SQL Server installed and have run the script SQLProgrammingChapter9.2Setup.sql.

Skill Check 1: Create a stored procedure named UpdateGrantEmployee which calls on the AddGrantAmount and AddBonusPoint procedures. It should accept the parameters @GrantID (which is a char(3)) and @Increase (money). Call on this procedure by passing in Grant 002 and an amount of 1000. Your Messages tab should resemble the figure below (Figure 9.58).

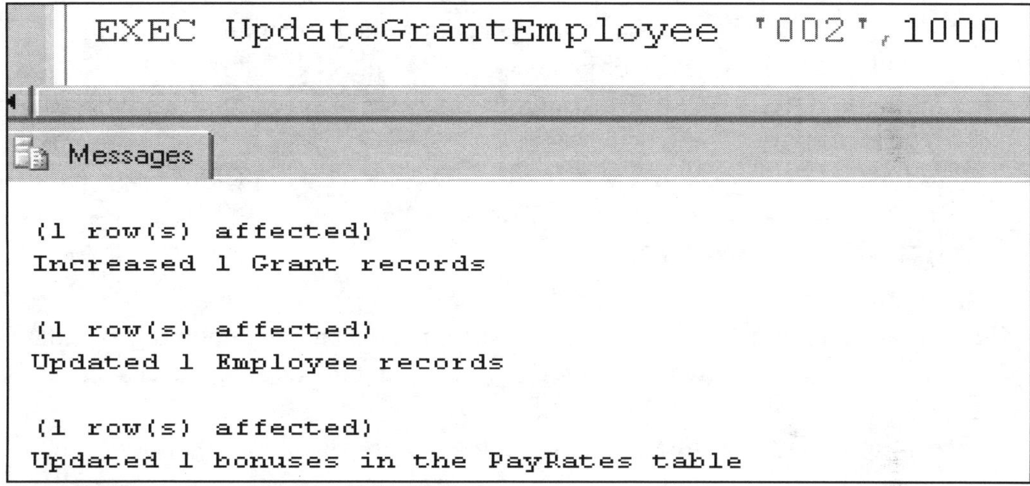
EXEC UpdateGrantEmployee '002',1000
Messages
(1 row(s) affected)
Increased 1 Grant records
(1 row(s) affected)
Updated 1 Employee records
(1 row(s) affected)
Updated 1 bonuses in the PayRates table

Figure 9.58 Result produced by Skill Check 1.

Skill Check 2: Call on the UpdateGrantEmployee stored procedure and decrement $1,000 from Amount for Grant 003 to bring the value down to $18,100. (Hint: Pass in a negative number for the second parameter.) When complete, your query of the Grant table should resemble the figure below (see Figure 9.59).

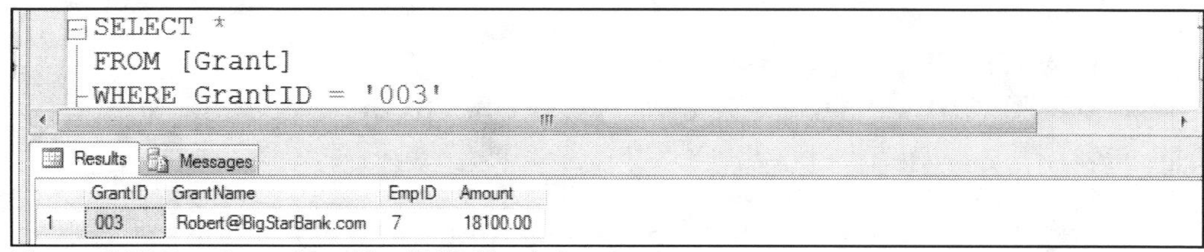
SELECT *
FROM [Grant]
WHERE GrantID = '003'
Results
Messages
GrantID
GrantName
EmpID
Amount
1
003
Robert@BigStarBank.com
7
18100.00

Figure 9.59 Result produced by Skill Check 2.

Answer Code: The T-SQL code to this lab can be found in the downloadable files in a file named Lab9.2_SQLErrorActions.sql.

SQL Error Actions - Points to Ponder

1. There are 4 possible actions SQL Server will take when encountering errors:
   a. ***Statement Termination*** – The statement with the procedure fails but the code keeps on running to the next statement. Transactions are not affected.
   b. ***Scope Abortion*** – The current procedure, function or batch is aborted and the next calling scope keeps running. That is, if Stored Procedure A calls B and C, and B fails, then nothing in B runs but A continues to call C. @@Error is set but the proc does not have a return value.
   c. ***Batch Abortion*** – The entire client call is terminated.
   d. ***Connection Termination*** – The client is disconnected and any open transaction is rolled back. This occurs when something really bad happens like a stack overflow or protocol error in the client library.
2. With the XACT_ABORT setting on, any error of severity 11-16 will result in batch abortion.
3. With the XACT_ABORT setting off, SQL Server will pick its error action.

Chapter Glossary

Batch abortion: the entire client call is aborted.
Connection termination: the client is disconnected and any open transaction is rolled back. This occurs when something really bad happened, such as a stack overflow or protocol error in the client library.
Informational notification: an error having an error level of 10, or lower, will simply produce an information notification. Any code looking for errors will ignore severity levels of 10, or lower.
RAISERROR( ): a function you can call if you want your procedure to raise an error defined by your own conditions, and not a system error.
Scope abortion: The current procedure, function or batch is aborted and the next calling scope keeps running. That is, if Stored Procedure A calls B and C, and B fails, then nothing in B runs but A continues to call B. @@Error is set but the proc does not have a return value.
XACT_ABORT: pronounced "transact abort."
SET XACT_ABORT OFF: SQL will choose those errors which are drastic enough to fail an entire stored procedure. In other words, SQL Server will pick the error action based on what error was raised.
SET XACT_ABORT ON: any error of severity 11-16 will result in batch abortion.
Severity Level: ranging from 0 to 25. Levels 1-10 are informative, whereas 11 and higher are actual errors.

SQL error action: a response taken by SQL Server in response to an error it encounters.
Statement termination: The statement with the procedure fails but the code keeps on running to the next statement. Transactions are not affected.
Sys.Messages: a table in the Master db containing the list of all error messages.
User error: an error having a severity level between 11 and 16.

Chapter Nine - Review Quiz

1.) Which SQL Server error action happens for errors with a severity of 11-16 when you set the XACT_ABORT setting to ON?

O a. You will get Statement Termination.
O b. You will get Scope Abortion.
O c. You will get Batch Abortion.
O d. You will get Connection Termination.
O e. SQL Server will pick the error action.

2.) Which SQL Server error action happens for errors with a severity of 11-16 when you set the XACT_ABORT setting to OFF?

O a. You will get Statement Termination
O b. You will get Scope Abortion
O c. You will get Batch Abortion
O d. You will get Connection Termination
O e. SQL Server will pick the error action

3.) You have many updates inside one transaction. You need to place an option at the top of the transaction that states if any errors in any updates are encountered, then the entire transaction should fail. Which option accomplishes this goal?

O a. ARITHABORT
O b. XACT_ABORT
O c. ARITHIGNORE
O d. DEADLOCK_PRIORITY
O e. NOEXEC

4.) When does SQL Server always raise an error message? (Choose two)

□ a. When a statement in SQL Server cannot run
□ b. When multiple records are updated in one table
□ c. When you issue a RAISERROR message

Answer Key

1.) c 2.) e 3.) b 4.) a, c

Bug Catcher Game

To play the Bug Catcher game, run BugCatcher_Chapter9_SQL_Error_Messages.pps from the BugCatcher folder of the companion files located at www.Joes2Pros.com.

Chapter 10. Error Handling

In everyday life, not everything you plan on doing goes your way. For example, recently I planned to turn left on Rosewood Avenue to head north to my office. To my surprise, the road was blocked because of construction. I still needed to head north, even though the signs told me that turning left was impossible. I could have treated the unexpected roadblock in the same way that SQL Server interprets a level 16 severity error. That is to say, I could have halted and simply abandoned my attempt to travel to the office. In the end, I came up with an alternate plan that was nearly as good. By using a detour route consisting of three right turns and traveling north on a parallel road, I was successfully able to avoid this unexpected disruption until the construction zone was cleared. When my Plan-A route didn't work, I tried and found a workable Plan-B.

Structured Error Handling in SQL Server is similar to the way we approach 'errors' in real life. When something does not go exactly as we expected, we adapt and find another way to accomplish our purpose. The job of a solution developer requires planning ahead and coding alternate pathways to keep our users and the application layer moving forward instead of stalling out when they encounter 'roadblocks.' As analysts and application users, we have come to expect that application architects anticipate the majority of errors which our input could generate. If a step we take within the application triggers a message or response from another program (e.g., from the underlying database program, from the operating system), then this is known as a bug – the developer has not adequately planned for this possibility and, as a result, the application appears broken to the user. Bugs which block the user from proceeding, or which force the user to exit and re-enter the application, are severe problems which should be caught and remedied during the test cycle.

This chapter will demonstrate structured error handling techniques in SQL Server.

READER NOTE: *In order to follow along with the examples in the first section of Chapter 10, please run the setup script SQLProgrammingChapter10.0Setup.sql. The setup scripts for this book are posted at Joes2Pros.com.*

Structured Error Handling

SQL Server introduced new and improved options for error handling beginning with SQL Server 2005. Prior versions did not include structured error handling.

Up until now, all the errors which we've seen have raised an error message which the client code must handle. However, what if you prefer SQL Server (and not the client) to handle the error? With structured error handling, unexpected events can be treated entirely within SQL Server. The client either does not know there was an error or simply receives a message. In other words, the client layer never sees the SQL Server error, and the user is unaware that a SQL Server error was generated.

Anticipating Potential Errors

We'll begin with an example from the Grant table. We've just learned that our current spelling for Grant 001 is incorrect, as shown in the JProCo database. The donor was actually "92 Per-cents %% team", not "92 Purr_Scents %% team."

```
SELECT * FROM [Grant]
```

Results | Messages

	GrantID	GrantName	EmpID	Amount
1	001	92 Purr_Scents %% team	7	4750.00
2	002	K-Land fund trust	2	16750.00
3	003	Robert@BigStarBank.com	7	18100.00

Figure 10.1 In the Grant table, the first Grant was made by "92 Purr_Scents %% team."

Let's first run an update statement correcting this GrantName. The data types are the same, so our update runs just fine.

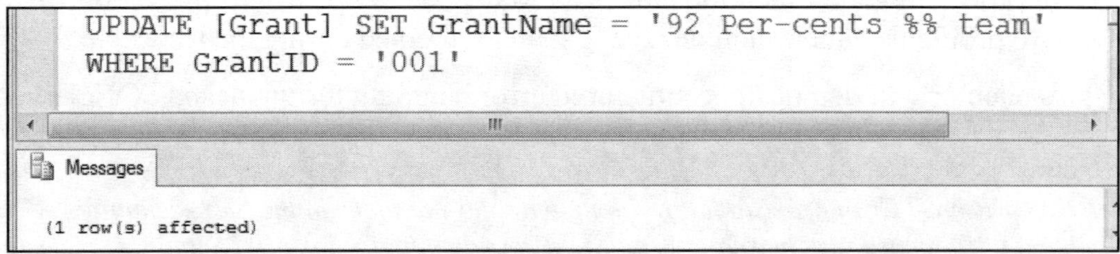

UPDATE [Grant] SET GrantName = '92 Per-cents %% team'
WHERE GrantID = '001'
Messages
(1 row(s) affected)

Figure 10.2 The GrantName of Grant 001 is updated to "92 Per-cents %% team" successfully.

Now we'll attempt to set a GrantName value to NULL. We expect to raise an error, since GrantName is a required field. The GrantName for Grant 001 fails to update to a value of NULL, since that field does not allow nulls.

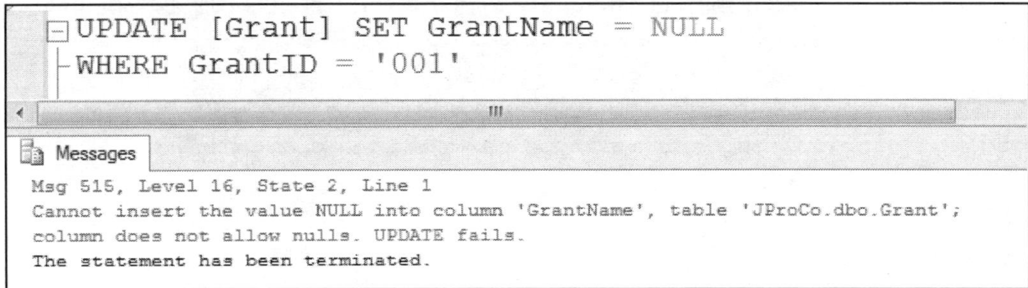

UPDATE [Grant] SET GrantName = NULL
WHERE GrantID = '001'
Messages
Msg 515, Level 16, State 2, Line 1
Cannot insert the value NULL into column 'GrantName', table 'JProCo.dbo.Grant';
column does not allow nulls. UPDATE fails.
The statement has been terminated.

Figure 10.3 The GrantName of NULL for Grant 001 fails to update, since that field does not allow nulls.

We can anticipate that updates might fail with an error. We can't prevent the occasional incorrect input from the client, but best practices require us to control or eliminate the error messaging and provide SQL Server instructions for how to behave when it receives incorrect input.

Let's next add code to our current example in order to catch these types of input errors. Structured error handling will help head off errors raised by incorrect inputs received from the client. We expect our users will send correct values and data types into the Grant table most of the time. However, for those few instances where a user attempts an incorrect value, seeing a message from anything besides the application or having to restart the application will not be comfortable experiences for our users. We will add code to deal with these types of errors and ensure that our users receive a message from the application layer (preferably one which gives them a hint they've attempted an incorrect value and providing guidance as to what the correct input should be).

The TRY Block

The Try Block is where you place code which you think may raise an error. A Try Block is a code segment starting with a BEGIN TRY statement and ending with END TRY. If a statement sits inside a Try Block and raises an error, then the error gets passed to another part of SQL Server and not to the client. The Try Block is aware that there is code which may fail.

The code which is vulnerable to potentially receiving bad input from the client should be enclosed within the Try Block. Think of your TRY block as Plan-A. This is what you are hoping works on the first try. If Plan-A does not work, we can tell SQL Server to try Plan-B instead of reacting with an error message. Our code which will handle contingency steps (i.e., Plan-B) for bad input will be enclosed in what's known as a Catch Block. *Only one of these two blocks will run to completion.* Think of the Try Block as "Plan-A" and Catch Block as "Plan-B."

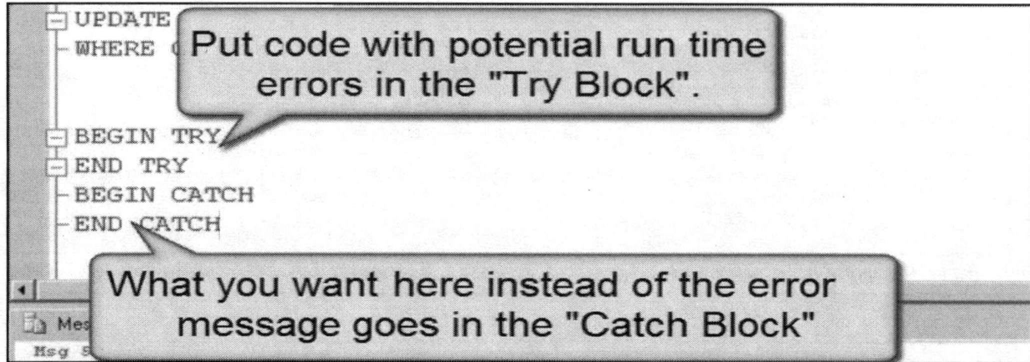

Figure 10.4 The code you want to run goes in the Try Block. The Catch Block will not run unless the code in the Try Block raises an error.

The CATCH Block

The Catch Block serves as a contingency plan for failed code from the Try Block. In other words, if any statement raises a level 11 or higher severity in the Try Block, it will not show the error from the calling code. It will run the code you have set up in the Catch Block. In Figure 10.5 the Catch Block never runs, since the Try Block ("Plan-A") runs fine. In other words, if Plan-A works then there is no need to try Plan-B.

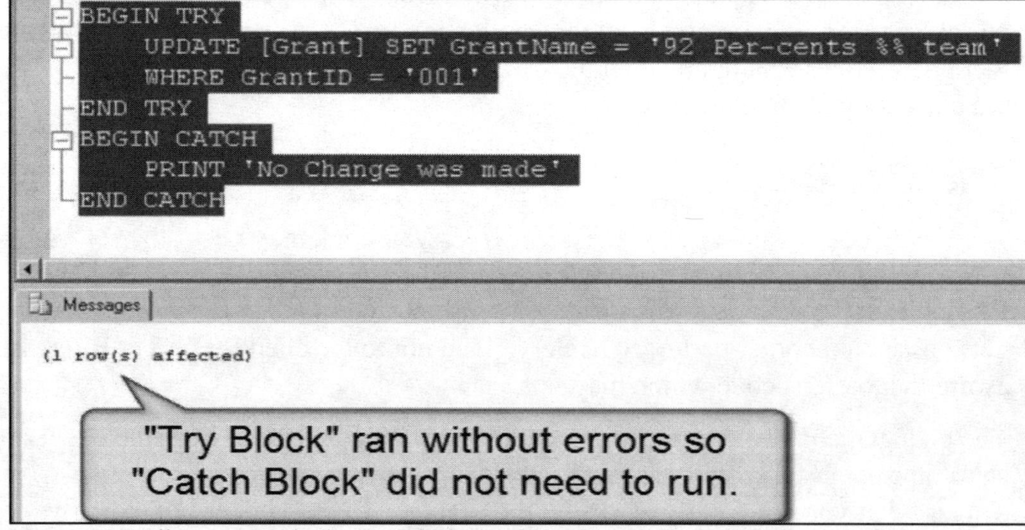

BEGIN TRY
UPDATE [Grant] SET GrantName = '92 Per-cents %% team'
WHERE GrantID = '001'
END TRY
BEGIN CATCH
PRINT 'No Change was made'
END CATCH
Messages
(1 row(s) affected)
"Try Block" ran without errors so "Catch Block" did not need to run.

Figure 10.5 All statements in the Try Block ran ok, so there was no need to run the Catch Block.

Notice in Figure 10.5 the Catch Block never runs, since the Try Block ("Plan-A") runs alright. Next let's observe an example where the Try Block will throw errors and not run successfully. Recall our previous example (refer back to Figure 10.3) where attempting to set GrantName to NULL threw an error. In using this same update statement, the Try Block encounters an error and thus will not run. The Catch Block will run instead.

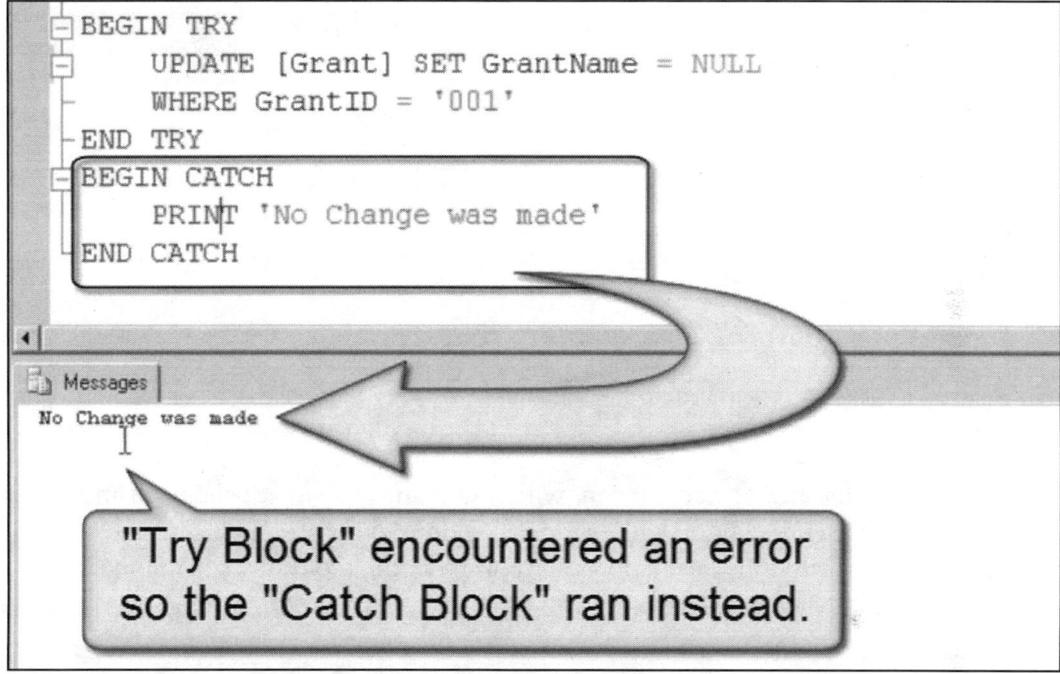

Figure 10.6 The Catch Block runs and the Try Block does not even show its error.

Let's review a few guidelines for getting the Catch Block to run. In general, the Catch Block will run if the Try Block encounters an error. However, there are some exceptions.

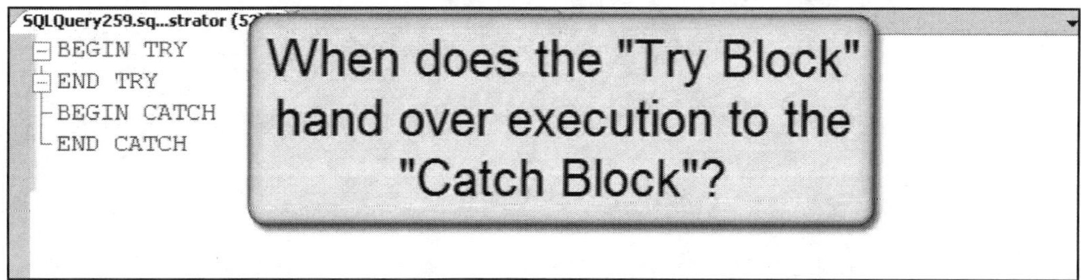

Figure 10.7 Under what conditions does the Try Block hand over execution to the Catch Block?

The Try Block in Figure 10.8 will always cause the Catch Block to run. Our RAISERROR function generates an error with severity level 16 and a state of 1. This means code in the Try Block encountered an error. When this happens, then the Catch block runs. The Catch Block in Figure 10.8 prints the confirmation "Catch Ran."

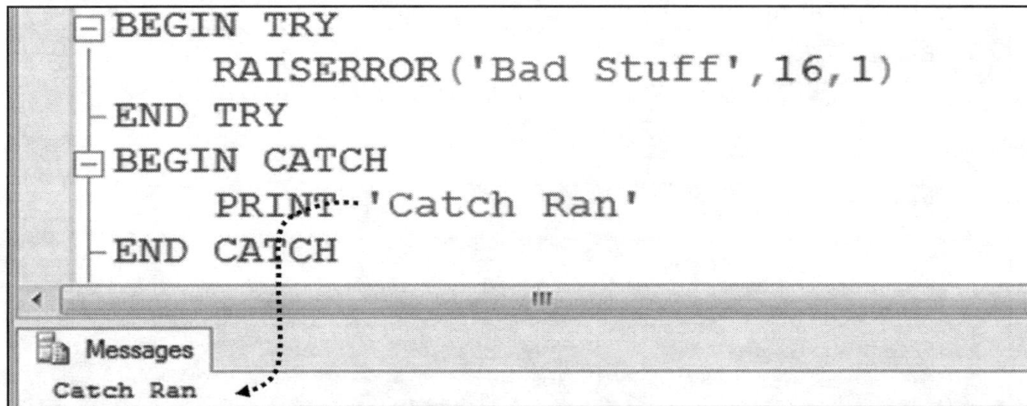

Figure 10.8 The RAISERROR function caused the Try Block to hand over execution to the Catch block.

We can add another print statement which will allow us to see the error message displayed. When the Try Block passes execution to the Catch Block, the system is fully aware of why this has happened. For example, the error causing the Try Block to fail is captured in the Error_Message system supplied function. In Figure 10.9 we have coded the Catch Block to print the error message generated by the Try Block.

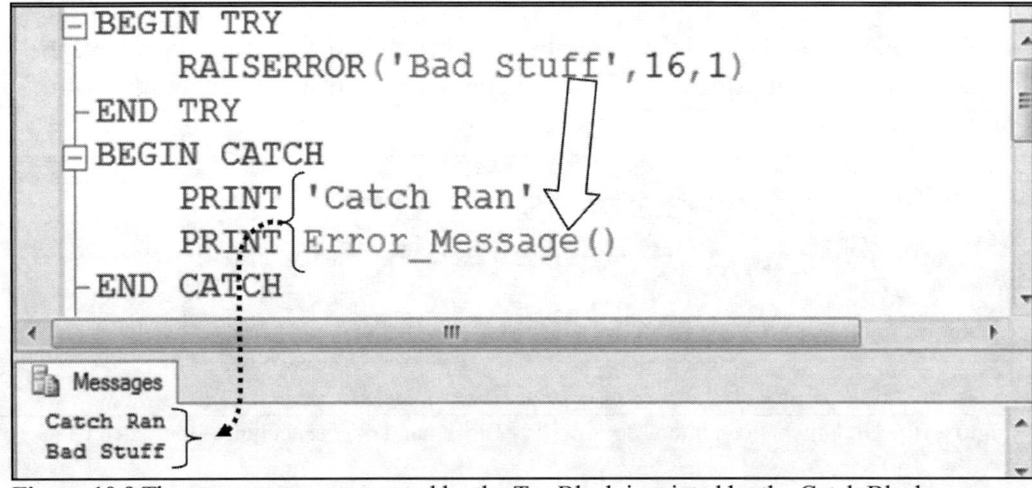

Figure 10.9 The error message generated by the Try Block is printed by the Catch Block.

We can extend this capability a bit further by capturing the severity of the error from the Try Block. By adding a print statement to display the severity level of the error, we see it in our Messages tab (see Figure 10.10).

```
BEGIN TRY
    RAISERROR('Bad Stuff',16,1)
END TRY
BEGIN CATCH
    PRINT 'Catch Ran'
    PRINT Error_Message()
    PRINT Error_Severity()
END CATCH
```

```
Messages
Catch Ran
Bad Stuff
16
```

Figure 10.10 The Error_Severity function gets the severity level of the error generated in the Try Block.

Notice that we get the value 16 because that is the level of the error severity that is generated by the Try Block (see Figure 10.10). In our next example, the Try Block has been changed to throw an error severity of 11 instead of 16 (see Figure 10.11).

```
BEGIN TRY
    RAISERROR('Sort of Bad Stuff',11,1)
END TRY
BEGIN CATCH
    PRINT 'Catch Ran'
    PRINT Error_Message()
    PRINT Error_Severity()
END CATCH
```

```
Messages
Catch Ran
Sort of Bad Stuff
11
```

Figure 10.11 This severity 11 error causes the Catch Block to run.

The Try will only hand over execution to the Catch for errors with a severity level of 11 or higher. Note that in the last example, we saw a severity 11 error invoke the Catch. However, a severity 10 error will **not** cause the Catch to execute. SQL Server treats errors of severity 10 or lower simply as informational messages (see Figure 10.12).

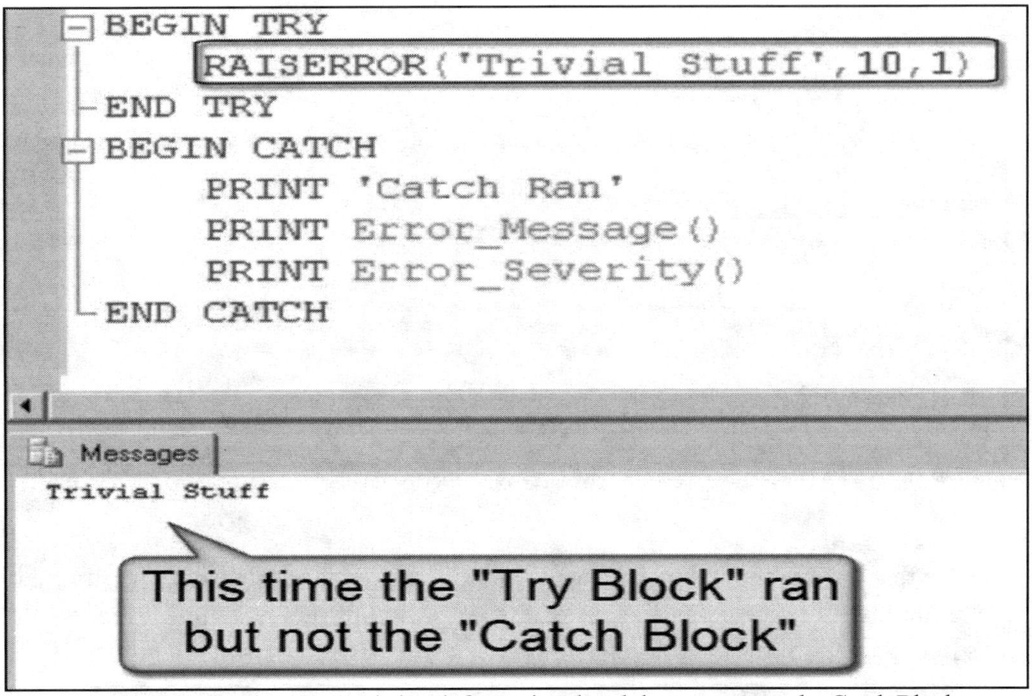

```
BEGIN TRY
    RAISERROR('Trivial Stuff',10,1)
END TRY
BEGIN CATCH
    PRINT 'Catch Ran'
    PRINT Error_Message()
    PRINT Error_Severity()
END CATCH
```

```
Messages
Trivial Stuff
```

This time the "Try Block" ran but not the "Catch Block"

Figure 10.12 This severity 10 error is just informational and does not cause the Catch Block to run.

The Try Block will pass execution to the Catch Block whenever it encounters execution errors of severity 11 or higher which do not close the database connection. If the severity is 10 or lower, then the Try Block will continue to run. Remember that it is just an informational message that is displayed when the severity is 10 or lower. Also, if the error severity is so high that it causes your database connection to close, then the Catch Block will never get the chance to run.

Structured Error Handling Summary

When you are using a Try Block together with a Catch Block to handle your errors, you are using what is known as "Structured Error Handling." The Try and Catch Blocks were introduced in SQL Server 2005 and are key tools for Structured Error Handling.

Transactions in Structured Error Handling

Our final topic will show error handling in the context of transactions, which use Begin Tran, Commit Tran, and Rollback Tran statements. Recall the stored procedure AddGrantAmount was used in Chapter 9 (refer to Figure 9.41).

```
ALTER PROC AddGrantAmount @GrantID char(3), @MoreAmount Money
AS
BEGIN
    DECLARE @GrantINT INT
    SET @GrantINT = CAST(@GrantID as INT)
    UPDATE [Grant] SET Amount = Amount + @MoreAmount
    WHERE GrantID = @GrantINT
    RAISERROR('Increased %i Grant records',10,1,@@ROWCOUNT  )

    UPDATE em SET Em.LatestGrantActivity = CURRENT_TIMESTAMP
    FROM Employee as em INNER JOIN [Grant] as gr
    ON em.EmpID = gr.EmpID
    WHERE GrantID = @GrantID
    RAISERROR('Updated %i Employee records',10,1,@@ROWCOUNT )
END
```

Figure 10.13 The AddGrantAmount sproc from Chapter 9 contains two UPDATE statements.

In Chapter 9, we saw that the second update statement sometimes runs, even if the first statement failed. This was a SQL error action called ***Statement Termination***. In some cases we saw a failure of the first statement cause the stored procedure to fail and not run the second update statement. The behavior after an error in the first update statement in Figure 10.14 is somewhat unpredictable.

```
ALTER PROC AddGrantAmount @GrantID char(3), @MoreAmount Money
AS
BEGIN
    DECLARE @GrantINT INT
    SET @GrantINT = CAST(@GrantID as INT)
    UPDATE [Grant] SET Amount = Amount + @MoreAmount
    WHERE GrantID = @GrantINT
    RAISERROR('Increased %i Grant records',10,1,@@ROWCOUNT  )

    UPDATE em SET Em.LatestGrantActivity = CURRENT_TIMESTAMP
    FROM Employee as em INNER JOIN [Grant] as gr
    ON em.EmpID = gr.EmpID
    WHERE GrantID = @GrantID
    RAISERROR('Updated %i Employee records',10,1,@@ROWCOUNT )
END
```

Figure 10.14 Sometimes a failure on the first statement will not prevent execution of subsequent statements within a stored procedure.

For an example on Statement Termination, please see Figure 10.15 below. When we attempt to update Grant 003 with an Amount value of NULL, we see the first update statement fails and disallows the NULL (recall that Amount is a non-nullable field). However, we get a confirmation message showing that the second update statement ran anyway. Thus, our database information is inconsistent because the Employee table now shows an updated timestamp for the employee who found GrantID 003 even though no change was actually made.

```
EXEC AddGrantAmount '003', NULL

ALTER PROC AddGrantAmount @GrantID char(3), @MoreAmount Money
AS
BEGIN
    DECLARE @GrantINT INT
    SET @GrantINT = CAST(@GrantID as INT)
    UPDATE [Grant] SET Amount = Amount + @MoreAmount
    WHERE GrantID = @GrantINT
    RAISERROR('Increased %i Grant records',10,1,@@ROWCOUNT  )

    UPDATE em SET Em.LatestGrantActivity = CURRENT_TIMESTAMP
    FROM Employee as em INNER JOIN [Grant] as gr
    ON em.EmpID = gr.EmpID
    WHERE GrantID = @GrantID
    RAISERROR('Updated %i Employee records',10,1,@@ROWCOUNT )
END
```

Messages

```
Msg 515, Level 16, State 2, Procedure AddGrantAmount, Line 6
Cannot insert the value NULL into column 'Amount', table 'JProCo.dbo.Grant'; colum
The statement has been terminated.
Increased 0 Grant records

(1 row(s) affected)
Updated 1 Employee records
```

The second update statement ran even after the first update failed.

Figure 10.15 The Null data type in the first update statement resulted in Statement Termination.

Let's also recall the result produced by passing the sproc two valid parameters. The valid inputs in Figure 10.16 cause one Grant Amount to increase and the corresponding Employee record to be updated. This is the ideal situation we expect to see in nearly all cases.

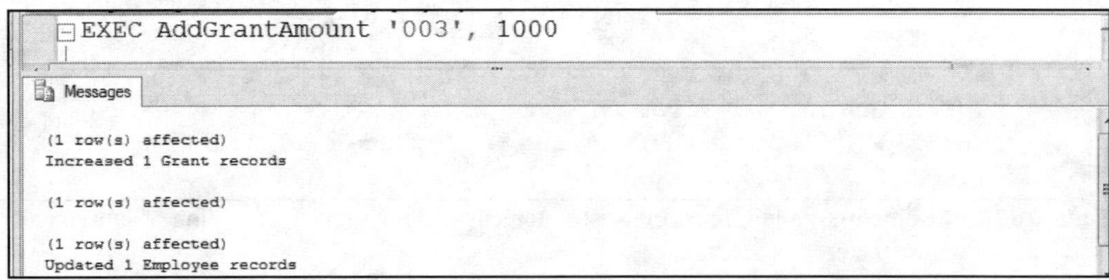
EXEC AddGrantAmount '003', 1000
Messages
(1 row(s) affected)
Increased 1 Grant records
(1 row(s) affected)
(1 row(s) affected)
Updated 1 Employee records

Figure 10.16 Calling on the AddGrantAmount stored procedure works with valid inputs.

Now we'll add the transaction keywords (BEGIN TRAN, COMMIT TRAN, and ROLLBACK TRAN) to enhance the robustness of our error handling. Previously in the *Joes 2 Pros* series (see *Beginning SQL Joes 2 Pros*, Chapter 9), we worked with updates and transactions which we wanted to either succeed or fail as a whole. If any part of the code failed, we wanted none of the changes to be committed. In Figure 10.17, we add a BEGIN TRAN and COMMIT TRAN statements at the beginning and end of our update code to put both statements into one transaction.

```
ALTER PROC AddGrantAmount @GrantID char(3), @MoreAmount Money
AS
BEGIN
    BEGIN TRAN
    DECLARE @GrantINT INT
    SET @GrantINT = CAST(@GrantID as INT)
    UPDATE [Grant] SET Amount = Amount + @MoreAmount
    WHERE GrantID = @GrantINT
    RAISERROR('Increased %i Grant records',10,1,@@ROWCOUNT )

    UPDATE em SET Em.LatestGrantActivity = CURRENT_TIMESTAMP
    FROM Employee as em INNER JOIN [Grant] as gr
    ON em.EmpID = gr.EmpID
    WHERE GrantID = @GrantID
    RAISERROR('Updated %i Employee records',10,1,@@ROWCOUNT )
    COMMIT TRAN
END
```

Figure 10.17 Both update statements are put inside of one transaction.

After running the stored procedure, we still seem to get an error on the first statement and an update on the second statement (see Figure 10.18).

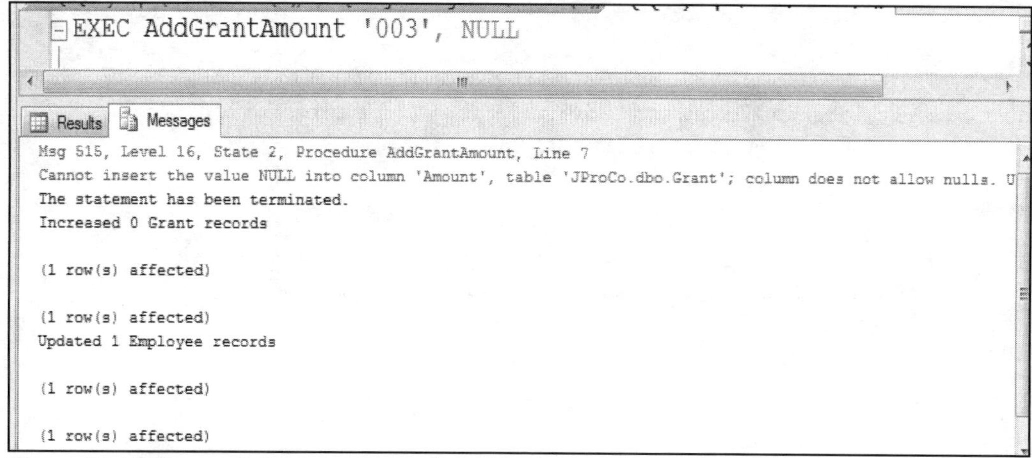
EXEC AddGrantAmount '003', NULL
Results
Messages
Msg 515, Level 16, State 2, Procedure AddGrantAmount, Line 7
Cannot insert the value NULL into column 'Amount', table 'JProCo.dbo.Grant'; column does not allow nulls. U
The statement has been terminated.
Increased 0 Grant records
(1 row(s) affected)
(1 row(s) affected)
Updated 1 Employee records
(1 row(s) affected)
(1 row(s) affected)

Figure 10.18 The explicit transaction code inside the stored procedure did not change the statement termination error action.

The query in Figure 10.19 confirms that no update was made to the Grant table, yet a new value shows in the Employee table.

```
SELECT * FROM [Grant] WHERE GrantID = '003'
SELECT * FROM Employee WHERE EmpID  = 7
```

Results | Messages

	GrantID	GrantName	EmpID	Amount
1	003	Robert@BigStarBank.com	7	19100.00

	EmpID	LastName	FirstName	HireDate	LocationID	ManagerID	Status	HiredOffset	TimeZo...	LatestGrantActivity
1	7	Lonning	David	2000-01-01...	1	11	On Leave	2000-01-01...	-08:00	2011-06-05 21:44:51.190

Figure 10.19 The update to the Grant table failed but the update to the Employee table succeeded.

While these statements are needed to change our code into a transaction, note that simply adding these statements doesn't produce a different result. This is because transactions ignore raised errors**.** In other words, before this code will accomplish our intended result, we first need to enclose all the code for our transaction within a Try Block. In Figure 10.20 we put the entire transaction inside its own Try Block. We then need to add a Catch Block just below it to react to the error.

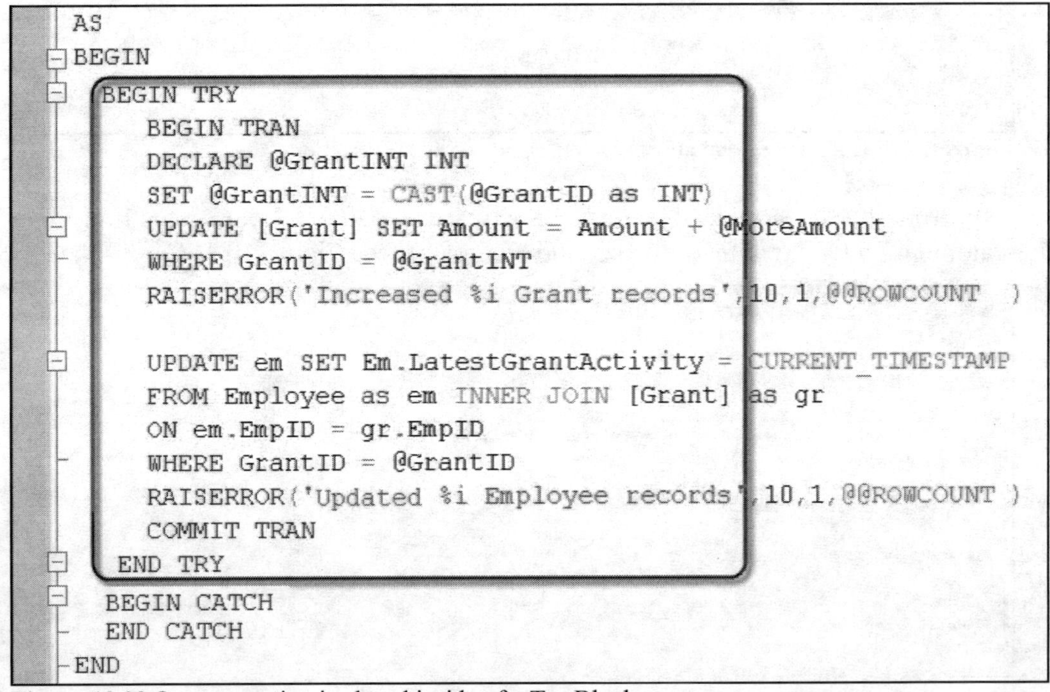

```
AS
BEGIN
 BEGIN TRY
    BEGIN TRAN
    DECLARE @GrantINT INT
    SET @GrantINT = CAST(@GrantID as INT)
    UPDATE [Grant] SET Amount = Amount + @MoreAmount
    WHERE GrantID = @GrantINT
    RAISERROR('Increased %i Grant records',10,1,@@ROWCOUNT  )

    UPDATE em SET Em.LatestGrantActivity = CURRENT_TIMESTAMP
    FROM Employee as em INNER JOIN [Grant] as gr
    ON em.EmpID = gr.EmpID
    WHERE GrantID = @GrantID
    RAISERROR('Updated %i Employee records',10,1,@@ROWCOUNT )
    COMMIT TRAN
  END TRY
  BEGIN CATCH
  END CATCH
END
```

Figure 10.20 Our transaction is placed inside of a Try Block.

What will we include in our Catch Block? Well if there is any error in the transaction, then we know there is a problem. We can simply have the Catch Block "Rollback Transaction", if the Try Block fails.

```
BEGIN TRY
   BEGIN TRAN
   DECLARE @GrantINT INT
   SET @GrantINT = CAST(@GrantID as INT)
   UPDATE [Grant] SET Amount = Amount + @MoreAmount
   WHERE GrantID = @GrantINT
   RAISERROR('Increased %i Grant records',10,1,@@ROWCOUNT  )

   UPDATE em SET Em.LatestGrantActivity = CURRENT_TIMESTAMP
   FROM Employee as em INNER JOIN [Grant] as gr
   ON em.EmpID = gr.EmpID
   WHERE GrantID = @GrantID
   RAISERROR('Updated %i Employee records',10,1,@@ROWCOUNT )
   COMMIT TRAN
 END TRY
 BEGIN CATCH
   ROLLBACK TRAN
 END CATCH
END
```

Figure 10.21 Our Catch Block simply rolls back the transaction if the Try Block fails.

```
ALTER PROC AddGrantAmount @GrantID char(3), @MoreAmount Money
AS
BEGIN
 BEGIN TRY
    BEGIN TRAN
    DECLARE @GrantINT INT
    SET @GrantINT = CAST(@GrantID as INT)
    UPDATE [Grant] SET Amount = Amount + @MoreAmount
    WHERE GrantID = @GrantINT
    RAISERROR('Increased %i Grant records',10,1,@@ROWCOUNT  )

    UPDATE em SET Em.LatestGrantActivity = CURRENT_TIMESTAMP
    FROM Employee as em INNER JOIN [Grant] as gr
    ON em.EmpID = gr.EmpID
    WHERE GrantID = @GrantID
    RAISERROR('Updated %i Employee records',10,1,@@ROWCOUNT )
    COMMIT TRAN
  END TRY
  BEGIN CATCH
    ROLLBACK TRAN
  END CATCH
END
```

Figure 10.22 All of the code contained in the ALTER PROC statement.

After running all of the code in the ALTER PROC statement (see Figure 10.22), observe that attempting to pass in the NULL parameter will have no effect on the database (see Figure 10.23). Not only is the incorrect value disallowed by the Grant table, but the Employee table similarly does not get updated since the entire transaction is rolled back.

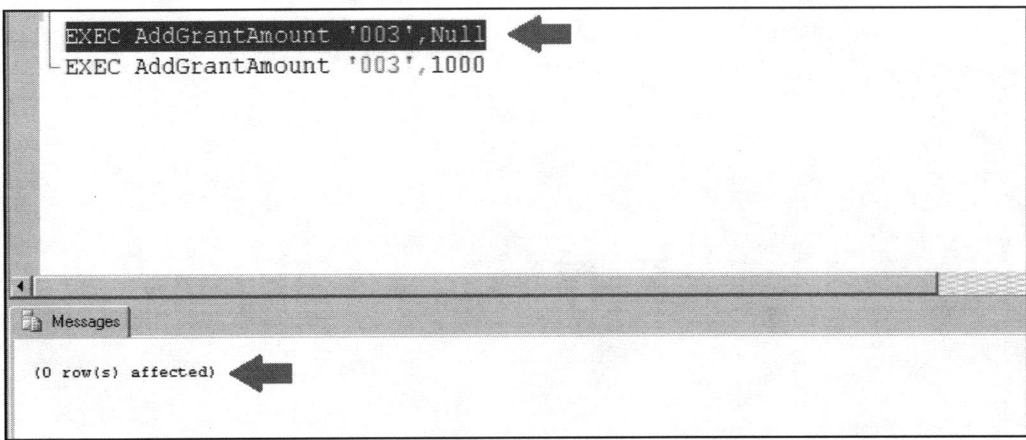
EXEC AddGrantAmount '003',Null
EXEC AddGrantAmount '003',1000
Messages
(0 row(s) affected)

Figure 10.23 When calling on the stored procedure creates an error, no records are affected.

Notice that passing in two valid parameters shows the result we expected to achieve: one Grant record was increased and one Employee record was updated (see Figure 10.24). The amount of Grant 3 is now $20,100.

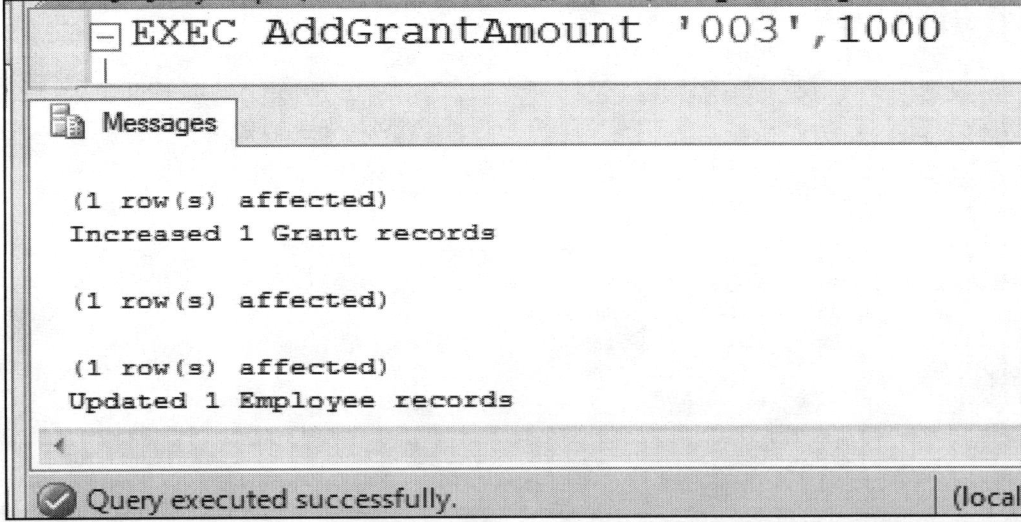
EXEC AddGrantAmount '003',1000
Messages
(1 row(s) affected)
Increased 1 Grant records
(1 row(s) affected)
(1 row(s) affected)
Updated 1 Employee records
Query executed successfully.
(local

Figure 10.24 When no error is encountered, then all statements in the transaction complete.

Before proceeding to Lab 10.1, we will spend a few moments on this example which reviews transactions and foreign keys. Figure 10.25 shows us all fields and records in the CurrentProducts table, which currently contains 486 records.

```sql
SELECT * FROM CurrentProducts
```

	ProductID	ProductName	RetailPrice	OriginationDate	ToBeDeleted	Category	SupplierID	OriginationOffset
1	1	Underwater Tour 1 Day West Coast	61.483	2006-08-11 13:33:09.957	0	No-Stay	0	2006-08-11 13:33:09.9570000
2	2	Underwater Tour 2 Days West Coast	110.6694	2007-10-03 23:43:22.813	0	Overnight-Stay	0	2007-10-03 23:43:22.8130000
3	3	Underwater Tour 3 Days West Coast	184.449	2009-05-09 16:07:49.900	0	Medium-Stay	0	2009-05-09 16:07:49.9000000
4	4	Underwater Tour 5 Days West Coast	245.932	2006-03-04 04:59:06.600	0	Medium-Stay	0	2006-03-04 04:59:06.6000000

Query executed successfully. | (local) (10.0 SP1) | Joes2ProsA10\Teacher (52) | JProCo | 00:00:00 | 486 rows

Figure 10.25 The CurrentProducts table has 486 records.

We want to obtain a list of the products which have never been ordered. Since the SalesInvoiceDetail table contains sales invoice data, joining it to the CurrentProducts table on the ProductID field (using a left outer join) will show us the list of products that are not present in the SalesInvoiceDetail table and thus which have never been ordered. There are 426 products that have never been ordered (see Figure 10.26).

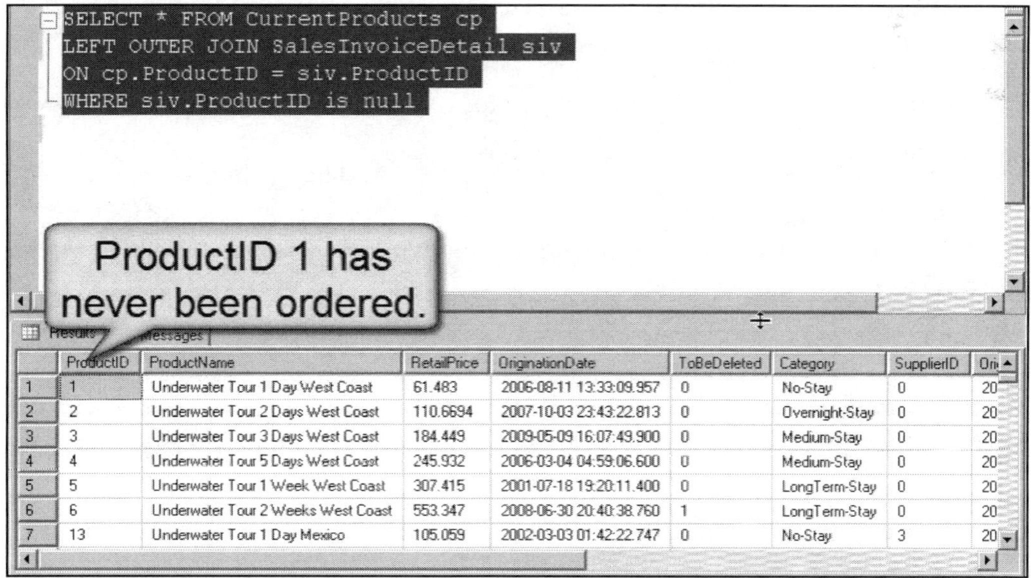

```sql
SELECT * FROM CurrentProducts cp
LEFT OUTER JOIN SalesInvoiceDetail siv
ON cp.ProductID = siv.ProductID
WHERE siv.ProductID is null
```

	ProductID	ProductName	RetailPrice	OriginationDate	ToBeDeleted	Category	SupplierID	Ori
1	1	Underwater Tour 1 Day West Coast	61.483	2006-08-11 13:33:09.957	0	No-Stay	0	20
2	2	Underwater Tour 2 Days West Coast	110.6694	2007-10-03 23:43:22.813	0	Overnight-Stay	0	20
3	3	Underwater Tour 3 Days West Coast	184.449	2009-05-09 16:07:49.900	0	Medium-Stay	0	20
4	4	Underwater Tour 5 Days West Coast	245.932	2006-03-04 04:59:06.600	0	Medium-Stay	0	20
5	5	Underwater Tour 1 Week West Coast	307.415	2001-07-18 19:20:11.400	0	LongTerm-Stay	0	20
6	6	Underwater Tour 2 Weeks West Coast	553.347	2008-06-30 20:40:38.760	1	LongTerm-Stay	0	20
7	13	Underwater Tour 1 Day Mexico	105.059	2002-03-03 01:42:22.747	0	No-Stay	3	20

ProductID 1 has
never been ordered.

Figure 10.26 ProductID 1 is present in our query and thus has never been ordered.

Any product missing from this result set has already been ordered by a customer. For example, we know Products 7 through 12 have been ordered because they are missing from this result set (see Figure 10.27).

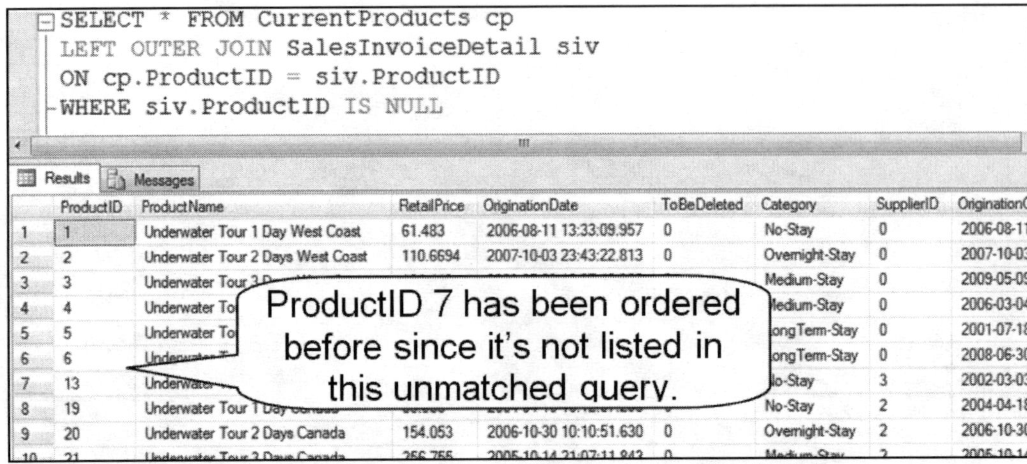

Figure 10.27 Any ProductID not listed in this result set has been ordered before.

Since Product 1 hasn't been ordered, we will delete it from the CurrentProducts table. SQL Server allows this deletion (see Figure 10.28).

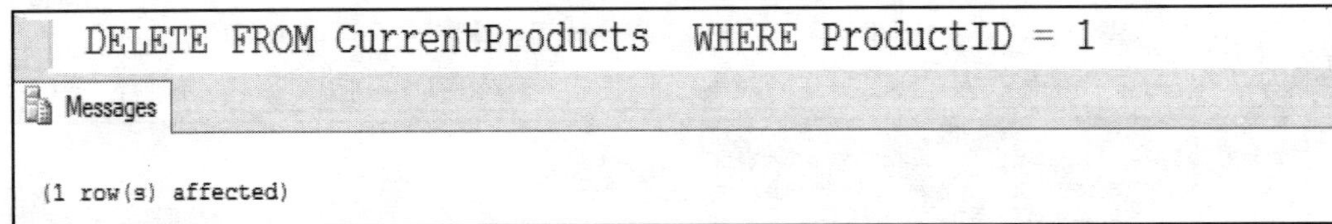

Figure 10.28 Since ProductID 1 has never been ordered, SQL Server allows deletion of this record.

However, SQL Server will not allow us to delete Product 7, since there are invoice records which depend on ProductID 7. Here we see an error message (severity 16) which references a foreign key constraint, and we see the statement has been terminated (see Figure 10.29).

```
DELETE FROM CurrentProducts  WHERE ProductID = 7
```

Messages

```
Msg 547, Level 16, State 0, Line 1
The DELETE statement conflicted with the REFERENCE constraint
"FK_SalesInvoiceDetail_CurrentProducts_ProductID".
The conflict occurred in database "JProCo", table "dbo.SalesInvoiceDetail", column 'ProductID'.
The statement has been terminated.
```

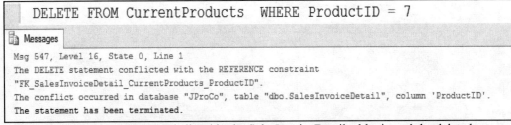

Figure 10.29 Since ProductID 7 is listed in the SalesInvoiceDetail table, it can't be deleted.

After we delete Product 1, suppose that we receive an order for this product. Our query (see Figure 10.30) attempts to insert a record reflecting this supposed order. Because Product 1 has been deleted, this insert statement will fail and terminate.

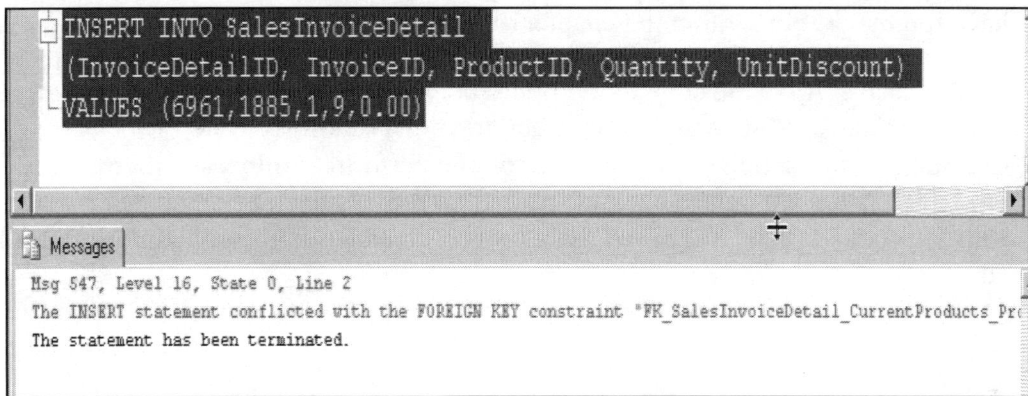
INSERT INTO SalesInvoiceDetail
(InvoiceDetailID, InvoiceID, ProductID, Quantity, UnitDiscount)
VALUES (6961,1885,1,9,0.00)
Messages
Msg 547, Level 16, State 0, Line 2
The INSERT statement conflicted with the FOREIGN KEY constraint "FK_SalesInvoiceDetail_CurrentProducts_Pr
The statement has been terminated.

Figure 10.30 Trying to insert an order for ProductID 1 fails since you deleted it in Figure 10.28.

This brings us to the scenario described in the Lab 10.1 Skill Check. Suppose that at the same time you are deleting Product 2, a sales order is received for Product 2.

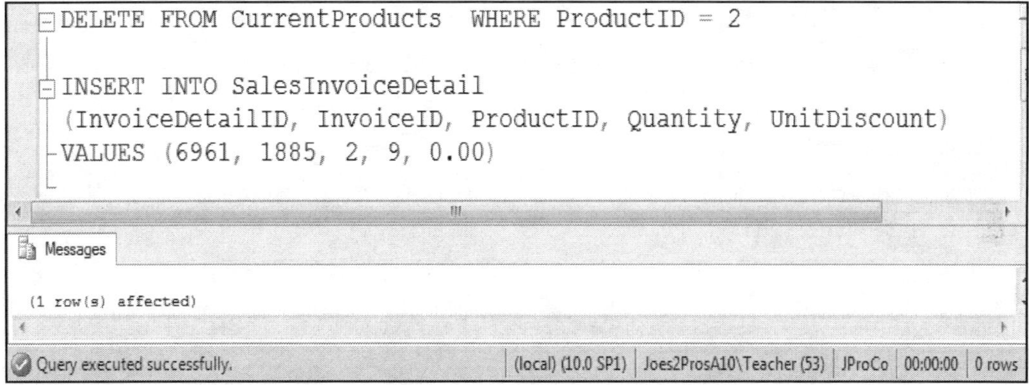
DELETE FROM CurrentProducts WHERE ProductID = 2
INSERT INTO SalesInvoiceDetail
(InvoiceDetailID, InvoiceID, ProductID, Quantity, UnitDiscount)
VALUES (6961, 1885, 2, 9, 0.00)
Messages
(1 row(s) affected)
Query executed successfully.
(local) (10.0 SP1)
Joes2ProsA10\Teacher (53)
JProCo
00:00:00
0 rows

Figure 10.31 This code would error out if you treat the insertion and deletion as two separate operations.

Lab 10.1: Structured Error Handling

Lab Prep: Before you can begin the lab, you must have SQL Server installed and have run the SQLProgrammingChapter10.1Setup.sql script.

Skill Check 1: Take the code in the figure below (see Figure 10.32) and put all of it into one transaction. Wrap the transaction with a set of Try/Catch Blocks. Commit the transaction if there is no error and perform a rollback if there is an error. When you are done, check to see that no records have been deleted from the CurrentProducts table, nor have any records been added to the SalesInvoiceDetail table.

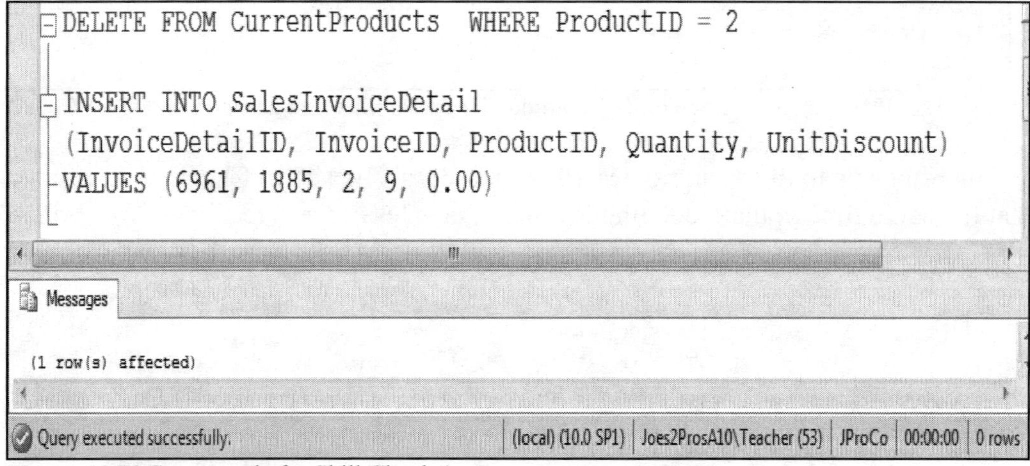

```
DELETE FROM CurrentProducts  WHERE ProductID = 2

INSERT INTO SalesInvoiceDetail
(InvoiceDetailID, InvoiceID, ProductID, Quantity, UnitDiscount)
VALUES (6961, 1885, 2, 9, 0.00)
```


Figure 10.32 Starter code for Skill Check 1.

Answer Code: The T-SQL code to this lab can be found in the downloadable files in a file named Lab10.1_StructuredErrorHandling.sql.

Structured Error Handling - Points to Ponder

1. Until SQL Server 2005, there was no way to prevent SQL Server from raising error messages.
2. In SQL Server 2005 and beyond you can use the TRY-CATCH approach for all the error messages trapped by your catch handler. None of this was possible with the old RAISERROR process.
3. The catch block supports six functions:
    a. Error_Number( )
    b. Error_Message( )
    c. Error_Severity( )
    d. Error_State( )
    e. Error_Procedure( )
    f. Error_Line( )
4. A TRY…CATCH construct catches all execution errors with a severity higher than 10 and which do not close the database connection.
5. GOTO statements cannot be used to enter a TRY or CATCH block.
6. In a trigger context, almost all errors result in batch abortion, except for errors which you raise yourself with a RAISERROR message.
7. Set XACT_ABORT to OFF. This sets your SQL Server instance back to the default set of rules for responding to errors.
8. Set XACT_ABORT to ON. This causes batch abortion on the first error (except for errors you raise yourself with RAISERROR).

Chapter Glossary

BEGIN CATCH…END CATCH: the CATCH block; serves as a contingency plan for failed code from the Try Block.
BEGIN TRY…END TRY: the TRY block; "Plan A" for what you would like your program to do. If the TRY block fails, it passes the attempted code to the CATCH block.
TRY…CATCH: a construct which catches all execution errors with a severity higher than 10 and which do not close the database connection.

Chapter Ten - Review Quiz

1.) You have tables named CurrentProducts and SaleInvoiceDetail. The CurrentProducts table has a foreign key relationship with the SalesInvoiceDetail table on the ProductID. All products in the CurrentProducts table are listed at least once in the SalesInvoiceDetail table. You use the following code:

```
BEGIN TRY
	BEGIN TRANSACTION
		DELETE FROM CurrentProducts WHERE ProductID = 1
		INSERT INTO SalesInvoiceDetail VALUES (778,1,0,DEFAULT)
	COMMIT TRANSACTION
END TRY
BEGIN CATCH
	ROLLBACK TRAN
END CATCH
```

You need to know the results of this batch. What will happen?

O a. 1 record is deleted from the CurrentProducts table and 1 record is added to the SalesInvoiceDetail table.

O b. 1 record is deleted from the CurrentProducts table but no records are added to the SalesInvoiceDetail table.

O c. No records are deleted from the CurrentProducts table but 1 record is added to the SalesInvoiceDetail table.

O d. No records are deleted from the CurrentProducts table and no records are added to the SalesInvoiceDetail table.

2.) SQL Server has many error severity rating levels. You notice a severity of 9 ran inside your TRY block and did not pass control to the CATCH block. What level of severity is the minimum that will cause the TRY block to pass control to the CATCH block?

O a. 11

O b. 12

O c. 16

O d. 17

3.) You have code that counts the number of rows in a given table by using the code below.

```
BEGIN TRY
	DECLARE @SQL Varchar(max)
	'SELECT Count(*) FROM' + @TableName
	EXEC (@SQL)
	SET @Total = @@ROWCOUNT
	--PUT CODE HERE
END TRY
BEGIN CATCH
	PRINT ERROR_MESSAGE( )
END CATCH
```

You want to insert a SQL statement right before the end of the TRY block that will send a notification and how many rows were affected. Which code do you use?

O a. RAISERROR ('Deleted %i records',10,1, @Total)
O b. RAISERROR ('Deleted %i records',11,1, @Total)
O c. RAISERROR ('Deleted %i records',16,1, @Total)

4.) You are using a TRY...CATCH block in your structured error handling. You need to raise an error in the TRY block that will pass execution to the CATCH block. Which severity level will do this?

O a. 0

O b. 9

O c. 10

O d. 16

5.) You have written multiple DML statements to modify existing records in your CurrentProducts table. You have placed these DML updates into an explicit transaction. You know that some errors will cause SQL to abort the whole batch while other errors will encounter statement termination and continue to run the remaining code. You need to set an abort option and roll back all changes if any error in the transaction is encountered. Which option should you enable?

O a. SET NOEXEC

O b. SET XACT_ABORT

O c. SET TRANSACTION ISOLATION LEVEL

6.) You have tables named CurrentProducts and SalesInvoiceHeader. The CurrentProducts table has a foreign key relationship with the SalesInvoiceHeader table on the ProductID column. You are deleting ProductID 77 from the Product table and then trying to insert a sale for Product77 into the SalesInvoiceHeader table.

```
BEGIN TRY
 BEGIN TRANSACTION
    DELETE FROM CurrentProducts  WHERE ProductID = 77;
    BEGIN TRANSACTION
      INSERT INTO SalesInvoiceHeader VALUES ( 95894, 77, 2 );
    COMMIT TRANSACTION
 COMMIT TRANSACTION
END TRY
BEGIN CATCH
 ROLLBACK TRANSACTION
 PRINT ERROR_MESSAGE( );
END CATCH
```

What will be the outcome when you run this query?

O a. 1) The product will be deleted from the CurrentProducts table.
  2) The order details will be inserted into the SalesInvoiceHeader table.

O b. 1) The product will be deleted from the CurrentProducts table.
  2) The order details will not be inserted into the SalesInvoiceHeader table.

O c. 1) The product will not be deleted from the CurrentProducts table.
  2) The order details will be inserted into the SalesInvoiceHeader table.

O d. 1) The product will not be deleted from the CurrentProducts table.
  2) The order details will not be inserted into the SalesInvoiceHeader table.

Answer Key

1.) d 2.) a 3.) a 4.) d 5.) b 6.) d

Bug Catcher Game

To play the Bug Catcher game, run the file BugCatcher_Chapter10_ErrorHandling.pps from the BugCatcher folder of the companion files located at www.Joes2Pros.com.

Chapter 11. Change Tracking

Right after I turned 18, my parents let my brother and I make the 100-mile holiday trek to our grandma's house in my bright yellow VW Rabbit. My parents took their own car. Both cars left at about the same time. However, my parents arrived about 20 minutes before me, because my brother and I took a few wrong turns and were circling around the rural neighborhoods until we figured out precisely where to go. We traveled from the same starting point and to the same destination as my parents, but we took very different steps to get there. Upon our arrival, my parents were a little worried and asked how we finally got to grandma's house.

Change Tracking can help you answer similar questions about your data. You can easily see what records are currently sitting in each of your tables. But oftentimes you will need to see a record as it was originally entered into the database, or the way it appeared before the most recent billing process ran. Imagine an HR analyst encounters an employee record with what seems to be an incorrect address and needs to see what changes were last made to that record. With Change Tracking, you can see the changes which brought your data to the current point. You can see how many and what types of changes have taken place on your records.

Change Tracking is a new and much anticipated feature in SQL Server 2008. Prior to SQL Server 2008, SQL DBAs had to code complex triggers and archive tables in order to track changes made to their database tables.

READER NOTE: *In order to follow along with the examples in the first section of Chapter 11, please run the setup script SQLProgrammingChapter11.0Setup.sql. The setup scripts for this book are posted at Joes2Pros.com.*

Change Tracking Basics

A SELECT statement displays just your current data. Change Tracking gives you visibility to the changes which have brought your table's data to its current point.

Prior to SQL Server 2008, the most common way to see changed data was with triggers sending data into archive tables that had similar fields to the tables you needed to track. Tracking with triggers not only requires complex code logic but it also incurs a performance hit.

With one select statement, it's easy to tell how many records any given table has. As we look at this first example with the Military table in the dbBasics database, let's ponder a scenario. Imagine we begin with a table containing 10 records. We delete one of the records then add one new record. Our table will contain 10 records and therefore appear similar to our original table. But those 10 records are not the same 10 records we began with – our table has undergone some changes along the way to its current state. At the beginning and end of the example, the Military table will contain 10 records (see Figure 11.1).

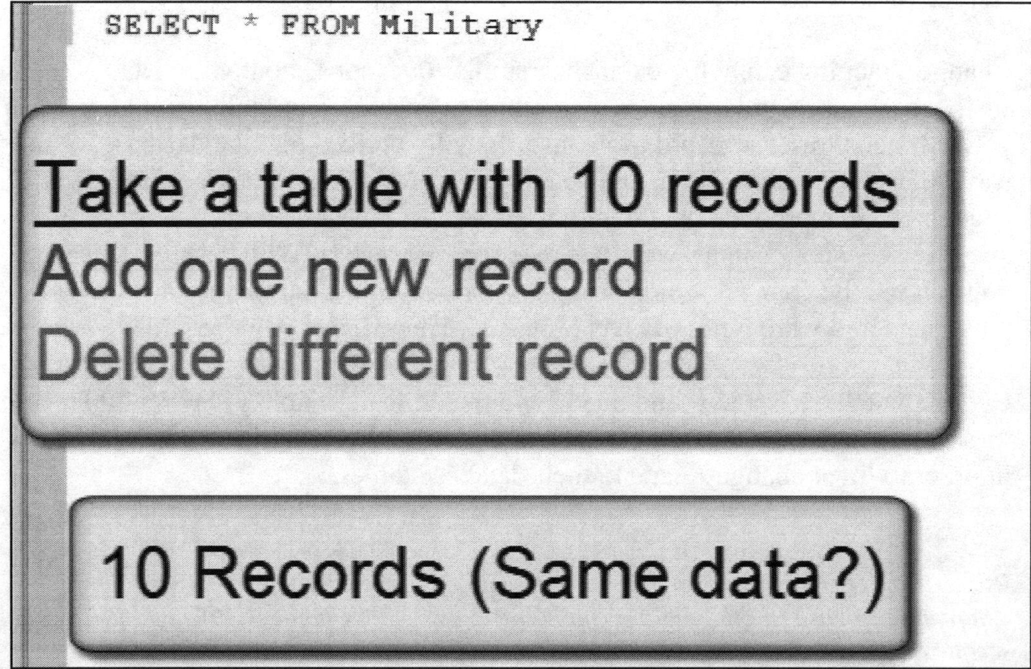

Figure 11.1 The Military table would contain 10 records before and after our changes.

The records of our Military table appear below. Private is the lowest level, and Colonel is the highest level shown. Notice we have two RankGrades which have multiple RankNames (see Figure 11.2).

	RankGrade	RankName
1	1	Private
2	2	Corporal
3	2	Specialist
4	3	Sergeant
5	4	First Sergeant
6	4	Master Sergeant
7	5	Lieutenant
8	6	Captain
9	7	Major
10	8	Colonel

Figure 11.2 The Military table in the dbBasics database contains ranks used by the U.S. Army.

After inserting one record (General), our table contains 11 records (Figure 11.3).

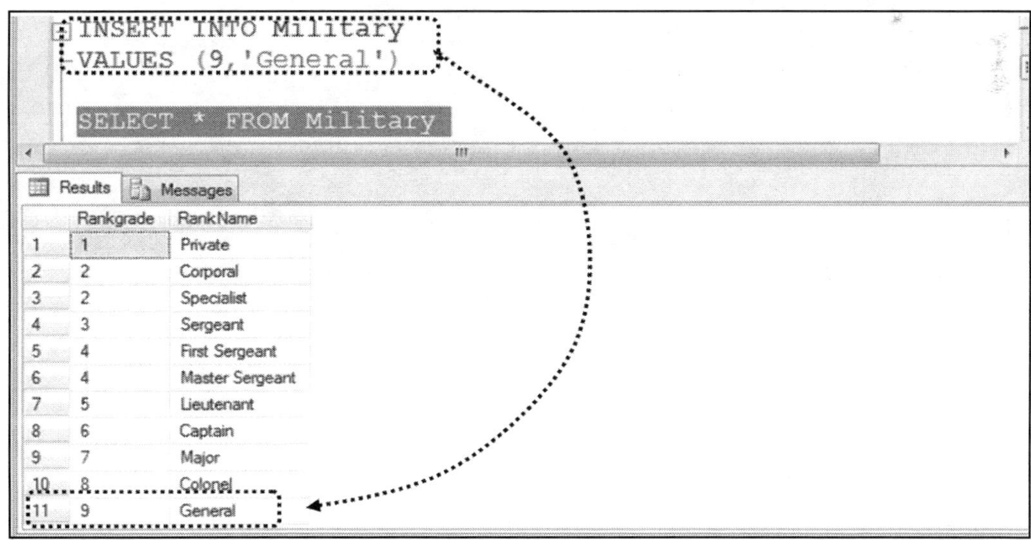

```
INSERT INTO Military
VALUES (9,'General')

SELECT * FROM Military
```

	Rankgrade	RankName
1	1	Private
2	2	Corporal
3	2	Specialist
4	3	Sergeant
5	4	First Sergeant
6	4	Master Sergeant
7	5	Lieutenant
8	6	Captain
9	7	Major
10	8	Colonel
11	9	General

Figure 11.3 The table now contains 11 records.

Next we will delete one of the records which are tied on RankGrade (Master Sergeant).

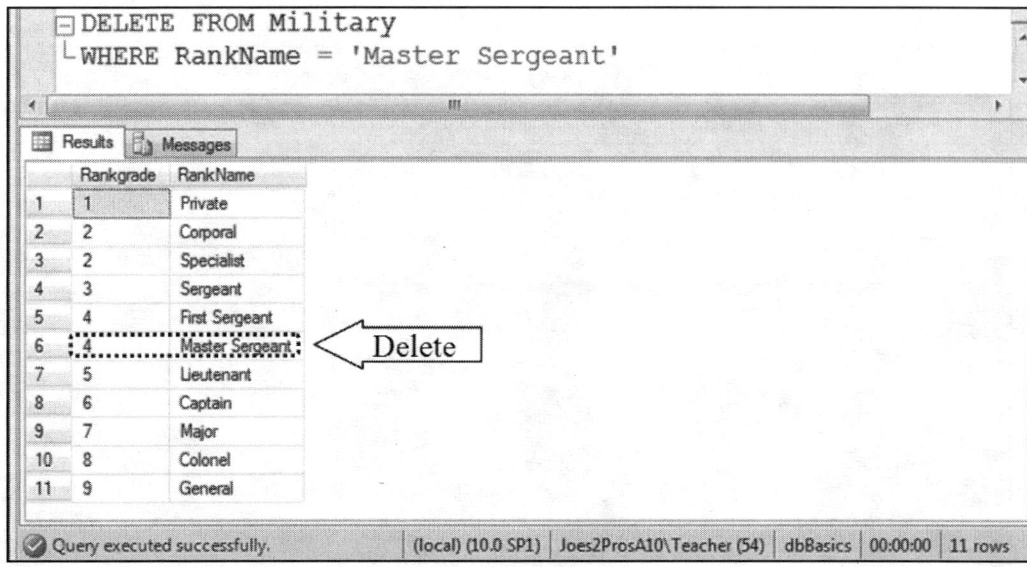

DELETE FROM Military
WHERE RankName = 'Master Sergeant'
Results
Messages
Rankgrade RankName
1 1 Private
2 2 Corporal
3 2 Specialist
4 3 Sergeant
5 4 First Sergeant
6 4 Master Sergeant
7 5 Lieutenant
8 6 Captain
9 7 Major
10 8 Colonel
11 9 General
Delete
Query executed successfully.
(local) (10.0 SP1) | Joes2ProsA10\Teacher (54) | dbBasics | 00:00:00 | 11 rows

Figure 11.4 Delete the Master Sergeant record from the table.

After the changes, the table again contains 10 records (see Figure 11.5).

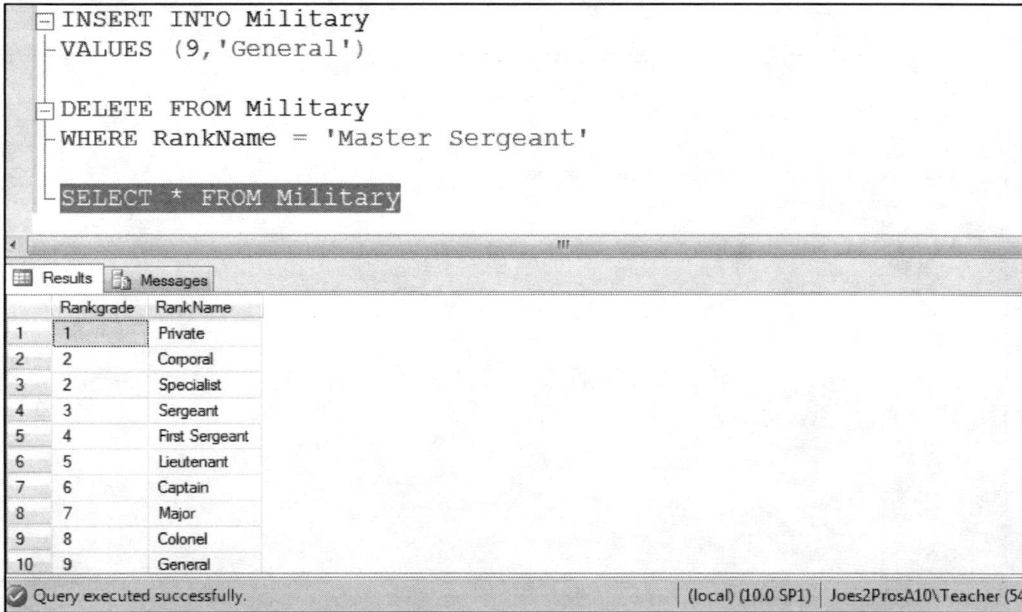

Figure 11.5 The table once again contains 10 records.

We had 10 records before the changes, and now we again have 10 records (as shown in Figure 11.5). But what has changed? And how can we – or another observer – know for certain what changes have been made to a table?

Prior to SQL Server 2008, you would have had to create a trigger in order to track changes. In this case an INSERT, DELETE, and UPDATE trigger would have been required to capture all DML changes and to send the information to another table, which you would then need to review.

Change Tracking keeps track of all DML changes which take place in the database table(s) for which you've enabled Change Tracking. *[For a review of DML (Data Manipulation Language), DDL (Data Definition Language), DCL (Data Control Language), or TCL (Transaction Control Language) statements, please refer to Volumes 1 and 2 in the Joes 2 Pros series.]*

Let's first take a look at our end product before we dive into the mechanics of Change Tracking and coding the queries which will show us our change metadata. In the figure below (see Figure 11.6), we see that Change Tracking kept track of the record we inserted (**I = Insert**) and the record we deleted (**D = Delete**) from the Military table.

	WhatHappened	RankGrade	RankName
1	I	9	General
2	D	4	Master Sergeant

Change Tracking: A way to determine what DML changes have taken place on a specified table or tables in your database.

Figure 11.6 Change Tracking keeps a record of our Military table inserts and deletes.

In order for our results to follow the steps necessary to arrive at the result shown in Figure 11.6, let's reset our data by running the SQLProgrammingChapter11.0Setup.sql script.

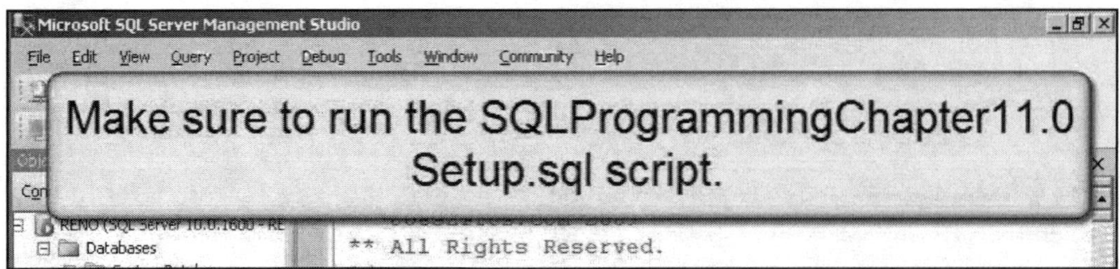

Figure 11.7 Before proceeding, run the Chapter 11.0 reset script (available at Joes2Pros.com).

Enabling Change Tracking on a Database

Before we can enable Change Tracking (often abbreviated as "CT") on a table, we must first enable Change Tracking at the database level.

When altering a database, the best practice is to run your ALTER statement while in the context of the Master database.

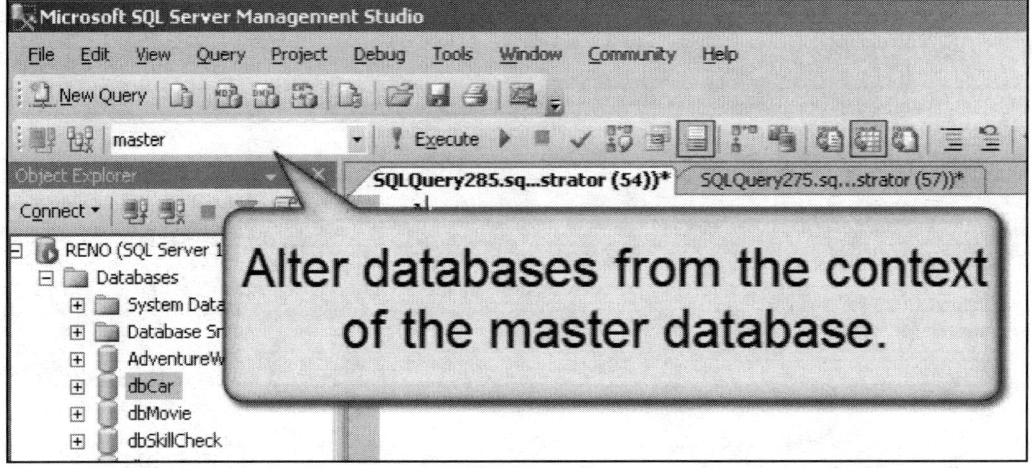

Figure 11.8 Change this dropdown or run "USE Master" to set your context to the Master db.

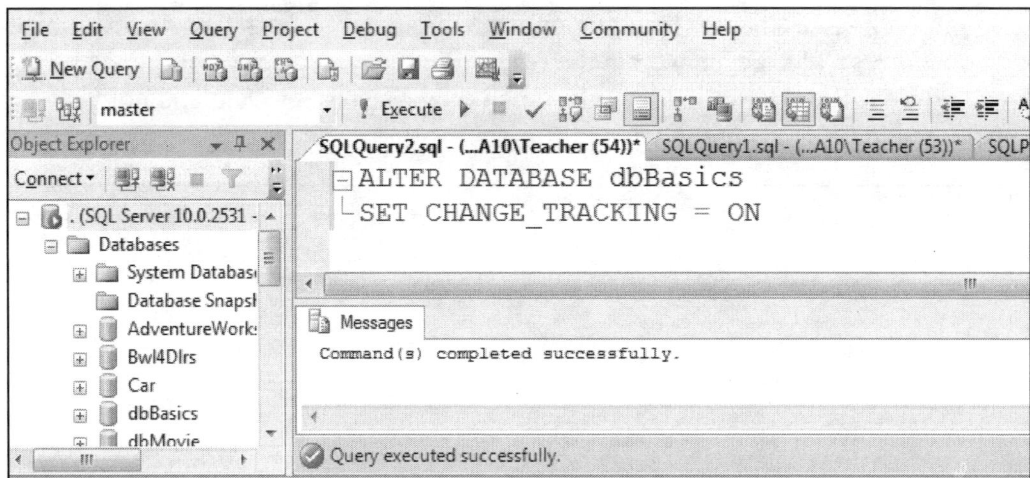

Figure 11.9 This T-SQL code enables CT at the database level.

While we have enabled Change Tracking on the dbBasics database (as shown in Figure 11.9), we still don't have any tables set for Change Tracking. Next we need to enable Change Tracking on a table in the dbBasics database.

Enabling Change Tracking on a Table

Before we can enable CT on the Military table, we first must reset our context to the dbBasics database (see Figure 11.10).

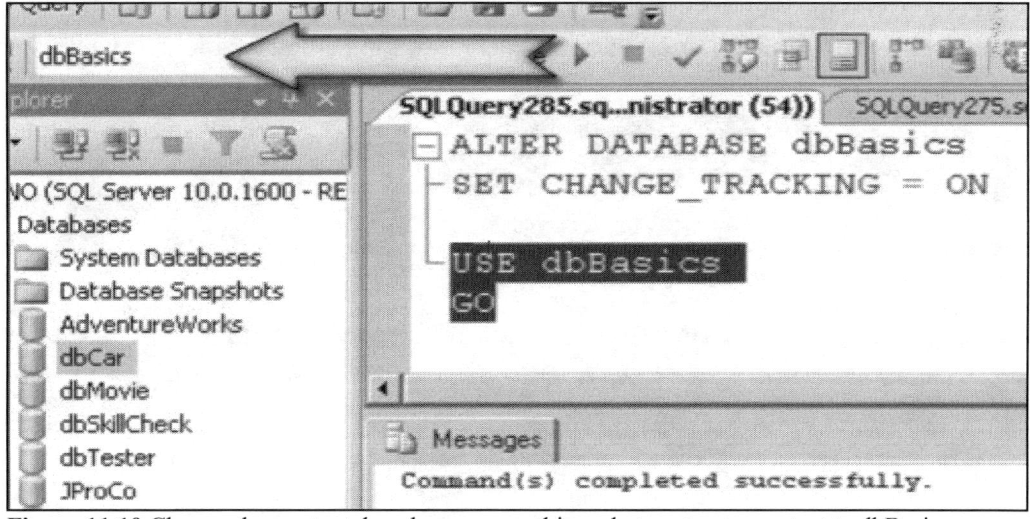

Figure 11.10 Change the context dropdown or run this code to set your context to dbBasics.

Before we enable Change Tracking on the Military table, let's first review the table (see Figure 11.11). Since we ran the reset script (shown earlier in Figure 11.6), we will now see the original 10 records – including Master Sergeant and not yet including the RankName of General.

```
SELECT * FROM Military
```

Results | Messages

	Rankgrade	RankName
1	1	Private
2	2	Corporal
3	2	Specialist
4	3	Sergeant
5	4	First Sergeant
6	4	Master Sergeant
7	5	Lieutenant
8	6	Captain
9	7	Major
10	8	Colonel

Figure 11.11 The Military table has been reset to its original 10 records (e.g., no General).

After you run the ALTER TABLE statement in Figure 11.12, all subsequent DML changes (Insert, Update, or Delete statements) to the Military table will be tracked.

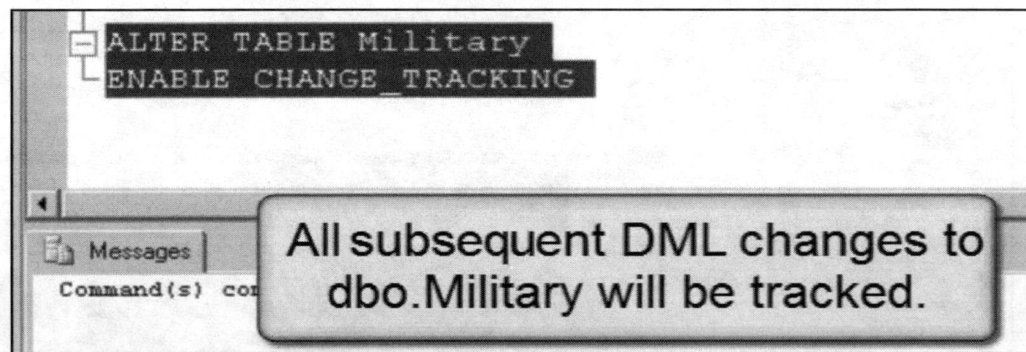
ALTER TABLE Military
ENABLE CHANGE_TRACKING
Messages
All subsequent DML changes to dbo.Military will be tracked.

Figure 11.12 This ALTER TABLE statement enables Change Tracking on the Military table.

As shown in Figure 11.13, our first change to the Military table will be the insertion of the General record.

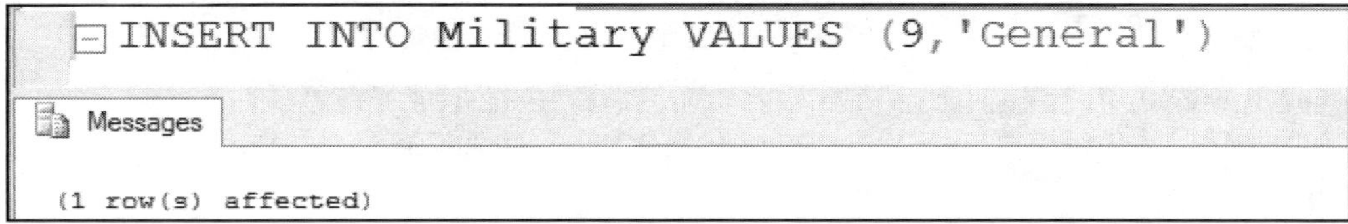
INSERT INTO Military VALUES (9,'General')
Messages
(1 row(s) affected)

Figure 11.13 The first change which Change Tracking will capture is the insert of General.

We now have 11 records in the Military table (see Figure 11.14).

```
SELECT * FROM Military
```

Results | Messages

	Rankgrade	RankName
1	1	Private
2	2	Corporal
3	2	Specialist
4	3	Sergeant
5	4	First Sergeant
6	4	Master Sergeant
7	5	Lieutenant
8	6	Captain
9	7	Major
10	8	Colonel
11	9	General

Figure 11.14 We now have 11 records in the Military table.

Our next change will be to delete the Master Sergeant record (see Figure 11.15).

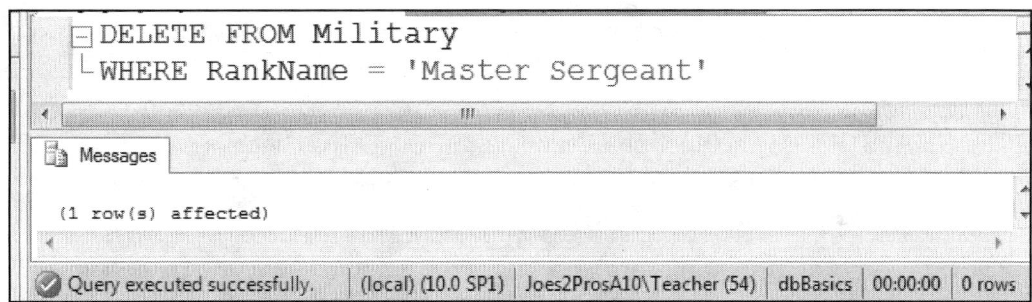
DELETE FROM Military
WHERE RankName = 'Master Sergeant'
Messages
(1 row(s) affected)
Query executed successfully.
(local) (10.0 SP1)
Joes2ProsA10\Teacher (54)
dbBasics
00:00:00
0 rows

Figure 11.15 We now have 10 records in the Military table.

When we re-check our select statement, we again see 10 records ranging from the rank of Private to General (see Figure 11.16).

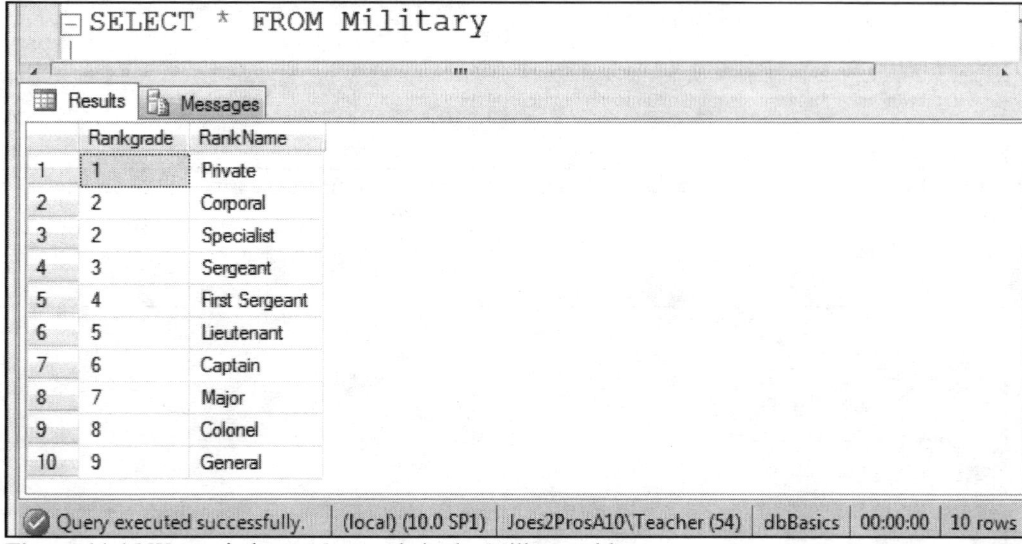
```
SELECT * FROM Military
```

	Rankgrade	RankName
1	1	Private
2	2	Corporal
3	2	Specialist
4	3	Sergeant
5	4	First Sergeant
6	5	Lieutenant
7	6	Captain
8	7	Major
9	8	Colonel
10	9	General

Figure 11.16 We again have 10 records in the Military table.

Using the CHANGETABLE Function

Let's review our steps so far. We began the chapter by looking ahead to our expected changes to the Military table (one insertion, one deletion). We then took a sneak-peek ahead to the results which Change Tracking (CT) would capture for us (Figure 11.6). After we reset the Military table back to its baseline, we then enabled Change Tracking and reran the two DML changes (one insertion, one deletion) against the refreshed table.

We're now ready to write the query which produced our "sneak-peek" results of the change data shown back in Figure 11.6.

The CHANGETABLE function contains all of the DML changes we've made to the Military table. This function requires two input parameters:

1) The keyword CHANGES + the table name (Military)
2) The starting point for the changes we want to see. If we made 10 changes to a table but only wanted to view the last change, then our input would be 9. The zero (0) here indicates that we want to see all changes made since Change Tracking began.

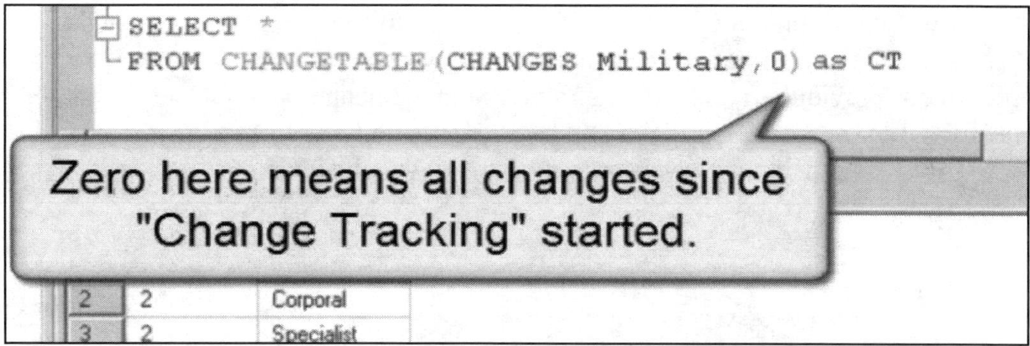
SELECT *
FROM CHANGETABLE(CHANGES Military,0) as CT
Zero here means all changes since "Change Tracking" started.
2 2 Corporal
3 2 Specialist

Figure 11.17 The CHANGETABLE function requires two input parameters.

Run this query for yourself and note the many fields and datapoints included in each CHANGETABLE record. While the CHANGETABLE records are quite wide, we can easily see that the Version 1 record reflects the first change we made and corresponds to the I = insert record (Record 1) in Figure 11.18. Recall that all we did was simply enable Change Tracking on the Military table. We didn't need to write any additional code to ask it to display the original data we changed (values for RankGrade and RankName) alongside the metadata returned by CHANGETABLE.

```
SELECT *
FROM CHANGETABLE(CHANGES Military,0) as CT
```

Results | Messages

	SYS_CHANGE_VERSION	SYS_CHANGE_C...	SYS_CHANGE_OPERATION	SYS_CHANGE_COLUMNS	SYS_CHANGE_CONTEXT	Rankgrade	RankName
1	1	1	I	NULL	NULL	9	General
2	2	NULL	D	NULL	NULL	4	Master Sergeant

Query executed successfully. | (local) (10.0 SP1) | Joes2ProsA10\Teacher (54) | dbBasics | 00:00:00 | 2 rows

11.18 The I = insert record shows the data we inserted for the new rank (General). The D = delete record shows the Master Sergeant data which we deleted.

Next let's run an update statement against the Military table to see how Change Tracking will handle an update. Let's change the current RankName "Private" to PFC (which stands for Private First Class) (see Figure 11.19).

```
UPDATE Military SET RankName = 'PFC'
WHERE RankGrade = 1
```

Messages

```
(1 row(s) affected)
```

Figure 11.19 Run an update statement to see how CHANGETABLE handles updates.

Next we will rerun our CHANGETABLE query to see the update reflected. We see a Version 3 change added, which is split over two CHANGETABLE records. From our previous studies (*Joes 2 Pros* Volume 2 chapters on OUTPUT and MERGE), you will recall that an update actually consists of two steps: the old record is deleted and a record containing the updated data is inserted.

```
UPDATE Military SET RankName = 'PFC'
WHERE RankGrade = 1

SELECT *
FROM CHANGETABLE(CHANGES Military,0) as CT
```

	SYS_CHANGE_VERSION	SYS_CHANGE_CREATION_VERSION	SYS_CHANGE_OPERATION	SYS_CHANGE_COLUMNS	SYS_CHANGE_
1	1	1	I	NULL	NULL
2	2	NULL	D	NULL	NULL
3	3		I	NULL	NULL
4	3		D	NULL	NULL

Figure 11.20 CHANGETABLE now shows Version 3, which is the update of Private to PFC.

Finally, let's itemize the fields in our select statement, so we can see our salient data in one shot without having to scroll through all of CHANGETABLE's columns. Each change Version is listed, alongside the type of change, and the actual data which was changed (see Figure 11.21).

```
SELECT sys_Change_Version,
sys_Change_Operation as WhatHappened,
RankGrade,
RankName
FROM CHANGETABLE(CHANGES Military,0) as CT
```

	sys_Change_Version	WhatHappened	RankGrade	RankName
1	1	I	9	General
2	2	D	4	Master Sergeant
3	3	I	1	PFC
4	3	D	1	Private

Figure 11.21 We refine our CHANGETABLE query to show just the columns we want.

While this won't be discussed until the next section, please be aware that one important reason we're able to enable Change Tracking on the Military table is because this table includes a primary key. *In order to enable Change Tracking on a table it must contain a primary key field.*

Disabling Change Tracking

The code to disable Change Tracking is similar to the code we used to enable Change Tracking (shown earlier in Figures 11.10 and 11.12).

You must first disable Change Tracking on your database table(s), then disable it on the database (see Figure 11.22).

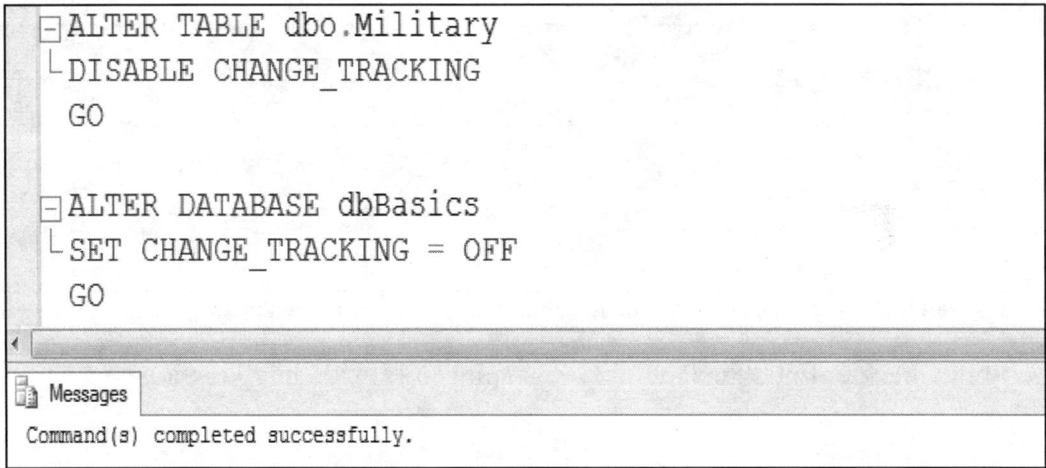

```
ALTER TABLE dbo.Military
DISABLE CHANGE_TRACKING
GO

ALTER DATABASE dbBasics
SET CHANGE_TRACKING = OFF
GO
```

Messages
Command(s) completed successfully.

Figure 11.22 The code to disable Change Tracking.

Lab 11.1: Using CHANGETABLE

Lab Prep: Before you can begin the lab, you must have SQL Server installed and have run the script SQLProgrammingChapter11.1Setup.sql.

Skill Check 1: Enable Change Tracking on the dbo.PayRates table in the JProCo database. Verify that Change Tracking is enabled by getting the properties of the dbo.PayRates table in SSMS (SQL Server Management Studio).

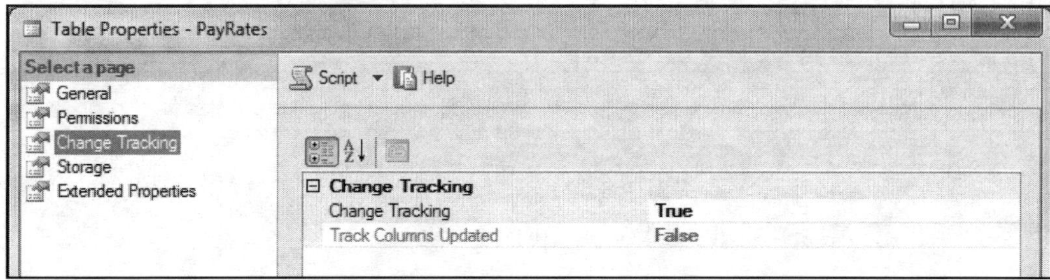

Figure 11.23 Use Management Studio to confirm the properties of the PayRates table.

Skill Check 2: Enter the PayRate for Employee 15 with the following code:

```
INSERT INTO dbo.PayRates
VALUES (15,55000,null,null,0)
```

Verify this insert was tracked by querying from the CHANGETABLE function. When you're done, your result should resemble this figure.

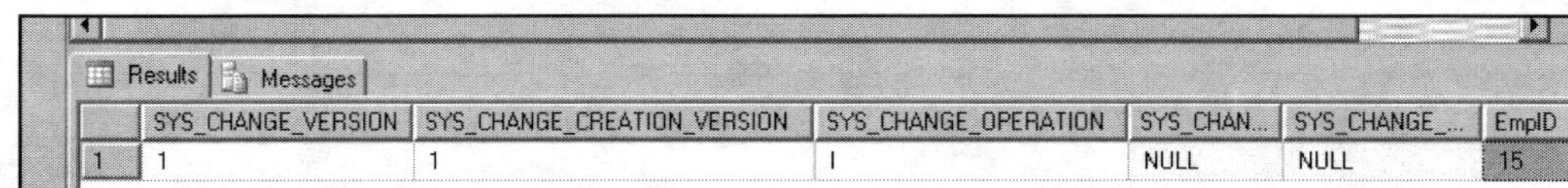

	SYS_CHANGE_VERSION	SYS_CHANGE_CREATION_VERSION	SYS_CHANGE_OPERATION	SYS_CHAN...	SYS_CHANGE_...	EmpID
1	1	1	I	NULL	NULL	15

Figure 11.24 Verify your insert is tracked correctly by using the CHANGETABLE function.

Answer Code: The T-SQL code to this lab can be found in the downloadable files in a file named Lab11.1_usingCHANGETABLE.sql.

Using CHANGETABLE - Points to Ponder

1. Tracking changed table data can be done by using triggers which feed the data from DML actions into archive tables.
2. Triggers come with known performance drawbacks.
3. The logic for keeping track of row versions or deletes gets complicated.
4. SQL Server 2008 offers a more clear-cut way to track changes versus using triggers with complex logic.
5. Before you can enable Change Tracking on a table, you must first enable Change Tracking at the database level.
6. The table you wish to track must have a primary key (PK).
7. Once Change Tracking is enabled, and enabled for a table, SQL Server keeps track of the primary key of the records inserted, updated, or deleted from that table.
8. All complexity of tracking and versioning is handled by the CHANGETABLE function. You just need to know how to call the function in order to see your change data.
9. You can use the CHANGETABLE function to find the latest version numbers and to return incremental changes which were made to your tracked tables.
10. Use the last_sync_version parameter of the CHANGETABLE (CHANGES) argument to choose how far back you want to see table changes.
11. You can use SQL Server Management Studio OR T-SQL code to enable Change Tracking on databases and tables.
12. Use the following code to enable Change Tracking on a table:
    ALTER TABLE Location ENABLE CHANGE_TRACKING
13. Use the following code to enable Change Tracking on the JProCo database:
    ALTER DATABASE JProCo SET CHANGE_TRACKING = ON
14. To get the changes for a table as a result set you can query the CHANGETABLE( ) function with a SELECT statement.

Change Tracking Options

In this section we will explore some additional options and tricks for working with Change Tracking and your tracked data.

Tracked Fields

Recall the code we ran for the last skill check, which reappears below (Figure 11.25). The insert statement added Employee 15 to the PayRates table. Run the select query and look closely at the values shown in CHANGETABLE for Employee 15.

```
INSERT INTO dbo.PayRates
VALUES (15, 55000,  NULL,   NULL,   0)

SELECT *
FROM CHANGETABLE(CHANGES PayRates,0) as ct
```

Figure 11.25 Our code written for the previous Skill Check.

We see the CHANGETABLE record for Employee 15. However, we don't see the pay amount we just added (i.e., the YearlySalary value of $55,000).

```
SELECT * FROM CHANGETABLE(CHANGES PayRates,0) as CT
```

	N	SYS_CHANGE_CREATION_VERSION	SYS_CHANGE_OPERATION	SYS_CHANGE_COLUMNS	SYS_CHANGE_CONTEXT	EmpID
1		1	I	NULL	NULL	15

Figure 11.26 Change Tracking keeps track of EmpID but not any other fields in the PayRates table.

This is because Change Tracking only tracks values which are associated with the primary key field. Change Tracking does not keep track of other data in the table on which you have enabled tracking. This is why the EmpID values are contained in CHANGETABLE but the other fields (YearlySalary, MonthlySalary, HourlyRate) are not.

Note: In the first section of the chapter, the field RankName is tracked by CHANGETABLE because it is associated with the primary key. Specifically, RankName is part of the clustered primary key. Fields which are included in a composite key are tracked by CHANGETABLE.

One way to see data from all the fields of our table is by joining it to CHANGETABLE on EmpID. In our join result, one side of the record will contain all fields of the PayRates table. The other side of the record will pull all fields from the CHANGETABLE function and will show all DML changes performed on each EmpID record (see Figure 11.27).

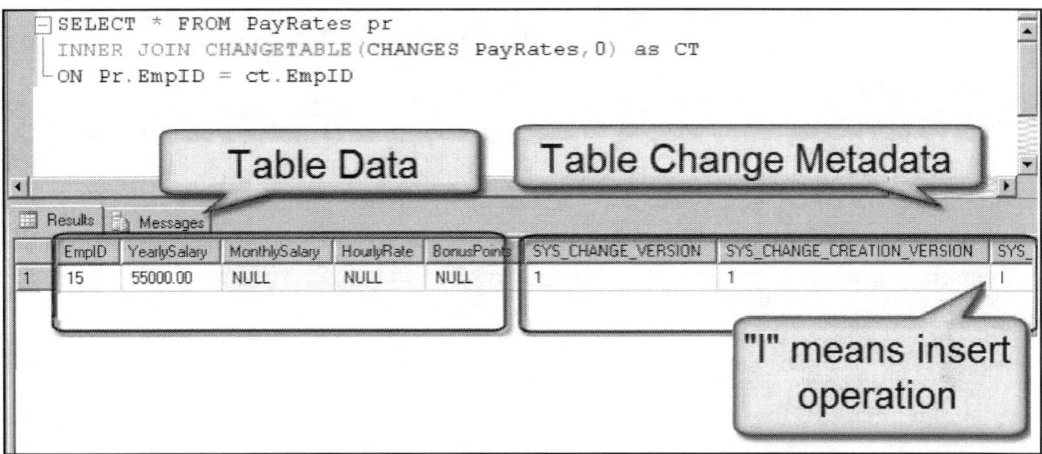

Figure 11.27 By joining the PayRates table to CHANGETABLE, we can see all the fields together. Each record will include the table data alongside the CHANGETABLE metadata.

Next let's perform an update on the PayRates table, which we still have enabled for Change Tracking. Since we're going to update the YearSalary field, let's bear in mind this is a non-primary key field. Employee 1 currently has a YearlySalary of $99,000. We will increase that amount to $100,000.

Recall our earlier example involving an update operation (Figures 11.19-11.21). Both fields of dbo.Military were associated with the primary key. The update statement was reflected by Change Tracking as one insert record and one delete record.

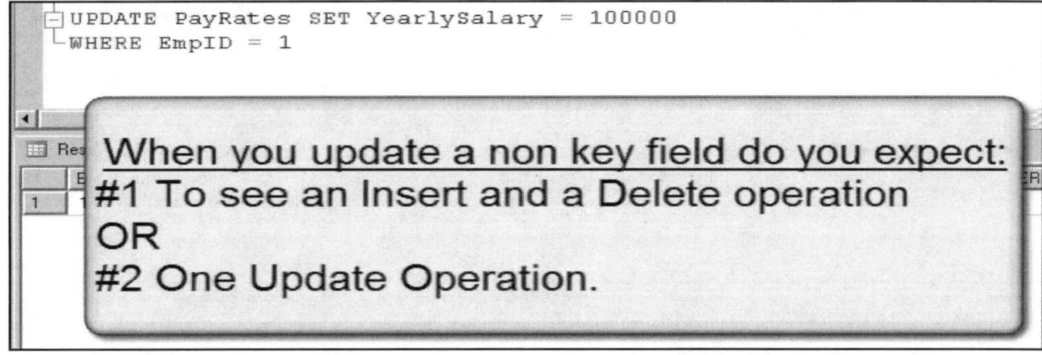

UPDATE PayRates SET YearlySalary = 100000
WHERE EmpID = 1
When you update a non key field do you expect:
#1 To see an Insert and a Delete operation
OR
#2 One Update Operation.

Figure 11.28 Our next step will be to update a non-primary key field of the PayRates table.

However, Change Tracking handles the update differently when we're updating a field not associated with the primary key. Let's run the update (Figure 11.29) and then see the **U = update** record in CHANGETABLE (see Figure 11.30).

```
UPDATE PayRates SET YearlySalary = 100000
WHERE EmpID = 1
```

Messages

```
(1 row(s) affected)

(1 row(s) affected)
```

Figure 11.29 Run the statement updating one of the non-primary key fields of the PayRates table.

Since our update doesn't affect the value of a primary key field, Change Tracking simply records the operation as an Update. CHANGETABLE will track only the metadata from the update – it will not contain either the old or new data from the YearlySalary field.

The only way for us to see the YearSalary data alongside the CHANGETABLE metadata is by running our JOIN query (see Figure 11.30).

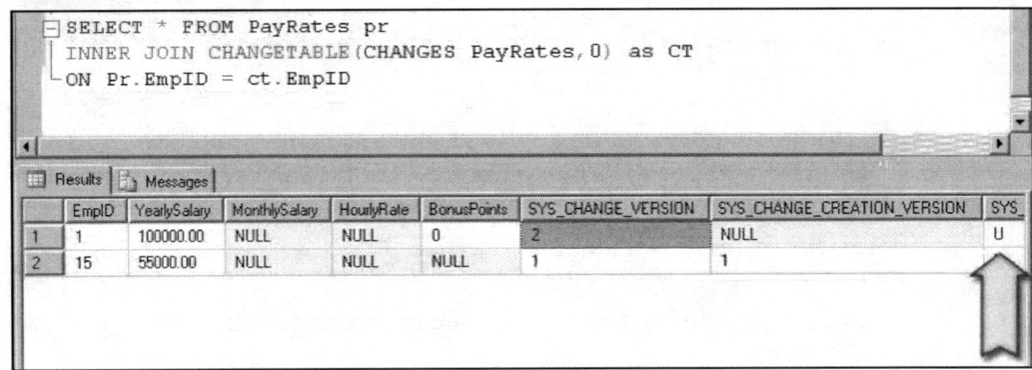

```
SELECT * FROM PayRates pr
INNER JOIN CHANGETABLE(CHANGES PayRates,0) as CT
ON Pr.EmpID = ct.EmpID
```

	EmpID	YearlySalary	MonthlySalary	HourlyRate	BonusPoints	SYS_CHANGE_VERSION	SYS_CHANGE_CREATION_VERSION	SYS_
1	1	100000.00	NULL	NULL	0	2	NULL	U
2	15	55000.00	NULL	NULL	NULL	1	1	

Figure 11.30 Change Tracking has tracked our update as a **U = update** operation.

Run this code to make two more changes to the PayRates table.

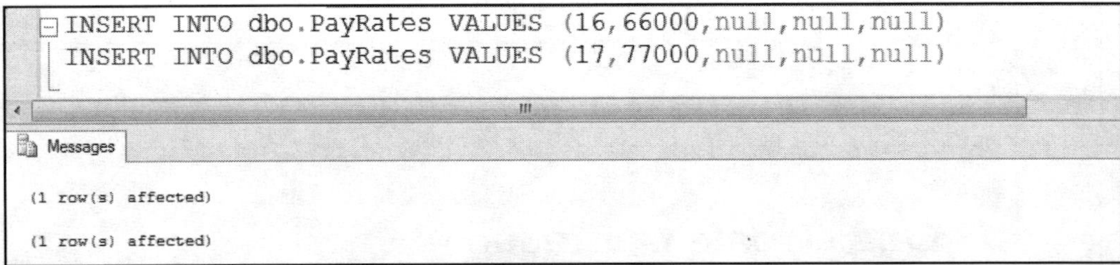

```
INSERT INTO dbo.PayRates VALUES (16,66000,null,null,null)
INSERT INTO dbo.PayRates VALUES (17,77000,null,null,null)
```


Figure 11.31 Insert two new records into the PayRates table.

Following the two inserts, we see two additional records (tracking Versions 3 and 4) returned by our query (see Figure 11.31). CHANGETABLE'S SYS_CHANGE_OPERATION field reflects **I = insert** for EmpID 16 and 17.

```
SELECT * FROM PayRates pr
INNER JOIN CHANGETABLE(CHANGES PayRates,0) as CT
ON Pr.EmpID = ct.EmpID
```

	EmpID	YearlySalary	MonthlySalary	HourlyRate	BonusPoints	SYS_CHANGE_VERSION	SYS_CHANGE_CREATION_VERSION	SYS_
1	1	100000.00	NULL	NULL	0	2	NULL	U
2	15	55000.00	NULL	NULL	NULL	1	1	I
3	16	66000.00	NULL	NULL	NULL	3	3	I
4	17	77000.00	NULL	NULL	NULL	4	4	I

Figure 11.32 Tracking Version 3 & Version 4 are now visible in our join query.

Tracking Range

The tracking version for each change is shown in the SYS_CHANGE_VERSION field. The version numbers are sequenced in the order in which the transactions were committed. Lower version numbers represent the oldest changes; records with higher version numbers contain the most recent changes.

Until now, we've used a 0 for the last_sync_version parameter in our queries pulling from the CHANGETABLE function. This parameter specifies the starting point for the changes we want to see. Each time we've used a 0, it's because we wanted to see every change made. When we specify 2 as the parameter value, we are saying we want to see only those changes which occurred after the second change. The query shown in the lower half of Figure 11.33 will return changes 3 and 4 (results shown in Figure 11.34).

```
SELECT * FROM PayRates pr
INNER JOIN CHANGETABLE(CHANGES PayRates,0) as CT
ON Pr.EmpID = ct.EmpID


SELECT *
FROM PayRates pr
INNER JOIN CHANGETABLE(CHANGES PayRates,2) as CT
ON Pr.EmpID = ct.EmpID
```

Figure 11.33 Until now, we've used a 0 when querying the CHANGETABLE function.

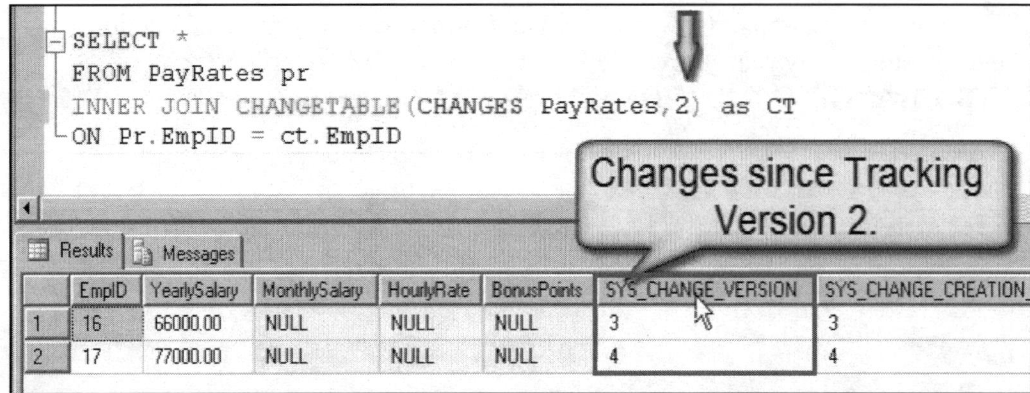

Figure 11.34 The 2 in the last_sync_version parameter returns only changes 3 and 4.

Note that, since we've only made four changes to the PayRates table, a parameter of 4 will return no records. SQL Server provides no error message if you choose an invalid parameter; it simply returns NULL (no records). In our current example, if we were to choose a parameter value which is too low (e.g., -1, -10) or too high (4, 5, 10), our query will return no records.

Change Tracking Functions

The **Change_Tracking_Current_Version( )** function will show you the SYS_CHANGE_VERSION value of the most recent change (see Figure 11.35).

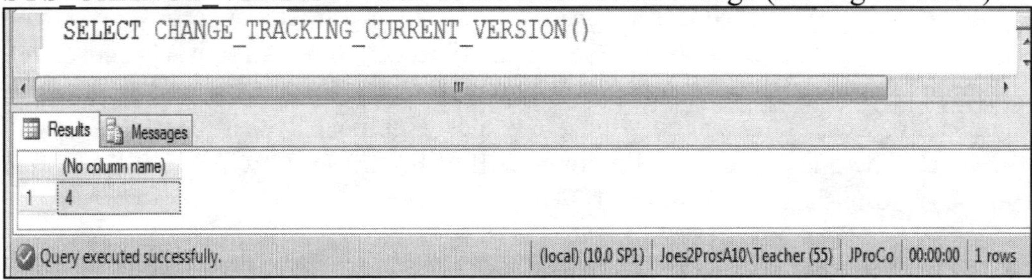

Figure 11.35 Syntax for the Change_Tracking_Current_Version( ) function.

Change_Tracking_Current_Version( ) may be used in conjunction with a variable.

```
SELECT Change_tracking_current_version()

DECLARE @SyncNum INT
SET @SyncNum = Change_tracking_current_version() - 1
```

Figure 11.36 The Change_Tracking_Current_Version( ) function shown with a variable.

Using a variable and the Change_Tracking_Current_Version( ) function in combination with our base query provides an easy way to dynamically return just the latest change without having to hardcode the parameter value.

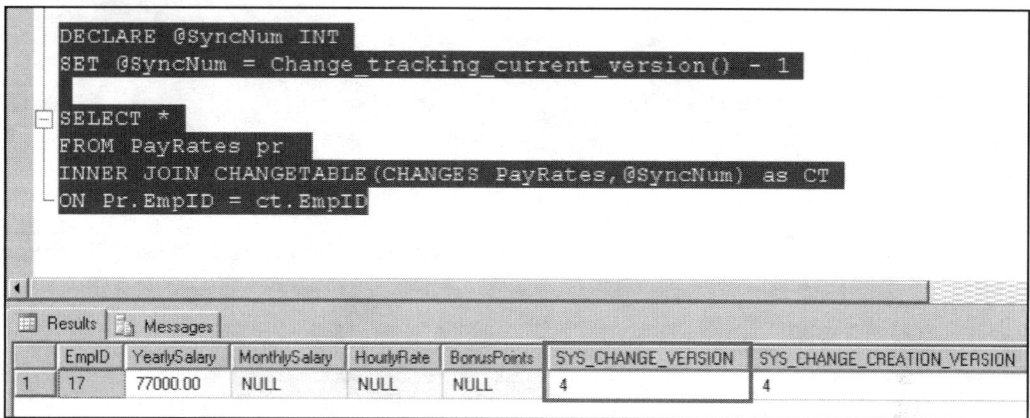
```
DECLARE @SyncNum INT
SET @SyncNum = Change_tracking_current_version() - 1

SELECT *
FROM PayRates pr
INNER JOIN CHANGETABLE(CHANGES PayRates,@SyncNum) as CT
ON Pr.EmpID = ct.EmpID
```

	EmpID	YearlySalary	MonthlySalary	HourlyRate	BonusPoints	SYS_CHANGE_VERSION	SYS_CHANGE_CREATION_VERSION
1	17	77000.00	NULL	NULL	NULL	4	4

Figure 11.37 Returning just the latest change record without hardcoding the parameter value.

Until now, all of our examples have had 0 as the minimum tracking version (SYS_CHANGE_VERSION). But we should be aware that 0 may not always be the minimum tracking version. Change Tracking uses Auto_Cleanup to periodically clean up the oldest data.

The **Change_Tracking_Min_Valid_Version( )** function will show you the lowest valid value for use in the last_sync_version parameter of the CHANGETABLE function. But unlike the current version function, this function requires that you pass in the ObjectID of a table as an argument (see Figure 11.38).

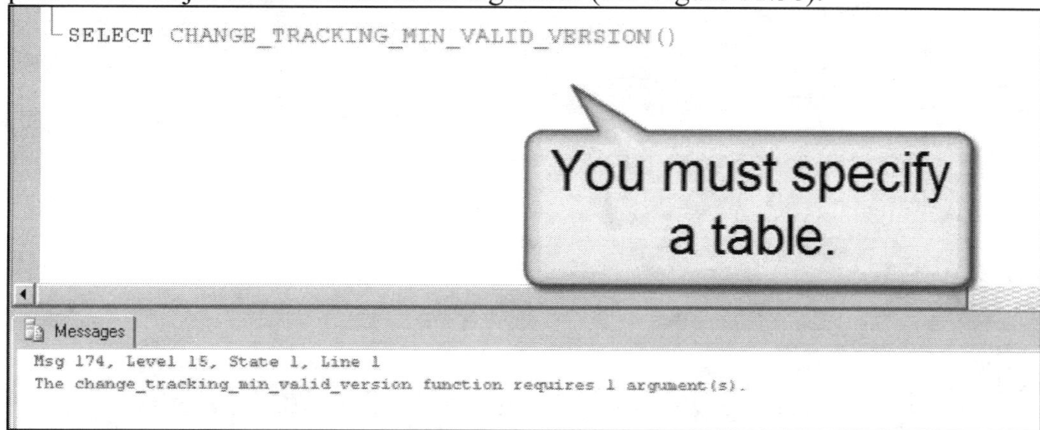

Figure 11.38 Incorrect syntax for the Change_Tracking_Min_Valid_Version( ) function.

```
SELECT CHANGE_TRACKING_MIN_VALID_VERSION()

SELECT OBJECT_ID('PayRates')
```

Results | Messages

	(No column name)
1	2105058535

Figure 11.39 Syntax for obtaining the PayRate table's OBJECT_ID value (which is 2105058535).

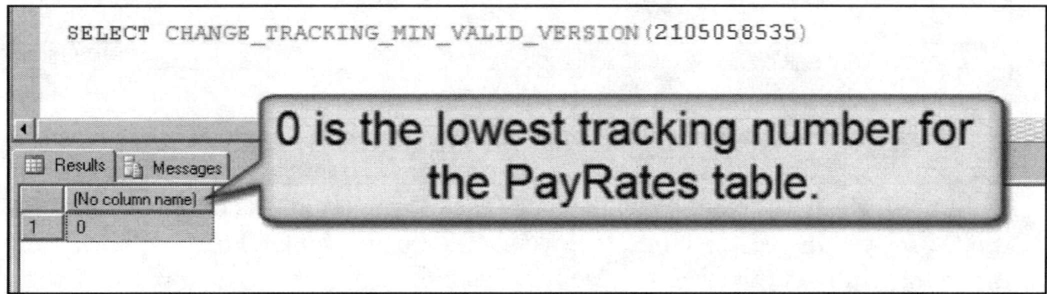

Figure 11.40 The ID can be supplied as an argument to Change_Tracking_Min_Valid_Version( ).

There is an alternative way to find the lowest tracking version without hardcoding (see Figure 11.41). The OBJECT_ID function call may be supplied as the argument to the CHANGE_TRACKING_MIN_VALID_VERSION( ) function, so as to find the lowest version without having to query or hardcode the actual OBJECT_ID of your table.

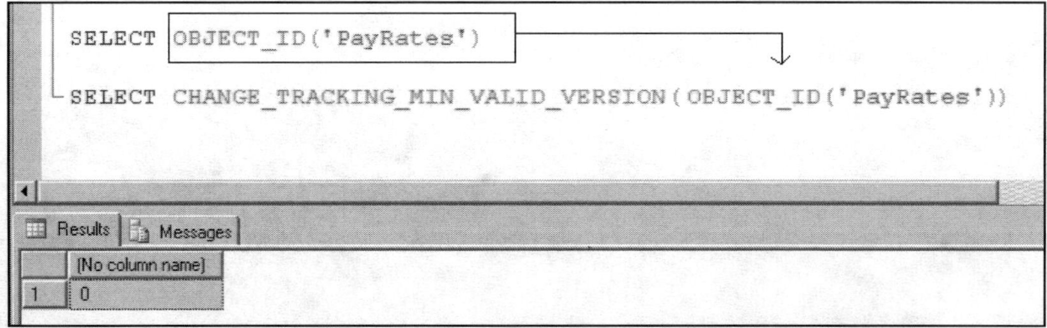

Figure 11.41 To avoid hardcoding the table's OBJECT_ID, use the call to the OBJECT_ID function as the argument to CHANGE_TRACKING_MIN_VALID_VERSION( ).

More on Tracking Version

Be aware that tracking versions apply database-wide. Our examples have thus far included changes made to just one table within one database. (The Military table in dbBasics and the PayRates table in the JProCo database.)

Recall the last change we made in the JProCo database (i.e., to the PayRates table) was change version 4.

If we enable change tracking on an additional table in the JProCo database (e.g., the CurrentProducts table) and make one change to that table, then the first available change tracking value in that table would be 5.

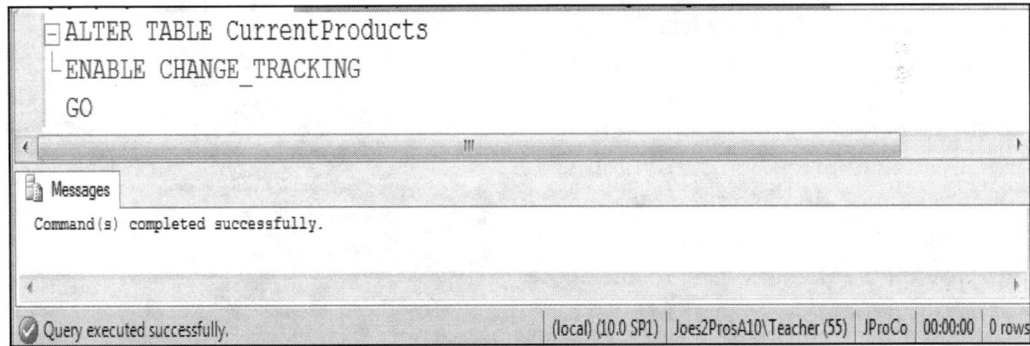
ALTER TABLE CurrentProducts
ENABLE CHANGE_TRACKING
GO
Messages
Command(s) completed successfully.
Query executed successfully.
(local) (10.0 SP1) | Joes2ProsA10\Teacher (55) | JProCo | 00:00:00 | 0 rows

Figure 11.42 Enable change tracking on the CurrentProducts table.

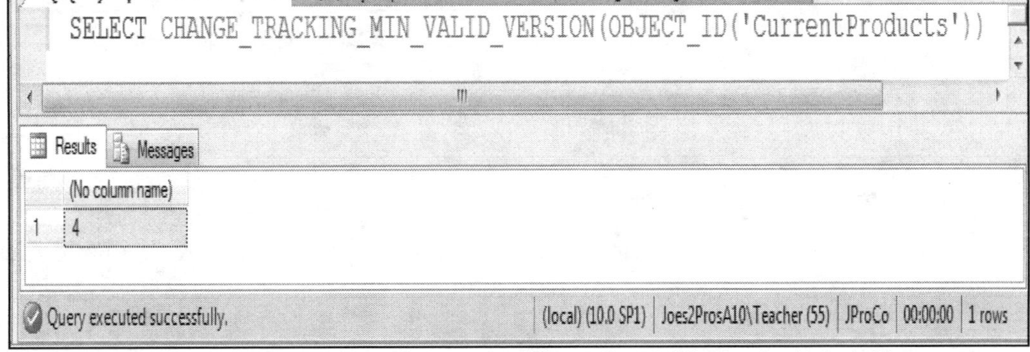
SELECT CHANGE_TRACKING_MIN_VALID_VERSION(OBJECT_ID('CurrentProducts'))
Results
Messages
(No column name)
1 4
Query executed successfully.
(local) (10.0 SP1) | Joes2ProsA10\Teacher (55) | JProCo | 00:00:00 | 1 rows

Figure 11.43 The value returned by Change_Tracking_Min_Valid_Version( ) is 4. If you make a change to the CurrentProducts table right now (and no other changes have been made to any tracked tables in the JProCo database), then that will be change version 5.

Lab 11.2: Change Tracking Options

Lab Prep: Before you can begin the lab, you must have SQL Server installed and have run the setup script SQLProgrammingChapter11.2Setup.sql.

Skill Check 1: Enable Change Tracking on the dbo.Movie table of the dbMovie database. Update Movie 6 (m_id = 6) to have a runtime of 99 minutes. After the update, show the tracking results data and metadata. Your result should resemble this figure (see Figure 11.44).

	m_id	m_title	m_runtime	m_Rating	m_Teaser	m_Release	SYS_CHANGE_VERSION	S...	SYS_CHANGE_OPER
1	6	Farewell Yeti	99	R	Ice and Terror find com...	2009	1	N...	U

Figure 11.44 Skill Check 1 result.

Skill Check 2: Show the minimum valid value to use when searching for changes to the dbo.Movie table, and the maximum tracking version value in the dbMovie db. Alias the first result as MinVer and the last one as MaxVer. When you're done, your result should resemble the figure here.

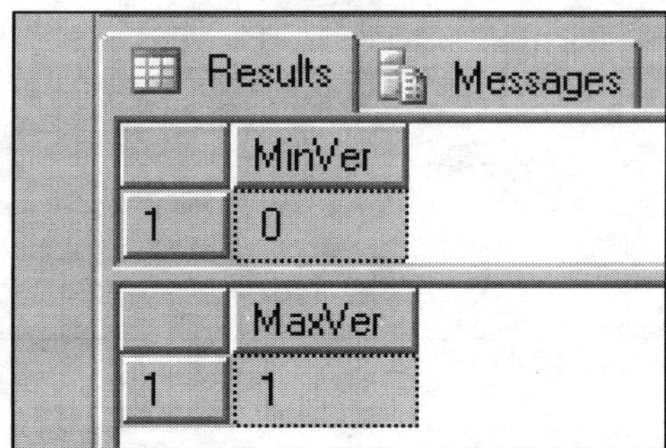

Figure 11.45 Skill Check 2 result.

Answer Code: The T-SQL code to this lab can be found in the downloadable files in a file named Lab11.2_ChangeTrackingOptions.sql.

Change Tracking Options - Points to Ponder

1. Use the last_sync_version parameter of the CHANGETABLE (CHANGES) argument to choose how far back you want to see table changes.
2. To SELECT from the CHANGETABLE function, you must alias the table.
3. The following syntax will show you all changes to the Invoice table that took place after change version 5:

   SELECT * FROM CHANGETABLE (CHANGES Invoice, 5) AS CT
4. In the example above (#2), you would not see changes 1-5 but would see changes 6 and beyond.
5. The last_sync_version parameter marks the beginning of where you want to retrieve your data from the CHANGETABLE( ) function.
6. If you want to get the most changes out of your CHANGETABLE( ) function, you would set the tracking version as low as possible.
7. Setting a higher last_sync_version means you don't want the older changes but only the newest ones. This would get fewer records from your CHANGETABLE( ) functions.
8. If you never truncate data from CHANGETABLE, then the minimum valid value of last_sync_version would be zero.
9. You can set Change Tracking to cleanup manually or automatically.
10. If you don't want your Change Table to get too big, you might set it up for AUTO_CLEANUP with a limited retention.
11. When your oldest changes get deleted, then the minimum valid version for your last_sync_version parameter goes up.
12. To get the minimum valid value for your last_sync_version parameter run the CHANGE_TRACKING_MIN_VALID_VERSION( ) function.
13. To get the tracking number of the most recently run transaction use the CHANGE_TRACKING_CURRENT_VERSION( ) function.

Chapter Glossary

CHANGE TRACKING (CT): SQL Server 2008 feature which provides visibility to the changes which have brought your table's data to its current point. Once Change Tracking is enabled, and enabled for a table, SQL Server keeps track of the primary key of the records inserted, updated, or deleted from that table.

CHANGE_TRACKING_MIN_VALID_VERSION( ): the function which will return the minimum valid value for your tracking version.

CHANGE_TRACKING_CURRENT_VERSION( ): the function which will return the Tracking number of the most recently run transaction.

Chapter Eleven - Review Quiz

1.) You have a table named dbo.SalesInvoiceDetail. You want to track the type of DML modification that was made. You don't need to track any of the changes to non-key field values. Which new feature of SQL 2008 should you use?

O a. Table Parameters
O b. Change Tracking
O c. Change Data Capture
O d. DML after Triggers
O e. DDL Triggers

2.) You have determined that your lowest valid tracking version is 4 and your maximum valid tracking version is 18. You specify a valid integer outside of this range with your CHANGETABLE function. What could you see? (Choose two)

O a. You could get an error message.
O b. You could get all changes in the change table.
O c. You could get none of the changes in the change table.

3.) You have determined that your lowest valid tracking version is 4 and your maximum valid tracking version is 18. You want to see all changes in the change table for your Location table. Which code will do this?

O a. SELECT * FROM CHANGETABLE (CHANGES Location, 3)
O b. SELECT * FROM CHANGETABLE (CHANGES Location, 4)
O c. SELECT * FROM CHANGETABLE (CHANGES Location, 17)
O d. SELECT * FROM CHANGETABLE (CHANGES Location, 18)
O e. SELECT * FROM CHANGETABLE (CHANGES Location, 19)

4.) You want to find the minimum valid version of your change table. Which function will do this?

O a. Change_Tracking_Current_Version( )
O b. Change_Tracking_Minimum_Version( )
O c. Change_Tracking_Min_Valid_Version( )
O d. Change_Tracking_Oldest_Valid_Version( )

5.) You configured Change Tracking on the Sales table. The minimum valid version of the Sales table is 12. You need to write a query to show data that changed since version 12. The results of this query will be show a view named vSales. If any rows were deleted from the table you want to see the primary key values of those deleted rows. Which method should you use?

O a. SELECT * FROM Sales
RIGHT JOIN CHANGETABLE (CHANGES Sales, 12) AS CT ...
ON ct.SalesID = Sales.SalesID

O b. SELECT * FROM Sales
INNER JOIN CHANGETABLE (CHANGES Sales, 12) AS CT ...
ON ct.SalesID = Sales.SalesID

O c. SELECT * FROM vSales
RIGHT JOIN CHANGETABLE (CHANGES vSales, 12) AS CT ...
ON ct.SalesID = vSales.SalesID

O d. SELECT * FROM vSales
INNER JOIN CHANGETABLE (CHANGES vSales, 12) AS CT ...
ON ct.SalesID = vSales.SalesID

6.) You have implemented change tracking on a table named Sales.SalesOrder. You need to find changes in your Change tracking table. Which function should you use?

O a. CHANGE_TRACKING_CURRENT_VERSION
O b. Change_Tracking_Min_Valid_Version( )
O c. CHANGETABLE with the CHANGES argument

7.) A database contains tables named Activity and ActivityArchive. ActivityArchive contains historical activity data. You configure Change Tracking on the Activity table. The minimum valid version of the Activity table is 10. You need to write a query to export only activity data that changed since version 10, including the primary key of deleted rows. Which method should you use?

O a. FROM Activity
RIGHT JOIN CHANGETABLE (CHANGES Activity, 10) AS C.

O b. FROM Activity
INNER JOIN CHANGETABLE (CHANGES Activity, 10) AS C

O c. FROM Activity
INNER JOIN CHANGETABLE (CHANGES ActivityArchive, 10) AS C

Answer Key

1.) b 2.) b, c 3.) a 4.) c 5.) a 6.) c 7.) a

Bug Catcher Game

To play the Bug Catcher game, run the file BugCatcher_Chapter11_ChangeTracking.pps from the BugCatcher folder of the companion files located at www.Joes2Pros.com.

Chapter 12. Change Data Capture

Another innovative new feature in SQL Server 2008 is **C**hange **D**ata **C**apture (abbreviated as CDC). The concept is similar to Change Tracking (see Chapter 11) but with a major difference. CDC tracks every field in your table(s) – not just the primary key fields. A set of system-defined functions have been created for your use with CDC.

The additional infrastructure of this robust CDC feature incurs a slight performance hit but one that is well worth this small cost. While the lightweight and low overhead Change Tracking has been eagerly anticipated by SQL developers, CDC has also generated excitement for the greater ease it offers in the ETL (**e**xtract, **t**ransform, **l**oad) process. Stated simply, ETL is the process of moving data (usually many tables) from one database to another. When you are moving data to a data warehouse, you will often merge many tables with many joins into one giant table. The combining or changing of the data (referred to as a Transform) happens after you extract the data but right before you load it into the destination. Therefore the order is Extract (from the source), Transform, and Load (to the destination). Regardless of whether you are an analyst, SQL DBA, or a developer, if your work involves **B**usiness **I**ntelligence (BI), you will frequently hear the shorthand term ETL in interviews and on the job.

ETL is a crucial area for those involved in the disciplines of data warehousing and BI. While the genius of CDC is best appreciated in settings involving ETL and massive amounts of data, our aim will be to cover the basic capabilities of this new feature using smaller scale examples so students to grasp the basic points of CDC.

READER NOTE: *In order to follow along with the examples in the first section of Chapter 12, please run the setup script SQLProgrammingChapter12.0Setup.sql. The setup scripts for this book are posted at Joes2Pros.com.*

Enabling CDC on a Database

Change Data Capture (CDC) reads the log file (.ldf) of your table and captures all of the change activity (metadata + data) in a Change Table.

Similar to Change Tracking, the first step in using CDC is to enable it at the database level. We want to enable CDC on the JProCo database. Let's first check the catalog view to confirm whether CDC has already been enabled on JProCo.

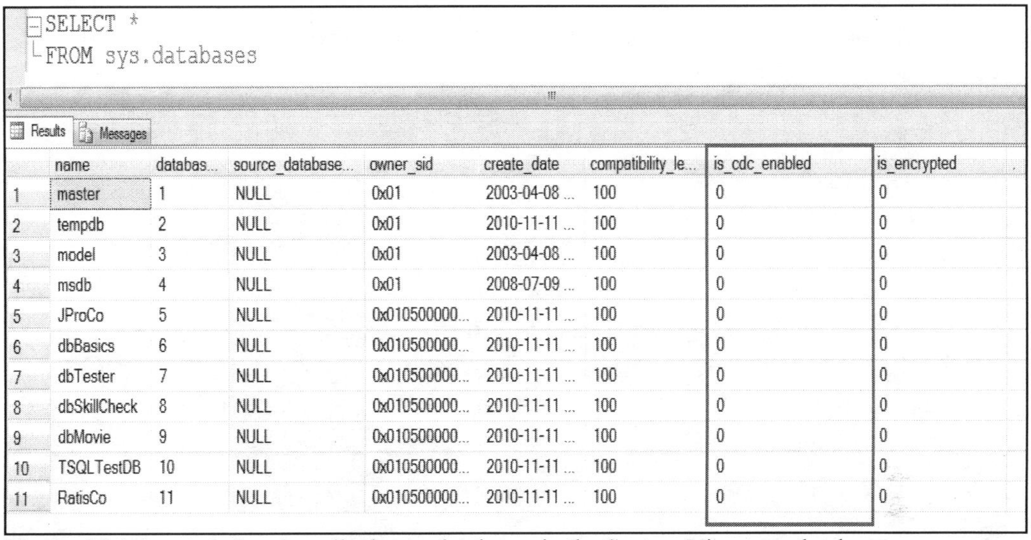

```
SELECT *
FROM sys.databases
```

	name	databas...	source_database...	owner_sid	create_date	compatibility_le...	is_cdc_enabled	is_encrypted
1	master	1	NULL	0x01	2003-04-08 ...	100	0	0
2	tempdb	2	NULL	0x01	2010-11-11 ...	100	0	0
3	model	3	NULL	0x01	2003-04-08 ...	100	0	0
4	msdb	4	NULL	0x01	2008-07-09 ...	100	0	0
5	JProCo	5	NULL	0x010500000...	2010-11-11 ...	100	0	0
6	dbBasics	6	NULL	0x010500000...	2010-11-11 ...	100	0	0
7	dbTester	7	NULL	0x010500000...	2010-11-11 ...	100	0	0
8	dbSkillCheck	8	NULL	0x010500000...	2010-11-11 ...	100	0	0
9	dbMovie	9	NULL	0x010500000...	2010-11-11 ...	100	0	0
10	TSQLTestDB	10	NULL	0x010500000...	2010-11-11 ...	100	0	0
11	RatisCo	11	NULL	0x010500000...	2010-11-11 ...	100	0	0

Figure 12.1 A query showing all of your databases in the System View, sys.databases.

Note: In this query of sys.databases, Figure 12.1 has been adjusted to display the **is_cdc_enabled** field. Since it is the 54th of the 56 fields contained in the System View **sys.databases**, when you run the query yourself you will need to scroll to the right to see the actual position of **is_cdc_enabled**. The System Views may be queried from any database context.

Next we will itemize our Select list to see whether any of our databases are currently enabled for CDC (see Figure 12.2). Since all of our databases currently show a 0 value for **is_cdc_enabled**, we know that none of them has been enabled for CDC.

```
SELECT [name], is_cdc_enabled
FROM sys.databases
```

Results | Messages

	name	is_cdc_enabled
1	master	0
2	tempdb	0
3	model	0
4	msdb	0
5	JProCo	0
6	dbBasics	0
7	dbTester	0
8	dbSkillCheck	0
9	dbMovie	0
10	TSQLTestDB	0
11	RatisCo	0

Figure 12.2 None of our databases has been enabled for CDC.

Shown in Figure 12.3 is **sp_cdc_enable_db**, the system stored procedure which enables CDC on the current database. First make sure you are in the JProCo database context and then execute this sproc in order to enable CDC.

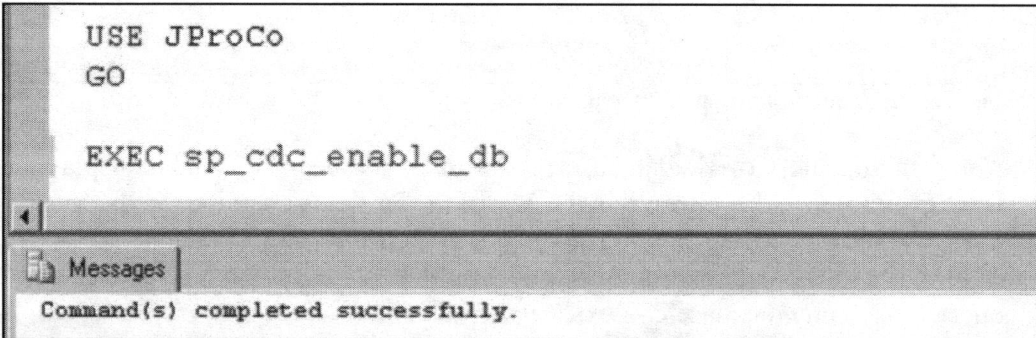
USE JProCo
GO
EXEC sp_cdc_enable_db
Messages
Command(s) completed successfully.

Figure 12.3 Enable CDC on the JProCo database.

Let's rerun our itemized query and see that is_cdc_enabled now shows a value of 1 for JProCo. The JProCo database is now enabled for CDC (see Figure 12.4).

```sql
SELECT [name], is_cdc_enabled
FROM sys.databases
```

Results | Messages

	name	is_cdc_enabled
1	master	0
2	tempdb	0
3	model	0
4	msdb	0
5	JProCo	1
6	dbBasics	0
7	dbTester	0

Figure 12.4 We have successfully enabled CDC on the JProCo database.

Enabling CDC on a Table

Now we can choose the table(s) in JProCo for which we want to enable CDC. The **sys.tables** System View is a handy way to check all tables in your database and see which ones are enabled for CDC.

```sql
USE JProCo
GO

SELECT [name],is_tracked_by_cdc
FROM sys.tables
```

Results | Messages

	name	is_tracked_by_cdc
1	PayRatesHistory	0
2	FormerEmployee	0
3	MgmtTraining	0
4	FormerPayRates	0
5	CurrentProducts	0
6	Employee	0
7	Test	0
8	Location	0
9	Grant	0
10	BosssIsCool	0
11	Customer	0
12	SalesInvoice	0
13	MgmtTrainingNew	0
14	SalesInvoiceDetail	0

Figure 12.5 Currently no tables have been enabled for CDC in the JProCo database.

We will create a new table, Department, to track our CDC changes.

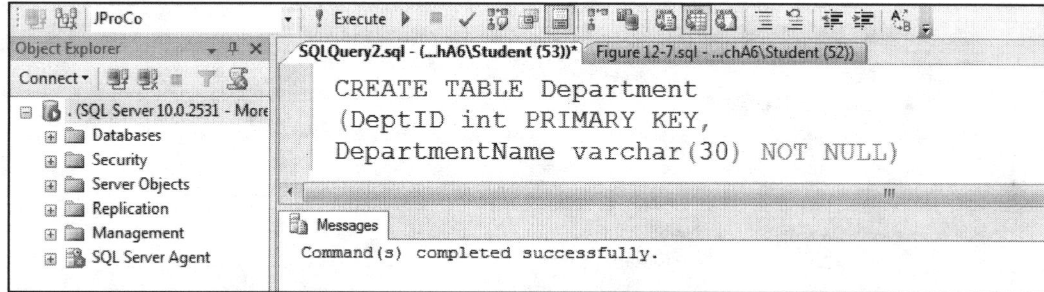

Figure 12.6 Create a new table in JProCo to track CDC changes.

Next we will execute **sp_cdc_enable_table** in order enable our new table for CDC. Since we've said CDC does a lot of heavy lifting, it should come as no surprise that enabling a table for CDC requires us to supply specifications for how we intend to track and access our table.

Our first three inputs specify the table being tracked: 1) the schema name (dbo); 2) the table name (Department); 3) the name of the tracking instance which CDC will use for this table (dbo_Department). (For a refresher on Schemas, see Chapter 2 of Volume 3, *SQL Architecture Basics Joes 2 Pros*.)

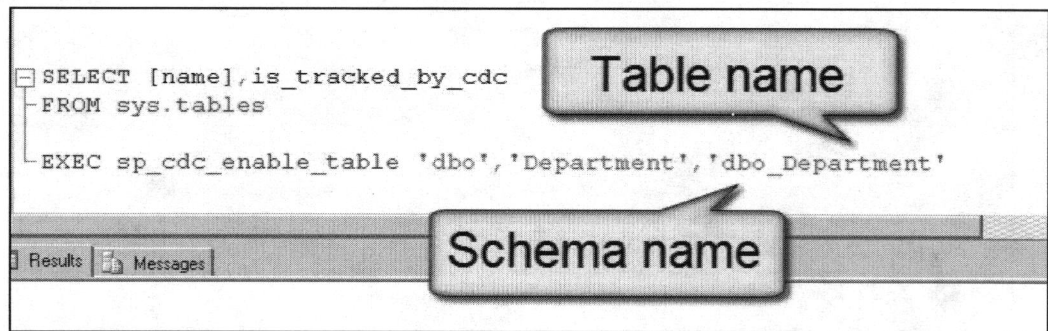

Figure 12.7 The first three inputs for the sp_cdc_enable_table system-supplied stored procedure.

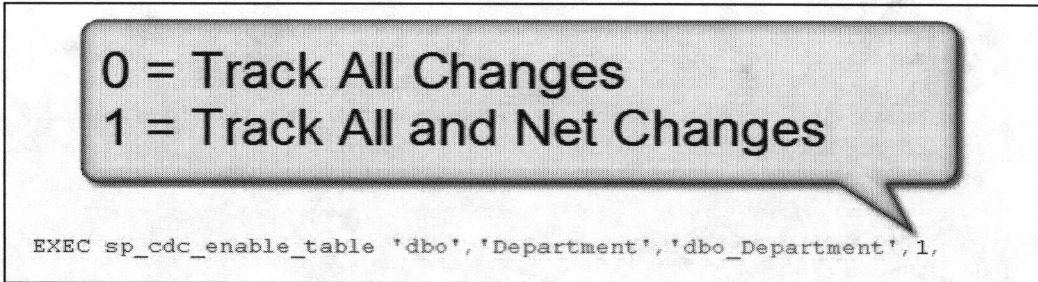

Figure 12.8 You must specify the types of changes you wish CDC to track.

The final input you must include is a role value. Here we are including a NULL input, since we don't want to restrict anyone from viewing the Change Table instance of the Department table. We want all system admins and all users with access to JProCo to be able to see this Change Table.

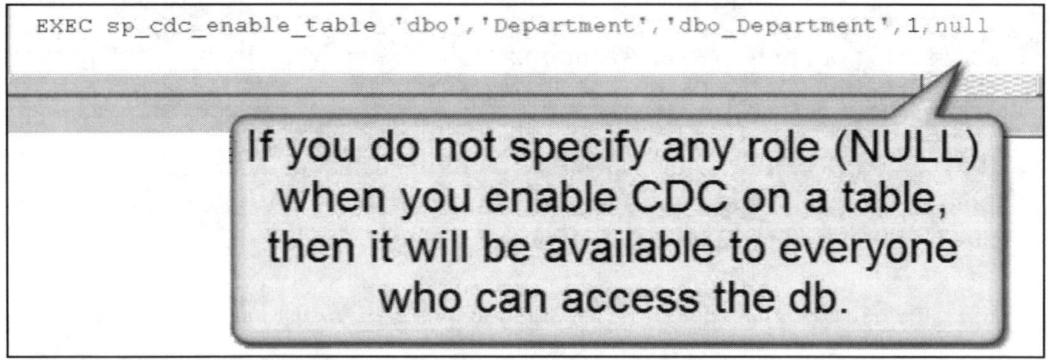

Figure 12.9 The final input for sp_cdc_enable_table is the role value.

Now you can run the sproc to enable CDC on the Department table. Notice that this will likely take at least 6-8 seconds to run, since it is creating additional security structures and new jobs (see Figure 12.10).

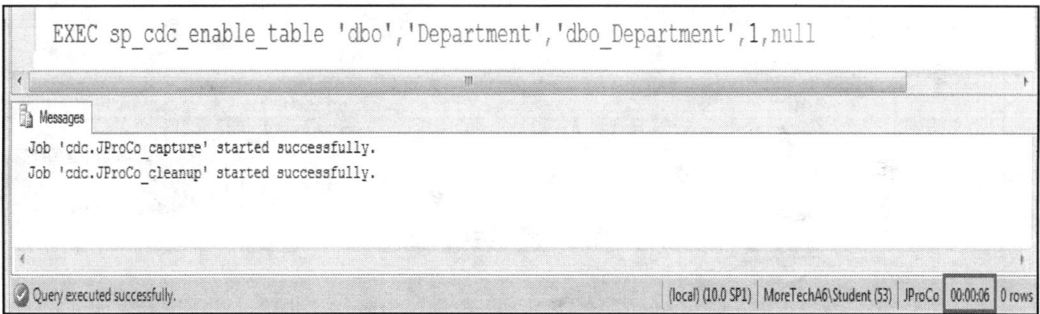

Figure 12.10 Run the sproc to enable CDC on the Department table.

Note: If your SQL Server Agent isn't running (as shown in Figure 12.11 with a red icon), then you will get this message when you try to run **sp_cdc_enable_table**. Right-click the icon and follow the prompts to start the service. You may also need to run the reset script, enable JProCo for CDC, and create the Department table.

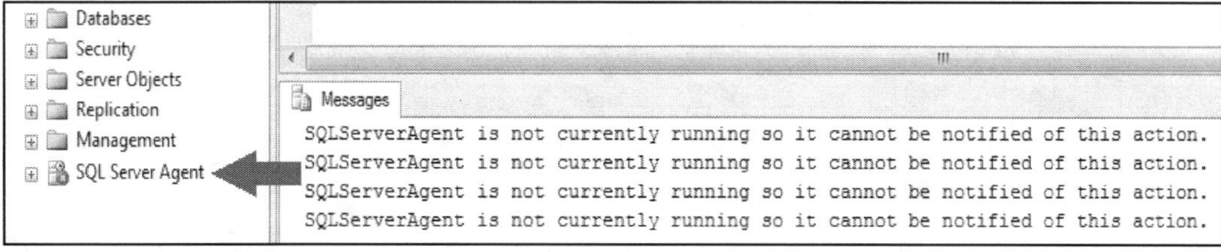

Figure 12.11 Your SQL Server Agent must be running in order to enable CDC on a table.

CDC Objects

Let's take a look at a few of the additional security structures and new jobs which CDC has established for us.

Navigate to your SQL Server Agent in the Object Explorer. Expand the Jobs folder and notice the two new jobs which CDC has created for you. The capture job is the one which reads the data from your table's log file (JProCo.dbo.Department.ldf) and stores all of the data and metadata in the Change Tables. The cleanup job runs once daily (at 2 a.m. by default) to cleanup your old data. By default, three days worth of changes are retained.

You can customize these settings to suit the needs of your business. For example, on a large table which receives a large number of transactions, three days worth of changes may be far more information than you want. Or perhaps your group policy is to retain at least 10 days worth of data in your Change Tables.

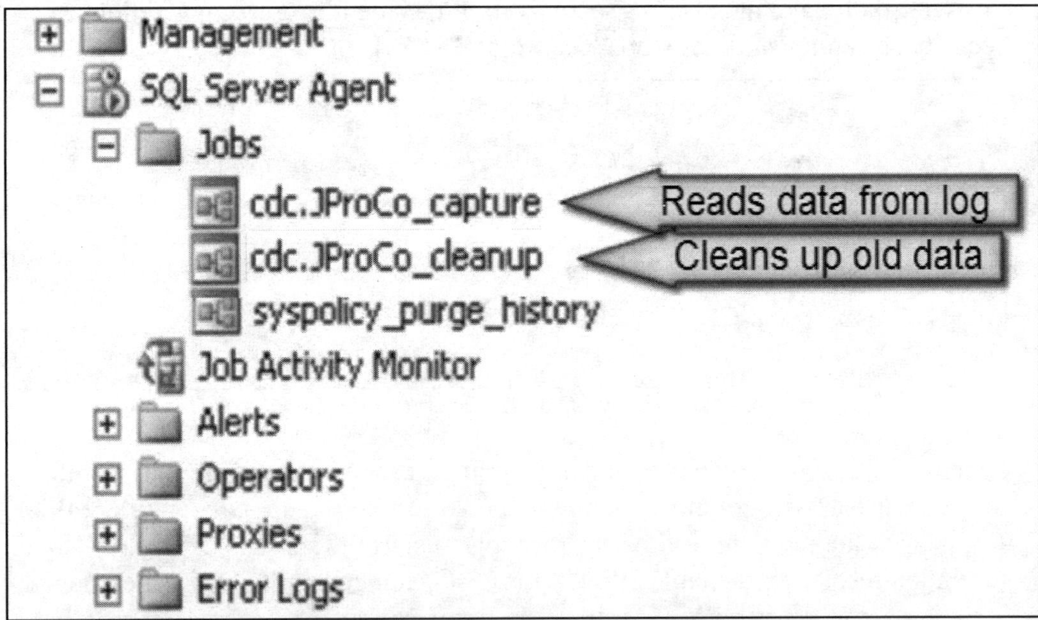

Figure 12.12 Your SQL Server Agent must be running in order to enable CDC on a table.

While still in the Object Explorer pane, scroll up to the Security folder in the JProCo database and observe the new **cdc** User and **cdc** Schema now available.

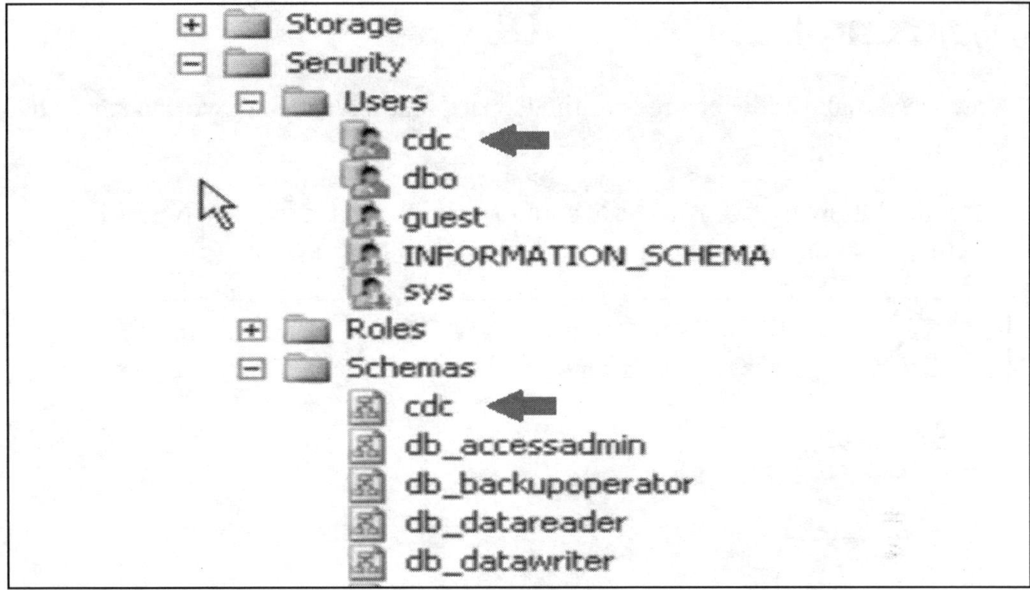

Figure 12.13 The JProCo Security folder now includes a cdc User and a cdc Schema.

In the System Tables folder of the JProCo database, we can also see that CDC has created several new tables. The Change Table for the Department table is called **cdc.dbo_Department_CT** (see Figure 12.14).

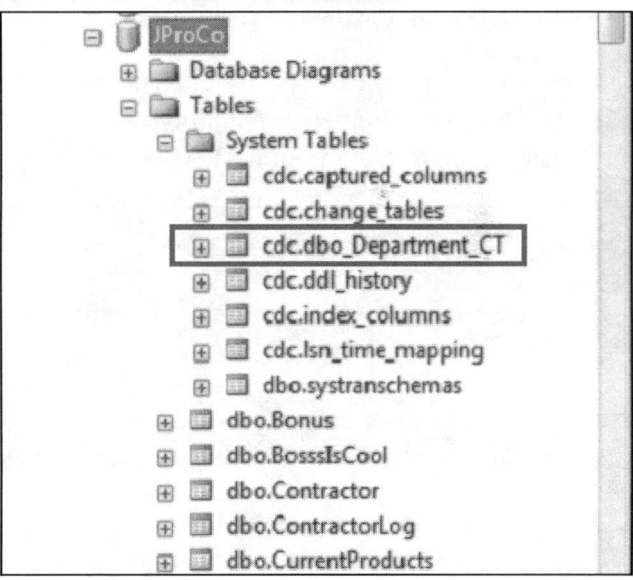

Figure 12.14 the Change Table for the Department table.

Tracking Data With CDC

Now we'll make a few changes to the Department table so that we can see CDC in action.

Insert the following two rows. Be sure to write them as separate INSERT statements, so that they are logged as two distinct transactions.

```
INSERT INTO Department VALUES (1,'Accounting')
INSERT INTO Department VALUES (2,'Security')
```

Messages

```
(1 row(s) affected)

(1 row(s) affected)
```

Figure 12.15 Insert two rows into the Department table.

Insert two more rows. Be sure to write these as a single INSERT statement, so that both changes are logged as a single transaction. (For a refresher on using Row Constructors, refer to Volume 1 (Chapter 4) or Volume 2 (Chapter 3).)

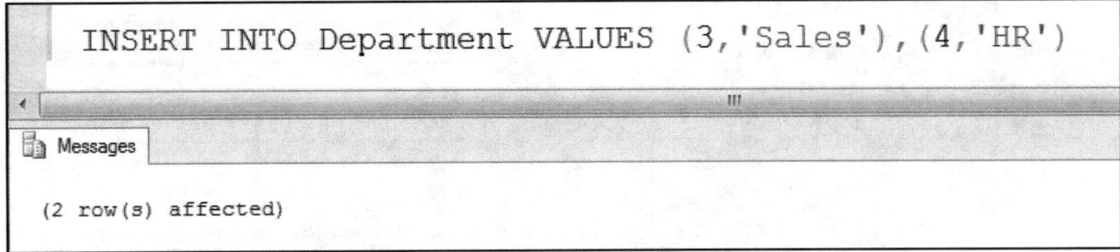
INSERT INTO Department VALUES (3,'Sales'),(4,'HR')
Messages
(2 row(s) affected)

Figure 12.16 Insert two more rows into the Department table using Row Constructors.

Next we will query the Department table, so we can see the four department name records that we inserted. We will also query the Change Table **cdc.dbo_Department_CT** and observe its contents (see Figure 12.17).

```
SELECT * FROM Department
SELECT * FROM cdc.dbo_Department_CT
```

Results | Messages

	DeptID	DepartmentName
1	1	Accounting
2	2	Security
3	3	Sales
4	4	HR

	__$start_lsn	__$end_l...	__$seqval	__$operation	__$update_mask	DeptID	DepartmentName
1	0x00000016000001050013	NULL	0x00000016000001050012	2	0x03	1	Accounting
2	0x00000016000001090003	NULL	0x00000016000001090002	2	0x03	2	Security
3	0x00000016000001900004	NULL	0x00000016000001900002	2	0x03	3	Sales
4	0x00000016000001900004	NULL	0x00000016000001900003	2	0x03	4	HR

Figure 12.17 The Change Table contains 5 fields of metadata and all of the data from the Department table.

The first field (_$start_lsn) contains the transaction number. Note the records we inserted as two separate transactions (see Figure 12.15) have different transaction numbers. The records we inserted as a single transaction (Figure 12.16) have the same transaction number. But note they each have a different value for _$seqval. Since the _$seqval field captures the order of events within a transaction, we can see that Record 3 was first in the transaction and Record 4 was second.

The _$operation field of the Change Table tracks the operation type. Since we've only inserted records thus far, all four records reflect operation type 2, insert statement.

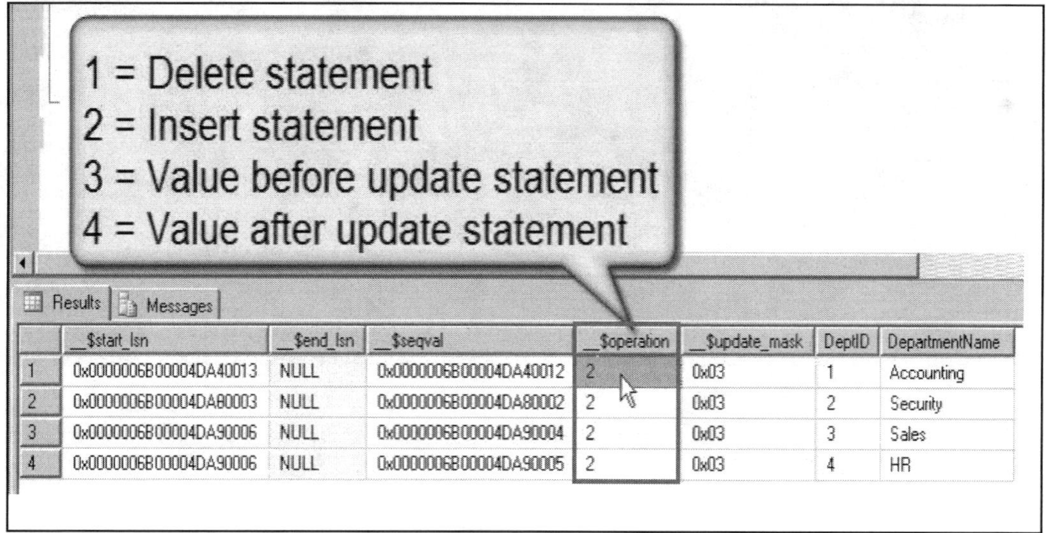

	__$start_lsn	__$end_lsn	__$seqval	__$operation	__$update_mask	DeptID	DepartmentName
1	0x0000006B00004DA40013	NULL	0x0000006B00004DA40012	2	0x03	1	Accounting
2	0x0000006B00004DA80003	NULL	0x0000006B00004DA80002	2	0x03	2	Security
3	0x0000006B00004DA90006	NULL	0x0000006B00004DA90004	2	0x03	3	Sales
4	0x0000006B00004DA90006	NULL	0x0000006B00004DA90005	2	0x03	4	HR

Figure 12.18 The _$operation field of the Change Table tracks the type of each operation.

We want to perform an update to see how CDC handles this change. Update the name of the Sales department to Marketing.

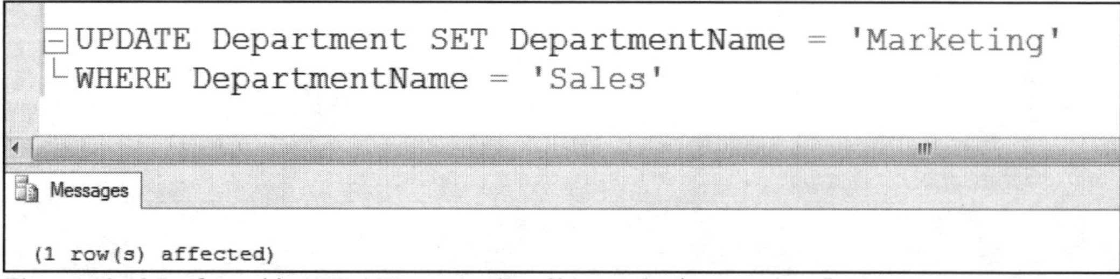

```
UPDATE Department SET DepartmentName = 'Marketing'
WHERE DepartmentName = 'Sales'
```

Messages

(1 row(s) affected)

Figure 12.19 Perform this UPDATE to see the effect on the $_operation field.

We still see four records in our updated Department table. However, the Change Table shows six records. Referring back to our list of operation types (Figure 12.18), we see that Record 3 contains the original insert of the record as the "Sales" department. Record 5's _$operation value is 3, which indicates that the data in this record contains the original values for all fields of Record 3 as they appeared prior to the update. Finally, Record 6's _$operation value of 4 tells us that the data in this record contains the new values for all fields of Record 3 as they appear after the update statement ran.

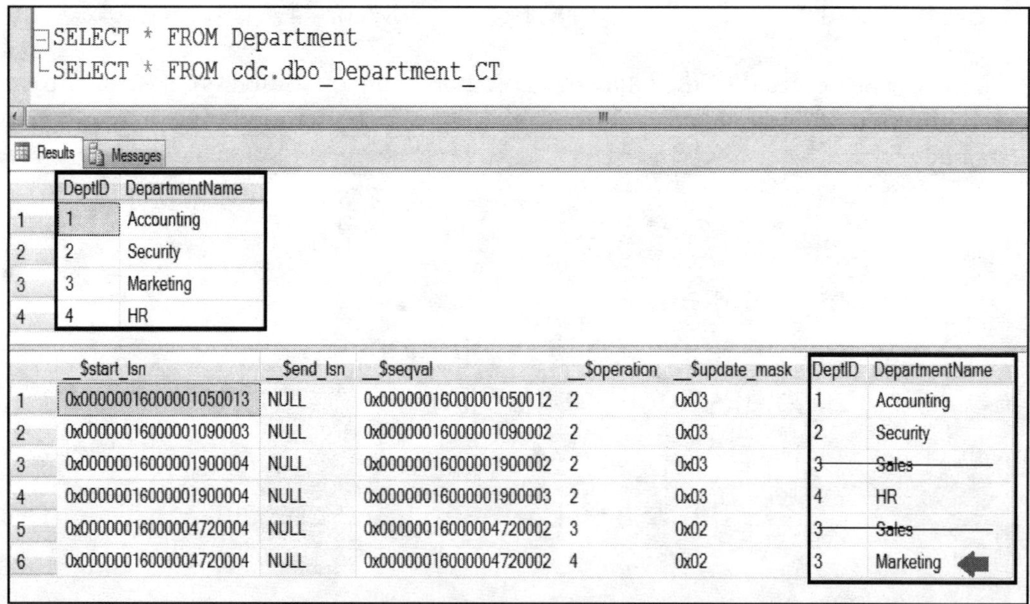

```
SELECT * FROM Department
SELECT * FROM cdc.dbo_Department_CT
```

Results | Messages

	DeptID	DepartmentName
1	1	Accounting
2	2	Security
3	3	Marketing
4	4	HR

	__$start_lsn	__$end_lsn	__$seqval	__$operation	__$update_mask	DeptID	DepartmentName
1	0x0000001600001050013	NULL	0x0000001600001050012	2	0x03	1	Accounting
2	0x0000001600001090003	NULL	0x0000001600001090002	2	0x03	2	Security
3	0x0000001600001900004	NULL	0x0000001600001900002	2	0x03	3	Sales
4	0x0000001600001900004	NULL	0x0000001600001900003	2	0x03	4	HR
5	0x0000001600004720004	NULL	0x0000001600004720002	3	0x02	3	Sales
6	0x0000001600004720004	NULL	0x0000001600004720002	4	0x02	3	Marketing

Figure 12.20 The Change Table records the values before and after the UPDATE.

Lab 12.1: Change Data Capture Basics

Lab Prep: Before you can begin the lab, you must have SQL Server installed and have run the script SQLProgrammingChapter12.1Setup.sql.

Skill Check 1: Enable Change Data Capture on the dbBasics database. Verify your work by querying the sys.databases table. When you are done, your result should look like this figure.

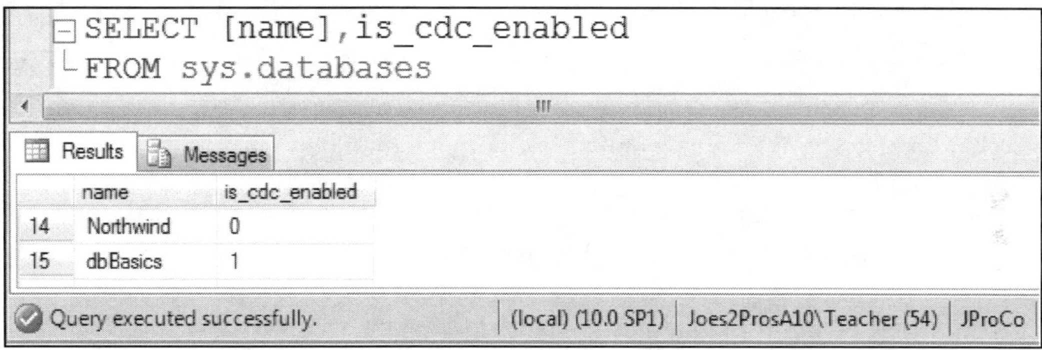

Figure 12.21 Skill Check 1 enables CDC on the dbBasics database.

Skill Check 2: Enable Change Data Capture on the dbo.ShoppingList table of the dbBasics database. Verify your work by looking at the records of the sys.tables catalog view.

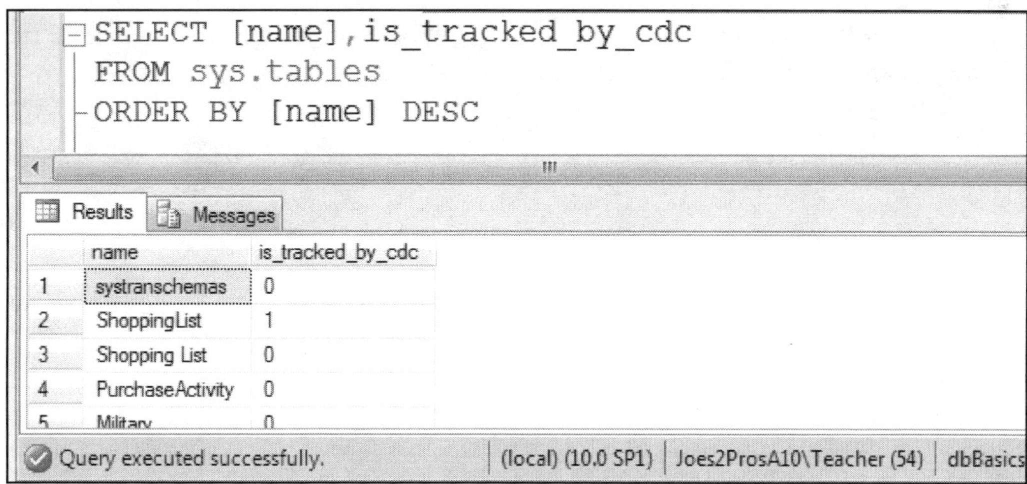

Figure 12.22 Skill Check 2 enables CDC on the ShoppingList table.

Skill Check 3: Add the following two records to the shopping list table using the code you see here:

INSERT INTO ShoppingList VALUES ('Juice',2.45)
INSERT INTO ShoppingList VALUES ('Mixed Nuts',4.66)

Verify the inserts by querying from your change table instance.

	__$start_lsn	__$end_lsn	__$seqval	__$operation	__$update_mask	ItemNumber	Description	Price
1	0x000000A0000000800004	NULL	0x000000A0000000800003	2	0x07	8	Juice	2.45
2	0x000000A0000000810004	NULL	0x000000A0000000810003	2	0x07	9	Mixed Nuts	4.66

Figure 12.23 Result for Skill Check 3.

Skill Check 4: Mixed nuts went on sale. Update the ShoppingList table using the following code:
UPDATE ShoppingList SET Price = 3.99
WHERE [Description] = 'Mixed Nuts'

Verify the update from your change table instance.

3	0x000000B00000001D0004	NULL	0x000000B00000001D0002	3	0x04	9	Mixed Nuts	4.66
4	0x000000B00000001D0004	NULL	0x000000B00000001D0002	4	0x04	9	Mixed Nuts	3.99

Figure 12.24 Result for Skill Check 4.

Answer Code: The T-SQL code to this lab can be found in the downloadable files in a file named Lab12.1_ChangeDataCaptureBasics.sql.

Change Data Capture - Points to Ponder

1. Change Data Capture (CDC) reads changes from the log file (ldf) to help you track changes based on a range of time.
2. The CDC feature is new to SQL Server 2008.
3. The sp_cdc_enable_db system stored procedure will enable CDC on the database context which you are currently in.
4. To support net changes queries, the source table must have a primary key or unique index to uniquely identify rows.
5. The is_cdc_enabled field of the sys.databases catalog view will tell you whether a given database is enabled for Change Data Tracking.
6. Once a database is enabled for CDC you can enable CDC on one or more tables in that database.
7. The is_tracked_by_cdc field of the sys.tables catalog view will tell you whether a given table is using CDC.
8. To enable CDC for a table, use the sp_cdc_enable_table system stored procedure.
9. The cdc schema and cdc user are created the first time you enable cdc on your database.
10. The first table you enable for CDC will setup the cdc.dbName_capture and cdc.dbName_cleanup jobs for SQL Agent.
11. An update to a record in your source table will result in two records being added to your tracking table. This is because we need to track the data both before and after the update.

CDC Options

To conclude our overview of Change Data Capture (CDC), we will look at a few more useful tricks for viewing change data and step through the process of disabling CDC on the table(s) and database(s) which you've enabled for tracking.

LSN (Log Sequence Number)

When transactions are committed, they receive a sequential number known as an LSN (**L**og **S**equence **N**umber). The LSN is like a transaction number and uses a binary format: 0x00000016000001050013.

Earlier we looked at LSNs contained in cdc.dbo_Department_CT (the Change Table tracking all changes made to the JProCo.dbo.Department table). In our previous Figures 12.17 and 12.20, the first field (_$start_lsn) contains the log sequence number.

We know your Change Table(s) contains potentially massive quantities of data. However, when actually viewing or handling this data, you will frequently need to narrow down the data by timeframe. For example, you may want to get the oldest change, the most recent change, changes which occurred in the last 12 hours, or those which occurred in the last day, etc.

Most CDC functions will not allow you to use datetime values in parameters. Instead you must pass in transaction numbers associated with those times. In other words, you must pass in the LSN(s) which most closely corresponds to the timeframe you need.

Mapping Times to LSNs

Suppose we want to see all changes which have occurred during the last 24 hours. Since we can't pass a datetime value (e.g., GetDate( ) -1) directly into a CDC function, we'll need to learn how to map our desired timeframe datapoints to the binary format which CDC will recognize.

We'll begin by declaring two variables corresponding to our target timeframe (@Begin_time and @End_time). We need two more variables to contain the binary equivalent of our beginning and ending timeframe datapoints (@From_lsn and @To_lsn). Since we want to see changes from the last 24 hours, our beginning time is GetDate( ) -1 and our end time is the time right now, or GetDate( ).

```
DECLARE @Begin_time datetime, @End_time datetime
DECLARE @From_lsn binary(10), @to_lsn binary(10)

SET @Begin_time = Getdate() - 1
SET @End_Time = GetDate()
```

Figure 12.25 The first part of the code segment needed to run **sys.fn_cdc_map_time_to_lsn**.

The next piece of code to add will be the two SELECT statements shown in Figure 12.26. By using the CDC function sys.fn_cdc_map_time_to_lsn, we are able to translate our timeframes to the nearest transaction number.

```
DECLARE @Begin_time datetime, @End_time datetime
DECLARE @From_lsn binary(10), @to_lsn binary(10)
SET @Begin_time = Getdate() - 1
SET @End_Time = GetDate()

SELECT @From_lsn =
sys.fn_cdc_map_time_to_lsn('smallest greater than or equal',@begin_time)

SELECT @to_lsn =
sys.fn_cdc_map_time_to_lsn('Largest less than or equal',@End_time)
```

Figure 12.26 The first part of the code segment needed to run **sys.fn_cdc_map_time_to_lsn**.

Finally, we'll add a SELECT statement to query all four variables. Run all the code you see below (in Figure 12.27).

We now see our target timeframe (i.e., the last 24 hours) expressed as datetime values (see A, B) and the two binary values (the LSNs in C and D) which will help us hone in on just the change data captured during the last 24 hours.

The datetime value labeled A is the time precisely 24 hours ago. This value corresponds to the LSN labeled C. The datetime value labeled B is the time right now, which corresponds to the LSN labeled as D.

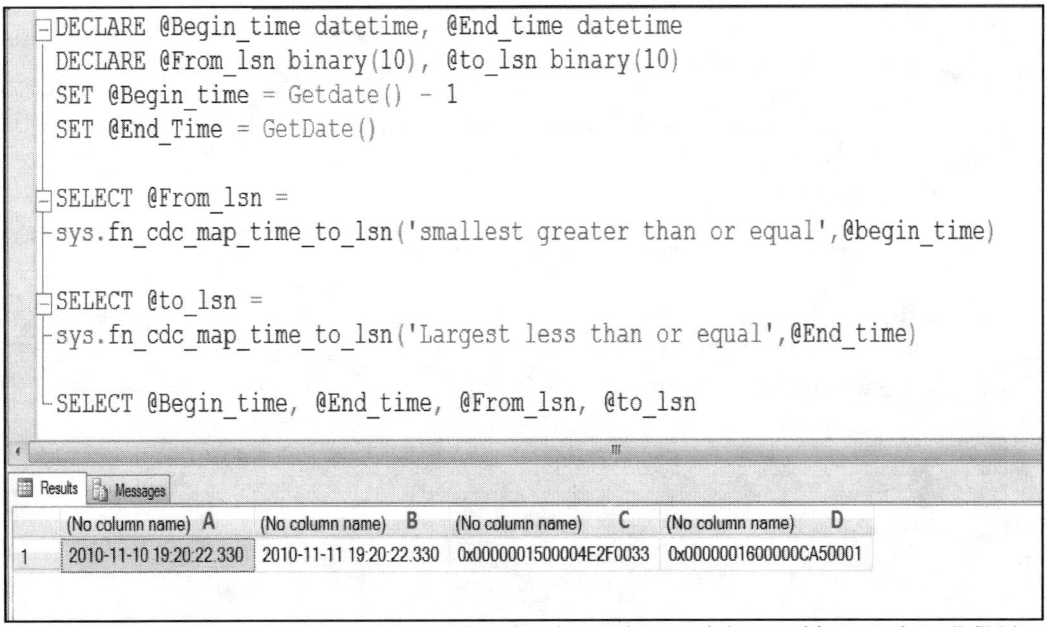

```
DECLARE @Begin_time datetime, @End_time datetime
DECLARE @From_lsn binary(10), @to_lsn binary(10)
SET @Begin_time = Getdate() - 1
SET @End_Time = GetDate()

SELECT @From_lsn =
sys.fn_cdc_map_time_to_lsn('smallest greater than or equal',@begin_time)

SELECT @to_lsn =
sys.fn_cdc_map_time_to_lsn('Largest less than or equal',@End_time)

SELECT @Begin_time, @End_time, @From_lsn, @to_lsn
```

	(No column name) A	(No column name) B	(No column name) C	(No column name) D
1	2010-11-10 19:20:22.330	2010-11-11 19:20:22.330	0x0000001500004E2F0033	0x0000001600000CA50001

Figure 12.27 Our target timeframe expressed as datetime values and the two binary values (LSNs).

Viewing Specific CDC Data

Next we'll combine our previous technique with the CDC function cdc.fn_cdc_Get_All_Changes, which will show us all changes to the table which we're tracking.

You can re-use all of the code you just ran (shown in Figure 12.27). As shown in the next figure (Figure 12.28), simply comment out the third SELECT statement so it won't run:
[SELECT @Begin_time, @End_time, @From_lsn, @to_lsn].

Now add this SELECT statement to pull from the function:
[SELECT * FROM cdc.fn_cdc_Get_All_Changes_dbo_Department(@From_lsn, @to_lsn, 'all')].

Recall that dbo_Department was the name we chose for the tracking instance of the Department table in the JProCo db. The lowercase 'all' argument specifies that we want to see all change data for the time period we specified (i.e., the last 24 hours).

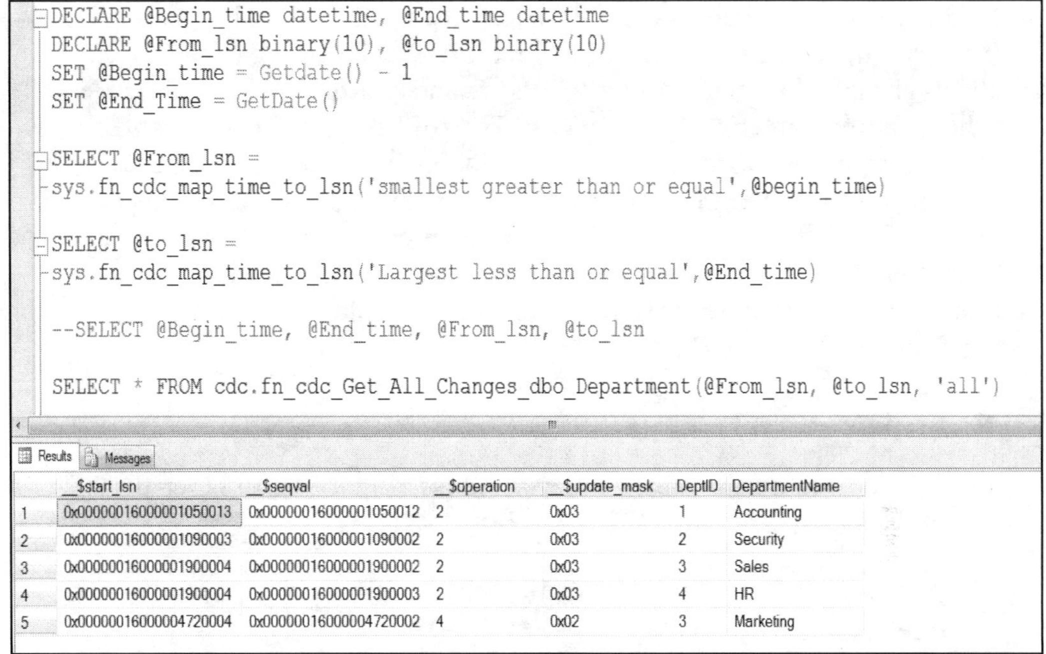

```
DECLARE @Begin_time datetime, @End_time datetime
DECLARE @From_lsn binary(10), @to_lsn binary(10)
SET @Begin_time = Getdate() - 1
SET @End_Time = GetDate()

SELECT @From_lsn =
sys.fn_cdc_map_time_to_lsn('smallest greater than or equal',@begin_time)

SELECT @to_lsn =
sys.fn_cdc_map_time_to_lsn('Largest less than or equal',@End_time)

--SELECT @Begin_time, @End_time, @From_lsn, @to_lsn

SELECT * FROM cdc.fn_cdc_Get_All_Changes_dbo_Department(@From_lsn, @to_lsn, 'all')
```


	__$start_lsn	__$seqval	__$operation	__$update_mask	DeptID	DepartmentName
1	0x00000016000001050013	0x00000016000001050012	2	0x03	1	Accounting
2	0x00000016000001090003	0x00000016000001090002	2	0x03	2	Security
3	0x00000016000001900004	0x00000016000001900002	2	0x03	3	Sales
4	0x00000016000001900004	0x00000016000001900003	2	0x03	4	HR
5	0x00000016000004720004	0x00000016000004720002	4	0x02	3	Marketing

Figure 12.28 Our result shows 'all' of the changes made to dbo.Department in the last 24 hours.

Use the **cdc.fn_cdc_Get_Net_Changes** function to see net changes for your CDC instance. The figure below (Figure 12.29) runs nearly the same code as our previous example.The only difference is the use of the Net Changes function.

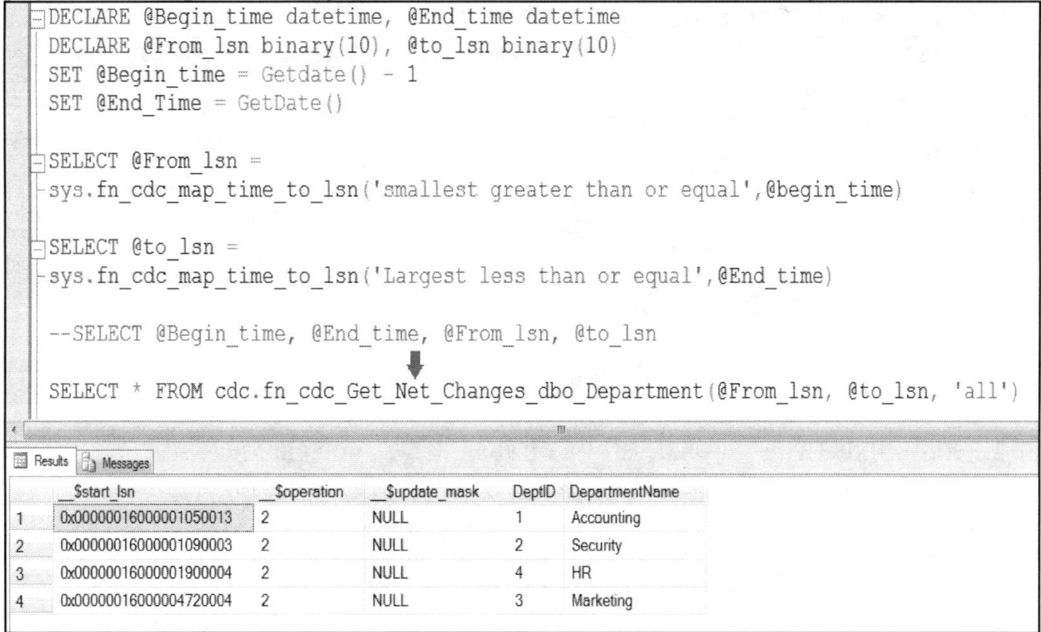

```
DECLARE @Begin_time datetime, @End_time datetime
DECLARE @From_lsn binary(10), @to_lsn binary(10)
SET @Begin_time = Getdate() - 1
SET @End_Time = GetDate()

SELECT @From_lsn =
sys.fn_cdc_map_time_to_lsn('smallest greater than or equal',@begin_time)

SELECT @to_lsn =
sys.fn_cdc_map_time_to_lsn('Largest less than or equal',@End_time)

--SELECT @Begin_time, @End_time, @From_lsn, @to_lsn

SELECT * FROM cdc.fn_cdc_Get_Net_Changes_dbo_Department(@From_lsn, @to_lsn, 'all')
```


	__$start_lsn	__$operation	__$update_mask	DeptID	DepartmentName
1	0x00000016000001050013	2	NULL	1	Accounting
2	0x00000016000001090003	2	NULL	2	Security
3	0x00000016000001900004	2	NULL	4	HR
4	0x00000016000004720004	2	NULL	3	Marketing

Figure 12.29 The 'net' changes query shows the latest changes to dbo.Department.

Be sure that you understand the difference between the "All Changes" and the "Net Changes" query results (Figures 12.28 and 12.29). The Net Changes function reflects changes between the start-time-state and end-time-state of the table, without all of the intermediate changes. The All Changes function exhaustively details every change made to the table, including all of the intermediate changes. Recall that the name of the Sales department was updated to Marketing (shown earlier in Figure 12.19). The All Changes function shows both the old name (Sales) and the current name (Marketing). However, the Net Changes function shows only the current records in the Department table. Thus, only the Marketing record appears for DeptID 3.

Disabling CDC

First disable CDC on any tables you enabled (see Figure 12.30), then disable CDC on your database (see Figure 12.31).

```
EXECUTE sys.sp_cdc_disable_table
@Source_schema = 'dbo',
@Source_name = 'Department',
@Capture_Instance = 'dbo_Department'
```

```
Messages
Command(s) completed successfully.
```

Figure 12.30 Run this code to disable CDC on the Department table (JProCo.dbo.Department).

Finally, run this code to disable CDC on the JProCo database.

```
EXEC sys.sp_cdc_Disable_db
```

```
Messages
Command(s) completed successfully.
```

Figure 12.31 Run this code to disable CDC on the entire JProCo database.

To confirm that you've successfully disabled CDC, you can query the sys.databases and sys.tables catalog views (shown earlier in Figures 12.2 and 12.5).

```
SELECT [name], is_cdc_enabled FROM sys.databases
SELECT [name], is_tracked_by_cdc FROM sys.tables
```

Lab 12.2: CDC

Lab Prep: Before you can begin the lab, you must have SQL Server installed and have run the script SQLProgrammingChapter12.2Setup.sql.

Skill Check 1: Declare two datetime variables, @Begin_Time and @End_Time. Set @Begin_Time to two days ago and @End_Time to the current time. Declare two binary(10) numbers called @From_lsn and @To_lsn. Set the values of both by calling the sys.fn_cdc_map_time_to_lsn function. Query all the changes of the dbo.ShoppingList table that have taken place in the last two days.

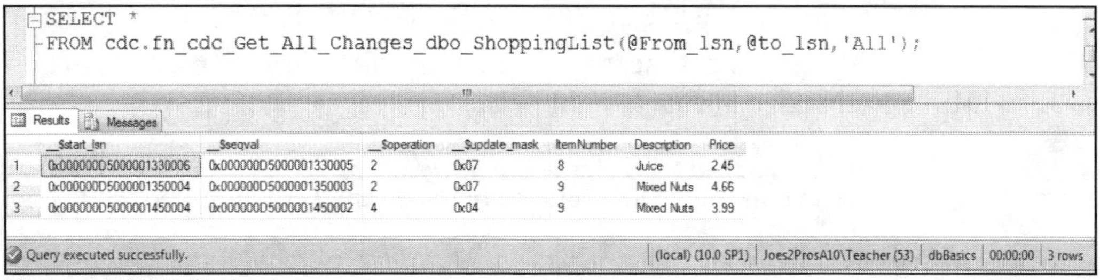

```
SELECT *
FROM cdc.fn_cdc_Get_All_Changes_dbo_ShoppingList(@From_lsn,@to_lsn,'All');
```

Results | Messages

	__$start_lsn	__$seqval	__$operation	__$update_mask	ItemNumber	Description	Price
1	0x000000D5000001330006	0x000000D5000001330005	2	0x07	8	Juice	2.45
2	0x000000D5000001350004	0x000000D5000001350003	2	0x07	9	Mixed Nuts	4.66
3	0x000000D5000001450004	0x000000D5000001450002	4	0x04	9	Mixed Nuts	3.99

Query executed successfully. | (local) (10.0 SP1) | Joes2ProsA10\Teacher (53) | dbBasics | 00:00:00 | 3 rows

Figure 12.32 Skill Check 1.

Skill Check 2: Disable Change Data Capture on the dbo.ShoppingList table in the dbBasics database. Confirm your result by checking the appropriate System View and seeing that this table is no longer enabled for CDC.

Skill Check 3: Turn off Change Data Capture for the entire dbBasics Database. Confirm your result by checking the appropriate System View and seeing that this db is no longer enabled for CDC.

Answer Code: The T-SQL code to this lab can be found in the downloadable files in a file named Lab12.2_ChangeDataCaptureOptions.sql.

CDC Options - Points to Ponder

1. If you enable change data capture on the dbo.Employee table you would notice the cdc.dbo_Employee_CT system table is created in your database. This is known as the tracking table.
2. The Tracking Table contains all the fields of the source table plus 5 metadata fields about the operation, log sequence and other information.
3. The Tracking Table's metadata is hard to read, so it is recommended that you use system supplied functions (which typically begin with sys.fn_cdc_ or cdc.fn_cdc_) to help you when querying this table.
4. The sys.fn_cdc_map_time_to_lsn function will return a binary LSN (**L**og **S**equence **N**umber) from a regular datetime field.
5. The cdc.fn_cdc_Get_All_Changes_dbo_*tablename* function will query your tracking table and return all changes between the LSN numbers you supply.
6. The cdc.fn_cdc_Get_Net_Changes_dbo_*tablename* function will query your tracking table and return only the net changes made to the table in question *("Tablename").*
7. If you were to update one record in a table three times, the most recent change would be the **net change**. When you query using the Net Change function, you get one instance of a changed record (i.e., the latest change) no matter how many times it has changed.
8. If you were to update one record in a table three times, the All Changes function would return all three updates made to that record. However, in this scenario, the Net Changes function would return just the latest version of that record.

Chapter Glossary

cdc.dbName_Capture: one of two jobs which SQL Agent sets up when you initially enable a table for CDC.

cdc.dbName_cleanup: one of two jobs which SQL Agent sets up when you initially enable a table for CDC.

cdc schema: SQL Server creates the cdc schema and cdc user the first time that CDC is enabled on a database.

CHANGE DATA CAPTURE (CDC): SQL Server 2008 feature which tracks every field in your table(s) -- not just the primary key fields. CDC eads the log file (.ldf) of your table and captures all of the change activity (metadata + data) in a Change Table.

LSN (Log Sequence Number): when transactions are committed, they receive a sequential LSN, which acts like a transaction number and uses a binary format: 0x0000001600000l050013.

sp_cdc_enable_db: the system stored procedure which enables CDC on the current database.

sys.fn_cdc_map_time_to_lsn: the CDC function which translates timeframes to the nearest transaction number.

Chapter Twelve - Review Quiz

1.) What does CDC stand for?

O a. Change Data Capture
O b. Call Data Changes
O c. Capture Data Calls

2.) What is the first version of SQL Server to support CDC?

O a. 7.0
O b. 2000
O c. 2005
O d. 2008
O e. It will be in a future version

3.) What code will enable CDC on the JProCo database?

O a.
```
USE JProCo
GO

EXEC sp_cdc_enable_db
```

O b.
```
ALTER DATABASE JProCo
SET CHANGE_TRACKING = ON
```

4.) What code will enable “all” and “net” CDC changes on the Sales.Invoice table and allow any role to view the changes?

O a. EXEC sp_cdc_enable_table ‘sales’,’Invoice’,’Sales_Invoice,0,null
O b. EXEC sp_cdc_enable_table ‘sales’,’Invoice’,’Sales_Invoice,1,null
O c.
```
ALTER TABLE Sales.Invoice
ENABLE CHANGE_TRACKING
```

5.) What code will disable CDC on the SalesDetail table of the sales schema?

O a.
```
EXEC sys.sp_cdc_disable_table
  @Source_Schema = 'sales',
  @Source_Name = ' SalesDetail',
  @Capture_Instance = 'Sales_SalesDetail'
```

O b.
```
ALTER TABLE Sales.SalesDetail
DISABLE CHANGE_TRACKING
```

6.) What code will disable CDC for the JProCo database?

O a.
```
USE JProCo
GO

EXEC sys.sp_cdc_Disable_db
```

O b.
```
ALTER DATABASE JProCo
SET CHANGE_TRACKING = OFF
```

O c.
```
ALTER DATABASE JProCo
SET CHANGE_TRACKING_ON = FALSE
```

7.) You have a table named dbo.SalesInvoiceDetail. You want to track all data changes made to values in this table. You also want to include the types of DML modifications that were made. Which new feature of SQL 2008 should you use?

O a. Change Tracking
O b. Geometry data type
O c. Geography data type
O d. Change Data Capture
O e. DML after Triggers
O f. DDL Triggers

8.) You need to maintain a history of all data modifications to a table. Which tracking method should you use?

O a. Database Audit
O b. Change Tracking
O c. C2 Audit Tracing
O d. Change Data Capture

Answer Key

1.) a 2.) d 3.) a 4.) b 5.) a 6.) a 7.) d 8.) d

Bug Catcher Game

To play the Bug Catcher game, run the file BugCatcher_Chapter12CDC.pps from the BugCatcher folder of the companion files located at www.Joes2Pros.com.

Chapter 13. Performance Tips by Pinal Dave

The phrase "It's the little stuff that counts" has many uses in life. It is through many such small ways and kindnesses that we show the people we care about how much they mean to us. A "please" or "thank you" accompanied by a genuine smile or a frequent helping hand means more to us than a disagreeable executive who tries to incentivize us through the promise of a Hawaiian vacation or a large bonus. If we want SQL Server to perform well for us, we need to know a number of little things that make its life easier. Too often people are seeking the big silver bullet to solve performance problems. Oftentimes it is just a matter of following several little performance tips that make the difference.

Some performance tips are well known and therefore asked in interviews to gauge how seasoned you are. Other tips are less known and are the ones which make you the one with the answers on the job. This section takes some of the basic knowledge of indexes, tables, and stored procedures you've learned in this book and in *SQL Architecture Basics Joes 2 Pros* and combines them into some performance skills and strategies.

Every time I go for SQL Server training or consultation, I always learn something from my attendees. Sometimes we find a simple concept we believe the whole world already knows when in fact it is actually known by very few people. This chapter will talk about many such tips relating to performance.

READER NOTE: *In order to follow along with the examples in the first section of Chapter 13, please run the SQLProgrammingChapter13.0Setup.sql setup script. The setup scripts for this book are posted at Joes2Pros.com.*

Please also note that, if you would like to reproduce the example shown in Figure 13.12, you will need the script SQLProgrammingChapter13CreateAndPopulateCompCol.sql to create the CompCol table, as well as the script PinalDaveStepsForFigure.sql in order to trace Steps 1-4.

Computed Columns

We are all familiar with the concept of why we have columns in a table. They are there to hold data for the table. The more columns you have, the more data each row can contain. Most columns have data that must be populated by some external means (like a user typing in a value or an ADO.net application inserting live data). However, sometimes columns will not need to be sourced externally (i.e., from outside of SQL Server) and instead will store data that is calculated from values residing in other columns. There are many ways to make data updates to these columns, such as using triggers that perform various DML statements to create new data. With **computed columns**, we don't need any new triggers or other programming objects, as the table will keep track of its own data value calculations. In other words, the table can keep some of its own data updated automatically. With any added convenience comes a tradeoff, namely the potential for added space usage or processing cost, both of which will be explored in this section.

Table Space Usage

SQL Server is pretty smart with most of its decision making algorithms. In fact, you could say it heeds a famous quote attributed to Albert Einstein, "Never memorize what you can look up in books." The point of the saying is that there rarely is a need to duplicate the same data yourself if it's already available to you. If SQL Server were to coin a similar phase, it might say, "Never materialize (store) data which you can already retrieve." In order to demonstrate this principle, we need to take a few steps to set the stage. Let's use dbo.SalesInvoiceDetail since it's the largest table in JProCo and we can easily track changes in stored (materialized) space usage (see Figure 13.1).

```
SELECT *
FROM SalesInvoiceDetail
```

Results | Messages

	InvoiceDetailID	InvoiceID	ProductID	Quantity	UnitDiscount
1	1	1	76	2	0.05
2	2	1	77	3	0.05
3	3	1	78	6	0.05
4	4	1	71	5	0.05
5	5	1	72	4	0.05
6	6	2	73	2	0.00
7	7	3	74	3	0.00

Figure 13.1 With 6960 records, SalesInvoiceDetail is the largest table in JProCo.

Figure 13.1 shows us some of the records of the SalesInvoiceDetail table. In this table we have 6960 records and five fields. The first record shows a Quantity of 2 and a 0.05 UnitDiscount. If you save five cents on each order, and you ordered a quantity of 2, then you should save 10 cents ($0.10). We are thinking about adding a new column called TotalDiscount that will store this calculated discount value for all records.

Adding a new field to SalesInvoiceDetail would add 6960 new values to this table. In other words, creating a new field would cause this table to consume more space. To test this out, let's see how much space the table is using before we make any changes. In Figure 13.2, we run the **sp_spaceused** system stored procedure to see that the data for the SaleInvoiceDetail table currently occupies 200KB.

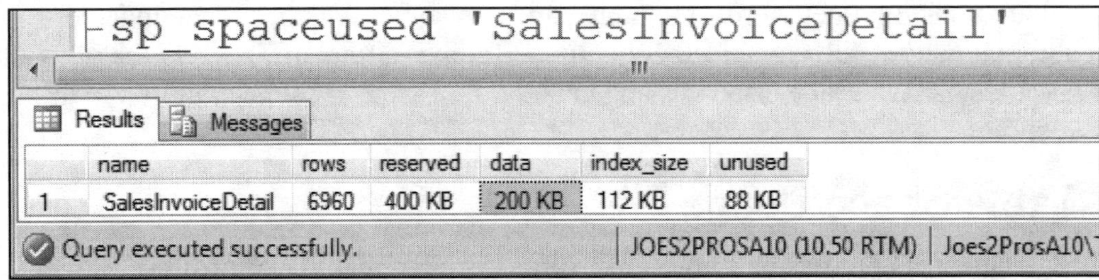

Figure 13.2 The records of JProCo's SalesInvoiceDetail table are currently taking up 200KB.

Please pay attention to the value in the [data] column which right now shows 200KB. As we will see, some changes will cause this value to grow and other changes will have no effect on the amount of materialized data in the table.

Expert Tip: Sometimes you may see a "SQL pro" running system-stored procedure without the EXEC command. Test this for yourself and notice that the code in Figure 13.2 runs ok with and without the EXEC command:

EXEC sp_spaceused 'SalesInvoiceDetail'

sp_spaceused 'SalesInvoiceDetail'

Standard Columns

Next we will add a new field, TotalDiscount, which uses the money data type. Once that field is in place, we will use an UPDATE statement to populate our new TotalDiscount column. A query from our SalesInvoiceDetail table shows us that this table now has six fields (see Figure 13.3). We can also see that this new field is populated with data calculated from the other columns of the SalesInvoiceDetail table.

```
ALTER TABLE SalesInvoiceDetail
ADD TotalDiscount MONEY
GO

UPDATE SalesInvoiceDetail
SET TotalDiscount = UnitDiscount * Quantity

SELECT *
FROM SalesInvoiceDetail
```

Results | Messages

InvoiceDetailID	InvoiceID	ProductID	Quantity	UnitDiscount	TotalDiscount
1	1	76	2	0.05	0.10
2	1	77	3	0.05	0.15
3	1	78	6	0.05	0.30

Query executed successfully. | JOES2PROSA10 (10.50 RTM) | Joes2ProsA10\Teacher (56) | JProCo | 00:00:00 | 6960 row

Figure 13.3 The TotalDiscount column has been added to SalesInvoiceDetail and then populated.

In Figure 13.4, **sp_spaceused** again shows us the amount of space used by the SalesInvoiceDetail table. It is very clear that the new column is taking up additional space in the database. In fact, we can see that the data in SalesInvoiceDetail has grown from 200KB and is now 400KB.

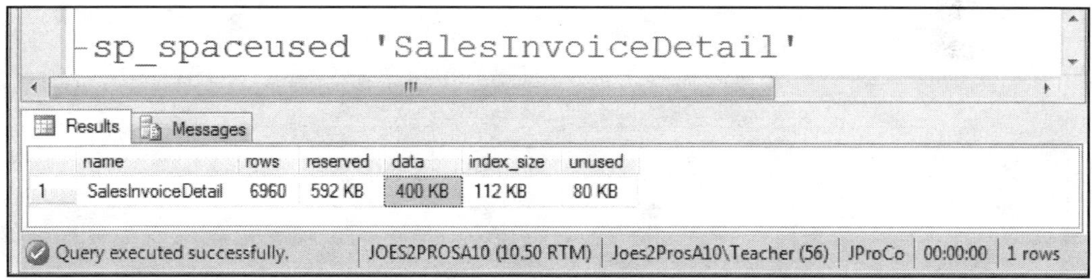

Figure 13.4 The data size for the SalesInvoiceDetail table has doubled from 200KB to 400KB.

Non-Persisted Computed Columns

Is it possible to add a new field to a table without using additional space? Since we already created the sixth field (the expression field TotalDiscount) in the standard fashion, we first must reset our table to remove this field and demonstrate a different approach. Close all query windows and then reset the database by running the SQLProgrammingChapter13.0Setup.sql script (as shown in Figure 13.5). After you run this script, your SalesInvoiceDetail table should again show just 5 fields.

```
/*
** Joes2Pros.com 2009
** All Rights Reserved.
*/

USE master
GO
```

Messages

Query executed successfully. | JOES2PROSA10 (10.50 RTM) | Joes2ProsA10\Teacher (53) | JProCo | 00:00:15 | 0 rows

Figure 13.5 To properly confirm that our table and db are reset, we must run the setup script. Simply dropping and re-adding the TotalDiscount column is insufficient for this demonstration.

Be sure to confirm that your SalesInvoiceDetail table has been reset and contains only the original five fields (refer to Figure 13.1). You can also use the sp_spaceused stored procedure to verify that the total data size is once again just 200KB. In our next step, we will create and populate the TotalDiscount field all at once. The ALTER TABLE statement (see Figure 13.6) creates this field as a **computed column**. A SELECT query of the table shows that the TotalDiscount field has been created and populated in one step.

```
ALTER TABLE SalesInvoiceDetail
ADD TotalDiscount AS (Quantity * UnitDiscount)
GO

SELECT *
FROM SalesInvoiceDetail
```

Results | Messages

	InvoiceDetailID	InvoiceID	ProductID	Quantity	UnitDiscount	TotalDiscount
1	1	1	76	2	0.05	0.10
2	2	1	77	3	0.05	0.15
3	3	1	78	6	0.05	0.30
4	4	1	71	5	0.05	0.25
5	5	1	72	4	0.05	0.20
6	6	2	73	2	0.00	0.00

Query executed successfully. | JOES2PROSA10 (10.50 RTM) | Joes2ProsA10\Teacher (56) | JProCo | 00:00:00 | 6960 rows

Figure 13.6 The TotalDiscount computed column is added and automatically populated.

More data means more space used, right? Notice that the space used data (see Figure 13.7) still shows just 200KB. Is this accurate? YES! Computed columns are computed at run time and therefore don't take up any more storage space in the table. Where is the data for the computed field coming from? The data contained in the Quantity and UnitDiscount fields are supplying the data being calculated by the TotalDiscount column. Be aware, however, that calculations made at runtime will slow performance. Each time you query the TotalDiscount column it will get the source data and run the calculation on the fly. This demonstration shows that SQL Server agrees with Einstein's rule…there is no need to memorize or store what you can easily look up!

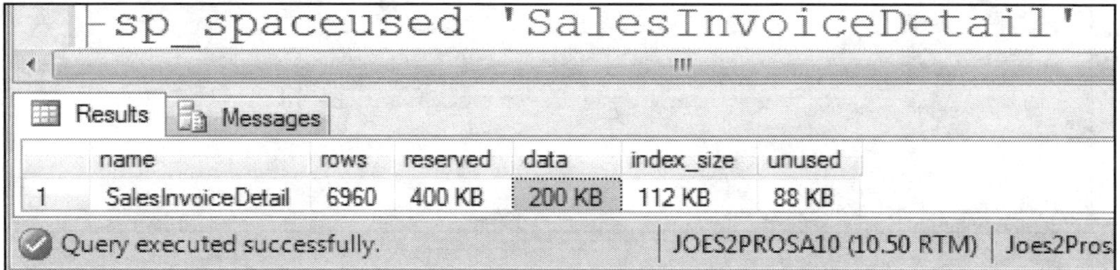
sp_spaceused 'SalesInvoiceDetail'
Results
Messages
name | rows | reserved | data | index_size | unused
1 | SalesInvoiceDetail | 6960 | 400 KB | 200 KB | 112 KB | 88 KB
Query executed successfully.
JOES2PROSA10 (10.50 RTM)
Joes2Pros

Figure 13.7 After adding and populating the TotalDiscount field as a computed column, the size of the table's data is unchanged.

Persisted Computed Columns

In a recent training session, I was surprised to discover that many people made assumptions about computed columns. They thought that as soon as computed columns are created, the column is materialized and the data is automatically stored in the new column. From our previous example, you can see that this assumption is not true by default. If computed columns are not marked in a special way, they are not materialized at the time they are created. Most computed columns are computed at runtime and thus are not **persisted data**. If computed columns are marked as persisted, the data will be materialized and stored when the column is created (see Figure 13.8).

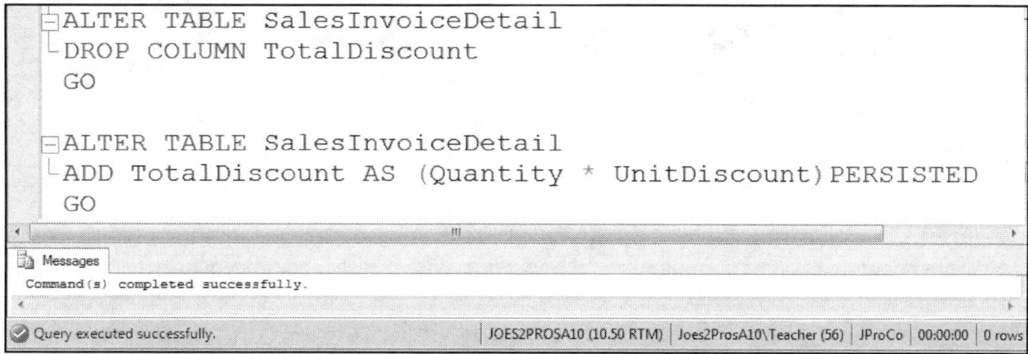
ALTER TABLE SalesInvoiceDetail
DROP COLUMN TotalDiscount
GO
ALTER TABLE SalesInvoiceDetail
ADD TotalDiscount AS (Quantity * UnitDiscount)PERSISTED
GO
Messages
Command(s) completed successfully.
Query executed successfully.
JOES2PROSA10 (10.50 RTM)
Joes2ProsA10\Teacher (56)
JProCo
00:00:00
0 rows

Figure 13.8 The TotalDiscount field is dropped and added back as a **persisted computed column**.

Once you designate a column PERSISTED, it is immediately computed and stored in the data table. Now that we have re-created TotalDiscount as a persistent computed column, let's run sp_spaceused to see the size of the data in the SalesInvoiceDetail table. The size has increased to 400KB. Thus, since we've created the computed column UnitDiscount and marked it as PERSISTED, it now consumes more space in the data table (see Figure 13.9).

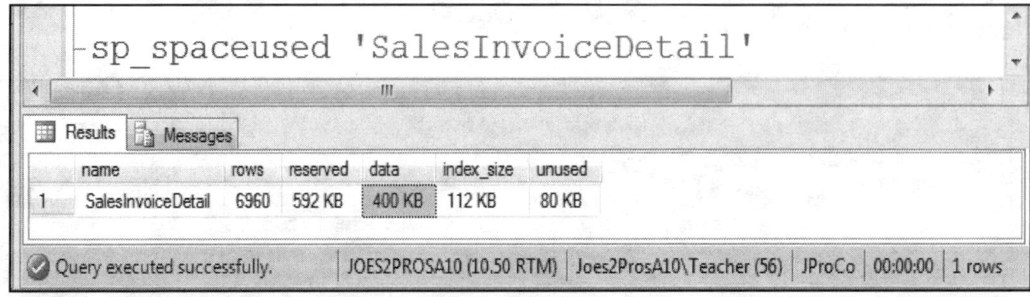
sp_spaceused 'SalesInvoiceDetail'
Results
Messages
name | rows | reserved | data | index_size | unused
1 | SalesInvoiceDetail | 6960 | 592 KB | 400 KB | 112 KB | 80 KB
Query executed successfully.
JOES2PROSA10 (10.50 RTM) | Joes2ProsA10\Teacher (56) | JProCo | 00:00:00 | 1 rows

Figure 13.9 Adding TotalDiscount as a persisted computed column means that the new column's data is materialized and stored in the table and thus consumes more space.

There is a tradeoff of advantages between having your computed column be persisted or non-persisted. If you don't persist the column, then it takes up less space but the need to calculate the numbers at runtime incurs a **performance cost**. If you persist the column, you use more storage space but the data is pre-calculated and stored and thus your query returns faster (i.e., a **performance savings**).

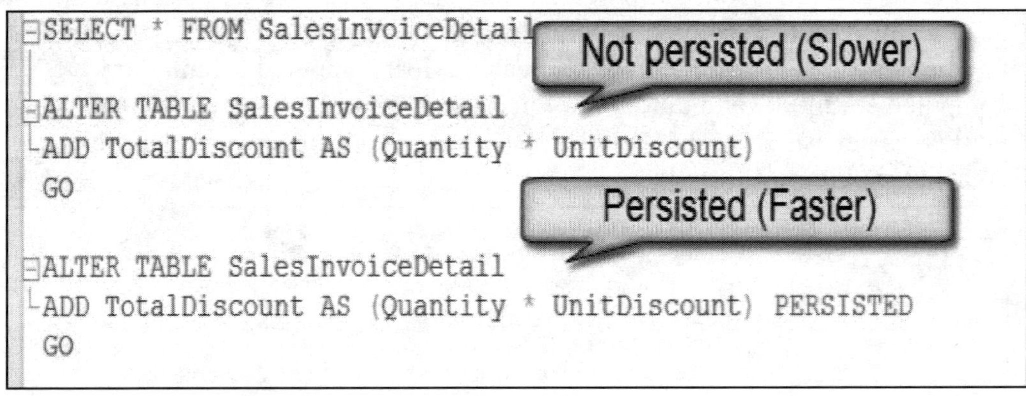
SELECT * FROM SalesInvoiceDetail
Not persisted (Slower)
ALTER TABLE SalesInvoiceDetail
ADD TotalDiscount AS (Quantity * UnitDiscount)
GO
Persisted (Faster)
ALTER TABLE SalesInvoiceDetail
ADD TotalDiscount AS (Quantity * UnitDiscount) PERSISTED
GO

Figure 13.10 You must consider the performance tradeoff when deciding whether or not you should persist a computed column. Columns which you query frequently should generally be persisted.

Let's compare the execution plan for a query including the computed column (upper half of Figure 13.11) versus one including the persisted computed column (lower half of Figure 13.11). *Notice that the same query will have a more expensive execution plan if the column is not persisted.* The plan for the non-persisted computed column contains an extra "Compute Scalar" step (see the upper half of Figure 13.11).

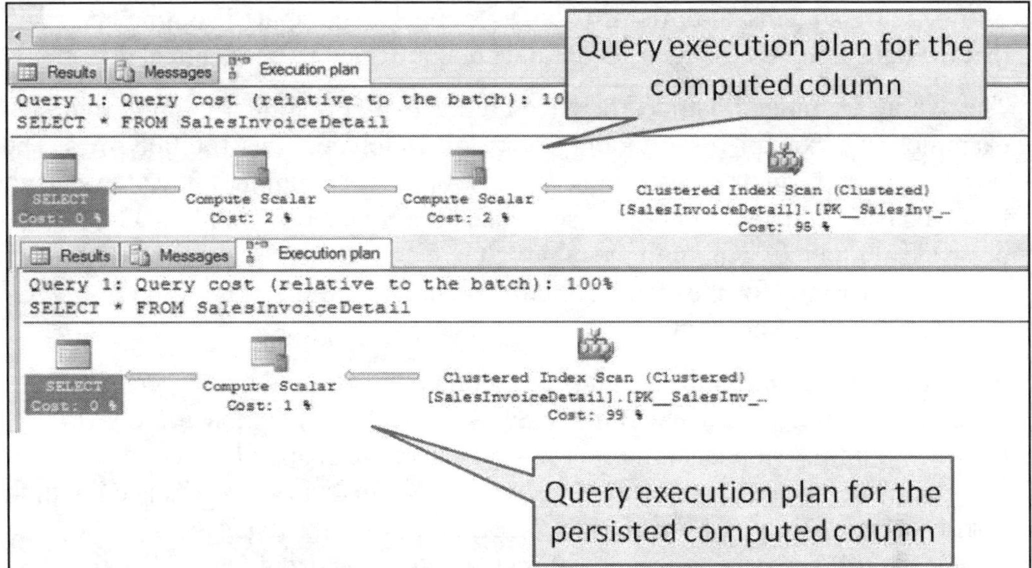

Figure 13.11 The execution plan on top is done against the non-persisted computed column and shows one extra step as compared to the persisted column on the bottom half of the figure.

Note: In order to compare the execution plans for a SELECT query on each of the two columns, I ran the steps from Figure 13.6 and captured the execution plan from the SELECT statement. The resulting plan is what you see in the upper half of Figure 13.11. I then repeated the process for the steps in Figure 13.8 (execution plan shown in the lower half of Figure 13.11). Please also note that the two query execution plans were not run at the same time. They are shown side-by-side (Figure 13.11) for illustrative purposes, namely to highlight the additional "Compute Scalar" step required when querying the table with the non-persisted version of the TotalDiscount column.

Indexing a Computed Column

This section actually originates from questions asked a few weeks ago by one of the smartest attendees I have ever met in training. He really impressed me with these good questions: "***If we create an index on a computed column, does it increase the data size of the original table? In other words, does the computed column become persisted if we create an index on it***?"

This is a great question and the answer is rather very simple: No. Adding an index will not increase the data size of the original table and it also will not automatically make the column persisted.

Notice that the top two items in the SQLAuthority.com figure (see Figure 13.12) are consistent with our own earlier example of a table before and after adding a computed column (see Figure 13.2 of the basic SalesInvoiceDetail versus Figure

13.7 after we added a sixth field, TotalDiscount, as a computed column and see that the data amounts for each scenario were confirmed to be identical at 200KB).

The overall example illustrated here (in Figure 13.12) is similar to our previous example. This example uses a table CompCol, which contains 100,000 rows. The first and second panels ("Basic table" and "Computed Column") trace the steps we followed earlier, namely to run sp_spaceused before and after adding a non-persisted computed column to the table. SQL Server reserves an identical amount of space (2696KB) for the CompCol table before and after the addition of the non-persisted computed column.

This example includes a third step (i.e., adding an index to the non-persisted computed column) not included in the SalesInvoiceDetail demonstration. However, its final step is similar to the step where we changed the computed column to become persisted (refer to Figure 13.8). Just as we experienced with the TotalDiscount column of the SalesInvoiceDetail table, the data size of the CompCol table increases after the column becomes persisted.

Notice that the third step answers the intriguing question posed by my very smart attendee. This third step of creating an index on the computed column has no impact on the size of the data contained in the table. SQL Server has reserved an additional amount of space to accommodate the index, but the size of the data remains constant. The only step which increases the size of the table data is when the computed column becomes persisted (see Figure 13.12).

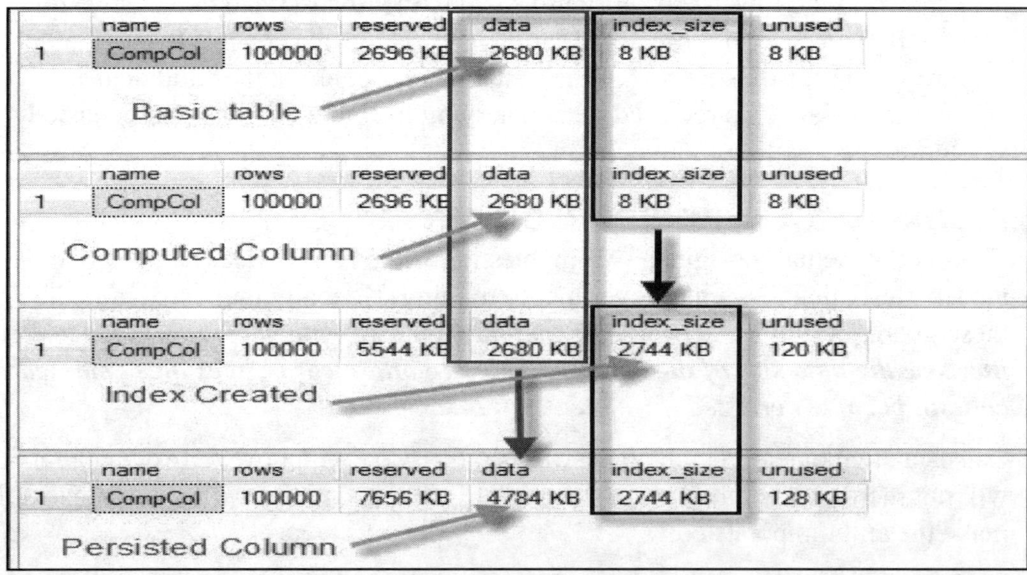

Figure 13.12 This SQLAuthority.com figure shows that adding an index to a table with a computed column does not automatically persist the data. The only impact of adding the index is to increase the index space used by the table. *Note:* Your result may vary slightly when run on your system.

Lab 13.1: Computed Columns

Lab Prep: Before you can begin the lab, you must have SQL Server installed and run the SQLProgrammingChapter13.1Setup.sql script.

Skill Check 1: The Retail price column in the CurrentProducts table includes the price after tax has been added. Only 95% of this price is the actual cost before tax. You need a column called PreTaxPrice, which is calculated as 95% the cost of the RetailPrice column. Add a computed column to this table so the new data is **not** stored in the PreTaxPrice.

```
SELECT * FROM CurrentProducts
```

Results | Messages

	ProductID	ProductName	RetailPrice	OriginationDate	ToBeDeleted	Category	SupplierID	OriginationOffset	PreTaxPrice
1	1	Underwater Tour 1 Day ...	61.483	2006-08-11 1...	0	No-Stay	0	2006-08-11 13:33:0...	58.408850
2	2	Underwater Tour 2 Days...	110.6694	2007-10-03 2...	0	Overnight-Stay	0	2007-10-03 23:43:2...	105.135930
3	3	Underwater Tour 3 Days...	184.449	2009-05-09 1...	0	Medium-Stay	0	2009-05-09 16:07:4...	175.226550
4	4	Underwater Tour 5 Days...	245.932	2006-03-04 0...	0	Medium-Stay	0	2006-03-04 04:59:0...	233.635400
5	5	Underwater Tour 1 Wee...	307.415	2001-07-18 1...	0	LongTerm-Stay	0	2001-07-18 19:20:1...	292.044250
6	6	Underwater Tour 2 Wee...	553.347	2008-06-30 2...	1	LongTerm-Stay	0	2008-06-30 20:40:3...	525.679650
7	7	Underwater Tour 1 Day ...	80.859	2007-04-07 0...	0	No-Stay	1	2007-04-07 08:25:4...	76.816050
8	8	Underwater Tour 2 Days...	145.5462	2005-06-11 0...	0	Overnight-Stay	1	2005-06-11 09:52:1...	138.268890

Query executed successfully. | JOES2PROSA10 (10.50 RTM) | Joes2ProsA10\Teacher (54) | JProCo | 00:00:00 | 486 rows

Figure 13.13 The CurrentProducts table should have a new field called PreTaxPrice.

```
EXEC sp_spaceused 'CurrentProducts'
```

Results | Messages

	name	rows	reserved	data	index_size	unused
1	CurrentProducts	486	224 KB	96 KB	48 KB	80 KB

Figure 13.14 The space used for the CurrentProducts table should be 96KB.

Answer Code: The T-SQL code for this lab can be found in the downloadable files in a file named Lab13.1_ComputedColumns.sql.

Computed Columns - Points to Ponder

1. The system stored procedure **sp_spaceused** will obtain space statistics for a table.
2. When computed columns are created, the default behavior is to not materialize the data, except at runtime. Therefore, computed columns do not take up any data storage space.
3. Along the same line as point #2, a computed column is only calculated if it is used in a query. Therefore, a query only incurs the additional performance cost of running the calculation if the computed column is included in that query.
4. Non-Persisted Computed Columns are computed at runtime when that column is listed in a SELECT query.
5. If you run a query execution plan against your computed column, you will see there is an additional "Compute Scalar" operation required when these columns are not persisted.
6. The query cost is lower for a persisted computed column compared to that of a non-persisted computed column.
7. Creating an index on a computed column does not increase the data size of the original table but there is an additional space occupied by that index. Columns made persisted are the only things that take up additional data space.

Stored Procedure Optimization Tips

Let's run through a few tips which can increase the performance of our stored procedures.

Using NOCOUNT

The NOCOUNT setting controls whether your system uses resources to count affected records during DML operations (i.e., SELECT, INSERT, UPDATE, and DELETE).

The default setting for NOCOUNT is OFF, meaning that the default is to always count records during DML operations. When you change the NOCOUNT setting, that change is in effect system-wide (i.e., across all databases and objects contained in your SQL Server instance).

To open the interface where you can find your default NOCOUNT setting (shown in Figure 13.15), launch SQL Server and follow this path from the main menu:

Tools > Options (interface launches) > expand Query Execution > expand SQL Server > Advanced

If "SET NOCOUNT" is unchecked, this is the equivalent of NOCOUNT being set to OFF: by default, the system will count records when running DML statements.

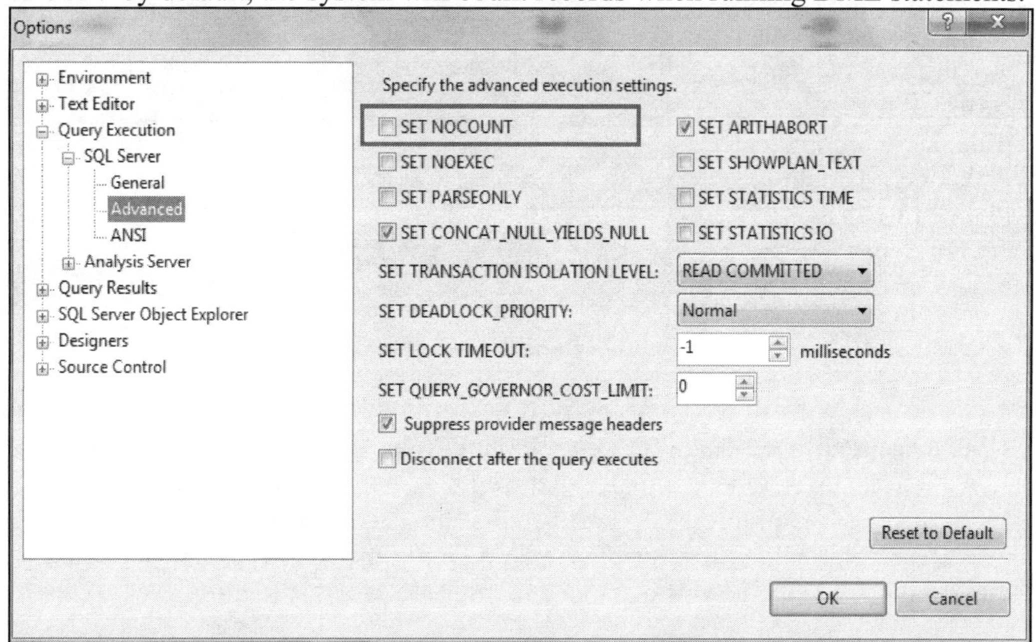

Figure 13.15 The default setting for NOCOUNT is OFF (shown here as unchecked).

Let's perform a simple query and observe this setting in action. Run this DML statement (see Figure 13.16) and toggle between the Results and Messages tabs to see that they both confirm that two rows are affected by this query.

```
SELECT *
FROM Employee
WHERE LocationID = 4
```

Results | Messages

(2 row(s) affected)

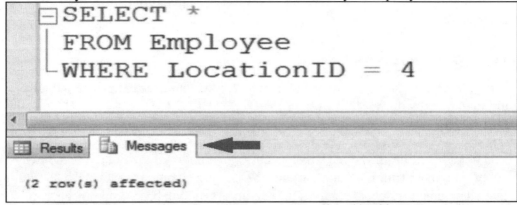

Figure 13.16 The Messages tab confirms that two rows are affected by this DML query.

For many readers, this will be the first time you've looked at the Messages tab instead of the Results tab following a SELECT query. When running a SELECT query, we're generally focused on the records our query returns and we are accustomed to looking at the lower right corner of the Results pane, if we are interested in the record count (see Figure 13.17).

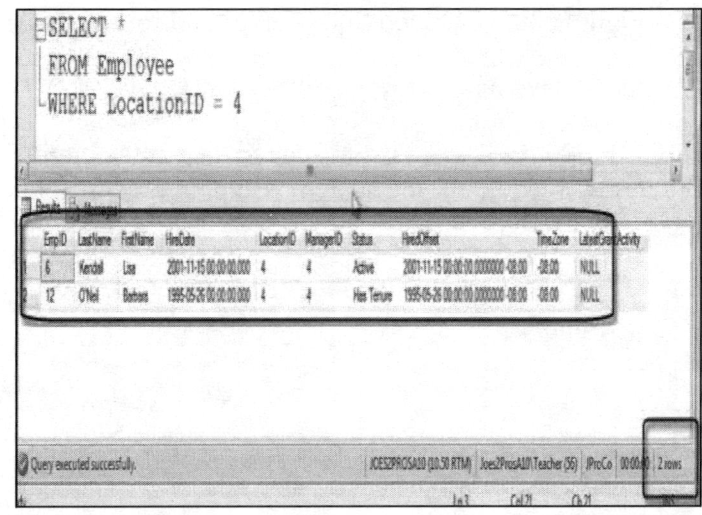
SELECT *
FROM Employee
WHERE LocationID = 4
Query executed successfully.
2 rows

Figure 13.17 Result set and row count shown for a SELECT query.

As is the case with all resources in SQL Server, tracking these record counts incurs some measure of overhead. Let's revise our current query to include a SET NOCOUNT ON statement and see that we no longer see a record count in the Messages tab (see Figure 13.18). Notice that the cell in the lower right corner of your Results tab will still show "2 rows", it's only the Messages tab which is impacted by the change you just made to your NOCOUNT setting.

SET NOCOUNT ON;
SELECT *
FROM Employee
WHERE LocationID = 4
Results
Messages
Command(s) completed successfully.

Figure 13.18 The Messages tab no longer displays the count of records.

Note: The optional semicolon delimiter for some T-SQL statements will be discussed at the end of this section. The examples in this section will run the same whether you do or don't choose to include this delimiter in your code.

Before we drop our code into a stored procedure, let's first expand our code to include three DML statements (see Figure 13.19). Just like our current example, notice that the record sets for all three SELECT queries appear in the Results tab and the count of records affected for each of the three transactions will appear in the Messages tab (shown in Figure 13.20).

```
SET NOCOUNT OFF;

SELECT *
FROM Employee
WHERE LocationID = 4

SELECT *
FROM Employee
WHERE HireDate > '1/1/2010'

SELECT *
FROM Customer
WHERE CompanyName IS NOT NULL
```

Figure 13.19 Set NOCOUNT to OFF and add two more transactions (queries) to your code.

Results
Messages
(2 row(s) affected)
(6 row(s) affected)
(2 row(s) affected)

Figure 13.20 The Messages tab displays a separate row count for each transaction.

When NOCOUNT is set to ON, the Messages tab displays one confirmation message for all DML transactions. Here we see the Messages tab displaying a single confirmation for three DML transactions (a SELECT, a DELETE, and an UPDATE query). ***Note:*** This example is included, so that readers can see that a combination of different DML statements produces results identical to our main demonstration, which uses only SELECT statements.

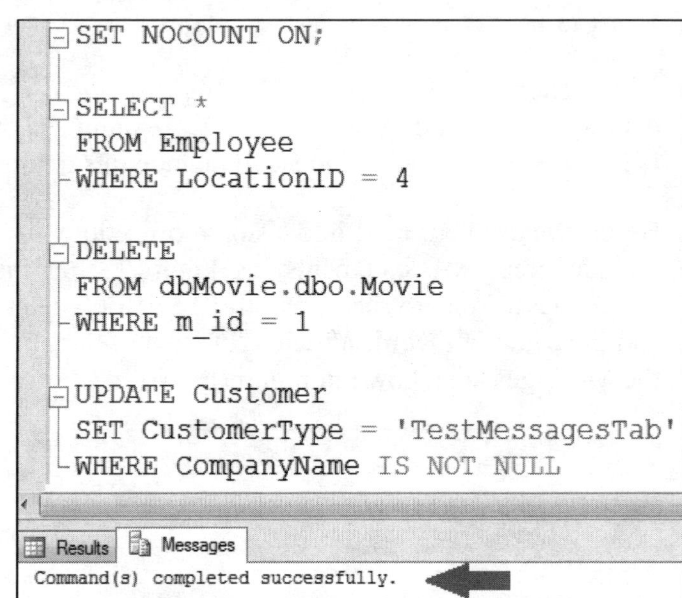
SET NOCOUNT ON;
SELECT *
FROM Employee
WHERE LocationID = 4
DELETE
FROM dbMovie.dbo.Movie
WHERE m_id = 1
UPDATE Customer
SET CustomerType = 'TestMessagesTab'
WHERE CompanyName IS NOT NULL
Results
Messages
Command(s) completed successfully.

Fig 13.21 With NOCOUNT ON, 1 message confirms all transactions.

Returning to our main demonstration, let's run our three SELECT queries (the same queries we ran in Figures 13.19 and 13.20) with NOCOUNT set to ON. Just one "Command(s) completed successfully" message appears to confirm our three separate transactions (see Figure 13.22).

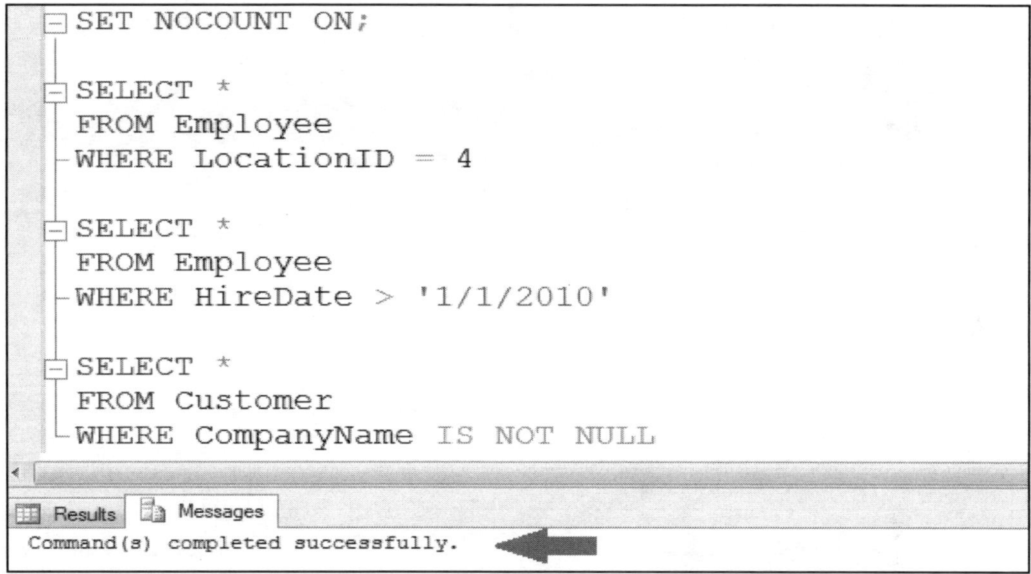
SET NOCOUNT ON;
SELECT *
FROM Employee
WHERE LocationID = 4
SELECT *
FROM Employee
WHERE HireDate > '1/1/2010'
SELECT *
FROM Customer
WHERE CompanyName IS NOT NULL
Results
Messages
Command(s) completed successfully.

Figure 13.22 With NOCOUNT ON, one confirmation message confirms our three transactions.

Once we've run the code and closed the session shown in Figure 13.22, our NOCOUNT setting reverts to our system default (this lesson assumes your default is OFF). Our next step will be to open a new query window and drop all of our queries into a stored procedure we will build called Test3Queries (Figure 13.23).

```
CREATE PROC Test3Queries
AS

SELECT *
FROM Employee
WHERE LocationID = 4

SELECT *
FROM Employee
WHERE HireDate > '1/1/2010'

SELECT *
FROM Customer
WHERE CompanyName IS NOT NULL
```

```
Messages
Command(s) completed successfully.
```

Figure 13.23 Build the sproc Test3Queries, which contains our three SELECT queries.

Execute this sproc (Test3Queries) and check the Messages tab.

Since NOCOUNT is off, we see row counts displayed for each separate transaction (see Figure 13.24).

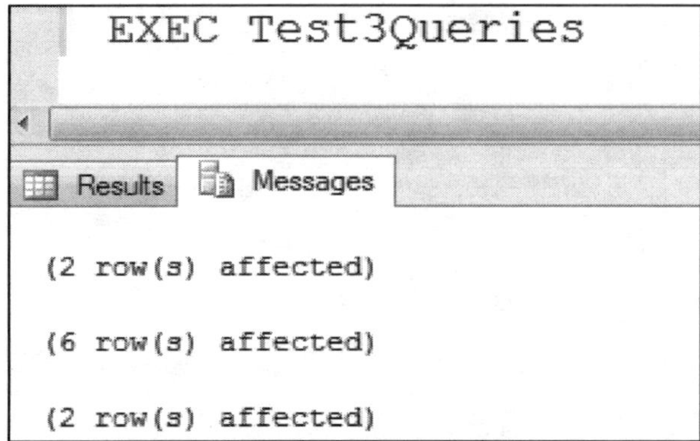
EXEC Test3Queries
Results
Messages
(2 row(s) affected)
(6 row(s) affected)
(2 row(s) affected)

Figure 13.24 Rows counts occur when we run our sproc.

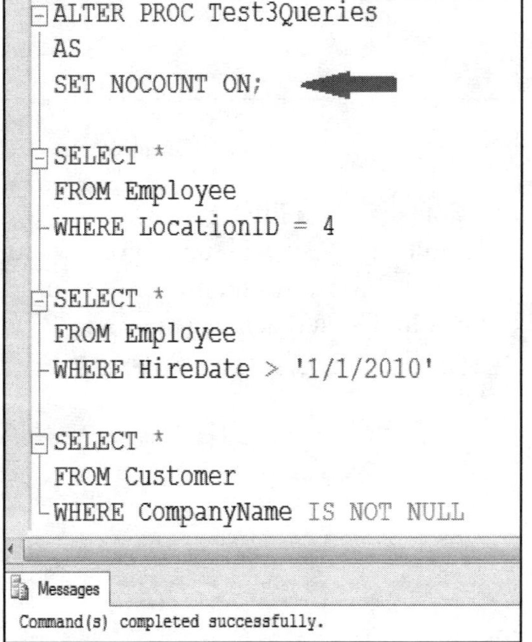
ALTER PROC Test3Queries
AS
SET NOCOUNT ON;
SELECT *
FROM Employee
WHERE LocationID = 4
SELECT *
FROM Employee
WHERE HireDate > '1/1/2010'
SELECT *
FROM Customer
WHERE CompanyName IS NOT NULL
Messages
Command(s) completed successfully.

Figure 13.25 Alter Test3Queries, NOCOUNT ON.

Our next step will be to rebuild this sproc with NOCOUNT set to ON (see Figure 13.25) and observe the affect on the confirmation messaging (see Figure 13.26).

When you set NOCOUNT ON as part of a sproc, that setting will remain in effect only for the duration of the sproc's execution. Thus, NOCOUNT turns on when we execute the sproc (as shown in the Messages tab - Figure 13.26). However, if you were to subsequently execute a different sproc, or run multiple DML statements, you will find that NOCOUNT is off. The SET NOCOUNT statement is in effect during the connection session (SPID) and then reverts back to the default.

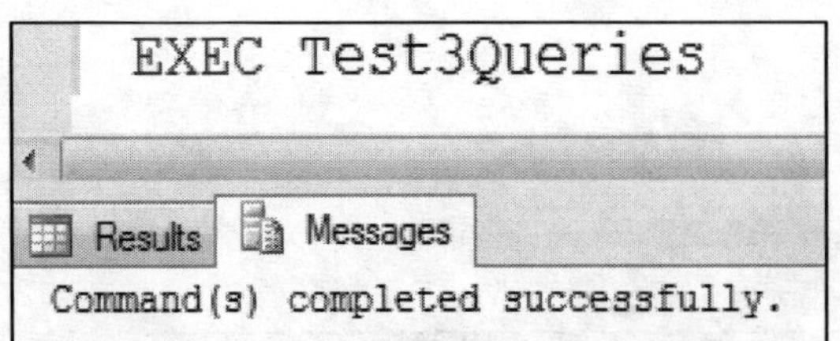
EXEC Test3Queries
Results
Messages
Command(s) completed successfully.

Figure 13.26 EXEC Test3Queries, NOCOUNT ON.

Setting NOCOUNT to ON can provide a performance boost because it reduces network traffic (i.e., the need for round trips to the server), particularly in the case of sprocs containing several statements or T-SQL loops.

Using Qualified Names

One easy performance-enhancing tip for your stored procedures is to always use the two-part name when invoking (calling) them. The same guidance applies to any objects referenced inside of your stored procedures.

Another term for the two-part name is the **qualified name**.

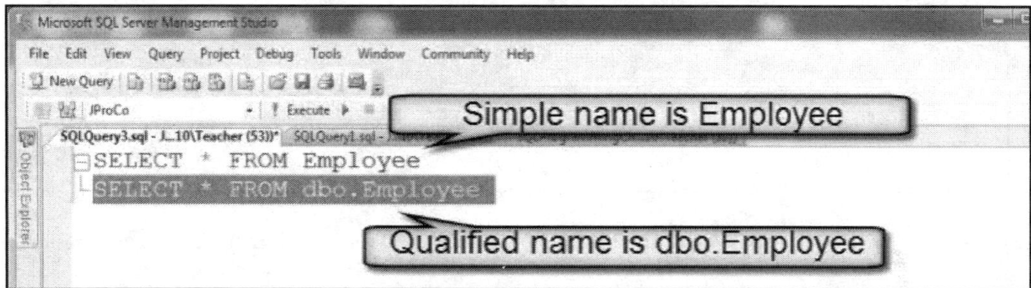

Figure 13.27 The qualified name (a.k.a., two-part name) for the Employee table is **dbo.Employee**.

In this series of *Joes 2 Pros* SQL books, we frequently use the simple name of objects in our small scale examples. For most objects, SQL Server can handle either the simple name or the two-part name (*SchemaName.ObjectName*), and SQL Server's error messaging will prompt you when a different name format is needed.

In the case of dbo.Employee, dbo is the schema name and Employee is the object name. In this case, the object is a database table (see Figure 13.28).

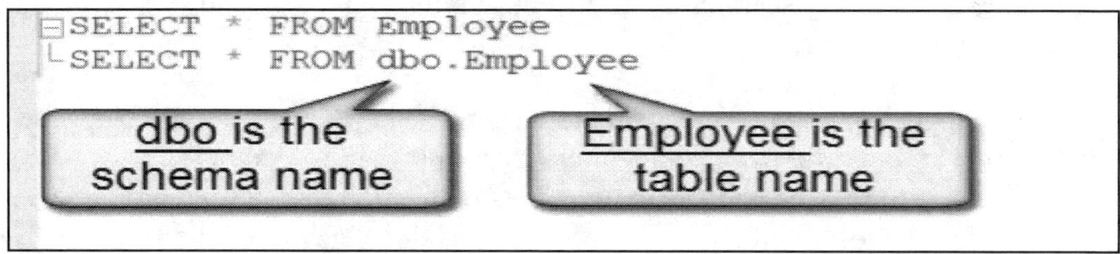

Figure 13.28 The qualified name (a.k.a., two-part name) consists of schema name and object name.

In our *Joes 2 Pros* work, we have encountered databases which have multiple schemas. AdventureWorks has numerous schemas. The JProCo database currently has two user-defined schemas and one default schema: HumanResources, Sales, and dbo (see Figure 13.29). In your SQL career, you are virtually guaranteed to encounter identically named tables (e.g., Employee, Product) within different schemas. In this figure, you can quickly spot the two different tables both having the simple name "Contractor" – dbo.Contractor and HumanResources.Contractor.

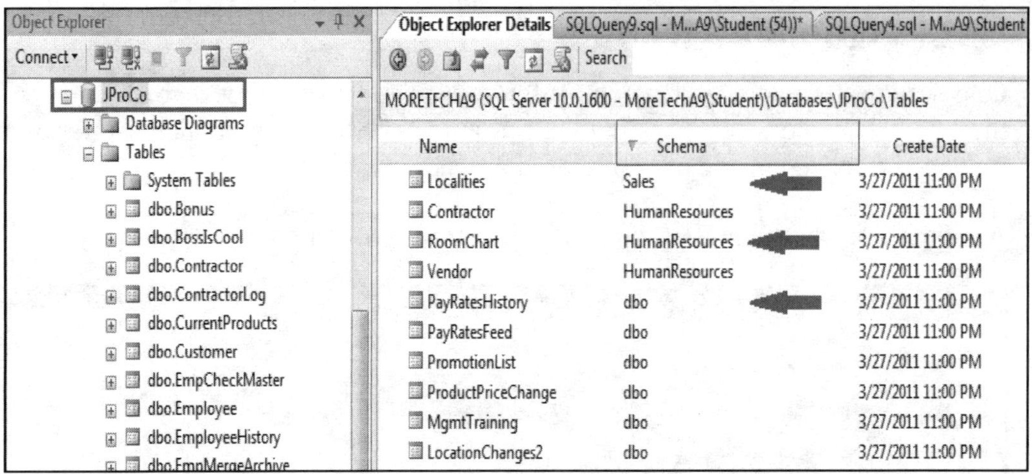

Figure 13.29 JProCo has two Contractor tables: dbo.Contractor and HumanResources.Contractor.

When SQL Server encounters a simple name (*ObjectName*), it searches the database to determine which object to use. With qualified names, SQL Server does not have to scan the database to reconcile the object name. This process of SQL Server having to search and decide an object's schema can lead to COMPILE lock and decreases the stored procedure's performance.

Recall that an advantage of the stored procedure is that an execution plan and statistics are cached from the time you first run the sproc. Thus, it's best to use two-part naming when calling your sproc (and the objects it contains) in order to eliminate unnecessary searching or delay at runtime and allow SQL Server to more rapidly run your sproc.

Earlier in this chapter, we created and ran a sproc called Test3Queries. Suppose we wanted to return to that example and rerun it using qualified naming. We know that JProCo's Employee and Customer tables belong to the dbo schema. So those tables should be referred to as dbo.Employee and dbo.Customer whenever we use them in a sproc. Since we didn't specify a schema for Test3Queries, SQL Server helped us out and interpreted our CREATE PROC and ALTER PROC statements as "dbo.Test3Queries" when we simply called it "Test3Queries" (see Figure 13.25). But suppose we didn't know what the default schema was, or we created a sproc a few months ago and can't recall the schema we used. The Object Explorer is a great resource and contains an exhaustive list of every user-defined object and every system-generated item contained in each of our databases (see Figure 13.30).

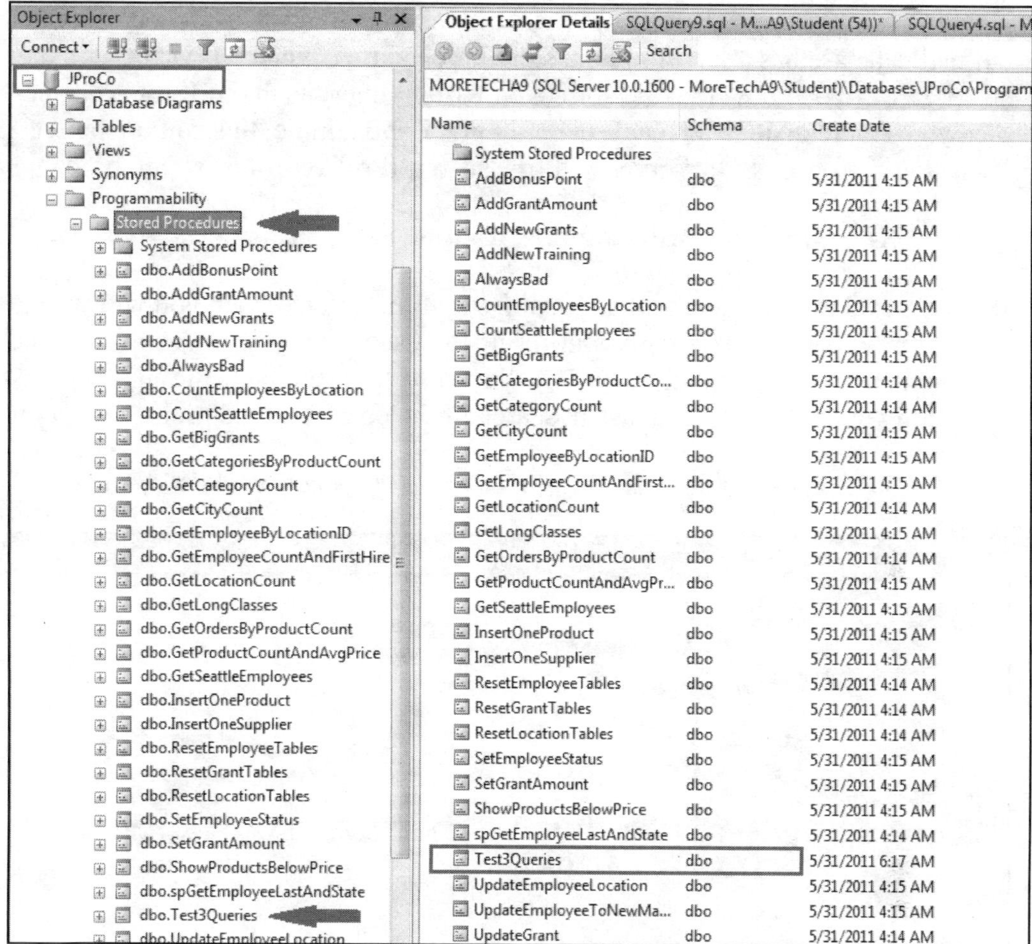

Figure 13.30 The qualified name (a.k.a., two-part name) for the sproc is **dbo.Test3Queries**.

The sp_ Prefix

In this book, we've used numerous system-stored procedures whose names begin with the prefix "sp_". For example, sp_spaceused, sp_cdc_enable_table, sp_help, sp_depends, and so forth.

When SQL Server encounters the prefix sp_, it always scans the Master database first, since that is where it first looks for system-stored procedures. The second place it looks is in your current database context. You want to avoid unnecessary searches of the Master database in your programming, since this incurs additional overhead.

Not all sp_ named stored procedures exist in the Master database. Each user-defined database has a list of system stored procedures, which also start with the sp_ prefix. If you know that the sproc you wish to query is in the JProCo database, then you should qualify the name accordingly. For example, this naming targets the local stored proc, so SQL Server will first search JProCo for this stored proc:

EXEC JProCo.sys.sp_columns 'Employee' *[recommended]*

If you instead ran the code without qualifying it for JProCo, then you will wait longer for SQL Server to return your result and use more system resources, since your non-specific name will cause SQL Server to first rummage through everything in the Master database in search of the correct stored proc:

EXEC sys.sp_columns 'Employee' *[not recommended]*

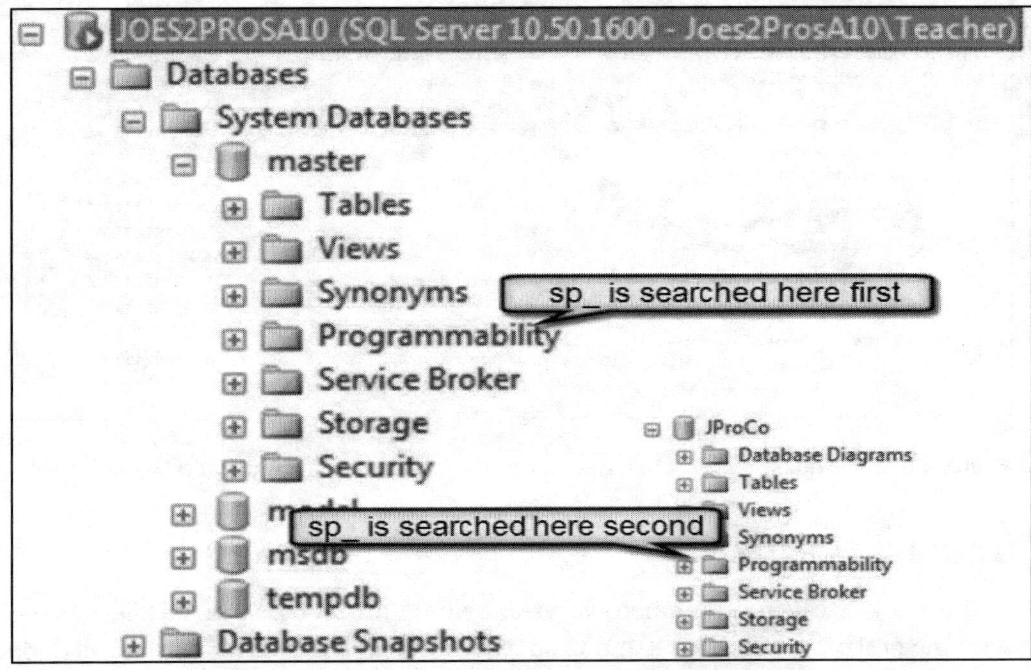

Figure 13.31 SQL searches for sp_ objects first in the Master db and then in the current db context.

Be aware that SQL Server will not stop you from using the prefix "sp_" to name objects that you create. Thus, you should avoid using that prefix for your own user-defined sprocs.

Note: In this section, we intermittently see a semicolon used as an optional delimiter with a few T-SQL statements. The semicolon is optional in every case where you find it in this chapter.

Only a handful of T-SQL statements currently require a semicolon delimiter (e.g., the MERGE statement). However, Microsoft Corporation (the publisher and manufacturer of SQL Server) has made it known via MSDN that a semicolon delimiter will be required for many more T-SQL statements in a future version of SQL Server.

Lab 13.2: Stored Procedure Optimization Tips

Lab Prep: Before you can begin the lab, you must have SQL Server installed and run the SQLProgrammingChapter13.2Setup.sql script.

Skill Check 1: Alter the ShowProductsBelowPrice stored procedure so that upon its execution you do not get the record count. You should instead get the "Command(s) completed successfully" message.

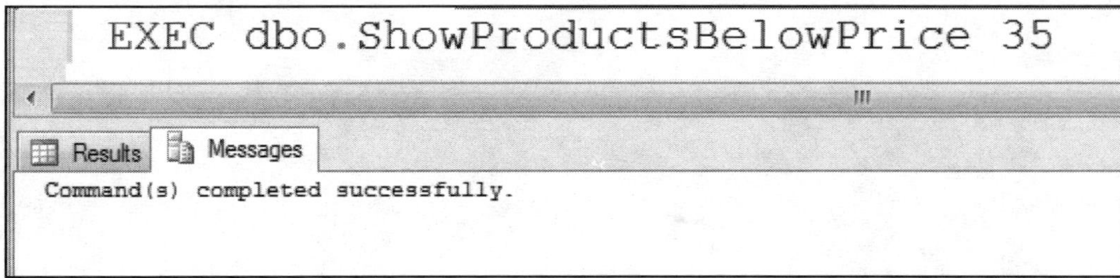

Figure 13.32 Skill Check 1 result.

Skill Check 2: Alter the CountSeattleEmployees stored procedure so that all object references use the qualified name(s). Call upon this stored procedure using the qualified name as seen in the figure below.

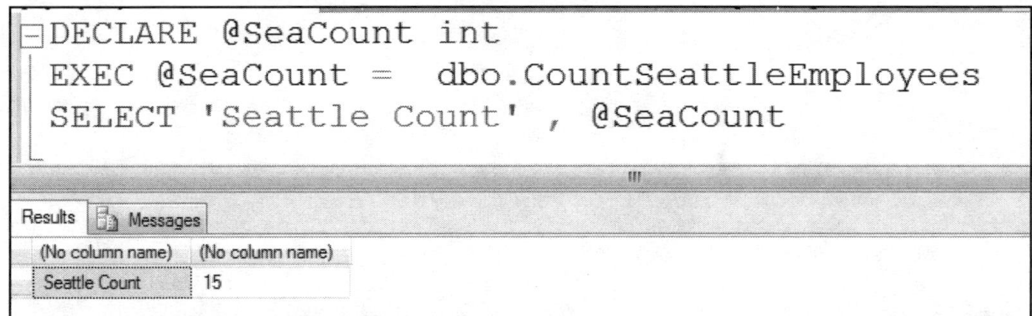

Figure 13.33 Skill Check 2 result.

Answer Code: The T-SQL code for this lab can be found in the downloadable files in a file named Lab13.2_StoredProcedureOptimizationTips.sql.

Stored Procedure Optimization Tips-Points to Ponder

1. With every SELECT and DML statement, SQL Server returns a message that indicates the number of affected rows by that statement.
2. If you use the SET NOCOUNT ON statement then returning this extra row(s) affected message information is not calculated by SQL server.
3. For stored procedures that contain several statements or T-SQL loops, setting NOCOUNT to ON can provide a performance boost because network traffic is greatly reduced.
4. An object name is considered to be qualified if it uses the format *SchemaName.ObjectName* (example: dbo.Employee).
5. When you provide the qualified name of an object, SQL Server no longer needs to search all objects in the database.
6. The process of searching and deciding which schema to use for a simple object name leads to COMPILE locks on stored procedures and decreases the stored procedure's performance.
7. Qualified naming helps SQL Server to directly find the compiled execution plan and statistics, instead of having to search the objects in other possible schemas.
8. If a stored procedure name begins with "sp_," then SQL server first searches in the Master database and then in the current session database which incurs extra overhead.

Stored Procedures vs. User-Defined Functions

On your next vacation do you plan to take a plane, boat, car, or train? If you want to travel to a secluded island, then odds are a train or car will not be capable of getting you there. How about a mountain getaway? If there is no airport nearby, then you might be limited to a car as your only option. If your trip takes you about 500 miles inland, then you can choose from a plane, car, or train. Based on what you want to accomplish, sometimes there is just one option that will work. In other cases, there may be several different options which will achieve your end result. In situations where you have multiple options, there will likely be timing or cost advantages to consider when deciding which option to utilize. The same holds true with respect to the choice of which SQL programming object will best meet your need.

SQL Server's user-defined functions and stored procedures offer similar functionality, in that they both involve bundles of SQL statements stored on the server for future use. They can both be used to convert Fahrenheit to Celsius or get the exact records or values from your database. The tasks that a function can't do, but that a stored procedure can, and *vice versa*, is very handy information to know before you begin coding. A common question that SQL professionals want answered about any tool or feature is when they should use one approach versus the other in situations when both will work. The goal of this section is to help you recognize when to use a function versus a stored procedure in your programming.

Using Functions

In general, I am against using a function in any case where a stored procedure will solve the same problem. However, there are a few areas where a stored procedure just won't work and you must use a function. You may remember in Volume 2 *(SQL Queries Joes 2 Pros)* we used a Table-valued function to join to a table using CROSS APPLY. Since you can't cross apply a stored procedure's result set with a table, you would need to use a function.

Stored procedures are called independently, using the EXECUTE (often shortened to EXEC) command, while functions can only be called from within another T-SQL statement. When using compiled code for processing data in a row-by-row manner, a function can be used but a stored procedure cannot. Let's look at one such example featuring two very similar pieces of code – one used within a function and the other used as a stored procedure.

We will create a stored procedure named sGetCelsius and a function named fnGetCelsius. They both include a formula that takes a Fahrenheit temperature value and converts it to Celsius. Create both of these objects using the correct DDL statements (shown in Figure 13.34).

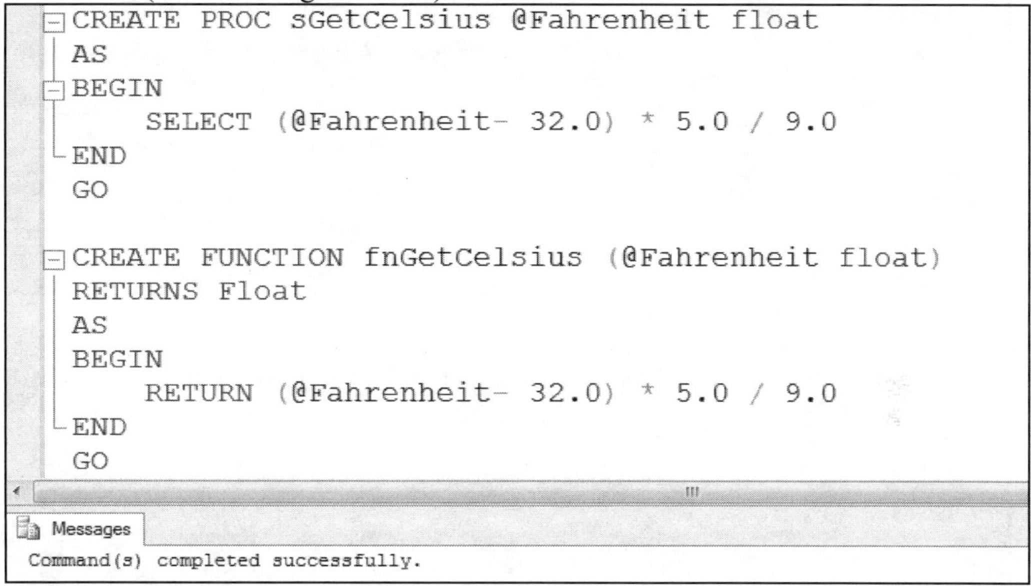

```
CREATE PROC sGetCelsius @Fahrenheit float
AS
BEGIN
    SELECT (@Fahrenheit- 32.0) * 5.0 / 9.0
END
GO

CREATE FUNCTION fnGetCelsius (@Fahrenheit float)
RETURNS Float
AS
BEGIN
    RETURN (@Fahrenheit- 32.0) * 5.0 / 9.0
END
GO
```

Messages

Command(s) completed successfully.

Figure 13.34 Use the same code to create a stored procedure and a function.

The average yearly temperature in Spokane is 47.3F degrees. What is that same value stated in Celsius? The answer is 8.5. Both the sproc and the function produce the same result (see Figure 13.35).

```
EXEC dbo.sGetCelsius 47.3
SELECT dbo.fnGetCelsius(47.3)
```

Results | Messages

	(No column name)
1	8.5

	(No column name)
1	8.5

Figure 13.35 Both the stored proc and the function produce the same result.

So far there appears to be no difference between these two approaches. The difference lies in how and where you can use each object. We want to use the conversion against the Location table to see both Fahrenheit and Celsius values for all locations. Figure 13.36 shows the Location table (if you ran the 13.2 or 13.3 setup script) with the average temperature displayed for each location.

```
SELECT *
FROM Location
```

Results | Spatial results | Messages

	LocationID	street	city	state	Latitude	Longitude	GeoLoc	AverageTempF
1	1	545 Pike	Seattle	WA	47.455	-122.231	0xE6100000010C0AD7A3703DBA4740105839B4C88E5EC0	52.3
2	2	222 Second AVE	Boston	MA	42.372	-71.0298	0xE6100000010C560E2DB29D2F4540EE5A423EE8C151C0	61.5
3	4	444 Ruby ST	Spokane	WA	47.668	-117.529	0xE6100000010C2FDD240681D5474060E5D022DB615DC0	47.3
4	5	1595 Main	Philadelphia	PA	39.888	-75.251	0xE6100000010C8B6CE7FBA9F14340F2D24D6210D052C0	63.9
5	6	915 Wallaby Drive	Sydney	NULL	-33.876	151.315	0xE6100000010CE3A59BC420F040C0AE47E17A14EA6240	55.3

Query executed successfully. | JOES2PROSA10 (10.50 RTM) | Joes2ProsA10\Teacher (58) | JProCo | 00:00:00 | 5 rows

Figure 13.36 Make sure that your Location table contains the new field, AverageTempF.

Let's use the function in a SELECT statement and have it create an expression field called AverageTempC (see Figure 13.37).

```
SELECT *, dbo.fnGetCelsius(AverageTempF) as AverageTempC
FROM Location
```

Results | Spatial results | Messages

	LocationID	street	city	state	Latitude	Longitu...	GeoLoc	AverageTempF	AverageTempC
1	1	545 Pike	Seattle	WA	47.455	-122.231	0xE61...	52.3	11.2777777777778
2	2	222 Second AVE	Boston	MA	42.372	-71.0298	0xE61...	61.5	16.3888888888889
3	4	444 Ruby ST	Spokane	WA	47.668	-117.529	0xE61...	47.3	8.5
4	5	1595 Main	Philadelp...	PA	39.888	-75.251	0xE61...	63.9	17.7222222222222
5	6	915 Wallaby Dri...	Sydney	NULL	-33.876	151.315	0xE61...	55.3	12.9444444444444

Figure 13.37 The function allows us to create a new expression field, AverageTempC.

Notice that you cannot use the stored proc in the same statement (Figure 13.38).

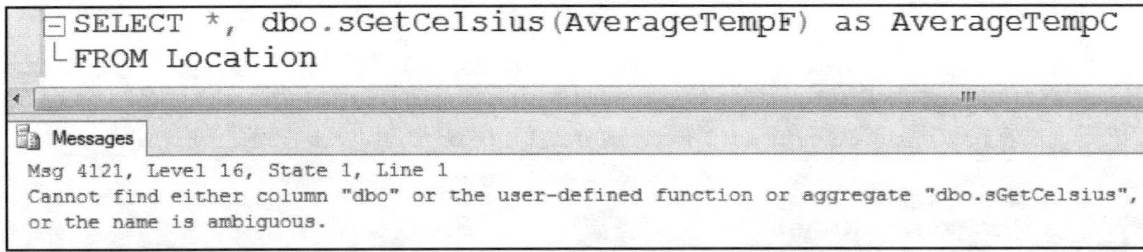

SELECT *, dbo.sGetCelsius(AverageTempF) as AverageTempC
FROM Location
Messages
Msg 4121, Level 16, State 1, Line 1
Cannot find either column "dbo" or the user-defined function or aggregate "dbo.sGetCelsius", or the name is ambiguous.

Figure 13.38 The same statement cannot run with the sproc. It simply won't work.

In summary, use functions within DML statements. Functions must be run as part of a DML statement (SELECT, INSERT, UPDATE, DELETE) and cannot run independently (i.e., can't run on their own).

Using Stored Procedures

In our *Joes 2 Pros* studies, so far it may seem like the function is more elegant than the stored procedure, which is a workhorse. In fact we have only talked about the area where you should use functions, namely in DML statements. In robust, well-planned SQL Server programming, you will likely use far more stored procedures than functions. Stored procedures are the reliable stalwarts of SQL Server, but they can also accomplish smart and fancy footwork behind the scenes. One important example is that the sproc is free from the encapsulation effect, which means Query Engine is free to access to all operations which can lead to a better query plan. (Read more about statistics and actual execution plans in Chapters 9-12 of Volume 3, *SQL Architecture Basics*.)

A stored procedure's query plan is kept in memory after its first execution so the code doesn't have to be optimized again on subsequent executions. This ability of stored procedures to pre-compile their code and cache the best execution plan reduces network traffic, since they do not need to be recompiled.

Stored procedures also have a security advantage. A user or a process can be granted access to execute a stored procedure without having direct permissions to the underlying tables. When connecting to SQL server with a .NET enterprise solution, you will want to use ADO.net as its connection to SQL Server. ADO.net's main built in classes can call upon SQL stored procedures (but not SQL functions). Yes, ADO.net can write a direct DML statement to SQL Server and use a function. However, this is considered a security risk, because you would need to give calling code processes elevated permissions to all underlying tables.

Sprocs are often better than functions for running similar code. There is still a longer list of tasks that functions can't do at all and stored procs can do just fine. If you need to run a DML, DDL, DCL, or TCL statement, a sproc can handle all statement types. However, functions can only run DML statements.

Have you noticed that every function needs to return something? Stored procedures can be created without any return values. Our last example (see Skill Check 1) has no return value for the sproc. It simply performs its work, which is confirmed by a "Command(s) Completed Successfully" message.

In short, my rule for using stored procedures is this: if a stored procedure solves your goal, then that is what you should use.

Lab 13.3: Stored Procedure vs. Functions

Lab Prep: Before you can begin the lab, you must have SQL Server installed and run the SQLProgrammingChapter13.3Setup.sql script.

Skill Check 1: Create the correct programming object that will set the Recursive Triggers of JProCo to the Off position.

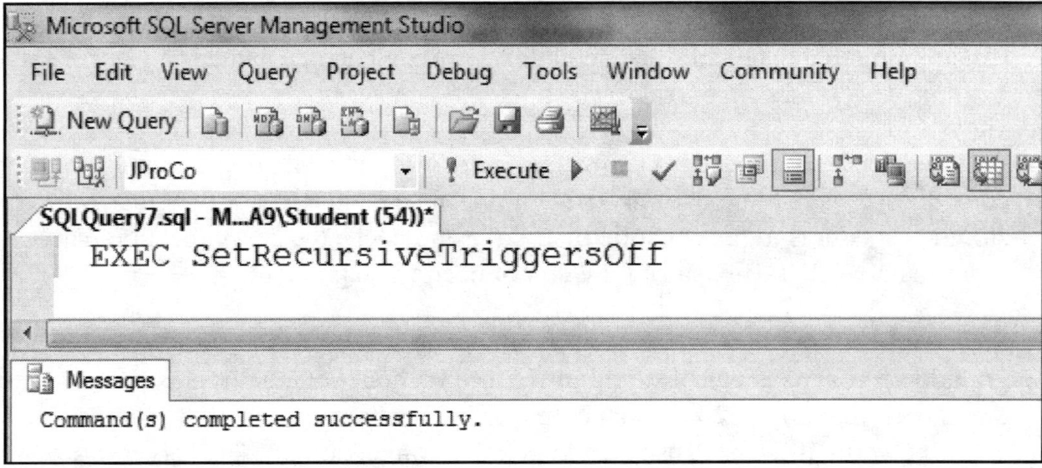

Figure 13.39 Skill Check 1 result.

Answer Code: The T-SQL code for this lab can be found in the downloadable files in a file named Lab13.3_StoredProcedureVsFunctions.sql.

Stored Procedures vs. Functions - Points to Ponder

1. Stored procedures are called independently, using the EXECUTE (often shortened to EXEC) command, while functions are called from within another T-SQL statement.
2. Use functions within DML statements. Functions must be run as part of a DML statement (SELECT, INSERT, UPDATE, DELETE) and cannot run independently (i.e., can't run on their own).
3. Stored procs can run DML, DDL, DCL, or TCL statements. Functions can only run DML statements.
4. Rule of thumb: if a stored procedure can solve your goal, then that is probably what you should use.

Chapter Glossary

COMPILE lock: a performance issue which arises when SQL Server has to search to locate a stored procedure or its dependent object(s); this problem can be prevented by always using qualified naming (a.k.a., two-part naming) when calling upon stored procedures and the objects they contain.

Computed column: a column built into the definition of a table. A computed column contains information calculated by an expression.

Materialized: a term meaning that the data was created and also stored. Data can be materialized to memory only (like a CTE), or it can be persisted to storage (like an indexed view).

NOCOUNT: a feature of SQL Server that lets you know the record count of a DML statement.

Persisted: a description characterizing data which has been materialized and which is saved to disk.

Qualified name: the combination of the schema and object name in a database. For example, if your Employee table is in the HR schema then the qualified name would be HR.Employee.

Simple name: the name of the object only (without the schema name before it).

sp_spaceused: a system stored-procedure which obtains space statistics for a table.

Chapter Thirteen - Review Quiz

1.) What types of changes to a table will result in increased data space used by a large table that has many rows? (Choose two.)

□ a. Adding a new field with all null data.
□ b. Adding a new field with populated data.
□ c. Adding a persisted computed column.
□ d. Adding a computed column with the default settings.
□ e. Adding a new index to the table.

2.) If NOCOUNT is set to OFF what type of statements will display a "Row(s) affected" message?

O a. DML
O b. DDL
O c. DCL
O d. TCL

3.) What are some performance tips relating to stored procedures?

□ a. Use qualified names for your referenced objects.
□ b. SET NOCOUNT OFF at the top of the stored procedure code.
□ c. SET NOCOUNT ON at the top of the stored procedure code.
□ d. SET NOCOUNT OFF at the end of the stored procedure code.
□ e. SET NOCOUNT ON at the end of the stored procedure code.
□ f. Always name your user-defined stored procedures with the sp_ prefix.

Answer Key

1.) b, c 2.) a 3.) a, c, d

Bug Catcher Game

Chapter 13 is a chapter on tips and does not have bug catcher game.

Chapter 14. Next Steps for Aspiring SQL Pros

Congratulations to those who have made it all the way through this book's lessons on programming, a vital leg on your journey to becoming a SQL Pro!

I have tried to write each book in this series to help anyone seeking knowledge about SQL Server – whether an intermediate looking to fill gaps in their knowledge, an expert looking for new features in the 2008 version of SQL Server, or even a developer picking up SQL Server as their second or third programming language. But the heart of my mission as an educator remains dedicated to the brand new beginner who learns about the power of SQL Server and becomes committed to mastering this awesome technology and 'making it their own.'

Those earnest seekers who have successfully studied these first four books in "cover-to-cover" fashion are well prepared for the final steps in their journey to becoming a SQL Pro. As my students and readers know, I believe strongly in the certification method of demonstrating your seriousness and expertise in SQL Server. I have designed the *Joes2Pros* curriculum to help prepare you on the journey toward becoming a Microsoft Certified Technology Specialist, and I recommend you consider this important step in building your SQL Server knowledge and career.

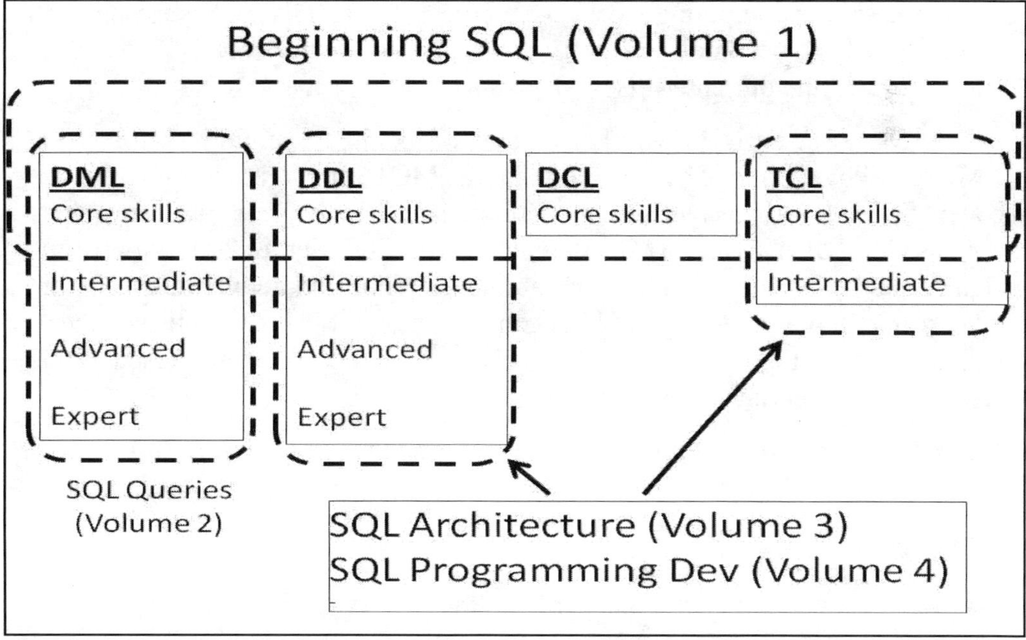

Figure 14.1 You have now mastered the knowledge in Books 1 through 4 and utilized expert level DML, DDL, and TCL concepts.

I've always had my students first become experts at both DML (Data Manipulation Language) and DDL (Data Definition Language) so they can use them together the way they will in the workplace. The DDL statements that build stored procedures, functions, or triggers often contain some very advanced DML statements to accomplish their complex work. With the error handling chapters of Volume 4, you used some more advanced topic of TCL (Transaction Control Language) with your explicit transactions. After the first two books you knew DDL and became an expert in DML. Volumes 3 and 4 taught you the concepts of object design and tuning to make you a DDL expert.

You will also need to work with DCL and TCL as a developer but often will find many of those advanced topics will fall into the job description of the SQL Administrator. SQL developers need to be experts in both DML and DDL statements, since these comprise 90% of what you will do on the job. All DDL statements contain code to define what is in them. Ten years ago, I would have told you your journey in the SQL world for development is done. After all, you have covered pretty much all the SQL programming topics.

The enterprise computing world and the internet made SQL Server (and not Access) the king it is today. Big interconnected systems now allow customers, workers, and partners to gain access to the data they need most. New delivery systems like C#, XML, and PowerShell continue to spring up and gain worldwide acceptance in the computing world. The more SQL can talk to these systems the more useful SQL becomes. SQL server continues to interoperate with more languages within your enterprise.

Nowadays, a true SQL Pro will know about SQL's interoperability with .NET, XML, and PowerShell. The final book in this MCTS preparation track series covers SQL Server's usage and interaction with other programming languages, such as C#, ADO.net, and XML. Beginning with SQL Server 2005, Microsoft has significantly enhanced SQL Server's ability to utilize and deliver data using these other programming languages. Skills combining SQL Server with these other languages are in high demand, and you also want to become well versed in this area before attempting the MCTS exam.

Best wishes for your continued progress in the realm of SQL Server databases!!

Rick Morelan

Find more detail on forthcoming titles (including a Business Intelligence series publishing in 2012) and keep in touch with the *Joes 2 Pros* community at ***www.Joes2Pros.com***. There you can find free downloads of each volume's table of contents, sample chapters of each volume, and other materials. Be sure to visit the excellent blog ***www.SQLAuthority.com***, a forum which is continuously updated with SQL tips, code examples, and questions answered by Pinal Dave.

Volume 1
Beginning SQL Joes 2 Pros: The SQL Hands-On Guide for Beginners
ISBN 1-4392-5317-X

Volume 2
SQL Queries Joes 2 Pros: SQL Query Techniques for Microsoft SQL Server 2008
ISBN 1-4392-5318-8

Volume 3
SQL Architecture Basics Joes 2 Pros: Core Architecture Concepts
ISBN: 1-4515-7946-2

Volume 4
SQL Programming Joes 2 Pros: Programming & Development for Microsoft SQL Server 2008
ISBN: 1-4515-7948-9

Volume 5
SQL Server Interoperability Joes 2 Pros: A guide to integrating SQL Server with XML, C#, and PowerShell
ISBN: 1-4515-7950-0

[THIS PAGE INTENTIONALLY LEFT BLANK]

[THIS PAGE INTENTIONALLY LEFT BLANK]

[THIS PAGE INTENTIONALLY LEFT BLANK]

[THIS PAGE INTENTIONALLY LEFT BLANK]

Index

T

U

V

W

X